PENG

MURD

M. M. Kaye was born in India and spent most of her childhood and much of her early married life in that country. Her ties with India are strong: her grandfather, father, brother and husband all served the Raj, and her grandfather's first cousin, Sir John Kaye, wrote the standard accounts of the Indian Mutiny and the first Afghan War. When India achieved independence her husband joined the British Army, and for the next nineteen years she followed the drum to all sorts of exciting places she would not otherwise have seen, including Kenya, Zanzibar, Egypt, Cyprus and Berlin. M. M. Kaye is best known for her highly successful historical novels, including the bestselling *The Far Pavilions*, *Shadow of the Moon* and *Trade Wind*, and for her detective novels, which include *Death in Zanzibar*, *Death in Kenya*, *Death in Kashmir*, *Death in Cyprus*, *Death in Berlin* and *Death in the Andamans*. All these titles are published by Penguin. Penguin also publish the first volume of her autobiography, *The Sun in the Morning*. M. M. Kaye has also written a children's story, *The Ordinary Princess* (1991).

M. M. KAYE

MURDER ABROAD

DEATH IN BERLIN
DEATH IN CYPRUS
DEATH IN KENYA

PENGUIN BOOKS

PENGUIN BOOKS

Published by the Penguin Group
Penguin Books Ltd, 27 Wrights Lane, London W8 5TZ, England
Penguin Books USA Inc., 375 Hudson Street, New York, New York 10014, USA
Penguin Books Australia Ltd, Ringwood, Victoria, Australia
Penguin Books Canada Ltd, 10 Alcorn Avenue, Toronto, Ontario, Canada M4V 3B2
Penguin Books (NZ) Ltd, 182–190 Wairau Road, Auckland 10, New Zealand

Penguin Books Ltd, Registered Offices: Harmondsworth, Middlesex, England

Death in Berlin
First published as *Death Walked in Berlin* by Staples Press 1955
Revised edition published as *Death in Berlin* by Viking 1985
Published in Penguin Books 1986

Copyright 1955 by M. M. Kaye
Copyright © M. M. Kaye, 1985

Death in Cyprus
First published as *Death Walked in Cyprus* by Staples Press 1956
Revised edition published as *Death in Cyprus* by Allen Lane 1984
Published in Penguin Books 1985

Copyright 1956 by M. M. Kaye
Copyright © M. M. Kaye, 1984

Death in Kenya
First published as *Later Than You Think* by Longmans 1958
Published as *Death in Kenya* by Allen Lane 1983
Published in Penguin Books 1984

Copyright © M. M. Kaye, 1958

This omnibus edition published in Penguin Books 1992
1 3 5 7 9 10 8 6 4 2

Printed in England by Clays Ltd, St Ives plc
Filmset in Monophoto Times

Contents

DEATH IN BERLIN

TO
all those Army wives who like myself
have followed the drum

Author's Note

This story is set in the battered Berlin of 1953 — eight years after the end of World War II and eight years before the infamous Berlin Wall went up, cutting off all free communication between the East and West sectors of the city.

My husband's British regiment was already serving in Germany when they received orders to move to Berlin, and within less than ten days of our arrival he himself was suddenly transferred to a new post in England, where there was no immediate accommodation available for his family — myself and our two small daughters. He departed alone, leaving us behind until such time as an army quarter could be found for us, and it was during the following few weeks of waiting that I thought up the plot for this book — largely as a result of long walks through the green, leafy suburbs between the Herr Strasse and the Grünewald where there were any number of ruined, roofless houses in which the Nazi élite had once lived, and wondering what their late owners had been like and what had become of them?

The Berlin I have described here is the Berlin I saw then. For being at a loose end I had plenty of time on my hands, and I spent a great deal of it exploring and taking notes for future use: scribbling down detailed descriptions of the ruined city, where the worst of the devastation was in the sector occupied by the Russians. Making rough sketches of the Maifeld, that vast, pretentious stadium-complex that Hitler had had built in the 1930s for the Olympic Games, and which later became the setting for innumerable Nazi rallies — and later still, after a brief period of Russian occupation, the headquarters of the British sector.

7

I also made notes on other things besides scenery and ruins. Small incidents that I thought might come in useful, such as the fact that only a few hours after our arrival at the original, ramshackle Families' Hostel, where we had to spend a night or two before moving into our army quarter, I happened to catch a glimpse of the woman who would be allotted to us as our cook-housekeeper. She had, it seemed, dropped in to visit a friend who worked at the hostel.

My husband, Goff Hamilton, says that his own clearest memory of his first brief stay in Berlin is of finding me standing in the dusk one evening beside the big outdoor swimming-pool in the Stadium area, staring down at the dark stagnant water with its 'anti-freeze' criss-cross of heavy straw cables, and replying (when he remarked a shade tartly that he presumed I was busy drowning someone in there?), 'Yes: I've had an idea about that straw ...' The trials of a man whose wife writes murder stories!

Goff was a major at that time, and when, six years later, he returned to command the British sector's Berlin Brigade, we lived in a lovely house complete with a heated swimming-pool and a spectacular view over the Havelsee; and I could barely recognize the city as the Berlin I had described in this book, for by that time most of the ruins had disappeared: from the British sector, at least. The Russians too had vanished from the Rundfunk; though they still mounted a guard on a memorial they had built on the western side of the Brandenburg Gate, and took their turn at garrisoning Spandau gaol, ostensibly to keep an eye on its three remaining Nazi inmates, but obviously because it allowed them to keep a foot inside the West Berlin door! The ruined Kaiser Wilhelm Kirche on the Kurfürstendamm, that had once seemed to me so strangely beautiful, had by now been pared down to a single broken spire which, in the guise of a war memorial, had been incorporated in a new and very modernistic church where it no longer looked like some romantic ruin from Angkor Wat, but regrettably like the stump of a blackened and rotted tooth that should have been pulled out long ago.

A few months before we left, The Wall went up. And with its rise many fond hopes for the future of humanity came tumbling down. I watched it being built: which is possibly why, when I look back, I think that I prefer the battered but more hopeful Berlin of 1953.

Prologue

With nightfall the uneasy wind that had sighed all day through the grass and the gorse bushes at the cliff edge died away, and a cold fog crawled in from the sea, obliterating the darkening coastline and muting the drag of waves on shingle to a rhythmic murmur barely louder than the unrelenting and monotonous mutter of gunfire to the west.

The hours crept by in silence until at last the moon rose, tingeing the fog with silver and bringing with it a night breeze that blew gently off the land and eddied but did not disperse the fog.

Something that appeared to be a bent whin bush moved and stood upright, and a low voice spoke in the patois of that lonely stretch of coast: a man's voice, barely above a whisper. 'It is good. Now we go — but without noise. I go first, and each one will put the hand on him who is ahead. It is better to carry the children. Now——!' There was a rustle that might have been the wind among the bushes and the harsh sea-grass as the little band of refugees, formless and without substance in the uncertain moon-light, rose from the shelter of the whins and began to creep forward along a narrow goat track that descended the low, sandy cliff.

But despite their desperate caution it proved impossible for them to move without noise, for the dry, sandy soil broke under their feet, sending little showers of earth and pebbles rolling and clattering down to the beach. A child whimpered softly, and there was a sudden harsh tearing sound as a woman's skirt caught and ripped on a length of rusty sheep wire. And when at last they gained the shore their stumbling progress across the rattling banks

11

of shingle was a torture to stretched nerves. But at least they had now reached the sea ...

Behind them the wolf packs of hate and destruction howled across Europe, while on either hand the smoke from the pyres of Rotterdam and Dunkirk blackened the sweet May skies; but ahead of them, beyond the narrow sea and the shifting fogbanks, lay the coast of England.

At the water's edge the shadowy bulk of a fishing boat loomed out of the surrounding fog, and despite the darkness it could be seen that the man who stood knee-deep in the creaming water, holding the prow to the shore, was tense and listening. His head was raised and he was not looking towards the stumbling line of refugees, but to the right, where the curve of the bay ran out in a huddle of weed-covered rocks.

He spoke in a harsh whisper and without turning his head: 'I am afraid. Be swift!' Then over his shoulder to a dim figure in the boat: 'Be ready with the sail, Pierre.'

A child began to cry in small gulping sobs: the sobbing of one who would normally have screamed its woe aloud, but who had been reduced by an adult experience of fear to the status of a terrified animal.

'Hush thou!' The whisper was savage with fear as the small figure was lifted over the gunwale. There followed three more children, the last of whom appeared to be clutching a large doll. The man who had been carrying her climbed in after her and turned to pull a shivering woman into the boat.

'Quick!' muttered the man in the water. 'Oh be quick!'

And then, with shocking suddenness, the darkness was ripped apart by a streak of flame, and the fogbanks and the low sandy cliffs that curved about the lonely bay echoed to the crash and whine of bullets, hoarse shouting voices and the clatter of running boots upon rock and shingle.

Without words the man who steadied the prow of the boat, and he who had led the refugees down the goat track, put their shoulders to the laden boat and thrust her off into deep water. The sail, invisible against the night and the drifting fog, rose and took the breeze and, slowly at first, the boat began to move away from the shelving beach. The two fishermen hauled themselves aboard and the remaining refugees, panic lending them strength, flung themselves screaming into the water, clawing at the receding prow, and were dragged on board.

A lone figure ran wildly across the shingle. It was the woman whose clothing had caught on the rusty tangle of sheep wire. She had paused in the darkness to free herself, appalled by the noise of the ripping material and the fear that she might dislodge stones and clods of earth if she dragged at the cloth, and so had arrived late upon the beach.

She rushed into the water, her feet stumbling among the treacherous pebbles as the waves snatched them from under her. But the boat had gone. The fog had closed behind it, and there was nothing to show that it had ever been there. She tried to scream: to shriek to them to come back for her, to save her and not leave her alone on that dark beach. But her throat was dry and her breath came in hoarse gasps.

The vicious chatter of a machine-gun added itself to the noise of running feet, and tracer bullets ripped brilliant orange streaks through the fog around her. Turning from the sea that had betrayed her, she ran back like a hunted animal towards the dark whin bushes, the low sandy cliffs and the hostile land . . .

1

Miranda Brand knelt on the floor of a bedroom in the Families' Hostel at Bad Oeynhausen in the British zone of Germany, searching her suitcase for a cake of soap, and regretting that she had ever accepted her cousin Robert Melville's invitation to spend a month with him and his family in Berlin.

There was something about this gaunt building, about the dimly familiar, guttural voices and the wet, grey miles that had streamed past the train windows all that afternoon, that had acted unpleasantly upon her nerves. Yet it could not be Germany, and the fact that she was back there once more for the first time since childhood, that was responsible for this curious feeling of apprehension and unease that possessed her, because she had been aware of it before she had even set foot in the country.

It had begun ... When had it begun? Was it on the boat to the Hook of Holland? ... Or even earlier, on the boat-train to Harwich? She could not be sure. She only knew that for some inexplicable reason she felt tense and uneasy, and ... And afraid!

Yes, that was it: *afraid*. 'Well then what are you afraid of?' Miranda demanded of herself. '*Nothing!* But you can't be afraid of nothing!'

I'm getting as bad as Aunt Hetty, thought Miranda ruefully, and was smiling at the recollection of that neurotic and highly strung spinster when the door burst open and Stella Melville rushed in and slammed it noisily behind her, causing Miranda to start violently and drop the lid of the suitcase on the fingers of one hand.

'*Ow!* What on earth is the matter, Stel'? I wish you wouldn't make me jump like that. It puts years on my life.' Miranda blew on her injured fingers and regarded her cousin's wife with affectionate indignation.

Mrs Melville drew a quivering breath and her hands clenched into fists: 'I *hate* the Army! *I hate it!* Oh, why did Robert have to be a soldier? Why couldn't he have been a farmer, or a pig-breeder, or a stockbroker or – or — oh, *anything* but a soldier?'

Stella flung herself face down upon the bed and burst into tears.

'Good heavens!' said Miranda blankly.

She stood up hurriedly and perching on the edge of the bed threw a comforting arm about Stella's shoulders: 'What's up, darling? — that tiresome Leslie woman been sharpening her claws on you again? Forget it! I expect all those seasick pills have upset her liver. Come on, sweetie, brace up!'

'Oh go away!' sobbed Stella furiously, attempting to burrow further into the unyielding hostel pillow: 'You don't understand. No one understands!'

'Well tell me about it then,' said Miranda reasonably. 'Come on, Stel', it can't be as bad as that. Tell your Aunt 'Randa!'

Stella gave a watery chuckle and sat up, pushing away a wet strand of blond hair with the back of her hand. 'Aunt 'Randa! I like that, when I'm old enough to be your mother.'

'Give yourself a chance, darling. I shall be twenty-one next month.' Miranda hunted through her coat pockets, and producing a passably clean handkerchief handed it over.

'*Twenty-one,*' said Stella desolately. 'Dear God! and I shall be forty!' She blew her nose and sat looking at Miranda; her pretty pink and white face blotched with tears, and the ruin of her carefully applied make-up suddenly revealing the truth of that last statement.

Miranda looked momentarily taken aback. 'Will you? Well I suppose if you'd been married at eighteen I could just—— Look, how did we come to be discussing our ages anyway? What has your age got to do with hating the Army?'

'Perhaps more than you think,' said Stella bitterly. She saw that

Miranda was looking bewildered, and laughed a little shakily. 'Oh, it isn't that! It's — well Robert has just met a man he knows, and — and oh 'Randa isn't it awful? He told Robert that the regiment is going to be sent to Malaya next year!' Stella's blue eyes brimmed over with tears that coursed slowly down her wet cheeks and dripped off her chin, making ugly dark spots on her smart grey dress.

'Malaya? But good heavens, Stella, why on earth should that upset you? If I were in your shoes I'd be thrilled to bits! Sunshine, palm trees, temple bells — not to mention masses of servants in lovely eastern clothes to do all the dirty work for you. Just think of it! No more washing up dishes or fuel economy: *heaven!* What are you worrying about? You don't have to worry about Robert, because he told me once that Malaya was a "Company Commander's war" — whatever that means. And anyway the papers all seem to think that this Templer man has got the bandits buttoned.'

'You don't understand,' repeated Stella impatiently. 'I know *you* think it would be lovely to go there, but I'm not you. People like you think of the East as exotic and exciting, but to me it's only uncivilized and frightening. Perhaps that's because I'm not an exotic or exciting person. I don't like strange places. I love my own bit of England and I don't want to live anywhere else.'

'But you can have it both ways,' urged Miranda. 'You can live in England and in between you can go off and see romantic foreign places.'

'It isn't like that,' said Stella drearily. 'When I married Johnnie — you never knew Johnnie, did you — I thought what fun it would be. Being married, I mean. I thought we'd live at Mallow, or somewhere near it in Sussex or Kent, and that everything would be lovely. I actually thought that I should "live happily ever after" just like they do in fairy stories!'

She gave a short laugh, startling in its bitterness, and getting up from the bed walked over to the window and stood with her forehead pressed against a pane, looking down at the narrow, darkening street and speaking in an undertone, almost as if she had forgotten Miranda's presence and was talking to herself.

'It didn't work out that way. Perhaps it never does. We had to go to India. He ... *I hated it!* The dirt, the dust, the flies, the dark, secret faces. The horrible heat and that awful club life. And I was ill; always ill.' She shivered so violently that her teeth chattered.

'It was heaven to come home again. To see green fields and cool grey skies—— Oh, the awfulness of that brassy sunlight! But then the war came and he had to go back there without me. And I never saw him again. When he — when the telegram came I thought I should never be happy again. But you can't go on being unhappy for ever. That's the merciful thing about it. And after the war I met Robert.'

Her voice rose again suddenly, and she turned to face Miranda, her pretty mouth working and her slim fingers clenching and unclenching against the suave lines of the grey travelling dress.

'But it was only the same thing all over again. They sent him to Egypt, and they wouldn't let me go with him. They said I hadn't enough "points". *Points!* As if love and marriage were things on a ration card! Later the families were all sent away anyway, but that didn't make it any better for me. And when he did get back, the regiment was in Germany so we get sent to Berlin! This, believe it or not, is a "Home posting". *Home!* And now to be told that it will be Malaya next. I can't *bear* it!'

Stella turned away to stare desperately down into the street once more.

'Stella, darling,' Miranda spoke soothingly as though addressing a fractious child, 'you're feeling tired and nervy, and I don't blame you. It's all this wretched packing and moving. But it isn't as bad as all that, you know. There won't be flies and heat and oriental faces in Berlin, and Robert says your house is one of the nicest ones. And you are sure to be allowed to go to Malaya with him.'

'You don't understand,' repeated Stella tonelessly. 'No one really understands. I don't want to live in Germany. I've dreaded the idea. When I was six I had a German governess and I loathed her. And mother insisted on sending me to a finishing school in Brussels, and I hated that too: every minute of it. I don't want to go to Malaya. I'm like that girl in one of Nancy Mitford's books who hated "abroad". *I* hate "abroad" too. I want to live in England. In my own home, with my own things around me. Not this awful endless packing and moving and separation, and living in soulless army-furnished quarters.'

'In that case,' said Miranda briskly, 'I can't see why you don't stay at home.'

'And be separated from Robert? I couldn't bear it! That's the awful part of it. I swore I'd never marry another soldier. But I couldn't help it. You don't mean to fall in love with people. You just do, and then it's too late and you find yourself being pulled in two between loving someone and hating the untidy, nomadic life you will have to live if you want to be with them. Oh well——! I suppose I shall just go on living the sort of life I don't like, in places I loathe, until I'm an old hag and Robert retires with a tummy and a pension! Never marry a soldier, Miranda.'

'Moral, never marry anyone,' said Miranda, hugging her. 'It sounds much safer and far more comfortable to remain a resolute spinster — like me!'

Stella gave a dreary little laugh and turned away from the window: 'What a mess I must look! I'm sorry, 'Randa. I've been behaving like a hysterical lunatic. I suppose it's seeing it all start again; and being older this time, and — oh forget it darling! I'm tired and I feel as if we'd been travelling for weeks instead of less than two days.' She turned on both washbasin taps and peered disconsolately at herself in the inadequate square of looking-glass above them. 'Do you suppose if I slosh my face with cold water it will do any good? I can't go down to the dining-room looking like this.'

'Would you like to have your supper sent up here?' suggested Miranda.

'No. I must go down. Robert has asked that Control

Commission man to have dinner with us. You know — the elderly man we met on the train. Brigadier something or other.'

'Brindley,' supplied Miranda.

'That's it. I don't think the poor man realized that he'd have to eat his meal with Lottie and Mademoiselle as well, or he'd probably have refused. He doesn't look the type who likes children. Those gossipy old bachelors seldom do. What time is this train supposed to leave for Berlin?'

'Well there's an extremely military notice downstairs which says it "departs 22.55 hrs", but I haven't taken time off to work that one out yet. You'd think they'd run a through-train from the Hook, wouldn't you? — instead of throwing us all off and dumping us in a hostel for hours on end.'

'Russians,' said Stella splashing her face with cold water.

'What do you mean, "Russians"?'

'Apparently they won't let us run trains through their zone except by night. I suppose they're afraid we'd hang out of the carriage windows clicking our Kodaks. Do I look any better?'

'You look marvellous,' said Miranda lightly, and turned quickly away, thinking, with a sudden sense of shock, that Stella looked more than middle-aged; she looked old.

Stella Carrell, who had then been Stella Radley and was now Stella Melville, had been a grown woman of twenty-seven when Miranda, a leggy and frightened six-year-old, had first seen her. Then, and for many years afterwards, she had seemed old to Miranda. It was only during the last two or three years that Miranda had begun to think of Stella as an attractive woman in her thirties, and to admire her looks and copy her taste in clothes and hats. Stella had seemed to grow younger as Miranda grew older, for there was a curious touch of immaturity about her character and outlook that somehow made Miranda feel protective and as though she were the elder of the two. Yet now, in the space of a few minutes, although the spoilt child had been

20

apparent in her recent outburst, she had suddenly seemed to age ten years in appearance.

Looking back, Miranda could not remember ever having seen Stella look anything but immaculately neat and beautifully dressed. There was a term for Stella that the glossier women's magazines were inordinately fond of, although Miranda had always considered it more suitable for horses: Stella was 'well-groomed'. Now, however, her blond hair hung about her face in damp disorder and Miranda noticed for the first time that its yellow fairness was touched with silver and that without benefit of powder and rouge her skin appeared faded and almost sallow, with a network of fine lines and spreading crowsfeet marking it about the eyes and mouth.

Miranda was suddenly reminded of the roses in the garden at Mallow: one day so beautiful in their velvety perfection, and the next, overblown and fading. Stella was like the roses, she thought; and like them, she would fade quickly. Her looks were not of the kind that will outlast youth, and soon there would be nothing left of that bright prettiness, and little to show that it had ever existed.

Seized by a disturbing thought Miranda turned quickly to stare at her own face in the looking-glass. It gazed reassuringly back at her with eyes the colour of a winter sky: wide of cheekbone, pointed of chin, framed in curling dark hair and set on a long slender throat the colour of warm ivory. A face startlingly like Thompson's portrait of Charlotte Brontë, that in Charlotte's day had been dismissed as 'plain' but which, allied to a slimmer-than-slim figure, had earned Miranda Brand a very comfortable income during the past two years as a fashion model.

I shall wear well, decided Miranda dispassionately. When I am seventy, people will say: 'Who is that distinguished-looking old lady?'

She laughed suddenly: being young enough to enjoy picturing herself in old age without believing in its possibility.

'What are you giggling about?' demanded Stella, completing her make-up with an expert hand before the mirror above the wash-

21

basin. She looked, once more, serene and poised, and as completely out of place in the dull setting of the hostel bedroom as an expensive orchid worn on the ample bosom of an elderly German *hausfrau*.

'Nothing,' said Miranda hastily. 'If you're ready let's go down and see if this caravanserai can produce some drinkable sherry.'

2

The dining-room of the Families' Hostel was large, long and high-ceilinged, and smelt strongly of past meals, floor polish and over-heated radiators. Miranda, seated at one of the larger tables between her cousin Robert Melville and a retired brigadier in the Control Commission, looked about it with interest.

The room was overfull of empty tables, but either the travellers who had been on the boat-train tended to huddle together, or else the German waiters, anxious to economize in time and labour, had shepherded them to conveniently adjacent ones.

The Melvilles' table was between one occupied by a Colonel and Mrs Leslie, and another shared by two of Robert's brother officers and their wives — Major and Mrs Marson and Lieutenant and Mrs Page.

Beyond the Leslies sat Mrs Wilkin and her five children. Mrs Wilkin, a small and sparrow-like woman on her way out to join her husband, a sergeant whose unit was stationed in Berlin, looked anxious and exhausted: and with good reason, since her offspring, who had been noisy and unmanageable for the past twenty-four hours, were now completely out of hand. The eldest Wilkin, addressed by his mother as 'Wally', was throwing bread. A demon-child, thought Miranda with a grin. Wally, intercepting the grin, paused in his bread-throwing and returned it. It split his plain, freckled face in an engaging though gap-toothed manner, and temporarily dispelled his striking resemblance to the Don Camillo imp. Conscious of an audience he threw an even larger piece of bread, and Miranda's gaze moved hurriedly on.

None of the other tables was occupied, and noting the fact, she felt childishly disappointed. And unreasonably annoyed with herself for feeling so. She had hoped to see someone else in that dining-room. Someone she had seen for the first time only the day before. But he was not there.

Miranda turned her attention to the soup, but as the meal progressed she became aware once more of that odd, indefinable prickling of apprehension. She wondered if perhaps she, like Stella, was overtired? Perhaps everyone in that echoing, ugly room with its depressing sea of empty tables was equally tired, and it was the accumulative effect of their weariness and taut nerves that created this inexplicable feeling of unease? Could tiredness, too, be the explanation of Mrs Leslie's odd behaviour? Miranda crumbled her bread and looked thoughtfully at the occupants of the table on her immediate left.

Colonel Leslie commanded one of the British regiments on duty in Berlin, and he and his wife Norah were returning there from three weeks' leave in England. Norah Leslie might well have stood for a model of the 'Army wife', for she was typed just as surely as though she had a placard about her neck proclaiming her status and occupation. One knew instinctively that she referred to her husband's regiment as 'My regiment', to the regimental wives as 'My wives', did her duty as to Welfare, and all that concerned the good of the battalion, played an excellent game of bridge, an adequate game of tennis and golf, read all the bestsellers, and was sincerely convinced that there was only one regiment in the British Army that counted.

The Melvilles' party had shared a carriage with the Leslies from London to Harwich, and it appeared that Norah Leslie had been a near neighbour of Robert's during their childhood and adolescence. But although Colonel Leslie had made polite conversation, Mrs Leslie had been curt to the point of rudeness. When, at Harwich, they had found the Harwich-to-Hook boat to be crowded and Stella, Miranda, Mademoiselle and seven-year-old Charlotte had been directed to a six-berth cabin, the other two occupants of which were Mrs Leslie and Elsa Marson, wife of

Major Harry Marson of Robert's regiment, Mrs Leslie had complained to the stewardess. She insisted that there had been a mistake, since her husband had expressly asked that a two-berth cabin should be reserved for them. The stewardess had been patient but unhelpful. She said that the boat was very full, and intimated that Mrs Leslie would have to make the best of it. Mrs Leslie had announced her intention of complaining to the authorities, taken several pills as a precautionary measure against seasickness, and retired to her bunk.

She was gracious to Miranda next morning as they waited in the Customs shed at the Hook, and inquired as to her reasons for coming to Germany. 'Oh, you're only coming for a holiday? A month? But what a very *odd* place to choose for a holiday! Now before the war——! But frankly, there's nothing worth looking at nowadays. Unless you are interested in mangled ruins, and even then, once you've seen the wreck of the Reichstag and a mass of rubble where the Chancellery and Hitler's bunker used to be, you've seen everything. Are the Melvilles relations of yours, or just friends? . . . You are Robert's cousin? I used to know Robert very well. His family lived almost next door to us for a great many years. I hadn't met his wife before. I didn't realize——' But at that point Robert and Stella had joined them, and Mrs Leslie had turned abruptly on her heel and walked away.

Robert had looked slightly surprised, and Stella hurt; she was unused to rudeness, and for a moment her blue eyes had widened and her mouth turned down at the corners like a snubbed child's. Miranda had felt both angry and curious: angry on her cousin's behalf, and curious to know what was behind Mrs Leslie's odd behaviour. Whatever the reason, it was patently clear that neither Robert nor Stella was aware of it.

Yes, mused Miranda, observing Mrs Leslie with a desultory interest from her place at the table in the Families' Hostel: there *is* something there. I wonder what? Norah Leslie was looking at her husband, but Miranda was sure in her own mind that her attention was not concentrated upon what he was saying, but on

25

the conversation at the Melvilles' table, and she was trying to decide why she should be so sure of this, when Mrs Leslie turned her head. It was not possible to tell whether she looked at Robert's squarely turned back, or his wife's face as she sat opposite him listening to Brigadier Brindley's views on growing sweetpeas. But the look itself did not require any interpretation. It is never possible to mistake naked hate.

Miranda turned away quickly; uncomfortable and more than a little startled. But no one else seemed to have noticed that smouldering stare. Brigadier Brindley had abandoned sweetpeas in favour of the ballet, and Robert and the elderly Swiss governess, Mademoiselle Marie Beljame, were occupied with Charlotte — Robert in answering his daughter's questions and Mademoiselle Beljame in fussily supervising her table-manners.

Charlotte, renamed 'Lottie-the-Devil-Cat' by Miranda, was a remarkably plain child who appeared to have inherited nothing of Robert's charm and outstanding good looks. Her mother, Robert's first wife, had been a beauty; but she had died giving birth to this plain little girl, and a year later Robert had married Stella Radley. Robert was younger than Stella by several years, though until now Miranda had never found it noticeable. But tonight, sitting in that unkindly lighted dining-room, it was suddenly apparent. Perhaps Stella's recent tears had something to do with it; or perhaps it was the contrast between Stella's carefully made-up face and the fresh, glowing prettiness of the girl who sat so near to her at the next table . . .

Sally Page had married a junior officer in Robert's regiment when she was barely eighteen, and despite four years of matrimony she still looked and behaved like a charming and giddy teenager. Andy and she had been stationed in Fayid during the two and a half years that Robert had been in the Suez Canal Zone, and now they too were rejoining the regiment.

If Stella looked like a florist's rose, thought Miranda, Sally Page looked like a wild rose: sweet and fresh, heartbreakingly young and essentially English. And from behind Stella's shoulder she was smiling now at Stella's husband. It was a revealing smile, as revealing as Mrs Leslie's look had been; and Miranda, observing it, was aware of a swift little jab of anxiety. No; perhaps it had not been such a good idea after all, this holiday in Berlin ...

'Number twenty-eight, did you say?' said Brigadier Brindley. 'Why, of course I know the house. And I can assure you that you will find it most comfortable. Quite one of the pleasantest houses in Charlottenburg. You have been fortunate.'

'That's what Robert says,' said Stella. 'But you know what army husbands are like. They tend to overdo the selling angle just to cheer you up.'

'Well, in this instance he is perfectly correct. A charming house, and quite undamaged. Interesting too: though only by association.'

'How do you mean?' Robert leant forward and joined in the conversation: 'Did it belong to some spectacular Nazi?'

'No, but it belonged to the mother of Herr Ridder — Willi Ridder. And I suppose one could almost call him a spectacular character. Or if not spectacular, at least mysterious and intriguing.'

'Do tell us,' begged Stella. 'I adore being mystified and intrigued.'

The Brigadier had a reputation as a raconteur, and was not at all averse to holding forth to an interested audience. He cleared his throat and took a small sip of wine.

'Willi Ridder,' began Brigadier Brindley, 'was a prominent member of the Nazi Secret Service. He was not one of those who took the spotlight at the front of the stage, but rather one of the puppet-masters who stayed in the background and pulled the strings. As far as outward appearances were concerned, he was merely a wealthy Berliner in high favour with the Nazi hierarchy.'

'And he lived in our house? It sounds as if it ought to be very Park Laneish,' said Stella.

'No, it was only his mother who lived in your house. He and his

27

wife lived in another house not so very far from yours, which is a ruin now: it stopped a stray bomb fairly early in the war, I believe. In spite of his wealth he lived comparatively simply. No large staff, just a married couple who lived in; one of them the cook-housekeeper and the other a sort of valet-cum-major-domo. There were the usual "dailies", I suppose, and reliable extra help who were called in only when required, for special occasions.'

The Brigadier paused as though he had made a point, and took another sip of Niersteiner, and Robert said; 'I don't suppose big shots in any Secret Service like having a lot of hangers-on around the house. Two dyed-in-the-wool trusties are probably preferable to a platoon of doubtfuls, even if it does mean that the soup is sometimes lukewarm and there is the odd spot of dust on the drawing-room chimneypiece.'

'Quite,' agreed the Brigadier. 'But in the light of after-events I am inclined to put a less obvious and more sinister interpretation upon it. In my opinion it was part of a plan.'

'What plan?' said Stella. 'How exciting you make it sound! Did you know this man Ridder?'

'I did,' said the Brigadier impressively. 'I met Herr Ridder in 1937 when he was over in England visiting the Gore-Houstons. Lady Gore-Houston was a cousin of mine, and she was, unfortunately — like some others I could name — inclined to be somewhat pro-facist in those days. In the following year I happened to be in Berlin for a short spell, and Herr Ridder invited me to stay with him. I spent only one night in his house, but my memory of that visit is most distinct — probably because I have thought of it so often since then . . .

'In the ordinary course of events I do not suppose I should have had occasion to recall it, and so the details would, in time, inevitably have become blurred in my mind. But owing to what happened afterwards I have frequently thought back over that brief visit with great interest.'

'What *did* happen?' begged Miranda, still young enough to wish to leap to the point of a story, and impatient of frills.

28

'All in good time, my dear,' said Brigadier Brindley, who disliked being hurried towards his dénouement and preferred to extract the full flavour of suspense from his story. He refreshed himself with another sip of wine before continuing.

'Perhaps you will remember — those of us who are not too young,' (here he made a courtly little bow in the direction of Miranda) 'that in the late spring of 1940 Germany made a savage and unprovoked attack upon Holland. Well, at that time there happened to be, in Rotterdam, a fortune in cut diamonds ready for transhipment to Britain and the United States. The Nazis were aware of this and their capture was an important part of the surprise attack. They knew exactly where they were, and they dropped special paratroops to surround the house. Only one of the men who was concerned in that operation knew what they were after, and that man was Herr Ridder, who was entrusted with the task of taking over the diamonds and bringing them back to Berlin. The plan worked admirably, and Ridder took possession of several million pounds worth of diamonds.'

Brigadier Brindley, well aware that conversation at the two neighbouring tables had ceased and their occupants were openly listening, paused to help himself with some deliberation to stewed fruit and custard.

'Oh, do go on,' urged Stella. 'What happened then? That isn't all, is it?'

'By no means!' said the Brigadier, accepting the sugar bowl handed to him by an interested German waiter: 'No, that is not all. *Danke*.'

A well-aimed bit of bread landed with a thump on the table, narrowly missing Brigadier Brindley's glass, and the Brigadier closed his eyes briefly and shuddered.

'May I eat my pudding at Wally's table?' asked Charlotte.

'*Mais non!*' said Mademoiselle firmly.

'Then I shan't eat my pudding,' said Charlotte, equally firmly: 'Why can't I? Wally's mother wouldn't mind. Daddy, can I eat my pudding at Wally's table?'

'You heard what Mademoiselle said, Lottie.'

'But she doesn't like Wally. She says he's a nasty, rude, rough boy. But I like him. Why can't I go? *I* shan't let him throw bread.'

'Oh, let her go,' said Stella impatiently, 'and then perhaps that child will stop heaving crusts. Don't let's have a scene. All right, darling, you can go and ask Mrs Wilkin if she'd mind your sitting at her table. But do behave nicely. No, there's no need for you to go too, Mademoiselle.' She turned back to Brigadier Brindley: 'Do go on. You were telling us about how Herr Ridder got the diamonds.'

'Ah, yes. The diamonds. Well, of course we knew — that is, our Intelligence Service knew — that the diamonds had fallen into German hands. And from our point of view that, so to speak, was that. We did not learn the end of the story — if indeed it can be said to have ended, which I doubt — until the war was over. It was only then, through the medium of captured documents and a certain amount of interested evidence, that we learned the rest of the story.'

The Brigadier paused and looked impressively about his audience, which now included all the occupants of the two adjacent tables.

'Willi Ridder, supposedly carrying the diamonds, returned to Berlin. He was flown in by night, and landed at Tempelhof airfield. His arrival was, purposely, as unobtrusive as possible. There he was met by his personal car and driven to his house. And neither he nor his wife was ever seen again.'

'You mean they were — liquidated, or purged, or whatever they called it?' asked Miranda. 'Because they knew about the diamonds?'

'No, they simply disappeared.'

'But what about the diamonds?'

'Those disappeared too.'

'You mean they skipped with the lot?' asked Robert.

The Brigadier gave him a reproving look, cleared his throat

again, and said: 'Possibly no one will ever know whether Herr Ridder and his wife had planned it carefully beforehand, or whether the fact that he suddenly found himself in possession of this fantastic fortune proved too much for him. But after reading some of the files on the case I am inclined to think that it was all planned. Ridder knew that Holland was to be attacked, and that he was to be sent in person to take over the diamonds. Then, you see, there was the new garage that was in the process of being built at the end of his garden ...'

The Brigadier paused expectantly, and Miranda did not disappoint him: 'What on earth had a new garage got to do with it?' she demanded, puzzled.

'Ah, what indeed! It was to be built of stone and brick, and large enough to take two cars. Stone needs mortar, and mortar needs quicklime. There was a pit of quicklime behind the garage so that the mortar could be mixed on the spot, and the building had been completed all except the roof. When Herr Ridder failed to report next day, a search was made of the house. There was no one in it, and no diamonds either. Later, the wreckage of the car and the body of the chauffeur were found in a town near the Dutch border. And later still the bodies of the cook and the valet were found buried in quicklime at the back of the unfinished garage in the Ridders' garden.'

There was silence for a moment, and Stella shuddered audibly.

'Did no one ever find out what had happened to the Ridders?' asked Robert.

'No. They could only guess. Their guess — and mine — is that Ridder and his wife murdered their two servants and used their passports and papers to conceal their own identity. The names of Herr and Frau Schumacher would have meant little to anyone; but far too many people in the S.S. knew Herr and Frau Ridder. The driver of the car was a picked S.S. man, but he would have thought nothing of being told to drive his employer and wife to some place outside Berlin. He would not have known about the diamonds — only a very few people knew. He obeyed Herr Ridder's orders,

31

while at the same time sending a detailed report of all Herr Ridder's movements to his chief in the S.S. The Ridders presumably shot him on a lonely stretch of road, and drove as far as they dared towards the Dutch frontier, leaving the car and the corpse in a town that was being bombed at the time. After that they ceased to be Herr and Frau Ridder and became Karl and Greta Schumacher, refugees.'

'But what do you suppose they meant to do?' demanded Robert. 'Where are they supposed to have gone? They couldn't have expected to get away. Why, I mean to say, the place must have been *crawling* with panzer divisions and all the rest of it at that time.'

'The supposition is that the diamonds never left Holland. That Herr Ridder managed to conceal them in some safe hiding-place and returned with an empty bag to Berlin. His intention being to go back and collect them, after which he and his wife would escape in the guise of refugees to England or Spain; and from there to America, which was not at that time in the war. With a fortune of such magnitude in their hands it must have seemed worth taking very great risks. And in the chaos of those days there were many people who escaped out of Europe. All the same, it should have been a fairly simple matter to trace them; and it is certain that the S.S. had no doubts as to their ability to do so.'

'And yet they got away.'

'They got away. And from that day to this they have never been heard of again; although ever since the war ended not only the German police but the police and Intelligence Services of four continents have been looking for them. They had a young child — a daughter I believe — who vanished too; though there was a story that the Ridders had sent her to relatives in Cologne some months before, and that she and her aunt had subsequently been killed with a great many other people when an air-raid shelter they were in received a direct hit. That may well have been true. Herr Ridder's mother was taken to a concentration camp and died there, but Willi and his wife and the diamonds apparently vanished into thin air.'

'Has nobody ever found a clue? Or heard even a rumour?' asked Stella.

'Yes, there was a clue. And though nothing ever came of it, I myself have always thought it provides the most intriguing part of the story. The unexpected and fantastic twist!' The Brigadier's voice was all at once less pedantic and almost eager, and it was obvious that the tale held a peculiar and recurrent fascination for him.

'In May 1940 a little band of refugees were landed in England from a small fishing boat. Among them was a child.'

'You mean you think it may have been the Ridders' child?'

'Oh no. This was an English child. Her parents had been in Belgium when the German attack came, and they had both been killed. None of the other refugees appeared to know anything about her and they had all imagined her to be French, for until an Englishwoman at the Centre spoke to her in English, and she replied in that language, she had only spoken French. She was sent with a batch of sick refugees — England was full of refugees in those days — to some hospital or home in Sussex, until she could be identified. She was carrying a large doll from which she refused to be parted.'

The silence about the table changed in an instant, and became curiously intent and charged with something far more than interest in an unusual story. But if the Brigadier noticed it he evidently put it down to his powers of narration.

'Some time later she broke the doll, and a kindly doctor offered to see if he could mend it for her. It was then discovered that the hollow body of the doll was stuffed with jewels and over five thousand pounds in high-denomination British and American banknotes. The child had no idea how they came to be there and could offer no explanation for their presence. She insisted that the doll had been given her for Christmas, and that nobody had touched it but herself. The jewels were later identified as being the property of Frau Ilse Ridder.'

There was a long, long silence.

Brigadier Brindley beamed complacently upon his audience, pleased at the sensation his dénouement had created. Robert was looking thunderstruck, Miranda's face had paled and she and Stella were staring at him literally open-mouthed.

'Well, I'm damned!' said Robert with explosive violence.

Stella's face flushed a vivid pink and she stuttered a little when she spoke.

'B–But – but — Oh, it can't be true! This is the most incredible thing I ever heard!'

'My dear lady,' said the Brigadier a little stiffly, 'I assure you ...'

'Oh, of course he hasn't made it up!' interrupted Miranda, her face pale and her eyes enormous. 'It's just a staggering coincidence. It's fantastic!'

'I am afraid I do not quite understand,' began the Brigadier, patently bewildered.

'No, of course you don't!' said Stella. 'How could you? It's just that your story has knocked all the wind out of us. You see it really is the queerest possible coincidence. That hospital you mentioned — the one in Sussex — well, it wasn't a proper hospital. It was only being used as a sort of nursing home during the war. It was my house — Mallow — and I was nursing there. And Miranda was the little girl with the doll!'

'Well, I'm damned!' said Brigadier Brindley, echoing Robert's words with equal fervour. He pulled out a handkerchief, and mopping his forehead looked a little wildly round the table. 'You are not by any chance pulling my leg?' he inquired suspiciously.

'No, I promise you we're not! It's quite true. Isn't it, Robert? Ask Miranda! She must remember it.'

'Of course I do,' said Miranda unsteadily. 'I dropped Wilhelmina — that was the doll — on the paving stones of the terrace, and her head came off. It had always been a bit wobbly I think. I was bathed in tears and despair, and a nice young doctor said he would mend her for me. He started in to see how she worked and before we knew where we were the place was a mass of diamonds and emeralds and banknotes. No wonder she was so heavy!'

Miranda shivered and made a little grimace, as though the memory was an unpleasant one.

'*Amazing!*' The Brigadier's voice was almost devout as he realized that he now had a story with which he could hold the attention of fellow diners for years to come.

'Wasn't it? I hadn't an *idea* how they got there, and I still haven't. To tell you the truth, I don't really remember much about what happened between the time the bombing started and arriving at Mallow. I don't think I wanted to remember it. But I do remember that they confiscated all Wilhelmina's stuffing, and I howled the roof off. I didn't mind about the banknotes, but the jewels sparkled, and I naturally thought that as they had come out of my doll I should be allowed to keep them. In the end they gave me a cheesy little chain bracelet to keep me quiet. It wasn't even gold or silver. Just a lot of thin links in some white metal, with a little Egyptian charm, an ankh, dangling from it. I lost the bracelet years ago, but I still have the charm. And what's more, I'm wearing it now! How's that for proof?'

Miranda held out her left hand with a flourish. About her wrist she wore a gold charm bracelet jingling with an assortment of miniature nonsense in the form of lucky coins, signs of the Zodiac, replicas of windmills, sailing boats and ship's lanterns, and among them, slightly larger than the rest, was a small ankh — the ancient Egyptian life-sign that appears again and again on the walls of tombs and temples in the Land of the Pharaohs, and can best be described as a loop standing on a capital T. It was fastened to the bracelet by a link attached to the top of the loop, and was made of some steel-grey metal that had been engraved on the flat surface with Egyptian hieroglyphics, and on the edge by deep parallel lines.

'I've worn it for years,' said Miranda. 'Stella gave me this bracelet for my tenth birthday, and I've added something to it almost every year. The ankh was the first thing to go on it, because at the time it was the only charm I possessed.'

'Really? This is most interesting,' said Brigadier Brindley. 'Extraordinarily interesting. Incredible! Might I have a look at that trinket?'

'Of course. Wait a minute and I'll undo the catch. It's a bit stiff. I've often meant to jettison that charm because it doesn't really go with the others, but now I shall cherish it as my prize piece.'

She struggled with the stiff clasp of the bracelet and having managed to remove it, handed it across the table to the Brigadier, who examined the ankh with absorbed interest and seemed disappointed.

'I'm afraid it's not very exciting,' apologized Miranda. 'It hasn't even got a date or a name or initials or anything on it. I remember a lot of men came and peered at it once, and one of them said it was modern and the signs on it were only for decoration, because they didn't make sense, but that it was made from some alloy that might be worth looking into. He tried to bend it, I remember. But it wouldn't bend, and because I thought he'd break it, I began to howl dismally, and one of the other men said, "Oh, let the kid have it!" and gave it back to me.'

The bracelet was passed around the table. 'It is very interesting, is it not?' said Mademoiselle, peering at it doubtfully before returning it to its owner.

'It's like a sort of fairy story, isn't it?' said Miranda pocketing the bracelet in preference to wrestling further with the clasp. 'A rather creepy one by the Brothers Grimm. I never did like their stories, anyway.'

'It is certainly a very remarkable coincidence,' said Brigadier Brindley. 'A most romantic story.'

'It is even more romantic than you think!' said Miranda with a laugh. 'In fact if it hadn't been for me, we should none of us be sitting here now. You see, I stayed at Stella's house while the authorities were trying to trace my next-of-kin, who turned out to be mother's brother, General Melville. Uncle David rushed over to see me, but he was just off to the battle, and as Aunt Frances was dead and their son — that's Robert here — was fighting

36

somewhere in the Middle East, he was in a bit of a flap as to what to do about me, and he simply jumped at Stella's noble offer to keep me for the duration. I never saw him again, because he got killed about a year later, but when the war was over Robert turned up to collect the family burden, and stayed and married Stella instead. And Stella and Robert asked me if I'd like to spend a month with them in Berlin — and so here we all are!'

'And there you have the end of your story,' said Stella.

Brigadier Brindley turned and looked at her, smiling. 'The end of *your* story, my dear Mrs Melville. But not the end of the story I have just told you. It is only another small piece of that story.'

'I see what you mean, sir,' said Robert. 'Your story won't end until the Ridders are discovered.'

'Perhaps they will never be discovered,' said Brigadier Brindley. 'And if so, no one will ever know the end. Perhaps they are dead — blown up by some bomb among the ruins of some broken city. I think it is very likely.'

'Why, sir?'

'Because if they were not dead, one of them at least should have been easy to trace. Frau Ilse had a deformity that was not a common one. The second and third fingers of her left hand were joined together. She had never attempted to have them operated on and was, curiously enough, rather proud of the fact, for she wore a specially made ring on the double finger. It was this ring that was largely responsible for establishing the ownership of the jewels found in — er — Wilhelmina.'

'But surely she could have had an operation performed?' said Robert. 'That sort of thing is not so unusual, after all. I've known of a case myself, a child who ...'

'Ah, a child,' interrupted the Brigadier with a tolerant smile. 'If it is done in childhood it does not leave quite so noticeable a scar. But to perform such an operation on a grown woman would be a more difficult matter, since it would undoubtedly leave scars that would be impossible to disguise. And that is why I feel sure that Frau Ilse, at least, is dead. A physical defect or peculiarity is like an illuminated sign: it attracts attention. And not only that. Once seen it is not forgotten. It sticks in the memory of the observer when all else has faded to a blur. One seldom fails to notice, or remember, a freak of nature.'

Miranda saw Mademoiselle's spine stiffen and her sallow face flush a painful shade of puce. The governess was one of those distressing persons who appear to be perpetually taking offence, and on this occasion she had obviously taken the Brigadier's words as a personal affront, since she herself possessed a noticeable physical peculiarity in that her eyes were of different colour — the left being blue and the right a grey that verged on hazel. A deviation from the normal that afforded Lottie and her young friends endless amusement. Mademoiselle had suffered a good deal from their uninhibited questions and comments, and Miranda, suspecting as much, smiled consolingly at her across the table. But Mademoiselle refused to be comforted. Her mouth narrowed into an offended line and she returned Miranda's smile with a frosty stare, and turned to Stella.

'If you will excuse, Madame, I would go now to find me some hot milk for the thermos. The little Charlotte will sleep better in the train if she drink the cup of hot milk when she is ready for bed.' She rose from the table and rustled away, wounded feelings in every line of her back.

Miranda suppressed her smile and turned again to Brigadier Brindley: 'What was she like?'

'Frau Ridder? Not a very remarkable woman in any way. Youngish, dark hair and eyes. Medium height, medium size, passably good-looking, but dressed in excruciatingly bad taste. I remember thinking that she must be colourblind. She favoured very bright colours. That peculiar and cruel shade of blue satin that sets one's teeth on edge.'

'And what about him? Herr Willi?'

'The same. A rather average Teutonic type. Blond and ordinary, except for a pair of very pale blue eyes that somehow gave you the impression that they could bore holes through the side of a battleship. A deceptive sort of chap. The kind who would always choose to be the power behind the throne rather than the man who sits on it.'

Stella said: 'Well, I've never been so thrilled in my life! I shall be able to dine out on this for the rest of my days. Robert, tell the waiter we'll have our coffee in the hall, will you, darling? Coming, Miranda?'

3

The train rocked and swayed to the clattering rhythm of the iron wheels, but Stella did not hear them for she was already asleep. She had borrowed two capsules of sleeping powders from Brigadier Brindley, who apparently never travelled without them, and these, combined with fatigue and the emotions of the earlier evening, had sent her into deep and dreamless sleep barely a minute or so after her head had touched the pillow. She had taken the upper berth, and the dim glow of the small reading-light at the head of Robert's berth below faintly illuminated her face and the blond waves of hair that were as neatly pinned for the night as though she had been in her own bedroom at Mallow.

Robert stood looking at her for a moment, swaying to the swing of the train. In that dim light she appeared strangely young and exhausted. Poor Stel', thought Robert, how she does hate it! But there was nothing he could do about it. He could not, as Stella wished, leave the Army. It was the only profession he knew and he had few illusions as to his abilities. If I'm lucky, thought Robert dispassionately, I may be able to retire as substantive lieutenant-colonel — but only if I'm lucky. That's about as far as I shall get. But if I chucked the Army now and tried for a civil job, I should probably end up as an office boy or a tout for vacuum cleaners. Stella doesn't understand. I'd retire tomorrow and try and farm the place myself, if we had the money. But we haven't, and that's all there is to it. It's a pity she hates this sort of life; it's not a bad one really, but I suppose you have to have some sort of vocation or a military background to enable you to follow the drum and like it.

He yawned tiredly and sat down on the edge of his berth to remove his slippers. He had not realized that the Pages would be on the same train. A bit awkward, their being in Berlin. He would have to be careful. Sally was a sweet creature, but ... Robert wriggled in between the sheets and switched off the light——

Fancy meeting old Brindley again! He hadn't seen him for over eight years — or was it nine? Not since before his father had been killed on the Anzio beaches. Queer story that. It had given Miranda a bit of a jolt. A fortune in diamonds, lost and perhaps still unclaimed. He could do with a handful of diamonds himself ... and who couldn't?

In the compartment next door Mademoiselle Beljame lifted a woollen dressing-gown of Edwardian design from an aged Gladstone bag, moving quietly so as not to wake Lottie who lay in the shadows of the upper berth. A flannel nightdress followed, and a pair of hand-knitted slippers. Mademoiselle laid them out upon the berth and half filled the small washbasin with warm water. The water sloshed to and fro with the movement of the train and made a soft, slapping sound that provided a counterpoint to the squeaks and rattles of the train. Mademoiselle peered at her watch and then held it to her ear to make sure that it was still going; it was late then! She placed the watch carefully on a little shelf over the basin and, catching sight of herself in the mirror above it, leant forward and peered intently at her reflection. It was time she gave herself another application of the dye. She lifted a bony finger and touched the centre parting of her severely dressed hair. Tomorrow, or the next day, she must see to it.

Before the war, thought Mademoiselle, you were a young woman. Yet now you are an old one. Old and ugly.

She drew a long, quivering breath, and began to undress. It was well that she had been able to procure hot milk for the child. And what luck that the elderly Englishman should have offered her a sleeping powder, for to sleep well on trains was not always possible. But tonight, thanks to the Brigadier, a sound night's sleep could be guaranteed.

'Well here we are, almost back in Berlin!'

Harry Marson yawned and pulled the blankets up about his chin: 'I shall be quite glad to get back to some central heating again. That house of Uncle Ted's is hellishly draughty — though I must admit that his port more than makes up for it!'

Major Marson ruminated for a moment or two, but his wife remained silent, and presently he spoke again.

'What did you make of that old bird's story this evening? Queer, wasn't it? I remember hearing about that chap Ridder when I was staying with Uncle Bill in Berlin before the war. I may even have met him. Odd coincidence about the Melvilles' kid cousin, wasn't it? If you read that in a book you'd say "too far-fetched". Except that when one comes to think of it, the Brigadier has probably told that story to so many people that the odds against his eventually telling it to another army chap like Robert are not so high as you'd think.'

There was still no sound from the lower berth.

'A fortune in diamonds!' mused Harry Marson. 'No wonder the blighter decided to stick to them. Any man of sense would probably have felt like doing the same. I wish to God I could get my hands on a fortune! In fact just now I'd settle for a thousand quid, cash down. How the hell we're going to—— Are you asleep, Elsa?'

But Elsa Marson was not asleep. She lay quite still, staring into the darkness and wishing with all her heart that the train was taking her anywhere but to Berlin. If only she need not have come back! If only Harry had allowed her to stay behind in England. But he would not hear of it: 'Not go back to Berlin? Don't be silly, darling! No housework, no servant troubles, no rationing; lovely house and loving husband. What more could you want? Besides I can't do without you — and anyway I can't afford to keep you at home.'

So here she was, with the train rushing remorselessly through the night and every mile bringing her nearer and nearer to the ruined, fear-haunted, faction-torn capital of Germany.

Elsa Marson, whose soft speaking voice with its slight broken accent so plainly proclaimed her foreign birth, turned on her pillow and wept for the safety of humdrum English towns with as passionate a longing as Stella had wept for Mallow: though her reasons for doing so were not entirely similar.

Odd seeing George Brindley again after all these years, thought Colonel Leslie. Wonder if he recognized me? Probably not. It's been a longish time. Just the same talkative ass. Sleeping pills! It used to be quinine. Never knew such a man for dosing himself. I wonder ... He climbed cautiously up into the upper berth.

Norah Leslie removed her hat, and taking off her gloves, frowned at the sight of their blackened palms and fingers. Continental trains were so dirty, and British ones almost worse. Perhaps if she gave them a quick wash now they would be dry before morning? The carriage was very hot and she could hang them near the pipes. She removed her coat and skirt and pressed the taps of the small fitted basin, wondering if her sons, left behind in England, would be asleep. Yes of course they would be. Hours ago! It must be very late ...

Her thoughts veered off at a tangent: Robert — Robert and that woman! Why had it got to be Robert? Why didn't men see through women like that? Selfish, spoilt, grabbing, dog-in-the-manger women. The kind who would always try and eat their cake and have it, and who so often succeeded in doing both.

Mrs Leslie reached for the soap and began to wash her gloves, scrubbing savagely at the inoffensive fabric.

Sally and Andy Page were quarrelling. They quarrelled too often these days and about too many trivial things. They were young, and had yet to learn that the strength of the matrimonial tie is not best proved by subjecting it to constant strain.

'All right then! You don't care a damn about him, and he's just a charming chap who dances like a dream! But is that any reason why you should look at him as though you were some frightful bobbysoxer goggling at the latest American crooner?'

'I did nothing of the sort!'

'Oh yes, you did! Everybody must have noticed it. It was quite blatant. You used to do it in Fayid, and now here you go again. One look at that glamorous profile, and you go weak at the knees.'

'The trouble with you,' said Sally furiously, 'is that you're small-minded and riddled with jealousy and inferiority complexes! Just because someone is better looking and better mannered and senior to you, you're jealous of him, and I'm not allowed to be even polite to him. If he were uglier and more junior, you wouldn't give a damn! I ought never to have married you. What do I get out of it? I pinch and scrape and save and wear old clothes and never have any fun, and when anyone under sixty speaks to me there's a vulgar, selfish, jealous scene!'

'Sally, you *know* that's not true!'

'It is! *It is!* You are jealous — and you're selfish too. You only think of yourself. You wouldn't let me have a fur coat, but you bought yourself that camera! You sit around and scowl and gloom, and when I talk to Bob Melville, who is amusing and interesting, you resent it and accuse me of behaving like a drooling bobbysoxer!'

'Sally, that isn't fair. You know it's not. You knew before you married me that we'd be very hard up. But you wanted us to get married at once ...'

'That's right! Blame it on to me. And I suppose *you* didn't want to marry me at all?'

'Darling, *don't*! You know I did. Desperately badly. Only I knew what it would let you in for. I can't buy you fur coats: and as for the camera, you know quite well that I swopped it with John Ellery for two quid and that set of hunting prints you liked. We shan't always be as broke as this, darling. And you do have fun, whatever you say. We never seem to stop going to parties. Or giving them — in fact that's what keeps us permanently in the red!

That, and the fact that you spend a small fortune on Chanel scent and Lizzie Arden make-up, and always having your hair done by the most expensive hairdresser you can find, even though you know quite well that it's "coals to Newcastle" and that you'd look every bit as good if you used no make-up at all and just left your face and your hair alone. No wonder we're always——'

'Oh, never mind,' said Sally drearily. 'Don't let's talk about it any more. We shall only start talking about bills again, and I can't bear it. I wish I had those diamonds that Brigadier was talking about. Millions! — just think of it! It isn't fair. I wonder who's got them now?'

But Andy did not answer.

Amazing! thought Brigadier Brindley drowsily. Quite extraordinary! Chance in a thousand ... He was asleep.

4

... clickety-clack, clickety-clack, clickety-clack. The train rushed on through the night towards Berlin, and Miranda began to put words to the monotonous song of the wheels as an alternative to counting sheep. It was long past midnight, but she could not sleep.

'I want to go home ... I want to go home ... I want to go home.' That would be Stella. Poor Stella! It must be cruel to have to live a life you hated in order to be with the man you loved. Well you can't have it both ways, thought Miranda. But why not? Millions of people did. Stella was just unlucky.

'Shan't go to bed! Shan't go to bed! Shan't go to bed!' 'Lottie-the-Devil-Cat'.

'Cela suffit! Cela suffit! Cela suffit!' Mademoiselle. A repellent woman, thought Miranda. Bony, greying and bespectacled: apparently suffering from a perpetual cold and given to nibbling caraway seeds like some desiccated Victorian spinster. It was difficult to realize that anyone like Mademoiselle had ever been young and lighthearted, yet traces of feminine vanity evidently lingered even in Mademoiselle's flinty bosom, for despite the fact that her scanty hair was obviously grey she persisted in secretly doctoring it with the contents of a small sticky bottle of dye; although the resulting jetty blackness, especially after a fresh application, added to rather than detracted from her years. She had been in Lille when the German Army had swept through France, and had been unable to return to her native Switzerland. Later, under suspicion of being involved with the Underground Movement, she had been sent to a concentration camp in which she had spent the greater part of the war. Mademoiselle was

46

fond of enlarging on her sufferings during that time, but although one could not help feeling sorry for her, it was impossible to like her.

Miranda yawned, wriggled, jerked irritably at her blankets, and wished fervently that she had accepted Brigadier Brindley's offer of a sleeping pill. She had refused them, watching with inward scorn as the Brigadier swallowed two with his coffee, and thinking that he was just the sort of man whom one would expect to carry about little boxes and bottles of capsules. 'Never travel without 'em!' said the Brigadier: 'Can't sleep in a train. I found that out years ago, so when I can't avoid travelling by night I take a couple of these. Works like magic. Like to try one? No after-effects I assure you. Excellent stuff.'

Mademoiselle, who had an incurable passion for pills in any form, had accepted one, and Stella had taken two, saying that she would try anything if only it would give her a decent night's sleep after the torture of the Harwich crossing. She had broken the small capsules in half, and stirring the powdered contents into her coffee, drunk it there and then. Miranda envied them their fore-thought.

There were not many passengers travelling to Berlin that night, and the train being half empty, Miranda and Brigadier Brindley had each been allotted a two-berth compartment to themselves. The Brigadier was next door to Miranda, and, she thought crossly, undoubtedly sleeping like a log. Somewhere down the corridor 'Lottie-the-Devil-Cat', soothed by hot milk, would be asleep and probably snoring (Lottie suffered from adenoids), while Stella and Mademoiselle, thanks to the Brigadier's pills, would also be sleep-ing soundly. Only she, Miranda, was awake ...

The narrow compartment was close and stuffy and she won-dered if she would do better on the upper berth, but a vague recollection that hot air rises caused her to abandon the idea. She threw off her blankets instead, and after a few moments discovered that it was, after all, colder than she had thought, and pulled them back again. She shut her eyes and tried to will herself to go to sleep,

47

but it was no use, and she opened them again and lay staring into the darkness.

A latch clicked somewhere near at hand and a faint thread of light showed under the locked door that lay between the two compartments. So much for the efficacy of the Brigadier's sleeping pills! thought Miranda.

The light vanished, and Miranda yawned and presently decided that she was thirsty. She would have a drink of water and read a book.

Almost on the heels of the thought she remembered that she had not got a book: she had lent it to Stella, and Sally Page had borrowed her only magazine during the afternoon and had failed to return it. Worse still, she had no drinking water, having upset the carafe while cleaning her teeth.

'Damn!' said Miranda, speaking aloud into the darkness.

She thought she heard someone pass down the corridor, and on a sudden impulse wriggled down to the other end of her berth, and groping for the handle of the door, turned it and pulled the door open. If the elderly and kindly faced sleeping-car attendant was patrolling the corridor to see if all was well with the passengers, he could probably get her a glass of water — or better still, a hot drink.

Miranda thrust her feet into her bedroom slippers and reached for her dressing-gown and having tied the sash round her slim waist, stepped out into the corridor and closed the door behind her. The attendant — if it had been him — had vanished, and the corridor stretched emptily away on either hand, bounded on the one side by a long line of closed doors and on the other by a blank wall of black window-blinds.

It was colder out here than it had been in her compartment. The train rocked and jiggled to the click and clatter of the flying wheels, but the corridor seemed uncannily silent, and for a fleeting moment Miranda had the disturbing fancy that behind every closed door there was someone who stood quite still, holding their breath to listen.

48

She shivered suddenly, and pulling the warm velvet folds of her dressing-gown closer about her throat, marched briskly off in search of the attendant.

The *Dienstraum*, the small cabin occupied by the sleeping-car attendant, was empty, and the lavatory beyond it boasted no drinking water. Miranda gave it up and decided to return to her own compartment: there was sure to be a bell there and it was stupid of her not to have thought of that before. Nevertheless she lingered by the open door of the attendant's brightly lit room, half hoping that he might return, and seized by an inexplicable reluctance to return down that long, cold, empty stretch of corridor.

What *is* the matter with me tonight? thought Miranda impatiently. Why do I keep imagining things? She would never have suspected herself of being a person subject to nerves or delusions, or even especially receptive to atmosphere; but even here, in a deserted corridor of the Berlin train, with a dozen people sleeping peacefully near at hand and twenty or thirty British troops not two coaches distant, she was conscious of a queer tremor of uneasiness: a prickling of the scalp as though unseen eyes were watching her, and a nervous desire to look over her shoulder.

Succumbing to that impulse, Miranda glanced quickly over her shoulder and started violently. But it was only the reflection of her own face in a looking-glass in the attendant's compartment that had startled her, and not someone standing behind her. Feeling exceedingly foolish and more than a little cross, and with her heart still beating uncomfortably fast, Miranda turned and walked rapidly back along the corridor.

The door of her compartment was ajar, and she pushed it quickly open and went in. It seemed very dark in there after the comparative brightness outside, and she groped for the electric light switch, but could not find it. Well, it did not matter, for she had lost all desire for a drink and could get back to bed quite easily in the dark.

The train rocked round a curve and Miranda's foot slipped

suddenly, and she stumbled and flung out a hand to feel for the edge of her berth.

But the berth appeared to be further from the door than she had imagined, and moving forward, she hit herself sharply against something hard and unyielding. Catching at the edge of it she discovered with surprise that it was one of the fitted basins with which each of the compartments was provided. But surely the basin had been on the opposite side of the carriage? Miranda took another cautious step and found herself touching a smooth wooden surface. Her berth seemed to have vanished.

And then suddenly she realized what had happened. She was in the wrong compartment!

The sleeping compartments on the Berlin train were in pairs, with a communicating door between each pair which could be opened if parents and children were travelling in adjoining compartments. The positions of berths and basins and light switches were reversed in each compartment, and Miranda, suppressing a strong desire to giggle, realized that she had invaded the bachelor sanctum of Brigadier Brindley.

Thank heaven for those sleeping tablets! thought Miranda fervently. At least she had not awakened him.

The door into the corridor was still ajar, and her eyes becoming accustomed to the darkness she could make out the Brigadier, lying imposingly upon his back with one arm hanging over the edge of the bunk and sleeping like the proverbial log. Miranda tiptoed to the door, and once in the corridor, closed it cautiously behind her.

A moment later she was back in her own compartment, sitting on the edge of her berth with the lights turned on and giggling helplessly.

What an idiotic thing to have done! How *could* she have been so stupid? How Stella would laugh!

All at once, and for the first time that night, Miranda felt relaxed and sleepy. She yawned largely and untied the sash of her dressing-gown. There was a wet smear on the velvet folds; she must have splashed some water on it from the basin in the next cabin. What a bore! thought Miranda, frowning. It was a new dressing-gown and its purchase had been an unwarrantable extravagance on her part. She brushed her hand over it. But it was not water ...

Miranda sat very still, staring down at the stain on her palm.

The carriage rocked and swayed in time to the clattering cadence of the wheels, and the harsh light of the ceiling bulbs threw a black, swaying shadow across the lower berth.

'It's the dye,' said a voice in Miranda's brain. 'It's only the dye from the velvet.'

But no dye was so richly red. So sticky ...

There was blood on the ruby-red folds of the dressing-gown. A wet, red patch of blood just above the level of her knee. Her stunned gaze moved slowly downwards towards the floor and her eyes widened incredulously, for there were marks upon the carriage floor that had not been there before. The dark, neat, damp prints of a shoe.

Miranda reached down with unsteady hands and pulling off her slippers sat staring at them in horrified unbelief. Both narrow leather soles were as wet and red as though they had walked through a pool of blood——

She dropped them onto the floor and stood up. There was only one possible explanation. The blood must have come from the Brigadier's compartment, and that meant the Brigadier had had a haemorrhage or broken a blood vessel. He might be bleeding to death! She must go to his help at once — surely there must be a doctor on the train?

Miranda jerked open the door of her compartment and stood once more in the cold, empty corridor. There were more marks on the floor of the corridor. The dark prints of her slippers, leading out of the door of the Brigadier's compartment.

This time she knew where to feel for the electric light switch, and it clicked under her hasty fingers.

The light seemed unnaturally bright and the clatter of the train wheels no more than a muted murmur like the sound of a sea shell held to the ear. The whole scene seemed to have taken on something of the detailed, lunatic quality of a Dali painting.

The train rocked and jolted and Miranda caught at the edge of the door to steady herself; staring, not at the silent figure on the narrow berth, but at the bright pool of blood upon the floor and the evilly stained knife that lay beyond it, half in and half out of the swaying shadow of Brigadier Brindley's overcoat.

She must fetch someone ... Robert ... Which was Robert's compartment? She could not remember. The attendant — surely the attendant would be back by now?

Miranda turned and fled wildly down the deserted corridor.

A man appeared at the end of the corridor: a slight young man wearing a heavy military overcoat and walking quickly towards her, and she had run into him and was clutching at him before she could stop herself. It was the man who had returned her bag to her at Harwich after she had walked out of the Customs shed, leaving it behind on the counter among the jumbled piles of hand luggage.

'Oh, it's you! *Do* something — quickly! He's dead!'

It seemed to Miranda that she had shouted the words aloud in the silent corridor, but to the man who steadied her with his arms against the sway of the train her voice was no more than a gasping whisper.

He put up his hands and caught her by her shoulders, his fingers gripping them painfully through the soft velvet, and stared down into her white, terrified face: 'What is it? Who's dead?'

'The Brigadier—— Oh, do come! Someone's killed him!'

The man did not speak, but for a moment his fingers bit into her shoulders. And then he had released them and caught her by the arm and jerked her round, and they were running down the corridor. He checked abruptly at the sight of the footprints outside the Brigadier's compartment, and pulled her to one side, his gaze moving swiftly from the prints to her bare feet, but he made no comment and pushed open the door.

Brigadier Brindley was lying as Miranda had left him: on his back and inclining slightly towards his right side, at the outer edge of the berth. His right arm hung down over the edge, the slack fingers touching the floor, and the blankets had been drawn back neatly as far as his waist.

The Brigadier had apparently worn dentures, and without them his face looked older and thinner. The breast of his lilac silk pyjamas was disfigured by a spreading stain, and blood from the wound in his chest had run down inside the sleeve on his right arm to form a pool on the floor.

The stranger stood quite still just inside the door of the small compartment. He appeared to have forgotten Miranda. He did not touch the body of the Brigadier or make any move to pick up the oddly shaped knife that lay on the floor, but his eyes, which were a queer pale grey that seemed to reflect the light like a cat's, were wide and bright and alight with some emotion that Miranda could not understand. They ranged slowly about the small, brightly lit compartment, noting, calculating, summing up and storing away detail after detail. Once he reached out and touched the dead man's cheek, but otherwise he did not move.

Miranda began to shiver, and her teeth chattered. It was a very small sound among the myriad noises of the train, but he must have heard it for he turned, and taking her by the arm went out into the corridor, closing the door quietly behind him.

Miranda spoke in a jerky whisper: 'Aren't you going to do anything? Get a doctor or – or something? He might not be dead.'

'He's dead all right. There's nothing anyone can do for him. Which is your compartment?'

'This one.' Miranda laid her hand on the adjoining door and saw a sudden flare of astonishment in the intent eyes.

'Who has the other berth in there?' The words were still spoken in an undertone, but this time they were clipped and hard.

'Nobody.' Miranda was shivering again and she found it difficult to speak. She saw her companion's eyes go once again from her feet to the prints on the floor of the corridor, and suddenly realized what he must be thinking: 'Those are mine,' she said unsteadily. 'But I didn't do it. I found him like that.'

The man looked at her oddly but made no comment, and pushing open the door of her compartment, he propelled her gently inside and said: 'Stay in there and don't move out of it until I get back.' He paused for a moment in the narrow doorway and glanced quickly about the small compartment as though assuring himself that there was no third person concealed there, and then without looking at her he closed the door softly and was gone.

Miranda sat down on the edge of her berth, her feet dangling just clear of the floor and jerking to the movements of the train and her hands locked tightly together in her lap.

A short time ago she had thought the compartment overheated. But now she was very cold, and she remembered that it was the first day of March. Outside the darkened windows the night air would be cold and sharp and tinged with frost, and that same cold air was seeping now through a hundred crevices into the warm atmosphere of the train, bringing with it a smell of wet earth and engine smoke.

It was very late. Soon they would reach Helmstedt, and after that the train would enter the Russian zone, where no window-blind might be drawn back, and guards would patrol the corridors. Miranda was seized with a sudden and passionate longing to be back in England; dear, safe, matter-of-fact England, where there were no Russian zones, sullen ex-Nazis or bullying 'People's Police', and trains did not keep closely drawn blinds over their windows by night or permit their passengers to be murdered in their sleep.

'... I want to go home ... I want to go home ... I want to go home,' chattered the wheels. But this time it was for her they spoke, and not Stella.

Because she had gone into the Brigadier's compartment would they think that she had killed him? It had been such a stupid thing to do. Would it sound like a story that she had made up ... a very thin story? 'I am so sorry, but I walked in by mistake——'

She wondered who that man was, and why he was going to Berlin? He appeared to be a person who knew what he was doing, and did it without fuss; an inordinately quiet-looking man. He had been on the boat, and on their train from the Hook. He had sat facing her, two tables away, in the dining-car, and she had thought that there was something about his face that was vaguely familiar. Once he had looked up, and encountering her speculative gaze, had smiled. Miranda had smiled warmly back at him; and had then been astounded and enraged to discover that she was blushing ...

There were footsteps in the corridor outside and subdued sounds of movement in the next compartment. People came and went, but always quietly, and the cold minutes seemed to stretch into hours. Then at last the handle turned and the man of the corridor was standing in the doorway.

He came in and closed the door behind him and stood looking down at her.

'Now, Miss Brand — that is your name isn't it? — do you mind answering a few questions?'

His voice was quiet and impersonal, and his face, thought Miranda, looked like the windows of the train — as though it had a blind drawn down over it.

'What were you doing in the next compartment?'

Miranda shivered.

'You're frozen!' His voice was suddenly kind and no longer impersonal and he reached up and pulled down the folded blankets from the upper berth, and wrapping one warmly about her unresisting shoulders, lifted her feet up onto the berth and tucked the second one about them.

'They'll dirty the blankets,' said Miranda childishly.

'What will?'

'My feet. They must be very dirty, because I took off my slippers. You see there was blood all over them and I ...' Her voice trailed away uncertainly.

He stooped and picked up the discarded slippers, and after examining them, dropped them back onto the floor.

'Do you mind if I sit down?' He took her permission for granted and seated himself at the far end of the berth, moving her feet over to make room; his head a bare inch from the low ceiling formed by the berth above them.

'Suppose you tell me all about it. What were you doing in there?' He jerked his head towards the locked door between the two compartments: 'Did you go in that way?'

'No. I went in by the door in the corridor. You see I couldn't sleep and I was thirsty, but I'd spilt my drinking water, and ...' Miranda was suddenly aware that there was more than a touch of hysteria in her voice, and she bit her lip and stopped.

'Go on.'

'I'm sorry. I seem to be behaving very badly. It's – it's the shock I suppose.'

'Don't let that worry you.' He smiled unexpectedly, as he had done once before on the train from the Hook. It was an extra-ordinarily pleasant smile that altered his face completely.

'Alec Guinness!' said Miranda abruptly. 'I knew you reminded me of someone!'

'Good God,' said the man absently, and Miranda flushed hotly, conscious that she had been gauche and schoolgirlish.

'As a matter of fact,' he said mildly, 'my name is Lang. Simon Lang. You were saying that you couldn't go to sleep ...'

Miranda took a deep breath and steadying her voice with an effort, told him exactly what she had done from the moment that she left her compartment in search of the sleeping-car attendant.

When she had finished Simon Lang said: 'Are you quite sure that's all? You don't remember anything else? No sounds from the next compartment or anyone moving in the corridor for instance?'

Miranda's eyes widened suddenly and she caught her breath in a little gasp: 'Yes. There was something else. I heard a door being opened and then I heard someone moving about in there. I thought it was funny — "funny peculiar", I mean.'

'What was peculiar about it?'

'Oh, nothing really, except that he had taken sleeping pills.'

'What's that?' Simon Lang's quiet voice had a sudden edge to it. 'How did you know that?'

'Because I saw him take them. We all did. He had dinner with us at the Families' Hostel in whatever the name of that place was, and he took them with his coffee. He said he couldn't sleep in trains unless he did. Mademoiselle and Stella took some too.'

'You say you all saw him take the pills. Who do you mean by "all"?'

'Well, all of us. That is, Robert and Stella — I mean Major and Mrs Melville, and the governess — Mademoiselle Beljame — and Lottie, Charlotte — she's only seven. But everyone else was having coffee in the hall too, and people were wandering in and out of that little office-cum-reception-desk thing in the hall, paying their bills and so on. I should think almost everyone must have seen him. He gave us a long lecture on sleeping tablets; apparently he had tried every known brand.'

'Let's have some names, please. Who else would you say was actually in the hall at the time?'

'Why? What does it matter?' Miranda was suddenly angry and completely exhausted. She had slept little during the crossing from Harwich and not at all during the past day. It was long past midnight, she had been subjected to a violent and horrible shock and she was very tired. So tired that she wanted to lean her head back against the wall behind her and sleep . . . and sleep . . .

Simon Lang said: 'I think we shall find that it matters rather a lot. Whoever killed the man in there must have known that he had taken a sleeping draught and was unlikely to wake. You can't just stab blindly at people in the dark. Or if you do, the chances are about a hundred to one against your hitting them in a vital spot. This was a quick stab straight to the heart, and whoever delivered it must have either turned on one of the lights or carried a torch. And known that it was safe to do so.'

'There was a light,' said Miranda tiredly. 'Mine was off, so I could see it at the edge of the door. It wasn't on for more than half a minute.'

'When was that?'

'I don't know. But only a few minutes before I went out in the corridor. I remember thinking "so much for the Brigadier's sleeping pills". And then I heard someone in the corridor and I thought it must be the sleeping-car attendant, so I got up and went out. But there wasn't anyone there . . .'

'This person you heard in the corridor — which way did they go?'

Miranda wrinkled her brow, and then shook her head. 'I can't remember. I don't think I knew at the time. It was such a soft sound; more an impression than anything else. Perhaps there wasn't anyone there after all.'

'Unfortunately we know only too well that there was,' said Simon Lang grimly. 'Now about the people who were in the hall of that hostel, please — and then you can go to sleep. Who else would you say was there at the time that the Brigadier took those sleeping pills?'

Miranda pondered the question. She tried to tick them off on her fingers as she spoke, and their faces seemed to float in front of her. Sally Page with her wild-rose face and her pretty shallow laugh, smiling that revealing smile at Robert. Andy Page, with his red hair and angry blue eyes. Elsa Marson, black-haired, dark-eyed, with her unmistakably foreign voice. Harry Marson, red-faced, cheerful, pugnacious and Anglo-Irish. Colonel Leslie, thin, tall and grey-haired, with an expression of dreamy boredom and a clipped military moustache. Mrs Leslie — dark hair streaked with grey, brightly coloured tweeds, Welfare and 'My wives' — who had looked at her, Miranda, with such hate . . . No, not at her . . . at someone else, surely? Who? She could not remember——

Who else? Mrs Wilkin, a bedraggled hedge-sparrow coping with a brood of unruly fledgelings. Wally, with his plain, freckled, pugnosed face and his endearing grin. A German waiter — several German waiters. And then there was Brigadier Brindley. Of course: he had been there too. But why had he forgotten to put back his teeth? He looked so very odd without them. Odd and old and pathetic . . .

Another face floated in front of her and blotted out the jumble of different faces. A strange face, and yet somehow familiar. It was someone she did not recognize, and yet felt that she had known all her life.

'It's time you got some sleep,' said the unknown face.

'That's a very sensible suggestion,' murmured Miranda. 'Good-night, Guinness.' She smiled drowsily at it, and was instantly asleep.

5

Miranda awoke to find the train at a standstill and cold grey daylight filtering into the carriage around the edges of the window-blind.

For a moment, between sleeping and waking, she thought that she was in her own bedroom and wondered why her bed seemed so narrow? Then almost in the same instant she remembered. She was in Germany — probably by now in Berlin — and on the other side of a door in her compartment lay the body of a murdered man.

Miranda's mind jerked away desperately from the memory of Brigadier Brindley as she had last seen him. She did not want to think of it. The thought of blood and that slack-mouthed dead face brought back too many things — forgotten and shadowy pictures of other dead faces; the sight and smell of death, and the horror and fear of that long-ago time when a small girl had been lost and alone in the terrible storm of war.

Pushing those memories resolutely back into a locked room of her mind from which they were threatening to escape, she sat up abruptly, knocked her head against the reading-light above her pillow, and pulling back the bedclothes was surprised to find that underneath them she was not only still wearing her dressing-gown, but was swathed in a cocoon of blankets.

That man — what was his name? — Simon Lang, must have pulled the bedclothes over her and subsequently tucked her in. Who was he? What was he? What had he been doing in the corridor so late last night and by what right had he questioned her? Why hadn't she refused to answer those questions and ordered him out of her compartment? She should have rung for the atten-

60

dant to fetch Robert. Instead of which she had sat meekly on her berth for hours on end waiting until a complete stranger should decide to come back and question her; and then, to make matters worse, she had made a gauche and personal remark about his appearance.

Miranda flushed hotly at the recollection and wriggled herself free of the enveloping blankets. He had probably thought that she was a gushing film-fan attempting to compliment him by comparing him to a popular actor, and had not realized that what had prompted her remark was less a matter of personal resemblance than the fact that it had suddenly occurred to her that he possessed an actor's face. A face that was in itself unremarkable, yet capable of altering completely to each change of its owner's mood; becoming a blank mask, or assuming a dozen different characteristics at will.

She bundled the blankets to one end of the berth and pulled aside the edge of the window-blind. It was daylight outside, and the train was standing at a station. There were several men who appeared to be policemen on the platform; one of whom stood with his back to the train, immediately outside her window.

Someone tapped on the door, and as it opened to admit Stella, Miranda saw that the blinds were no longer drawn over the corridor windows, and that beyond them a grey morning sky dripped a thin drizzle of rain onto railway tracks and gaunt buildings.

'You're awake,' said Stella. 'We were told to let you sleep for a bit. 'Randa, what a ghastly thing to happen! You found him, didn't you? Hurry and get your clothes on. They want to see us. No, don't pull up the blind. The platform is cordoned off and crawling with policemen. I'll turn the light on. Here's a cup of tea for you. It's not very hot, I'm afraid.'

She turned on the light, and closing the door behind her, sat on the edge of the berth and continued to talk while Miranda swallowed the lukewarm tea, washed in cold water and dressed in a hurry.

Stella looked both excited and resentful, and her voice had an injured edge to it as she explained that their section of the train had been shunted into a side platform on arrival at Charlottenburg station, and that no one had as yet been allowed off it — although all the passengers from the other coaches had left. A police guard had been placed on it, and hot tea and sandwiches produced by a uniformed member of the W.V.S. But they had already been stuck there for over two hours while police and special service officers had, according to Stella, swarmed all over the train taking photographs and hunting for clues and fingerprints.

'And they've taken all our luggage off,' complained Stella indignantly. 'They wouldn't let us keep a thing. They just came and took everything, and said that we'd find it all ready for us when we left. A man called Lang seems to have arranged it all. He was on our train from the Hook and he seems to be something to do with police or intelligence or M.I.5. He told Robert what had happened and explained that since you'd been kept up pretty late over all this, you might as well be allowed to sleep. He says that we shall all have to answer a few questions and then they'll let us go. It's only a matter of routine, or something silly. He let Robert and Colonel Leslie talk to some people who had come down to meet us. Oh, and he said to tell you to leave all your things in the carriage. He'll see that you get them back.'

'So I should hope!' said Miranda crisply. 'Switch off the light, will you, Stella.' She pulled up the blind and let in the wet daylight. 'Have I got to leave my bag as well? It's got my passport and all my papers and things in it.'

'No. We're allowed to keep those. But I gather they'll want to have a look at them too before they let us leave.'

'Well, I think it's a lot of nonsense,' said Miranda unreasonably. 'I suppose it's just that officious Guinness creature throwing his weight about!'

'Who?' inquired Stella, puzzled.

Miranda flushed and bit her lip. 'That man Lang. Why on earth can't he just let us go off to our own houses and answer questions later on?'

'But don't you understand?' said Stella impatiently. 'They think one of *us* did it!'

'Don't be silly,' begged Miranda, shivering. 'Of course they can't. It was obviously some thief who got into the carriage at one of those stations we stopped at during the night. It *must* have been.'

'They say it couldn't have been. I don't know why, but they seem to be quite sure. They say it must have been someone in this coach.'

Stella gave a little shudder that was half disgust and half unwilling excitement, and Miranda, looking at her, realized suddenly that none of this was real to her. It was merely some fantastic story in which she did not believe and had no part. She might resent the temporary inconvenience that it caused her, but her resentment was to a certain extent offset by interest in what was, to say the least of it, an unusual situation.

But then Stella, thought Miranda, had not seen the dead face of Brigadier Brindley, or that hideous, sprawling stain across his breast and on the carriage floor.

Miranda shivered again and turned away to touch up her mouth with lipstick, annoyed to find in the process that her hand was not entirely steady, and that the face that looked back at her from the square of mirror was unnaturally pale in the cold light: the grey eyes with their lovely tilting lashes wide and frightened. She pulled the collar of her soft squirrel coat close about her throat and said: 'I'm ready. What do we do now? Just wait here until someone comes to put the handcuffs on us?'

Stella said: 'Darling, you *are* upset! I'm so sorry. What a pig I am: I forgot how utterly hellish it must be for you. I ought to have been distracting your attention instead of talking about this sordid mess. Leave all this clutter and come and sit in our carriage. I daresay the police are very neat packers.'

'What about the children?' asked Miranda, closing the door

behind her. 'Lottie and the Wilkin kids? It's a bit tough on them being kept hanging about like this with no breakfast.'

'Oh they're all right. A charming W.V.S. girl turned up and took them all off to have a meal in some refreshment room or other. I don't envy her the job; the Wilkin gang are a bit of a handful. Mademoiselle is madly upset because she wasn't allowed to go with Lottie. She's soaking herself with smelling salts and muttering in French. What a trial foreigners are! Robert darling, here's Miranda, and we're both famished. When do you suppose they're going to let us off this beastly train?'

Robert, who had been staring out of the window with his hands in his pockets, swung round and smiled at Miranda, and she thought fleetingly, and for perhaps the hundredth time, how astonishingly good-looking he was. It was what most people thought when they looked at Robert, and some of them added as a mental note 'too good-looking'.

'Hullo, 'Randa. I hear you had a pretty hectic night?' He put his arm about her slim shoulders and gave her a friendly hug. 'What exactly happened? Why didn't you call me?'

'I meant to,' admitted Miranda, sitting down tiredly on the edge of the lower berth, 'but I couldn't remember which compartment you two were in. How much longer are we going to stay here, Robert?' She did not wish to discuss the happenings of the past night and hoped that the question might sidetrack him.

'Not much longer, I imagine,' said Robert, turning back to the window again. 'They appear to be taking the Brigadier away at last: can't think why they didn't do it earlier.'

Stella went to stand beside him and their bodies shut out the view of the grey platform so that Miranda did not see the stretcher-bearers carry a blanket-covered burden past the window.

A few minutes later a military policeman walked along the corridor and told them they were to leave the train, and Stella slipped into a silver-grey musquash coat and picked up her handbag: 'Ready, Miranda?'

They left the compartment and were ushered, with the other

64

passengers of the coach, along endless yards of wet platform under the curious gaze of the police guard and a sprinkling of unidentified bystanders, down a flight of steps, along a chill, vaulted passageway and, eventually, into a hastily cleared waiting-room where several officials and three British officers in uniform were grouped about a table. Suitcases, hatboxes, and other pieces of hand luggage that had accompanied the passengers on the sleeping coach, were neatly arranged against the wall.

'Isn't it thrilling?' whispered Sally Page, catching at Miranda's arm. Her blue eyes were wide and excited and she looked impossibly fresh and dewy — in marked contrast to the majority of her fellow-passengers, who appeared jaded and travel-worn: the men unshaven and the women weary.

Mrs Leslie, huddled inside a shapeless coat of purple tweed and wearing a muffler and fur gloves, was looking cold and cross and managing to convey without words that in her opinion the wife of a commanding officer of a regiment should be entitled to more consideration. She said acidly, for the benefit of anyone who might be listening: 'I can see no reason why we should be kept here. It's not as if I had even seen the man before.'

Colonel Leslie was looking bored and resigned, Major Marson amused and Andy Page sulky, while Elsa Marson and Mrs Wilkin were talking earnestly together in undertones; discussing, incongruously enough, the respective merits of gas and electric cooking stoves. Mademoiselle, wearing an expression of the deepest suspicion, had ostentatiously taken up a position by her own and Charlotte's luggage as though she feared that at any moment it might once again be reft from her.

There was no sign of Lottie or the young Wilkins, but Simon Lang was there, standing with his back to the window; his slight figure dark against the grey daylight and his bland, actor's face entirely expressionless. His eyes seemed to be focused on nothing in particular and he appeared to be relaxed and almost lethargic. He did not look at Miranda, or indeed appear in the least interested in the proceedings, but she had an uncomfortable conviction that he missed no word or gesture or fleeting expression from anyone in that room, and that he was in fact about as relaxed as a steel spring.

The proceedings were mercifully brief. Each passenger in turn produced a passport or identity card, gave the address to which they were going, and, in the case of the women, handed over their handbags for a cursory inspection. Sally Page's, Mrs Leslie's and Stella's each contained a cigarette lighter, and these were taken away and put into envelopes marked with the owner's name. Robert, Andy Page and Colonel Leslie also handed over lighters, which were treated in the same manner and added to a row of six torches that lay on the table and had evidently been removed from the passengers' luggage.

A small snapshot had fallen unnoticed from among the jumbled contents of Sally Page's bag, and Miranda, seeing it, stooped and picked it up: 'Here, Sally, you've dropped this.' She held it out, and Sally turned, and glancing at it, snatched it from her hand and crumpled it swiftly in her own.

'Oh ... thank you.' Her cheeks were scarlet, and Miranda was seized with a sudden and uncomfortable suspicion as to who had been the subject of the snapshot. She looked thoughtfully across the room to where Robert stood talking in an undertone to one of the British officers, and as though he felt her gaze, Robert looked up at that moment, and catching her eye grinned at her. Miranda flushed guiltily, ashamed of her suspicions, and Simon Lang saw the flush and misinterpreted it.

The last handbag was returned to its owner and the passengers were informed that they could now remove their luggage, with the exception of the torches and the lighters which would be returned as soon as possible. There were cars outside to take them to their several destinations.

A middle-aged man wearing a dark blue uniform with the crown and star of a lieutenant-colonel apologized charmingly for any inconvenience they might have suffered and thanked them for their patience and co-operation. Mrs Wilkin was led away to collect her offspring, and Mademoiselle hurried off in search of Charlotte, clutching a piece of luggage in each black-gloved hand and refusing all offers of assistance. Only Miranda was still luggageless.

'When do I get my things?' she inquired of the affable gentleman in the blue uniform. 'I was told to leave everything in my carriage and I've left two suitcases and a hatbox in there.'

'Well — er—— It's Miss Brand isn't it? I am sure your luggage will be along soon. If you would not mind waiting——' The affable gentleman looked suddenly less affable, and Simon Lang abandoned the contemplation of his shoes and spoke for the first time.

'I'll send them along to the hostel. There's no need to wait for them. I expect you could all do with some breakfast.'

He looked directly at Miranda, but voice and look were as blankly impersonal as though he were addressing someone he had never seen before.

'I'll wait,' said Miranda flatly. She was both annoyed and frightened. Why had they kept all her hand luggage? Why was Simon Lang behaving as though she were some complete stranger?

'I wouldn't advise it,' said Simon Lang softly. 'We are a little busy just now and it might mean waiting an hour or so. You shall have them as soon as possible.'

Miranda wanted to cry out to him: 'You mean when you have looked for bloodstains! But you know there are bloodstains — you saw them last night! I showed them to you myself. Why do you have to look again?' She choked back the words with an effort that made her hands tremble, and turning blindly away, caught at Robert's arm, and clinging to it, walked quickly out of the room.

Stella, following, said: 'Darling, don't look so upset! I'm sure they'll let you have your stuff soon, and if there's anything you need in the meantime I can probably lend it to you.'

'He's a suspicious, soft-spoken, officious little man!' said Miranda furiously; unaccountably near to tears.

Robert said: 'Who? Lang? I think he's rather a decent type. He

67

went quite a bit out of his way to be helpful this morning. Why have you got your knife into him, Miranda?'

'I haven't. I mean . . . is this the car?'

'Yes. Get in. This is a Volkswagen. The Families' Hostel, please, Corporal.'

Stella said: 'What about Lottie and Mademoiselle? We can't all fit into that.'

'I've sent 'em on ahead with the Leslies. Colonel Leslie very decently offered to drop them at the hostel. The Pages are going there too, so Andy will keep an eye on them.'

Robert bundled them into a small khaki-green beetle of a car driven by a corporal in battledress, and they drove away from Charlottenburg station in the thin, drizzling rain.

Looking back on it, Miranda could never remember much of her first sight of Berlin. She had stared out with unseeing eyes at grey buildings and grey rain. At blocks of shops and houses, interspersed with open spaces where only a rubble of bricks and stone and blackened, twisted steel remained to show where other houses had once stood. At unfamiliar notices that said *Fleischerei*, *Friseur*, *Bäckerei*, *Eisengeschäft* . . .

Robert, who had been in Berlin for several months before he had returned to fetch Stella and Charlotte, pointed out various places of interest as they passed.

'That's the Rundfunk, Stella; the Soviet-controlled wireless station, the one the Russians still keep in our zone. It's a bit of a mystery still. Looks as dead as a morgue, doesn't it? You never seem to see anyone going in or coming out of it, and I've never met anyone who has even seen a face at one of the windows. But I suppose there must be a collection of comrades circulating around somewhere inside it. That? . . . That's a circus that's doing a season here. Very good one. I went with a party one night. We must take Lottie, she'd love it. That's the Funkturm. Sort of Eiffel Tower effect. You can go up it in a lift and have a look at Berlin from the top, or eat in the restaurant in that bulgy bit halfway up — if you can afford it. It's supposed to be the highest building with the highest prices in Berlin; one of those places where they soak you ten bob for a cup of tea and fifteen-and-six for a biscuit to go with it. That's the Naafi building, where you'll do a good bit of your shopping; this used to be called Adolf Hitler Platz, but it's now called the Reichskanzler Platz. Here we are; out you get. Down that paved path and the door's straight ahead of you. Run, or you'll get wet.'

Robert had decided that it was better for them to spend the first night at the Families' Hostel, so that Stella need not bother with meals and housekeeping while taking over the new house, which they would move into on the following day.

The hostel was a large, tall building where they were taken up in a lift and then down a long passage, vaguely reminiscent of a hospital, to two rooms on the third floor. There were sounds of splashing from an adjoining bathroom, and Lottie's voice and Mademoiselle's singing *'Malbrouck s'en va t'en guerre'*.

The Melvilles' luggage was carried into the larger bedroom, the smaller one being already strewn with toys and redolent of caraway seeds. Stella went off to talk to Lottie, and Robert turned to the German who had carried up the suitcases: 'Where is this lady going? We need another room. A single room for the *fräulein*.'

The man nodded cheerfully. *'Ja, ja.* The *fräulein* will come with me, please.'

He led Miranda back down the passage, and after several turnings ushered her into a small room that looked down upon an open concrete space and the ruined shell of a bombed building, and departed.

Miranda pushed open the window and stood looking out at the grey sky and the falling rain, and down at the ruined walls.

So this was Berlin! It had sounded so exciting. 'Where are you going for a holiday this year, Miranda?' 'I'm going to Berlin!' *'Berlin?* My dear, what fun! Bring us back some lovely cut-glass and don't get arrested by the Russians!'

Well, she was here; and she wished passionately that she was back again in the tiny flat near Sloane Street. Oh, how right Stella had been! Travelling in foreign countries was all very well when things went smoothly, but when everything went crazily awry, as they had last night, it was an additional horror that one was in a strange land and surrounded by unfamiliar things and people. She had not felt like this — frightened and unsure and lost — since she was a small girl wandering through terrible, ruined streets and crying for parents whom she was never to see again.

It was not only the sight of a murdered man that had brought those days back, dragging them out of that dark attic in her mind into which her conscious and subconscious mind had thrust them. She should never have come here, to this shattered city where the very language in the streets tugged at shadowy memories that were better forgotten.

6

Robert had left for the barracks, and Stella, Mademoiselle and Lottie had all gone off to see the new house. There had not been room for Miranda in the Volkswagen.

'Are you sure you don't mind being abandoned like this?' Stella had inquired anxiously. 'I'd leave Mademoiselle and Lottie instead, but I know Lottie would only rampage up and down the passages with that awful Wally, and Mademoiselle may as well start making herself useful in the new house.'

'No, of course I don't mind,' said Miranda untruthfully. 'In fact I'd far rather stay quietly here and have a hot bath.'

But she did mind. She did not want to be left alone in this large, strange, impersonal building with its rabbit-warren of passages and stairways that smelt faintly of disinfectant, hot pipes and stale cooking, and its windows that looked out upon grey rain and grey, bomb-scarred buildings.

Her own luggage had still not arrived, but the Melvilles had left a cake of soap and a bath towel in the bathroom adjoining their rooms, and Miranda lay and soaked until the water cooled, and then dressed slowly. But there was still an hour and a half to fill in before the others would return for lunch.

She combed back her dark, shining waves of hair, pinning them so that they curled above her ears, and wondered if the Pages were still in the hostel — only to remember that Andy too had left for the barracks and Sally had announced her intention of taking over her new flat, which was less than five minutes' walk away. And neither the Leslies nor the Marsons would be at the hostel, for they had driven direct to their own homes.

Miranda decided to go down to the lounge and see if there were any papers or magazines she could read.

She did not use the lift, but walked down by the stairs, and turning left at the first landing found that she had lost her way. There was no lounge or dining-room here: only a narrow hall with bedrooms leading off it. She paused, at a loss. Should she have turned to the right, or was she on the wrong floor? As she hesitated, she heard the lift come up from below and stop at the landing that she had just left. There was a subdued clash of metal as the doors slid back, and someone began to talk swiftly and urgently in German.

Once, long ago, Miranda had spoken German with a child's fluency; but she had forgotten it, with much else, and the conversation on the landing, even if she could have heard it clearly, meant nothing to her. But the voice that spoke in an undertone barely above a whisper held an unmistakable ring of desperation that was oddly disturbing.

It was a woman speaking; a woman not far from tears, who was answered by another; a sullen voice this time, clearer and harsher. 'Not so loud!' begged the first voice, unexpectedly in English. There were footsteps on the stairs above the landing and Miranda heard one of the women gasp in alarm, and realizing that she herself would seem to be eavesdropping she turned and walked around the corner and back onto the landing.

A dark-haired woman, hatless and wearing a wet raincoat, was standing with her back to Miranda, and a second woman was entering the lift. The steel gates clashed together and the lift sank out of sight as the woman in the raincoat turned on her heel, and brushing past Miranda disappeared round the corner into the passage.

Miranda stood on the narrow landing and frowned into the darkness of the empty lift-shaft, thinking that she must have been mistaken. She had only caught a brief glimpse of the back of the woman who had entered the lift, but the colour and cut of the coat had been familiar, for Mrs Marson had worn a similar one during the journey to Berlin. But Mrs Marson spoke no German. She had said as much on the platform at Bad Oeynhausen, when there had been some difficulty over a porter, and Stella, whose German was halting and rusty from disuse, had had to act as interpreter.

The woman on the landing had spoken fluent German, so obviously it could not have been Mrs Marson; there were probably plenty of women in Berlin who wore dark red coats with black *passementerie* on the collar and cuffs, and small black hats. All the same, it was odd and unsettling, and of a piece with the strange, uneasy atmosphere of the past forty-eight hours. But it was not to be the only unexpected incident of that morning.

As Miranda reached the turn of the stairs leading down to the next floor, a man coming from the direction of the dining-room and the lounge passed quickly along the landing below her and vanished down the staircase leading to the ground floor. It was Robert. Then it must be later than she thought, and Stella would be back!

Miranda reached the lower landing and turned to her left, and this time she was on the right floor for the lounge lay before her. But the hands of the clock stated that it was barely fifteen minutes to twelve, and standing alone in the middle of the lounge, facing the door, was Sally Page.

'*Oh!*' said Sally Page on a half gasp. 'Oh—— Hullo, Miranda.' Her flower face flushed pinkly.

'Hullo,' said Miranda, surprised. 'I thought you were taking over your flat?'

'I am — I mean I was. But it all seemed such a muddle that I thought I'd wait until Andy could give me a hand. There's a corporal there now checking lists, and the carpets are old and dirty and hideous and none of the curtains seem to match——' Sally's voice was a little breathless and she appeared to be talking for the sake of filling an awkward silence — 'so I just gave it up and thought I'd come back here and see if I could get a cup of coffee or something. But as there doesn't seem to be anyone about, I think I'd better run back. Perhaps I shouldn't have walked out on them.'

Miranda did not attempt to dissuade her, and with a childish toss of her head and a heightened colour, Sally walked quickly out of the room.

Miranda looked after her thoughtfully. Surely Robert couldn't be such a fool as to ...? There you go again! she accused herself. Imagining things. Making mountains out of molehills like some gossiping old spinster. What if Sally *has* got a schoolgirl crush on Robert? A good many far more mature women had experienced something of the same emotion when looking at him, and those same women probably cherished a sentimental admiration for some glittering and unobtainable hero of the screen, which in no way impaired their affection for their own far less spectacular husbands!

As for Robert, he had probably had some perfectly legitimate reason for making a brief return to the hostel, and there was no need to suppose that he had been keeping a sentimental assignation with Sally.

Miranda picked up a dog-eared copy of a women's magazine and determinedly embarked on a story that turned out, maddeningly, to be the first instalment of a full-length novel.

Mademoiselle and Lottie returned at lunchtime with a message from Stella to say that she was having lunch with the Marsons, whose house was near hers, and would probably return for tea. And a few minutes later Robert rang up to say that he was lunching at the Mess; adding that they would be moving into the house next morning.

Miranda's luggage was delivered at the hostel after lunch and carried up to her room with the assistance of Mademoiselle and Lottie. Mademoiselle's offer to stay and help unpack being refused, she swept Lottie off to rest, and Miranda was left alone.

Whoever had examined the contents of her suitcases had re-packed them with incredible neatness but a complete disregard for the cut of feminine clothes. Even her rolled underwear had been folded into small squares the size of a man's handkerchief.

Miranda removed only what she would need for the night and left the suitcases on the floor.

The thin drizzle of the morning had turned to a steady rain that drummed on the window ledge and spattered up against the panes. But except for the sound of the rain, the room and the rambling building and the wet afternoon seemed very quiet.

A hinge creaked faintly in the silence, and reflected in the dressing-table mirror Miranda saw the door behind her opening very softly, an inch at a time, as though a draught swung it slowly inwards.

Something moved in the widening gap — a face. A hideous, idiot face of white and scarlet blotches with a wide grinning mouth. And for a brief moment Miranda's heart seemed to jerk in her breast and her breath stopped. The next moment she had swung round and leapt at the door.

The head dodged back and its owner fled down the passage with Miranda in pursuit.

The small figure darted round the turn of the passage, and Miranda, rounding it a split second later, crashed full tilt into someone coming from the opposite direction; and for the second time in less than twelve hours found herself in the arms of Simon Lang.

'Oh!' gasped Miranda furiously, tears of fright and rage in her voice: 'Now look what you've done! I'd have caught that little horror if it hadn't been for you!'

'What little horror? The small boy who just streaked past me?'

'Wally Wilkin! I'd like to murder that child!'

Her voice broke on a sob; and then a sudden realization of what she had said, and to whom she had said it, struck her like a slap in the face, and she jerked herself away from Simon Lang's supporting arm, her white face flushing scarlet. 'And that doesn't mean I murdered the Brigadier last night, so you needn't look at me like that!' she said, her voice unnaturally high and unsteady.

'Take it easy,' advised Simon Lang mildly. 'What's the matter? You seem a bit upset.'

'So would you be if that sort of thing came peering round a corner at you!' She gestured to where a brightly coloured cardboard mask, cut from the carton of a well-known brand of breakfast cereal, lay on the floor.

Simon Lang's lips twitched and Miranda said tremulously: 'You needn't laugh! It scared me.'

'I can see it did. And I'm not laughing. You're feeling pretty jumpy, aren't you? Is it that business of last night, or is it something else?'

'I don't know.' Miranda's anger had suddenly evaporated and she felt tired and bewildered. 'Partly last night, I suppose. But it's not only that. I just wish I'd never come to Berlin. I thought it was going to be such fun, but it's been hateful instead. Hateful and frightening. What are you doing here?' she finished abruptly.

'I wanted to talk to you. Has your luggage arrived all right?'

'Yes, thank you. Is that all you wanted to talk about?'

'No. Do you mind if we go along to the lounge? There isn't anyone there just now, and I think it would be more comfortable than standing talking in the passage — and more in keeping with the conventions than using your bedroom.'

The lounge looked gloomy and inhospitable in the grey light of the wet afternoon. There was no one else there and the whole hostel appeared to be empty and deserted.

Simon Lang selected two armchairs farthest from the door and offered Miranda a cigarette. He lit it for her and she looked up from leaning down to the lighted match and met his eyes. The flame was reflected in them, turning them to an odd shade of amber and there was a curious look in them very like surprise.

Miranda sat back in her chair and said uncertainly: 'Why do you want to see me? Who are you?'

'The Officer Commanding 89 Section Berlin, if that means anything to you; and in the regretted absence of the D.A.P.M. Security and Intelligence Branch, who is at present incarcerated in an isolation ward with mumps, this murder is my pigeon.'

76

'Oh,' said Miranda, and was silent for a moment. 'What do you want to talk about?'

'About you,' said Simon Lang amiably: 'I'd like you to tell me again just exactly what happened last night. Try and remember everything, however trivial it may seem.'

Miranda thought for a moment. 'I couldn't go to sleep,' she began ...

She told the story as accurately as she could, trying to relive it exactly as it had happened, and Simon Lang listened without interruption, and when she had finished, said: 'You say that you felt nervous and on edge the first time that you went out into the corridor, and as though you wanted to look over your shoulder. Any particular reason why you should have felt like that? Are you sure that you hadn't heard or seen something that had frightened you?'

'Quite sure. There wasn't anything to be frightened of. Not then. That's what made it all so silly. Anyway, it wasn't just on the train. I'd been feeling a bit Aunt Hettyish all day.'

'A bit *who*?'

Miranda flushed. 'I'm sorry. It's a sort of family catchword of the Carrells — that's Stella's — Mrs Melville's — family. They've got an aunt who detests cats, and she's always saying: *"I have a feeling in my bones that there is a cat somewhere about!"*'

'I see. And you had a feeling in your bones that there was something wrong somewhere. Is that it?'

'Well ... not quite,' said Miranda, moving restlessly in her chair. 'It's a little difficult to explain. I just felt a bit scared and on edge and — oh, I can't describe it. It isn't a thing you can pin down!'

'All right,' said Simon equably, 'leave it for the moment. Can you tell me instead if there was any particular moment at which you began to feel — *um* — Aunt Hettyish?'

Miranda considered the question. 'I don't think so,' she said at last. 'I felt in terrific form when I went off to meet Stella and Robert at Liverpool Street station. We had tea at the Station Hotel and it was quite a party. It was only later on that there seemed to be a sort of queer feeling about things.'

'When you arrived at the Hook? Or while you were still in England?'

Miranda wrinkled her brows: 'In England, I think. I'm not quite sure. Why? Is it important?'

'Perhaps it isn't. It merely struck me as an interesting point that, according to your own story, you should have felt scared and uneasy before you had any reason to be so, and that possibly you may have seen or noticed something — perhaps without knowing it — that would account for it. Was there anything at all, at any time, that struck you as unusual?'

'No,' said Miranda flatly. She had no intention of telling him of those two looks, so utterly different from each other, that she had surprised on the faces of Sally Page and Mrs Leslie on the previous evening. 'I expect it's only Germany. Coming back here, I mean. You see I used to live in Germany when I was a child. My father had a job here, and when the war came we moved over into Belgium. Then Belgium was attacked, and my parents were killed and I got over to England somehow with a batch of refugees. I thought I'd forgotten about it — or very nearly. But coming back here seems to have stirred it all up again. And then of course there was that impossible coincidence of the Brigadier's story.'

'What story was that?' Simon Lang's voice was deceptively casual, but his eyes, which appeared to be able to change colour — or did they reflect colour? — were suddenly bright and intent.

Miranda repeated the story that the Brigadier had told on the previous evening — abridging considerably — and her own connection with it.

Simon Lang did not appear unduly interested. He wanted to know when Miranda had met the Brigadier and if she had ever, at any time, known him or seen him before? He asked a great many questions in that quiet, casual voice, some of which appeared to have little point. How had they been seated at the dinner table? Who had been sitting at the next tables, and would they have been

78

near enough to overhear what was said? At what time had they moved into the hall? What had they done there and who had been standing where? When had they gone back to the station and in what order? What exactly happened when they boarded the train? Had there been much visiting between the various compartments before or after the train started?

Miranda answered his questions to the best of her ability, and when there appeared to be no more, asked one of her own: 'Why do you want to know all this? Is it — was it one of us?'

Simon Lang did not pretend to misunderstand her.

'Yes.' The monosyllable was curt and uncompromising.

'How can you possibly know? There were so many people on that train. Dozens of others!' Once again there was a thin edge of panic to Miranda's voice.

'It's quite simple,' said Simon Lang softly. 'He was killed with a knife that had been taken off the reception desk at the hostel at Bad Oeynhausen. It belonged to the manager who used it as a paperknife and for sharpening pencils, and it was on his desk during the earlier part of the evening, because one of the staff remembers using it to cut a piece of string. Someone must have picked it up between then and the time that the passengers left for the train. And it could only have been one of the people who had used the Families' Hostel. Which rules out everyone except the people you have mentioned.'

'But – but one of the Germans — a waiter at the hostel — one of the staff could have taken it.'

'None of them were on the train.'

'But they could have given it to someone! The attendant . . .'

'The attendant was with a sick man in the next coach at the time the murder was committed; and five people can prove it.'

Miranda said: 'How do you know when it was committed?' Her voice had wavered a little for she could not believe — she would not — that one of the people who had sat near her at supper only last night could be capable of that savage act.

'Blood,' said Simon Lang. The single, softly spoken word

sounded horribly loud in the quiet room. 'It clots and dries very quickly. You had brushed against it; there was a wet stain on your dressing-gown and your slippers were soaked with it. When I reached the carriage it was still wet, but it was beginning to coagulate and the body was warm. Brigadier Brindley cannot have been killed more than ten to fifteen minutes at the most before you entered his compartment. Possibly less. If the murderer had only had the sense to leave the weapon in the wound instead of pulling it out, we should probably not have discovered the murder until the attendant went round calling people in the morning; and by that time it might have been a little more difficult to fix the time of death. As it was the murderer pulled out the knife, which would have served to plug the wound, and the resulting rush of blood was the cause of your discovering it. I imagine that the first idea was to get rid of a weapon that could be traced, and then the difficulty of carrying it away without getting smeared with blood resulted in its being dropped on the floor and left.'

'It can't be true!' said Miranda. 'There must be some other explanation. I've talked to these people. They are all three perfectly nice and very ordinary people.'

'Three?' Simon Lang's expressive eyebrows lifted slightly.

Miranda said quickly: 'If you think Robert could possibly murder anyone it shows that you don't know the first thing about him. Well I do. I've known him for years, so I know he couldn't conceivably do it.'

'Calm down, my child,' said Simon equably. 'No one is casting doubts upon your cousin. Although I imagine that given sufficient incentive, more people are capable of murder than one would suppose. In fact some of the world's most notorious killers have been mild little people whom their families and friends were convinced "wouldn't hurt a fly".'

'You've forgotten Stella,' interrupted Miranda scornfully. 'If Robert had left the compartment during the night, Stella would have heard him.'

'But Mrs Melville had taken sleeping powders,' said Simon

Lang gently. 'Quite a few people saw her take them, including yourself. It might have given him just the opportunity he needed.'

'You can't believe that!' said Miranda. 'You *can't*!'

'Oh, don't worry. I wasn't advancing it as my opinion. At the moment I'm keeping an open mind. No, I was merely interested in your arithmetic. Why "three"? I make it eleven. Or a round dozen, if we are to include the young dead-ender you were pursuing down the passage earlier on.'

'You mean you think a woman...? It *couldn't* be!'

'Why not?' There was a distinct glint of mockery in his eyes. 'Don't tell me you think women are frail flowers incapable of violence? We have it on record that *"The female of the species is more deadly than the male!"* My dear, anyone could have done the job — in the circumstances.'

'What do you mean? In what circumstances?'

'Brigadier Brindley had taken two capsules of a particularly effective sleeping powder, and we can take it the murderer was aware of the fact. The weapon was exceedingly sharp and had a double edge and a point like a needle. Whoever used it walked calmly into the Brigadier's compartment, either turned on the small reading-light over the top berth or used a torch or a cigarette lighter, drew down the blankets to make things easier, and stabbed the knife home to the hilt. Given those advantages — a doped man and a knife of that type — a child could have done it. And I mean that quite literally. Even young Wally could have done the job; granted he had the nerve and some elementary knowledge of anatomy. However I think we can safely count him out, which leaves us with eleven suspects. Two Marsons, two Melvilles, two Pages, two Leslies, Mademoiselle Beljame, Mrs Wilkin — and Miss Miranda Brand.'

'"And the last shall be first,"' quoted Miranda flippantly, an angry sparkle in her eyes. 'Is that what you mean?'

'Not necessarily,' returned Simon Lang without heat. 'I told you that I'm keeping an open mind. So far, I will admit, you are our most promising suspect. Whoever killed Brigadier Brindley either wore gloves or wrapped the handle of the knife in a handkerchief, and we haven't found anything among the luggage that shows signs of having had bloodstains on it. But the chances are that whoever killed him got some blood on him — or her. On their hands if nowhere else.'

'But – but *I* had blood on my hands,' whispered Miranda: 'I rubbed my hand over the mark on my dressing-gown ... That was how I – I saw what it was.'

'I know,' said Simon Lang quietly.

He reached out and took both her cold hands in his and held them for a moment in a warm clasp that was curiously comforting: 'Don't let it worry you. You'll be quite safe as long as you stick to the truth.'

'I've told you the truth,' said Miranda shakily.

'I believe you have. With reservations——! He released her hands and smiled a little crookedly. 'Anyway, you would appear to have no motive. Not that that is much help in the present instance, since the same seems to apply to all of you. What we need are a few really reliable alibis.'

'*I'm* the only one who needs an alibi,' said Miranda with an uncertain laugh. 'Everyone else has got one, because they were all sleeping two to a compartment. That's an alibi in itself.'

'Not always. Husbands and wives are odd in that way. They will alibi each other for any number of reasons, ranging from devotion to a desire not to be involved, in any way whatever, with anything as socially damning as murder.'

Miranda said: 'Well, you can cut Stella off your list, for one.'

'Why?'

'You told me a minute ago that Robert hasn't an alibi because he knew that Stella had taken the same amount of dope as the Brigadier and was therefore out like a light. And you can't have it both ways.'

'But I can,' Simon Lang assured her, 'I can merely look at it

82

from another angle. Suppose Mrs Melville merely pretended to take the pills? It's perfectly possible.'

'Why should she do anything so silly?'

'To fake an alibi perhaps? It would be quite a good one and very difficult to disprove.'

'And I suppose Mademoiselle was also faking up an alibi?' said Miranda coldly.

'Not such a good one,' said Simon, unruffled. 'She only took one capsule.'

'Or pretended to take one!'

'Or pretended to take one,' agreed Simon. 'So you see we still have eleven suspects and not one watertight alibi among them.'

'That's where you're wrong,' declared Miranda. 'Stella has one, and I'll tell you why. She *did* take those sleeping pills and I can prove it. She hates swallowing pills. She always powders them up first. She didn't swallow the capsules; she broke them open and stirred the stuff into her coffee and drank it. And we all saw her do it. So unless you think that the Brigadier deliberately palmed off two fake capsules on her, and she knew it, and knew that she was taking something that wouldn't make her sleep, you've lost one suspect.'

'Are you telling me the truth, the whole truth and nothing but the truth?' inquired Simon Lang seriously.

'I don't have to say that until you've got me in the witness-box,' retorted Miranda bitterly. 'And I'm not there yet. Yes, of *course* I'm telling you the truth! Ask Mademoiselle if you don't believe me. Ask Robert. Ask Lottie! Telephone Bad Oeynhausen and ask the waiter who served the coffee!'

'All right, all right, all right,' said Simon Lang pacifically. 'The point is taken. And disabuse yourself of the idea that I am trying to pin the crime on some innocent person merely for the sake of collecting a victim.'

Miranda's tense attitude relaxed and she sank back in her chair and gave a shaky laugh.

'That's better,' approved Simon.

There were voices in the hall beyond the lounge, and he glanced at his wristwatch and stood up.

'Well, that's about all for the moment. I'm afraid you'll probably be asked to go over the same ground again during the next few days, so I shall be seeing you. Thank you for bearing with me so well.'

He smiled down at her. A slow smile that broke up the planes of his face and transformed him into an entirely different and very likeable person.

The next moment the lounge was full of people and Simon Lang had gone.

Miranda went out onto the landing where she found Lottie and Wally Wilkin playing in the lift.

Wally turned to fly at the sight of her, but this time Miranda was too quick for him.

'Listen to me, you young menace,' said Miranda, retaining a firm grip upon the writhing child. 'If I ever catch you creeping into other people's rooms wearing paper masks again, I'll – I'll bastinado you!'

Wally's eel-like struggles ceased and an unexpected look of interest came over his freckled face: ''Ow could you do that? Mum's got 'er marriage lines: I seen 'em.'

'What on earth——?' began Miranda, puzzled; then the sudden realization that he had confused the word with one more familiar to him betrayed her into a laugh.

'You ought not to know the meaning of words like that!' she said with attempted severity. '*Bastinado*, you precocious little imp. It's a Chinese torture!' Miranda put a slim forefinger to each temple, drew her lovely eyes up into an oriental slant and pulled her curving mouth into a grimace that would have done credit to any cereal package.

'*Coo!*' said Wally, a wealth of admiration in the tone. 'D'you know any more Chinese tortures?'

'Lots!' said Miranda mendaciously. 'So just you watch your

step, young Wally, or you'll find yourself on the receiving end of them one of these days!'

Wally favoured her with a wide and gap-toothed grin. *'Garn!'* he said, 'yer too soft-'earted!'

Miranda tweaked his nose and released him: 'And now get out of that lift, both of you, or you'll have the manager after you. What are you doing down here anyway, Lottie? Waiting for your mother to come back?'

'She's back,' said Charlotte. 'She came back a long time ago. Hours 'n hours.'

'Oh. Well I'd better go and find her.'

Stella was in her bedroom. And looking remarkably pretty, thought Miranda, for a woman who had travelled non-stop for over forty-eight hours, been interviewed by the police over a murder case, and worked hard taking over a new house and a foreign staff in a strange city. She had lost all trace of weariness, and her manner was almost feverishly gay. A brilliant colour burned in her cheeks and her eyes were over-bright.

'Hullo, Miranda darling. *What* a day! I hear you've been spending the afternoon being third-degreed by the police? They were around asking endless questions half the morning. They had a session with Mademoiselle too, and another with Lottie. Let's get Robert to take us out on the town tonight. We may as well eat, drink and be merry while we have the chance, just in case they throw us all into jail tomorrow——

'Mademoiselle had a *crise de nerfs*. She said that they were all picking on her because she was a poor, defenceless foreigner, and they would send her to the guillotine — innocent as she was — solely in order to save the head of a guilty Englishman! And Lottie said it wouldn't be the guillotine because we don't chop people's heads off in England, we hang them (how *do* they learn these things?) and Mademoiselle rushed wildly out of the room in a cloud of smelling salts . . .

'The cook can't speak any English, and Robert's batman is in hospital with jaundice and won't be out for another week. Where is Robert, by the way? I haven't seen him all day. Harry Marson brought me back. Let's send for a bottle of champagne, 'Randa: I feel we should do *something* to celebrate our first, gay, glorious day in Berlin!'

Her laugh held a note of hysteria, and Miranda said: 'What you need is a cup of tea and some aspirin. We'll try the champagne later. Let's see what happens if we press a bell. Or do you suppose they only serve tea in the lounge?'

It was well after six o'clock before Miranda returned to her own room.

Sally Page had suggested that they should all go over to the Officers' Club for dinner, and Stella had enthusiastically seconded the idea and gone upstairs to change and say good-night to Lottie.

Miranda turned on her bedroom light and drew the curtains over the rain-spattered windows.

The room looked much the same as when she had left it earlier that afternoon in pursuit of Wally Wilkin, but for one difference: someone had visited it in her absence. Someone who had searched through her suitcases and had not had time to repack the contents neatly, but replaced them in a haphazard manner so that shoes, stockings, underwear and toilet articles were inextricably mingled. The drawers of the dressing-table had been opened, and in the cupboard her squirrel coat hung crookedly on its hanger. Even the bed was rumpled, as though someone had searched under the pillows and the mattress and then hurriedly drawn the coverlet straight above the disarranged bedding.

So *that's* why he wanted me to go down to the lounge! thought Miranda. So that some of his ham-handed underlings could go through my things again. Why, when they've done it once already? What did they think they might have missed? Something that I might have had on me? A handkerchief or gloves with stains on it?

Another thought slid into her mind like a thin sliver of ice. The searching of her room meant something else. Simon Lang had not

86

believed her. He had been kind and friendly and had made her feel that he was on her side. But he was on no one's side; unless it was the dead man's.

Once again she seemed to hear his voice saying: 'Whoever killed him must have got some blood on them — on their hands at least.' But there was only one person who had had blood on their hands: Miranda Brand.

'Circumstantial evidence'. Why had she suddenly thought of that phrase? What exactly did it mean?

Miranda turned slowly away from the disordered suitcases and began to take off her coat and skirt with stiff, unsteady fingers. And as she dressed for the Club, and all through the evening that followed, a mocking little rhyme seemed to beat in her brain with the same monotonous cadence as the train wheels on the previous night: *Miranda Brand had blood on her hand ... Miranda Brand had blood on her hand ... Miranda Brand ...*

7

The sky was a clear spring blue full of small white clouds, and the sun was shining as Robert drove the car down Bundes Allee, and turned left into the long sweep of the Herr Strasse.

On either side there were widely spaced houses standing back from the road; some of them set among pine trees and the pale green of new spring leaves, and others — a good many others — only ruined shells standing among a wilderness of stunted bushes, weeds and tangled briars.

'Not bombs — Russians,' said Robert in answer to a query from Miranda. 'They burnt them. "Houses of the bloated enemy capitalists" and all that sort of thing. Or so I am told.'

He turned the car off the Herr Strasse, and after crossing one or two parallel and smaller streets, pulled up in a quiet, tree-lined road before a red-roofed house flanked by budding lilacs and approached by a short flagged path.

'Here we are: bundle out. I'm late. See you at lunch.' He kissed Stella, released the brake and went on his way to the barracks which lay some half-dozen miles distant.

The house, though sparsely furnished, was comfortable and not without charm. A white painted staircase led up from a wide hall to a narrow landing that ran round three sides of the stairwell and gave access to four bedrooms. A large drawing-room and a smaller dining-room looked out on half an acre of garden that lay at the back of the house and consisted mainly of a lawn surrounded by a hedge and more lilac bushes and ending in a high reed fence. There were two pine trees in the garden, a few cherry trees and some sad, sandy-looking flowerbeds. A single almond tree provided a gay splash of colour and the cherry trees were already in bloom.

A shallow alcove off the hall held a telephone, and to the right an archway and a short passage led to the kitchen quarters and the back staircase. There was a small study for Robert and a smaller cloakroom.

'The cellars are about the largest part of the house,' said Stella. 'A ghastly waste of space, as there's nothing down there but a boiler and piles of coke and coal. But thank heavens we have two bathrooms! This is your room, and Robert and I are in here and Lottie next door to you. Mademoiselle's in there. There's another bathroom and two servants' rooms in the attic, but only the house-maid sleeps in; she seems a nice woman and mercifully can speak quite good English. My German is pretty rusty. When you've gone, I'll turn your room into a schoolroom-cum-playroom for Lottie, but until then she'll have to use that little room downstairs. Robert will never really use it.'

A woman wearing a starched white apron passed along the landing carrying a pile of clean linen, and Miranda caught at Stella's arm:

'Who's that?'

'That's Friedel.'

'Madam?' The woman turned, thinking she had been addressed.

'Es ist nichts, Friedel,' Stella waved a hand in dismissal. 'What is it, 'Randa?'

'I've seen that woman before. She was at the hostel yesterday.'

'Was she? Probably collecting her papers or a reference or something. She used to work there once. Now I'm going to leave you to your unpacking while I go down to wrestle with the cook. What's the *Deutsch* for "braised"?'

Stella ran down the stairs to the hall, but Miranda stood gazing into space. There was no reason why Stella's explanation of the woman Friedel's presence in the hostel should not be the right one. It seemed obvious enough. And yet standing there in a square of bright spring sunlight in Stella's house, Miranda had a swift and fleeting impression that she was looking at part of a pattern.

It was as though everything that had happened since she had left Liverpool Street station less than three days ago was all part of the same pattern, and that if she could only stand back from it, and see it from far enough away, she would be able to see a shape and a meaning. But she could not do so, because she herself was part of it. A small, coloured thread caught up in the machinery and woven in and out, willy-nilly, with other threads of other colours ...

I'm being Aunt Hettyish again, thought Miranda ruefully. I'm worse than Aunt Hetty! At least when she had a feeling that there was a cat about, there always was, while I keep peopling the place with imaginary cats. I must need a dose or a tonic or something.

Towards twelve o'clock a Mrs Lawrence arrived to call, and Friedel produced coffee and cakes in the drawing-room.

Mrs Lawrence, the wife of Robert's commanding officer, was a tall woman with auburn hair and an energetic personality. She was, Miranda surmised, more interested in the murder than in Stella's possible domestic problems, for having accepted their assurances that they were in no immediate need of assistance, she turned to the more interesting subject of Brigadier Brindley's death.

According to Mrs Lawrence, the B.B.C. had mentioned the murder in a news broadcast, a London daily had headlined it, and several German newspapers had already printed columns on the subject. But both Stella and Miranda had made their accounts as colourless as possible. Stella because she had slept throughout the entire proceedings, and Miranda because she had been too closely and unpleasantly involved to relish discussing the matter.

Mrs Lawrence was thrilled and sympathetic, but a little disappointed. She gave it as her opinion that the police would undoubtedly discover that the poor man had committed suicide after all, urged them once more to call upon her if they needed anything, mentioned that there was a Wives' Meeting at her house on Monday at three o'clock which she hoped Stella would attend, refused the offer of a glass of sherry, and left.

During the afternoon two members of the Public Safety Branch called at the house, and once more Stella, Miranda and Mademoiselle were interviewed in turn. The two men were friendly and pleasant and managed to give their visit the atmosphere of an informal call rather than that of a police inquiry, so that even Mademoiselle thawed and remarked after their departure that they were *'très gentils, très comme il faut'*.

The remainder of the day passed quietly enough except for one small, disturbing incident that occurred in the late afternoon. Stella, who was lining her dressing-table drawers with paper, looked up from the task to ask Miranda if she would telephone Robert and remind him to bring back ration cards for them. There was a telephone extension on the bedside table, and Miranda, who had been lying on Stella's bed reading a new copy of *Vogue*, reached out and idly lifted the receiver.

Someone was talking on the other end of the line: a quick, low voice speaking in German. The girl at the exchange, thought Miranda, turning a page of the magazine and waiting for the voice to ask what number she wanted.

The voice changed suddenly to a mixture of German and English.

'Speak then in English! *Es wäre mir sehr angenehm?* I must meet with you this night. If you come not I come myself upstairs to your house, and that will make trouble for you! ... *Nein, danke!* ... *wie du willst* ... By the third house then, where the light is not ... *Das ist gut!* ...'

Miranda broke firmly into the conversation: 'Exchange?'

There was an indescribable gasp at the other end of the line, followed by a sudden click as a receiver was replaced. And then silence.

'Exchange!' repeated Miranda impatiently.

Stella looked up from cutting lengths of paper and said: 'Don't be silly, darling. It's a dial phone.'

'But someone was speaking in German.'

'I expect you got a crossed line or something. Robert's number is at the top of that pad.'

91

Miranda reached out, and turning the telephone to face her, dialled a number; but with no result.

'It's not working. I can't get a sound out of it.'

'What an idiot I am!' said Stella, dropping the scissors and standing up. 'This is only an extension of course, and it won't work unless you switch it up here from the hall. Don't bother. I'll run down and put in a call from the one downstairs.'

She left the room and Miranda sat looking thoughtfully at the telephone ...

The downstairs telephone. Of course, that was it. She had been listening to the conversation of some person in the house. And that person could only be the woman Friedel, for the cook spoke no English.

Who had Friedel been talking to in that half-whispered, threatening voice?

Robert returned about six o'clock bringing Major Marson with him. The Marsons lived in the same road, their house being separated from the Melvilles' by that of Colonel and Mrs Leslie, who were next door.

Robert mixed gin and vermouth and he and Harry became immersed in regimental shop.

Harry Marson's usually high spirits seemed to have temporarily deserted him. He looked tired and morose, and his comments appeared to be mainly confined to criticism of the Army. Presently Stella smothered a yawn with nicely calculated effect, and the conversation became more general.

Harry, who before the war had spent three weeks' leave in Berlin with an uncle in the British Embassy and knew the city reasonably well, described it in the days of its Nazi glory when the flags had flown and panzer divisions and steel-helmeted, goose-stepping ranks had paraded down the great stretch of the Kaiserdamm.

The house that Brigadier Brindley had talked of, from which Herr Ridder and his wife had disappeared, was, said Harry, less than half a mile away. It was only a burnt-out shell now, but the unfinished garage still stood. He had driven past it only that day and had stopped out of curiosity to look through the rusted iron gateway. 'Tell you what — I'll take you round on Sunday,' offered Harry. 'That is, if you're interested.'

He, too, it appeared, had been interrogated by the S.I.B. on the subject of the murder, as had Elsa, Colonel and Mrs Leslie, the Pages and Mrs Wilkin. Elsa Marson had apparently not taken the inquiries in good part. She had wept and been what Harry described as 'a bit upset'. In other words, had behaved on the same lines as Mademoiselle, thought Miranda. Stella caught her eye and pantomimed *foreigners!* and Miranda's attempt to turn a fit of the giggles into a cough was not entirely successful.

Next morning Robert had rung up from the office to say that he could get three seats for a bus tour of Berlin on the following day, and would they like to go? It would, he said, take the best part of four hours, as the buses toured the British, American and Russian sectors of the city. Shortly afterwards, Mrs Leslie made an unexpected appearance and offered — somewhat surprisingly in view of her attitude during the journey from England — to take Miranda to see the shops. An offer that Miranda accepted with alacrity, since Stella, who was far more interested in overseeing the hanging of her newly unpacked curtains, plainly did not need her help.

Norah Leslie drove up the Herr Strasse, circled the Reichskanzler Platz and proceeded by way of Masuren Allee and Kant Strasse, to the Kurfürstendamm, the luxury shopping street of Berlin.

She parked the car not far from the fantastic ruin of the Kaiser Wilhelm memorial church, and Miranda stood in the clear spring sunlight and looked up at the broken towers and the vivid colours of the mosaics that could be glimpsed through the shattered walls, and marvelled that a ruin could look so beautiful. Before war and bombs had blasted it, it could not have been a particularly impressive building, but now, lifting against the pale sky out of a surge of shops, cinemas, hotels, apartments and the clatter of trams and traffic, there was something strangely ancient and oriental about its shattered silhouette; as though it were some beautiful, lost ruin from Angkor Wat — instead of the wreckage of a late-nineteenth-century Christian church.

Mrs Leslie touched her arm, and Miranda turned away and followed her through a maze of traffic and hurrying pedestrians, across the busy street. But it soon began to dawn on her that there had been an ulterior motive in Mrs Leslie's offer to take her to see the shops, although she certainly fulfilled the letter of her promise. Together they gazed at china shops and antique shops, admired hats, dresses, shoes and glass, and wandered through the crowded aisles of the KaDeWe, a hive-like multiple store. But this window-shopping was only a background and an opportunity for talk, and the talk was almost entirely on the subject of the Melvilles ...

Mrs Leslie, it seemed, had known Robert for many years. They had played together as children, and the families had only lost touch when Robert's father had sold his house on his wife's death in 1935. Norah had been in India then, newly married. But it was obvious that she did not wish to talk of herself: it was the Melvilles who interested her, and Miranda was as yet too young and inexperienced to be able to parry her questions with much skill. Besides, the questions themselves appeared to be harmless enough, and no more than one might have expected from someone who had once known the family well and took an interest in their affairs. Yet Miranda felt vaguely uncomfortable. There was something behind Mrs Leslie's questions. A hint of animosity? An undertone of spite? Miranda could not quite place it, but she gained the impression that Norah Leslie would not have been displeased to hear that Robert and Stella were unhappy, and their marriage a failure.

She was especially curious about Stella: her character, her interests, her clothes. She had heard of Stella, but had never met her until Robert had introduced them at Liverpool Street station. 'She's very pretty,' said Mrs Leslie in a brittle voice. 'You would hardly know that she was older than Robert. Somehow I had not expected her to look so — soft. I had imagined something harder. But appearances are very deceptive, aren't they? Of course women have a sort of instinct about these things, but men only go by appearances.'

She stopped to look at a window containing an exquisite display of modern porcelain, and added in a bright, conversational voice: 'She killed Johnnie, of course.'

'What?' Miranda checked, unable to believe that she had heard aright, and a stout German *hausfrau*, hurrying along the pavement behind her, cannoned into her and muttered crossly under her breath before continuing on her way. But Miranda had not even noticed. She was looking at Mrs Leslie with eyes that were bright with anger, and she said the first thing that came into her head. 'So you knew him well enough to call him by his Christian name, did you? Then why did you pretend that you had never met him before?'

Mrs Leslie turned to stare at her. 'What *are* you talking about?'

'Brigadier Brindley. You've just accused Stella of killing him.'

'*Brigadier Brindley?* You must be mad! I said she'd killed Johnnie Radley, her first husband. And it's quite true.'

'I don't think you know what you're talking about,' said Miranda icily. 'Stella's first husband was killed in Libya in 1941. He got a posthumous V.C. I've read the citation. I think it is you who must be mad!'

Mrs Leslie gave a short mirthless laugh.

'It's odd how women like that can always get people to stick up for them. And people like Johnnie — and Robert — to marry them . . .'

Her voice cracked a little on the last word, as though she was suddenly near tears, and all at once Miranda was sorry for her. There was some tragedy in Norah Leslie's past; a tragedy that was still real and alive and unforgotten. Perhaps she had once loved Robert, or Johnnie Radley, or both, and had lost them in turn to this unknown Stella?

Miranda thrust her hand impulsively through the older

woman's arm and said quickly: 'You don't really know Stella at all. How could you, when you only met her for the first time about three days ago? She's a darling. Really she is; wait until you know her better, and then you'll see for yourself.'

Mrs Leslie smiled. It was a smile that did not quite reach her eyes, but her voice had lost its hard, brittle tone when she spoke: 'I'm sorry. I should not have said that. You are her cousin and her guest. It was unpardonable of me to discuss her with you. I don't know why I—— Oh well, shall we forget it? There's a shop near here where they sell all sorts of odds and ends of china and glass. Let's go in and poke about.'

The Melvilles were not mentioned again and the remainder of the morning passed pleasantly enough. Mrs Leslie dropped Miranda back at the house a little before one o'clock, and actually accepted an invitation to come in for a drink.

Stella was in the drawing-room arranging sprays of cherry blossom in a green celadon vase. She had hung her own cream brocade curtains in place of the somewhat uninspired cretonne ones supplied by the Army, her own pictures were on the walls, and the room already looked individual, elegant and essentially Stella's. She dispensed sherry and admired the tiny china roses that Miranda had bought at a junk shop, and Mrs Leslie, possibly in an effort to atone for her outburst in the Kurfürstendamm, was friendly and pleasant until Robert arrived home, when she rose abruptly, and with something of a return of her former manner said she had no idea it was so late, and left.

'You know, she's really quite a nice woman,' said Stella. 'I thought she was utterly beastly when we first met her.'

'Oh, Norah's all right,' said Robert easily. 'I wonder why she married old Leslie? Nice chap, but a bit of a bore. Funny, I always had an idea that she'd married a foreigner. But perhaps that was Sue, her kid sister. I wonder what happened to Sue? I must ask Norah.'

8

The two buses, both full of sightseers and provided with English-speaking guides, left for their tour of Berlin from the Naafi building in the Reichskanzler Platz, and rolled off down the magnificent sweep of the Kaiserdamm towards the Charlottenburg Gate and the Victory Column.

The guides began to point out places of interest. The Opera House. The heap of rubble that had been the Technical University, from the battered steps of which Hitler had stood to review his bombastic military parades. The Charlottenburg Gate ...

Miranda looked out at the shattered ruins and began to wish that she had not come. It was interesting no doubt, but also appalling. The magnificent work of men's hands — the colleges built to increase knowledge and the boastful monuments to commemorate past glories, the golden-winged Victory atop a towering column whose decoration consisted of the gilded barrels of guns captured in the Franco-Prussian war — all pockmarked and disfigured by man-made weapons of destruction, or blasted into senseless heaps of rubble.

The stupidity of it all! The waste and horror of man's inhumanity to man.

She gazed at the scowling statues of Moltke and Bismarck and Roon, joint architects of this ruin, and, a few hundred yards away, at the new Russian war memorial — a signpost pointing the way to more and greater destruction — and she shivered in the airless warmth of the overheated bus.

Above the Brandenburg Gate flew a great red flag, flapping out against the sky. 'We are now entering the Russian sector,' said the guide: 'To the left you will see the ruins of the Reichstag that the Nazis burnt as an excuse for a purge of the Communists.'

The palace of Marshal Blücher; the French Embassy; the Adlon Hotel — more ruins. Mile upon mile of ruins. The skeletons and skulls and bones of houses. The evil birds let loose on Rotterdam and Coventry, London and the Loire, Malta and Crete, and a thousand towns and hamlets of Europe, coming home to roost ...

It will take years and years to clear all this away and build it up again, thought Miranda with horror.

'Well, they asked for it, and they certainly got it!' commented a stout lady in a puce coat and a magenta hat who was sitting next to Miranda: 'Serve 'em right, I says. But it's a proper mess, ain't it. Seems a pity some'ow.' She sighed gustily and relapsed into silence.

Marx–Engels Platz. A noticeable absence of pictures of Stalin. Lenin Allee and the headquarters of the People's Police. Stalin Allee and the First Socialist Road — the New Utopia and the New Hope personified by a long canyon of newly built and half-built apartment houses; block upon block of 'Workers' flats', identical, yellow-tiled, ugly. The Unter den Linden, that once-gay thoroughfare, now a drab street where the famous linden trees were smashed and stunted and the few pedestrians wore sullen and unsmiling faces. The Waterloo Memorial, ironic reminder of the days when the great-grandfathers of the *Luftwaffe* and the S.S. had been the admired allies of Britain.

The buses drew up outside a pair of ornamental park gates and the guide said: 'We are now at the Soviet Garden of Remembrance. It is the burial place of many hundreds of their soldiers. We may dismount here and enter the park. It is requested that you do not light cigarettes or make jokes in the sanctuary, and gentlemen who enter must remove their hats.'

Stella and Robert, who had been sitting together just behind Miranda, waited for her by the door.

'You're looking very seductive, Miranda,' commented Robert, tucking her hand under his arm. 'Isn't she, Stella? Who would have believed that such a hideously plain kid could grow up into such a delectable eyeful? When I left for Egypt she was a scruffy schoolgirl with a perpetual sniff and a gym tunic; and now look at her!'

'She looks marvellous,' agreed Stella, taking her other arm and giving it a little squeeze.

'You look pretty good yourself, darling. But far too expensive for this sort of party,' said Miranda. 'With so many red-hot comrades surging around, you look almost offensively capitalist.'

Stella laughed. 'Then it only goes to show how deceptive appearances can be!'

Her words brought back an echo of Mrs Leslie's conversation of the previous day, and Miranda frowned at the memory, and turned to look at her. She has changed, she thought; but could not be sure in what way or even why she should think so. Perhaps it was something to do with the way in which Stella looked at Robert. It was, thought Miranda, a new look and one that she had only noticed during the last few days: a strange compound of anxiety and strain; a look at once protective and possessive.

Had Sally Page been the cause?

Sally was there now, walking buoyantly on the other side of Robert and chattering in her clear, high voice; her inexpensive teenage clothes making Stella's tiny grey-feathered hat and silvery-grey fur coat appear sophisticated and expensive and mature.

Miranda looked up at Robert and was conscious of a sudden pang of anger and resentment. It wasn't fair, she thought. Robert would continue to look outrageously handsome when Stella was old and grey-haired and Sally middle-aged and faded. When Robert was sixty there would still be women who would sigh when they looked at him. His hair would be grey at the temples but they would think it added to his attractions, for the clean, beautiful planes of his face would still be there and his grey eyes would still crinkle at the corners when he smiled — as he was smiling now at Sally Page.

Robert was a darling. Good-tempered, indolent, charming and

entirely lacking in vanity, and Miranda had a deep affection for him. Nevertheless she was suddenly sorry for Stella.

Turning a corner, they stopped in involuntary admiration at the sight before them. They had been walking along a wide path between neatly kept flowerbeds towards a large statue of a dejected and drooping woman — 'Mother Russia mourning for her children,' murmured the guide behind them — that stood at a convergence of paths and faced a long, wide, stone-paved causeway that ended in a short flight of stone steps. Flanking the steps on either side rose a wall of polished red marble that had once formed the floors of Hitler's Chancellery, but had now been fashioned into the shape of two vast, stylized red flags, half lowered in salute to the dead.

Below each flag, and at the top of the steps, was a statue of a kneeling Russian soldier, his bared head bent in homage — statues, steps and the towering expanse of red marble dwarfing the stream of sightseers to pigmy proportions.

Robert gave a low expressive whistle, and Andy Page said, 'Crippen!'

The expression might have been inappropriate, but the tribute was none the less sincere.

From the top of those steps they looked down upon a sunken garden with stone-paved paths that skirted grassed lawns, each lawn bearing an immense iron laurel-wreath and flanked by large blocks of stone sculptured in low relief with scenes depicting Soviet soldiers in battle, Soviet citizens being bombed by German planes and Soviet troops liberating cities. At the end of each block were inscriptions in Russian, evidently extracts of speeches by Stalin, and at the far end of the sunken garden stood a tall, grassy mound.

A steep flight of stone steps led up the face of the mound to the sanctuary; a small, circular building on its summit that was topped, and entirely thrown out of proportion, by a gigantic bronze statue of a Russian soldier, sword in hand, holding a 'liberated' child and crushing a huge broken swastika under one booted foot.

'They certainly do things in a big way,' said Andy Page, busy with a camera. 'How long do you suppose this will stand?'

'Until about five minutes after the Russians move out of East Germany, whenever that is,' said Robert. 'A pity, because it would make a magnificent ruin. Something that future ages would run tourist trips to see — like Karnak and Luxor and the Acropolis. Let's go and take a look inside that sanctuary arrangement.'

They moved down the steps towards the sunken gardens, and Miranda released Stella's arm and fell back. She did not in the least want to join the slow-moving queue of people who were filing up that steep stairway towards the tiny building on top of the mound. It gave her an unpleasant claustrophobic feeling even to look at it, for the small sanctuary seemed a wholly inadequate pedestal for the colossal bronze figure it supported, and strongly suggested that it might collapse at any moment under the strain of the weight above it.

Miranda preferred to remain outside in the sunshine and the cold spring wind.

She walked slowly round the sunken garden, looking at the bas reliefs, and presently turned into a shaded path between shrubs and flowerbeds that led away from that part of the garden.

The path was deserted except for a solitary woman wearing a small black hat and a dark red coat trimmed with black *passementerie*. And this time there was no mistaking Elsa Marson.

There was no reason why Mrs Marson should not be there. She had obviously travelled in the other bus, which accounted for the fact that Miranda had not noticed her before. But why was she behaving so oddly?

She stood at the junction of two intersecting paths and peered furtively down them, first on one side and then on the other; quivering anxiety in every line of her body and turn of her head; and when footsteps sounded from the path to her right, she shrank back, stiff and tense, until they died away again.

An entirely natural and unmentionable reason for her display of agitation occurred to Miranda, and stifling a laugh she moved discreetly back round the angle of the path where a cluster of bushes and young trees provided a thin screen of leaves between herself and Mrs Marson. If anyone approached them from this direction she could at least cough loudly to warn her!

But she had been wrong about Elsa Marson.

Quick, light footsteps crunched the gravel of one of the paths, and a man wearing a shabby raincoat and a dark, peaked German cap appeared beside her.

Miranda saw him look swiftly over his shoulder to the right and left as Mrs Marson had done: a frightened, furtive look. It seemed impossible that he should have failed to see Miranda when she herself could see him so clearly through the thin screen of leaves, but he obviously did not do so, and there was that in his face, and in Elsa Marson's white-faced fear, that kept her from moving.

The man spoke quickly, but in so low a tone that she could not make out what he said or even in what language he had spoken. She saw Elsa Marson's stiff lips move in reply, and once again the man threw a swift, hunted look around him. Then drawing a small packet from under his coat, he handed it to Mrs Marson, and turning on his heel walked quickly away.

Elsa Marson opened her capacious handbag and stowed the packet away with trembling fingers. Even at this distance Miranda could see that her hands were shaking uncontrollably. She managed to shut the clasp, and then with another hunted look up and down the paths, she turned and hurried away in the opposite direction to which the unknown man had gone.

Miranda remained where she was, staring down the deserted path. What *had* Elsa Marson been up to? Stories of the notorious Berlin black market flashed across her brain: was that why she had looked so frightened? Had Harry Marson accompanied his wife on the conducted tour, and if so, where was he?

A bank of cloud had come over the sun and the day was suddenly cold and drab. Miranda shivered.

'Bird's nesting?' inquired a gentle voice behind her. Miranda started violently and whipped round.

'Captain Lang!'

'Simon, to you.'

'What are you doing here?'

'Oh, just seeing the sights you know.'

'And keeping an eye on your suspects at the same time, I suppose!' said Miranda angrily.

'That, of course — among other things.' He met her indignant gaze with a bland look that held a trace of amusement; though whether the amusement was directed against her or himself she could not be sure.

She said abruptly: 'Why did you go in for a job like this? Being a policeman. Did you have to?'

'Frankly, because I like it. For an unspectacular type with a morbid taste for drama and the seamy side of life, it offers a pleasurable escape from monotony. Or were you merely inquiring as to whether I have an adequate private income? It's all right. I have.'

Miranda turned and began to walk rapidly away down the path, Simon Lang beside her.

'What are we training for?' he inquired after a moment. 'The quarter mile, or London-to-Brighton?'

Miranda's sense of the ridiculous overcame her temper, and she laughed.

'That's better,' approved Simon. 'Now suppose we walk gently back to the bus at a normal pace.' He glanced at his wristwatch and said: 'We've got about five minutes more here.'

'How did you get here?' demanded Miranda.

'The same way as you did. As a matter of fact, in the same bus.'

'But I didn't see you!'

'Why should you? I'm a very unobtrusive sort of chap,' said Simon Lang regretfully.

'Only when it suits you!' retorted Miranda tartly. And stopped suddenly to turn to look at him: 'Why is it,' she demanded, puzzled, 'that I always seem to quarrel with you?'

Simon Lang looked slightly surprised. 'Do you? I can't remember quarrelling with you.'

'Oh, *you* don't quarrel,' said Miranda impatiently. 'I can't imagine you quarrelling with anyone. You're too – too——'

'Dull?' offered Simon Lang.

'I was going to say "lazy". Or too detached.'

'Let's just say that I have a nice, peaceable disposition.' He took her arm and turned her into a long, gravelled path that ran parallel with the paved way that led up to the red marble flags: 'You only try to quarrel with me because you feel on the defensive. There's no need for you to be you know. I'm not your enemy.'

'Then why do you behave like one?' said Miranda with a quiver in her voice. 'If you don't suspect me, why don't you tell me things straight out?'

'What sort of things?' asked Simon gently.

'Things like why you had my room searched, and why you have followed me here and——'

'What's that?' Simon's voice was suddenly sharp and he stopped dead and pulled Miranda round to face him: 'When was your room searched?'

'While you were so conveniently interviewing me in the lounge of the hostel, I imagine,' said Miranda bitterly. 'Or are you going to pretend that you didn't know anything about it? Surely your underlings don't do anything like that without orders, or a search-warrant or something?'

'Wednesday afternoon ...' murmured Simon Lang. He was looking directly at Miranda but his eyes appeared curiously blank and opaque as though they did not see her but were looking inwards at some picture in his mind.

A knot of East Berliners in the drab clothes and shabby raincoats that seemed to be almost a uniform of the sector passed by and stared at them curiously, but Simon did not move.

'What is it?' asked Miranda uncertainly.

His eyes seemed to focus her again and his fingers tightened about her arm. 'I don't know. That's the devil of it. Listen to me,

Miranda, if anything like that ever happens again — or anything odd or unusual — will you tell me at once? I mean that. This isn't just a social gesture of the "let me know if there's anything I can do to help" variety. This is important.'

He did not wait for an answer, but releasing her arm, took a small flat leather-bound notebook out of his pocket, and having scribbled something on a leaf of it in pencil, ripped the page out and gave it to her: 'That's my personal telephone number. If I'm not there myself there will always be someone who is and who can contact me.'

He glanced at his watch again and said: 'If we don't get a move on, we shall find that the bus has got tired of waiting for us and we're stranded behind the Iron Curtain. In fact here, I think, is a search party.'

Sally Page ran towards them, waving. 'Where on earth have you been?' she panted. 'We're all waiting for you and the driver is fuming. We thought you'd been kidnapped by the Kremlin or something. Do hurry!'

The remainder of the tour was uneventful. They did not again leave the bus, but were driven through the American sector, past the Tempelhof airfield where something like a huge, curving, three-fingered hand groped helplessly at the impersonal sky, and was, the guide explained, a memorial to the Airlift: an 'abstract' in concrete, symbolizing the three air corridors by which West Berlin had been fed and fuelled during the Russian blockade of the Allied sector.

More ruins; a honeycomb of roofless, ruined walls like a modern stage setting for hell.

The Kurfürstendamm; the Haffensee Brücke; the tall, steel trellis work of the Funkturm. The Reichskanzler Platz once more, and the parked cars waiting to take the sightseers to their homes in the swiftly gathering dusk.

9

It was raining again next morning, and Robert drove his family to morning service at St George's in a steady downpour.

Stella huddled the collar of her fur coat about her ears, its delicate silver-grey exactly matching the heavy rain outside the car windows. She looked cold and tired, and the eye-veil of her smart little hat failed to disguise the dark shadows of sleeplessness under her blue eyes.

Mademoiselle, lean and taciturn in black, also appeared to be in poor spirits. She had discovered, with considerable annoyance, that the Wilkins lived in a small house less than a quarter of a mile from the Melvilles, and Wally, exploring the neighbourhood, had been caught by Mademoiselle on the previous afternoon plastering Charlotte's face with coal dust in the Melvilles' boiler-room. Mademoiselle had pursued him, armed with one of the boiler-room pokers, but Wally had been too quick for her.

The three houses now occupied by the Melvilles, Leslies and Marsons had previously been lived in by three families whose children had been inseparable friends, and gaps in the hedges and the wire that separated each garden from the next had been made for their convenience, so that they could go from one garden to the next without running out into the road. These gaps still remained open, and Wally had darted through the one in the Melvilles' hedge and escaped across the Leslies' lawn and by way of the Marsons' garden into the no-man's-land beyond.

Mademoiselle had been forced to abandon the pursuit, and had not been appeased by Charlotte's assertion that she had *asked*

Wally to make her face black, as how could she be Eliza crossing the ice with a white face?

Despite the rain there was a large congregation, and Miranda, glancing surreptitiously around her during the singing of the psalm, saw that they were all there — Simon Lang's eleven suspects. We ought to get up a cricket team, thought Miranda wryly: 'Suspects versus the Rest'.

She did not realize that Simon was also present until the service ended and the congregation were streaming out of the church. She had not seen him out of uniform before and thought how different and unfamiliar he looked in a dark suit.

I suppose he's keeping an eye on us, even in church! she thought bitterly; and then remembered what Simon had said of her only the day before. She was being on the defensive again.

Stella stopped to speak to him while Robert went to fetch the car, and Miranda said sweetly: 'I didn't recognize you without your uniform.'

'I practise being a plain-clothes man on Sundays,' explained Simon Lang, straightfaced. He turned back to Stella, and Miranda walked quickly over to the car, feeling both snubbed and childish.

The rain had stopped and there were patches of blue sky overhead, and a rainbow drew a gleaming arc over the distant skeleton tower of the Funkturm. The air held a fresh, clean smell as of newly mixed mortar — that characteristic smell of Berlin on a wet day, that has its origin in rain falling on mile after mile of rubble.

They did not go straight back to the house, but drove instead to the Lawrences: Mrs Lawrence having buttonholed Robert and asked them to come in after the service for drinks.

Colonel Lawrence, in contrast to his wife, was small, thin and vague, and looked more like the popular idea of an atom scientist than the commanding officer of a regiment. He obviously did not know who Miranda was, or catch her name, but he smiled kindly, pressed a glass into her hand and made a few observations on the weather before drifting off to meet more of his wife's guests.

'What did you think of old Snoozy?' inquired Robert, exchanging Miranda's pink gin — a form of drink that she detested — for a tomato juice. 'The Colonel. He always behaves like that on social occasions, but don't let it fool you. It's protective colouring. He loathes large gatherings, unless they are strictly in the way of business.'

'Like Simon,' said Miranda thoughtfully.

'Like who? Oh, you mean Lang? I shouldn't have thought he hated large gatherings.'

Miranda flushed. 'I didn't mean that. I meant what you said about protective colouring. He seems to have quite a lot of that.'

Robert looked interested. 'I think I see what you mean. You don't notice him unless he wants you to.'

'That's it,' approved Miranda. She slipped her hand through his arm and smiled at him. 'Oh Robert, you are such a comfortable person! I don't have to explain things to you.'

Robert grinned affectionately at her. 'Probably something to do with blood being thicker than water,' he suggested. 'Are you by any chance getting interested in young Simon Stylites?'

'He's interested in me!' said Miranda bitterly. 'And not in the way you mean, either!'

'You mean you think he suspects you of having bumped off the Brigadier? Don't you believe it! If he's given you that impression you can take it from me that he's after something quite different. That young man has not acquired a reputation as the best poker player in the combined British, French and American sectors for nothing. You should hear "Lootenant" Decker on the subject. Hank Decker says it's plumb against all the laws of nature that a limey should be able to clean out a bunch of boys who cut their teeth on poker chips and could say "I'll raise you" before they could say "Da-da"!'

Miranda did not smile. She was silent for a moment, and then she said abruptly: 'Robert, who do *you* think did it?'

Robert did not answer her. He was looking past Miranda to someone behind her, and she saw his mouth tighten queerly as

Sally Page's clear voice cut through the babble of talk and the clink of glasses.

'I'm so sorry we're late, but Andy had to go down to the office about something.'

Robert's eyes came back to Miranda. 'I'm sorry — what did you say?'

Miranda repeated the question.

'Stuck a knife into the Brigadier, you mean? God knows! Some nasty little ex-Nazi I suppose. I'd stop worrying about it if I were you 'Randa.'

'But Simon Lang says it could only have been one of the people who went to the Families' Hostel in Bad Oeynhausen; because of the knife. And that means us — those of us who dined there I mean.'

'Oh yes, I heard that too. But I don't believe it means a thing. Look at that bunch of kids for instance. Any one of them might have walked off with the paperknife — you know what a fascination knives have for children — and then got bored with it and dropped it on the platform or in the corridor or the loo. Forget it sweetie!'

He smiled down at her anxious face and covered the hand on his arm with one of his own in a brief and comforting pressure.

Miranda grinned at him affectionately, and looking away, encountered Simon Lang's coolly observant gaze.

She had not realized he was here and the discovery came as something of a shock. He was standing at the far side of the room near the door that led into the hall, and he did not make any attempt to disguise the fact that he had been watching her. His face was unsmiling and his eyes, across the width of the room, were very bright. He looked, thought Miranda, as though a new and interesting idea had suddenly occurred to him.

She tried to stare calmly back at him, but could not do it; and after a moment her gaze wavered and turned aside. Her hand tightened convulsively on Robert's sleeve and Robert said: 'I can't think why we should be having such a gloomy conversation at a

Sunday morning beer party. Let's talk about something cheerful ... Hullo, Norah!'

Miranda released his arm and turned to see Mrs Leslie, wearing a distressingly sensible tweed suit, standing beside her.

'We saw you in church,' said Robert. 'Is your husband here?'

'Yes. He's gone into a huddle with your C.O. and one or two others in the dining-room. They appear to be talking shop as usual. Good-morning, Miranda.'

Mrs Leslie smiled at Miranda and sat down on the arm of a chair. 'Do you think you could get me a glass of sherry, Robert? I do so dislike beer before luncheon.'

Robert departed in the direction of the dining-room, and Mrs Leslie turned to Miranda.

'Well, what do you think of Berlin? I hear you went on a conducted tour yesterday.'

'Interesting, but very depressing,' said Miranda. 'It looks as if it would take a hundred years to clear up the mess. It must have been a beautiful city once.'

'It wasn't. Imposing perhaps — bits of it — but not beautiful. And you're wrong when you say it will take a hundred years to restore it. You don't know the Germans! Frankly, they terrify me.'

'Terrify you? Why? Do you think they'll go Nazi again?'

'Oh, I'm not worrying about their politics. It's their industry that frightens me. Haven't you noticed it yet? My dear, in our last army house at home we had to have the place painted and a few odd jobs done. It took over a month; and a large proportion of that time was spent making and drinking tea. It took three full days to put a gate up, and a fourth morning to come back and fetch the tools that had been left behind because it was a nuisance carrying tools in a bus during the rush hour!'

'At least you weren't paying for it yourself,' said Miranda with a laugh.

'My dear girl,' said Norah Leslie tartly, 'you miss the point. *Someone* was paying for it. And it was pretty slipshod work at that, let me tell you! I could have done most of it myself single-handed

110

in half the time and for a quarter of the money. Our country is still too intent upon its tea-breaks and its next pay rise to buckle to. But not the Germans! Have you watched them build a house out here? I have and it scares me. No tea-breaks or "go slow", or a good workman being forbidden by his union to lay more bricks than a mediocre one. No five-day week either! They are willing and eager to work flat out. I watch a gang of German workmen spitting on their hands, and I get a cold feeling in the pit of my stomach. These people are finding their feet again and bursting with confidence. They know where they are going, and just exactly how soon they'll get there. And that's going to be too soon for a lot of us! Oh, thank you, Robert!'

'I seem to have slopped it about a bit,' apologized Robert.

Mrs Leslie removed her gloves and accepted the glass gingerly.

'It's nice to see you again, Norah,' said Robert leaning on the back of the chair: 'I thought I'd see something of you in Fayid, but you went home to take a child to school or something, and I never saw you at all; except once in the middle distance. Amazing really how families who live next door to each other for years can lose touch completely as soon as one of them moves away. The war had a lot to do with it I suppose.'

'Partly that; and of course I was abroad a great deal,' said Mrs Leslie. 'I heard news of you from time to time, and I saw the announcement of your marriage in the *Telegraph* of course.'

'That's where women have the advantage of us,' said Robert with a laugh. 'Not many men read the Births, Marriages and Deaths columns — or not until they reach the age when it's only the last of those that interests them! When were you married, Norah?'

'I married Edward in 1948,' said Mrs Leslie.

'Good Lord! You're a mere bride! I imagined you'd been married for years.'

'My first husband was killed in the war. You and I, Robert, have both married twice.'

'Oh! . . . Oh — er — yes,' said Robert. He appeared momentarily disconcerted. 'That reminds me,' he said after a perceptible pause, 'where's Lottie, 'Randa? I hope she's not creating mayhem somewhere?'

'She's in the garden with the Lawrence children. They're being policed by Mademoiselle,' said Miranda.

'Thank God for that!'

Mrs Leslie laughed. 'The penalties of fatherhood catching up on you, Robert?'

'You're telling me!' said Robert. 'By the way, how are your parents, Norah? And Sue?'

There was an infinitesimal pause before Mrs Leslie answered. Then: 'They're dead,' she said flatly.

She stood up abruptly and handed him her empty glass, and Robert said: 'I'm sorry, Norah.'

'You needn't be,' said Mrs Leslie. She nodded at Miranda, retrieved the gloves that had fallen off her lap onto the chair, and walked quickly away across the crowded room.

'That was obviously an unfortunate question,' said Robert slowly. 'But how the hell is one to know? Oh, well——' He shrugged his shoulders and turned away, and a little later Miranda saw him talking to Sally Page. He was looking young and gay and insufferably handsome, and once again, as in the Soviet Garden of Remembrance, Miranda was conscious of a sudden pang of irritation and anxiety.

She was for the moment alone and could allow her attention to wander, and it was perhaps because of this that she became aware that from different parts of the room three other people were also watching Robert. Stella with a little anxious frown on her white forehead, Andy Page with a sullen scowl, and Norah Leslie with a curiously speculative look. And that from the open doorway that led into the dining-room Colonel Leslie was watching his wife; his expression a mirror-image of her own.

With a confused idea that she should do something about it, Miranda edged her way through the chattering guests towards

Stella, but just before she reached her an unknown man claimed her attention and Miranda turned instead to Andy Page.

Andy Page was a slim young man who looked as though he should have been an artist or a writer, or a newspaper correspondent. Almost anything but a soldier. A stray lock of hair was perpetually falling over his forehead, giving his thin features something of the look of a young stage genius, and even when in uniform there clung about him a vaguely Bohemian air.

But Andy Page was anything but a genius. He was in fact a fairly ordinary and rather likeable young man of no more than average intelligence, and people were apt to wonder why such an outstandingly pretty creature as Sally Barclay had ever married him: forgetting that he was probably the first man she had had a chance to fall in love with; Sally being barely seventeen when she met him, and having married him, in the teeth of parental opposition, three days after her eighteenth birthday.

'Hullo, Andy,' said Miranda gaily. 'What did you think of the conducted tour yesterday? Do you think you got any good photographs?'

Andy turned quickly. He would really be quite good-looking if he didn't look so sulky, thought Miranda — and smiled at him.

Miranda's long lashes tilted charmingly when she smiled, and the ghost of a dimple accented the lovely curve of a mouth that Rossetti might have painted. Her shining hair curled about an absurd little hat that was no more than a triangle of topaz velvet that matched her deceptively simple woollen frock and brought a glint of sherry-coloured light into her grey eyes. Andy Page was only human. His scowl vanished and he smiled back at her.

'I hope so. It's quite a good camera. A bit elderly, of course, but I can't afford a better one just now. You know, Miranda, if I thought I could get away with it I'd go into the black-market racket in a big way, if only to get my hands on some of those new German cameras. They're marvels! Do you know what I'd like to do?'

His face was suddenly animated and his eyes bright, and for a moment he looked as young, or younger, than Sally: 'I'd like to

113

chuck the Army and take up photography. The sort of thing Beaton and Schiavone and Olins do. It fascinates me! I buy up all the fashion magazines I can get my hands on just to gloat over those photographs. I saw some Italian ones the other day — outdoor ones of cottons, taken in Rome, in a wind. All movement and light. Terrific!'

He sighed, and the enthusiasm drained out of his face and his voice went flat again: 'Oh, what's the use? I shall never do it.'

He looked Miranda up and down and said abruptly: 'Your clothes always make everyone else's look too fussy. Even that bundle of junk you wear on your wrist looks all right on you, though I detest jangling charm bracelets on most women.'

Miranda laughed. 'Thank you, Andy. I expect it's because I can afford so few clothes that I have to choose really plain ones that not only look good, but wear well.'

'I wish you'd tell Sally that,' said Andy moodily. 'God knows I can't afford to give her a decent dress-allowance, but she will buy things that look all right the first time she wears them and pretty dreadful ever after.'

'When you are as pretty as Sally it doesn't matter what you wear,' said Miranda firmly. 'If she wore a sugar sack she'd look lovely in it, and you know it!'

'Sugar sacks are about what she'll be reduced to at the present rate,' said Andy bitterly. 'That is if——' He stopped suddenly in mid-sentence and flushed, and Miranda, in a praiseworthy attempt to change the conversation, asked after the new flat. But the topic was not a success. Andy replied morosely that it was sordid and uncomfortable, but that he supposed that they would just have to pig it there for a year.

Miranda was saved the necessity of commenting upon this gloomy statement by the appearance of Stella. Mademoiselle and Lottie, said Stella, were already in the car, and Robert was waiting to drive them home. Miranda gave Andy what she hoped was an encouraging smile, and departed.

*

114

Rain fell again during the afternoon, but towards evening the sky cleared and sunlight glittered on the wet rooftops.

'Who's for a walk?' asked Robert. 'We could all do with some fresh air after stuffing indoors the entire day. Lottie and Mademoiselle can come too.'

They set off down the road, choosing the direction at random and taking any turning that seemed promising, and some five minutes later met the Leslies, who turned and walked with them along the clean-washed streets that glistened with rain.

Early cherry blossom and deep pink almond frothed among the wet spring leaves in the late evening sunlight, and at first, in contrast to most of Berlin, the roads down which they went seemed to be singularly untouched by war. But presently between the neat houses with their white-painted gates and green gardens there appeared gaping, weed-grown spaces where other houses had once stood and where only ruined walls and fallen rubble now remained.

'What's that?' inquired Miranda, pointing to a long, low hill just visible above the distant treetops. 'Were there houses on there once?'

Colonel Leslie, to whom the question had been addressed, shook his head. 'It is houses.'

'I mean the hill over there.'

'So do I. It wasn't there before the war. It has been made from the rubble of bombed houses. Every day lorry-loads of rubble are brought from the ruins and dumped there. And that is the second hill! The first one already has grass and greenstuff growing on it. In winter the Berliners ski on them, and there will come a time when people will have forgotten how they came to be there and accept them as natural features of the landscape.'

'How gruesome!' said Stella.

'Why? The London that we know is built on the ruins of many earlier Londons.'

'"Cities and Thrones and Powers stand in Time's eye almost as long as flowers——"' quoted Miranda under her breath.

115

' "—which daily die".' Colonel Leslie finished the quotation for her. 'Yes, one must not take the close view of these things, but try to look at them with the eye of history.'

'But that's so cold-blooded,' protested Stella.

'One should be cold-blooded,' said Colonel Leslie. 'Hot-blooded people are responsible for two-thirds of the world's tragedies. An action done in hot blood is merely violent and frequently messy. Those performed in cold blood are at least calculated, and probably, in the long run, necessary.'

'I'm no good at arguing,' said Stella, 'so I'm not going to try. Lottie, darling, don't walk through all the puddles, there's an angel-chick. Isn't that the Marsons, Robert?'

They had turned into a quiet street overshadowed by trees. Along one side ran a high wall with the tops of trees showing above it, while on the other was the gutted ruin of a house standing in what must once have been a large and well-kept garden bounded by a shoulder-high wall and a tangle of laurels. Gazing in at the ruin through a rusty wrought-iron gate were Harry and Elsa Marson.

Harry Marson turned and waved as they approached: 'Hullo, have you come to see the cross that marks the spot where the accident occurred? Elsa wanted to see it too.'

'What accident?' inquired Miranda.

'*The* accident, of course. Do you mean to say you didn't know? This is it. Herr Whatisname's house. The character who bumped off his domestic staff and decamped with a Rockefeller's ransom in Dutch diamonds.'

'Is it really? What a thrill! Let's go in and have a look.'

They pushed open the rusty gate and walked up a sunken, weed-grown path to where a short flight of steps led up to the gaping space where a front door had once been. The button of the doorbell was still there, a white china circle incongruously bright and unbroken against the blackened stone.

The bomb that had hit the house had caused less damage than the fire that had followed, and the greater part of the building was

116

still standing. 'No. Don't go in!' warned Colonel Leslie sharply, pulling Miranda back. 'It isn't safe to go exploring this sort of ruin. Everything might cave in at any moment. That's why most of these bomb-damaged buildings carry warning notices — like that one ...' He pointed with his walking-stick at a weather-worn noticeboard, half-hidden by weeds, near the foot of the steps.

Sun had blistered and faded the once-bright letters, and wind, rain and snow had combined to make them barely legible. But it was still possible to read the red-printed warning *ACHTUNG!* that headed it, and, further down, another favourite and all-too-familiar word *Verboten*. Though exactly what was forbidden was by now in doubt.

'Not that it matters,' concluded the Colonel, commenting on that fact, 'because no one who's been in this country for longer than half an hour could fail to realize what those two words mean. And in this case it's sound advice — "Keep out!"'

'Yes, *do* let's!' agreed Stella with a shudder. 'Besides, it's getting late. Mademoiselle, will you start back with Lottie? Come on, 'Randa.'

She tugged at Miranda's arm, and as they went back down the steps to the path, the others following, Harry Marson suggested a visit to the garage.

Weeds had grown up about it and weather and rain had left their mark on the walls that the builders had left unfinished before the fall of France. 'But you can still see where the lime pit was,' said Harry Marson, poking about interestedly among the weeds and rubble.

No one else appeared to share his enthusiasm. They stood in silence, looking at the discoloured walls and the tangle of weeds.

The sun had been moving swiftly down the sky and now, as they stood in the deserted garden, it dipped behind the long hill of rubble that rose behind the far trees, and left the weed-grown garden and the shell of the ruined house to the cold spring twilight.

'I wonder if they'll ever come back?' mused Harry Marson. 'The Ridders, I mean.'

'To haunt it?' said Stella with a shiver.

'Oh Lord, no! I mean, if they're still alive. They say that murderers always return to the scene of their crime. It has some fatal attraction that draws them back like a trout on a long cast. For all we know they may be here now, in Berlin. Perhaps they walk down this road and peer furtively over the wall in the dusk and picture it all happening again.'

His voice had dropped to a half-whisper and, involuntarily, Miranda looked quickly over her shoulder, as though she thought that someone might even now be peering through the rusty gates.

And there was someone — a shadowy figure, barely distinguishable in the deepening twilight, standing just within the gateway and half-hidden by the straggling laurels.

The next moment it had gone; so swiftly and noiselessly that Miranda wondered for a moment if there had really been anyone there, or if some trick of the fading light had made her imagine it.

'Harry, stop! I do not like it!' said Elsa Marson with sudden violence. 'Let us go away now. This is not a good place.'

'Yes, let's!' said Stella fervently. 'I couldn't agree with you more. Come on, or it will be dark before we get home.'

She took Robert's arm and they turned and walked away across the silent garden and out into the quiet road.

10

'Did I tell you that I'm having tea with Mrs Lawrence this afternoon?' asked Stella, helping herself to cheese: 'It seems she's having several of the wives over. Some sort of committee meeting of Welfare, I gather. And we shall be cook-less this evening because Frau Herbach wants to leave early today. I told her we'd have hot soup with a cold supper and she can leave it ready. Friedel can deal with that. It's your half-day isn't it, Mademoiselle? What are you going to do?'

'I shall go me to the British Centre,' said Mademoiselle. 'One tells me that they have the books there and many lectures.'

'How nice,' said Stella absently. 'All right, Lottie darling, I'm sure Mademoiselle won't mind your getting down if you've finished. Now don't be a nuisance this afternoon, there's a sweetie, because Mademoiselle and I are both going to be out.'

Stella left the house shortly before three o'clock: 'I have to be there at three,' she explained, 'but I shan't be back late — unless I get arrested for bad driving! Robert left me the car, but as I've never had to drive on the right-hand side of the road before I shall proceed at a slow crawl. If you don't hear of me before eight o'clock you'd better ring up the police and tell them that they've got another body on their hands!'

She went out of the front door, banging it behind her, and Miranda, reminded of something, plunged her hand into the pocket of her grey suit. Yes, it was still there; the small square of paper on which Simon Lang had written down his telephone number in the Soviet Garden of Remembrance. Miranda smoothed it out and stared at it for a moment, frowning, and then crumpling it into a small pellet tossed it into the waste-paper basket with the air of one who is mentally saying 'So there!'

The drawing-room door opened behind her and Norah Leslie walked into the hall.

'Oh, there you are! I hope you don't mind me walking in on you like this, but it's so much shorter to come through the gap in the hedge. I came over to ask if you'd have supper with us this evening. We're having a few of our subalterns in, and I want some pretty young things to entertain them. Sally Page is coming because Andy has to dine in some Mess, and I've got the General's niece. Now don't say you won't come! I'm sure the Melvilles would like an evening to themselves.'

Miranda laughed. 'I expect they would. Thank you. I'd love to come.'

'Good. Then that's fixed. See you at about a quarter to eight. Short frock.'

Mrs Leslie turned and left by the way that she had come, through the open french window in the drawing-room, and Miranda was about to settle down with a book when she was once more interrupted; this time by the ringing of a bell. She put down her book, wondering idly if it was the telephone or the front door, and hoping that Friedel had heard it, when she heard Mademoiselle come out of the cloakroom and lift the receiver.

' *'ullo? Oui!* . . . Ah, Major Melville! . . . Madame is not here. She takes the tea with Madame Lawrence . . . Law-rence. The wife of Monsieur le Colonel . . . That I know not. M'selle Brand is here . . . *Oui . . . Merci.*'

The receiver was replaced and Mademoiselle appeared in the drawing-room, gloved and hatted and clasping a tightly rolled umbrella.

'It is Monsieur le Major,' she announced. 'He reports him that he will not be able to return for supper this evening, but must work late at the office. He will try to inform Madame.'

'Thank you, Mademoiselle. Just tell Frau Herbach that there'll only be one for supper tonight. I shall be out too, I'm having supper with Colonel and Mrs Leslie.'

'*Bien.*' Mademoiselle withdrew, and a few minutes later Miranda heard the front door close behind her.

The house was quiet and peaceful and Miranda stretched out on the window-seat and relaxed in the warm afternoon sunshine, feeling pleasantly drowsy and temporarily free from that haunting sense of uneasiness that had twitched furtively at her nerves ever since she had started on the journey towards Berlin.

Her eyes closed, and she was on the verge of sleep when a sound from outside the window aroused her.

There were bushes immediately below the drawing-room windows, except in front of the single french window, and something or someone was crawling between those bushes and the wall. Miranda knelt up cautiously on the window-seat and looked out. The next minute she had leaned out over the sill and grasped the belt of a grubby pair of corduroy shorts.

There was a shrill squeal, and Miranda jerked her captive to its feet.

'Wally Wilkin! What are you doing here?'

Miranda shook him, and the large crêpe-hair moustache and beard with which his countenance was adorned fell off and was lost among the bushes.

'*Now* look wot you done!' said Wally indignantly.

'Never mind about those whiskers. What do you mean by crawling round the house like this, young Wally?'

'I'm detecting,' replied Wally sulkily.

'You're what?'

'Lookin' fer cloos.'

'Oh you are, are you. What sort of clues? And why here?'

' 'Cos I 'av to keep an eye on me suspecs. That's why.'

'Oh, I see. This is a game you're playing.'

'Game? *Naw!*' said Wally indignantly. 'I jus' told you: I'm seein' if I can solve this 'ere case.'

'What case?'

121

'Why the murder, o' course!' explained Wally in disgust. 'That old bloke on the train.'

'Well, Dick Barton, would it be too much to ask you to take your magnifying glass and go and detect somewhere else? I hate to seem inhospitable, but I could do with a bit of sleep this afternoon.'

Miranda relaxed her grip, but Wally made no move to escape. He leant his grubby elbows on the windowsill and lowering his voice to a hoarse and confidential undertone, informed her that it was his ambition to join the secret service when he grew up, and that this being so, it was necessary to put in a bit of practice.

'That's the stuff!' approved Miranda. 'And have you solved this case yet?'

A sudden look of caution came over the grubby, freckled face, and the blue eyes were all at once shrewd and wary: 'Maybe I 'av, and maybe I 'aven't,' said Wally slowly. 'I ain't talking yet. But I gotta cloo.'

'Have you, indeed! And what have you done with it?'

'It ain't that sort of cloo. It's a thing I knows; not somethink I 'as.'

'Is that so?' said Miranda, politely. 'And what are you doing crawling round in the bushes, Detective Inspector? Collecting more clues?'

Wally nodded, and remarked with satisfaction that it was very useful having most of his suspects living next door to each other. Adding a rider to the effect that he could crawl round all three houses without showing up at all.

'Do you mean you've been snooping round our houses?' demanded Miranda. 'Wally, you're going to land the father and mother of a walloping one day if Colonel Leslie or Major Marson catches you!'

'They're out,' said Wally smugly. 'I can get up to that balcony, too. An' Mrs Leslie's! I did yesterday. S'easy!'

'You *what*? Why, you little horror! Don't you ever do it again!'

'I may 'av to,' said Wally darkly.

'Then let me tell you, Inspector Wilkin,' said Miranda energetically, 'that if ever I find you've been climbing up to the balconies and snooping in at the bedroom windows again, I shall go after you with a good stout stick. So now you know!'

'Women!' said Wally bitterly.

'I'm sorry,' said Miranda, softening. 'But I can't have you snooping round people's rooms, Wally. It isn't' — she hesitated for a word and finished rather lamely — 'British.'

'The secret service 'as to snoop,' said Wally austerely. 'Where'd us British be if we didn't? Beat by the Russians an' the Japs, and the F.B.I., that's wot!'

'It's quite a point,' conceded Miranda. 'But even a detective inspector has to have a search-warrant before he can search anyone's house, you know.'

'Okay,' said Wally resignedly. He scrambled about in the bushes, and having retrieved the crêpe-hair beard, regarded it doubtfully, remarking that it couldn't be much good for she had recognized him at once.

'Try something a bit less conspicuous next time,' recommended Miranda.

'I *could* try paintin' myself green so I wouldn't show up in the bushes?' suggested Wally. 'Camyflage — like them "commandos" use. There's a big tin o' green paint in the garidge of the Marsons' 'ouse: I saw it when I was detectin' this morning — I could swipe a bit o' that, easy.'

'Don't attempt it,' advised Miranda earnestly. 'Just think how you'd show up against things like walls and gravel. If I were you I'd stick to plain-clothes detecting. All the real experts do.'

'P'raps you're right,' conceded Wally, stuffing his unsatisfactory disguise into his pocket.

'Hullo, Wally. What are you doing behind there?' inquired Lottie, appearing round the corner of the house.

'I bin talkin' to your aunt,' said Wally with dignity.

'She isn't my aunt. She's my cousin,' contradicted Lottie.

'She isn't, neither! *"She's"* the cat's mother!' retorted Wally

123

triumphantly. He wriggled through the bushes and they disappeared in the direction of the sandpit, wrangling amicably.

Friedel brought in tea on a tray at 4.30, and an hour later Stella phoned to say that she would not be back for supper: 'Robert has to work late, so we thought perhaps we'd have supper at the Club,' explained Stella. 'You don't mind do you, darling? Oh, and another thing: Friedel asked me if she could go out for an hour or two this evening and I said she could. Of course, I didn't know I'd be out then. You won't mind keeping an eye on Lottie, will you? Friedel will put her to bed. It's just that someone has to be in the house ... Sweet of you, darling. I must fly. I'll try not to be too late.'

There was a click and Stella had rung off.

'Well, that's that!' said Miranda. She would have to let Mrs Leslie know that she couldn't come, for if Stella had already given Friedel permission to go out, she, Miranda, could hardly countermand it. She opened the phone book and dialled Mrs Leslie's number, but it was Colonel Leslie who answered the phone and accepted Miranda's explanation and apologies without demur.

Miranda put down the receiver and went in search of Friedel.

'I go out when I have put Lottie to bed,' said Friedel. 'And your supper I put ready at a quarter to eight, yes? I am not gone more than the one hour. By nine o'clock I am back. I will make the back door to lock and then only the front door needs by itself stay open.'

'Will you tuck me in please?' requested Lottie. 'I don't think I like German mattresses, do you? They only tuck in in bits.'

'They aren't German mattresses,' said Miranda. 'No self-respecting German would dream of sleeping on one. They're army-issue mattresses. Biscuits.'

'Biscuits?' said Lottie, fascinated. 'Do you mean you can *akshually* eat them?'

'No, of course not, silly! It's only because they look like big square dog biscuits.'

'Oh. Why doesn't the Army have proper mattresses?'

'Goodness knows!' said Miranda. 'Now are you all fixed?'

'No. Rollerbear has fallen out.'

Miranda stooped and retrieved the small white china bear that was Lottie's chiefest treasure. Rollerbear measured some three inches in length and had once decorated the top of some forgotten Christmas cake, and for some unaccountable reason Lottie loved him above all her other toys. He accompanied her everywhere and spent every night tucked under her pillow.

'Rollerbear doesn't like these mattresses either,' said Lottie. 'He falls down the sides, over'n over. Good-night, Cousin 'Randa.'

'Good-night, puss-cat. Sleep tight.' Miranda switched off the light and went out, leaving the door ajar.

Across the landing was the big double bedroom that was Robert's and Stella's. The door was not quite shut and Miranda noticed that the bedroom light had been left burning.

She walked across the landing and pushed open the door, but either her eyes must have played a trick on her or else the headlights of a passing car had flashed across the windows, for the room was in darkness.

Miranda closed the door, turned off the landing light that shone too strongly into Lottie's half-open door, and more from habit than for any other reason, changed her grey suit for the dress of topaz-coloured wool that she had worn the previous day, before going downstairs.

The drawing-room curtains had not been drawn and the room was in darkness, but beyond the windows the garden was full of cold spring moonlight and black shadows. Somewhere in the house a door shut quietly and Miranda turned away and went into the hall.

Friedel came out of the kitchen and said that the soup was on the table and that she had put cold meat and salad on the sideboard. She had locked the back door, and would be back soon.

Miranda went into the dining-room and sat down to her solitary meal, and presently she heard light footsteps crossing the hall and the click of the front door as it closed. Friedel had gone, and she was alone in the house.

Alone in the house ... Now why should that thought suddenly disturb her and bring with it a return of the vague, troubling feeling of apprehension that had been absent from her all that sunny afternoon and quiet evening?

Besides she was not alone; Lottie was asleep upstairs.

Miranda turned her attention resolutely to the cooling soup, and having finished it, carried the empty plate to the sideboard and helped herself to cold meat and salad, making as much noise about it as possible as a protection against the silence.

The clatter of plates and knives comforted her in some obscure fashion; they made a pleasant, ordinary, everyday sound. She mixed herself a french dressing from the ingredients that Friedel had left on the table, and was pouring them over her salad when she heard soft footsteps on the landing upstairs.

For a fleeting moment her heart seemed to leap into her throat; and then she realized who had caused them and was correspondingly annoyed. She got up from the table, marched over to the door and called up to the top landing: 'Get back to bed, Lottie! It's quite time you were asleep. If I hear you out of bed again I'll come up and spank you. That's a promise!'

There was the sound of.a hurried, surreptitious movement and then silence.

Miranda waited for a moment or two and then returned to her interrupted meal.

The sound of her own voice and the realization that someone else was awake in the house, even though it was only a child of seven, had temporarily dispelled her feeling of disquiet. But it did not last.

The uneasiness crept back again, and grew and spread with the silence of the quiet house. The tick of the dining-room clock seemed absurdly loud, for the noise it made was the only sound in that silence; and once again, as in the corridor of the Berlin train, Miranda found herself fighting an impulse to look over her shoulder.

126

She put down her knife and fork and was angrily aware that she had laid them down softly and with exaggerated care, and that she was holding her breath. Why should she suddenly feel that she must not make a sound — that any sound would seem frightening and overloud in that waiting silence? What was she listening for?

A board creaked overhead and Miranda's teeth clenched on her lower lip.

The quiet house, despite the stillness — or perhaps because of it? — began to fill with noises. The ticking of the clock; the sudden inexplicable creak of floors and furniture that becomes audible only by night; a moth fluttering against a windowpane, and an occasional stealthy scrabbling that sounded as though someone or something was crawling up the gutters, but that came from the central-heating pipes.

But Miranda was listening for none of these things.

She turned quickly and looked behind her; but there was no one there, and beyond the open doorway of the dining-room the hall stretched emptily away to the shadowed alcove where the telephone stood.

Miranda picked up her knife and fork again, feeling ashamed of herself for having given way to that foolish impulse, but she could not force herself to eat, and after a moment or two she laid them down once more and stared around her.

The dining-room furniture seemed to stare back at her, remote and uninterested, its varnished immobility mocking her tense and quivering awareness. She could see herself reflected dimly in the smooth panels of the sideboard, the polished table-top and the gleaming surface of a silver salver: a white, heart-shaped face with wide, terrified eyes, red mouth and dark wings of hair. A frightened girl in a sleek topaz-coloured dress.

The hideous hanging lamp above the dining-room table filled the room with harsh light, and there was no possible hiding-place in it. Even the curtains reached only as far as the window-sill, and their thin cotton folds could not have concealed a kitten.

Nevertheless, from somewhere someone was watching her. She did not know why she knew it. She only knew that she did know it; and with an absolute certainty that left no room for doubt.

Miranda stood up suddenly, pushing her chair back so violently that it fell with a crash to the floor. The noise, with its suggestion of uncontrolled hysteria, steadied her and made her realize that she was behaving in a panic-stricken and unadult manner, and that if she were not careful, would presently be rushing out of the house screaming. The house was locked up and no one could enter it except by the front door into the hall, which was clearly visible from the dining-room.

She forced herself to pick up the fallen chair and replace it, and feeling unaccountably fortified by the act, walked firmly across the room and out into the hall.

There was no one there. The staircase leading up to the shadowed landing was empty and nothing moved on or above it. Miranda turned towards the darkened drawing-room.

After the brightly lit hall and dining-room, the moonlight beyond the drawing-room windows appeared faint and wan, but as Miranda's fingers groped for the switch she thought she saw a flicker of movement outside the french window.

The switch clicked under her fingers, and as light flooded the room the windows were once again dark. But in that fraction of a second she had ceased to be frightened: 'Wally!' said Miranda, speaking aloud in the silence. 'I bet it's Wally!' Her curving mouth set itself in a determined line that boded no good for Master Wilkin, and switching off the light she tiptoed to the french window, unlocked it and slipped out into the garden.

The night was cold and very still. No breath of wind stirred the branches of the fir trees and not a leaf rustled, and Miranda too stood motionless; waiting until her eyes were accustomed to the uncertain light and listening for sounds of stealthy movement that would betray the whereabouts of that fervent embryo detective, Master Wallace Wilkin. And this time, vowed Miranda, I shall tell his father, and I only hope that Wally will have to take his meals off the mantelpiece for the next week as a result!

She held her breath to listen, but the garden was quiet and nothing moved. Perhaps Wally — if it had been Wally — had run for it as soon as he saw the drawing-room light go on. Or had that faint flicker of movement been only an owl or a bat? One thing at least was certain; she could not stand here indefinitely. She would walk once round the garden and then, if she found no one, would go in and lock the front door and turn on the wireless and every light in the house until Friedel or Robert and Stella returned.

Miranda walked down the sandy path that led past the dining-room windows and turned right-handed to skirt the lawn, but when she reached the cherry trees at the far end of the garden she paused, and on an impulse sat down on the wooden seat that encircled a tree near the path.

The windless night was full of stars and lights: stars in the sky and the red stars that warned aircraft away from the tall steel radio pylons. Twin stars, green and red, that moved across the sky and were the wing lights of an aircraft heading for Tempelhof airfield. A spangle of coloured lights that outlined the distant Funkturm ...

The path was a tangle of moonlight and tree-shadows, and the garden was fragrant with the faint, elusive scent of spring. The silent night was not frightening and hostile as the silent house had been, for the Leslies' drawing-room windows made friendly squares of soft, orange light against the blue of the moonlight, and Miranda could hear voices and laughter and the sound of a radio playing dance music.

She leant back against the rough bark of the cherry tree, and a few pale petals, dislodged by the slight movement, drifted down like snowflakes into her lap.

For no reason at all she found herself thinking of Simon Lang, and the discovery gave her the same feeling of resentment that Simon Lang himself seemed to produce in her. She had not meant to think of him, but it was as though he had walked across the garden and stood in front of her, blocking out the moonlight and the white ghosts of the cherry trees, and refused to go away.

Miranda shut her eyes, and found that she could not picture him clearly. She could make a list of features, but none of them added up to the same Simon. He was, as he had told her, an unobtrusive person. He was certainly a singularly quiet one; his voice and manner and movements providing a gentle and pleasant façade that concealed the real Simon Lang.

The real Simon Lang, Miranda suspected, was a person who knew exactly what he wanted and invariably got it; and who, as a general rule, simply did not find it necessary, and could not be bothered, to use force or noise in any form in order to achieve it. He had interested her from the first moment she had set eyes on him, though she had not paused to discover the reason for this. And at the present time there was a more important question: why was he interested in her?

Had he been almost anyone else, Miranda would have instantly supplied an obvious answer. But in the case of Simon Lang she was regretfully compelled to reject that simple solution, since she did not in the least believe that Simon was attracted by her personal charms. Did he, then, believe that she knew more about the murder of Brigadier Brindley than she had admitted? Or was he, as Robert suggested, using that as a blind? — allowing someone else to suppose that he suspected her, in order to put that someone off their guard?

It was a possible solution, and an unpleasant one. But why should she, Miranda, be interested in Simon Lang?

Miranda frowned at the shadows of the cherry trees and was unable to find an acceptable answer.

Someone turned off the radio in the Leslies' house, and a few minutes later their lights went out, leaving the house in darkness. Presently Miranda heard the sound of cars being started up and realized that the Leslies must have decided to take their party on to the Club or to some Berlin nightspot. Three cars, one after another, purred down the road on the far side of the house. And as the sounds faded and dwindled away into silence, Miranda shivered and awoke to the fact that she was wearing a thin woollen frock and the night was cold.

A chill breath of wind sighed across the garden, bringing down a shower of white petals and bearing with it the threat of a stronger wind to follow, and she stood up to brush the fallen petals from her lap and resume her interrupted tour of the garden.

11

Once or twice Miranda stopped to peer left and right into the shadows, but the gesture was a purely perfunctory one.

If Wally had been there, he had gone, for the garden was so still that she would have caught the slightest rustle of movement. But all she could hear was the sound of her own breathing and the faint, faraway purr of traffic from the distant Herr Strasse.

Overhead the white pencils of Russian searchlights, paled by the clear moonlight, swept across the sky and picked out scattered, drifting shreds of cloud, as Miranda walked quickly along the path by the hedge that formed a boundary between the two gardens. She was cold, and anxious to get indoors once more to the comfort of the friendly lamplight, for now that the Leslies' house was in darkness, the moonlit garden seemed darker and somehow daunting.

The sandy path was bone white in the moonlight except where an oddly shaped shadow blotted it near a clump of lilacs by the gap in the hedge. A shadow that, when she reached it, was not a shadow at all ... but the body of a woman who lay face downwards with her feet towards the house and her head hidden by the darkness of the gap——

For a long moment that seemed to have no beginning or end, Miranda stood staring down at the sprawling, silk-clad legs and the blur of silvery-grey fur; numb with horror, and caught once more in the web of a waking nightmare. Then all at once she was on her knees beside it, tugging at it, trying to lift it, her voice a harsh scream.

'Stella! Stella! What's happened? ... Oh no! ... Oh God, no! ...
Stella ...!'

The limp arms were outstretched, fingers clawed in the damp
earth, and the body was slack and unbelievably heavy as Miranda
put her arms about it and dragged it, panting, up and away from
the black shadow of the hedge.

The head lolled back against her shoulder and the moonlight
bathed it in white light. And it was not Stella. It was Friedel ...

Miranda's immediate reaction was one of violent relief. It
wasn't Stella! That, for the moment, was all that mattered, and she
let the heavy head drop back onto the grass, and laughing a
cracked, hysterical laugh of relief, fell on her knees again beside
it.

A thin wet trickle, black in the moonlight, crept across the white
face from some wound concealed by the woman's hair, and
reached and darkened one staring eye. But the eye did not blink
or close, and it was only then that Miranda realized that she
was looking at a dead body. She had known it when she had
first laid a hand upon it, but she had not really believed it until
now.

A sudden, shuddering horror brought her to her feet: and then
all at once she was running. Running desperately across the lawn
and to the shelter of the house.

She had no clear recollection afterwards of entering the house
or of fastening the french window behind her, but she had done
so, and reached the telephone and had somehow managed to dial
a number.

The distant muffled bell purred only twice and then someone
lifted the receiver. 'Lang here,' said a quiet voice.

'Simon!' the word was a sob. Miranda's voice was shaking and
she could barely control it. It seemed to her that she had shouted
his name but to Simon it was no more than a soft, indistinguishable sound.

'Who is it? I can't hear you.'

Miranda fought to steady herself, gripping the receiver in both

133

hands until the fingernails of her left hand cut into the flesh below the thumb.

'Miranda. Simon, please come quickly! Friedel's dead, and I'm all alone — *Simon!*'

Simon did not waste time asking questions. He said: 'I'll be along as soon as I can. Ring Dr Elvers, that'll save me time. You'll find his name in the book. Or get any doctor.'

'It's no good!' said Miranda frantically. 'She's dead! The blood went into her eye and——' But Simon had rung off.

Miranda stood shivering, still clutching the receiver to her ear. And as she stood there, she heard a sound. It was a very soft sound, but quite unmistakable, and she stopped shivering and stood rigid; staring with widened, terrified eyes at the receiver in her hand.

She had told Simon Lang that she was alone in the house. But it was not true. There was someone else there. Someone besides herself and Lottie. Someone who had listened to her conversation with Simon and then very quietly replaced the receiver of the telephone extension that stood beside Robert's bed in the big front room upstairs ...

Miranda dropped the receiver and whirled round to stare up at the landing above the hall, her heart beating suffocatingly. But the landing was in shadow and from where she stood she could not see the door of Stella's bedroom.

She backed away towards the cloakroom. There was a bolt on the inside of the cloakroom door. She could shut herself in and wait until Simon came.

And then, suddenly, she remembered Lottie. Someone was hiding upstairs in one of the darkened rooms — and Lottie was up there too, asleep.

Miranda ran across the hall and raced up the staircase, heedless of what might be awaiting her in the shadows above the lighted hall, and flung open the door of Lottie's room. She found the switch and pressed it, and the room was flooded with soft light.

Lottie was sound asleep, curled up with her hands folded under her chin. She did not move or wake, and Miranda pulled the key from the outside of the door with trembling fingers and locked herself in.

She knew that she should turn off the light again in case it should wake Lottie, but she could not bring herself to wait in the dark, and she found a small green cardigan and draped it over the light instead. The effect was dim and eerie, but at least it was better than darkness, and she leant weakly against the door, struggling to steady herself and regain control over her breathing.

Once she thought she heard a stair creak and someone moving somewhere in the house, but though she strained her ears to listen she could not be certain of the sound or its direction.

Whoever had been in Stella and Robert's bedroom would not stay there: that much was certain. And it would be quite simple for anyone to leave, for they had only to walk down the stairs and out of the front door. Or if that was too public, the drop from the balcony outside the bedroom windows was not so great, and the small back landing, from which one flight of stairs ascended to the attic and another descended to the kitchen quarters, lay only a few yards to the right of the bedroom door. Once down the back staircase there would be no difficulty in leaving the house, since the locks were Yale ones and could be opened from inside.

Oh, why didn't Simon come?

Miranda left the door and went quickly to the window, but there was no sign of any approaching car. Only the moonlight, and the yellow glow of the street lamps gleaming intermittently through the fretted branches of the trees that a rising wind was beginning to sway and shiver.

She dropped the curtain back into place and as she turned away her eye was caught by her own reflection in the looking-glass above the small dressing-table. There were marks on the pale topaz-coloured wool of her dress. A dark stain near the shoulder.

Miranda put up an unsteady hand and touched it.

So it had happened again! The pattern had repeated itself. Once again there was blood on her dress — and now there was blood on her hand too . . . *'Circumstantial evidence'*.

135

She could not let it happen again! She could not. Who would believe her this time? She must change her dress ... hide it ... burn it! She began to tear at the fastenings with frenzied, frantic hands.

A fingernail caught and tore agonizingly in the catch of the zip-fastener, and her hair tangled about the dangling charms on her bracelet and wrenched free as she pulled the dress over her head and threw it from her as if it had been something alive and crawling. Her breath was coming in sobbing gasps and her hands were wet with sweat.

A car turned into the road and its headlights licked the windows with brief, brilliant light; and then it had jerked to a stop outside the house. Quick footsteps sounded on the flagged path below and Miranda heard the front door open.

Simon Lang! And she had sent for him herself. She had lost her head and sent for the one man who already had reason to suspect her of murder. She must have been mad! She should have said nothing; pretended to know nothing; changed the stained dress and waited for someone else to discover the murder. Instead of which she had run headlong into suspicion and danger as once before she had run wildly down the corridor of the night train to Berlin ...

'Miranda!' Simon's voice echoed strangely in the silent house. She heard him cross the hall and jerk open the drawing-room door.

'Miranda!'

Lottie stirred and murmured in her sleep and once again the instinct to protect the sleeping child overcame the nightmare numbness that had held Miranda in its grip. She turned the key in the lock and went out onto the landing, closing the door softly behind her.

Simon was standing in the hall immediately below her, his body, seen from above, looking curiously foreshortened by the drop, and the pupils of his eyes so dilated that his eyes looked black, like a cat's that has come in from the dark. He stood quite still for a

136

moment, looking up at her; and then she saw his face change and he came up the stairs, taking them three at a time, and was standing in front of her, his hands gripping her shoulders, as he had stood in the corridor of the train on the night that Brigadier Brindley had died.

He said sharply: 'Are you all right?'

'*Ssssh!* You'll wake Lottie,' said Miranda automatically. She swayed and would have fallen but for Simon's grip on her shoulders.

Simon shook her savagely. The action was so unexpected that it acted upon Miranda's numbed faculties like a dash of cold water, and she gasped and jerked herself away.

'That's better,' said Simon ungently.

He caught her arm and pulled it through his, and holding it tightly against him, turned and walked her down the stairs and into the hall.

'Now let's have it,' said Simon, swinging her round to face him.

His eyes narrowed suddenly. In the dimness of the unlighted landing he had not noticed her unorthodox attire, and had imagined her to be wearing some form of evening dress. Miranda looked down, following the direction of his startled gaze, and her white face coloured hotly. She had forgotten that she wore no dress and was standing in the full light of the hall clad in the scantiest possible underwear.

She tried to pull away, but Simon's fingers tightened about her arm as his eyes took her in from head to foot — the tangled disorder of the dark curls, the white arms and shoulders, the absurd wisps of lace-trimmed, apricot-tinted transparency, long slender legs and small high-heeled slippers. And suddenly there was a cold anger in his eyes that frightened her.

'What on earth,' said Simon softly, 'are you dressed like that for? Come on — out with it!'

'I – I meant to burn it.' Miranda's voice was a jerky whisper despite her effort to control it, and her eyes were wide and enormous.

'Burn what?'

'My dress. There was blood on it. You see I – I touched her. And – and it was like the other time; and I thought you would think — that everyone would think ...' Miranda's voice trailed away hopelessly and stopped.

Simon said: 'I see.' There was, curiously enough, relief in his voice. He released her arm and Miranda sat down abruptly on the bottom step of the stairs.

Simon turned on his heel, and going over to the coat rack by the cloakroom door, took down a coat at random and returning, tossed it at Miranda.

'You'd better put that on.'

It was a Burberry of Robert's and far too large for her, but Miranda struggled into it, wrapping it about her as she sat on the hall stair.

Simon said curtly: 'Where is she?'

'In the garden.' Miranda jerked her head towards the open door of the drawing-room and the moonlit windows beyond. 'By the gap in the hedge near the lilac bushes.'

He turned and walked quickly across the hall and into the drawing-room, and she heard him open the french window and go out. After that there was silence for what seemed a very long time ...

Miranda leaned her head against the newel post and shut her eyes. She felt utterly exhausted and strangely apathetic. None of this was real. It could not be real, because things like this did not happen to ordinary people like herself. They only happened to strange beings whose faces adorned the pages of the more sensational Sunday papers. She would wake up presently and find that the whole thing was a nightmare.

A slight sound aroused her and she opened her eyes. Simon Lang was standing in front of her, frowning down at her, and he did not look in the least like a nightmare.

'She's dead all right,' said Simon. 'Who is she?'

'Friedel. The housemaid.'

Simon leant down and pulled her to her feet and walked her across to the dining-room.

The lights still burned above the table and the room was in every way as Miranda had left it halfway through her supper. It seemed as if months of time must have passed since she had last sat here, and yet her half-eaten meal was still on the table and the hands on the clock-face pointed to five minutes past nine. Friedel had said she would be away only an hour. She would be back by nine. But Friedel was dead and her body lay in the cold spring moonlight beyond the curtained windows of the dining-room.

Miranda began to shiver again, and Simon pushed her down into a chair and held a glass to her mouth. She drank obediently and choked as the fiery liquid caught her throat.

He stood looking down at her with a frown in his eyes, and after a moment or two he pulled up a chair, and sitting down facing her said: 'Tell me what happened.'

'I was alone in the house,' began Miranda haltingly. 'It was Mademoiselle's day out, and Robert phoned to say he wouldn't be back until late, and then Stella rang up and said she would have supper with him at the Club and would I look after Lottie as Friedel wanted to go out for an hour or two. I said good-night to Lottie, and Friedel said that my supper was ready, and then – then she went out.'

'What time was that?'

'About a quarter to eight I think. I don't think I looked at the clock ...'

She looked at it now. Not much more than an hour ago! It wasn't possible — it wasn't possible——

Simon's voice jerked her back to the present.

'What happened then?'

'I heard someone moving about upstairs and I thought it was Lottie. I called up to her to get back into bed. And then ...' She stopped.

'And then?' prompted Simon.

'I – I was afraid.'

139

'Why? What were you afraid of?'

'I don't know. I thought that someone was watching me. I was quite sure of it. I didn't hear anything, it was just a – a feeling. And after a bit I couldn't bear it any longer, so I went into the hall to see if anyone was there; but there wasn't anyone. And then I thought I saw something move outside the drawing-room window, and I thought it was Wally . . .'

'The Wilkin child? Why?'

'Because he had been playing round here before, and I'd caught him only this afternoon crawling through the bushes under the windows. I thought he was at it again and that this time I'd catch him and give him a good smacking, so I went out and – and found her.'

Miranda's voice wavered uncertainly and her hands tightened on the arms of her chair.

'Where?'

'Near the lilac bushes, in the gap by the hedge. I told you.'

'She was on the edge of the lawn,' said Simon. 'Did you move her?'

'Yes . . . I forgot that. I tried to lift her. I – I thought it was Stella.'

'*Stella?* You thought it was Mrs Melville? Why?'

'She was lying face downwards, you see. And – and her head was in the shadow and she was wearing Stella's coat.'

Simon Lang did not say anything for what appeared to be a very long time. He sat quite still and looked at Miranda, his face entirely expressionless and his eyes intent and unreadable. And once again, as earlier in the evening, she became aware of the clock, chipping off splinters of time into the silence.

She put up a hand to loosen the enveloping folds of Robert's Burberry from about her throat, jerking at it as though it impeded her breathing.

Simon said: 'So you thought it was Mrs Melville. What did you do when you found out that it wasn't?'

'I dropped her, and ran in and telephoned you.'

'Why? Why not a doctor? Or Major Melville?'

140

'I don't know,' said Miranda wearily. 'I suppose because I knew that she was dead and I remembered your number. You gave it to me. I can't quite remember what I thought.'

Simon Lang looked away from her for the first time and his speculative gaze travelled over the table.

'What time was it, would you say, when you went out into the garden?'

'I don't know. I didn't look.'

'But you must have some idea. It can't have taken you very long to drink a plate of soup — put it at five minutes. When did you think you heard Lottie moving?'

Miranda pressed her hands to her face, trying to think back. 'I put the soup plate on the sideboard and helped myself to meat and salad and – and I mixed some dressing. It was after that I thought I heard Lottie.'

'Let's say another five minutes. And then?'

'I told you. I went to the door and called up to her.'

'And came back to the table but did not touch your food. Why?'

'I told you,' repeated Miranda. 'I felt — I felt jumpy and frightened, so I sat here for a bit and – and listened, I suppose.'

'For very long?'

'Not very. Not as much as five minutes. Five minutes is a very long time when you're sitting quite still and you're frightened.'

'Then it was probably about eight o'clock — five past at the most — when you went out into the garden. But it was almost half-past eight when you telephoned me. What were you doing in the garden for twenty minutes, Miranda?'

Miranda stared at him, her eyes wide and frightened, and once again she put up a hand to tug at the cloth about her slender throat. 'Nothing. I mean I – I looked for Wally. I stood and waited for a bit, thinking I would hear him move. Then I listened to the party in the Leslies' house until I saw their lights go off and heard them leave.'

Simon let his breath out in a curious little sigh. He said: 'So you knew that there was no one in the next house.' It was more in the

141

nature of a statement than a query, but Miranda did not appear to notice that. The brandy that Simon had given her was taking effect and she was feeling less tense and considerably more at ease.

'Yes. And I began to feel cold and I couldn't hear anyone moving, so I decided that I would go round the rest of the garden and then lock myself into the house and play the radio until the others came back. So I walked round and ... I've told you the rest.'

Simon said: 'Twenty minutes is a long time, Miranda. Too long. Are you quite sure that you've told me everything?'

'Yes,' said Miranda flatly. She could feel the colour flooding up into her face; it was a childish and Victorian habit that she had failed to outgrow and over which she had no control.

'And that's all you did in the garden? Just walked once round it?'

'I sat on the seat under the cherry tree for a bit. I was thinking.'

'What about?'

'Nothing,' said Miranda quite definitely. 'Just thinking.'

Simon gave a little shrug and dropped the question.

'Are you quite sure that there was no one else in the house?' He saw the look on Miranda's face and said: 'So there *was* someone. Who was it?'

'I don't know,' said Miranda in a shuddering whisper that made her teeth chatter: 'It was when I was telephoning you. You rang off, and just afterwards I heard someone put down the receiver of the extension in Stella's room. There must have been someone up there, listening.'

'And you've no idea who it was?'

'No. I was too frightened to think. I tore upstairs to Lottie's room and locked myself in; and then you arrived. That's all.'

'You didn't hear anyone leave the room?'

'I'm not sure. I thought I did. They could have gone down the front stairs — or the back ones. But – but then I saw that I'd got blood on my dress and I suppose I lost my head.'

Miranda laughed: a dreary little laugh with no mirth in it. 'I thought what a fool I was to have sent for you — or for anyone!

It was exactly the same all over again you see. That's what made it so awful. And so – so horribly impossible. It was a sort of repeat performance. Do you remember saying that whoever killed the Brigadier must have had blood on them? Well I was the only person who had blood on them. And now I've got it again! Silly, isn't it?'

She laughed again, loudly, and Simon said curtly: 'Stop it, Miranda!'

'I'm sorry. I feel a little odd.'

'You're tight,' said Simon unkindly.

He got up and stood looking down at her for a moment, his hands in his pockets. 'You'd better go upstairs and take that coat off, and get back into your dress,' he said. 'I'm going to do some telephoning and there will be quite a few people round here soon. You'll have to answer a good many questions, and if your story is true there's no point in your not wearing the dress you had on when you found that woman. In fact, it won't look so good if you're not. Do you know where I can contact Major Melville?'

Miranda didn't answer the question. She stood up quickly; so quickly that for the second time that evening she knocked over her chair, but this time she did not notice it. She said breathlessly: 'It *is* true! Why should you say it isn't true?'

'I haven't said so,' said Simon evenly. 'Where is Major Melville?'

'I don't know. Yes I do. Stella said they'd probably have supper at the Club.'

Simon walked past her and out of the room, and Miranda stooped mechanically and replaced the fallen chair. Her heart was hammering again and once more she felt as though she was in the grip of a nightmare. *'Twenty minutes is a long time, Miranda ...'*

Were innocent people ever hanged for murders they had not committed? *'If your story is true.'* How could you prove a thing like that if people would not take your word for it? She had read books in which people who discovered murdered bodies instantly panicked and either attempted to dispose of them, or concealed evidence and were, on that account, suspected of committing the crime. And she had always thought scornfully that of course any innocent person would instantly ring for the police, and only a hysterical or a guilty person would keep quiet about it. But perhaps those panic-stricken characters had been right after all. She, Miranda, had sent for the police, in the person of Simon Lang. But she might well have been better off if she had done nothing, concealed evidence, and professed blank ignorance of the whole affair.

12

Miranda awoke next morning with an aching head and a dull sense of disaster.

She sat up wearily and frowned at the clock by her bedside, wondering if it had stopped, for the hands pointed at ten minutes to eleven. But the small strip of bright sunlight that pierced between the curtains confirmed the lateness of the hour, and she crawled out of bed and crossing to the basin turned on both taps and splashed her face with water.

Her eyes felt heavy from lack of sleep; her head ached abominably and her brain seemed singularly sluggish. She began to dress slowly, remembering as she did so the details of the past night ...

Friedel Schultz was dead; murdered. Someone had hit her over the back of the head with one of the iron pokers from the boiler-room. Her death must have been more a matter of chance than judgement, for had the blow fallen an inch higher it would have stunned but not killed her.

Within an hour of her death a wind had risen and blown steadily and with increasing force until shortly before midnight, when it had culminated in a brief and violent storm. There would be no trace of footprints on the sandy paths or by the lilac bushes on this bright morning to betray where the murderer had stood, or come, or gone; and Miranda herself had dragged Friedel's body from where it had originally lain ...

They had questioned her about that for hours: Simon Lang and the grey-haired man who had spoken to them in the waiting-room at Charlottenburg station, and a third man whom she could not remember having seen before, but who had evidently interrogated Stella and Mademoiselle on their first morning in Berlin.

There had been a doctor too, and a couple of medical orderlies with a stretcher who had carried the body of Friedel away from the house. There had been people with lights and cameras; though by the time these had arrived the little breeze that had driven Miranda from her seat by the cherry trees had freshened to a wind that had blown the sandy paths clean, and there was nothing to photograph except Friedel herself, lying on her back at the edge of the lawn where Miranda had left her.

Simon had failed to contact either Robert or Stella, and they had returned in the middle of it all, though not together: Stella arriving shortly after ten o'clock and Robert half an hour later.

Mademoiselle had returned at half past eleven. She had been to see a film at the A.K.C. cinema in the Reichskanzler Platz, and had walked home after coffee and biscuits at a café.

It had all been a nightmare. The lights above the dining-room table shining down on the remains of Miranda's supper and the faces of the three men who questioned her. The arrival of Stella, who had walked into the hall just as Friedel's limp body was being carried in from the garden.

Simon had gone out to intercept her and explain the ugly situation in as few words as possible, but Stella had not appeared to hear him. She had only stared at Friedel and said in a queer high-pitched voice: 'But she's wearing my coat! Why is she wearing my coat? Where's Miranda?'

'I'm here,' said Miranda shaking off the hand of the grey-haired man who would have detained her, and running into the hall: 'She must have borrowed it Stel', and thought she could put it back before you got home. But I thought it was you who'd been killed ... I saw the coat, and I thought it was you!' Miranda's voice wavered.

Stella's eyes widened until they were violet circles, and the last vestige of colour drained out of her pale face leaving it a dreadful greenish white. She put up a hand to her throat and said in a dry whisper: 'You thought it was me!' And then she had fainted, falling to the floor in a sprawling, untidy heap.

Hours later — or was it only minutes? — she had been carried up to her room, where she had been very sick, and finally the doctor had given her an injection of morphia and she had gone to sleep. But that had not been until after Robert had arrived back.

Robert, it appeared, had intended to work late at the office and dine in the Mess, but the Colonel had rung him up shortly before seven-thirty and suggested that he bring the work over to his house for discussion since another matter relating to it had just cropped up, and stay to supper there: whereupon Robert had borrowed a fellow officer's car and had driven to the Lawrences' house.

He had listened to an account of the evening's happenings with incredulity. Then he had seen Miranda sitting pallid and exhausted, facing her interrogators over the dining-room table, and he had lost his temper.

'What the hell do you mean by devilling the girl? Can't you wait to do your bullying in the morning?' stormed Robert. He strode over to the table and put his arms around her, and Miranda, turning, had clung to him and burst into overwrought tears.

Robert picked her up bodily, and having favoured the assembly with an unprintable opinion of them, carried her out into the hall and up the stairs. Stella's bedroom door stood open, and Stella was facing it, her fair hair dark with water where the doctor had bathed her forehead and face, and looking as though she was about to be sick again. Robert put Miranda roughly on her feet and left her at a run, and she saw him catch Stella into his arms. Then the doctor closed the door on them, and she was alone on the landing and Lottie had awakened and was demanding a drink of water.

Miranda dried her wet cheeks with the back of her hand and attended to the matter, and having retrieved Rollerbear from the floor and succeeded in settling Lottie off to sleep again, went slowly downstairs once more.

Simon Lang was still sitting in the dining-room, but the others

147

had gone. He was engaged in playing patience with a doll-sized pack of cards that Lottie had left on the windowsill, and he looked up briefly as she came into the room and then thoughtfully placed the queen of diamonds on the king of clubs before speaking.

'I think some of these must be missing,' he said. 'Why did you come down again? Your cousin is quite right. As far as you are concerned there is no real reason why you should answer any more questions until the morning.'

'I don't intend to,' said Miranda wearily. She sank into a chair, resting her elbows on the table and her chin in her hands. 'But I can't go to bed yet. I shouldn't sleep. Besides, Mademoiselle isn't back yet. Someone will have to let her in.'

'Someone will. I'm afraid that I must break it to you that I shall have to stick around here until the governess turns up.'

'Why?'

'Oh just a matter of routine you know. Someone has got to ask the usual questions: where was she, what was she doing at such-and-such a time, and all the rest of it.'

'Why can't you ask her that in the morning?'

Simon Lang looked along the lines of cards, added a three of clubs, and said softly: 'She might have a different story by the morning.'

Miranda got up abruptly and went over to the sideboard, returning a moment or so later with a glass in her hand.

Simon lifted an expressive eyebrow. 'Do you usually drink whisky with lemonade?'

'No. I don't drink it with anything,' said Miranda bleakly, 'but I'm going to drink it now. Robert says it's the world's best pick-me-up, and I need one.'

'Robert was not aware that you would ever try it out on top of a straight double-brandy,' observed Simon. 'Leave it alone, Miranda, and go and get yourself some hot milk instead; or some black coffee.'

Miranda drank off the contents of her glass with deliberation

148

and suppressing a grimace of distaste, pushed it away from her and said: 'Where are the others?'

'They've gone.'

'And – and Friedel?'

'She's gone, too. Miranda——'

'My name,' said Miranda stiffly, 'is Brand.'

'But then I don't know you well enough to call you by your name,' said Simon gently, his attention still apparently on the array of cards spread out before him. 'Don't be childish, Miranda. Who introduced you to Brigadier Brindley?'

The question was so unexpected that for a moment Miranda wondered if she had heard aright. Simon looked up and waited, his eyes on hers.

'I – I don't remember. Robert, I suppose — or Stella. No it wasn't. It was Colonel Leslie: I remember now. It was in the dining-car of the train from the Hook. He was sitting opposite the Leslies and I sat next to him because we could only sit four to a table, and as Mademoiselle and Lottie were with Stella and Robert, I sat at the next one.'

'Did you get the impression that they had known each other before, or had only just met?'

'I don't really know. It's very difficult to tell with army people, because even if they have only just met they know so many people and places in common that they sound as if they know each other well. Mrs Leslie must have known him before, because she said that Stella——' Miranda stopped, frowning. 'No, it wasn't that of course.'

'What wasn't which?'

'Nothing really. Only something I got the wrong way round. I thought she meant the Brigadier but she didn't. It was Johnnie she meant.'

'Who meant? And who is Johnnie?' inquired Simon patiently.

'Johnnie Radley: Stella's first husband. He was killed at Tobruk.' Suddenly she found herself telling Simon of that curious conversation in the Kurfürstendamm. Perhaps it was the unac-

149

customed effects of a stiff whisky on top of the brandy that Simon had given her, or perhaps she only wished to talk in order to keep herself from thinking of Friedel's dead face in the moonlight and the feel of that slack, heavy body in her arms — and of her own perilous position.

Simon listened without comment and without once raising his eyes from the tiny coloured playing-cards before him. He continued to deal and place them, and when she had finished he swept the cards together and remarked in an abstracted voice that there were two missing.

There were low voices in the hall, and Robert and the doctor came down the stairs and into the dining-room. Robert looked bewildered and angry, and his handsome face was unusually pale. He ignored Simon and asked Miranda why on earth she wasn't in bed?

'Mademoiselle isn't back yet,' said Miranda tiredly. 'And I thought that Stella ...'

'Stella's asleep. And it's quite time you were too. Run along now, darling; I want to talk to Lang. I'll see to Mademoiselle.' He turned to the doctor. 'Can't you give her something? Not a knock-out drop, just something that will help her sleep.'

'She won't need it,' said Simon dryly. 'All she needs is a couple of aspirins to ward off a hangover.'

Robert said furiously: 'What the hell do you mean by that?'

'Only that the kid has about a quarter of a pint of mixed whisky and brandy inside her at the moment,' said Simon equably, 'and as she appears to be unused to spirits it should prove a fairly effective soporific.'

The doctor silently handed over two aspirins and Miranda swallowed them obediently and stood up. Robert put an arm around her slim shoulders: 'I'll see you up to your room.'

Miranda smiled a little crookedly and said: 'I'm all right,' and turning her head saw that Simon had risen too and was watching her. She thought that she had never seen a blanker or more expressionless face. And yet there was something there — perhaps in the eyes that met hers so steadily — something watchful and intensely interested and, yes, angry . . .

She freed herself gently from Robert's hold and turned and went out of the room.

But she had not gone to sleep until long after midnight. She had not even undressed. She had sat on the edge of her bed with her chin on her hands and stared ahead of her, and listened to the murmur of voices from the dining-room. She had heard Mademoiselle return, and Mademoiselle's excitable tones raised in angry expostulation — the governess became exceedingly foreign when agitated, and her speech became a mixed torrent of English and the German-French of St Gallen.

Miranda, listening to her, gave a little shiver of distaste. She found Mademoiselle repellent, and felt towards her much as Aunt Hetty did towards cats. Even the smell of the caraway seeds that Mademoiselle would nibble between her strong yellow teeth could make her nerves curl in disgust.

Mademoiselle had been with Stella for three years, ever since Lottie was five. She had proved a hard worker, and willing to help with housework, mending and laundering; she never seemed to take holidays, had no near relatives, and in a day when reliable household help was difficult to obtain, had turned out to be worth at least four times her modest salary. Stella frequently said that she did not know how she would manage without her, and blessed the chance that had brought her to their door inquiring for employment.

Three years ago Miranda, who had recently left school, was living in a girls' club in London, having obtained work with a model agency. And later, when she was earning a steady income, she had taken a small flat with a girl of her own age who was studying at R.A.D.A. So she had not seen very much of Stella, and little or nothing of Mademoiselle until she had accepted the Melvilles' invitation to go out with them to Berlin, and had met them all in the lounge of the Station Hotel at Liverpool Street. But since then her first instinctive dislike of the elderly Swiss spinster,

151

with her dyed hair, her peculiar eyes and perpetual aroma of caraway seed, had grown into aversion. And tonight, sitting in her bedroom with her aching head in her hands, Miranda listened to Mademoiselle's plangent tones echoing up from the hall below and shivered with distaste.

Presently Mademoiselle had come upstairs and gone to her room, and later Robert had crossed the hall with the doctor and Simon Lang. Miranda could not make out what they were saying, but Robert's voice sounded weary and cross, the doctor's soothing, and Simon's unendurably placid.

It was past one o'clock before Miranda again removed the topaz-coloured dress that was smeared with Friedel's blood, and fell into an exhausted and uneasy slumber; but the hall was bright with mid-morning sunlight when she came downstairs again.

She could hear Stella's voice behind the closed door of the drawing-room, and as she hesitated someone crossed the landing above and came quickly down the stairs. It was Mrs Leslie, hatted and gloved and carrying a small suitcase. She stopped when she saw Miranda and looked surprised.

'Hullo, my dear. They told me you were asleep. Have you had any breakfast? It was kept hot for you. I've been helping the governess to pack.'

'Pack what? Is she leaving?' inquired Miranda, wishing that her head did not ache so.

'Oh no. It's only the child. Lottie is going over to the Lawrences' for a day or two until this horrible business is cleared up. Katy Lawrence rang me up this morning and asked me to arrange it. She didn't like to ring this house in case Mrs Melville or you were asleep, so I came over and fixed it with Robert. Of course it's the obvious thing to do — get the child right out of the way. The governess is to sleep here and bicycle over every morning to look after her during the day. It's no distance, really.'

Miranda said: 'Who's Stella talking to?'

'Captain Lang — or some other man from the local equivalent of the Gestapo,' said Mrs Leslie with a trace of acid. 'We've had a swarm of them all over the place this morning, including the German police. They had Edward and myself answering a lot of idiotic questions before breakfast; *and* the servants and the batman! They even wanted a list of our guests last night, and in what order they had arrived. I never heard such nonsense! I'll tell the cook that you're up and she can bring you something to eat in the dining-room.

'I don't want anything to eat,' said Miranda with strong revulsion.

'Nonsense! You'll feel far better once you've had some food and hot coffee,' said Mrs Leslie bracingly. 'You're looking a wreck. At least twenty-four!'

Miranda smiled and Mrs Leslie said: 'That's better,' and went off to the kitchen to speak briefly and with authority to Frau Herbach.

'Silly woman!' said Mrs Leslie, returning. 'Scared out of her wits and wants to leave. Says she'll be the next victim. And this is the nation that ... well, never mind. Ah, here's the coffee: have some of that at least. I'll take the suitcases over to my house.'

'Is Lottie at the Lawrences' already?' asked Miranda, following Frau Herbach and the tray into the dining-room.

'No, she's over at my house playing with that child with the freckles who was on the train with us. Katy Lawrence is going to fetch her later. I expect I shall be seeing you. Brace up!'

She turned away and left Miranda to her belated breakfast.

Someone had forgotten to turn off the central heating in the dining-room, and since the room was full of sunlight and very hot, Miranda went over to the nearest window and opened it. The drawing-room windows, a yard or so to the left, were also open, and Stella's voice was clearly audible. There was a break in it, as though she had been crying.

'... Oh, I know I behaved like a fool! But I *had* to know. I couldn't bear not knowing! You see, he'd known her in Egypt and I knew that she had written to him.'

Simon Lang asked a question, but Miranda only caught the

intonation of his quiet voice and did not hear the words.

Stella said: 'It was Mrs Marson. She was there too — at the Lawrences'; I think all the wives were — and she said something to Sally — Mrs Page — about her being a grass-widow for the evening because her husband was dining out at some Mess in the American sector. So then Mrs Bradley asked Sally if she'd like to come up to their flat for supper, but she said she already had a date, and Mrs Bradley laughed and said: "Trust you for that!" And – and — when Robert, my husband, rang up and said he wouldn't be back to supper because he would be working late on some scheme, I ...'

There was a brief pause, as though Stella were striving to control herself, and when she spoke again, it was in a flat, level voice.

'I didn't mean to do anything silly. It was just that I didn't want to go back to the house because ...' Her voice wavered momentarily. 'Because Miranda was there, and I wanted to be alone and think. So I rang up and said I wouldn't be back, and I drove out somewhere — to that place where the swimming-pool is — and parked the car and walked about the grounds and thought about everything. And then I suddenly decided to ring up the office and – and make sure. I drove to the Officers' Club and telephoned from there. But there was no answer from his office and he wasn't in the Mess either.'

Simon Lang must have moved nearer the window, because this time Miranda heard him say: 'What time was that?'

'Just after half-past seven.'

'Quite sure?'

'Yes. I looked at the clock when I'd finished telephoning. It was about a minute past the half hour.'

'And then?'

'Then I went out and got into the car and drove to the road where the Pages' flat is,' said Stella in a hard, defiant voice. 'I parked the car where I could watch the entrance. And I saw Sally — Mrs Page — come out and get into a taxi — and I followed it. But I lost it at the traffic lights.'

'Had you waited long?' Simon's voice was entirely matter-of-fact, and he might have been discussing the weather. It evidently had a steadying effect upon Stella, for her voice sounded less taut and more normal.

'No. Only a minute or two. It's not far from the Club, so it must have been about twenty to eight.'

'Mrs Page was dining at the Leslies',' said Simon. 'So by that reckoning she must have arrived at their house not later than ten minutes to eight.'

'I know,' said Stella wretchedly. 'I've made a complete fool of myself. I see that now.'

'What did you do when you lost sight of the taxi?'

'I parked the car in a side street and just sat.'

'For how long?'

'I don't know. It didn't seem very long, but it may have been an hour — or two hours!' She gave a dreary little laugh. 'And then I had something to eat at a café in one of the back roads and came home, and ... Well, you know the rest.'

Simon said: 'Did you see anyone you knew? Or anyone you think might be able to identify you, between the time you left the Club and eight o'clock? That's almost the only time we're interested in.'

'No,' said Stella wearily. 'No one at all. So you see I haven't got an alibi. Captain Lang ...'

'Yes?'

'Does Robert have to know?'

'Not unless you tell him yourself,' said Simon. 'It might not be a bad idea you know,' he suggested, gently deprecatory.

'I can't!' Stella's voice had a hard edge to it. 'He asked me this morning and I said that I had just decided to see Berlin and have supper at a German café for – for fun. I only told you because ...' She stopped, and then said in a voice that was puzzled and a little angry: 'I don't know why I should have told you.'

Because people do tell him things, thought Miranda wryly. Things they don't mean to tell him——

She leaned against the windowsill and looked out across the sunny strip of lawn. Last night's rain had battered the cherry trees, but though the ground below them was strewn with fallen petals, new buds were opening to take their place, and the garden looked fresh and clean and a little smug. It did not seem possible that a woman had died a violent death in it only a few hours ago.

Mademoiselle came round the corner of the house wheeling her bicycle, and seeing Miranda at the window, paused and inquired if she had slept well. She herself had not closed her eyes, so great was her alarm, and her sorrow for the poor, poor woman so foully done to death — without doubt by the agents of the Soviet. Always there were killings and kidnappings in Berlin by the Russians: one had told her so only yesterday.

She was interrupted by Stella who leant out of the window to ask if she was sure she knew the way to the Lawrences' house?

But yes, said Mademoiselle. She knew quite well the direction and would have departed earlier had it not been for the time wasted by the imbecile gendarmes and their so foolish questions. Mademoiselle concluded her remarks with a resounding sniff and wheeled her bicycle away, and Stella said: 'Hullo, 'Randa. I didn't realize you were up. How are you feeling?'

'Terrible! Come and have some coffee.'

'I can't,' said Stella with an attempt at a smile. 'I'm being given the third degree.'

'Do you mean to say that the imbecile gendarmes haven't finished with their so foolish questions yet?' inquired Miranda, raising her voice with intent.

Stella frowned and said sharply: 'Don't be silly, Miranda!' She drew in her head and Miranda heard Simon Lang laugh, and then the window shut with a bang.

Miranda poured herself another cup of black coffee and sipped it slowly. She was trying to explain something to herself. She, Miranda, had for a brief space behaved like that fictional character who plays into the murderer's hands by concealing evidence instead of yelling for the police. Which was understandable, since

156

she had, after all, received a series of violent and unpleasant shocks, and could be forgiven for reacting to them a little wildly.

What was not understandable was why, in the bright light of morning, an uncomfortable proportion of the panic that had driven her to tear off the stained dress, and had whispered the words *'Circumstantial evidence'* in her ear, should still remain with her? Because, of course, it was nonsense. Suspicion could not possibly rest on her for the simple reason that unless they suspected her of homicidal mania, she had no shadow of motive for killing Brigadier Brindley or Friedel Schultz; and no possible connection with either of them. And yet she was still afraid. Why?

Because of Simon Lang! The answer presented itself to her as suddenly as though someone had spoken the words aloud.

Simon Lang could see a possible reason why she might have committed both crimes. A motive that had escaped Miranda herself, but was, none the less, a feasible one; since she did not believe that he would waste time on impossibilities. It followed, therefore, that somewhere in all this there was some connection between Brigadier Brindley, Friedel and herself, and a possible motive for the murder of both Brigadier Brindley and Friedel by Miranda Brand.

She heard the drawing-room door open and Stella walk quickly across the hall and run up the stairs, and a moment later the sound of her bedroom door being shut with a bang. Miranda put down her coffee cup and, leaving the room, walked resolutely across the hall and into the drawing-room.

Simon Lang was leaning against the window frame, his hands deep in his pockets, looking out into the garden. He turned his head as she entered and acknowledged her presence with something that might conceivably have been called a smile, and when she did not speak, turned back to his contemplation of the garden.

Miranda seemed suddenly to have forgotten what it was she had wanted to say. She crossed the room slowly and stood beside him, looking out on the green, sunlit space and trying to imagine it as it had looked last night; and would look again when the sun had set: a place of darkness and mystery and shadows.

Something of what was passing in her mind seemed also to be in Simon Lang's, for he said under his breath: ' "*Is the day fair? Yet unto evening shall the day spin on ...*" ' He did not finish the quotation, and Miranda spoke the next two lines almost without knowing that she had done so: ' "*And soon thy sun be gone; then darkness come, and this, a narrow home.*" '

Simon turned and looked at her, his eyebrows up and an odd gleam in his eyes.

Miranda shivered suddenly in the bright sunlight and said: 'It all looks so ordinary, and so safe. It doesn't seem possible that anything like that could have happened out there.'

Simon said: 'You've forgotten the first line of that poem.'

'No, I haven't. You left it out. *"O passer-by, beware!"* I was the passer-by: but how is one to know?'

Simon did not reply and the room was very silent; as silent as the quiet garden outside.

Miranda sighed and turned away from the window. 'I wanted to ask you something,' she said slowly. 'You have a theory about me, haven't you? A possible reason why I might have murdered two people who were complete strangers to me.'

She looked directly at Simon Lang, but her eyes were dazzled by the bright sunlight beyond the window, and his face seemed to be oddly out of focus and once again entirely without expression: as though a blind had been drawn down over it. He did not trouble to deny or confirm her statement, but returned her gaze evenly and in silence.

'What reason could I possibly have had?' urged Miranda. 'I didn't know either of them.'

Simon said quietly: 'That might not have been necessary.'

'I don't understand.'

'Don't you? I wonder.'

Simon was silent for a moment or two, then he said meditatively: 'Men commit murder for a variety of reasons. But generally

158

speaking, there are only two reasons why women do; and they frequently commit them for a combination of the two. It is just conceivable — only just — that you might qualify on account of those reasons.'

'I don't understand!' repeated Miranda angrily.

'If you don't, then there's no need for you to worry,' said Simon.

'But I tell you, I'd never even met Brigadier Brindley before that afternoon on the train,' insisted Miranda.

'No, I don't think you had,' said Simon unexpectedly.

'There you are then! As for Friedel, I hadn't spoken more than a dozen words to her.'

Simon looked at her speculatively for a moment or two, then he said quietly: 'Whoever killed the Brigadier need not have known him for more than a few hours.'

'And Friedel?'

'That was, I think, a mistake,' said Simon. He glanced at his watch and said: 'I must go,' and turned and walked to the door.

Miranda ran after him and caught at his arm: 'But you haven't answered my question!'

Simon looked down at the slim fingers that clutched his sleeve. 'No,' he said reflectively. 'I don't believe I have.'

He detached her fingers quite gently, as though he were removing some small creeping object that he did not wish to harm, and the hall door closed quietly behind him.

Miranda made a sound like an infuriated and frightened kitten, and turning her back on the door, ran upstairs to find Stella.

13

Stella's bedroom door was not only closed, but locked. Miranda knocked softly, and receiving no answer, tried the handle.

A voice that she did not immediately recognize as Stella's said sharply: 'Who is it?'

'It's me,' said Miranda with a fine disregard for grammar. 'I only wanted to see how you were bearing up.'

A key turned in the lock and the door opened. Stella said: 'I'm sorry. I didn't hear you knock. Come in. Has Captain Lang left?'

'Yes,' said Miranda uncommunicatively.

Stella moved over to her dressing-table, and sitting down in front of it began to fidget aimlessly with bottles and brushes, and Miranda, watching her reflection in the glass, saw with something like horror that she looked old. Sallow-skinned and haggard, and desperate. Stella looked up, and catching sight of Miranda's face in the glass, started violently. The bottle she had been touching overturned and spilt a stream of scented lotion over the table, and Miranda ran to her and put her arms about her.

'What is it, Stel'? What's the matter?'

Stella flinched at her touch and then sat still, submitting to the embrace. But Miranda could feel that her body was tense and trembling, and see that she was staring at her own reflection in the mirror as if it were some stranger she saw there. She said in a hoarse whisper: 'I'm afraid, 'Randa. *I'm afraid!*'

Miranda's arms tightened about her and she tried to think of something to say that would convince Stella that Robert would never leave her for Sally Page or anyone else. She said to gain time: 'What have you got to be afraid of, darling?'

'Of being murdered,' said Stella in a whisper.

The answer was so unexpected and so shocking that Miranda released her and took a quick step backward.

'What on *earth* do you mean?'

Stella's hands clutched at the edge of the dressing-table. 'Someone meant to kill me. *Me* — not Friedel!'

Miranda opened her mouth to say 'Don't be ridiculous!' but a sudden recollection of what Simon had said to her less than ten minutes ago checked the words on her tongue. At the time, preoccupied with her own angle, she had not stopped to think what he had meant when he said that Friedel's death had probably been a mistake.

After a moment she said: 'Nonsense!' but the word lacked conviction and Stella brushed it aside.

'It isn't nonsense! It was night, and she was wearing my coat. Don't you see — someone thought it was me! Even *you* did. You said so! Someone thought I should be here alone, as you were. You should have been out — Mrs Leslie told me so — but I ought to have been here. I tell you, someone meant to kill me, 'Randa!'

Miranda said: 'Darling, why? *Do* be sensible! Why should anyone want to kill you? Surely it's obvious that someone had it in for that wretched woman, and the fact that she had borrowed your coat had nothing whatever to do with it?' She was trying to be reasonable and comforting, but she did not believe her own words, because if Simon Lang thought that Friedel's death was a mistake, he must have a very good reason for thinking so. But who would want to kill Stella? Surely you would have to hate someone very much to wish to kill them? Simon had said that women usually killed for one of two reasons; though he had not specified those reasons. Was one of them hate? Who hated Stella? Who would want her out of the way?

Two names leapt to Miranda's mind: Norah Leslie and Sally Page . . .

'No!' said Miranda aloud. *'No!'*

'You can believe what you like,' said Stella in a shaking voice, 'but I know that someone meant to kill me. I tell you I *know!*'

But Miranda had been speaking to herself — or to Sally Page: pretty, young, foolish Sally, who imagined herself to be in love with Stella's husband. Or to Norah Leslie, who hated Stella for some hidden reason of her own. But neither of them was capable of murder, and it was all nonsense that Stella had been the intended victim. It *must* be! Simon was wrong, and Friedel had been killed for some reason unconnected with either or any of them.

She tried to make Stella see this, but Stella was frightened beyond the reach of reason. Her insular dislike of foreigners and foreign countries, her jealousy of Sally Page, and the shocking reality of the two brutal murders with which she had been brought into contact, had combined to bring her to the verge of a complete physical and mental collapse. She would only repeat, 'I know that it was meant to be me,' in reply to all Miranda's soothing arguments.

Miranda said patiently: 'How can you be so sure? Do you know of any reason why anyone should want to kill you?'

'Yes . . .' Miranda barely caught the whispered word. Stella was not even looking at her; she was staring in front of her as though she saw someone or something that Miranda could not see, and there was a stark terror in her eyes that made Miranda's heart miss a beat.

Miranda said quickly. 'If you mean Sally Page, I think . . .'

'Sally?' interrupted Stella, her gaze returning to Miranda. 'What on earth has Sally Page to do with it?' Her voice sounded genuinely startled.

'Nothing,' said Miranda hastily. 'Stel', this reason you know of — why someone should want to kill you — what is it?'

Stella's face changed. It became blank and expressionless, and her violet-blue eyes were no longer terrified, but guarded and wary. She did not answer for a moment, and then she picked up a powder puff from the dressing-table and spoke to Miranda over her shoulder.

'Of course I don't know of any reason. How should I? It's just that that woman was wearing my coat. That's all. Don't let's talk about it any more for heaven's sake, 'Randa. Oh God, what a mess I look! I must do something to my face before Robert gets back.'

'Where is he?' asked Miranda, only too glad to change the subject.

'Seeing a lot of people about this Friedel business. He'll be back for luncheon. You might go down and see if the cook is doing anything about it. She's been behaving in a most peculiar manner. Where the Germans acquired their reputation for toughness I can't imagine. They seem to me to collapse into tears and hysteria at the drop of a hat! Oh well, I suppose I can't talk. Go and see about it will you, darling? Robert should be back any minute now!'

But Robert had already arrived, for Miranda found him in the drawing-room with Harry and Elsa Marson. The three had been talking together in low tones, but they broke off as she entered and turned quickly to face her.

Standing together in the cool cream and green of Stella's drawing-room, they seemed to Miranda to look curiously alike, despite their wide physical dissimilarities. And for a brief moment that fleeting impression of likeness puzzled her, until she realized that it was solely a matter of tension. They had turned simultaneously, and as they stood facing her in silence, their three faces bore the same look of strained wariness. It lasted only for a moment, and then the tension relaxed and Robert said: 'Oh, it's you, 'Randa. I thought——' He bit off the sentence and turned to Mrs Marson: 'Elsa, have a brandy and soda instead of that sherry. You look as if you could do with it. We all could.'

'Thank you, no,' said Mrs Marson. 'I think it is time we go now.'

She looked shockingly ill, thought Miranda. Something had happened to her face since they had first met on that fateful journey to Berlin. It seemed to have aged, as Stella's too had aged. Yet that was not all. Her face seemed thinner and somehow more un-English, and she had taken to a lavish use of make-up, as though to provide a mask with which to conceal that change. But the bright patches of rouge on her cheeks only served to accentuate their thinness and the curious grey pallor of her skin, and no amount of paint and powder could disguise the dark patches under her eyes or dim their feverish glitter. She too looked as Stella had looked — haggard and raddled and afraid. Miranda wondered if her own face bore that same look of fear?

Harry Marson said: 'Hullo, Miranda. This is a bloody business isn't it — in more senses than one.' He finished the contents of his glass at a gulp. 'We've had the *Polizei* and the F.B.I. and the Gendarmerie and old Uncle Sherlock-Holmes-Cantrell and all swarming over us since early dawn. Or that's what it feels like. The entire allied police force appears to be interested in the demise of your late parlourmaid, and it's probably only a matter of time before we're all lined up answering questions for a squad of comrades from the N.K.V.D. as well!'

Robert said quite pleasantly: 'Shut up, Harry,' and Harry Marson shot him a quick look and reddened under his tan. He cleared his throat uncomfortably and said: 'Well I suppose we'd better be getting along. Give you a lift to the office after lunch — fair exchange and all that.'

'Make it about three,' said Robert.

'Okay. Come on, Elsa.'

They went out through the french window and took the short cut across the Leslies' garden to their own house.

Stella came down to luncheon looking smooth and poised and soignée. It did not seem possible that this was the same woman who had crouched before her looking-glass, hysterical and terrified, so short a time ago. She had changed into a leaf-brown suit that brought out the copper tints in her blond hair, and had made up her face with care. But her hands still trembled slightly and the carefully applied mascara could not hide the redness about her eyes.

Robert went to the foot of the stairs to meet her. He took her into his arms and held her close to him for a moment, her head thrown back so that he could look into her eyes. Then he kissed her gently and released her.

164

'Well done, darling,' said Robert approvingly.

A little flush of colour rose to Stella's cheeks and the tension in her face and body seemed to relax. She smiled at him warmly and lovingly, and tucking her hand through his arm, turned towards the dining-room.

A little after three o'clock a horn sounded in the road. 'That'll be Harry,' said Robert. 'Darling, I'm going to be late again this evening. I'm sorry. It's specially beastly just now, but there is a bit of an international flap on, and the C.O. is up to his eyes in work and worry. I'll be back as soon as I can, but it may not be until around eight o'clock. Goodbye, my sweet. Try not to worry too much. Everything is going to be all right, and as soon as all this has blown over I shall see if I can't scrounge a bit of leave and we'll go down to Italy for ten days. Would you like that?'

'No,' said Stella with a crooked smile. 'Frankly, darling, I'd prefer ten days in a boarding-house at Blackpool or a cosy chalet in some Butlin holiday camp. Bracing Britain is good enough for me, and I feel I never want to see another hysterical foreigner in my life!'

Robert laughed and stooped to kiss her. 'Butlins it shall be! And if only I were a man of means instead of an impecunious chap who has still to qualify for a minimum pension, I'd hand in my papers and take to breeding pigs tomorrow! Never mind, my sweet, one day we shall retire to some nice, safe semi-detached on a bus route, and keep hens in the back garden.'

'It sounds heavenly,' said Stella with a laugh. 'But why the semi-detached? Why not Mallow?'

'My dear girl,' said Robert, reaching for his hat, 'by the time I can afford to retire or am heaved out — whichever comes first — the local housing committee will have grabbed it under some by-law and converted it into Workers' flats. And about time too! With the cost of living well over the roof, the place is a mark one white elephant.'

The car horn tooted again impatiently and Robert pulled Stella to him and kissed her again, holding her for a moment with his

165

cheek against hers. He looked past her to Miranda, his eyes anxious, and said: 'Look after her, 'Randa.'

Stella released herself with a little laugh. 'It's Miranda who needs looking after darling, not me. 'Randa was in the thick of it all.'

'Well, look after each other then.' He reached out and ruffled Miranda's dark hair affectionately, kissed her cheek, and was gone.

Two men came to interview Stella during the course of the afternoon: one of them Colonel Cantrell, whom Miranda had first seen in the waiting-room of Charlottenburg station, and the other a German policeman. But they did not ask to see Miranda, and she returned to the garden and sat on the edge of Lottie's sandpit with an anxious eye on the drawing-room windows.

Why were they worrying Stella again? Was it because she could produce no alibi for the previous night? But Stella of all people would not kill someone in mistake for herself. Unless Simon was wrong and there was no question of a mistake? Or did they perhaps think that for some reason of her own Stella might have killed Friedel and had the brilliant idea of dressing her in her own coat in order to create the impression that she herself had been the intended victim — thereby providing herself in some sort with an alibi, to compensate for the fact that she could produce no evidence to prove where she had been during that short margin of time in which Friedel must have met her death? They might reason like that; but then they had not seen her, as Miranda had, in her bedroom that morning. Stella was afraid. Afraid for her life. Genuinely and terribly afraid. And despite her subsequent denial, it was quite obvious that she had a special and secret reason for that fear.

Mrs Marson . . . ? *Had* it been Elsa Marson who had spoken to Friedel on the landing in the hostel that first morning in Berlin? Where had she been last night, and what had she been doing in the Soviet Garden of Remembrance? Miranda sighed and abandoned the problem in favour of wishing herself back once more in the tiny, comfortable flat off Sloane Street.

Colonel Cantrell and the German policeman left after half an hour, and towards five o'clock Stella suggested a visit to the swimming-pool at the Stadium, where Lottie and the Lawrence children were to have a swimming lesson. She had not referred to the afternoon's interview, but her eyes were over-bright and there was a hectic flush of colour in her cheeks that made Miranda feel anxious. Stella was making an obvious effort to appear her normal self, and was gay and talkative and had confined her conversation to an amusingly malicious account of the Wives' Meeting at the Lawrence house.

'I wonder if we need any petrol?' said Stella, starting the car and backing it out cautiously. 'I think there's a spare gallon somewhere.'

Miranda leant forward and peered at the gauge: 'No. You've got two gallons in the tank. It isn't far, is it?'

'Only a couple of miles, I think. If that.' Stella sighed and said: 'Do you remember when we bought this car? It was in 1950, for Robert's leave. We went to Dorset. Oh, those peaceful English lanes and hedges! And here I am, driving it down an autobahn in Berlin. It seems all wrong, somehow.'

'Don't worry, darling,' comforted Miranda. 'You'll drive it down a lot more English lanes one day. It's done a nice, comfortable wodge of British mileage — 17,332 miles no less — so I see no reason why it should not tot up a few on autobahns before getting back to hedges again.'

'It won't be hedges,' said Stella gloomily. 'It will be some beastly bamboo forest or a rubber plantation, and I expect we'll be made to paint it a dreary shade of jungle green.'

The eastern entrance to the Stadium area, where Hitler's Youth Rallies and the Olympic Games of the Nazi era had been held, led into a road that skirted a vast amphitheatre and passed between green playing fields to a large block of buildings, one of which housed the big indoor swimming-pool.

Stella parked the car, and they walked between tall gates and along a wide path, and turned down a short flight of stone steps and past a large outdoor pool which was three parts full of dark, stagnant water and flanked by a bronze bull and his mate, wading knee-deep in rigid bronze ripples, and eventually reached the huge indoor pool.

After the sharp evening air outside the atmosphere seemed to them intolerably steamy and stifling, for the pool was a heated one. But they endured it for an hour, after which Mrs Lawrence, who had also been watching her offspring having a swimming lesson in the pool reserved for children and beginners, invited them back to her house for a drink so that Stella could say good-night to Lottie.

The house lay not more than half a mile from the west entrance of the Stadium area in a quiet, tree-lined road, and it was after half-past six by the time they reached it and were ushered into the drawing-room by Katy Lawrence, who hunted the children off to supper in charge of Mademoiselle and apologized for the absence of the Colonel.

'He's having a foul time, poor pet,' said his wife, dispensing sherry. 'There's some terrific flap on. George thinks I don't know a thing about it, but of course I do. They're all getting a lecture, or a "briefing", or whatever they call it, this evening by someone from the Headquarters — Toddy Pilcher. Rather a pompous little man, I always thought. And then there's this talk by the C-in-C tomorrow night. George says Toddy insisted on a projector in the lecture room. Lantern slides — I ask you! Sounds madly Women's Institute to me. Was that the doorbell? Let's hope it's Monica Bradley with that stuff for the Thrift Shop at last!'

But it was Sally Page who was ushered in by a whitecoated batman. Sally wearing that same look of strain and weariness that Miranda had seen on Stella's face; and Mrs Marson's. And on her own as it looked back at her from a mirror. Yet on Sally it was neither ugly nor ageing: she merely looked fragile, childlike and pathetic, and the faint smudges of sleeplessness under the forget-me-not blue eyes only served to enhance their size and colour.

Sally had only called to say that she could not, after all, help in the Thrift Shop the following week, but that she had swopped weeks with Esmé Carroll and did Mrs Lawrence mind? She stayed to drink a glass of sherry and press Stella and Miranda to go back with her to her flat that evening.

'*Do* say you'll come!' begged Sally prettily. 'I do so want you to see my flat. And Andy would simply love to see you: he wants to show you some photographs he's taken of me. And besides I want your advice about what colour to have the drawing-room painted. I hear that your drawing-room is lovely, Mrs Melville. You *will* come, won't you?'

Miranda saw Stella's face pale and her mouth tighten, and noticed that her voice was distinctly metallic as she said crisply: 'I know Miranda would love to go, but I'm afraid I can't manage it this evening.'

Left with no option — since she could hardly refuse in face of Stella's positive statement that she would love to go — Miranda accepted, and Sally smiled disarmingly at her, and having got her way, turned to the subject of Friedel's murder. Whereupon Stella stood up abruptly saying that she would run up and say good-night to Lottie, and left the room. Miranda endeavoured to change the subject, but without success, since her hostess was far too interested in the whole affair to discourage such an entertaining topic of conversation.

'We had the police round this morning,' said Sally, ending a long and enthusiastic dissertation on the latest murder. 'Well, not really the police I suppose, but that nice Lang man, and another creature who just sat there and never uttered — rather good-looking, with dark hair. They wanted to know what we were doing last night. I mean to say — *honestly*! As if any of us were likely to go round hitting German housemaids on the head with pokers! Not that I haven't thought it mightn't be a good thing, because you've no idea what a clueless creature the Labour Exchange people have foisted on us ...

'She says her name's Sonya, and I'm quite sure she's a Russian spy. I mean, she wears Russian boots and stumps about in them all day and simply *never* washes. She's supposed to be a cook, but she can't even boil a potato, and when I complained she said she didn't understand English cooking — only German. So of course I said, "*Let's* have some German cooking," because I'm all for fancy foreign dishes. But it seems that German cooking is just the same as English cooking, only worse: I mean all you do is to pour masses of grease over everything and that's it.'

She paused for breath and Miranda, fearful of the conversation returning to the subject of Friedel, said: 'Well, personally, I think you're very lucky to have cooks and housemaids at all. If there is one thing I do detest, it's peeling potatoes and washing up greasy dishes.'

Mrs Lawrence, however, was not to be drawn into a discussion of the servant problem. She said: 'But why were you questioned about last night, Sally? Did they explain?'

'Oh yes. But it wasn't very exciting, really. It was just in case either of us had seen anyone lurking about, or noticed anything like a car standing at the end of the road. Things like that. And alibis of course. Simon Lang said it would help to clear up things if we could each produce an alibi.'

'Why "each"?' inquired Mrs Lawrence, puzzled. 'Surely Andy was dining in the American sector?'

'Well, he was,' said Sally, 'but it was *too* stupid — I can't think how he could have made such a silly mistake — but it seems it was the wrong night, so he came back and went to bed.'

'Does that mean he hasn't got an alibi?'

'Oh no; I'm afraid that as suspects we're both out of the running,' said Sally regretfully.

Miranda, noting the tone, thought with some irritation that Sally, whose reading seemed to be entirely of the escapist variety, would rather have enjoyed appearing as a witness in a murder trial: she probably saw herself as the frail and sensitive heroine of this type of fiction, and would have found it pleasurably exciting to be a suspect.

'Andy couldn't get the lift to work,' explained Sally, 'so he routed out the caretaker, who is rather an old sweetie, and the old boy fixed it for him. Andy asked him in for a beer, and very fortunately noticed that the time was just eight o'clock by that dining-room clock of ours; because he told Herr Hübbe that he could only have missed me by about a quarter of an hour or so and now he would have to cook his own supper.'

'And what about you?' inquired Mrs Lawrence. 'Did you have to produce an alibi too?'

'Oh yes. Mine's all right too. I arrived at the Leslies' at ten to eight and I said, "I do hope I'm not late" — not that I thought I was, but you know how one says that sort of thing — and Colonel Leslie looked at his watch and said, "You're about dead on time; it's ten to eight." And the good-looking man with the dark hair wrote something in a notebook and said, "That agrees with Colonel Leslie's account," so I suppose they were checking on the Leslies as well.'

'But *why*?' demanded Mrs Lawrence. 'What possible reason can they think any of you could have for murdering an unknown German servant-girl? The thing's absurd!'

'I couldn't agree more. But Andy has a theory that the police, or the S.I.B. or M.I.5, or whoever it is who is doing all the fussing around over this, think that there is some connection between the murder of that Brigadier and this German woman's.'

'Quite ridiculous,' pronounced Mrs Lawrence firmly: 'Of course they don't think anything of the sort!'

'Then why is it that they have questioned all the same people?'

'What people?'

'"Lang's Eleven",' put in Miranda; and instantly regretted having spoken.

'Lang's eleven? What *do* you mean? What eleven?'

'Nothing really,' said Miranda unhappily. 'Only that there were eleven people who might have murdered the Brigadier, and most of them seem to have been questioned again over this murder.'

'Not most of them,' corrected Sally Page. 'All of them.'

'How do you know that?'

'I asked,' said Sally, simply. And ticked them off one by one on

171

the fingers of her rather large, schoolgirlish hands. 'Myself and Andy, Elsa and Harry Marson, the Leslies, Miranda and that Swiss female, Mademoiselle something-or-other, and Mrs Melville and Bob, and——'

'Bob . . . ?' for a moment the unfamiliar name puzzled Miranda.

Sally flushed. 'Robert. We used to call him Bob when he was in Egypt. Then there's Mrs Wilkin of course. They even checked up on her, believe it or not!'

She laughed her pretty, shallow laugh, and Mrs Lawrence said: 'Wilkin? *Not* the mother of that frightful freckled child?'

'You mean Wally,' said Miranda. 'The original Giles cartoon, isn't he? Where have you come across Wally?'

'My dear, he has been infesting my house all day! It seems he's a special friend of Lottie's. Mademoiselle did her best to chase him off the premises, but I think he came back over the wall.'

Sounds of woe from above penetrated to the drawing-room and Stella reappeared looking worried. 'That was Lottie,' she said apologetically. 'She's left that tiresome little china bear of hers behind at the swimming-pool, and she won't go to sleep without it.'

'Oh dear,' exclaimed Mrs Lawrence, 'and I'm afraid the car has gone off to fetch George. But I'll get the driver to go up and look for it as soon as he gets back.'

'Please don't bother. I could go, if it comes to that. But Mademoiselle has offered to run up on her bicycle. It's no distance at all, really, and I do think she might have seen that Lottie had that toy. It's all right for her to go, isn't it? I mean, they will let her in?'

'Of course. She'll probably be stopped at the gate and asked what she's doing, but they know her. She took the children there for a walk this afternoon and George gave her a pass in case anyone asked questions. In a month or two, when they've moved all those offices and things into the Stadium area, they'll probably get madly security-minded. But no one bothers much at the moment. They stop a car with a German registration number and ask questions, I believe. But all our cars go through on sight, because of the B.Z. on the number-plates — for British Zone.'

'Then that's all right,' said Stella, thankfully. 'I must admit that the last thing I want to do is to drive back to the baths and hunt around for twenty minutes or so for a minute china toy. But thank goodness Mademoiselle is made of sterner stuff. I only hope she's got a bicycle lamp. It's getting dark. 'Randa, if you're going to see Mrs Page's flat, I think I'll get along home and have a hot bath before Robert gets back. Good-night, Mrs Lawrence, and thank you again for having Lottie. It's really very good of you.'

Mrs Lawrence saw her to the door, while Sally Page went off to telephone Andy and tell him that she was bringing Miranda back to the flat. She appeared to take an unconscionable time over it, and when at last she returned she looked flushed and defiant: the reason for this becoming immediately apparent on their arrival at the flat, when Miranda realized, too late, that Sally's only object in asking her there had been to use her as a buffer between herself and Andy. There had apparently been a major matrimonial row between the two young Pages, but owing to Miranda's presence, Andy was compelled to play the willing host and dispense drinks and social smalltalk.

The flat proved to be large, dim and depressing, and Sally seemed to have made little effort towards improving it. The drawing-room, which was chilly and uncomfortable, smelt strongly of turpentine. 'The painters have been in,' explained Andy gloomily.

Sally urged Miranda to stay to supper or, alternatively, to accompany Andy and herself to the Club. But Andy made no attempt to second the invitation, and when Miranda firmly excused herself, he said that he would drive her back; adding curtly that as it was Sonya's day out, Sally had better get down to cooking something for supper.

He was morose and monosyllabic on the journey to the Melvilles', and to Miranda's relief he refused her half-hearted invitation to come in for a drink, and having dropped her at the gate drove away at speed without waiting to see her to the door.

The bell had been answered by Robert.

'Hullo, 'Randa, you're just in time for supper. Frau Herbach insisted on leaving before it got dark, so I've been trying my hand at a bit of amateur cookery. However, not to worry; it will be quite edible. All I've actually done is to heat up the stuff she left ready. Tell Stella to get a move on while I dish up the result.'

He vanished in the direction of the kitchen, and Miranda started up the stairs. She was halfway up when she remembered that earlier in the evening she had left her handbag in the front pocket of the Melvilles' car; and since it contained her lipstick and powder puff, she turned and went down again to the hall, lifted the garage key off its hook near the hall door, and went out, leaving the door open behind her.

A wandering gust of wind blew down the road, momentarily shaking the branches of the trees before the street lamp near the gate and sending leaping shadows across the house wall. The road looked long and dark and deserted, and Miranda shivered and walked quickly down the short path to the left of the house.

The garage was cold and airless and smelt unpleasantly of petrol and mildew, and the single overhead bulb only served to throw the interior of the car into deep shadow. Miranda reached in and switched on the dashboard lights, but the bag was not there, and she realized that Stella must have taken it in when she returned from the Lawrences'.

Switching off the dashboard light she slammed the car door behind her, and in the same moment thought she heard a sound behind her: a swift, stealthy, scrambling sound. Miranda whirled round, her hand still clutching at the door of the car, and stood rigid, listening. But the gust of wind that had blown along the street had died away, and the night was quiet again and nothing moved.

The car threw a dense black shadow across a pile of empty wooden packing-cases stacked against the far wall, above which a small window, its panes festooned with cobwebs, cut a dark square in the whitewashed brick. Beyond the open doorway the path lay dark and empty, and the light streaming out from the garage caught the lilac bushes lining the short, concrete ramp that sloped up to the level of the road, and silhouetted their motionless leaves against the surrounding shadows, as though they had been canvas scenery lit by stage footlights.

Miranda did not move. Her fingers, clenched about the metal door handle, felt stiff with cold, and her heart was beating in odd, uneven jerks. Had she really heard a sound, or had it only been an echo from the slamming of the car door? Was there someone crouched among the empty packing-cases, or waiting outside behind the lilac bushes? — waiting until she switched off the light and turned to lock the door? Waiting for her as they had waited for Friedel?

The silent garage and the quiet night outside seemed to be waiting too, and in the silence she could hear the sound of her own uneven heartbeats.

A swift, flickering shadow swept across the small, cold walls and brought a choking gasp to her throat, but it was only a large moth attracted by the naked light. And suddenly the taut thread of terror slackened and she took a deep breath, and walking quickly over to the garage door, turned off the light with shaking fingers, and locking the door behind her, fled back up the path to the house.

Stella was coming down the hall stairs, but she checked at the sight of Miranda's white face; one hand gripping the banister and the other suddenly at her throat, her eyes wide with terror: *'What is it? What's happened?'*

'Nothing. I – I went down to the garage to get my bag out of the car, and I thought I heard someone or something. Probably only a cat or an owl. But my nerves are in poor shape these days, and I panicked and ran back here at the double. That's all.'

Stella swayed and Miranda ran up the stairs and put an arm about her.

'I'm sorry,' apologized Stella: 'But you gave me a fright; rushing

175

in like that. I thought for a moment that something awful had happened.'

'Something awful has,' announced Robert, appearing abruptly from the direction of the kitchen: 'I've let the soup boil over. You've no idea the mess it's made. For God's sake, darling, come and mop up the ruin!'

The strain left Stella's face and she laughed, and releasing herself from Miranda's arm ran down to him: 'Let's have supper in the kitchen. Then we can serve everything out of saucepans and save on the washing up.'

'Let's not,' said Robert. 'There's burnt soup all over the top of the stove, and it smells hellish. Let's eat in the dining-room, and stack.'

'It does smell horrid, doesn't it?' said Miranda, wrinkling her nose. 'Rather like petrol.'

'That's me,' said Robert. 'Only it's turpentine. I spilt about half a pint of it over my trousers. Our dear governess uses it to discourage moths, and she had left her bottle, improperly corked, on the bathroom windowsill. I knocked it for six.'

'It goes well with burnt soup,' commented Miranda lightly, going upstairs to tidy herself for supper.

Apparently a modicum of soup had survived, for by the time she reappeared in the dining-room Robert had produced three plates of it and Stella was already sipping hers cautiously.

'What were you panicking about in the garage for, Miranda?' inquired Robert.

'I was looking for my bag. And I wasn't panicking — or at least not much.'

'Well the next time you want to go scouting around in the dark, call me first, and I'll go along as bodyguard — heavily armed with the offensive weapon which is at present nestling in my cupboard under a discreet pile of underpants. I have even taken the precaution of loading the thing since last night.'

Stella's face was suddenly white. 'Robert! You don't mean — you don't really think——'

'Of course not, darling. It was only a weak attempt at humour. All the same, I'd rather you both laid off wandering around after dark — for the sake of your nerves if nothing else. Did you find your bag, 'Randa?'

'No. I turned on the dashboard light and hunted around, but——'

'I took it in,' interrupted Stella. 'I meant to tell you, only Robert and his soup put it out of my head. It's in the drawing-room.'

'That's a relief. It's got my only lipstick in it — which accounts for my rather pallid appearance at the moment.'

'Rubbish!' said Robert, turning to look at her. 'If you did but know it, Miranda my pet, yours is one of the few faces that looks better the less you do to it. It's the planes or something. I suppose that's why you photograph so well. As for lipstick, you don't need any. You have a mouth like that plummy pre-Raphaelite female in the Tate Gallery — Mona something. The one dressed up in a pair of brocade curtains and ropes of red beads, clutching a hideous feather fan.'

'Robert, this is most unexpected of you!' said Miranda, surprised. 'I'd no idea you frequented the Tate!'

'I don't,' admitted Robert, clearing away the soup plates and proceeding to carve cold mutton: 'The comparison is not my own. I was idly gazing at a reproduction of the masterpiece in question, "courtesy of the Tate", on the cover of some arty-crafty publication at Katy Lawrence's on Sunday, and happened to mention that the damsel reminded me dimly of someone. It was your friend Lang who remarked that she had your mouth. And how right he was! She has.'

Miranda coloured and Stella looked at her sharply, but forebore to comment.

'Which reminds me,' said Robert handing round the mutton, 'How was it that you knew that chap's telephone number, young 'Randa? I gather you rang him up and yelled for help.'

'He gave me his number,' said Miranda shortly, angrily conscious of her heightened colour.

Robert lifted an amused and mocking eyebrow. 'And you carried it about clutched in one hand ever after, I suppose?'

'No,' said Miranda coldly. 'I didn't need to. I've got a freak memory for numbers. If I've seen them written down, I can visualize them again as if I was looking at a photograph.'

'Oh damn!' interrupted Stella. 'Now I've spilt the mayonnaise! Quick Robert, get me a cloth from the kitchen!'

In the ensuing tumult Simon Lang was forgotten, and Miranda, profoundly grateful for Stella's timely interruption, hastened to change the subject.

14

'Where's Mademoiselle?' inquired Robert, stacking dirty plates in the serving-hatch. 'Is she having supper with the Lawrences? I thought she was supposed to eat here.'

'So she is,' said Stella. 'I hope you've left her some soup.'

'Not a drop — unless she cares to scrape some off the linoleum. But there's any amount of cold mutton and salad left.'

Stella looked at the clock and frowned. 'It's nearly ten o'clock,' she said in a troubled voice: 'I'd no idea it was as late as that! She *must* be back by now. She's probably in the kitchen.'

'No she isn't,' reported Robert, peering through the hatch.

'Then I think I'll just run up and see if she's in her room. You know how she sulks sometimes.'

'I'll go,' said Miranda. 'You put your feet up on the sofa while Robert brews some coffee. You look all in.'

Miranda tapped on Mademoiselle's door, and receiving no answer turned the handle and went in. The room was in darkness and she turned on the light and stood looking about her curiously. It was meticulously neat; the bedcover drawn smoothly and without a wrinkle and the dressing-table almost bare — a severely utilitarian hairbrush and comb, a solid pin-cushion and a small box of hairpins being all that lay upon it. There were no photographs or any form of personal souvenirs, and it might have been a hotel bedroom for all the impression that its owner's personality had left upon it.

Miranda switched off the light and went downstairs again. 'She's not there,' she reported.

'I think perhaps I'd better ring up the Lawrences',' said Stella anxiously.

But Mademoiselle was not at the Lawrences'. She had not returned there and Lottie had eventually gone to sleep without Rollerbear.

'Damn the woman!' said Robert crossly. 'I suppose she's punctured a tyre or something of the sort, and hasn't got the sense to ring up and let us know. I suppose I'd better go out and hunt her up.'

He collected a coat from the hall and went off to the garage; to return an hour later, but without Mademoiselle. The German sentries on the Stadium's gates had been changed about the time she would have left, and the ones now on duty had no recollection of seeing any woman on a bicycle. 'She's probably met a pal, or gone off to some lecture,' said Robert irritably. 'After all, there's no particular reason why she should come home early now that Lottie isn't here. She's probably going to seize the opportunity and take every evening off!'

'But Rollerbear!' said Stella unhappily. 'She knows how Lottie feels about that creature. Surely she would — Robert don't you think we should do something?'

'Such as what?' inquired Robert shortly.

'I don't know,' said Stella helplessly. 'Ring up the hospital perhaps. She might have had an accident or – or something.'

'Nonsense!' said Robert crisply. 'We should have heard soon enough if anything like that had happened. No, the blighted woman has undoubtedly gone on the toot for the evening. We'll leave the front door unlocked and she can let herself in. And I hope you'll rub it into her tomorrow that the next time she takes an impromptu evening off she rings up first!'

But in the morning Mademoiselle's room was still empty and her bed had not been slept in, though the coverlet was rumpled as though someone had sat on it. Her brush and comb, toothbrush and nightdress were missing, and the hall door, which Robert had left on the latch, was now locked. Mademoiselle had apparently returned sometime during the night, collected a few necessities, and left again as quietly as she had come. But she had left behind her one memento of her arrival. On the centre of the bare dressing-table, where her brush and comb had previously lain, stood a small china bear.

There was something white lying in the shadow just behind the door, and Miranda stooped mechanically and picked it up, but it was only a much crumpled face-tissue. 'Elizabeth Arden', noted Miranda with a mild sense of surprise. She had not suspected Mademoiselle of such expensive tastes. Somehow one connected her complexion more with face flannels and carbolic soap.

'I don't understand!' said Stella angrily. 'If she wanted to go, why didn't she say so? Why didn't she explain? She might at least have given me a month's notice instead of going off like this and leaving me in the lurch. Besides, we owe her for nearly three weeks. Robert, you don't think there's anything behind it, do you?'

'Of course there's something behind it,' said Robert crossly. 'She's tired of being interrogated by the police, and someone has offered her a better job at a considerably higher salary. We weren't paying her much, and you can bet your bottom dollar that some dame in the French or American sector has been advertising for a governess at three times the amount, and the old witch saw it and has snapped it up.'

'But to go off being owed money!'

'My dear girl, if she'd told you she wanted to go, you'd have insisted on her giving a month's notice — you know you would! And the chances are she couldn't wait. I hold no brief for the woman, but I can follow her line of reasoning.'

'Well I think it's beastly of her!' burst out Stella angrily. 'After we've paid her fare out here and everything! Can't we report her to the police or something, and at least get the money for her fare refunded?'

'I doubt if we'd have a leg to stand on,' said Robert moodily. 'The employee is always right in these days. Anyway I have no intention of wasting time and money in prosecuting the woman. Let her go — and the hell with her!'

But it appeared that the authorities took an entirely different view of the matter.

The following day, answering a ring at the doorbell, Miranda was confronted by Simon Lang. He walked in without ceremony, tossed his hat onto the hall table and said without preamble: 'What's this about the Melvilles' Swiss governess having run out on them?'

Miranda stiffened. 'Hadn't you better ask my cousin?' she asked coldly.

'I tried to, but he's out on some conference. I'd like to see Mrs Melville, please.'

'She's out,' said Miranda briefly.

'Then you'll have to do instead. *Has* the governess disappeared?'

Miranda said carefully: 'Mademoiselle Beljame has left. Yes.'

'When?'

Miranda hesitated, frowning, and Simon said with unwonted terseness: 'Don't be silly, Miranda! This is serious.'

'Why?'

'*Why*? Well apart from anything else we have two unsolved murders on our hands, and your Mademoiselle Beljame is a possible suspect.'

'Do you — do you really think that she might have done it?'

'What I think is beside the point,' said Simon Lang. 'At the moment I want to know when Mademoiselle Beljame went, where she is, and why the hell it wasn't reported immediately!'

'But we don't *know* where she is,' said Miranda breathlessly. She sat down somewhat abruptly on a hall chair and explained the circumstances, and when she had finished he asked to be shown Mademoiselle's room. It had, however, been swept and dusted only that morning, the bed-linen removed and the blankets neatly folded.

'Who did this?' demanded Simon.

'We did. Stella and I. We do the rooms now that Friedel — until

182

we can get a housemaid. Mademoiselle did her own of course, but as she wasn't here we did it. Her trunk is under the bed. I thought we ought to pack her things in it, but Stella said to leave them as they were, and if she wanted them she could jolly well come and pack them herself.'

Simon opened the cupboard, and looked into the drawers, but Mademoiselle's scanty possessions had little to tell him.

'Why wasn't this reported at once?'

'I don't think it occurred to us,' said Miranda candidly. 'We just thought she'd heard of a better job and left. It happens pretty often in Berlin, I gather; you just ask any of the wives! Stella wanted to tell the police. But only because of having paid her fare out, not because she thought there was anything fishy about it.'

Simon made no comment. He sat down on the edge of the bed and looked about the room with the shadow of a frown between his brows, and after an appreciable interval he said: 'If she went into the Stadium area last night we ought to be able to fix the time she went in and the time she left, because of the guards on the gates. Except that it is possible — though damn difficult — to get out of that place without using one of the entrances, providing one is prepared to risk taking a bit of skin off oneself.'

He stood up. 'Where can I find Mrs Melville? I'd like to see her.'

'She went out to do some shopping at the Naafi,' said Miranda, following him out onto the landing and watching indignantly while he locked the door behind him and calmly pocketed the key. 'I think she was going to the Lawrences',' she added as an afterthought as they reached the hall. 'You might find her there.'

'Thank you,' said Simon, picking up his hat. He paused by the hall door and looked at the catch of the Yale lock, and then said: 'How many other exits are there from this house? Apart from the windows, of course?'

'Two; the back door and the french window in the drawing-room. But we bolt those every night.' Miranda looked at his still face and said breathlessly: 'But if Mademoiselle did it — the murders I mean — she couldn't get away! No one can get in or out of Berlin

183

without endless passports and identity cards and bits of paper.'

Simon Lang transferred his speculative gaze from the Yale lock to Miranda's face and said: 'You've forgotten the Russian zone. It provides an admirable bolt-hole for every variety of bad hat.'

'Then you think she's in East Berlin?'

'No,' said Simon meditatively, 'I think she's——' He stopped and gave a slight shrug of his shoulders and said: 'No matter,' and turning away, opened the door and went down the short path that led to the gate, and drove away.

Stella returned just before lunch. She had met Simon Lang at the Lawrences', and she seemed cheerful and almost exhilarated. 'He thinks Mademoiselle may have had something to do with the murders,' she explained, 'and that she's taken fright and made a bolt for it. I only hope it's true!'

'Why?' demanded Miranda, startled.

'Because if only it *is* her it means that it wasn't——' Stella broke off abruptly and bit her lip. 'I mean,' she said carefully, 'that if it was Mademoiselle, then the whole matter is cleared up and we won't have any more of those ghastly police inquiries and people snooping around the house asking questions. It means that it's all over, and we can breathe again and enjoy ourselves, and nothing else frightening can happen.'

Miranda said quickly: 'For goodness sake cross your fingers when you say things like that! We don't know yet that she was the one.'

'She must be!' insisted Stella passionately. 'She's *got* to be! If she isn't, why did she run away?'

'Perhaps because she had heard of a better job — as Robert suggested. It may still be that, you know.'

'I don't believe it,' said Stella obstinately. 'Of course she's the murderer! Why don't you want it to be her?'

'I do want it to be her,' confessed Miranda. 'That is, if it has to be one of us, I can't think of anyone I'd rather it was. I've never liked the woman. She gives me the creeps; I don't know why. Like spiders! The whole house feels a better place now that she's out of it. Those awful caraway seeds! Do you remember the time your

184

mother gave me a slice of seed cake when I was about twelve — the day we took a picnic to the Roman camp — and I was instantly sick all over the chocolate éclairs?'

Stella made a grimace and laughed. 'Yes I do. Beastly child! But that was years before Mademoiselle arrived on the scene. I wasn't even married to Robert then. Lottie wasn't born.'

'Oh, I know: I wasn't suggesting that I disliked caraway seeds because of Mademoiselle. Only that I probably disliked Mademoiselle because of the caraway seeds! I hope that she just disappears into the Russian zone and that we never hear of her again. The Russians are welcome to her! All the same, we may well hear that she is merely pursuing her governessing in some innocuous home in the American sector; and if so we are right back where we started from and still under suspicion.'

But by tea-time no trace had yet been found of the errant governess, and a representative of the K.R.I.P.O., the German police force, speaking correct but halting English, had called to ask more questions and to interrogate Frau Herbach, the cook.

Robert returned shortly after tea in a bad temper. He had not seen Simon Lang, but Colonel Cantrell, the A.P.M., had apparently rung him up at his office and been brusquely outspoken on the subject of his failure to report the disappearance of Mademoiselle Beljame. Robert was normally an easy-going and even-tempered person, but Colonel Cantrell's comments having been forceful in the extreme, he was feeling sore and sulky, and Miranda hastened to accept an unexpected invitation by the Leslies to go swimming, and hoped that by the time she returned the atmosphere in the house would be less electric.

There were not many people at the indoor pool, for although the water was kept at a comfortable temperature and the big building was warmed throughout, it was still too early in the year, and too cold, for people to think of swimming.

Sally Page, her pretty figure showing to advantage in a brief swimming suit of white satin, was sitting at the far side of the pool, her feet dangling in the water, talking to Elsa Marson.

Mrs Marson, wearing a gaily coloured bathing-dress and a scarlet cap, was obviously in better spirits, and it occurred to Miranda that this was the first time that she had ever seen her laugh. Elsa Marson had always seemed pale and anxious, but this evening there were patches of bright colour in her cheeks, her eyes were sparkling and she looked as though some load of anxiety had been lifted from her shoulders. Catching sight of Mrs Leslie and Miranda she waved, and slipping into the water swam across to them.

'What's the water like?' asked Norah Leslie, peering cautiously over the edge.

'Too warm,' said Elsa. She turned to Miranda: 'Sally says that it was the Melvilles' Swiss governess who did the murders, and that she has run away to hide herself in East Berlin. Is it true?'

'What's that?' said Mrs Leslie sharply. She swung round to look at Miranda, her face pale and startled.

Miranda inquired tartly as to where Sally Page had obtained her information, but Norah Leslie was not to be deflected: 'Is it true?' she demanded. 'Did that woman really do it? Who said so? How did they find out?'

'We don't know that she did,' said Miranda briefly. 'Sally's only guessing.'

'Then she *has* disappeared?'

'Yes,' admitted Miranda reluctantly. 'But we think she may have merely gone off to some better-paid job. You know what it's like in Berlin. I gather that in spite of all the talk of unemployment, anyone who hears of a better job, or feels peevish for any trivial reason, is apt to walk out without a word of warning, and the first their employer knows of it is when the cook or the housemaid or the nurse fails to turn up. Mademoiselle may have found it catching.'

'But she *has* disappeared?' insisted Mrs Leslie.

Miranda did not answer. She looked across the pool to where Sally Page dangled her pretty feet in the vivid blue water and wondered where Sally had obtained her information. There was a quick way of finding out.

Miranda stepped back, took two running steps and dived cleanly into the pool. But it seemed that Sally had no desire to speak to her, for when Miranda surfaced Sally had already risen and was running lightly along the edge of the pool towards the diving-boards. Miranda swam to the side and sat watching her as she climbed one ladder after another until she reached the highest board, thirty feet or more above the water. Her tall, slender figure seemed absurdly small seen from below, and Miranda, who had no head for heights, shuddered and felt a little sick as young Mrs Page walked calmly out upon the narrow plank and looked down at the clear blue depths below, her hands at her sides.

Sally tested the spring of the board, waiting, it seemed deliberately, until the attention of the other bathers was focused upon her. Then she turned and walked back again, swung round and ran lightly along it, and springing upwards and outwards, somersaulted once in the air and finished with a perfect swallow dive. Her body entered the water like a silver arrow, so smoothly that it appeared to cause only the slightest splash, and one or two spectators applauded vigorously.

It was a surprisingly competent performance, and Miranda felt a glow of admiration. She was a tolerably good swimmer herself and could dive prettily, but she knew that she would never have dared walk out upon that slender plank so near the high ceiling, and that she did not possess either the nerve, judgement or co-ordination of brain and muscle to execute such a dive.

Sally rose to the surface, shook the water out of her eyes and swimming easily to the edge of the pool hoisted herself out of the water and walked quickly away in the direction of the changing-rooms.

Colonel Leslie, employing a stately breaststroke, swam across to Miranda and paused beside her, keeping himself afloat by duck-paddling. 'Norah tells me that your cousin's governess has bolted, he remarked. 'Very useful of her. I should imagine that this lets us all out. Well, no one can say that it has not been an interesting experience.'

'What has?' asked Miranda bleakly.

'Being a murder suspect.'

'I don't think they know yet that it was her.'

'No. But provided she doesn't turn up again, the supposition will be that it was. The various police forces of this city are fairly efficient, my dear, and as they have been unable to trace her as yet, we can be reasonably sure that she is well and truly behind the Iron Curtain.'

Miranda looked at him in some surprise, but he appeared to be unaware of any discrepancy in his words. Yet if it were true that he had only just this moment heard of Mademoiselle's disappearance, how could he know that she might not already have been traced? However, as she did not want to talk of Mademoiselle, she said: 'I expect so,' in a colourless voice. Mrs Leslie swam across to join them, and after a few minutes of desultory conversation, offered to race Miranda a length, and having lost by a couple of yards, left the water and went off with her husband to talk to some friends on the steps at the far end of the pool.

It was almost an hour later that Miranda, who had become involved in a game of water-polo, strolled down from the changing-rooms in the wake of the Leslies, who had gone on ahead some ten minutes earlier in order to collect their car, which they had parked a good distance away, telling her that they would pick her up by the gate that gave access to the swimming-pools. The air outside felt very cold after the overheated atmosphere inside the building, and the clear spring evening was faintly scented with fruit blossom and the fumes of petrol.

A reclining nude in bronze, several times larger than life, stood near the edge of the open-air pool against an angle of the wall that bore the word *Herren* largely lettered upon it — the word apparently directing attention not to the bronze statue, but to a shadowy flight of steps that descended to a door in a narrow area behind it. The bronze itself, like the wall and the stone-paving below, was pockmarked with bullet holes, and Miranda looked at it critically as she passed.

The entire Stadium was littered with similarly pockmarked

statuary, and she was pondering over the Nazi passion for outsize representations of the unclothed male and female body, when she was surprised to see that the Leslies had gone no further than the other side of the open-air pool — the one flanked by the bronze cattle — where they seemed to have been waylaid by one of the swimming instructors, a Herr Kroll.

Herr Kroll, talking excitedly, was gripping the Colonel's arm with one hand and gesturing with the other, and presently all three of them bent to peer down into the dark, stagnant depths of the water below. Miranda heard Colonel Leslie say, 'Rubbish!' and Herr Kroll retort, '*Nein*! I tell you, no! It is not the rubbish!' and presumed that the instructor had been explaining how the sea-green tiles of the pool were protected from cracking in the winter frosts by a grid of ropes, each the thickness of a man's body, that were made from bales of straw and lay, partially submerged, on the surface of the water, where they moved sluggishly to every breath of wind and thus prevented ice from forming. Either that, or he was telling them a tale that Harry Marson had told her; about how the Russians, when they had first occupied Berlin and used some of the nearby buildings as stables for their horses, had found no better use for this huge, pale-tiled pool than to use it as a dumping place for manure.

A last ray from the setting sun gilded the flanks and tipped the long, curving horns of the bronze bulls with gold, and across the dark green water of the pool the ruined columns of a bomb-damaged wing of the building began to take on the outlines of some pyloned temple of the Nile Valley. Miranda quickened her steps, and joining the group at the pool side, demanded to know what all the excitement was about?

Colonel Leslie, who had been bending down to peer short-sightedly into the water, straightened up and said irritably: 'Herr Kroll here thinks there's something down there — a body; or something equally ridiculous. He swears he saw a face. Well, if he did it isn't there now, for I'm damned if I can see anything. Come along, Norah.'

'No, wait a minute, Ted. I believe I can ... *There*! Over there! I'm sure I ...' Mrs Leslie gripped Miranda's arm and pointed: 'Look — down there, just below that ... No. It's only a hank of straw. Funny, I could have sworn I saw a face too.'

'Probably your own reflection,' grunted her husband, bending again, hands on knees, to peer in the direction in which she had pointed. 'Your eyes are better than mine, Miranda. See if *you* can see anything.'

The sun slid below the horizon, and a little breeze awoke and sighed through the branches of a group of pine trees that stood near the edge of the lawn behind them, momentarily ruffling the quiet surface of the pool so that a half-submerged rope of straw immediately below Miranda drifted a little way and disclosed the pale, distorted reflection of her own face looking up at her, Narcissus-like, from a patch of dark water.

The breeze passed and the water steadied again ... And it was not her own face that was staring up at her from the pool, but another face. A ghost out of the terrifying, shadowy past. A pallid face, open-mouthed, with wide, staring eyes and lank, straw-coloured hair. Suddenly and horribly familiar ...

A second catspaw of wind ruffled across the pool, and the heavy blond hair drifted before it and was once again only a swathe of sodden straw. And below it lay the grey face and black, scanty locks of Mademoiselle Marie Beljame.

Miranda did not know how long she stood there looking down at that drowned face, for she had stepped back into the past and was a child again — several hundreds of miles and fifteen years removed from the battered city of Berlin.

Every sound of the quiet evening came clearly to her ears with an unnatural distinctness; but now each one possessed a different and terrifying meaning. The muffled shouts and laughter of the few remaining bathers from the indoor swimming-bath were the cries of fleeing, panic-stricken people. The whisper of the breeze through the pine needles was a frightened man whispering orders in the shadow of fog-shrouded whin bushes. A passing car was the drone of an enemy bomber, and the faint lap of water against the sea-green tiles at the far side of the wide pool was the lap of waves against a pebble beach ...

She became aware that the swimming instructor was shouting, 'You see now how I am right?' That Colonel Leslie was swearing and that Norah Leslie had screamed — though mercifully only once — and that other departing bathers were hurrying up to swell the group and add their voices to the babble of sound.

The sky behind the tall, spidery lines of the wireless masts had turned to a clear green flecked with gold and the bronze cattle that stood at the head of the pool were no longer warmly gilded, but dark and clear-cut in the gathering twilight.

Miranda stepped back from the rim of the pool, moving very carefully, as a person may move on a surface of ice. Edging her way through the rapidly growing crowd, she reached the top of the flagged steps, and turned down the wide path towards the entrance gates, past the shell of the ruined, roofless wing where the budding boughs of young trees thrust up through the fallen rubble around a small, white, concrete square that was a newly built fire-station.

A car was coming up the road past the hockey field, and as it reached the junction of the road opposite the gates to the swimming-pool, and slowed for the turn, Miranda broke into a run.

Simon Lang jammed on the brakes, and after one quick look at her face threw open the car door, and she stumbled in and sank down beside him.

Simon did not ask any questions. He leant across her and shut the door, and turned the car into the road that ran past the Sports Centre; bringing it to a stop by the curb a few yards from the gates to the pool, with the engine still running.

There was a babble of voices from the path beyond the gates, and as Colonel and Mrs Leslie and a tall woman in a persian lamb coat came into view, Miranda said with stiff lips: 'They're looking for me.'

There was a queer singing sound in her ears and she felt cold

191

and oddly light-headed. She was aware of Simon calling across the road something about giving her a lift home, and the car moved forward again before she heard the reply.

Simon said lightly : 'I imagine, from their expressions, that they are all under the impression that I have arrested you.'

Presently he brought the car to a standstill by some trees and switched off the engine. He turned to look at her and said abruptly: 'Do you want to be sick?'

Miranda shook her head. The gold had faded from the sky, and dusk was gathering over the scattered lawns and gardens and buildings of the Stadium. Simon lit a cigarette and sat relaxed and silent, leaning back against the worn leather seat and letting her take her own time, and after a while Miranda said jerkily: 'Mademoiselle Beljame——' and he turned his head and looked at her; his face indistinct in the twilight and his quiet eyes reflecting the faint glow of his cigarette.

'I *knew* her!' whispered Miranda: 'I didn't realize it before. I never recognized her. I don't know why I never recognized her. It was the hair, I suppose: and she looked so old, and – and I never thought of it. I only knew that I didn't like her. I suppose that was why I didn't like her.'

She stopped, and after a moment or two Simon said quietly: 'Who was she?'

'I don't know. But years ago, when I was a child, my parents were killed in Belgium, while we were trying to reach the coast. The road we were on was bombed and our car was wrecked, but I must have been thrown clear. I don't remember much after that; except how Mother looked, and – and my father. I wasn't very old, but I knew they were dead. There were a lot of other people who were dead too. There was a head in the middle of the road; only a head. It had its eyes open and it was looking at me. It's funny that I should have forgotten that until now. I thought — I thought I didn't remember it. But it's come back again . . .

'I was frightened of the head, and I picked up my doll and ran away screaming. Then sometime later on — or perhaps it was days

192

later, I don't remember — a woman spoke to me in French. There was a man with her and they took me with them and gave me some food, and the woman pointed to my doll and said: "That is how we will do it." I thought she meant to take it away, but she didn't. I was afraid of them; but there was no one else. I think we must have walked a long way, but we only walked at night and hid in the daytime. Then we joined some other people, and one night we got into a boat and there was a lot of shooting and it was dark and misty, and the woman got left behind . . .

'When we got to England the man was ill, and I was left on my own. I heard people talking in English so I spoke in English too, and I remember someone saying: "Good God — the child's English!" I didn't see the man again: I think he died. I'd forgotten about the woman, but – but now I've remembered her again. It was Mademoiselle Beljame . . .'

'Why have you remembered now?' asked Simon quietly.

'Her hair,' said Miranda in a whisper. 'She had a lot of thick yellowish hair, and she wore it banded across her forehead; not strained back and dyed black, like Mademoiselle's. The straw looked like hair, and – and her face was puffy, and not so old. And then I remembered where I had seen eyes like that before. They weren't the same colour: I don't know how I could have forgotten that. Someone – someone only the other day — said that you never forgot a physical defect. But I had forgotten it. Until – until now.'

Simon said: 'Where is she?'

Miranda turned to look at him, her face no more than a small white blur in the shadows, and tried to speak and could not.

Simon reached out a warm hand and laid it over the two cold ones that were clutched together so tightly in her lap, and her chilled fingers turned and clung desperately to his. He said: 'Tell me, dear.'

'In – in the open-air pool near the swimming-bath.'

She felt rather than saw the sudden involuntary movement of Simon's body, but his hand remained steady and his voice unhurried.

'She's dead then.' It was a statement and not a query.

Miranda nodded dumbly, and when she spoke again he had to bend his head to catch the words.

'The swimming instructor, Herr Kroll, found her. Or – or perhaps it was Mrs Leslie ... I don't know. They were arguing and pointing, and Colonel Leslie told me to see if I could see anything ... and – and at first I thought it was only the reflection of my own face, but then the wind moved some straw and ... And I saw her face——'

Simon did not ask any further questions. He released her hands and restarted the car, and before the sudden flood of light from the headlights the violet evening turned to night as the car swept down a long curving road bordered by trees, and turned in the direction of the Herr Strasse.

There was a rigidly enforced speed limit in Berlin, but Simon must have disregarded it, for in an astonishingly short time the car drew up before the Melvilles' house. He had not spoken during the swift journey from the Stadium, but now he turned to look at Miranda; his face unwontedly grim in the reflected glow of the headlights.

'You are not to say a word of this to anyone — about recognizing her. Anyone at all. Do you understand?'

Miranda nodded wordlessly. He studied her face for a moment or two, and what he saw there evidently satisfied him, for he laid the back of his hand against her cheek in a brief gesture that was somehow more intimate than a kiss, and then leant across her and jerked open the door of the car: 'And another thing,' said Simon. 'Don't go out of the house until I've seen you again. No matter who asks you. And if for any reason you are alone in the house, lock yourself into your room. Is that understood?'

Miranda nodded again and stepped out into the dark road, and Simon gave a little jerk of his head in the direction of the gate: 'Go on. I want to see that you get safely into the house.'

Once again it was Robert who opened the front door for her, and turning to look back, she saw the car move away down the road.

194

'Who was that?' inquired Robert, shutting the door behind her. 'That wasn't the Leslies' car, was it?'

'No,' said Miranda, looking curiously dazed. 'Captain Lang gave me a lift back. He – he wanted to ask me some questions.'

Robert laughed — he appeared to have recovered his good temper. 'Still Suspect Number One, are you? Don't worry, darling! It's my guess that Lang is merely using this business as an excuse for enjoying your society. And who can blame him? Cheer up, 'Randa!' He put an arm about her shoulders and gave her a companionable hug as Stella leaned over the landing rail to ask if Miranda had brought the Leslies in for a drink.

'No,' said Miranda; and was spared explanations by the ringing of the telephone bell. Robert released her and went over to answer it, and she saw his face stiffen and after a moment relax again. He said: 'Yes. She's here,' and turned towards Miranda holding out the receiver: 'It's for you.'

It's Simon, thought Miranda, her hands suddenly unsteady, but he can't have got there as soon as this: he can't have found her yet!

She took the receiver and steadied her voice with an effort, glad that Robert had walked quickly away. But it was only Sally Page, ringing up to ask if she would like to make a fourth to dine and dance at a nightclub on Grünewald Strasse with Andy and herself and a young American; they could pick her up in about twenty minutes.

Miranda, feeling weak from a mixture of shock and emotional reaction, murmured excuses and thanks, and rang off. She went to bed early that night, but could not sleep. The past that she had buried deep in oblivion for so long had returned to her, and when at long last she dropped into an uneasy sleep it was to dream of a blond woman with curious eyes, who smelt of caraway seeds and dragged her by the hand through a clinging fog down a long road pitted with shell holes . . .

15

'Pssst!'

The bushes underneath the drawing-room window rustled, and
a twig, accurately aimed, flipped against the pages of the morning
paper that concealed Miranda's face.

Miranda lowered it hurriedly.

'Pssst!' said Wally Wilkin, his flaming hair and excited eyes
appearing briefly above the level of the sill.

'Hullo, Inspector. On the trail again?' inquired Miranda, folding away the paper.

'Sssh!' begged Wally frantically, casting an agonized look
towards the half-open door into the hall. Miranda rose and shut
it and returned to the window-seat: 'Well, Rip Kirby — what is
it now?'

'That there governess,' hissed Wally. 'They found 'er!'

Miranda's hands clenched suddenly on the window ledge. 'Who
told you? How do you know?'

'Cos I was there! In the water she was. I saw 'em pull 'er out.
Coo, it were a treat!'

'Wally, *no!*'

'Dad takes me up to see the 'ockey, an' 'e thinks I gorn 'ome
in the other lorry. But I nips off to 'ave a bathe. Then up comes
a chap wot tells everyone to clear off, and I sees there's a guard
on the gate and that 'tec's there with 'is busies; so I 'ides, and I
seen 'em fish 'er out. Drowned she was, and all tangled up in that
grass — and 'er bike too. An' listen — I know oo done it, cos I——'

There was a sound of women's voices from the hall, and Wally
disappeared with the speed of a diving duck as the drawing-room

door opened and Elsa Marson came in, followed by Stella carrying a sheaf of cherry blossom and white lilac.

'Do look, 'Randa! Aren't they lovely? Mrs Marson has just brought them over. Isn't it sweet of her? Would you be an angel and put them in water for me? She's offered to give me a lift to the Lawrences', because Robert has the car this morning and I have to take over some clean clothes for Lottie.'

Elsa Marson looked curiously at Miranda, and from her to the window, and her eyes were all at once wide and wary. She walked quickly across the room to lean on the windowsill and look out into the garden, and said with an attempt at a laugh: 'I see that I have only brought coals to Newcastle. I did not realize that you had cherry trees in your garden.'

'But no white lilac,' said Stella. 'Our lilac isn't out yet, and it will be several days before we can pick any. I think your garden must get more sun than ours.'

'Perhaps,' said Elsa Marson, her gaze roaming quickly about the garden. Miranda looked out, but Wally had vanished and the leaves were unmoving in the morning sunlight.

A bell rang in the hall and Stella deposited her fragrant burden on the coffee table and said: 'With any luck that will be a new housemaid. The Labour Exchange swore they'd send round a few suitable applicants. Or do you suppose it's someone ringing up to ask us to forward Mademoiselle's belongings?'

She went out into the hall, shutting the door behind her, and Elsa Marson said in a bright, conversational voice: 'You know, I really thought that you were talking to someone in here when we came in!'

'Did you?' Miranda's tone expressed polite interest and Mrs Marson coloured and turned away from the window to walk aimlessly about the room, fingering photographs and ornaments and talking at random of the weather and the recent kidnapping by the Russian police of a German from West Berlin: 'It says in the papers that they have their agents everywhere — all through the city. Why do we not put a stop to it? Why cannot we protect these people? *Why?*'

Her voice rose unnaturally, and a small porcelain horse that she had been fidgeting with slipped from her fingers and smashed in pieces on the parquet floor. Mrs Marson stared at it in horror and plunged down upon her knees to gather up the broken bits.

The door opened and Stella was back, her face white and excited. Mrs Marson began to apologize for her clumsiness, but Stella said: 'The horse? It doesn't matter,' and looked across the room at Miranda: 'Captain Lang is here.'

Simon had been up all night, and had not slept for over twenty-four hours. But there was nothing in his face or manner to betray the fact. Stella said abruptly: 'He says that they have traced Mademoiselle.'

There was a little crash as the broken pieces of china that Mrs Marson had gathered up fell back onto the polished floor.

Simon said: 'Can I help?' He crossed over to her and stooping down began to pick up the pieces, an expression of polite concern on his face.

Stella said urgently: 'Where is she, Captain Lang? Don't keep us on tenterhooks! Has she only gone to another job? Or did she make a bolt for it to the Russian zone after all?'

Simon straightened up and placed the small white pieces neatly into an ashtray. 'She's dead,' he said laconically.

Stella said: 'No! Oh, no!'

She pressed the back of one hand against her teeth as though to stop herself from screaming, and did not notice that Miranda had shown no surprise at the news.

'Why do you not stop it?' cried Elsa Marson hysterically. 'Why is there no protection? It is the Russians, I tell you! The *Russians*!'

Her voice rose to a scream and Stella took her hand away from her mouth and said desperately: 'Please don't, Mrs Marson!' She turned to Simon Lang.

'How did she — die?'

'She was drowned.'

The rigidity went out of Stella's body. 'Oh, thank God!' she said on a long breath of relief.

She took an uncertain step towards the nearest chair and sinking down into it, hid her face in her hands, and after a moment or two let them drop and looked up: 'I'm sorry. That was a beastly thing to say. But I didn't mean it like that; I thought for a minute it was another murder.'

'It was,' said Simon Lang briefly.

Stella's hands tightened on the arms of her chair until the knuckles showed white, but she did not move or speak.

Simon said: 'She was hit over the head with something like a spanner, and either fell, or was pushed, into the water, somewhere around Tuesday evening or Tuesday night.'

He turned away to gaze abstractedly at an excellent reproduction of Velasquez's 'Lady with a Fan' that hung on the wall beside him, and added as though as an afterthought: 'Her hands were covered with green paint.'

For a moment no one spoke and then without warning Mrs Marson began to laugh. She rocked to and fro in shrill, hysterical mirth that grated abominably upon their taut nerves and went on, and on ...

Stella came to her feet in one swift movement and crossing over to her, grasped her by the shoulders and shook her. Mrs Marson gasped, gulped and dissolved into tears, and Stella put an arm about her and glared defiantly at Simon Lang: 'I'm going to take her home,' she said: her face was quite white and her eyes were blazing.

'A very good idea,' said Simon politely. 'Perhaps you wouldn't mind staying with her until her husband or some responsible person can keep an eye on her? And after that I'd like to see you: we'll have to go over the details of Tuesday evening again, I'm afraid.'

'Of course. Come along, dear, I'll take you home.' Stella led the sobbing Mrs Marson from the room and the door closed behind them.

Miranda said in a shaking voice: 'What did that mean?'

'What did what mean?'

'The green paint. Why did it frighten her so?'

'Because there is a can of green paint in Major Marson's garage. They have been painting their garden furniture.'

Miranda said helplessly: 'I don't understand!' and sat down abruptly on the window-seat as though her legs could no longer support her: 'Simon, what is it all about? Please tell me! You know, don't you?'

'Yes,' said Simon slowly. 'I know. Not quite everything yet, but enough to go on with.'

He looked at her thoughtfully for what seemed a long time. His eyes were slightly narrowed and there was an expression on his face that puzzled her — though it was probably familiar to Lieutenant Hank Decker of the United States Army and other devotees of poker.

After a moment or two he sat down beside her, and thrusting his hands in his pockets said: 'What is it that you want to know? I'll try and answer at least some of the questions.'

'I want to know about Mademoiselle. I've been thinking and thinking about her. I even dreamt of her last night! Was she really the woman I think she was, or did I only imagine it?'

'No. She was the same woman.'

'How do you know? Perhaps – perhaps I was mistaken?'

Simon shook his head. 'No you weren't. We spent most of last night and a good bit of this morning going through endless files and records and documents and dossiers. It was all astonishingly simple really, and one wonders why on earth no one spotted it before. Do you remember the story Brigadier Brindley told you at Bad Oeynhausen?'

'About the Nazi couple who murdered their servants and got away with millions of pounds worth of diamonds?'

'The Ridders. Yes. But it was not the Ridders who murdered their cook-housekeeper and valet. It was the cook and the valet — Karl and Greta Schumacher — who murdered the Ridders. They probably planned it for weeks beforehand. We shall never know about that, but the chances are that the building of the new garage and

200

the lime pit at the bottom of the garden gave them the idea——

'On the night that Herr Ridder returns to Berlin with the diamonds he is killed by the Schumachers. Frau Ridder is probably already dead and her jewels, plus any other available loot, packed in a small suitcase. The Schumachers dress the bodies in some of their clothes — they were much of a size — making sure that a few identifiable metal objects are included with them for the purpose of identification; the buttons off the valet's coat for instance, and his wristwatch, and a locket and chain and ring belonging to the cook, and one or two similar things that lime would not destroy—— Greta Schumacher probably shaves Frau Ridder's head and chops off a hank of her own hair to bury with her, just in case.

'Then they bury the bodies in quicklime, and make their getaway. Once the lime has destroyed the flesh that deformed hand of Frau Ridder's will not show, since the bone formation was apparently normal. But even then the imposture might well have been discovered if it hadn't been for the tremendous events that were taking place at the time. The British Army was in full retreat, Belgium suing for an armistice, and France crumbling to pieces. The authorities had a great many things on their hands in those days!'

Miranda said: 'Brigadier Brindley said there was a child. Did they kill it too?'

'No one knows. There seems to be no evidence to show that it was even in Berlin at the time. But its body was never found. I think myself that they may have taken it with them and that it died or was killed on the road, which is why they picked up a stray child as a substitute. They may have needed a child; it was probably part of the plan.'

Miranda said slowly: 'Then it was the housekeeper — Frau Schumacher. How did they get away?'

'I don't suppose anyone will ever know that. The chauffeur may conceivably have been in the plot. Or they may have stuck a gun in his ribs, or had some convincing lie ready. They probably meant to get across Europe to Lisbon, and so to South America, but

201

found that it was too dangerous and decided to try for England instead. I don't suppose they ever realized you were British. You say the woman spoke to you in French, so the odds are that you answered her in the same language.'

Miranda nodded. 'I expect so. I spoke more German and French than English in those days.'

'Then that's the answer. You were a stray child and they needed a child. But your chief attraction was undoubtedly the fact that you were clutching a large doll. What better way to smuggle out a lot of stolen valuables than for a child to carry them inside a toy?'

'But the Dutch diamonds?' said Miranda.

'No one knows what they did with those, or even if they knew anything about them. They may not have done. The stuff they got away with was a sufficiently spectacular haul! Well, there you are. Some of that is guesswork, but there's quite a bit of evidence to support it, and it all adds up. Do you mind if I smoke?'

Simon drew out a flat gold cigarette case and offered it to Miranda, who shook her head. He lit a cigarette himself and flicked the spent match out of the open window.

'Go on,' said Miranda impatiently. 'That isn't all.'

'You told me some of the rest yourself. Greta Schumacher was left behind when you and her husband escaped across the channel. Karl Schumacher died of double pneumonia, and no one connected a dying refugee with an obviously English child. The jewels and money were not found until some time later, and by the time their ownership was proved the trail was cold and there was nothing to connect the Ridders with you, or you with an unknown dead man: you apparently insisted that the doll was yours and that no one had touched it. In the end it was decided that the Ridders had at one time been among the refugee party, and had hidden the stuff there temporarily, meaning to retrieve it, but had probably been killed in an air raid. Various trails were followed up, but none of them led anywhere.'

Miranda said: 'But Mademoiselle — Frau Schumacher? How did she—— What happened to her?'

'We haven't got much of a line on her yet,' confessed Simon. 'But as far as can be made out she ended up in a prison camp where one of her cell mates was a Swiss woman called Beljame, who either died or was assisted to die, and Mademoiselle — Frau Schumacher — eventually turned up in England with her papers and calling herself by that name. She was, of course, looking for a husband and a child, and a doll stuffed with jewels. And also, possibly, a fortune in Dutch diamonds! She must have struck a trail at last, for your cousin Robert says she turned up on the doorstep one day with some story about having been told that they needed a governess-cum-household help.'

'Supposing they hadn't?'

'Domestics were pretty rare in those days,' said Simon. 'She drew a card to an open straight and pulled it off.'

'She did work well,' said Miranda, slowly. 'And they paid her so very little: that was the main reason why they kept her on.'

'When did you first meet her — as Mademoiselle?' asked Simon.

Miranda frowned, trying to think back. 'Only about two years ago, I think. And then only for very brief intervals. I hardly spoke to her. I had a job in London and didn't get to Mallow often. But I never liked her. She looked quite different — thin and old and black-haired. I couldn't have recognized her. But she still ate caraway seeds, and I suppose, without knowing it, the smell of them must have reminded me of that awful time. It wasn't until I started for Berlin that I really began to feel on edge and to feel — oh, I don't know!'

'Aunt Hettyish?' supplied Simon with a grin.

'Yes!' Miranda turned a surprised look on him. 'How did you know that?'

'You explained the expression to me once,' said Simon. 'I thought it very apt.'

'Well, it's true. I didn't connect it with Mademoiselle. I only knew that for some reason or other I felt on edge and – and frightened. It was a horrid feeling. I suppose it came from being boxed up with her for so long, and my subconscious or something

203

getting uneasy about it. But how could I be expected to guess at such a fantastic coincidence?'

'It wasn't a coincidence,' said Simon. 'It was a careful piece of planning by Mademoiselle Beljame, *alias* Greta Schumacher. But what we *don't* know is why did she stick to the Melvilles after she found out that the jewels had gone? — which she must have done fairly soon. However, the chances are that the answer to that is quite simply because it was a job, and since she had nowhere else to go she might as well live that way as any other. It was what followed that was the fantastic coincidence. Your cousin Robert meets a man who had known his father, and asks him to have supper with you all at the Families' Hostel. And during the meal Brigadier Brindley, who had actually stayed at the Ridders' house, told the story — probably for the five-hundredth time — of the missing diamonds.'

Miranda shivered in the warm spring sunlight. 'And she had to sit there and listen to it!' she said in a whisper.

'Yes. It can't have been very pleasant. But there was worse to come. He mentioned, didn't he, that Frau Ridder had a physical defect, and added that of all things a physical defect was the one thing one did not forget?'

'Yes,' said Miranda. 'But he was wrong. I forgot.'

'You were only a child, and very frightened; so to you it was only an unimportant detail in a welter of horrible things. But I think that the ex-housekeeper thought that the Brigadier's remark was aimed at her — remember, she had actually seen and spoken to him in the Ridders' house! Supposing he had recognized her? She may even have thought that he told the story in order to surprise some reaction from her. I think that she must have decided then and there to take precautions against his denouncing her when she reached Berlin, and his talk of sleeping tablets gave her the opportunity.'

Miranda said: 'Then it *was* Mademoiselle who killed him!'

'I think so,' said Simon, slowly. 'You all told me that she and the Brigadier and Mrs Melville each took sleeping powders. But though a good many people saw the Brigadier and Mrs Melville take theirs, no one seems to have seen the governess take hers. My guess is that she put it in the hot milk that she gave to Lottie, to ensure that the child slept soundly.'

'But — Friedel?' said Miranda. 'Why Friedel? There was no reason for that.'

'That's something else I don't know yet,' admitted Simon. 'I think that it's perfectly possible that she did kill Friedel, but that she killed her by mistake — and in mistake for someone else.'

'Stella,' whispered Miranda.

'It could be. On the other hand — always supposing she did do it — she may have mistaken her for you.'

'*Me?*' Miranda's face was suddenly white and startled. 'But why me? You're joking!'

'You know, this doesn't strike me as being a joking matter,' observed Simon pensively.

'But why me? It doesn't make sense!'

'I think you may have had something that she — or someone — wanted. *That*——' Simon reached out and touched the charm bracelet that encircled Miranda's slim wrist: 'The ankh. It was one of the items inside your doll, if you remember. I don't suppose she realized that you had it until you drew attention to it yourself.'

Miranda stared at the little metal charm with a shrinking distaste. 'But why should she want it?'

'I don't know. I'm not even sure that she did. It's just a theory as yet. But I'm interested in that charm; because you weren't wearing the bracelet when you arrived in Berlin. *Or* when I spoke to you that afternoon at the Families' Hostel.'

Miranda wrinkled her brows. 'I must have been! I always wear it. No ... You're right. I couldn't make the catch work; it's stiff. So I put it in my pocket.'

'And someone noticed that you were not wearing it, and searched your room for it.'

'How can you know that?'

'I don't. It's just an idea. But since I knew that your room hadn't been searched officially, I realized that you obviously had something that someone wanted badly. And having heard at least half a dozen versions of the Brigadier's story, and its sequel, I made a guess at what it was.'

Miranda looked from the little metal charm to Simon's face, and back again. 'It can't be true! Why try to kill me when it would be so much simpler to steal it?'

'Perhaps it wasn't so easy to steal?' suggested Simon. 'You've just told me that you always wear it. And possibly time was short.'

Miranda said: 'No, you can't be right. You've forgotten the coat. Friedel was wearing Stella's coat.'

'Yes, I know. But your coat is squirrel, isn't it? By moonlight the difference in colouring would be negligible. And there's another point that appears to have escaped general notice. Both you and Friedel had dark hair, but Mrs Melville is a blonde.'

Miranda said in a low voice: 'Stella thought that someone had meant to kill her.'

'I know she did. She was almost scared out of her wits, wasn't she? I realized that. But it was better to let her go on being scared, in order to allow the murderer to think we were off on a false trail.'

'Stella said that there was a reason — ' began Miranda and stopped.

Simon looked up quickly. 'What's that? What did she say?'

'Very little,' said Miranda slowly. 'She said that she knew that someone had meant to kill her, and when I told her not to be silly and asked her if she knew of any reason why anyone should want to kill her she – she said "Yes".'

'Are you sure of that?' demanded Simon.

'Quite sure: she said it in a sort of whisper, as though she were talking to herself. Afterwards she said she hadn't said anything of the sort; but she had — I heard her. And she was more than just frightened. She was terrified!'

Simon Lang said 'Oh' in a preoccupied voice, and remained silent for a moment or two, watching a thin spiral of smoke curling up from his cigarette, and presently Miranda said: 'If it was

Mademoiselle who killed the Brigadier and Friedel, then the case is over.'

'That's where you're wrong. Because now Mademoiselle herself has been killed.'

'I was forgetting that,' said Miranda unhappily. She turned to stare out of the window and said abruptly: 'Is it Elsa Marson?'

'Now why should you say that?' inquired Simon with an odd note in his voice.

Miranda turned to face him: 'Because I saw her at the hostel the day we arrived, talking to Friedel in German. I wasn't sure then, but I am now. It *was* Mrs Marson. And I saw her again in that Russian cemetery place. She had gone there to meet someone, hadn't she?'

'Yes,' said Simon slowly. 'She had. And for that reason it's possible that Friedel was killed by someone who had no connection with the murder of Brigadier Brindley, and who killed her knowing quite well who she really was.'

'Who was she?'

'She was Mrs Marson's sister,' said Simon surprisingly.

'Her *sister*!' Miranda stared at him, open-mouthed. 'How long have you known that? Did she tell you?'

'Since yesterday. She told us everything. Elsa's mother was French and her father German. They parted in 1938 and the mother took the younger child with her and resumed her maiden name. Elsa's elder sister and brother remained in Germany with their father. When the war broke out the mother's family supplied her with falsified identification papers that mentioned a French father, deceased, and got them away to England. The mother died in the last year of the war, and Elsa got a job as private secretary to the head of a firm of importers.

'Major Marson met her and married her, thinking that she was French and an only child. She was afraid to tell him that her father was a German and a Nazi. Then last year the regiment was sent to Berlin, where Friedel saw her by chance and was struck by her resemblance to a photograph of their mother; and also to their elder brother. She stopped her in the street one day and taxed her with it, and Elsa lost her head and admitted it. After that, Friedel blackmailed her.'

'Threatened to tell Harry, I suppose. Beastly woman!'

'Yes. After paying over various odd amounts, Mrs Marson borrowed money and paid Friedel a large sum, in return for which her sister had promised to leave Berlin. But when the Marsons returned from leave Friedel was still here. She rang up Mrs Marson and arranged to meet her at the hostel, which is where you saw them. You interrupted them, and so Friedel, who had got a job with Mrs Melville, arranged another meeting that night. She told Mrs Marson that their brother was in East Berlin. He had played ball with the Communists and risen to a position of some importance, at a shady level, but he was getting frightened and wanted to escape to the West. He also wanted money. More money than Elsa could supply. And he thought he knew how to get it. He had something to sell that he thought the Americans or ourselves would be prepared to pay pretty highly for. And he was right!' added Simon grimly.

'What was it?' inquired Miranda.

'That, my dear Miranda, is still a Top Secret: and likely to remain so. But I think you saw Mrs Marson take it over.'

'Yes I did. I thought she was doing a bit of black-marketing. But why go to all that bother? Why didn't he just walk out with it himself? It seems quite easy to go from one zone to the next.'

'Because he hadn't the nerve,' said Simon. 'By chance, and a talent for lock-picking that must amount to genius, he knew he could get his hands on a bit of pure dynamite. He didn't mind walking into West Berlin with empty hands, but he was scared of a good deal worse than death if he was caught trying it with that packet on him. And I can't say that I blame him. He and his sister made a deal with Mrs Marson. She was to go on that bus tour, collect the goods, and hand it to Friedel. We kept an eye on Elsa Marson, because for all we knew she might have been working for the Russians. It looked like it, and we wanted to see who contacted her.'

Miranda said: 'I thought I saw someone, the evening we were all looking at the ruin of the Ridders' house. Was that one of your people watching her?'

'I expect so,' said Simon without interest. 'When Friedel was killed, Mrs Marson lost her nerve and made a clean breast of it. As it turned out, she and her brother had done us a signal service.'

'Then he *has* got away?'

'Not as yet; which leads me to believe he has been liquidated.'

'Poor Elsa — what hell she must have been through! So she didn't have anything to do with Mademoiselle or the Ridders after all?'

'Apart from confusing the issue, no.'

Miranda said: 'But there's something else, isn't there? The green paint. If there hadn't been, you wouldn't have suddenly brought it up like that.'

'Like what?' inquired Simon softly.

'You said it on purpose,' said Miranda accusingly 'Didn't you? You wanted to see what she'd do.'

'I must be getting very obvious in my old age,' said Simon regretfully. 'Or else you are too acute for your tender years.'

'Then I *was* right?'

'Almost. You see that picture?' Simon gestured with his cigarette towards the dark Velasquez print. 'It makes a very adequate looking-glass, and people are more likely to display their emotions when they think they are unobserved. It is beginning to dawn on Mrs Marson that the Russians may get to hear of her part in taking that package out of East Berlin, and the mention of green paint in connection with Mademoiselle instantly suggested to her that the governess and her killer had been lurking round her house. I wasn't interested in Mrs Marson's reactions. But I *was* interested in Mrs Melville's. I wanted to know if green paint meant anything to her. It did.'

'Nonsense!' said Miranda sharply. 'You're imagining things!'

'Am I?' said Simon softly. 'I don't think so.'

Miranda stood up abruptly. 'What are you hinting at?' she demanded breathlessly.

Simon leaned out over the windowsill and dropped the end of his cigarette into the bushes. 'That wasn't a hint, it was a statement of fact.' He leant his head against the window frame and looked up at Miranda, his hands deep in his pockets.

'That mention of green paint meant something to Mrs Melville. It gave her a clue to something that had puzzled her, and it frightened her badly — so badly that I thought for a moment that she was going to faint. But she hid it very well. Mrs Marson's hysterics helped her out there, and I have no doubt at all that had I been facing her she would have kept a better control over her features. But I had my back to her, and you and Mrs Marson were both looking at me and not at her.'

Miranda said angrily: 'Why are you trying to make her out to be a hypocrite?'

'My dear Miranda,' said Simon mildly, 'there is a considerable difference between being an actress and a hypocrite. A good many men and women can act very well if they have to. Some are better than others; that's all.'

'You don't know Stella!' said Miranda shortly.

'Do you, I wonder? Sit down and be sensible.' Simon reached up and caught her wrist, and pulled her down again onto the window-seat. 'How can you be sure that you know anyone well enough to tell what they might not be capable of under pressure? I'm not accusing your Stella of anything. I am merely pointing out that she knows something, or thinks she knows something, about that green paint on Mademoiselle's hands. She may decide to tell. I can only hope so. To possess a vital piece of knowledge in connection with murder is a very dangerous thing. After all, a murderer can only hang once.'

Miranda stared at him, whitefaced. 'You mean that – that anyone who knew something that might point to the murderer might be murdered too? That's what you mean, isn't it?'

210

'Of course. It occurs in almost every detective story, and you'd be surprised how often it also happens in real life.'

Miranda put out a shaking hand and clutched at his sleeve.

'*Wally!*' she said breathlessly.

Simon's brows twitched together in a sudden frown. 'The Wilkin brat? What about him?'

'He was here this morning. He said he saw the body being taken out of the pool last night——'

'I know he did,' said Simon grimly. 'And the bicycle, too! It had green rubber hand-grips that had been daubed with fresh green paint — Wally's work! He'd done it to get his own back on Mademoiselle, who'd caught him lurking round the Lawrences' house on the evening that she disappeared. He was looking for Lottie it seems, and Mademoiselle, who also had a score or two to settle, went after him with a stick and evidently landed a few shrewd shots on target. The paint was Wally's revenge.'

'Then why,' demanded Miranda hotly, 'didn't you say so at once, instead of scaring the daylights out of Stella and poor Elsa Marson with your sinister hints?'

'I've already told you why,' said Simon patiently. 'I wanted to know if by any chance green paint meant anything to anyone here. It ought not to have done, since only the police — and Wally of course — knew anything about it. You see, it wasn't applied until dusk on the evening of the day Mademoiselle disappeared. And as it was dark when she set off for the swimming-baths to look for Lottie's china bear, she wouldn't have noticed it; though she must have realized that there was something sticky on the handles, once she got started. But then rubber is apt to become tacky with age, so she probably thought it was that; or if she did drive up to the fact that it was paint, she obviously decided to deal with it when she got back. Only she never did get back.'

'I still don't see why you should have thought that Stel'——'

'Use your head, Miranda!' interrupted Simon brusquely. 'No one except Wally, Mademoiselle, and the murderer — who presumably touched the handles when the bicycle was tipped into the pool — could have known anything about that paint. Unless someone else brushed against it by accident, either when it was parked at the Lawrences', or by the gate into the swimming-pool area.'

'Wally may have told someone!'

'I doubt it. I caught the young demon watching us fish the body out of the pool. Which was when he owned up about the paint — he hadn't much option, as his clothes were liberally bespotted with it! I tore a king-size strip off him in more senses than one, and told him that if he said one word about the affair, he'd be for the high-jump!'

'He didn't tell me that,' said Miranda. 'But he said he knew who had killed her. Supposing he was hiding there on Tuesday night too—— Supposing ...'

Simon stood up as swiftly as though he had been jerked to his feet and his quiet voice had an unexpectedly harsh ring to it: 'Did he give you a name?'

'No,' said Miranda, her own voice unsteady. 'We were interrupted and he bolted.'

Simon said a single wicked word in a tone that held so much concentrated rage that Miranda flinched and her eyes widened with shock. But it seemed that his fury was directed neither at her nor Master Wilkin, but against himself. 'Why didn't I think of that?' whispered Simon. 'It ought to have occurred to me that there might be some particular reason for that kid's interest in the pool and why he should happen to be hanging about there. I should have jollied the little blighter along — instead of scaring him into clamming up like an oyster. I ought to be hung, drawn and quartered——!'

'But you can't ... but you don't think that he *really* knows, do you?' quavered Miranda.

'We can always find out,' said Simon briefly. He turned and walked quickly across the room, but at the door he stopped suddenly and came back to her.

'What I told you last night still goes. You are not to tell anyone

212

anything of all this until I give you permission. *Anything*, do you understand?'

'Yes,' said Miranda unsteadily.

He stood looking down at her with an odd mixture of doubt and irresolution on his normally blandly expressionless face, and said something under his breath that Miranda could not catch. And then he swung round, and she was alone.

16

Stella returned, looking white and exhausted, barely five minutes after Simon's departure. She seemed surprised that he had gone. 'I thought he wanted to see me,' she said, sinking wearily onto the sofa. She leaned her head on her hand and shut her eyes.

'Why don't you take a couple of aspirins and have a day in bed?' suggested Miranda. 'You're looking like a ghost.'

'Am I?' Stella got up and went to peer at herself in a little Venetian-glass mirror that stood on the chimneypiece. 'I do look a bit of a hag, don't I? I feel as if I'd aged ten years since I arrived in Berlin. Oh dear, that Marson woman!'

'How is she?'

'I telephoned her unfortunate husband and he came right over. I should think Colonel Lawrence must be going crazy, what with his officers' time being gummed up by police inquiries and hysterical wives.'

'Was she very tiresome?'

'Awful!' said Stella feelingly. 'She appears to have got a bee in her bonnet about Soviet spies. She thinks Mademoiselle may have been one. She also thinks that the Russians mean to kill her in revenge for something or other. I think she must be out of her mind!'

She leant tiredly against the chimneypiece, her back to Miranda, and said: 'It's because of the green paint. Captain Lang said something about green paint, and Mrs Marson seems to think that this proves that Mademoiselle had been snooping around their house.'

The words were said casually enough, but Miranda was suddenly aware, with a startled sense of shock, that Stella was watching her in the Venetian-glass mirror: watching her with an inexplicable and furtive intentness. Miranda flushed hotly and looked quickly away. It was true then, what Simon had said! Stella did know something about that green paint — and she wanted to know if Miranda also knew. She had mentioned it deliberately while watching Miranda's face reflected in the little mirror, as Simon Lang had watched hers in the glass of the Velasquez print.

Stella ... Miranda stared blindly out of the window and thought about Stella, and all that she knew about her. She had said so confidently to Simon: 'You don't know Stella!' and he had replied, 'Do you?' *Did she?* She had known Stella for so long, yet how well did she really know her?

Stella had been there, part of the background of her childhood and schooldays — taken for granted. She was in many ways a curiously childlike person; a charming, rather spoilt child, simple, direct and not particularly clever. Gay and lighthearted when things went well, tearful and dazed at the unreasonable injustice of life when they went wrong. She was pretty without being beautiful, and always well dressed; always smooth and scented and shining. She had been widowed and remarried, and although she hated army life and the prospect of living in foreign countries she had again married a soldier. She loved England and Mallow — and Robert.

A sudden thought took root in Miranda's mind and grew swiftly into a certainty. Robert! Stella adored Robert. She would, thought Miranda, quite literally die for him if it were necessary. She would certainly lie for him and scheme and fight for him, and protect him. Simon had said that most people could act if circumstances forced them to it, and Miranda had thought instantly and scornfully 'Not Stella!' But even a bird will pretend to a broken wing and act a part to perfection, limping and fluttering, in order to lure an enemy away from its nest.

For some obscure reason Stella was afraid for Robert. Far more afraid than she had been for herself. She had been convinced that someone had meant to kill her: and been reduced by that knowledge to helpless and shuddering terror. But she was not helpless now. She was wary and alert and watchful.

Turpentine! thought Miranda suddenly. Robert had spilt some turpentine . . . when was it? — on Tuesday evening, of course! Was that what Stella had thought of? Had it puzzled her, and had the mention of green paint made her think that he had perhaps used it to clean stains from his clothes? What did Stella know, or think that she knew?

Whatever it was, she was wrong! Robert could not possibly have been involved in the murder of Mademoiselle. And for a very simple reason. He had no means of knowing that Mademoiselle would be at the swimming-pool late that evening, since her presence there was purely fortuitous. He had been at a conference that had not ended until about seven-thirty, and had been given a lift home by Harry Marson: and from then, until they had gone up to bed, he had been with Stella or herself or both of them.

But even if Robert had not possessed an alibi and had actually been seen near the pool that evening, Miranda would still have been sure that he could not possibly have murdered Mademoiselle. It was not a question of proof, but of instinct. There was no hard core to Robert. He was charming and attractive, and despite an occasional display of temper or irritability, essentially easy-going — she would not use the word 'weak' even to herself.

Robert wouldn't *care* enough to commit murder, thought Miranda, trying to explain her conviction to herself. Things don't matter enough to him. He will always avoid something unpleasant rather than face it — if facing it means taking any drastic action. He loves Stella, but not as Stella loves him. He lets himself be loved. He will always let things happen, never do them — or even do anything towards making them happen. Why is it that I can see that, thought Miranda, and Stella can't? The answer presented itself to her almost before the question had formed in her mind. Because Stella was in love with him and wore the bandage of her love across her eyes. She could not reason; she could only feel.

216

Stella's voice cut sharply across the silence.

'What are you thinking about, Miranda?'

Miranda turned quickly and said in some confusion: 'Nothing. I mean I was just thinking about all this ghastly business, and——' The sound of voices and laughter from the hall interrupted her, and she realized gratefully that Robert was back. It must be later than she had thought.

'I only hope there's some beer,' said Stella anxiously. 'He seems to have brought someone back with him. I wonder——' She stopped suddenly and Miranda saw her stiffen. The door opened to admit Colonel and Mrs Leslie, Robert, and Sally and Andy Page.

'Stella darling, have we a spare can of petrol?' demanded Robert, crossing to her side and kissing her lightly. 'Andy very kindly offered me a lift home, and then ran out of petrol about a quarter of a mile back. We were forced to abandon ship, and Colonel Leslie picked us up. There's a two-gallon can in the garage, isn't there?'

'Yes, I think so,' said Stella.

'Good. Well let's have a drink first. What about a glass of beer, sir? Or there's gin if you prefer it. Sherry for you, Norah?'

'Thank you.' Mrs Leslie looked across at Stella and said: 'I must apologize for this invasion, but your husband insisted.'

Stella smiled a stiff, social smile that did not reach her eyes, and murmured some polite formula as Norah Leslie accepted a cigarette and sat down on the sofa and Sally Page perched gracefully on the arm of a chair, one long slim leg swinging from the knee, and said, smiling appealingly at Stella: 'It's our fault really, Mrs Melville. I can't get Andy to have the petrol-gauge mended, and so this sort of thing keeps on happening.'

'Nonsense,' said Andy irritably. 'It's only happened once before — on the day we first discovered that the thing was bust. I can't understand it happening again. I filled the tank up only a day or two ago. It's all this coffee-partying of yours that eats up the petrol.'

'Far more likely to be a leak in the tank,' retorted Sally. 'I don't see what else we can expect with a museum piece like that.' She turned again to Stella: 'I keep telling Andy that a fifth-hand pre-war car is a false economy. A decent car might cost a good bit more to start with, but it would save pounds in the end! Don't you agree, Mrs Melville?'

Stella was saved the necessity of replying by the unexpected appearance of Harry Marson.

'Hullo,' said Harry, checking in the doorway and looking about the room, 'I seem to have gatecrashed a party.'

'Not at all,' said Robert hospitably. 'This is purely impromptu. The more the merrier. Have some beer?'

'Thanks, I will.' He turned to Stella. 'Elsa sent me over to ask if you could lend her something to read; magazines for choice. I've bunged her off to bed. She was feeling a bit mouldy.'

'Of course I will. I haven't got much in that line, I'm afraid, but she can have what there is.'

'Good of you,' said Harry Marson, and raised his tankard. 'Well — here's to crime!' He drank deeply and did not appear to notice the sudden strained silence that followed upon his words.

Miranda looked around the room. At Sally, sitting suddenly still, her slim foot in its neat shoe no longer swinging. At Mrs Leslie, with the cigarette ash falling unnoticed onto her skirt. At Andy Page, holding his tankard so tightly that the knuckles stood out white against the tanned skin. At the little muscle that twitched nervously at one corner of Colonel Leslie's mouth and belied the habitual boredom of his expression. At Stella, whose frightened gaze had darted momentarily to Robert and then away again, and at Robert, whose handsome mouth had tightened to a hard line ...

The silence was becoming oppressive when it was broken by Mrs Leslie.

'You're spilling sherry all over the chair, Sally,' she said briskly.

Sally righted the glass that she had been holding at an acute angle, and stood up hurriedly: 'Oh dear! I *am* sorry, Mrs Melville.

How messy of me!' She produced a face-tissue from her handbag and scrubbed anxiously at the stain.

'That,' said Robert, 'will be ninepence. And if you go on scrubbing at it Sally, it will cost you an additional two bob for having the hole invisibly mended.'

Sally laughed and tossed the crumpled tissue in the general direction of the fire. The tension was eased and a babble of conversation broke out again. But Miranda was not deceived. In the short space of silence that had followed upon Harry Marson's ill-chosen toast she had realized that the Pages too knew of Mademoiselle's death: the Leslies must have told them. They were all attempting to behave as though nothing had happened, but sometime during that morning each one of them had heard that there had been a third murder, and they were acting — discussing trivialities in gay, artificial voices.

'Fiddling while Rome burns!' thought Miranda, exasperated, and she said in a hard, bright voice: 'Well, what do you think about our latest murder?'

Seven faces turned swiftly towards her as though they had been pulled on one string. Seven faces that were all at once blank and unsmiling.

Stella said: 'Miranda — please!'

'Why? What's the matter?' demanded Miranda crisply. 'Why shouldn't we talk about it? It's what we're all thinking about, isn't it?'

Robert got up quickly, and coming over to her put an arm about her. 'Take it easy, darling. We all know how you feel. And we all feel much the same.'

Miranda jerked herself away angrily. 'I'm not having hysterics, if that's what you mean. I just think that it's silly to put on an act and pretend, when – when we all know what's happened.'

Robert returned to his chair and poured himself out some more beer, and sat down again.

'Of course we all know,' he said deliberately. 'We've all been on the carpet again; separately and severally. But what you do not realize, Miranda my pet, is that there is a limit to what one can take in this line. We have all been surfeited with horrors of late, and this is in the nature of a last straw. It's not that we are being ostriches and burying our heads in the sand, but that we just do not feel like discussing it any more. So for the time being, darling, we'll just lay off it if you don't mind.'

'Hear! Hear!' approved Harry Marson. 'Speaking for myself, I have gone over and over it until my brain is bubbling, and I now propose to lay off it for good — God willing and the gumshoe boys permitting.'

He finished his beer and set down his empty tankard with a thump.

'I'm sorry,' said Miranda contritely. 'You're right, of course. It's only that I——' She checked herself with an effort.

'Forget it, darling,' said Robert lightly. 'Have some more beer, Harry.'

'No thanks. Time I was getting back.'

Stella routed out some magazines and a novel for Elsa Marson, and the party broke up: Harry and Mrs Leslie leaving through the garden and Robert accompanying the Pages to the garage in search of petrol.

Colonel Leslie, who had offered to drive the Pages to where they had abandoned their car, lingered for a few moments in the hall, waiting for them to return, and said kindly to Miranda: 'Cheer up, my dear. Don't let this get you down. It's a terrible business, but perhaps not as bad as Lang and his lot, and the *Polizei*, seem to think. She could have taken the bicycle in with her, instead of leaving it unattended outside the entrance gate, and been wheeling it along the edge of that pool when she tripped, or the bicycle skidded and took her in with it, and she hit her head as she fell. Those sagging great ropes of straw would have let her through, but held her down if she tried to struggle up. Pity that instructor fellow, Kroll, didn't spot her earlier — or later, after we'd left! He called us over to show us, you know. If it hadn't been for him, we wouldn't have been involved in it. And if we hadn't asked you to go swimming with us, *you* wouldn't have been either. I'm sorry about that ...'

'You needn't be,' said Miranda sadly. 'We'd still have been involved even if she'd been found by the Bürgermeister of Berlin and his entire family! Because she was Lottie's governess, and employed by Robert and Stella, and we all lived in this house.'

'I suppose so,' admitted the Colonel. 'Still, it was unfortunate that—— Ah! here, I think, is the petrol.'

Stella and Robert accompanied the salvage party to the gate, and Miranda, left alone in the empty hall, went back into the drawing-room. It was quiet and warm and still, and in the silence she could hear through the open windows the voices of Harry Marson and Mrs Leslie talking in the next garden.

The green and white room was heavy with the scent of flowers, and Miranda looked guiltily at the wilting sheaf of cherry blossom and lilac, and realized that she had forgotten all about Elsa Marson's offering. A wisp of damp face-tissue had been wrapped about the stalks, but the petals of the cherry blossom were limp and fading for lack of water, and as she picked them up a small shower of white petals fell from the flowers in her arms onto the carpet, and she thought with a touch of irritation that if Elsa Marson needed an excuse to call on the Melvilles in order to find out what was going on, she might at least have refrained from bringing over cherry blossom, when she must have been able to see quite clearly from her own house that the Melvilles' garden was full of it!

Miranda bent down to gather up the fallen petals and stopped with her hand an inch away from the fender.

Presently she straightened up slowly, leaving the petals untouched, and having laid the flowers carefully on the table, sat down on the sofa, her brain whirling. She had remembered something that had happened in this room during the last half-hour. Something that her mind must have subconsciously noted at the time, but put aside. And a fantastic, impossible theory began to form in her head ...

221

She sat quite still, staring blindly ahead of her while another small, unregarded incident, and another and another, detached themselves from the memories of the past few days and fitted themselves together, like pieces of a jigsaw puzzle, to form a picture.

I have been looking at it the wrong way round, thought Miranda. It's like looking in a mirror. You see something quite clearly, but you see it the wrong way round.

Even Simon had seen it the wrong way round. No, that was not true. He had seen it both ways. If Friedel's death was a mistake, then the first guess was the right one after all, and it should have been Stella who died in the garden. The diamonds had only muddled it: they, and the package that Elsa Marson brought out of East Berlin. They sounded more important and more interesting, and so the more ordinary thing was overlooked. And if that were true, then Mademoiselle was only the excuse and the opportunity. She was dead now, and her story was finished. But the other story had not finished yet——

I must tell Simon, thought Miranda. I must let Simon know.

There was still no sound from the hall and the house was so quiet that Miranda could hear a faint clatter of pots and pans from the kitchen where Frau Herbach was preparing lunch.

Seized with a sudden panic she jumped up and ran quickly across the drawing-room and into the hall, and dialled Simon's number.

A strange voice answered her. No, Captain Lang was not in, and the strange voice had no idea when he would return; who was speaking? Oh, Miss Brand. Would Miss Brand care to leave a message?

Miranda hesitated. She could hear Robert's voice from the path outside the drawing-room windows.

She said hurriedly: 'Yes. Tell him I want to speak to him.' And rang off.

17

The long afternoon wore away, and still Simon did not phone.

Stella flipped over the pages of a magazine and Miranda forced herself to read a book, and struggled to keep her thoughts from the impossible theory that had occurred to her that morning. I won't think of it! she told herself desperately. I *won't*. I won't think of it until Simon comes. He will know what to do about it.

It was half-past three when a bell cut shrilly through the silence, and Miranda threw aside her book and was at the drawing-room door before Stella could rise. 'I'll answer it,' she said quickly.

She ran across the hall and lifted the receiver. But it was not Simon Lang.

'Who was it?' asked Stella as she returned to the drawing-room.

'It wasn't the telephone,' said Miranda. 'It was the front-door bell. One of the Wilkin children asking if we'd seen Wally.'

'He's probably up at the Lawrences' playing with Lottie,' said Stella.

'That's what I told her,' said Miranda, and shivered. Wally! Was he really at the Lawrences', or was he——? She pulled up her thoughts with a frightened jerk as they approached the edge of a yawning gulf into which she dared not look. I won't think of it, she told herself frantically. I won't think of it! *Wally* . . . ! Oh, not Wally!

'Only the Germans,' said Stella bitterly, 'would install a doorbell that is practically indistinguishable from a telephone bell. Oh, what wouldn't I give to be home! The daffodils will be out in the orchard at Mallow, and the primroses . . .' She got up suddenly and went out of the room, and Miranda heard her slam the door of her bedroom behind her and knew that she was crying.

At four o'clock Miranda rang Simon's number again. But he was still out, and the same voice assured her politely that Captain Lang would telephone her as soon as he came in: and with this she had to be content.

Robert returned an hour later with the unwelcome information that he would have to have an early supper, and leave again immediately afterwards to attend a talk by the Commander-in-Chief Northern Army Group on 'Allied Strategy in Europe'.

'I ought to have told you before,' apologized Robert, 'but what with all this flap on I'd completely forgotten about the damn thing. It's at eight-thirty, so I should be back by eleven at the latest; but don't wait up for me.'

Stella said: 'Are you taking the car, or is someone fetching you?'

'No, I'm certainly not taking the car! I don't see why the hell I should use my own petrol for this sort of show. One of the Volkswagens is calling for me.'

He lifted Stella's hands and kissed them. 'I'm sorry, my love. I don't like having to go out and leave you two alone in the house. Thank God we shall have a batman again tomorrow. The M.O. says Davies is fit for duty again, and until this business is cleared up he can live in. I shall feel a lot better when I know that there is a large and trustworthy chap around the place to discourage the criminally-minded when I'm not on the premises!'

He turned to Miranda and said: 'Keep an eye on her for me, 'Randa. She's just about all in.'

'I will.'

Robert put his hands on Miranda's shoulders and turned her about to face the light.

'You aren't looking too good yourself,' he said frowning. 'This has been one hell of a holiday for you, hasn't it dear? I wish we hadn't had to drag you into all this ghastly business.'

'Don't be silly, Robert,' said Miranda crisply. 'As if anyone could have known what was going to happen! And if I had known, I should probably have thought it sounded thrilling and insisted on coming. It's only when one is actually involved in a murder case

224

that one realizes that it isn't thrilling at all, but only very terrifying and quite beastly.'

Robert said: 'When this is all over, you and Stella had better take the next boat back to England and spend a month or two recuperating in some nice, safe, rural spot where the only problem on the hands of the local constable is who pinched the postmaster's prize marrow off the lectern during the Harvest Festival!'

He kissed Miranda affectionately and went out into the cold spring night.

Stella shivered suddenly. 'Cold, darling?' asked Miranda. 'Why don't you go and have a hot bath and get to bed?'

'I'm not cold. It was only a goose walking over my grave; and if I did go to bed I shouldn't sleep, so what's the use?' She closed the hall door, released the catch of the Yale lock and pushed home the heavy bolts above and below it. Miranda saw that her hands were shaking so that she could hardly control them, and that her face was white and frightened. She looked up and seeing Miranda's expression, smiled a little uncertainly.

'I know it's stupid of me, but I feel better with the doors locked. Robert locked both the other ones and any windows large enough for a cat to crawl through! If only I'd known that he was going to be out, I'd have asked a couple of people in to play bridge.'

'Well, let's do it now,' suggested Miranda. 'Let's go over and collect the Leslies.'

'No, don't let's,' said Stella with another shiver. 'Nothing would induce me to walk through the garden, and I don't intend to let you go over, and be left on my own in this house even for two minutes! Anyway, Colonel Leslie is sure to be going to this lecture affair too, and I couldn't stand Mrs Leslie solo just now. Let's turn on every light in the drawing-room and see if we can find a good programme on the wireless instead.'

The drawing-room looked larger and less friendly with all the lights burning, and the wireless offered them a choice between a mournful and wailing concerto by a popular modern composer, a drama about racketeers on the New York waterfront, a reading from *Murders in the Rue Morgue*, a political broadcast, and a variety of excitable gentlemen declaiming passionately in French, German, Italian and Russian.

Stella switched off impatiently and fetched a book. She seemed disinclined for talk, but Miranda noticed that although she kept the open book in her hands and occasionally turned a page, her eyes were unmoving and fixed in a blind stare as though they were turned inward on some frightening mental vision, and that every now and again she would shiver as if a cold intermittent draught blew through the warm room.

The house seemed strangely empty now that Robert had gone, but Miranda could not rid herself of a conviction that they were not alone, and that from somewhere near at hand an unseen pair of eyes was watching their every movement. Yet the curtains were closely drawn and gave no glimpse of the moonlit garden, and the door into the hall was shut. Could there be someone outside that door, waiting and listening? No, that was absurd! Every window and door was barred and bolted and there was no one in the house but Stella and herself. Nevertheless she found herself listening intently for sounds in the empty house or from the silent garden. Stella seemed aware of it too, for twice she turned her head and glanced uneasily over her shoulder. Her frightened tension reacted unpleasantly upon Miranda's own taut nerves and the thoughts that she had striven to keep at bay for so many hours came circling and swooping back again, closing in upon her like vultures gathering above a kill.

Had Stella too seen the thing that she had seen, and put the same interpretation upon it? Was she facing the same picture that had taken shape before Miranda earlier that day, and finding it equally feasible and frightening?

Why hadn't Simon telephoned? Had he ever received her message? If he had, surely only something urgent and alarming could have prevented him from getting in touch with her? He had gone to find Wally ... *Wally!* She had forgotten all about Wally! Supposing he too had – had disappeared?

Miranda's hands felt cold and unsteady. Like Stella's, she thought. We are both sitting here pretending to read and slowly scaring ourselves into idiocy. It's almost as if we were waiting for something horrible to happen. She looked across the room and saw Stella's desperate eyes upon her and tried to smile and could not.

Stella dropped her book to the floor and stood up abruptly. 'It's no good trying to read tonight,' she said in a high, strained voice. 'I can't concentrate. I think I'll get some knitting. It's a nice, soothing occupation!'

She went quickly out of the room leaving the door ajar behind her.

Miranda lowered her own book and thought, shall I try and ring Simon again? No. What's the use? I've done all I can.

She could hear Stella's footsteps in the hall, and a faint draught of cold air swung the drawing-room door open a little wider and ruffled the pages of the daily paper that lay on the window-seat. The faint rustle of the paper seemed absurdly loud in the silent room and Miranda started violently and bit her tongue, and closing her book with an impatient bang she reached for a cigarette. She very rarely smoked but at the moment, to smoke a cigarette, like Stella's knitting, seemed a soothing occupation.

The telephone bell rang shrilly in the hall and the cigarette box jerked from her grasp and fell to the floor, scattering its contents over the carpet.

Simon! thought Miranda with a gasp of relief. She jumped to her feet and started for the door, but Stella was already at the telephone.

'Hullo? . . . Yes, speaking.'

Miranda lingered near the open doorway hoping to hear Stella call her. But it was not Simon.

'Who?' Stella's voice sounded unnaturally high-pitched. 'Oh! Yes, of course I remember.' There followed an audible gasp and a long minute of silence. Miranda knew she should close the door and not listen to a private conversation, but she did not move.

There was something in Stella's voice that frightened her; and Stella was speaking again.

'*No!* ... No, I can't! not at this time of night! ... But *why*? ... Why not tomorrow? ... It's no good, I daren't! I tell you, I daren't ... not alone. Is Robert there? ... Can I speak to him? ... Oh. Oh, I see.'

There was another long pause and then Stella's voice; trembling and shrill, and completely unnatural.

'How do I know it is you? It might be anyone! ... Oh ... All right then. I'll ring you back.'

There was a click as the receiver was replaced and Miranda heard Stella ruffle through the leaves of the telephone book and presently dial a number.

'Hullo? — Oh it *is* you. I – I had to be sure ... Very well then. I'll do it ... Yes, as soon as I can.'

She rang off and came swiftly across the hall and into the drawing-room. Her face was colourless and her eyes feverishly bright, and she was breathing unevenly. She said: 'I have to go out. I don't think I shall be very long. You – you won't mind staying here alone, will you? You could ring up Mrs Lawrence or someone?'

'*Going out?* But where? Who was that on the phone? What's happened, Stella?' Miranda's voice was sharp with alarm.

'It was Colonel Cantrell. He says he has to see me at once. I said I wouldn't go, but he says it's a most important matter and that it can't wait. He wouldn't say much on the phone, but Robert is there; and so is Captain Lang, and I think one or two of the others. He said I was to take the car and drive over at once.'

Miranda said: 'But *why*? What's happened? Surely no one else is dead?' She heard the note of hysteria in her voice, but could not control it.

'I tell you I don't know! I'll try not to be too long.'

Stella turned away and went quickly across the hall to the cloakroom where the coats hung, Miranda at her heels. She took down a dark tweed coat from its peg, struggled into it, and reached for the garage key.

Miranda saw that her hands were trembling so that she could not fasten the heavy coat buttons, and she caught at Stella's arm.

'Don't go, Stel'! Let them come here. You can't go alone! It isn't safe, I tell you. It isn't safe!'

'I must,' said Stella, briefly. 'I'll be all right; Robert's there.'

'No!' said Miranda. *'No!'*

Stella must not go out alone into that dark, spring night. It was dangerous; Stella did not realize how dangerous!

But Stella only pulled away from her clutching hand and moved towards the door.

Miranda gave it up. 'All right, then; but I'm coming with you.'

Stella turned, relief and a tense anxiety on her white face. 'No, 'Randa! You keep out of this. Robert was right — we've let you in for too much already. You stay here and lock yourself safely into the drawing-room until I get back.'

'Don't talk nonsense!' said Miranda, hurriedly getting into a coat. 'If you go, I go! I'm not going to let you go running off by yourself. It isn't safe. Besides, I promised Robert that I'd keep an eye on you. Come on — have we got a torch?'

'Yes. But——'

'I'm not going to argue with you darling,' interrupted Miranda firmly, 'but if you think for one moment that I'm going to be left alone in this house, you're crazy!'

Stella laughed a little hysterically. 'All right then — on your own head be it!'

She turned away to unbar the door, and a little chill wind breathed against Miranda's cheek. She turned her head, puzzled, for the front door was still shut. And it was only then that she noticed that the tiny, narrow window alongside the door stood open to the night air.

The window was no more than a slot in the wall; a narrow slab of thick plate glass in a steel frame, that opened inwards and had probably been placed there so that anyone pressing the doorbell could be seen from inside, and letters, small parcels, or messages could be taken in without the necessity of unlocking the door.

229

Possibly it had been a useful and necessary precaution in the days of the Nazi régime, and even now Frau Herbach, the cook, would peer anxiously through it before admitting a visitor.

It was seldom opened and it had certainly not been open when Robert had left — of that Miranda was quite sure, for she had watched Stella lock and bar the door and neither of them could have overlooked an open window directly beside it. But Frau Herbach had left before dark, and there was no one in the house except herself and Stella. Then who had opened it?

The window was too narrow for even the smallest child to squeeze through. Yet supposing someone had thought that by reaching in an arm they could unlock the door? It was not possible, for the window opened to the left and even a double-jointed person could not have touched so much as the edge of the door. But someone standing outside might not know that . . .

Stella pulled back the last bolt, and turning saw Miranda's fixed and frightened stare.

'What is it? What are you looking at?'

'The window,' said Miranda, in a shaking whisper. 'Did you open it?'

Stella shook her head. Her eyes were wide and terrified.

'Someone did. It wasn't open when you shut the door after Robert had left.'

Stella licked her dry lips: 'Perhaps – perhaps the catch is loose and the wind blew it open.' She caught at Miranda's arm. ''Randa, you don't think — you don't think——?'

Miranda said: 'I don't know. Shut that door again and wait here a minute.' She turned and ran back across the hall.

'Where are you going? *Miranda! Where are you going!*' Stella's voice rose to a scream.

'I'm going to get Robert's revolver!'

A minute later, panting and breathless, she was back again, the heavy service revolver in her hand.

Stella shrank back at the sight of it. She looked as though she

230

were going to faint. 'Wha – what are you going to do with it?' she whispered.

'Heaven alone knows. But it may come in useful. We can always wave it at anyone we don't like the look of!'

Stella looked from the ugly weapon to Miranda's face, and broke into sudden hysterical laughter. The glazed look of terror left her eyes and they glittered with excitement. 'I never thought of that gun,' she said.'Dare we use it if – if——'

'Of course,' said Miranda, with a confidence she was far from feeling. 'Any idiot can pull a trigger. We'll fire first and ask questions afterwards. At the worst they can only bring it in as justifiable homicide! Let's go.'

There was a misty halo about the moon and once again the little chill wind that drifted through the branches of the trees threw slow-moving shadows from the nearest street lamp over the walls of the house and the path that led to the garage.

The lilac bushes made a dense pool of blackness about the garage door, and as Stella switched on the torch and fitted the key into the lock, the bushes stirred and rustled and a twig cracked sharply in the shadows. It's only the wind, Miranda assured herself desperately. It's only the wind!

She kept her back to Stella and the garage door, facing the dark tangle of the lilacs with Robert's gun in her hand, and said in an urgent whisper: 'Be quick, Stella!'

'I'm being as quick as I can; it's stiff.' The key grated in the lock and a moment later the hinges creaked complainingly as Stella pushed the doors wide.

Once again a twig cracked in the darkness, and a shadow that was not thrown by the street lamp slipped across the narrow path near the house and merged with the deeper shadows of the walls ...

Stella opened the car door and switched on the headlights. A blaze of warm light filled the garage and drove back the blackness from around the doors, and in the noise of the engine the small night noises were swallowed up and lost.

231

'Get in, 'Randa.' Stella backed the car out into the road and turned it in the direction of the city.

As the purr of its departure died away down the quiet road, a figure that had been standing in the deep shadow formed by an angle of the wall ran lightly up the path towards the hall door. It paused for an instant and looked intently at the open window, and then slipped through the door that Stella had forgotten to lock, and closed it again.

A moment later, had there been anyone in the empty house, they might have heard the faint click of the telephone receiver being lifted softly from its cradle, and the sound of a number being dialled.

Miranda sank back against the car seat breathing quickly as though she had been running. The palms of her hands were wet and clammy and she put the revolver down carefully on the seat beside her and rubbed them mechanically against her coat.

Now that they had left the house she was asking herself questions; foolish, frightening questions to which there were no answers.

Who had opened the window by the hall door, and why? Had there really been anyone among the shadows of the lilacs by the garage, or was it only the wind or a prowling cat? Why had Colonel Cantrell only wanted to see Stella, and not her, Miranda, as well? Was it really Colonel Cantrell who had telephoned, or someone who wanted to get Stella out of the house? She would not have recognized his voice.

Miranda said suddenly: 'How do you know that it was Colonel Cantrell who telephoned? It may have been someone pretending to be him.'

Stella turned her head to look at her and the car swerved a little on the road. 'I didn't know. That's why I told him I'd ring him back.'

'So you did: I forgot that. Then it must be all right.'

'Of course it is,' said Stella impatiently, her eyes on the road again.

But was it? Supposing it was possible for someone to use Colonel Cantrell's telephone? Someone who might have reason to know that he was out? And yet if anyone had wanted to get Stella out of the house, why had the window been opened? That looked more as though someone had intended to get in.

Yet another idea — a cold, horrible idea — slid into Miranda's mind. If Stella had gone without her, she, Miranda, would have been left alone in the empty house. Had someone intended that, and had she spoiled some carefully laid plan by insisting on going with her?

Miranda shivered and shut her eyes tightly, as though by doing so she could blot out the ugly pictures that were tormenting her: and instantly she saw again, as if it had been flashed on some screen of the mind, the open window by the hall door.

That window ... if only she could stop being frightened and think clearly for a minute, it could tell her something. She did not know why she should suddenly be so certain of that, but she was certain. There was something simple and obvious about that open window that shouted itself aloud, but she could not hear it because fear was scurrying to and fro in her brain like some terrified animal in a trap.

Miranda became aware of darkness and opened her eyes to find that Stella had switched off the headlights and that the car was cruising slowly down a long, tree-lined road, sparsely lit by two widely distant street lamps that made only small pools of light in the long stretch of moonlit darkness.

There were no lighted windows behind the screen of trees, but against a night sky made luminous by the lurid, reflected glow of the city's lights, rose the black outlines of ruined walls and gaping, eyeless windows.

The car slid softly to a standstill, and in the brief moment before Stella switched off the side lights, Miranda caught a glimpse of a pair of rusty iron gates that were vaguely familiar.

There was a soft click and the engine was silent. The dashboard light vanished and they were sitting in darkness.

Miranda felt Stella shiver beside her and then open the car door and slip out quietly into the road. She stood there for a moment, listening, the glow from a distant street lamp drawing a faint gold aureole about the dark outline of her blond head.

Miranda scrambled out of the car and stood beside her. 'Where are we?' She had meant to speak aloud, but the words came out as a whisper. And even as she spoke them, she knew where they were. 'This is the Ridders' house! Stella——!'

Stella turned her head: 'I know. He said I was to come here.'

She turned her head again, listening; peering down the dark, moon-splashed road, and said in an urgent whisper: 'There isn't anyone here is there? Can you see anyone else? Any car?'

'No,' Miranda caught at Stella's arm: 'Let's go back! I don't believe that anyone else is here. Or if they are, it's a trap. Stella, don't!'

Stella jerked away her arm and said: 'He told me not to be afraid. I was to walk up the path and into the house, and I would understand when I got there. You can stay here if you like, but I'm going.'

She turned towards the gate and Miranda said: 'No — wait! Stella, wait for me!' She groped about in the darkened car. 'I can't find the gun.'

'It's all right,' said Stella, 'I've got it.' They were still speaking in whispers.

The iron gates squeaked open under Stella's hand, and Miranda passed through and stood beside her in the black shadow of the laurels, fighting a terrifying conviction that they had been followed.

Clouds had drifted over the moon, but the glow of the night sky silhouetted the gaunt shell of the house above them and they could neither see nor hear any sound or sign of movement. The house and the ruined, weed-grown garden were silent and deserted. A breath of the night wind stirred the laurels, making the lacquered leaves click and rustle, and Stella clutched at Miranda's arm and shuddered.

'Go on,' she whispered.

They moved out of the shadow of the laurels down the sunken path towards the house, their feet stumbling among a tangle of weeds and broken paving stones, and it seemed to Miranda that the wind died away and the night held its breath to listen to them, and that every shadow held an unseen watcher . . .

The clouds thinned and faint, watery moonlight filled the garden as Miranda reached the bottom of the short flight of stone steps that led up to the empty, gaping doorway, and took one hesitant step upwards. She could hear Stella's quick breathing a pace behind her and the heavy beating of her own heart. She took another step upward, feeling for it with her foot. Her eyes were becoming accustomed to the uncertain light and the face of the house was clear above her. The empty doorway yawned on blackness and beside it a fragment of broken glass in a narrow, slotted window gleamed palely in the faint moonlight.

Miranda reached the top step and her groping hand touched a circle of rusted metal in the centre of which lay a smooth, shallow knob of china; the doorbell of Herr Ridder's house.

For a fleeting, hysterical moment she wondered what would happen if she pressed it? Would some mouldering bell tinkle a shrill summons in the black depths of the ruined house, and bring the ghost of a housekeeper called Greta Schumacher, who had also been Mademoiselle Beljame, to peer suspiciously through that narrow slotted window before opening the door?

The window!

Miranda's hand fell to her side and she stood quite still.

The window! Of course, that was the answer! That was what had nagged at her brain. Not from the outside — that was impossible. From the *inside*! Someone had opened the window from the inside. But that could only mean——

She turned quickly, her back to the blackness of the empty doorway.

'Stella! *You* opened that window, didn't you? That was where the draught came from! No one else could have done it.'

235

She heard Stella catch her breath in a gasp. 'What window? Why should I open it?'

'To reach the bell. You wanted to reach the bell——'

Miranda's voice died suddenly and her eyes stared down at the thing that Stella held in her hand.

Stella's hand was not shaking any longer. It was quite steady, and the moon, sliding clear of the clouds, glinted on the barrel of Robert's revolver.

Miranda lifted her eyes slowly and looked into the face of a stranger. A white, haggard mask with lips drawn back over the teeth in a purely animal grimace below wide eyes, glittering and enormous. She could no more mistake the look on that face than she could have mistaken the hate that she had once seen on Mrs Leslie's. It meant only one thing — *murder*.

Stella laughed. A gay, clear, cold-blooded little laugh that echoed strangely in the hollow shell of the house. She said: 'You gave me the idea yourself. You thought it was the phone bell. I could have done it in the house, of course, but there might have been traces. And you are too heavy to carry. This was so much simpler.'

She laughed again, and said: 'I know you so well you see! I knew if I could make you overhear a telephone conversation you'd fall for it. I did it very well, didn't I? If I'd said someone wanted to see us both you might have been suspicious. But because I pretended it was only me, and that I was frightened, you rushed into the trap and I got you here without any bother at all!'

She sounded as naïvely pleased with herself as a child displaying its first efforts at handicrafts.

Miranda tried to speak, but found that she could not. Her mouth was dry and there appeared to be a constriction about her throat. She could only stare at that ashy-white, unfamiliar mask as though mesmerized.

Something in her petrified immobility seemed to infuriate the older woman. She said shrilly: 'You thought you'd been very clever, didn't you? *Didn't you!* Pretending you thought you'd left

236

your bag in my car, so you could sneak back to the garage and take a look at the speedometer to see how many miles I'd done. You and your "freak memory for numbers"! I didn't know that I'd left a smear of green paint on that door handle, but you saw it, didn't you? You were spying on me in my own house! Spying on me, and trying to get Robert away from me. Letting him kiss you in front of me! That's how sure of yourself you were! Well, you won't get him! Neither you nor that two-faced slut, Sally Page! Once I've got the money I can get him away from the Army and from her. And no one will ever know what happened to you. You'll just disappear and they'll think you've run away because you're afraid of being arrested!'

She paused for breath, gasping and shaking with rage, but only one word of the incomprehensible tirade made sense to Miranda.

She struggled with a nightmare sense of suffocation and said thickly: 'Paint — then it was you who——'

'Oh yes,' said Stella, her voice once more childlike and casual. 'I drowned her. I waited for her by the pool and hit her with the spanner. It was quite easy, and there was no one about. She'd tried to kill me, you see. She wanted to keep all the money for herself. She deserved to be killed.'

Miranda said numbly: 'What money?'

'The diamonds, of course,' said Stella, impatiently. 'They're here — in this house. That's why I had to bring you here. It was easier if you came with me. And then you actually insisted on bringing a gun with you!'

She laughed again and for a moment the barrel of the revolver wavered and Miranda took a step towards her.

'Oh no, you don't!' said Stella, sharply. 'Turn round. Go on — turn round and go into the house. I couldn't miss you at this range, so don't try and do anything silly.'

'Stella, you can't!' gasped Miranda. 'Don't you understand? It's too dangerous. You *know* no one is allowed inside these houses! Colonel Leslie said so ... he said they could fall down at any moment, and that it was even dangerous to go anywhere near them. He said ... he said ...'

'*I* said you were to go inside,' said Stella. 'And you'll do as I say!'

Her voice was the voice of a stranger — as changed as her face — and Miranda turned obediently and walked through the gaping doorway into the silent house. Nothing made sense any more. This could not possibly be real. It was only some fantastic and melodramatic nightmare from which she would presently awake.

A torch flashed on behind her and the thin, yellow pencil of light played on the rubble-strewn space that had once been a hall, and a dark ruined archway beyond.

A cold ring of metal pressed against Miranda's neck and she walked forward, following the beam of the torch that Stella held in her left hand. They passed through a gaping doorway and then another one, into a room where the moon peered down from a roofless square above them. A curving flight of steps, choked with debris, descended into blackness and Miranda groped her way down them, following that inexorable bar of light, into what appeared to be part of a ruined, vaulted cellar, with other cellars opening off it.

Loose bricks, rubble and bomb debris slid and clattered under their feet, every step dislodging miniature landslides that continued to rattle down even after they had reached the foot of the stairs. The crash and patter of falling odds and ends filled the darkness with echoes, so that it almost seemed as though not two, but ten or a dozen people were descending in Indian-file to the ruined cellar, following the two women down ...

Moonlight lay in one small, cold patch at the foot of the broken steps, but in the blackness beyond and around them the torch light seemed to gather strength.

Stella said: 'Now take off that bracelet and hand it to me. No, don't turn round!'

Her high, gasping voice reverberated hollowly around the unseen, empty spaces, and a Greek chorus of ghostly voices re-

238

peated *'don't turn round... turn round... round...'* And once again there came a soft, ominous clatter of falling debris——

Miranda's fingers fumbled with the stiff clasp, but the instinct of self-preservation was strong enough to keep her own voice calm and reasonable: 'You can't use that revolver, Stella, because if you do, you'll die too. The noise and the explosion, in a ruin like this, will be enough to bring the roof down on us — and the walls as well. If you fire, you may kill me. But *you'll* be buried alive!'

But it was no use. Stella was beyond the reach of reason, and though she must have heard that deadly rustle and fall of displaced rubble, it conveyed no warning to her obsessed brain. Her voice shot up and she said: 'If you think you can frighten me, you're wasting your time. Stop talking and give me that bracelet!'

If I turn quickly, thought Miranda, I might be able to knock the torch out of her hand ... she couldn't do anything in the dark. She's never fired a gun in her life. She'd miss except at short range. If the torch went out I'd have a chance ...

But she could not do it. She seemed to be gripped by a deadly inertia that prevented her body from obeying her will; it could only obey that high, unnatural voice that was, unbelievably, Stella's.

The bracelet slipped off her wrist and she held it out behind her and felt it taken.

'Now go and stand over there.'

Miranda moved forward again and turned, her eyes dazzled by the full glare of the torch.

'I told you not to turn round!' cried Stella, shrilly. 'I won't have you looking at me! I can't do it while you look at me!' Her voice broke suddenly into a high, childish babble: 'It's not my fault! I can't help it! You shouldn't have spied on me. I wouldn't have touched you if it hadn't been for that. But you'd have told. And I won't hang for Mademoiselle. I won't! And you tried to get Robert, so it serves you right ... it serves you right!'

She lifted the revolver in a shaking hand; and as she did so Miranda saw a movement in the blackness behind her.

There was someone else in the cellars. Someone who had followed them down. Two people — three——

'No one will know!' gabbled Stella. 'No one found the diamonds, and no one will find you.'

She steadied the wavering revolver, and a hand came over her shoulder and twisted it out of her grasp.

'I'll take that please, Mrs Melville,' said Simon Lang gently.

Stella screamed. A high, horrible scream like a trapped rabbit, and the torch fell to the floor and went out.

Someone brushed past Miranda in the dark, and then the blackness was rent by a flash of flame and the crashing reverberations of a shot.

Miranda heard Simon say savagely: *'You bloody idiot!'* and then there was another sound; a slow, ominous mutter like a growl of thunder; and a slither and rumble of falling stone.

The vaulted darkness was suddenly full of dust and torch beams and someone was shouting: 'Get on up those stairs!' and someone else had caught her arm and was dragging her, stumbling and running across the uneven floor and up the slippery, broken steps and through the rubble-strewn, roofless rooms to the safety of the moonlit garden.

The rumble grew to a roar and the gaunt black shell of the house appeared to sway and dissolve against the night sky as one wall leaned tiredly inwards and slowly, very slowly, collapsed upon itself.

The ground shook as though it had been hit by an earthquake, and for a minute or two the moonlight was thick with dust and mortar and flying splinters of stone. And when the garden was silent again only one wall of the house remained, and a gasping voice was saying over and over again: 'I tried to get her, sir, but she twists away and runs back. She twists away and runs back ... I tried to get her ...'

18

'It was the German, of course,' said Simon. 'I should have remembered that a continental cop is apt to be a bit quick on the draw. He imagined that she could escape and fired at her. But you can't go loosing off firearms in a building of that description without asking for trouble.'

Miranda said: 'Was she — was she alive?'

Simon looked down at her and glimpsed something of the horror that lurked behind the small white face.

He looked away again and spoke in a completely matter-of-fact voice.

'Yes. For a time. Long enough to make some sort of a statement. It was the best way out for her, you know. She knew it too. The last thing she said was: "I never thought I'd live to be grateful to a German."'

Miranda's mouth twisted and she bent her head hurriedly over the suitcase to hide the fact that there were tears in her eyes.

Over two days had passed since the night that Stella had died, and although Miranda had been questioned and asked to make and sign statements, and been interviewed exhaustively by a number of persons in authority, she had not spoken to Simon until this morning, when he had walked unannounced into her bedroom at the Lawrences' house and found her kneeling on the floor packing a row of shoes into the bottom of a suitcase.

Simon said dryly: 'There is no need to be sentimental over her just because she's dead. She wasn't an admirable character. She connived at one murder and committed another. And would have committed a third if we hadn't prevented it. It's her unfortunate

241

husband you can be sorry for. This has just about broken him up. He loved her very much: more than she knew, I think. I hear he's going home on compassionate leave.'

Miranda nodded without speaking, and Simon looked down at the bent head and the hands that were attempting to wrap a shoe in tissue paper and bungling the job because they trembled so, and realized that talking might ease that intolerable strain. He sat down on Miranda's bed and said in a casual and conversational tone: 'When did you realize that it was Mrs Melville?'

Miranda dropped the shoe onto the floor and sat back on her heels.

'It was the window,' she said. 'The little window by the front door in the hall was open, and I knew quite well that it hadn't been open before. It scared me stiff, because I knew that there was no one but Stella and myself in the house, so I thought that someone must have tried to get in. I couldn't stop thinking about it. And when I saw the window of the Ridder house I suddenly realized that of course it couldn't *possibly* have been opened from the outside. It could only have been opened from the inside. And I knew just when it had been opened, because the draught from it had blown into the drawing-room. But Stella had been in the hall then, and she would have seen if anyone else had been there. So she must have opened it herself. And then all at once I remembered that the doorbell and the telephone bell sounded alike, and I – I don't know why, but I had a sudden picture in my mind of Stella reaching out and pressing the bell, and then going quickly to the telephone. And I blurted it out, and——' Miranda stopped and gave a hopeless little shrug of her shoulders.

She picked up another shoe and began to wrap it mechanically in paper, but her hands were steadier and presently she spoke again, and without lifting her head.

'Simon, why did it have to happen? I don't understand!'

'What is it you don't understand, dear?'

'Anything! Anything at all. It's all such a ghastly muddle.'

'Not now,' said Simon. 'We've sorted it out by now.' He leant

242

back against the bed-head with his hands behind his head. 'Lottie helped us there. Lottie and Wally.'

'Lottie!' Miranda turned swiftly: 'Why how could she——'

'Ssh! Don't interrupt. Mademoiselle, who was Frau Schumacher, thought that Brigadier Brindley might possibly have recognized her, and when he took those sleeping pills she saw her chance. She took one herself you remember; intending, I'm fairly certain, to give it to Lottie. But Lottie poured her hot milk down the back of the basin while Mademoiselle was out of the carriage for a few minutes.'

Miranda said quickly: 'So she wasn't asleep after all!'

'No. She only pretended to be. She was still awake when her governess left the carriage that night, and she saw her come back. She saw something else as well. Mademoiselle had worn a pair of black gloves, and when she returned to the carriage she rinsed those gloves in the basin and the water turned red.'

Miranda caught her breath in a hard gasp. 'But why didn't she tell?'

'For a very simple reason — from a child's point of view,' said Simon. 'She had been told so often that hot milk at night made her sleep that she was afraid to admit that she had not slept, for fear that it would give away the fact that she had thrown away her milk instead of drinking it! All the same she did tell someone: she told Wally. And then a little later she told her stepmother — that was just before Mrs Melville walked into your room at the Berlin hostel and found her governess rifling your suitcases.'

'So you were right about that! Was it my bracelet she wanted?'

'It was. And for a very odd reason. We all thought that she and her husband murdered the Ridders for the sake of the diamonds, but it turns out that they knew nothing whatever about them. They had planned the murder for the sake of the money and the jewels alone. They knew there was a safe in the cellar, and had once seen it open; but they thought it only contained special wines. They had no idea that it concealed a second safe.

'Herr Ridder had mentioned on arrival that night that he had managed to acquire some Napoleon brandy, and he carried it directly down to the cellar. They must have killed him when he came up. When they came to strip his body they found the bracelet with the Egyptian charm.'

'Why did they keep it? Did they think it meant something?'

'No. They threw it in with the other stuff merely because it had to be removed, since Herr Ridder was known to have worn it. Schumacher escaped to England, where he died, but Greta Schumacher was left behind and ended up in a concentration camp under a false name. And in that same camp she met someone she knew: a distant cousin, Rosa Müller, who with her husband, Kurt, used to be called in to help as extra staff whenever the Ridders entertained — Rosa as parlourmaid and Kurt as footman-cum-waiter ...

'The Müllers had no idea why they had been arrested, for the Ridder story was not public property at that time — or for some considerable time afterwards — but I presume it was known that they worked regularly for Herr Willi and his wife. Poor Kurt was interrogated on arrival and died in the process: apparently he had a heart condition, and had been poorly for some time. Because of their kinship, the two women, Greta Schumacher — or whatever she was calling herself then — and Rosa Müller naturally gravitated together, and one presumes that Greta swore Rosa to secrecy in the matter of her identity, and cooked up a good story to account for it ...

'They liked to talk over old times together, and one day, in the course of conversation, Rosa told how her husband, who had been helping clear up after a late party at the Ridders', took several unopened bottles of wine back to the cellar, and surprised Herr Willi opening a safe in the back of the one in which he kept his special wines. He'd already opened the back of that safe; and was fiddling with the dials of an inner one: reading off the numbers, or the code or whatever, from a small, oddly shaped key attached to a chain bracelet. When he heard Kurt he whipped round so that his back hid the safe, and told him off like a pickpocket. Fortunately, Kurt had the sense to play the idiot-boy so convincingly that it all blew over, but Willi's fury had scared him so badly that he didn't even dare tell his Rosa about it until over a year later — by which time Hitler had marched into Poland and the incident didn't seem in the least important——

'Greta certainly didn't think anything of it. She had always known that Herr Ridder had a wine safe built into a wall in the cellar, and if there was a second safe concealed behind it, she supposed that he kept his top secret documents there. And since she was not interested in official documents, she never gave it another thought. Until Brigadier Brindley came out with that talk about the diamonds, and you told him about the Egyptian charm — and actually handed it around so that everyone could have a good look at it! It was only then that "Mademoiselle Beljame", née Greta Schumacher, remembered cousin Rosa's story and started putting two and two together; and came up with the right answer.'

'Was it really a key?' demanded Miranda, leaping womanlike from the general to the particular: 'And have you found the diamonds?'

'It was. And we have — though we had to shift a mountain of rubble to get at them. There were two keys to that safe, and your charm incorporated both of them. The stem of the ankh fitted into a tiny slot that opened a thick slab of steel at the back of the outer safe, and behind it were three sets of combination locks that worked on that series of hieroglyphics that were engraved on the back and front of the charm. Very ingenious. What's more, it still works. If it hadn't, I suppose we'd have had to blow the safe open. Which wouldn't have done the contents much good.'

Miranda said: 'How did you find out about all this? About Rosa Müller and Mademoiselle — I mean Greta Schumacher? Is Rosa still alive?'

'No. She died in the camp about a year later. The information came from Mademoiselle. She told Mrs Melville. And Wally Wilkin, in his role of Dan Dare, Detective, was hiding under the bed!'

'What!'

' "What" indeed! You know, it will always rile me to think that between them those two kids knew almost everything there was to know, right from the start, and kept it under their hats because Wally wanted to play a lone hand and solve the case without the help of the "grown-ups". And that I was fool enough to give him such a telling off for snooping that he shut up like a clam.'

'But why on earth should Mademoiselle tell Stella?' demanded Miranda.

'That's where Lottie comes in. Lottie had told Mrs Melville about Mademoiselle's doings in the night, and Mrs Melville, horrified, had rushed along to your room to consult you. She caught the governess going through your boxes and told her that she was going straight to the police.'

'But why didn't she, Simon?'

'Because Mademoiselle bribed her silence. Being desperate, she told her the whole story and offered her a half share in a colossal fortune to hold her tongue.'

Miranda stood up suddenly and went over to the window to stand with her back to Simon, staring blindly out into the garden.

'*Stella* did that? For *money*?'

'For Robert,' corrected Simon.

Miranda swung round. 'What do you mean?'

'It's rather an involved story,' said Simon slowly. 'We got part of it from Mrs Leslie.'

Miranda said quickly: 'Mrs Leslie hated her! You can't go by that.'

'She had her reasons,' said Simon gently.

'Robert?'

'No. Johnnie Radley. Stella's first husband. When Radley returned to India after his first leave, Stella refused to go back with him. She disliked the East and all foreign countries, so she tried to eat her cake and have it. But it didn't work out that way. Radley got fed up with a wife who preferred what she termed "civilization" to him. He was hurt and lonely, and he fell in love with another girl and asked Stella for a divorce. She wouldn't hear of it; and finding no way out, he volunteered for a particularly dangerous mission and was killed. The girl — who was young and impressionable and very much in love — shot herself when she heard the news. She was Norah Leslie's sister.'

'Oh!' said Miranda on a gasp. 'I see. Then that was why ... Go on.'

'Stella posed as a heartbroken widow, and after the war she met Robert. But Robert was different from Johnnie Radley. She was in love with Robert. Really in love.'

'I know,' said Miranda, almost inaudibly. 'I was thinking about that only the last — the last morning, and that Stella would die for him if she had to.'

'She did die for him; indirectly. She was prepared to risk death by hanging rather than lose him. When Robert was sent abroad she would have gone with him, but was not allowed to. She became terrified that history would repeat itself and that because she could not be with him he might leave her for someone else. She was older than Robert, and that didn't help. Then, on the journey out here, she realized that he knew Sally Page rather too well, and it frightened her. She began to see that she must live Robert's life or lose him, because they could not afford to leave the Army and live at Mallow ...

'Mademoiselle's story and her offer came at just the right moment. The sight of Sally Page and the way she had looked at Robert had scared Mrs Melville badly, and the news that the regiment was to go to Malaya put the lid on it. Money was the only way out. A lot of money, that would enable her to live at Mallow and keep Robert with her.'

Miranda said with a bitter little laugh: 'And I thought it was Sally! Did you know that? I worked it all out.'

'Did you? Why?'

'Several things. I remembered that just after Mademoiselle left to look for Lottie's bear, Sally went off to telephone someone and that she was away for simply ages. Quite long enough to do what they say Stella did. And then – then on the morning after Mademoiselle's body was found, Andy and Sally were given a lift by the Leslies because their car had run out of petrol, and Andy made a great fuss about it. He insisted that he'd filled up the tank only a few days before and that Sally must have been using it a lot since then: and – and I wondered. I thought perhaps she'd been using it up seeing Robert, and that Mademoiselle ...'

Miranda sketched a quick, impatient gesture with one hand, as though brushing away a too persistent fly, and changed course abruptly: 'And then there was the time when she spilt the sherry ...'

She paused for so long that finally Simon said: 'I'm not with you; what sherry, and who spilt it? Mademoiselle?'

'No. Sally. It was the morning after Mademoiselle's body had been found, and most of your team had dropped in for a drink.'

'My *what*?' exclaimed Simon, bewildered.

Miranda's pale face was suddenly pink. 'I'm sorry. It just slipped out. I'd forgotten you wouldn't know about that.'

'About what, for heaven's sake?'

' *"Lang's Eleven"* — there were eleven of us, you see. — Suspects,' translated Miranda, as Simon still looked puzzled. 'The ones in that sleeping-car coach from Helmstedt to Berlin. Two Melvilles, two Marsons, two Leslies, two Pages, Mademoiselle, Mrs Wilkin and myself.'

Simon laughed and said that he hadn't considered Mrs Wilkin, but that she was right about the rest, and would she please go on about Sally and the sherry?

Miranda's flush deepened and she said hastily: 'It sounds very silly now, but she spilt some on a chair and mopped it off with a face-tissue that she took out of her bag and threw away afterwards into the fire, but it missed and fell inside the fender instead. And after they had all gone I began to pick up some petals that had fallen on the floor, and I noticed the face-tissue: it was an Elizabeth Arden one, and that gave me a horrid shock, because there

248

had been an Elizabeth Arden tissue on the floor of Mademoiselle's room on the day that——'

She saw the expression on Simon's face and said quickly: 'You knew about that?'

'Yes. Mrs Melville put it there. She'd borrowed one from Sally.'

'*Stella* did? But why?'

'Because Mrs Page used them, and she wanted to throw suspicion on her. She reasoned the way you probably did: that some people might think that Sally Page had a motive for getting Robert's wife out of the way — the people who thought that Friedel had been killed in mistake for Mrs Melville. But it was Mademoiselle who killed Friedel — in mistake for you.'

'*Me?* Why me?'

'She was expecting you to go over to the Leslies' — she wasn't in when you cancelled that, remember? I imagine she only meant to knock you out and steal the bracelet, thereby doublecrossing Mrs Melville. But she hit harder than she intended, and Mrs Melville was convinced that her governess had meant to murder her ...

'She palmed that toy of Lottie's, sent Mademoiselle off on a wild-goose chase, and went after her in the car. All very simple. It was late evening and the numbers of cars with British zone licence plates are not taken, nor are the cars stopped. But she didn't reckon on the green paint.'

Miranda said: 'Did she — did she get some on herself?'

'She couldn't very well avoid it, after sliding both Mademoiselle and her bicycle into the water. She got it all over her gloves and smeared a little on the car door in the dark. She didn't notice it until she got home and hadn't any idea where it came from. But Wally knew. He was snooping through the garage window when she arrived back and he saw her pull off her gloves and look at the green stains. She fetched Mademoiselle's bottle of turpentine, and cleaned off some that was on her wrist, and burnt the gloves.'

'Robert spilt the turpentine,' said Miranda slowly.

'Did he?'

249

'Yes. I – I even thought once that he might have arranged it with Sally.'

Simon looked a question.

Miranda said: 'I – I thought that she, Mademoiselle. might have seen them together, or found a love-letter, or something of the sort, and tried to blackmail them. I had a horrid moment or two before I realized that Robert couldn't possibly have done it — not in a million years. Robert's not — he isn't ...'

'Ruthless enough?' offered Simon.

'*Yes*. He's too easy-going, and I don't think that anything has gone really deep with him. Until now. Poor Robert! Did you know that he's going to send in his papers and use his gratuity to turn Mallow into a home for handicapped children? The Leslies are going to help him run it as soon as Colonel Leslie retires ... one of their boys is a spastic. I didn't know that. It's to be called the "Stella Melville Memorial Home" ...'

Miranda shivered and pushed her hands into the pockets of her skirt to hide the fact that they were trembling again. She said: 'You knew it was Stella, didn't you? You knew all the time.'

'No. Not for a long time,' admitted Simon.

'When did you know?'

'Not until the very last day, I'm afraid. I knew that someone in the house must be involved when I heard that the governess had come back in the night and left that china bear and removed some of her belongings. I was sure it wasn't true; because though no one had heard her, the front door was locked. And that type of door will only lock from the outside if it's banged fairly hard. It seemed to me more likely that for some reason of their own, someone inside the house had faked that return and just slipped the latch. You see both the back door and the french window were bolted at night. And there was no key missing. I checked on that.'

'When did you begin to think it was Stella?'

'When I mentioned the green paint,' said Simon soberly. 'I saw her face in the glass, and I was sure. There are some expressions you cannot mistake.'

'No,' said Miranda in a low voice, and shuddered. She pushed the thought away from her and said quickly: 'You told me as much as you dared, to try and put me on my guard, didn't you?'

For the first time since she had known him Simon looked disconcerted. 'Well — not exactly,' he said.

'Why, then?' demanded Miranda, surprised. 'Was it because——' She checked herself and coloured.

Simon laughed. 'No, dear. It was not for the sake of your *beaux yeux*. It was because you are one of the many exceptions that prove the rule. Where your feelings are concerned you are a darned bad actress, and I wanted you to know too much in order to ensure that you would behave in the guilty manner of one who knows too much!'

Miranda flushed angrily and her chin went up with a jerk. 'And why should you want me to do that?'

'Because I needed proof. I thought that if Mrs Melville could be brought to believe that you knew more than you should, she might be goaded into showing her hand.'

'Thank you,' said Miranda in a voice that trembled in spite of herself.

'I'm sorry, my sweet. It was a rotten trick to play on you, but I needed evidence and I had only theories and guesswork. I didn't know then about Wally. And even now I doubt if the unsupported stories of a nine-year-old boy and a girl of seven would have been accepted in court: a good lawyer would have made mincemeat of them. I didn't know that Mrs Melville suspected you already. But I knew that she was afraid of you.'

'Of *me*?' said Miranda astounded. 'Why should she be afraid of me? I'd always been fond of her.'

Simon examined his fingernails with careful attention and said without looking at Miranda: 'Robert.'

Miranda coloured hotly. 'But that's absurd!'

'Is it? There was a time when I myself wondered if there might not be something in it. You could have wanted money and Robert. The two went together.'

251

Miranda whipped her hands out of her pockets and clenched them into a pair of admirable fists. She seemed to be having some difficulty with her breathing. 'You dared! You actually dared to think that I . . .'

'Calm down, darling. It was only a theory — one of many. But he had a habit of putting an affectionate arm about you on every possible occasion, and——'

'He *is* my cousin!' interrupted Miranda stormily.

'Oh, quite. All the same it put you under suspicion when Friedel died; and it upset his wife. Besides, you were too pretty and too young, and Mrs Melville began to fear the constant contrast that your youthful charms offered to her more mature attractions. She was, in the words of an ex-cook of my mother's, "in a state". What with her unbalanced passion for her husband, a dislike of foreigners and foreign countries that amounted to a phobia, jealousy of Sally Page, suspicion that you were also on the way to an affair with her Robert, and the conviction that her governess had intended to murder her, she cannot have been quite sane. That's the kindest view to take of it, anyway.'

Miranda said helplessly: 'But even if you are right, why should she want to kill me? There was still Sally.'

'Oh, it wasn't that. I thought you knew. From your own account of that night, she told you herself.'

'She said something about spying on her, and – and a speedometer. I didn't understand.'

Simon looked at her curiously. 'Then you didn't notice anything about the car on the night that Mademoiselle disappeared?'

'No. What was there to notice?'

'She was convinced that you had, and that there was only one way to make sure that you didn't eventually tell someone. It seems that you went down to the garage that evening just after she had got back from the swimming-pool, and that there were three things you might have noticed. First, that the engine was still hot although the car was supposed to have been back well over half an hour. Secondly, that the handle of the door on the driver's side was smeared with green paint — she cleaned it off next day with petrol, still without knowing that it had any connection with Mademoiselle. And lastly, that the speedometer had clocked up a higher figure than it should. You evidently made some idle remark during supper that night about always remembering numbers, and a guilty conscience suggested to her that you were hinting that you had spotted it.'

Miranda said bitterly: 'Then she had it all planned!'

'Oh, no,' said Simon gently. 'She was afraid of you giving her away; and then when her husband left that night, he kissed you. That's right, isn't it?' Simon lifted an interrogatory eyebrow.

'Yes. But it was only ...'

'It was only the last straw. She told us that it all jumped into her mind then and there. Her husband had gone out and there was no one else in the house. But the next day there would be a resident batman. If she could just get her hands on the bracelet and the diamonds, and dispose of you at the same time, it would all be over and she would be safe. If you disappeared, suspicion might point to you. And if you were never found you might be supposed to have bolted behind the Iron Curtain. But she had to get you out of the house and just where she wanted you without fuss. And then she remembered that the doorbell sounded like the telephone. She was nearly off her head with fear and jealousy, and the cunning of near lunacy suggested it all to her in the space of a few minutes.'

Miranda said stormily: 'And you knew what she might do - - and you let me go through all that – that horror! You're nothing but a cold-blooded, scheming ...' She searched for a word and failed to find one sufficiently opprobrious for her purpose.

'You weren't in any danger,' said Simon mildly. 'I'd run Wally to earth by then, and had a pretty clear idea of the form. The place was crawling with cops and you were more or less under observation from the second you walked out of the front door. You see we couldn't be sure where she was heading for — though we had a shrewd idea. So we had to tail you. Once you got to the Ridders' house. we knew we were right; and after that we were practically on your heels. Fortunately for us, and thanks to all that loose rubble, your descent to the cellar was so noisy that we were able to sneak down behind you without any trouble, and, after listening to what she had to say, step into the picture in a nice melodramatic manner at the last moment.'

'And I suppose,' said Miranda furiously, 'that it didn't occur to any of you that she might have pressed the trigger a second before you got it away from her?'

'It wouldn't really have mattered very much if she had,' said Simon, placidly.

Miranda stared at him unbelievingly: rigid with a sudden sense of outrage that had, illogically, nothing whatsoever to do with her terrors of that past night.

Simon observed her reaction with a half smile. There was a gleam of complete comprehension and a warm, dancing malice in his eyes.

'One of the things I like about you, Miranda,' he remarked gently, 'is that you are so beautifully uncomplicated. Don't worry, my darling. I wasn't being callous about your personal safety. I only meant that I had taken the precaution of unloading that weapon and removing all live ammunition from the house, just in case of accidents.'

'Oh!' said Miranda explosively. 'Well if you're quite sure that you've said all you want to say, I think you had better go! I've got a lot of packing to do. And I don't know what you mean by walking calmly into my bedroom in the first place, and I'm not your darling!'

'Aren't you?' said Simon softly. 'Well I won't argue the point, but you are wasting your time over that packing. You'll only have to unpack it all again. As for my walking into your bedroom, I'm afraid you will have to get used to it. I understand it is one of a husband's privileges.'

'Oh!' said Miranda again, on a long breath: 'You – you're very sure of yourself, aren't you?'

'Very,' agreed Simon placidly. 'I generally get what I want.'

'Miranda,' said Mrs Lawrence, walking briskly into the room a few moments later, 'do you know if Captain Lang has left yet, or ... Oh, I'm so sorry!'

She retreated hurriedly and closed the door.

'Well, really!' said Mrs Lawrence, addressing the empty landing, a bundle of laundry, three regimental prints of unusual hideousness and her immortal soul: 'You wouldn't think that after three murders and ... Oh well, perhaps they are right. Life is more important than death.'

She shrugged her shoulders tolerantly and went downstairs to explain to her cook in what she confidently imagined to be German, that *der Herr Polizisten Capitan Lang* would be remaining to luncheon.

DEATH IN CYPRUS

To
MAXINE
and the Enchanted Island

Author's Note

Back in 1949, while my husband's regiment was stationed in Egypt, and we were living in an army quarter at Fayid in what was then known as the 'Suez Canal Zone', a friend and I decided to spend a painting holiday in Cyprus. We went there on a ship sailing from Port Said to Limassol, and once on the Island, hired a self-drive car for the duration. (Incidentally, cars in those days were still build with running-boards, and had a luggage-grid instead of a boot!) We stayed in the enchanting house in Kyrenia that I have described in this story, and the plot was practically handed to me on a plate by a curious series of incidents that occurred during our stay. But owing to the fact that I was too busy painting and, later, because of a multiplicity of army moves, I did not get around to writing it for almost five years. Reading it now, I am interested to see that even during that halcyon holiday I must have been aware that the Cyprus I was living in and painting was much too good to last, and that one day greedy quarrelling factions were bound to destroy it. That day came sooner than I thought; and nowadays the Island is divided into two hostile sections. Kyrenia and Hilarion, lovely Aiyos Epiktitos and beautiful Bellapais, and most of the places I knew best, are now held by the Turkish Cypriots, while the Greek Cypriots, who hold the remainder, have turned their sleepy little coastal towns into roaring tourist resorts, complete with vast holiday hotels and 'recreation complexes'. *'O world! O life! O time!'* ... Shelley said it all.

1

Amanda had not been really frightened until she found the bottle. Horrified certainly: shaken by incredulity and shock, but not with fear. Not with this cold, crawling apprehension of evil ...

One minute Julia Blaine had been alive and talking in that high, hysterical, sobbing voice. And almost the next minute she was dead — sprawled on the floor of Amanda's cabin in an ungainly satin-clad heap.

It had all happened so suddenly, and without a word of warning. Or had there been a warning? Somewhere in the happenings of the past few days or weeks had there been nothing to suggest that such an ugly and fantastic thing might possibly occur ...?

Amanda Derington had been staying with an aunt at Fayid in the Suez Canal Zone while her uncle and guardian, Oswin Derington of Derington and Company, looked into his business affairs in the simmering stock-pot of the Middle East.

A night raid on London during the autumn of 1940 had left Amanda an orphan, and she had been subsequently and arbitrarily annexed by her Uncle Oswin. This despite the fact that there had been several sympathetic aunts only too ready and willing to take charge of the child. But then Oswin Derington, a bachelor and a misogynist, had little or no opinion of any of them, and a great many opinions on everything else: including the upbringing of children.

The head of Deringtons — that ubiquitous firm whose name and multitudinous activities crop up like measles spots wherever the shoe of the white man has managed to gain a foothold — was a stern moralist in whom the blood of Calvinistic ancestors ran strongly. He was, in addition, successful, egotistical, selfish and frequently inclined to pompousness, and it was his firm conviction that the majority of his fellow-men led sinfully immoral lives. Anyone hearing him holding forth on his favourite subject might well gain the impression that, in the mind of the speaker at least, the entire population of the world was given over to sinful and riotous living with the solitary exception of that pillar of uprightness, Oswin Greatorex Derington.

Uncle Oswin apparently included Amanda's aunts among the ranks of the ungodly, for his action in assuming sole charge of his brother Anthony's only child was prompted as much by a desire to save a tender brand from the burning, as to put into practice various long-held theories on the correct method of bringing up the young. And Anthony having left a will in which he had light-heartedly named his brother as trustee and sole guardian of his daughter, there was nothing that anyone else could do about it.

The outlook for Amanda might well have been bleak, had it not been for the fact that she had inherited her mother's physical beauty, together with much of her father's gaiety and courage. Three useful legacies that a series of strict boarding schools, constantly changed, and her Uncle Oswin's selfish and Victorian ideas on the correct behaviour of young ladies, had done nothing to diminish.

In the years that followed on the heels of Hiroshima, and saw a startling shrinkage of those pink-tinted portions of the map that depicted territories governed by or owing allegiance to the Crown of Great Britain, the trading empire of Derington and Company saw many changes. A number of branches, mainly in the Far East, had been compelled to close down with unexpected suddenness. But other and newer branches had sprung up to replace them, and there came a time when Oswin Derington (whose harassed but resourceful medical adviser had recommended him to take a long sea voyage) decided to combine business with the pursuit of health, and personally inspect a few selected Outposts of the Derington Empire.

He had taken Amanda, now aged twenty, with him; in pursuance of a favourite and often expressed theory that women have an instinct in the matter of irregularities, and that no Branch Manager however efficient occupied — at least in Mr Derington's opinion — the position of Caesar's wife.

He intended to visit Alexandria, Cairo, Aden, Mombasa and Nairobi, and to return via Tripoli. But finding that travel in or to various of these cities was likely to prove full of unpleasant surprises, he had, on reaching Cairo, ordered his niece to return to England forthwith, while he continued the journey alone. There being no return passage immediately available, and as he had a rooted objection to flying (except on those occasions when it happened to suit his convenience) he had packed her off to the temporary care of one of his sisters whose husband, a Brigadier, was stationed in Fayid.

Amanda enjoyed Fayid, and had ultimately administered an even more unwelcome surprise to her Uncle Oswin than his discovery of a strange tendency among certain coloured races to take an actively unappreciative view of Empire builders. She had announced her intention of remaining in Fayid for several months and, later, of visiting the Island of Cyprus.

Since she had in the meantime celebrated her twenty-first birthday and come into control of a small but adequate income, there was little that her Uncle Oswin could do about it beyond losing his temper, which he had done to exhaustion and no effect. His niece had remained sweetly adamant; aided and abetted by her aunt, who had waited a good many years for a chance to repay Oswin for a few forceful criticisms he had uttered on the subject of her choice of a husband, in the days when the Brigadier had been a high-spirited subaltern in the Horse Artillery.

265

Amanda had extended her stay in Fayid, and eventually carried out her intention of visiting Cyprus, where she had planned to put up in some hotel in Kyrenia. But here, after several weeks of sulky silence, Uncle Oswin had once more intervened:

Deringtons, it appeared, owned a wine business in Cyprus: a post-war venture that was not of sufficient importance to warrant a personal visit from Derington of Deringtons. The management of the business was in the hands of a Mr Glennister Barton, and — wrote Uncle Oswin — if Amanda insisted on gallivanting all over the Middle East in this unmaidenly and unladylike manner, it was only right that she should have some consideration for his good name, if not for her own, and, as an unmarried female, stay in some respectable private house rather than in a public hotel. He had therefore taken it upon himself to appraise the Bartons of his niece's arrival, and demand that they should put her up for the duration of her stay, offer her all facilities and see that she came to no harm. He had already received a favourable reply, and Mr and Mrs Barton would meet Amanda at Limassol ...

'You are on no account to fly. I hear that there was an accident only last week. I am further informed that anti-British feeling runs high among those Cypriots who support Enosis and wish the Island to be united to Greece. If you had the slightest consideration for the name of Derington you would abandon this rash and unwomanly project and return to Hampshire,' wrote Uncle Oswin — but without much hope.

Amanda read the letter and sighed. She would have much preferred a hotel and independence, but although she could not be fond of her Uncle Oswin, she felt a certain sense of duty towards him. Despite his selfishness and pomposity, and his conviction that he had been sent into the world to reprove Vice and restore Victorianism, he was — or had been — her legal guardian. And if he had arranged for her to see Cyprus under the auspices of these Bartons, she did not feel like pouring oil on the smouldering embers of his disapproval by refusing to be their guest. She therefore wrote dutifully to say that she would be delighted to accept their kind hospitality.

To the dismay of her aunt and uncle, who pointed out that it would entail travelling to Port Said with an armed convoy and going through the Egyptian Customs, Amanda booked a passage on the S.S. *Orantares* sailing from Port Said to Limassol. They were, however, relieved to discover that others from Fayid, also bound for a holiday in Cyprus, had decided to travel the same way, and that she would be accompanied by Captain Gates, Major and Mrs Blaine and Persis Halliday.

Captain the Hon. Tobias John Allerton Gates was a pleasant young man whose more engaging qualities were at present somewhat obscured by the state of his emotions. Toby was in love — not for the first time — and his failure to make the present object of his devotion, Miss Amanda Derington, take him seriously was casting a deep gloom over a hitherto volatile nature.

Toby had not intended to go to Cyprus for his leave. He had had other plans that included Roehampton and Cowdray Park. But on hearing that Miss Derington meant to visit Cyprus, he had hurriedly cancelled these arrangements and booked a room at the same hotel in Kyrenia that his divinity had intended to patronize. And now it seemed that she was not to stay there after all. She would not even be staying in Kyrenia. She was staying instead at Nicosia with the manager of the Cyprus branch of some Derington & Co. enterprise, and Captain Gates wondered gloomily if it would be possible for him to cancel his room at the Dome Hotel and obtain one in some hotel in Nicosia instead?

Major Alastair Blaine of the 6th Hussars and his wife, Julia, were to spend three weeks with cousins who had a house in Kyrenia. They had intended to go by air, but the only passages available had been on a plane leaving on the 13th of the month, and Julia, a superstitious woman, had refused to fly on such an inauspicious date and had insisted on going by sea. The fifth member of the party from Fayid was Persis Halliday.

Mrs Halliday, although perhaps not so well known outside her own country, would have needed no introduction to anyone living within the bounds of the United States. Persis was a writer of romances, and unlike most of that sisterhood managed to look it. Her books sold by the hundred thousand and her name on the cover of any woman's magazine could be guaranteed to boost its circulation into astronomical figures. She had been widowed by an air disaster three years previously, and her presence in Fayid was accounted for by the fact that she had been on a world tour collecting material for Love in an Eastern setting, and was a friend of Amanda's aunt.

Persis, having heard Amanda mention that Venus-Aphrodite was supposed to have arisen from the foam off the coast of Cyprus, had immediately decided to visit the Island.

'Why, honey — it's a natural for me,' declared Persis. 'The birthplace of the Goddess of Love! Say, that's wonderful. You can count me in on the tour. I just can't miss it!'

'When one thinks of the money you must have made out of the woman,' commented Julia Blaine acidly, 'I suppose the least you can do is to pay her birthplace a visit.'

That had been at a dance at the Fayid Officers' Club, and Persis had raised her brows in real or affected astonishment at the vehemence of Julia's tone, and then laughed and drifted away on a wave of expensive scent.

'Twaddle!' said Mrs Blaine angrily, watching her go.

'What is?' inquired Amanda, startled.

'Her books. Silly, sloppy, sentimental twaddle with a nasty, slimy streak of sex. I can't think why anyone ever reads the stuff.'

'Escape,' said Amanda promptly. 'Just think what life must be like for millions of girls? A deadly, boring grind. Then they read something by Persis and they think, "That might be me!" and feel a lot better.'

'Do you mean to say that *you* read them?' demanded Mrs Blaine incredulously.

'I used to. My last headmistress banned them on the strength of one about a poor but honest hat-check girl who got mixed up with racketeers, dope peddling and white slavery. She emerged spotless of course — all Halliday heroines do — but the ban was enough to make us smuggle them into the dormitories by the dozen.'

Julia Blaine produced a sound uncommonly like a snort and said sharply: 'That merely bears out what I have just been saying. Only giggling schoolgirls would read them!'

She rose abruptly and walked away, angrily jerking at a long chiffon scarf that she wore about her plump, bare shoulders, the end of which had caught on the back of her chair.

'Sour grapes, I'm afraid,' said Amanda's aunt regretfully. 'Poor Julia. She used to write herself — or at least she tried to write. She once had a short story accepted by a magazine and thought that she had really arrived. But nothing came of it and she gave it up. Nothing has ever gone quite right for Julia.'

'Whose fault is that?' grunted the Brigadier, mopping the sweat from his brow and trying to edge his chair round so as to get a more direct blast from the nearest electric fan. 'I know she's your cousin, but the woman's a fool.'

'I know,' sighed Amanda's aunt. 'She is difficult. Poor Julia! She's always angry about something — usually something that doesn't matter at all, like Persis Halliday's books. If she hadn't anything to be angry about I believe she'd invent it. It's a habit of mind. Such a pity that she's never had any children. Alastair's father was one of a family of eighteen I believe, but only two of them married. Alastair is the very last of the Blaines of Tetworth and I think Julia feels it rather. Perhaps that's why she's turned so sour. She shouldn't be sour. Stout people are usually rather placid and jolly.'

'Probably the result of all those pints of lemon juice and iced water that she drinks,' said the Brigadier. 'Enough to sour anyone. Can't think why she does it!'

'To make her thin,' said Amanda's aunt. 'Not that it seems to do much good. All the same it's really very stupid of her to be rude to Persis. Persis may seem gay and good-tempered, and her books may drip with sentiment. But underneath all that she has a good hard streak of vanity and cast iron. She wouldn't have got where she has without it. And because she makes fun of her own books, it doesn't necessarily mean that she takes kindly to other people doing so.'

'Julia,' said the Brigadier, 'is jealous.'

'I know, poor dear. But then she's always been like that ever since she was a child. She's pretty — or she was pretty — and she's got plenty of money. But she would so like to have been fascinating and famous and filthy-rich. And she's automatically jealous of anyone who has anything she hasn't got.'

'I didn't mean that,' remarked the Brigadier. 'I meant Alastair.'

'Oh *that!*' said Amanda's aunt, and sighed. 'That's just an occupational disease with her. She wouldn't speak to Amanda for days just because he started giving her those riding lessons, and she still sulks every time he asks Amanda for a dance.'

Amanda laughed. 'I can't think why,' she said. 'He's very nice and he has charming manners. But he's as dull as — well I don't believe that ditch water is dull. Isn't it supposed to be simply teeming with weird and peculiar and wriggly forms of life? I don't believe that you'd find anything weird or peculiar about Alastair Blaine if you pushed him under a microscope. He's just a nice reliable glass of water — slightly chlorinated. The sort of thing you drink at every meal without thinking about it, and pass up at once if anything better offers.'

'Such as what?' demanded the Brigadier. 'Champagne? Seen anything yet that looks like champagne to you, Mandy?'

'Yes,' said Amanda, her dimples suddenly in evidence.

They had been sitting, all three of them, in a corner of the ballroom, and Amanda's aunt had turned in her chair to watch Persis Halliday and Major Blaine, who were dancing together.

Alastair Blaine was not a particularly good-looking man, but he possessed a pleasant tanned face, the lean lines of a cavalryman, thick blond hair and a pair of frosty blue eyes. He was forty, but did not look it, and was frequently taken to be at least five years younger than his wife's stout and embittered thirty-eight. He was popular, especially with men, and his manner towards his nagging, discontented wife was generally admitted to be beyond reproach, for Julia Blaine cannot have been an easy woman to live with. She had been the spoilt only child of rich and elderly parents, and as a plumply pretty debutante with a more than adequate income she had fallen in love with young Alastair Blaine, home on leave from India, and had married him.

Julia had not liked India. Alastair, a junior officer in an Indian Cavalry Regiment, knew too many people and had too many friends there, and Julia was jealous of anyone and anything that distracted his attention from her. It was there that she first tried out a gambit that was in time to wreck her peace of mind and all prospects of a happily married life. At any party, picnic, ball or social gathering where Alastair appeared to be enjoying himself, she would develop a headache or feel suddenly unwell, and ask to be taken home.

It became her way of demanding his attention and demonstrating her possession of him, and satisfied some hungry, jealous, grasping instinct in her that could not bear to see him entertained or interested by anything or anyone but herself. She loved him with a bitter, jealous love that drove her to almost pathological extremes of behaviour in order to prove to herself that she had at least the power to wound him, and which only served to drive him further from her. The nerves and ill-health that had at first been imaginary, she pandered to and coaxed into reality. And there had been no children to direct her energies and emotions into more normal channels. The plumpness which had been pleasing in youth had turned in her thirties to fat, and the uncharitable were quick to decide that it was only his wife's money that kept Alastair

Blaine from running off with some younger and more glamorous charmer. Not that gossip had ever been able to name one. Everyone liked Alastair, but despite his wife's unreasonable jealousy no one could accuse him of taking any particular interest in any other woman, and he had perhaps paid as much attention to Amanda Derington as he had ever been known to pay to anyone.

At the moment he was dancing with Persis Halliday, and Persis, slim and spectacular in flame-coloured chiffon, was flirting with him with a deliberate and malicious ostentation that was undoubtedly aimed at annoying his wife.

'I can only hope that Persis changes her mind about going to Cyprus,' murmured Amanda's aunt, watching Mrs Halliday with a troubled frown. 'Julia isn't going to like it a bit, and she really does need a holiday. The heat has been very trying and she is not at all fit.'

'You mean she's too fat,' said Amanda with the callousness of youth and a twenty-two-inch waist. 'If she took a bit more exercise, instead of sipping all that diluted lemon juice, she'd feel far better. Who are these people she and Alastair are staying with in Cyprus?'

'The Normans. He's Alastair's first cousin, and next in line to inherit Tetworth if Alastair doesn't come up with any children — which seems highly likely at this late date. I met them when I was over there last year. They have a fascinating house in Kyrenia. I rather think that Claire Norman is delicate — lungs probably — and that is why they have to live in a warm climate. They must have plenty of money, as George Norman does nothing. Julia tells me that they'll be crossing on the same boat as you are, as they've been staying with friends in Alex. You'll probably be seeing quite a lot of them.'

'I do *hope* not,' said Amanda feelingly. 'Not if it means seeing much more of Mrs Blaine. The proper place for her is flat on her back on some psychiatrist's couch being de-complexed. You can't blame Mrs Halliday for trying to take a rise out of her — she's been consistently rude all evening. That's no way to keep a husband!'

'When you have acquired one of your own, Mandy, you will be able to show us how it should be done,' said the Brigadier dryly.

Amanda laughed and made a face at him. 'If you really want to know, darling, I've decided to be a spinster.'

'What? Do you mean to say that in all this seething mob of males you see nothing that attracts your eye?'

'Only one,' said Amanda reflectively. 'Present company excepted, of course.'

'Ah!' said the Brigadier. 'That champagne you were referring to a moment or two ago. Don't tell me that young Toby has at last succeeded in making a dent in your affections? — where is he by the way?'

'He had to rush off and turn out a guard, or something equally martial,' said Amanda. 'He'll be back. No, Toby isn't my idea of champagne, poor lamb.'

'Not Andrew Carron I hope? — or is it young Haigh? or the Plumbly boy or — no it *can't* be Major Cotter! I won't believe it of you.'

'It isn't anyone you know,' said Amanda regretfully. 'In fact it isn't anyone I know either.'

She indicated by a brief gesture of the hand a lone gentleman who was lounging in a chair on the terrace just beyond the nearest door that led out of the ballroom, his long legs stretched out before him and his hands deep in the pockets of a pair of burnt-orange slacks of the type worn by Breton fishermen.

'Good God!' said the Brigadier, revolted. 'The *Artist?*'

'That's right,' agreed Amanda. 'Don't you think he looks rather intriguing?'

'No I do not. Needs a hair-cut! Where did you meet the feller?'

'I didn't. I mean I haven't. I've only seen him here and there. And as I'm off to Cyprus on Monday, I don't suppose I shall ever meet him now. A pity. He looks precisely my cup of tea.'

'You are mixing your drinks,' observed the Brigadier, hitching his chair round so as to obtain a better view. 'He probably wears sandals and manicures his toenails and thinks Picasso is terrific.'

'Well so do I, if it comes to that.'

'*Tacha!*' said the Brigadier. 'All you women are alike. Hand you a lot of nice clean-living normal chaps on a platter, and you won't look at 'em! But you fall over your feet at the sight of the first long-haired blighter who dabbles in art. What's he doing here anyway?'

'Painting the pyramids,' sighed Amanda's aunt. 'They will do it!' She turned an affectionate smile upon her niece: 'You are quite right, Mandy. Such a change from chlorinated drinking water or gin and lime. I must get to know him at once.'

'What on earth are you talking about?' demanded the Brigadier, bewildered.

'Champagne, of course,' said Amanda's aunt. 'So much more exciting and stimulating than — well, beer.' She rose to her feet in a swirl of grey draperies and turned towards the door.

'Muriel!' said the Brigadier, scandalized, 'even at your age you cannot go accosting strange men!'

'Watch me,' said Amanda's aunt, and left them.

It was perhaps half an hour later that her niece, leaving the ballroom for the cooler air of the terrace, was hailed by her aunt.

'Amanda dear, come over here. I want to introduce you to Steven Howard. Mr Howard — my niece, Amanda Derington.'

Mr Howard rose and Amanda held out her hand and found herself looking up into a pair of coolly observant hazel eyes that held a curious glint of speculative interest. There was no trace of admiration in that level gaze, or any recognition of the fact that Miss Derington was an exceptionally pretty girl. Only that oddly speculative interest.

Brown hair ... light brown eyes ... sun-browned face ... thirtyish; he isn't really good-looking, thought Amanda confusedly: his face is out of drawing. But that's what makes it so intriguing ...

A muscle twitched at the corner of Mr Howard's mouth and Amanda suddenly awoke to the fact that her hand was still in his and that she had been studying his face for a full minute. She snatched her hand away, blushed vividly, and was instantly furious with herself and — illogically — with Steven Howard.

'Mr Howard is an artist. He paints,' said Amanda's aunt helpfully. 'He is collecting material for an Exhibition in the autumn.'

'Oh,' said Amanda briefly.

Mr Howard said: 'I am afraid that your aunt gives me credit for more zeal than I possess. To tell the truth, I find art an admirable excuse for avoiding work and loafing around in the sun.' His voice was slow and pleasant and contained the hint of a laugh.

Amanda said: 'Really?' in the tone of one who is not amused, and the band launched into '*La Vie en Rose*'.

'I'm sorry I can't ask you to dance,' said Mr Howard, 'but as you see, I am improperly dressed. Perhaps some other time——?'

'I shan't be here,' said Amanda flatly. 'I'm leaving on Monday. Toby, isn't this our dance?'

She turned abruptly away and left him, and when the dance was over and she and Toby returned to the terrace, he was gone.

'But I thought you wanted to meet him, Mandy!' said Amanda's aunt plaintively. 'Why did you snub the poor man after I'd gone to all that trouble?'

'I don't know,' admitted Amanda ruefully. 'Because I felt I'd make an exhibition of myself, I suppose. Or else because I don't like being laughed at. And he wasn't in the least snubbed. He was amused — and I don't think I like him at all.'

'Oh well,' said Amanda's aunt, 'I don't suppose you're ever likely to see him again.'

But in this she was entirely wrong. Amanda was to see him again not five minutes after Julia died.

2

The decks of the S.S. *Orantares*, which was due to leave Port Said for Limassol, were hot and crowded, and the party from Fayid had taken refuge in the lounge where they had turned on all the fans and ordered iced drinks.

They had been joined there by Mr and Mrs Norman, who had arrived from Alexandria earlier in the day.

Claire Norman was a petite, small-boned and magnolia-skinned woman who possessed a pair of wide grey eyes fringed with silky black lashes, and a cloud of short dark curls cut like a child's. She was not particularly pretty, but her lack of inches and look of slender delicacy somehow suggested the drooping fragility of a snowdrop bending before a harsh wind, and managed to make every other woman appear, by comparison, buxom and oversized. She owned in addition a sweet, soft little voice, and her beautifully cut dress of pale green linen, small white hat and the faint scent of lily-of-the-valley that clung about her, strongly emphasized the First-Flower-of-Spring motif.

Her husband, George Norman, appeared by contrast almost aggressively solid and beefy as he fussed about his tiny wife like some large and over-anxious St Bernard dog. His square, homely face was burnt brick-red by the sun and his thick brown hair was streaked with grey, and he looked completely out of place in the hot, garish and cosmopolitan setting of the crowded lounge. One felt instinctively that he would have been more at home wearing old tweeds and a hat with salmon flies stuck into the band,

276

drinking draught beer at some English country pub, rather than wearing thin tropical duck and accepting an iced gin sling from a coffee-coloured gentleman in a red tarboosh.

'Oh, this heat!' sighed Claire Norman, 'I'm exhausted!'

'Claire tires so easily,' explained George Norman to the assembled company. 'Darling, don't you think you should go and lie down? It's probably a lot cooler in the cabin.'

'And leave dear Julia? — and Alastair — just when we've met? Of course not! Why I've been *longing* to see them again. It's been such *years!*'

'January,' said Julia blightingly. 'Six months.'

'So it is. But it *seems* like years. It's dreadful the way one misses one's real friends . . .'

' ——and before that, September,' continued Julia as though Mrs Norman had not spoken.

'And now again. It's so wonderful to see you Julia — and you too Alastair . . .' Claire Norman laid a small white hand caressingly on Alastair Blaine's lean brown one and Amanda saw him flush, and saw too that for a brief moment there was a queer, unreadable look on his face.

Julia put down her glass with a grimace of disgust and said: 'They've put sugar in it! Alastair, make that man get me another. I particularly said only lemon and water, *not* lemon squash. They don't listen!'

Major Blaine dutifully hailed a passing steward and Claire said: 'It's so good of you both to come and stay with us, Julia. I get so lonely in Cyprus — so far from home and friends.'

'Then why stay there?' demanded Julia.

Claire Norman drew a soft, quivering breath and smiled wistfully. 'The doctors,' she said gently. 'They tell me that I could never . . . But don't let's talk about me. Let's talk about something more interesting. *You!* You're looking so well Julia darling. I only wish I could put on a little weight too. George makes me drink pints

277

of cream and eat pounds of butter, but it's no good. I cannot seem to gain an ounce. Daddy always said I was a changeling — too small for a mortal.'

Persis choked into her gin and lime, dabbed her mouth with a vast chiffon handkerchief and muttered something into its folds that sounded suspiciously like '*Teeny weeny me!*' and Amanda's dimples were suddenly visible. She turned hurriedly away, and looking out of the window said: 'We must be going to sail. They seem to be getting the gangway in.'

There was a burst of shouting and invective from over the side as two more passengers, late arrivals who had almost succeeded in missing the boat, scrambled up the gangway and stood panting and breathless on the deck.

They were an ill-matched couple. The attractive, dark-haired woman in the pink linen suit was as smartly and expensively dressed as Persis, and her white shoes and gloves, despite the heat and the coal dust, were fresh and spotless. She carried a small white leather dressing case in one hand, and what appeared to be an easel in the other. Her companion, by contrast, appeared hot, grubby and dressed with deliberate carelessness. He wore a pair of exceedingly dirty blue linen slacks topped by an orange sports shirt that could also have done with a wash, and sported a scanty ginger beard and a black beret.

Artist, thought Amanda; and was suddenly reminded of Steven Howard. No one meeting Mr Howard for the first time could have typed him, she thought. He had, it is true, worn brightly coloured slacks; but then a good many members of the Sailing Club affected them too, and there was nothing else about him to suggest his profession. He might have been anything: *Tinker, tailor, soldier, sailor*, mused Amanda; and wondered why it was that she should remember everything about him, and every line of his face, so clearly?

The blatantly artistic gentleman on the deck dropped two suitcases and an untidy paper parcel containing canvases, and said crossly and as though continuing a previous conversation:

'Of course I declared them. What a country! Not a tube of usable paint in the place. Students' Water Colours — *Bah!* Put that down, you frightful coolie! Put it *down* — it's not dry yet! *God in heaven*——!'

George Norman, his attention attracted by the howl of fury from the deck, stood up and peered through the window over Amanda's head.

'I thought so,' he said. 'It's that chap Potter.'

Claire turned quickly. 'Lumley? Why, whatever can he have been doing over here?'

'Painting the pyramids, I suppose,' said her husband in an unconscious echo of Amanda's aunt.

'Tell him to come in and join us,' said Claire. She turned to Major Blaine: 'You remember Lumley Potter, don't you Alastair? He has a studio-flat in Famagusta. You met him once or twice at our house when you and Julia were staying with us last year. I think I took you over to see his paintings.'

'You did,' said Julia. '*Lumley!* That wasn't what his mother christened him. I met a Mrs Deadon in Cairo last winter who knew *all* about Mr Potter. I'm not surprised that he decided to settle in Cyprus. As for his paintings, I could do as well with my eyes shut — better! If that's art——'

'But Julia darling, it *is* Art' — Claire pronounced it as though it had a capital A. 'You mustn't be conventional, darling. Lumley doesn't paint what ordinary, conventional people see. He paints the *soul* of a place — the spiritual aroma.'

'Spiritual garlic you mean!' snapped Julia. 'Don't be such a humbug, Claire! The man's a flop, a failure and a fake, and you know it. He can't paint well, so he dresses himself up in what is practically fancy dress, grows a beard, talks a lot of rubbish and paints as badly as he can in the hope of fooling a lot of credulous artistic snobs into thinking he's a genius. And so I told him!'

'Yes, I remember,' said Claire dryly. 'And lost him a great deal of money by doing so. That new-rich Australian couple had

279

practically bought eight of his canvases, but when they heard you they took fright and backed out. However Alastair at least did not agree with you. He bought one — "Sea Green Cypriots" — didn't you Alastair?'

'Only because he felt he had to, to make up for the Blaggs backing out of buying those dreadful daubs,' said Julia unpleasantly.

'Oh darling! You *do* misjudge Alastair so. He has a real, deep-down feeling for truth in Art.'

'I understand Alastair perfectly, thank you Claire,' said Julia acidly.

Alastair Blaine flushed uncomfortably and Persis rose with determination: 'Well, I don't know about you, but I guess I've had all that I can take of the ship's gin,' she remarked cheerfully. 'Alastair honey, how about leaving the girls to sort out your artistic sensibilities while you escort me on deck? I'd like to take a slant at the waterfront before we pull out. Will you spare him, Julia?'

Major Blaine rose with alacrity and assisted Persis to collect her handbag and gloves, while Claire Norman watched them with a sudden frown on her white forehead. After a moment she turned abruptly to her husband and said: 'George dear, I asked you to call Lumley.'

George Norman looked embarrassed and spoke with obvious hesitation: 'Er – well – I thought perhaps I had better not. He had someone with him.'

'Oh?' Claire Norman's soft voice sharpened a little. 'Who was it? Anyone we know?'

'Anita.'

'*Who?*' said Major Blaine, turning sharply. 'But I thought——' He glanced at Amanda, but did not finish the sentence, for Persis took his arm and said: 'Let's go,' and they turned away together and disappeared through the doorway.

'Anita!' said Claire Norman. There were suddenly two bright

patches of colour in her pale cheeks. Her small mouth tightened into a hard narrow line, and for a moment it was as if the frail, pliant snowdrop had been transformed into something made of steel.

The impression was only a fleeting one, and then the corners of her small mouth drooped childishly and once more the sense of wistfulness and fragility was back, and Mrs Norman was saying in her soft, apologetic voice: 'I think after all that I will go and lie down for a while, George dear. I feel so tired. I'll see you at dinner Julia — if I feel strong enough.'

She bestowed a faint smile upon Amanda, directed another at Toby Gates, tucked her small hand confidingly through her husband's arm and moved gracefully away.

Julia Blaine sat staring after her in silence and Amanda saw with surprise that her face was colourless and her eyes wide and fixed and filled with something that looked uncommonly like fear. It was a disturbing expression, and Amanda tried to think of something light and casual to say that would break the spell of that uncomfortable silence. But before she could speak Mrs Blaine stood up, pushing her chair back so violently that it overturned on the thick carpet, and walked quickly out of the lounge.

The ship had sailed some ten minutes later, and Amanda and Toby had gone out on to the deck to watch the garish waterfront of Port Said with its blaze of flame trees slide past them, shimmering in the heat haze.

Feluccas with their squat prows and huge triangular sails drifted by among a clutter of shipping from almost every nation in the world: a British destroyer bound for Colombo and the Far East; oil tankers from England, America, Holland, France, Scandinavia; a P & O liner, white and glittering in the hot sunshine; a troopship returning from Singapore; a dhow from Dacca and a cargo boat from Brazil.

They passed the long stone mole where the statue of de Lesseps gazes out upon that narrow ribbon of water that is his memorial for all time. Beyond and far behind the green-bronze figure, a fleet of fishing boats lay motionless on the shallow waters that curve away towards Damietta and the Delta of the Nile, their sails ghostly in the haze. A cool breath of wind from the open sea blew gently across the sun-baked deck as the ship turned her bows towards Cyprus, and when the white roof-tops and garish domes of Port Said had vanished into the heat haze, Amanda went down to her cabin to wash off the dust of the journey from Fayid.

The long, white-painted ship's corridor was hot and airless and smelt strongly of food, disinfectant, engine oil and that curious all-pervading and entirely individual smell of shipboard. A small but voluble group of people were standing halfway down the corridor and Mrs Blaine's voice made itself heard above the babble:

'I don't care, you'll just have to find me another cabin. I didn't notice it before, or I would never have let you move my things in. I won't sleep in there, and that's all there is to it!'

Mrs Blaine, looking flushed and angry, pushed her way through the group and caught sight of Amanda.

'Really, these people are impossible!' she announced heatedly. 'There must be dozens of other cabins!'

'What's the matter?' inquired Amanda. 'Is there something wrong with yours?'

'Only the number,' said Julia bitterly. 'It's thirteen. I won't travel in it. I'd rather sleep on deck. It isn't even as if the ship were full. Why it's half empty! And it's no good just saying that I'm superstitious. I am. Not about some things — like cats and ladders — but I am about thirteen.'

'Well I'm not,' said Amanda cheerfully. 'I'll swop with you if you like. They've given me a two-berth cabin all to myself.'

'Would you? Would you really?'

'Of course. I haven't unpacked anything yet so it won't take a minute. Mine's fourteen — right next door to you.'

The stewardess, a cabin steward, a hovering Cypriot deck-hand

282

and a man who was evidently the purser, expressed voluble relief, and the transfer was accomplished in a matter of minutes.

'It's very good of you,' said Julia Blaine awkwardly, lingering in the doorway of her late cabin and speaking in a halting, difficult voice. 'I know it sounds silly to be so superstitious, but – well I've wanted to get away from the heat and – and Fayid so badly, and I – I do so want this leave to be a success. But when I saw that number on the door it – it seemed like a bad omen, and I . . .' Her voice trailed away and stopped.

Amanda smiled sympathetically at her, but Julia Blaine did not return the smile. She was not looking at Amanda. She was staring instead at her own reflection in the narrow strip of looking-glass behind Amanda's head, and her plump, ageing face was once again white and frightened.

Amanda had tea in the lounge with Toby Gates, and when the sun had set in a blaze of gold and rose and amethyst and the sky was brilliant with stars, they had all dined in the saloon: Amanda, Toby, Julia and Alastair Blaine, the Normans and Persis Halliday.

The saloon was far from crowded and Amanda caught sight of the ginger-bearded painter of spiritual aromas dining at a small table with his companion of the afternoon, who had changed her linen suit for a short, strapless dinner dress of scarlet lace.

Amanda had exchanged one cotton frock for another, and Julia Blaine had not bothered to change at all. But Claire Norman was looking cool and ethereal in white chiffon and pearls, while Mrs Halliday, despite the heat, had elected to wear gold lamé and some astonishing emeralds. The glittering cloth brought out the gold lights in her copper hair and the emeralds turned her eyes to a clear, shining green. She looked stunning and knew it, and was amusing herself by flirting outrageously with George Norman.

Alastair Blaine was sitting next to Amanda, but Claire Norman, seated on his right, monopolized most of his attention, and for once Julia's acid tongue was silent. She was watching her husband and Claire Norman with a furtive and almost frightened intentness, but if Alastair was aware of this he certainly paid no attention to it. Major Blaine, for the first time since Amanda had known him, appeared to be the better — or worse — for drink. His face was unnaturally flushed and his blue eyes overbright, and he appeared to be slurring his words a little.

They were half-way through the meal when Claire leant across and spoke to Amanda:

'Alastair tells me that you've never been to Cyprus before, Amanda? — I may call you Amanda, mayn't I? Are you staying long?'

'Only ten days,' said Amanda regretfully. 'It doesn't seem nearly long enough. Ten days is such a little time.'

'Oh, but it's a very little Island. Where are you staying? In Kyrenia?'

'No, I'm afraid not. I'd much rather have stayed somewhere near the sea, but my uncle arranged for me to stay with some people in Nicosia.'

'Army people I suppose. They're nearly all stuck in Nicosia, poor things.'

Amanda shook her head. 'No. They're something to do with wine. People called Barton.'

'Barton! You can't mean *Glenn* Barton?'

'Yes, I think that must be it. Glennister Barton. Do you know them?'

'Yes, of course I know them; but you can't possibly be staying at the Villa Sosis. Why——' She stopped suddenly and bit her lip.

'But I am staying with them,' said Amanda with a laugh. 'Did you think they were away?'

'No. I mean——' Once more Claire Norman did not finish the sentence. She laughed instead; a light tinkling laugh that somehow gave Amanda the impression that she was both disturbed and angry. 'Oh well — we shall see. It will be very interesting. But personally I should have thought that Glenn would have had more respect for the convention. He is such a stickler for propriety.'

With which cryptic remark she turned her attention to Toby Gates, and Amanda had no further opportunity of reopening the subject, for it was at that point that the artistic Mr Potter and his companion rose to leave the dining saloon and paused beside their table. Amanda, looking round, saw the painter pull at the woman's arm as though he would have hurried her past, but she disengaged herself deliberately and spoke in a clear high voice:

'Hullo Claire. Hullo Mrs Blaine. Alastair! — fancy seeing you here again!'

Alastair Blaine stood up quickly. He was swaying a little. 'Hullo Anita. What are you doing here?'

'As if you didn't know!' mocked Mr Potter's companion. 'However if you don't, you soon will. Claire will see to that. Won't you, Claire?'

Claire Norman stiffened where she sat. She turned slowly and it seemed a full minute before she spoke:

'Hullo Anita. I'm not sure that I expected to see you here either. I should have thought—— ' She broke off with a shrug of her white shoulders and gave her tinkling little laugh: 'Oh well, it's no concern of mine, is it? Hullo Lumley. You remember Major and Mrs Blaine, don't you?'

She made no attempt to introduce the woman she had addressed as Anita, but turned instead to the three men at her own table: 'Do sit down, darlings. There's no need for you to stand around while your food gets cold. They're just going.'

Mr Potter's face, which had acquired a fiery glow that reduced his beard to luke-warm proportions, turned an even richer shade of puce and he said hurriedly: 'Yes, we – we were going on deck. Come on Anita.' He grabbed his companion's arm and almost dragged her from the dining-room.

'Say, who was that dame?' inquired Persis, interested.

'Just someone we have the misfortune to know,' said Claire in a small, cold voice, and instantly changed the subject.

Persis raised her eyebrows but did not press the question. And presently they left the table and went up to drink coffee in the lounge, and later someone turned on a gramophone and they danced on deck under a blaze of stars.

It was almost eleven o'clock by the time Amanda went down to bed, and except for a passing Cypriot deck-hand the long brightly lit corridor was silent and deserted. Her cabin was hot and stuffy after the cool night air on deck and she was pleasantly surprised to see that a thoughtful stewardess had placed a brimming frosted glass, with ice and a long strip of lemon peel floating in it, on a small stool near her berth. A moment or two later she realized that the drink must have been ordered by Julia, and placed in error in the cabin that Julia should have been occupying: she would have to take it in to her, but as she had already removed her dress it could wait until she was ready for bed. She put on a thin silk nightdress, washed in cold water and removing the pins from her hair, brushed out its long, shining length.

Amanda's hair — a deep golden brown with glints in it the colour of the first chestnuts in September — was a glorious anachronism. In the sunlight there were other colours in it too; purple and green and bronze; and it fell far below her slim waist in a rippling, glinting cloak that might well have rivalled Montezuma's fabled cloak of feathers. Yet as she brushed it she regretted — not for the first time since the advent of the hot weather — that she could not summon up the moral courage to defy her uncle and chop it off.

But Oswin Derington did not approve of short hair for women, and although Amanda was now of age and had demonstrated her independence in a drastic manner, the habit of years made her shrink from the prospect of Uncle Oswin's scandalized wrath should she cut off what he persisted in referring to as 'Woman's Crowning Glory'.

Amanda sighed and rummaged in her suitcase for a length of ribbon with which to tie it back, and she was pulling the bow tight when the door of the cabin burst open without any preliminary knock to disclose Julia Blaine, arrayed in a pink satin dressing-gown liberally trimmed with lace, a tight pink satin nightdress and feathered mules.

Mrs Blaine banged the door shut behind her and subsided heavily on the end of Amanda's berth. She was trembling violently and her teeth chattered as though she were cold.

'What's the matter?' demanded Amanda sharply; appalled by the sight of the older woman's ravaged face. 'Are you ill? Shall I call the stewardess?'

'No,' said Mrs Blaine hoarsely. 'It's – it's Alastair——'

'Alastair? You mean he's ill?'

'No. But he hasn't come to bed. He – he was dancing to that gramophone, and I told him that I wasn't feeling well and would have to go to bed, but he wouldn't come with me. He wouldn't even come as far as the cabin with me! He said I could find the way myself. I waited and waited; and then I sent the stewardess to tell him to come as I was feeling very unwell, and he – he sent back to say that I'd better take an aspirin and that he couldn't come just now. Couldn't come ...! It's that woman! I should have known it. I've always known that this would happen one day. Alastair ... *Alastair ...!*'

She broke into gulping, hysterical sobs.

'Mrs Blaine,' said Amanda gently, 'don't you think you'd better go back to your cabin and lie down? You shouldn't say these things to me — really you shouldn't. You'll feel quite differently about it in the morning. It's only because it's been a hot, tiring day that you're feeling upset. You don't really mean it. *Do* lie down.'

But Julia Blaine was beyond the reach of reason. She had to talk, and if it had not been to Amanda it would have been to someone else — anyone else — the stewardess, or a stranger.

She said violently: 'I shall say it! I do mean it! I shall tell everyone. *Everyone!* I've always known that he'd leave me one day. I've felt it; *here*——'

287

She struck her billowing breasts with her clenched fists, while the tears poured down her plump, faded cheeks:

'Only he couldn't leave me! I had the money and he needed that. He might have managed in an Indian cavalry regiment, but when he had to transfer into a British one he had to have money. And I had more than the others. A lot more. There might have been prettier women, and younger and – and slimmer ones, like Anita, but they couldn't give him the horses and cars and comforts that I could. But now it's different. That American woman. She's rich. You saw those emeralds! They must have cost a fortune. And Claire — it isn't George's money. It's Claire's. That's why George has to stay in Cyprus. He hates it — he's always hated it. But if he left her he wouldn't have a penny, and he's grown used to doing nothing. When she got him to give up the Army she told him that they'd buy a farm in England. But she didn't; and he hadn't even qualified for a pension. She's got him where she wants him. But I didn't realize that she wanted Alastair. He can't do this to me! — he can't!'

She wept noisily, rocking her stout body to and fro, and Amanda sat down beside her and put her arms about the fat, satin-clad shoulders, wondering desperately what she could say to comfort this hysterical, despairing woman.

'I'm – I'm sure you must be imagining it,' said Amanda helplessly.

'I know him and you don't,' sobbed Julia, 'and I've never known him behave like this before. But she shan't have him! I'll kill myself first! I'd be better dead than having to go through all this – this awful agony.'

Amanda began to wonder if she ought not to ring the bell for the stewardess and ask for sedatives or the ship's doctor. She said anxiously: 'Wouldn't you like a – an aspirin or something?'

Mrs Blaine turned her head slowly and looked at Amanda as though she was awakening from a deep sleep or an anaesthetic. Her blotched and tear-disfigured face coloured a slow, ugly red and she jerked herself free of Amanda's arm and stood up abruptly:

'That's what Alastair said. He said to take some aspirin. The stewardess brought me some. The one who – who brought me the message.'

She opened her hot, plump hand to show two small white tablets that were already beginning to crumble.

Amanda said: 'You take those and get into bed. They'll make you sleep, and you'll feel much better in the morning.'

'Yes,' said Julia slowly. 'Perhaps it's the heat. I always feel so dreadful in the heat. It's horrible, having to live so much in the East. I've always hated Army life ... but Alastair likes it. Perhaps if I sleep ...'

She put the tablets into her mouth and reached out one plump beringed hand for the glass that stood beside the berth. The diamonds on her fingers winked and sparkled in the light of the ceiling bulbs as she lifted it to her lips and drank deeply.

She made a wry grimace and drank again, swaying a little as she stood, and presently said in a harsh whisper: 'I've been a fool. I should never have let him go back to Cyprus. But I never suspected ... Claire's too clever. We stayed with them last year, you know. And then they came and stayed with us, and we all spent Christmas and New Year together in Alex. He never seemed to pay any special attention to her. He – he always said that he didn't like little women. But tonight – tonight—— '

She swayed again and put up a hand, catching at the edge of the upper berth to steady herself. Holding it, she drew herself erect and said in a voice that was no longer trembling with hysteria but cold and venomous: 'Well he can't divorce me! And I'll never divorce him. *Never!* He knows that. I'd kill myself first — I'd kill myself!'

She clung to the edge of the berth, breathing stertorously and shivering, her eyes staring blindly across the small cabin. There were great beads of sweat on her forehead that trickled down and mingled with the tears that smeared her cheeks, and the silence in the cabin, broken only by the sound of her hoarse panting breath, began to grow oppressive.

Amanda watched her anxiously and presently said: '*Do* go to bed. You're only upsetting yourself. I'm sure your husband will be along soon.'

Julia Blaine looked at her as though she did not know who she was or could not focus her, and lifting the glass that she still held, drank again, thirstily.

A minute or two later she suddenly swayed and staggered and seemed to gasp for air, and releasing her hold on the berth, doubled up, retching; her face suffused and her eyes starting from her head.

The glass dropped from her hand and rolled on its side, spilling what little remained of its contents on to the floor in a scatter of melting ice, and Julia gave a curious, choking cry and fell forward to sprawl face downwards on the narrow cabin floor.

3

She's fainted, thought Amanda frantically. What on earth does one do for a faint? Oh, *bother* the woman!

She leapt for the bell and pressed it hard. The stewardess would know what to do.

Amanda bent and attempted to lift the limp body, but the task was beyond her. She managed to turn Mrs Blaine over. But at the sight of that contorted face her heart gave an odd lurch: Julia Blaine's mouth had fallen open and her eyes were wide and fixed and staring.

'It isn't a faint. She's had a fit,' said Amanda, unaware that she had spoken aloud. She reached for the unbroken glass, and filling it with water from the cold tap, splashed it over Mrs Blaine's face and neck: the water streamed over Julia's contorted features and across her staring eyeballs. But her eyelids did not close ...

Amanda straightened up, cold and trembling. She sprang to the bell and pressed it again, frantically, and then seized by a sudden, shuddering horror, jerked open the door and ran out into the corridor. It stretched away on either side of her, blank, brightly lit and empty, and she had no idea at which end of it the stewardess had her cabin, or where to find her. But she must fetch help, and quickly.

Julia's own cabin was empty, and there was no one in No. 12, for it was a darkness and the door stood open. She turned in desperation to the one beyond it and hammered on the door.

'Who is it?' demanded a man's voice impatiently.

Amanda tried to speak and found that she could not. The next

291

moment the door opened and Steven Howard, pyjama clad and sleepy, was staring down at her with a mixture of amusement and unqualified surprise.

'Well, well!' said Mr Howard cordially, his interested gaze missing no detail of her unorthodox attire. His eyes went to her white face and his own face changed abruptly, so that all at once it was an entirely different person who was standing there in the white, brightly lit corridor of the S.S. *Orantares*. His hand shot out and gripped Amanda's shoulder, steadying her:

'What is it?'

'It's Mrs Blaine,' said Amanda, shuddering. 'She's in my cabin. I – I think she's had a fit and I can't bring her round. And I rang and rang, but no one has answered the bell, and ... and ...'

Mr Howard said briskly: 'Just a minute.' He reached for a dressing-gown, put it on and said: 'Where is she?'

Amanda led the way to her cabin and stood back for him to enter, and he went quickly past her and dropped on one knee beside the sprawling figure whose pink satin attire was blotched and stained with water.

After a moment or two he lifted his head and said curtly: 'She's dead.'

He came to his feet rather slowly and looked at Amanda. It was a long, measuring look that held that same curious suggestion of speculation and intentness that she had seen in his eyes on the terrace of the Club at Fayid.

'No!' said Amanda in a whisper. 'Oh no! She can't be — she was talking to me! Why don't you get a doctor? Why don't you do something? If it's a heart attack a doctor——'

Mr Howard cut her short: 'I'm not too sure that it was a heart attack.'

'What else could it *possibly* be?'

'Well, it could be suicide.'

'No,' said Amanda loudly and definitely. 'She wouldn't have

done that, because it would mean that he could——' She stopped abruptly.

'Mean that who could what?' inquired Steven Howard softly.

'Nothing,' said Amanda confusedly. 'I didn't mean ... it was just something that she said.'

Mr Howard reached across her and shut the cabin door.

'I think you'd better tell me just exactly what happened,' he said. 'Quickly, before anyone comes. If you rang for the stewardess she may be along at any moment, so let's have it.'

He spoke quite quietly, but with an unconscious note of authority which, for some reason, it did not occur to Amanda to question, and she found herself telling him exactly what Julia Blaine had said and done: repeating the substance of that hysterical outburst almost word for word.

Mr Howard said: 'Then you saw her take the tablets herself?'

'Yes. She put them in her mouth and then drank some lemon-water, and a little while later she seemed to feel ill, and then she fell down like – like she is now, only on her face.'

'Is that the glass?'

'Yes.' Amanda's teeth chattered a little and she clenched them on her lower lip.

Mr Howard reached out and picked it up, holding it by the extreme edge of the rim. He smelt it, put it down again and said: 'Where did all that water on her clothes come from? It didn't all come out of this glass, did it?'

'I filled it again at the basin and poured it over her. I thought it might bring her round.'

'I see.' He went down on his knees again and examined the contorted, staring face and then lifted the slack hands one after another. A few coarse grains of white powder clung damply to the palm of one hand. Steven Howard sniffed it, and rubbing the tip of his finger over it, touched it to his tongue with infinite caution, and frowned.

293

He sat back on his heels and looked around at the floor and presently said: 'What was the last thing she said again?'

'She said she'd kill herself. But I didn't think she meant it. I thought she was only – only——'

'Quite,' said Mr Howard curtly. 'All the same it looks as though she may have meant it.'

He frowned thoughtfully down at the plump-fingered hands with their glittering rings and then stood up abruptly:

'It doesn't look as though anyone is going to answer that bell. You'd better see if you can find someone. See if you can rout out a steward or a stewardess; or grab the first ship's officer you see and tell him to send along a doctor.'

He looked Amanda over and added dryly: 'And if I were you, I'd put on a dressing-gown.'

An hour later Julia Blaine's body had been removed to the sick bay and the water had been mopped off Amanda's cabin floor. Amanda herself, having repeated her story — with several reservations — at least half a dozen times, was at last left in peace.

The ship's doctor had seemed puzzled by the cause of death and he too had suggested the possibility of suicide, but the stewardess had sworn with fervour and a touch of hysteria that she had given Mrs Blaine two aspirins and nothing else. She had produced the bottle in evidence, and the doctor had taken charge of it and after careful examination pronounced the tablets to be innocuous.

Alastair Blaine, white-faced and incredulous, had agreed that his wife had been in poor spirits of late; that she was highly strung and, though her health had not been of the best, there had never been any suggestion of heart trouble, and he did not know how she could have obtained poison.

'In the East, that is easy,' commented the Captain dryly. 'A little money, and the thing is done' — he had pantomimed a sly, expressive Oriental gesture.

Amanda, prompted by Steven Howard, had agreed that Mrs Blaine had talked of taking her life. And looking at Alastair

Blaine's haggard face, she had refrained from any mention of names or motives; allowing it to be inferred that a combination of nerves, ill-health and the heat had been responsible for Mrs Blaine's state of mind. She had not looked at Steven Howard, and to her relief he had failed to point out that this version differed considerably from the one that she had given him so short a time ago. He had, in fact, barely spoken. But Amanda had the odd impression that in some way that she could not define, he had directed the course of the inquiry and headed it away from dangerous ground. He had eventually, and still without appearing to do so, managed to get rid of the Captain, the First Officer, the doctor, the stewardess and sundry other spectators who had crowded in and asked questions and talked in unison. He had been the last to leave, and had stood in the doorway, his hands thrust into the pockets of his dressing-gown, frowning down at her.

'Are you sure you're all right? You wouldn't like me to knock up Mrs Halliday or get one of the stewardesses to sleep on that top berth?'

'No thank you,' said Amanda wearily. 'I'm all right. You wouldn't think that anyone could feel sleepy after all that, but I do. I feel very stupid and dopey.'

'Reaction from shock,' said Mr Howard. 'Well if anything scares you, don't wait for someone to answer that bell. Come out into the corridor and yell!'

'*Scares* me? What is there to be scared of?' asked Amanda, puzzled.

'I don't know,' said Steven Howard slowly. 'Nothing, I hope.'

He looked round the narrow cabin almost as though he were making certain that no one could be concealed there, and the frown line deepened between his brows. Then he shrugged his shoulders, smiled briefly, and was gone.

Amanda yawned. She felt unbelievably exhausted. She slipped out of her dressing-gown, leaving it in a heap on the floor, and climbing into her berth, switched off the light.

After a minute or two she became aware that there was a small hard lump either in or under her pillow, and she put up a sleepy and impatient hand to investigate.

And that was how she found the bottle.

It was a small bottle, and there was something in it that rattled. Amanda lay for a time in the semi-darkness, turning it over in her hand and wondering how it could have come there. Presently she reached out to switch on the light again, and sat up to look at it.

It was an ordinary glass bottle of the type that usually contains aspirins. There were three small tablets in it and it bore a bright red label with a single warning word printed blackly across it. POISON.

All at once Amanda was frightened. She had been shocked and horrified by Julia's collapse, and frightened by the staring, sightless eyes that had not blinked when the water splashed across them. But this was a different sort of fear. A cold, creeping fear that seemed to chill her blood and slow down the beat of her heart. For the bottle had not been there earlier that evening. She was quite sure of that. And for a very good reason.

She had sat down on the centre of the berth to read some letters before changing for dinner, and, reaching for the pillow, had tucked it between her shoulders and the back of the berth. There had been no bottle under it then.

That meant that someone had placed it there some time after eight o'clock. Julia? But Julia had not come near the pillow. She had sat on the foot of the berth and had not moved from there until she had stood up and put those tablets in her mouth and reached for the glass. Amanda had been between Julia Blaine and the pillow and it was quite out of the question that Mrs Blaine could have reached across her and put anything under it without her knowledge.

Who then? And why?

Quite suddenly an answer slipped into Amanda's head as though someone had whispered it very softly into her ear.

Julia Blaine had neither died of a heart attack nor killed herself. She had been murdered. And that small bottle with the poison label proved it—— !

The tablets that Julia had put into her mouth had been aspirin tablets given to her by the stewardess. The poison had been in the glass. In that innocent iced drink whose unsweetened tartness would serve to disguise any additional acidity.

Someone who knew that Julia Blaine drank lemon juice and water, but who did not realize that she had changed cabins with Amanda, had laid that deadly trap for her. Julia should have drunk from that glass in her own cabin, and she would have been found there, dead. And presently the bottle would have been found under her pillow, to ensure a verdict of suicide.

Fate had been on the murderer's side, for chance had brought Julia to her former cabin and she had, after all, drunk from the glass and died. But it was Amanda who had found the bottle. And its presence under the wrong pillow was no longer a pointer to suicide, but proof of murder.

'No!' said Amanda, speaking aloud in the hot, silent little cabin. 'No!'

Almost without realizing what she meant to do, she slipped out of bed. The carpet was still damp and faintly sticky under her bare feet, and she groped for her dressing-gown and putting it on rang the bell. This time it was answered promptly.

Amanda could hear the stewardess rustling down the corridor, her stiff, starched uniform sounding brisk and reassuring.

'What is it, dear? Can't you sleep?' The stewardess was stout, middle-aged, motherly and, by some miracle, English.

Amanda said: 'Did you – did you put a glass of water and lemon juice in here for Mrs Blaine, by mistake?'

The stewardess looked bewildered. 'A lemon squash dear? No. Would you like one?'

'No thank you. But there was one here. It was on that stool when I came in. Did you put it there?'

'Me? Oh no, dear. We don't provide drinks for the passengers unless they ask for them. But you'd only have to ring.'

'*Did* Mrs Blaine ask for one? This was her cabin before, and I – I thought perhaps it was put in here by mistake.'

'She didn't ask me for one, poor lady. And no one who has to do with the cabins would have made such a mistake, I assure you. They were all aware of the exchange. So it must have been put there by one of your friends. Now what is it that you want, dear?'

'Nothing,' said Amanda, white-faced. 'I – I only wondered ... You see when she — Mrs Blaine — swallowed those tablets she drank out of a glass that was on that stool; and I – I wondered who had put it there.'

'I'll tell you what's the matter with you, dear,' said the stewardess kindly. 'You're sufferin' from shock. That's what it is. You mustn't let it worry you. The poor lady must have bin out of her mind. Now just you try and forget all about it and go to sleep. I expect she had a drink out of that tooth glass over there.'

'No she didn't,' said Amanda. 'It was another glass.'

'Then where is it now?'

Amanda turned and looked about her, but the glass had gone. It was nowhere in the cabin.

'There now!' said the stewardess cosily. 'You're lettin' your nerves run away with you, dearie. An' no wonder! I'll fetch you a nice cup of hot milk, and you'll soon be asleep.'

'No thank you,' said Amanda in a small unsteady voice. 'It's very kind of you, but I don't want anything. I'm sorry to have bothered you.'

'That's all right,' said the stewardess. 'Now you get back into bed, and I'll turn the light out, and if you should want me you only have to ring.'

She tucked Amanda into her berth and went out, switching off the light and closing the door behind her. Her starched skirts rustled crisply away down the passage, and from somewhere near-by a door latch clicked softly.

A faint light from the passage outside filtered in through a narrow open grill above the door and thinned the darkness of the small cabin, and beyond the open porthole the sky was bright with moonlight.

Except for the soothing swish of the sea and the muffled, rhythmic throb of the engines, the night was still and silent and Amanda had heard no sound of footsteps. But suddenly her cabin door opened and closed again. And someone was there, standing beside her; a dark shape against the faint light from the transom.

Amanda's heart seemed to jerk and turn over sickeningly. She sat up, shrinking back against the head of the berth, and tried to scream — and could not, because her throat was dry and constricted with terror; and because there was a hand across her mouth.

A voice spoke in a whisper: 'Don't make a noise. It's I — Steve Howard.'

Amanda crumpled up in a small sobbing heap against him, and he put an arm about her, holding her hard, and sat down on the berth.

'I'm sorry. I didn't mean to frighten you' — his voice was barely a breath against her ear. 'But I had to talk to you. Come on, dear — take a pull on yourself.'

Amanda lifted her head from his shoulder and said in a sobbing furious whisper: *'Get out of my cabin!'*

'That's more like it,' approved Mr Howard. He produced a handkerchief and dried her eyes. Amanda snatched it from him, and having completed the operation for herself, reached for the electric light switch.

Steve Howard's hand shot out and caught her wrist. 'No! Don't turn on the light. I don't want the stewardess coming in here to find out why you're still awake. What were you telling her about a glass? I heard you talking to her. Your door was open. What about that glass, Amanda?'

Amanda shivered and her teeth made a small chattering sound in the silence. She said in a halting whisper: 'There was a glass of water in here – with – with lemon in it, when I came to bed. Mrs Blaine always drinks – drank – lemon and water. She did it to make her thin. And she changed cabins with me.'

'When was that?' the whisper was suddenly sharp. 'Why did you change cabins?'

'This afternoon. Just before tea. This was her cabin. But she wouldn't go into it when she saw the number. It's thirteen, and she was superstitious about thirteen. So I told her that she could have mine.'

'Who knew about it?'

'I don't know. The stewardess said that – that the ship's people would all know. But I don't suppose anyone else would. Except Alastair of course — her husband. The – the stewardess said that it must have been one of the passengers who put that glass there.'

'Yes I know. I heard her. What made you ask her about it?'

'I – I was frightened. Mrs Blaine drank out of it. And now it's gone. Someone must have taken it.'

'I did,' said Steven Howard softly.

'You! But why? I don't understand.'

'Don't you? Why were you frightened because Mrs Blaine drank out of it?'

'Because of the bottle,' breathed Amanda tremulously. 'There was a bottle hidden under my pillow, and I thought——'

'What's that!' The whispered question cracked like a whip in the silence.

Amanda turned and thrust a shaking hand under the pillow, found the bottle and held it out.

Mr Howard took the bottle from her gingerly, holding it with extreme care, and turned to face the light that filtered in through the grill above the door. The little cabin that had seemed so dark

300

when the light had first been switched off no longer appeared dark now that Amanda's eyes had grown accustomed to the dim light, and the single word printed across the red label was clearly readable.

He turned back to her and said: 'How did you come to find it?'

'I told you. It was under my pillow. But it hadn't been there before.' She told him about that, and why she knew that it had not been there before eight o'clock.

'You don't think Mrs Blaine could have put it there while she was talking to you.' The words were less a query than an assertion.

'I know she didn't.'

'Then what *do* you think?'

Amanda did not answer him. She stared down instead at the small bottle that he held so carefully with a corner of his handkerchief.

'Why were you frightened, Amanda?'

Amanda's eyes lifted slowly to his face. His back was to the light from the passage and his face was in deep shadow, but she could see the gleam of his eyes and the line of his mouth and jaw.

She said: 'You know, don't you? That's why you took the glass.'

'*Ssh!* Quietly. Yes I know. You don't think that she died from a heart attack. Or that she killed herself either. That's it, isn't it?'

'What else can I think?' said Amanda shivering. 'If – if it was something in the glass and not the tablets in her hand, then it must have been – have been——'

'Murder,' finished Steven Howard softly. 'Of course. And I think you're right. Mrs Blaine took two tablets of aspirin. The stuff that killed her was in that glass.'

'How – how can you know?' demanded Amanda in a shaking whisper.

'There are only two sets of finger-prints on the glass, and both of them are quite clear.'

Amanda said: 'But of course there are only two! Only two people touched it. Myself and Mrs Blaine. Oh, and you.'

Mr Howard shook his head. 'I lifted it by the rim. Those marks are there too. But what about the person who brought it here in the first place? There should have been at least three sets of prints on it.'

Amanda put her hands to her throat. It seemed oddly constricted. 'Then she *was* murdered. No! No, it can't be true!'

Her voice rose and Steven Howard's hand was instantly over her mouth. Amanda twisted her head away and said in a shuddering whisper: 'But – but don't you see, that would mean that it was someone she knew. Someone *I* know! — Persis or Toby—— No, it can't be. It couldn't possibly be!'

'It must be. Unless——'

He stopped, and Amanda said breathlessly: 'Unless what?'

Mr Howard did not answer her. His eyes had not moved from her face, but he appeared to be listening intently and his hand closed warningly about her wrist.

There was someone in the passage outside. Amanda did not know how she knew it, or how Steven Howard had known it, for her ear had caught no sound of approaching footsteps. Perhaps someone had brushed against the door in passing, or a shadow had flickered briefly across the white wall of the passage.

Steve Howard sat between her and the door so that she could only see the edge of it. The door did not quite fit and there was a thin sliver of light where age had warped the wood. But even as she looked, the slit of light vanished.

Steve saw her eyes widen, and for a brief moment his fingers tightened on her wrist. He turned his head and drew something out of the pocket of his dressing-gown, moving with infinite caution. Amanda saw the light from the transom glint on the barrel of the gun he held, and thought with a stunned illogicality, 'He's left-handed.'

302

Booted feet clattered noisily down a companion-way at the far end of the passage and instantly the thin sliver of light reappeared at the edge of the door. Whoever had paused outside Amanda's cabin had gone as silently as they had come.

Someone, a ship's officer by the sound, passed quickly down the passage, and a distant door banged shut. Mr Howard slid the small gun into his pocket and sighed.

'I was afraid of that,' he said softly.

'Of what?' breathed Amanda.

Mr Howard turned to look at her. 'Without wishing to be an alarmist,' he said, 'I think you would be advised to walk extremely warily for the next few days. In fact I would suggest that you send yourself an urgent telegram and take the next available plane for England?'

'Why?' said Amanda. 'I don't understand——'

'Don't you? I should have thought it was obvious. It looks as though somebody planned a murder that was to pass as suicide. That someone has either realized already, or will shortly realize, that the thing has blown a fuse, in that you and not Mrs Blaine are occupying Cabin No. 13, and that you will therefore be in a position to know — or at least suspect — that Mrs Blaine was murdered. That being so, whoever planted that bottle may go to considerable lengths to get it back.'

'Then what are you going to do with it?' demanded Amanda in a dry whisper.

'Dispose of it.'

'But you can't! The Captain must see it — the police. If you don't tell them, I shall!'

Mr Howard stood up. 'I wouldn't do that if I were you,' he said quietly. 'Not unless you want to find yourself under arrest.'

Amanda shrank back against the pillow, her breath coming short. 'What do you mean?'

He stood looking down at her, his hands in his pockets, and

303

after a moment he said softly and very deliberately: 'You see, there is always the possibility that you might have worked the whole thing yourself.'

There was a long silence in the little cabin. A silence that seemed to stretch out into interminable minutes. Outside that silence the quiet night was once again full of sounds: the rustling wash of water along the sides of the ship, the monotonous throb of the engines and the hundred and one tiny creaks and squeaks and rattles that the shudder of the screw set up in the fabric of the ship.

Amanda spoke at last. 'You can't believe that. You can't!'

'Perhaps not. But there'll have to be a post-mortem, and the police may — if this turns out to be a case of murder. You see, they would have only your own word for what happened in this cabin, and of how you came to be in possession of that bottle. If it turns out to contain the same poison that killed Mrs Blaine, they may even think that you invited her in to talk to you. And since her husband presumably inherits anything she had to leave, Major Blaine will now be an exceedingly eligible widower — and you saw quite a lot of him in Fayid, didn't you?'

Amanda caught her breath in a hard gasp. She said in a furious whisper: '*Get out!* Get out of my cabin before I call someone to put you out!'

'Don't be silly, Amanda;' Steven Howard had not raised his voice, but the words held a cutting edge that was as effective as a slap in the face. 'You are in no position to behave stupidly. You have no idea at all what it would be like to get yourself involved in a police inquiry out here. It's no joke anywhere. With this set-up it would be hell. If you have any sense in that charming head you will keep your mouth shut about that bottle and the glass and let it be supposed that Mrs Blaine committed suicide. Any other course is likely to prove very sticky for you, if not downright dangerous. And you are in a sticky enough position already, without that.'

Amanda said: '*Who are you?*'

Mr Howard grinned unexpectedly. 'The name is Howard. Steve to my friends. I paint indifferent pictures and have a passion for meddling in other people's affairs. Anything else you'd like to know?'

'Yes,' said Amanda. 'Who are you really? Why do you carry a gun? What are you doing in all this? Don't tell me that you're just out here to paint pictures, because I don't believe a word of it!'

Mr Howard laughed. 'All right. Let's say that I happen, for reasons of my own, to be interested in one or two people who are on this boat.'

'Are you in the police?' demanded Amanda abruptly.

'No.'

'Then why are you taking a hand in this?'

Steve Howard grinned. 'Pure knight-errantry. Or mere meddling — take your choice. And now I think you'd better get some sleep, if you think you can manage it. There's a bolt on that door. I suggest you use it. Goodnight Amarantha.'

The door closed softly behind him.

4

Amanda shot the bolt on the inside of her cabin door with unsteady fingers, and returned to her berth to sit rigidly upright with her arms about her knees, straining to listen and starting at every unidentified sound.

The full import of Steven Howard's statement that sooner or later someone must inevitably realize that Amanda, as the present occupant of cabin number thirteen, was bound to obtain possession of evidence that pointed to murder, had only just come home to her. It was a singularly unpleasant thought; and even more unpleasant was the sudden realization that but for Julia's arrival, she would have carried that glass into Julia's cabin. Her fingerprints would have been found upon it, and there would only have been her own word for why she had handed a glass of poison to Alastair Blaine's wife.

Alastair's wife ... Was that the key to this cruel murder? Had Alastair—— ? But no, that was absurd! It could not be Alastair because he at least would know of the exchange of cabins. Who then? Someone who knew Julia well enough to be aware of her lemon-and-water slimming fad, and who had made a note of the number of her cabin but had not realized that she had subsequently moved into Amanda's. Mrs Norman—— ? George Norman? Persis? Toby? No, it could not be! There must be some mistake. Julia must either have had a heart attack or committed suicide after all, and there must be some other explanation for that bottle. There *must* be!

Why, oh why, thought Amanda desperately, had she ever

offered to exchange cabins with Julia Blaine? But for that, no one need ever have suspected that there had been a murder. No one would ever have known. Yet because she had made that exchange, she knew — and someone else must suspect that she knew — that Julia's death was not suicide, but a carefully planned murder.

The sky was paling to the dawn, and the swish of hoses and a thump of holystones betokened the arrival of a new day before Amanda fell at last into an exhausted sleep, from which she was eventually awakened by a loud knocking on her door. Starting up with her heart in her mouth, she found the cabin full of reflected sunlight, and the stewardess demanding entrance with a lukewarm cup of tea.

In the gay morning sunlight Amanda could not remember for a moment why she should have been frightened. Her first impression was that she must have had a particularly vivid and unpleasant dream. But this was quickly dispelled by the stewardess, who on being admitted, announced with relish that the police were already on board and that the captain wished to see Miss Derington in his cabin as soon as possible.

Amanda was suddenly aware that the sea was no longer swishing past the ship and that the engines were silent.

'Have we arrived?'

'Half an hour or more ago,' said the stewardess. 'We're at Limassol. I would have woken you before, but the gentleman in number eleven said to let you sleep. *Such* a nice man! So thoughtful. It's not many that are these days. Shall I get you some breakfast, dear? You looked a bit peaked — an' no wonder.'

'No thank you,' said Amanda. 'Just coffee, if you would. What does the captain want to see me about?'

'I'm sure I don't know, dear. I expect they just want you to tell the police what happened last night — just as a matter of form as you might say — before they bury the poor lady. Very cut up her husband is. Looks like a ghost he does. As for the little lady in 31, she came over all queer when she heard the news. The dead lady

307

and her husband were going to stay with her. Fancy! Cousins or something. Very delicate she is — Mrs Norman, that is. The sensitive kind I should say. *Dreadfully* upset she was. "Why, Mrs Norman," I said—— '

A knock on the door mercifully stemmed the flow and Toby Gates' voice inquired anxiously if Amanda was all right and wasn't it ghastly?

Amanda replied in the affirmative to both, adding that she would be out in five minutes; and while the stewardess went in search of coffee she dressed hurriedly, plaiting her hair into two thick braids and pinning it swiftly about her head instead of coiling it into the heavy knot at the nape of her neck that took considerably more time and care to achieve.

The yellow cotton frock that she had worn on the previous day seemed too gay a garment in which to attend an inquiry into sudden death (she would not say the word 'murder' even to herself), and she rummaged hastily in her suitcase and found a silver-grey poplin with a narrow white belt. Gulping down the coffee that the stewardess had brought, she slipped her feet into white sandals and found Toby Gates waiting for her at the end of the passage.

'They want to see all of us,' said Toby, taking her arm and hurrying her up the stairs. 'Those of us who knew her. She must have had a brain-storm. I always thought she was a spot peculiar. Rotten for Alastair, poor devil; utter hell I should think.'

Amanda said anxiously: 'What do they want to see us for, Toby?'

'Oh, just to give them some sort of a picture of the whole thing I suppose. Matter of form an' all that. They've already had poor old Alastair answering questions for the odd half-hour or so. Jolly kick-off to a holiday for all of us, I must say!'

The ship was anchored near a town whose white-walled houses were set among green trees and the silver-grey of olives, against a backdrop of low, barren hills. The sun blazed down from a cloudless sky and glittered on the dancing water, and the blue shallow sea was streaked with bars of vivid emerald, clear cerulean and a soft, milky jade. There was an exhilaration and a sparkle in the air and once again Amanda found that it was impossible to believe that any of the events of the past night had really occurred, or that Julia Blaine was dead.

Toby said: 'Up this ladder. Left turn. Here we are.'

The captain's cabin appeared to be filled to overflowing. Besides the captain, the first officer, the doctor, purser and stewardess, there were three unidentified men in uniform, presumably police officers, one of whom, at least, was British. Alastair Blaine, the Normans and Persis Halliday were also present, and Steve Howard was standing at the far side of the room, leaning on the window-sill and looking out across the sunlit deck towards the little town of Limassol. He glanced round as Amanda and Toby Gates entered, but he did not speak and presently returned to his idle contemplation of the view.

Alastair Blaine was looking drawn and grey. He appeared to have aged ten years, and the merciless morning sunlight showed unexpected traces of silver among his thick blond hair.

Persis Halliday, looking, as ever, as if she had that moment been unpacked from an expensive bandbox, was sitting on the arm of a chintz-covered chair swinging one silken foot in a neat alligator shoe and fidgeting with an unlighted cigarette. She looked up as Amanda came in and said: ''Lo, honey. This is a pretty set up, I'll say! Did you sleep at all?'

Claire Norman said: 'Sleep? I am sure none of us did! How *could* we? Poor Julia! I shall never forgive myself. Never! Dancing, while she was dying . . .!'

Her voice was tragic and quivering and she had managed to find among her suitcases a deceptively simple and most becoming frock in black linen that made her appear smaller and whiter and more fragile than ever.

George Norman patted her shoulder with awkward tenderness

and Persis, turning to face her, said: 'So you knew about it last night? Now that's very interesting. I didn't get in on it until the stewardess spilt the beans this morning. How did you hear about it?'

For a brief moment two small patches of colour appeared in Claire Norman's ivory cheeks, and she was all at once very still; her grey eyes no longer limpid with tragedy but curiously alert and guarded. She did not answer Mrs Halliday's question and it was George Norman who broke the brief silence:

'We didn't hear until this morning,' he said. 'Claire was only speaking figuratively. She's a little upset.'

The rigidity went out of Claire Norman's small body. She did not contradict her husband's statement, and there was no further chance for conversation, for the captain, clearly impatient to be done with the whole affair, was introducing the police officers and hurrying on with the business in hand. This proved to be merely a repetition of last night's questions and answers, with the sole difference that four of the late Mrs Blaine's friends and acquaintances were also present, each of whom gave their individual opinion as to her state of nerves and mind.

Amanda was asked to repeat her story, and did so; making the same reservations that she had made the night before. Mrs Blaine, said Amanda, had been overwrought and hysterical. She felt the heat badly, had complained of the East and Army life in general and had talked of taking her own life. She had been holding some tablets in her hand — no, Amanda could not say how many — and had eventually swallowed them——

Amanda's voice wavered suddenly, and looking beyond the captain's shoulder she encountered Steve Howard's deceptively lazy gaze. He shook his head very slightly. It was only a fractional gesture but in the circumstances plainly readable. Amanda turned her eyes away and looked at the ring of silent faces — the red, impatient face of the captain; the avid gaze of the stewardess; the weary resignation on the face of the ship's doctor and the alert concentrated gaze of the three police officers — and closed her lips without mentioning the glass in her cabin. She did not look at Steven Howard again but she had the impression that he had relaxed.

The police were courteous and sympathetic and the captain only too eager to wash his hands of the lot of them, and after leaving their names and addresses and completing various other formalities, the passengers were hustled out of the cabin and told that they could now go ashore.

It was perhaps twenty minutes later that they descended the gangway and were rowed away from the ship over water so crystal clear that as they neared the shore every rock and pebble and shell on the sea floor was clearly visible, and they could see the shell markings on the back of a huge turtle that flippered its way lazily through the water beneath them.

There was a man waiting on the water steps by the quay; hatless and presumably British, since he wore a thin, well-cut and very English tweed coat. He was a slim man in the late thirties, of medium height and with a face so deeply tanned by sun and wind as to make his eyes and his crisp, sunbleached and slightly greying hair seem light by contrast. But despite its brownness it gave an impression of being pale under the tan. A paleness that gave a curious greyish tint to the shadows on his face. It was a thin, pleasant face that would have been handsome except that just now it looked desperately tired and was scored with lines of weariness and anxiety.

'There's Glenn,' said George Norman. 'Do you suppose he's—— ' He checked suddenly and coughed in an embarrassed manner. The prow grated upon stone and a moment later the passengers were on shore and Claire Norman was holding out a small white hand to the man in the tweed coat:

'Glenn. How nice to see you! I suppose you are here to meet Miss Derington. Or did you come to meet ... someone else?'

There was the faintest pause before the last two words, and Mr

Glennister Barton's pleasant tanned face flushed deeply and the muscles about his mouth tightened. Claire Norman said: 'Amanda, this is Glenn Barton. Your host in Cyprus.'

Amanda held out her hand and found herself looking into a pair of grey eyes that were unmistakably desperate and unhappy. And she was suddenly unreasonably angry with Mrs Norman, who had said something which, though meaningless to Amanda, had undoubtedly possessed a hidden and hurtful meaning for this pleasant, rather diffident man.

Glenn Barton barely touched her hand, was introduced to her companions and exchanged a few civilities. He inquired after her Uncle Oswin and, having taken charge of her luggage and seen her through the customs, led the way to a long grey saloon car that was parked near the customs' shed. Amanda had expected to see Mrs Barton, but there was no sign of any other woman, and Glenn Barton, having piled Amanda's suitcases on to the back seat held open the front door of the car for her.

Persis called out: 'See you in Kyrenia, honey!' and Toby Gates, looking like a spaniel puppy that is being left behind from a walk, said in an urgent undertone: 'You *will* let me come over and see you, won't you?'

Amanda glanced over his shoulder, but Steve Howard, his back to her, was leaning lazily against a pillar with his hands in his pockets, talking to Claire Norman. Amanda got into the car feeling unaccountably annoyed and said: 'Why, of course, Toby,' with unnecessary cordiality and emphasis, and a moment later Glenn Barton released the clutch and the car slid out of shadow into the bright sunlight of the road to Nicosia.

The countryside, once they had left the coast and the incredible sapphire, turquoise and jade of the shallow waters that fringed it, was bleached and colourless in the hot sun. The earth was brown and stony and dotted with small shrubs, and except for an occasional olive grove there was little green and almost no shade as the road wound and twisted through barren hills and past dried-up watercourses where the heat haze shimmered on the stones and boulders.

It was all new and strange and different to Amanda, and she might well have found it fascinating but for the fact that her host was strangely silent and was driving much too fast. She wondered if he were shy or if there was something in that seemingly innocent remark of Claire Norman's that had goaded him to this silence and speed? The big car was moving with dangerous velocity, shaving corners with a screech of tortured tyres and singing down the straight stretches of road with the speed of a steel-shafted arrow, while Amanda, who was not normally of a nervous disposition, found herself unconsciously clutching at the edge of her seat with rigid fingers and watching the flickering needle of the speedometer with fixed and apprehensive eyes.

She turned her head away with an effort and covertly studied her prospective host. He was sitting hunched forward a little, as a man will sit who steadies a nervous horse at the approach of a dangerous fence, and there was a look of nervous strain and tension in every line of his brown face and slim body. His hands were gripping the wheel so tightly that the knuckles stood out white against the tanned skin and there was a deep crease between his brows. Amanda thought that she had never seen anyone look so unhappy, and she looked away quickly, embarrassed and disturbed.

The needle of the speedometer wavered on ninety and she tightened her clutch on the seat, shut her eyes briefly and swallowed hard. Making a valiant effort she attempted a few polite observations on the scenery, to which Mr Barton returned equally polite but brief replies. The car whipped between an ox cart and a bus load of Cypriot peasants on their way to market, avoiding both by a hair's breadth; flashed past a string of camels on to a narrow bridge, and missed a small boy on a donkey by a matter of millimetres.

Amanda shut her eyes again and Mr Barton inquired if she had had a pleasant trip from Fayid.

'No,' said Amanda with feeling. 'It was perfectly beastly!' She found herself telling him about Julia Blaine's death, and Mr Barton expressed concern but no surprise.

Amanda said: 'Did you know about it then?'

'Yes. You see we ship a good bit of our wine from Limassol, so there are always several of our people on those boats or at the docks and most of them had heard. There was a lot of talk about it. The Blaines were over here for a couple of weeks last year, staying with Claire and George Norman. They're related I believe. I was away on business at the time so I didn't meet them myself, but my — wife knew them slightly.' He was silent for a moment or two and then said apologetically: 'Of course I had no idea that Mrs Blaine had died in your cabin, or I should not have asked such a stupid question. It must have been a most unpleasant experience. I'm sorry that you should have had such a horrible introduction to Cyprus. I wish I could do something to make up for it.'

He turned to look at her and his tired, unhappy face broke into a smile. It was an extraordinarily pleasant smile and Amanda found herself returning it with frank friendliness.

He's nice, she thought. But he's got something on his mind. He's tired and badgered and worried sick about something — and then he has to come and meet me and put me up and look after me!

She said quickly: 'It's very kind of you and your wife to have me to stay. I do hope it hasn't been an awful nuisance. I feel rather bad about it — inflicting myself on you like this. I don't imagine that Uncle Oswin gave you much choice, did he?'

'Well — no,' said Glenn Barton with a rueful smile and a return of the anxious crease between his brows. 'But—— '

He slowed the car down and said abruptly: 'Look, would you like something to eat? There's an inn just ahead. We could get some bread and cheese and olives and some goat's milk if you'd like it.'

'I'd love it!' said Amanda, suddenly remembering that she had had no breakfast. Mr Barton removed his foot from the

314

accelerator and brought the car to a stop before a small shabby building half hidden by trees.

The little inn consisted of one large room furnished with rough wooden chairs and tables and decorated with portraits of the King and Queen of the Hellenes, torn from some illustrated paper and tacked against the walls. The charming, elfin face of Fredricka smiled out from a wreath of green leaves, reminding Amanda that this was an island where many of the inhabitants resented the British occupation and were demanding union with Greece.

The room was crowded with black-haired, dark-eyed Cypriots and redolent with garlic and the spilled lees of wine, but the proprietress, a buxom red-cheeked woman who seemed to know Mr Barton well and addressed him in rapid Greek, found them a table and fetched coarse bread, grapes, figs and lumps of cheese made from goat's milk. At Mr Barton's request she added a bottle of some colourless liquid that appeared to be gin, a carafe of water and two glasses.

Amanda ate the simple food with relish and Glenn Barton poured a small portion of the liquid into each glass and added water, whereupon the mixture turned a cloudy white.

'What is it?' demanded Amanda, intrigued.

'*Ouzo*. The national drink. Do you see that old man over there by the door?' Amanda turned and observed an ancient and decrepit greybeard who appeared to be dozing comfortably in his chair. 'He's our hostess's husband. He used to be a tough upstanding chap when I first came to Cyprus, but he took to drinking his *ouzo* straight. If you drink enough of it it's supposed to send you off your head. But it's quite harmless in small quantities. Try it.'

Amanda picked up the nearest glass, sniffed at it and wrinkled her nose expressively. Glenn Barton laughed. 'It smells pretty pungent, doesn't it? Aniseed. Don't you like it?'

'No,' said Amanda frankly, 'I've always detested the smell of aniseed ever since my kindergarten days when there was a small

315

boy who used to sit next to me in class and suck aniseed balls. I hated him — and them.'

'It tastes better than it smells,' said Glenn Barton. He raised his glass to her. 'Here's to your first visit to Cyprus. May it be a very pleasant one.'

'Thank you,' said Amanda, and smiled at him.

Mr Barton drank and pushed away his glass. The frown was suddenly back in his forehead and Amanda saw that his hands were not quite steady and that there was a tinge of whiteness about his mouth. He offered her a cigarette, and when she refused, lit one himself and said in a jerky and difficult voice: 'I – I'm afraid that I – we – shall not be able to put you up after all. You see – my wife is not well, and I couldn't ask you to stay in the house while – while——'

He stopped and pushed his hands through his hair in a gesture that was somehow boyish and despairing.

'But of course you can't!' said Amanda, moved by a sudden warm feeling of compassion. 'Don't give it another thought — please. I'm terribly sorry to hear about your wife. Are you sure that there is nothing I can do to help?'

'No, nothing,' said Glenn Barton wretchedly. 'It's very good of you to take it like this. I feel pretty terrible about it — saying that we'd put you up, and then letting you get here and failing you like this.'

'Nonsense!' said Amanda cheerfully. 'It doesn't matter a bit. I can easily go to a hotel.'

'Oh no. I couldn't let you do that!' Glenn Barton lifted his eyes from the table and looked at her earnestly. 'I've arranged all that. A friend of mind in Kyrenia, a Miss Moon, is going to put you up instead. She's a bit eccentric, but very kind. I know you'll like her.'

'But I can't go sponging on your friends,' said Amanda dismayed. 'It was quite bad enough Uncle Oswin pushing me on to you like this, but——'

'Please!' interrupted Glenn Barton with a twisted smile. 'You're being kind and letting me down gently, but I'd be very grateful if you'd add to your kindness by agreeing to stay with Miss Moon. I'd feel much better about it. Besides, she's expecting you. She's a dear and is delighted at the idea of having you. She likes young people — specially pretty ones.'

His smile pointed the compliment and Amanda laughed and capitulated. She had been disappointed at the prospect of staying in Nicosia instead of on the coast, and Persis and Toby would be in Kyrenia. She would have preferred to be independent and stay at a hotel, but she could hardly treat Mr Barton's arrangements in a cavalier fashion.

Mr Barton said: 'Then that's fixed. We'll have to stop in at the office in Nicosia just for a minute or two I'm afraid, but we should be in Kyrenia in time for lunch. If you really won't try the *ouzo* we'd better be getting along.'

5

The buxom proprietress of the inn presented the bill and embarked on an animated conversation with Mr Barton that, judging from her laughing glance, referred to Amanda.

'What is she saying?' asked Amanda.

'She was asking where you'd come from, and she says that you are a very beautiful young lady and wishes to know if you can sit on your hair when it is unbound,' said Glenn Barton with a smile.

Amanda laughed. 'Tell her, only just!'

'You come on *Orantares*, yes? From Port Said?' said the woman in halting English. 'My man too. Is fine ship.'

She smiled broadly at Amanda, swept up the handful of small coins that Mr Barton had counted out onto the table, and hurried away to deal with an impatient patron.

'Are all the people here as friendly and cheerful as that?' asked Amanda.

'A good many of them. Why? You sound surprised.'

'I suppose I am,' admitted Amanda. 'The only things that ever get into the papers about Cyprus are articles about how discontented they are with the whole set-up.'

Glenn Barton smiled and said: 'I think you'll find them cheerful enough.'

He dropped the end of his cigarette into Amanda's glass, where it hissed out and disintegrated slowly, and sat watching it abstractedly for a moment or two with his own face anything but cheerful. Presently he gave a sharp sigh and stood up.

'Let's go, shall we?'

They walked out into the bright sunlight to the car and continued their journey towards Nicosia; but at a less dangerous speed. The interlude at the inn appeared to have lessened Glenn Barton's nervous tension, and he was more talkative and at ease; but he did not refer again to his wife's illness and it was obvious that he did not wish to discuss it.

Amanda found herself wondering what Mrs Barton was like, and if she would meet her — and passed from that to wondering whether she would meet Steven Howard again, and why it should be a matter of concern to her whether she did or not? Mr Howard had been brusque and arbitrary and rude, and had had the incredible effrontery to hint that she might have planned the murder of Julia Blaine as the result of an intrigue with Julia's husband Alastair. True, he had said nothing to suggest that he himself believed it. But that such an idea could even enter his head, infuriated and frightened her. She ought by rights to be thankful that she need have no more to do with him and could put him out of her mind and forget him.

But she found that she could not stop thinking about him. Who was he? Why had he been on the *Orantares*? What had he been doing in Fayid and who was it that he had followed to Cyprus?

The road twisted downwards through the sun-bleached hills and ran out upon the wide, flat, dusty central plain of Cyprus, and it was midday by the time they came in sight of the green trees, jostling rooftops, Byzantine churches and Gothic mosques of Nicosia.

The heat danced in the narrow, crowded streets; on minarets and domes and fretted balconies, the concrete walls and roofs of innumerable newly built suburban-style houses, petrol pumps, jeeps, Army lorries and creaking carts drawn by oxen.

Presently the car turned in between white-washed gateposts shaded by flamboyants and oleanders, and drew up before a small bungalow.

319

'This is our Nicosia office,' explained Glenn Barton. 'Would you like to come in? I won't be more than a few minutes.'

The office walls were bare and white-washed. There was coarse matting on the floor, and green wooden jalousies over the windows kept out the midday heat and made the rooms cool and dim. A woman who had been seated at a littered desk rose quickly as they entered and Glenn Barton said: 'This is Miss Ford — my secretary. Monica, this is Miss Derington.'

Miss Ford was plain, solidly built and verging on middle age. She had slightly protruding teeth and her hair — of that indeterminate shade that is usually described as 'mouse' — was drawn loosely back from her forehead and confined in a small hard bun at the nape of her neck.

Glenn Barton said: 'I didn't think you'd be here today, Monica. Sure you're all right? You needn't have come you know.' There was concern in his voice and he put a hand on the thick shoulder and pressed it affectionately, and turning to Amanda said: 'Monica's not only my secretary. She's my right hand — and my left one! I don't know what I'd do without her. She practically runs the business.'

Miss Ford's sallow face flushed with pleasure and for a moment she looked almost girlish. 'That's nonsense, of course,' she said to Amanda. 'Glenn works far too hard. I'm always telling him that he'll have a breakdown if he doesn't let up a bit. How is your uncle, Miss Derington? I haven't seen him for over a year. He got me this post you know. I used to work in his London office.'

'Uncle Oswin is fine,' said Amanda. 'He's ramping round the Middle East putting the fear of Derington into Deringtons, which is his idea of bliss.'

Glenn Barton laughed. 'Then we can consider ourselves very lucky that he has sent us such a charming representative instead of paying us a personal visit.'

'Oh, I'm not a representative,' said Amanda, smiling back at him. 'I'm merely having a holiday on my own. Uncle Oswin would have come himself if he could have fitted it in, but he couldn't, and once he's worked out a programme nothing will induce him to alter it by an hour — let alone a day. So he decided that you would have to get along without a personal pep-talk for another year or so.'

'It's a pity he couldn't come,' said Glenn Barton with a sigh. 'We have a lot of problems to contend with that I don't think your uncle fully understands. They lose a lot of force when they are reduced to official reports, but a few days on the ground would have brought them home to him. Perhaps you could persuade him to come over on his way back?'

'I'm afraid not,' said Amanda lightly. 'He'll be in Kenya now, and he flies to Tripoli for a few days this week-end, and goes back to London from there for a conference. I don't believe he'd alter a schedule for the H Bomb. That is, not unless you could think up something that would really lure him; like flagrant immorality among the staff! Uncle Oswin is very hot on the Purity of Deringtons. It's his hobby.'

Amanda laughed, but there was no answering smile on the faces of her two companions. It was, on the contrary, instantly and painfully obvious that she had made an exceedingly tactless remark, for once again there was a white line about Glenn Barton's mouth while Miss Ford's sallow face had flushed a dull and unbecoming shade of red.

There was a brief uncomfortable silence and then Miss Ford turned hurriedly to Mr Barton:

'Kostos is here, Glenn. He arrived just before you did. I don't know why he didn't see you in Limassol and save himself the journey. These people never think.'

'He couldn't,' said Mr Barton. 'They had a bit of trouble on the ship. One of the passengers died, and things got a bit held up. I'll see him now. Will you look after Miss Derington?'

'Yes, of course. Wouldn't you like a wash, Miss Derington? I — I know how dusty that road is. And what about some orange juice or sherry or something? Or there's some iced coffee if you'd prefer that? Glenn will be here about ten or fifteen minutes; there are some invoices he'll have to look at.'

'Iced coffee sounds wonderful,' said Amanda gratefully. 'And so does a wash. I'm stiff with dust and parched with thirst.'

Glenn Barton said: 'I'll be as quick as I can,' and Monica Ford led Amanda away. 'Come on to the verandah when you're ready,' she said. 'It's through that door over there. I'll have the coffee ready for you.'

The verandah was wide and shady but it seemed intolerably bright after the cool dimness of the shuttered rooms. Monica Ford had set out two chairs and was pouring out iced coffee from a frosted jug.

'Lovely!' said Amanda, drinking thirstily. 'I needed that!'

She smiled gratefully at Miss Ford and noticed that in the full light of the verandah the sallow, sensible face looked older, and somewhat ill. There were dark shadows under Miss Ford's eyes that the wide pink plastic rims of her glasses failed to hide, and Amanda suspected that she had been crying. The square, plain face with its pale blue eyes, sandy lashes and entire absence of make-up, looked sensible and efficient. An impression that was somewhat belied by Miss Ford's choice of costume, for she wore a gaily coloured and full-skirted cotton frock which did nothing to improve either her thick waist or her unadorned complexion. To this she had added as a final incongruous touch a necklace and ear-rings of large plastic flowers and a liberal application of some cheap scent that smelt like violet hair oil.

Amanda suspected that the ear-rings at least were a recent and unusual adornment, for Monica Ford could not keep her hands from them. She kept touching them while she talked, as though they worried her; loosening the screws and tightening them again; her strong, square-fingered, sensible hands with their short un-varnished nails providing a sharp contrast to the glittering trans-parent petals of the plastic flowers.

She had arrived in Cyprus less than a year ago, she told Amanda, at the instigation of Mr Oswin Derington in whose office she had previously worked for over five years: 'He thought that Mr Barton needed someone to help him,' explained Miss Ford. 'Things were not going so well at first, and these little local typists are often worse than useless. There was a great deal of work. You've no idea what Glenn has had to contend with. Labour troubles and customs troubles and local prejudice, and no one to give him any help or encouragement. It's been an uphill fight. He ought to go on leave, but he won't. He works himself until he drops. He doesn't know how to spare himself. Some men are like that — Bobby was like that too ...'

Her voice suddenly broke and stopped and Amanda saw to her horror that the pale eyes had filled with tears.

Miss Ford fumbled in one of the large pockets that ornamented her skirt and producing a damp handkerchief blew her nose fiercely. 'Do forgive me. I – I'm not quite myself today. I – Hay fever you know—— '

'How horrid for you,' said Amanda politely. 'But I'm not surprised, with all these gorgeous flowers around.'

'They are lovely, aren't they?' said Miss Ford recovering herself. 'It's odd to think that I didn't want to come out to Cyprus at all.'

'Then you like it here?'

'Oh *yes!*' said Monica Ford clasping her hands together in a sudden convulsive gesture. 'It's – it's a beautiful island. I couldn't bear to leave! I won't leave! – I *won't* – I—— '

She stopped abruptly and the colour flamed up into her sallow cheeks. There was a brief embarrassed pause and Amanda said sympathetically: 'I suppose Uncle Oswin is trying to drag you back to London or Liverpool or somewhere? He is an old bully, isn't he? Pay no attention to him! I was scared stiff of him for years and then one day I suddenly realized that I wasn't a schoolgirl any longer, and I staged a token strike and got away with it. All you've got to do is to stand up to him '

323

Monica Ford smiled uncertainly and said: 'Have some more coffee?'

'I'd love some.' Amanda held out her glass and said: 'I'm sorry to hear that Mrs Barton is ill. What's the matter with her? I didn't like to ask her husband; he seemed rather upset about it. Is she really bad?'

Inexplicably the hot colour deepened in Monica Ford's plain face and she fumbled with the jug so that the coffee spilt in a pale brown stream down the skirt of her gaily patterned cotton frock. She sprang up hurriedly, her face crimson, and said in a muffled voice: 'Oh dear! — and it stains so! Excuse me just a minute—— ' and fled.

Amanda looked after her in considerable surprise. What *was* the matter with Mrs Barton? Had she perhaps gone off her head? Or contracted some illness like poliomyelitis that the authorities wished to hush up for fear of creating a panic? It was all rather mysterious and Amanda was suddenly intensely sorry for Glenn Barton. What with work and worry, a wife who was ill — or worse — and a secretary who was quite obviously suffering from nerves (Amanda did not believe the hay fever story) her own arrival at this juncture must have seemed to him like the proverbial last straw.

A door at the far end of the verandah opened and Mr Barton himself walked quickly towards her.

'I'm sorry to have kept you waiting. I hope that Monica kept you entertained. Where is she?'

'She spilt some coffee down her frock and she's gone to mop it off,' said Amanda, rising. 'I don't think she's feeling very well.'

A shadow crossed Glenn Barton's pleasant face and he glanced towards the door and lowered his voice:

'I know. Poor Monica. She's had a ghastly shock, but she's taking it splendidly. She's got lots of guts. She only heard yesterday that her brother was shot by Mau Mau terrorists in Kenya. He had a farm out there, and they attacked the place and wiped

324

it out. He was all the family she had. There don't seem to be any other relations, and she was devoted to him.'

'I *am* sorry!' said Amanda, smitten. 'How dreadful for her. No wonder she seemed so upset.'

She turned to look out across the sun-drenched garden with its blaze of flowers, and all at once, in that hot, quiet verandah, she shivered as though she were cold.

'What is it?' asked Glenn Barton, his voice suddenly gentle.

'Nothing. I – I was only thinking that – that it's such a lovely day, and it doesn't seem possible that awful, tragic things can happen to people. And yet they do. To ordinary, nice people like Alastair Blaine — and Miss Ford—— '

'I shouldn't have told you about it,' said Glenn Barton contritely. 'I'm sorry. You've had quite enough to upset you already. Tragedy is not for the young. Forget it and enjoy yourself. It *is* a lovely day!'

He held out a hand to her: 'Come on, or you will be late for luncheon and Miss Moon will never forgive me.'

6

The road from Nicosia to Kyrenia runs for a few miles across the plain and then begins to climb the long narrow barrier of the Kyrenia range that forms a rampart between the plain and the north coast of the Island.

The car topped the pass and began to descend, swinging and turning to the curves of the winding road, and there below them lay the sea — an impossible cerulean blue streaked with sapphire and viridian, with the white, beautiful coastline fading away into the heat haze until sky and sea and coast seemed to merge and melt into one.

Olive groves, the tree trunks so gnarled and twisted with age that some of them must surely have seen the Crusaders come and go, stood dark against the glittering expanse of blue, and below them the little white town of Kyrenia lay basking in the noonday sun like a handful of pearls and white pebbles washed up by the sea.

They drove down a long road that wound and curved between olive, carob, cypress, mulberry and mountain fir, and which finally ran straight from the foot of the hills to the sea.

A quarter of a mile short of the harbour the car turned off into a side road and drew up before a large, square, two-storeyed house that was separated from the road by a white wall, a line of cypress trees and a tangle of oleanders.

'Here we are,' said Glenn Barton. 'This is the Villa Oleander. Andreas will bring in your suitcases.'

The house was high and old, weather-worn and beautiful. Its walls had been colour-washed a flaking and discoloured pink that

326

had bleached to a warm, uneven shade of apricot, and the wrought-iron balconies and wooden shutters at the windows were a soft, faded, dusty emerald green. The roof tiles had probably come from the South of France, for they were not red, but a deep beautiful pink, each one curved and marked with the outline of a heart.

A short, flagged walk and six shallow stone steps led up to a massive front door whose heavy bronze knocker was green with age, and the garden was a neglected tangle of orange and lemon trees, figs, plum trees, oleanders, roses, and cascades of yellow and white jasmine. A vine grew along the wrought-iron of a balcony to the right of the front door, and water trickled from the mouth of a bronze dolphin into a deep pool full of lily pads and reeds; the sound of its fall providing a tinkling counterpoint to the cooing of pigeons from among the warm shadows of a gnarled olive tree.

Amanda stood with her hands on the gate and looked about her with a feeling of awe. It was all so right. So exactly right — the quintessence of serenity and enchantment.

Glenn Barton, watching her, said a little anxiously: 'I'm afraid it's a bit neglected. But Miss Moon says that she can't be bothered with keeping up the garden and that she likes it like this.'

'So do I,' said Amanda on a breath of rapture. 'It's beautiful! It's just exactly like a picture I've always had in my mind of what a house on a Mediterranean island should look like, but I've always been afraid that it wouldn't. It's like a dream!'

Glenn Barton looked relieved but uncomprehending, and it was obvious that he himself saw little to admire in the shabby house and neglected overgrown garden. He led the way up the short flight of stone steps to the front door and banged on the knocker. There was a sound of quick footsteps and the door swung open on well-oiled hinges to show a stout black-eyed woman who wore a voluminous and rather dirty apron and a brightly coloured cotton handkerchief tied over her abundant greying hair.

'Ah! Kyrie Barton! Kalossorisis. Ti habaria. Kopiase messa!'

327

'This is Euridice,' said Glenn Barton turning to Amanda. 'She's the cook and housekeeper and housemaid and everything rolled into one.'

Amanda smiled at her, and the woman beamed back and breaking into a flood of unintelligible speech, led the way across a wide hall into a large dim drawing-room full of old, beautiful furniture and dusty curio cabinets, where the shutters had been closed against the hot sunlight.

'Can't she speak English?' whispered Amanda apprehensively.

'Quite a lot. You'll find that she speaks enough to manage on. But Miss Moon has always refused flatly to speak to her in Greek, so Euridice, who has been with her for over thirty years, refuses to admit to any English. It's a point of honour with both of them.'

'How do they manage?'

'They both speak to each other very slowly and at the tops of their voices in their own languages. Here, I think, is your hostess——'

High heels clicked rapidly on the hall staircase: there was a jingle of jewellery and a strong scent of heliotrope, and Miss Moon was with them.

Miss Moon was small and bony and birdlike, and somehow managed to suggest a homely British sparrow that has gone to a fancy dress ball dressed as a peacock. Her thin hair, which she had thought fit to dye an improbable shade of scarlet, was dressed in innumerable frizzy curls and decorated with a bow of violet gauze. Her dress, also in shades of violet and mauve, was of the type known to an earlier generation as a 'tea gown', and she had confined it at the waist by a wide belt of silver filigree adorned by an enamel buckle in a design of irises. She wore a number of necklaces and bracelets of silver filigree, amethysts and opals, and a pair of amethyst ear-rings of rococo splendour.

'Glenn! Dear boy. How it warms me to see you! And this is Amanda? Let me look at you, child. Beautiful! You refresh my eyes. How *good* of you to come and stay with me. So few young people care to do a kindness to the old these days, alas! It will be delightful to have you in the house. Quite delightful — it needs cheering up, and so do I. You are looking at my dress. Not *quite* the thing to welcome a guest in. It should have been pink for that. Pink for joy! But it's Tuesday you know, and so it had to be mauve. I always wear mauve on Tuesdays. Monday is my pink day. I do so resent it when people speak of *black* Monday. Why, Monday is a new start! A fresh week — anything might happen! And so, of course, I always wear pink. In welcome. I think that colours are *so* important, do not you? But here I am keeping you talking when you must be quite famished! Glenn, dear boy, will you not change your mind and stay to luncheon?'

'I'm afraid I can't. Nothing I would have liked better, but I have to meet Gavriledes at the Dome. He's giving me lunch and we can get through our business at the same time.'

'Oh dear. How disappointing. You know, of course, that Lumley Potter has taken the top floor of one of the houses on the harbour, don't you? He arrives today.'

'Potter — who told you?' Glenn Barton's face was suddenly white.

'So you did *not* know! I think Anita should have told you. So awkward if you met. Lady Cooper-Foot told me. The flat — if you can call it that — belongs to her cook's second cousin. Mr Potter intends to set up a studio.'

'But – but I thought he was staying on in Famagusta.'

'He wishes to paint in Kyrenia. Famagusta has not enough spiritual essence. I could have told him that.'

Glenn Barton's eyes were wide and blank. He turned to Amanda as though he were about to say something, and checked. After a moment he said instead, in an uncertain, rather formal voice: 'I must go now, I hope to see you again soon. If you are by any chance writing to your uncle, let me have the letter and I will see that it is sent with the office mail. It will go quicker that way. I will see that someone calls every day in case you should want to send anything. I am sure Miss Moon will look after you well. I won't say good-bye. Only *au revoir*.'

He took Miss Moon's withered, be-ringed hand and kissed it in an affectionate gesture that was entirely without affectation, and went quickly away.

Miss Moon drew a gusty sigh. 'Poor boy! How that woman *can*—— But I must not stay gossiping here all day, must I? I will show you your room. Andreas will have taken up your luggage. And then we will have luncheon and hear all about each other. So stimulating!'

She led the way back through the high, dark hall and up a wide, shallow stepped staircase. 'This is the bathroom, dear, and there is a lavatory. That is my room, and here is yours——'

She opened a door and Amanda found herself in a large, high-ceilinged room that was painted a soft green and carpeted with coarse matting. There were flowers in tall jars and the furniture, like that in the drawing-room, was old and beautiful and dusty from neglect. A portrait of a girl in a green satin dress of the Restoration period hung on one wall, while on another a vast silvery looking glass, spotted with age and wreathed with garlands, ribbons and cupids of tarnished gilt, hung above a small painted French bureau that served as a dressing-table. A graceful Venetian glass chandelier, not entirely innocent of cobwebs, hung from the ceiling, and only the bed struck an incongruous note. It was a narrow cheap iron bedstead that supported, on four poles of varying size that had been lashed to it with string, a somewhat darned mosquito net. The shutters were closed against the heat of the day and the room was dim and green and smelt of lilies and syringa, dry rot and dust.

Amanda turned to her hostess with shining eyes:

'It is so good of you to have me. This is the most *beautiful* house!'

'Oh, I *am* so glad that you should feel like that!' said Miss Moon, suddenly embracing her. 'I knew the moment I saw you that you were *right*, and that the house would like you. So many people are wrong. Such a pity! It is indeed beautiful — the whole island. I came here with dear Papa forty-three years ago. That is a very long time, is it not? I cannot have been much older than you are now. He died here, and I meant to go back to Norfolk. But somehow I never did. I had walked through the looking-glass like Alice, and I could not get back. The enchantment had got me. I bought this house and I have been here ever since. And when I die I shall be buried among the lemon trees and the oleanders in the garden. I have it all arranged. Ah, Kyrenia——! The very name sings, does it not? Like a warm wind through the olive trees. How delightful that you should feel it too. Are you ready, dear? Euridice will be waiting to serve luncheon.'

The dining-room looked out across a froth of lemon trees to an old stone wall with deep, arched embrasures, crumbling into ruin, in which fantailed pigeons strutted and cooed, and the meal began with fruit. Purple and green figs, melons, oranges, grapes, and tiny plums like balls of blue velvet: ice-cold and piled in careless, colourful profusion on shallow dishes of Venetian glass. There were tall green glasses flecked with gold, also Venetian, into one of which Miss Moon poured a white wine of local manufacture:

'It is quite harmless, dear. A child could drink it. Glenn lets me have it. The firm exports it in bottles, but bottling seems to spoil the flavour, and it is never so good afterwards. This is straight from the cask, and really very pleasant. Or so I am told. I myself never take anything but barley water. Euridice makes it for me after breakfast, fresh every day.'

Amanda said: 'You know, I think I am going to be very grateful to Mrs Barton for being ill.'

'Ill?' said Miss Moon sharply. 'Who told you that she was ill?'

'Mr Barton. That's why I'm here. I was to have stayed with the Bartons in Nicosia. My uncle arranged it. But they couldn't have me after all because Mrs Barton was ill. Didn't he tell you?'

'Yes he did, now that you mention it, dear. But I never thought that he would really do it. Pretend that she was ill, I mean. So *much* better to stick to the truth, however unpleasant. I cannot see why Glenn should try and shield his wife at his own expense. He did ask me not to tell you, but now that they will actually be here in Kyrenia of course you are bound to find out.'

'Find out what?' inquired Amanda, puzzled. 'Isn't Mrs Barton ill?'

'She most certainly is not!' said Miss Moon with an indignant clash of bracelets. 'On the contrary, it is her poor husband who appears to be heading for a nervous breakdown. I cannot understand it — she seemed such a nice girl. But in my young days there was a good old-fashioned word for people who behaved as Anita Barton is behaving. We called them trollops.'

'Anita?' — the name struck a sudden chord of memory.

'That is her name,' said Miss Moon, and sighed. 'I should never have thought it of her. But I suppose that she found Glenn dull. He has been sadly overworked. And she is so good looking. Perhaps she felt the need for more excitement and attention and admiration than he could offer. No, she is not ill. She has merely left Glenn and run away with a painting person who calls himself Lumley Potter. She has not even left the Island. They are living together quite brazenly, and she has attempted to justify her flagrantly immoral behaviour by spreading scandal about her husband and his secretary, Miss Ford.

'*Oh!*' gasped Amanda, her eyes wide with horrified dismay. 'So *that* was why——' She was remembering her light-hearted remark of that morning on the subject of Uncle Oswin and flagrant immorality. Could they possibly have imagined that she had said anything so cruel and unkind on purpose? A hot wave of colour mounted to her cheeks at the very thought.

'What is it, dear?'

'Nothing,' said Amanda hastily. 'I was just thinking of – of something I said to Miss Ford.'

'You have met her then?'

'Yes. We stopped at the office on our way through Nicosia.'

'Then you will know what I mean when I say that Anita must have taken leave of her senses. If she felt that it was necessary to slander Glenn in order to justify her own quite unjustifiable behaviour, she should have picked on a more plausible story. Monica Ford is a nice, sensible woman and a most efficient secretary — and she worships Glenn. But speaking entirely without malice, she possesses no feminine charm whatsoever. There are plenty of pretty girls in Cyprus, and if that was what Glenn Barton was after he could have taken his pick. But Monica Ford——!'

Amanda was suddenly reminded of Julia Blaine and her equally senseless suspicions, but she pushed the thought quickly from her, and said lightly: 'She isn't exactly glamorous.'

'Glamorous! The poor girl is *Plain!* If she had even been ugly she might have stood more chance. Ugliness is at least arresting. The trouble with Glenn Barton is that he is too *soft.* You need to be hard if you marry a girl like Anita — as hard or harder than she is. She has accused him of carrying on with all sorts of people. Claire Norman for one. I would put nothing past Claire, and I am well aware that she cast a handkerchief in Glenn's direction — oh very discreetly of course; Claire is always discreet — and that she is not likely to forgive him for not picking it up. Dear me! What a lot of scandal I have been talking. *So* stimulating! You know, dear, there are a great many people — women of course — who will assure you that they *never* gossip, and that in fact they detest and abominate gossip. It is hardly ever true (the ones who say that are *always* the worst I find!) but if it *were* true, what a lot they must miss! Just think how much we should *all* have missed if people like Somerset Maugham had refused to listen to gossip? What would you like to do this afternoon, dear?'

'Sleep,' said Amanda promptly. 'I know that sounds very dull of me, but I feel as if I could sleep for hours. So much has happened, and – and I didn't get much sleep last night.'

'Not a rough crossing, I hope?'

333

'No,' said Amanda slowly; and for the third time that day told, with reservations, the story of Julia.

'You poor, *poor* child!' exclaimed Miss Moon in horrified sympathy. 'But how terrible! How too shocking. How fortunate that it should be a Tuesday. I should never have forgiven myself if I had been wearing orange or yellow when you arrived. So upsetting for you. Blue perhaps — blue is so soothing. But *not* orange. Certainly you must sleep. So sensible.'

She accompanied Amanda to her room at the conclusion of the meal. 'Just come down whenever you wake up,' urged Miss Moon. 'We pay no attention to the clock in this house. Time is our servant here, Amanda. We are not the servants of Time. *Amanda!* such a pretty name. So unusual. Amanda — "worthy to be loved".'

Amanda said abruptly, following a sudden train of thought: 'Did you ever hear of anyone called Amarantha?'

'Now I wonder who has been calling you that!' said Miss Moon, beaming. 'A man, of course. And one with a very pretty taste in compliments. Not Glennister Barton; he is *lamentably* unread. Amarantha was the subject of a charming poem by a cavalier named Richard Lovelace. He addressed some verses *To Amarantha, that she would dishevel her hair.* I am not sure that I remember them aright. My memory is *not* what it was, alas. Let me see — "*Amarantha sweet and fair, braid no more that shining hair. As my curious hand or eye hovering round thee, let it fly*—— " something like that. Ah, I see that you are blushing! *Such* a charming accomplishment. You must tell me all about him when you wake up.'

Miss Moon withdrew, leaving behind her a scent of heliotrope to mingle with that of the lilies, the syringa, the dry rot and the dust. And Amanda, barely pausing to remove her dress and kick off her shoes, wriggled in under the mosquito net and was instantly and deeply asleep.

7

Amanda had awakened too late to be able to see anything of Kyrenia that day, but shortly after breakfast on the following morning Toby Gates called at the Villa Oleander.

'I heard you were here,' he told Amanda. 'Mrs Norman told us. They asked us all to dinner at their house last night; those of us who were on the boat; and she'd heard that you were staying here. We came here from Limassol in their car. The hotel had a car laid on for us, but a jeep ran into it just outside Nicosia, so we all piled into the Normans' car.'

'Who's "we"?' asked Amanda, sniffing ecstatically at a foaming torrent of jasmine that tumbled over the edge of the verandah rail outside the french windows of the drawing-room.

'Claire and Persis and Howard and myself. Claire — Mrs Norman — said that she was sure you wouldn't be staying at the Bartons' house, because Mrs Barton has run off with that painter chap and you couldn't very well stay in the house with just Barton there. Funny that we should have seen them on the boat.'

So Steve Howard was staying in Kyrenia! Amanda said quickly: 'What happened to Mr Norman? Or did he have to come by bus?'

'Oh he stayed behind to help out Alastair Blaine. They didn't get in until late last night. I gather the body was taken to a hospital in Nicosia for a post-mortem, and he'll have to go over there this afternoon for some sort of an inquest. But they had the funeral yesterday evening.'

'So soon?' said Amanda, startled and distressed. Somehow, although she could have not explained why, Julia had not seemed

335

really dead until this moment. Now that she was buried — hidden under six feet of foreign soil in an alien country — the fact and the finality of her death came home to Amanda with a renewed sense of shock.

'It's a hot country,' said Toby uncomfortably. 'You have to bury people pretty quickly in this sort of climate.'

'What is he going to do? Alastair, I mean.'

'He's staying on with the Normans. No point in his doing anything else, really. He and Norman got in about ten o'clock and he went straight off to bed. Claire met Barton in the town yesterday afternoon and he told her you were here, so we rang up to ask you to join us, but the Moon woman said that you were asleep, and she wouldn't wake you. I say——' Toby sank his voice to a conspiratorial whisper — 'she's a bit peculiar, isn't she? She told me that I shouldn't be wearing a blue shirt because it was Wednesday. Do you suppose she's all there?'

'She's not dangerous, if that's what you mean,' said Amanda laughing. 'She just has a theory about wearing different colours on different days. If you'd turned up in cerise you'd have been dead right.'

Toby looked relieved. 'Oh I see. I thought the old girl was bats. She asked me if I had called to see Aramathea — sounded rather Biblical to me — must be one of her servant girls I suppose. I said no, as a matter of fact I'd called to see Miss Derington, and she said "Ah, I thought not. You do not look at all the sort of man who could quote loveless to the point." I began to think I'd got into the local looney bin. What on *earth* do you suppose she meant?'

'I haven't an idea,' said Amanda shamelessly.

'By the way,' said Toby diffidently, 'I – er – asked her if she'd mind if I took you out to luncheon and she said not at all. So would you come? It's not really just me — I wish it were — I mean, we arranged last night to have luncheon together at the Dome. Claire — Mrs Norman — thought it would cheer Alastair up, and it's

336

their cook's day off. I said I'd like to ask you along too, and——
You will come, won't you?'

'I'd love to.'

'That's marvellous,' said Toby enthusiastically. 'Let's go now!'

'It isn't ten yet,' pointed out Amanda, 'and there are lots of things I want to do this morning. I want to prowl around and explore.'

'I'll come with you. I must get hold of a car. Howard's hired one. A pound a day and you drive yourself; something like that. You know he's really an astonishingly good type, for an artist.'

'What do you mean — for an artist?' demanded Amanda, unaccountably annoyed.

'Oh I don't know. So many of them look like that bearded blighter in sandals; the one Barton's wife ran away with. Well I mean to say! if you're any good, surely you don't have to go about practically in fancy dress just to show what you are?'

'Nonsense!' said Amanda briskly. 'Look at you when you're on duty. You wear a weird khaki outfit with pips here and badges there and a peculiar hat with feathers that would make a man laugh his head off if he saw his wife wearing it. If you can go around in fancy dress just to show what you are, why can't he? It's the same idea. Which reminds me — wait while I get a sun-hat and I'll be with you!'

They spent the morning exploring Kyrenia, and towards twelve o'clock came down to the little harbour where the pastel-coloured houses, the ancient, glowing walls of Kyrenia castle, the minaret of a mosque and the white walls of the Greek Orthodox Church reflect themselves in the clear, luminous greens and blues of the harbour water and look as though they had been designed by an inspired artist as a Mediterranean mural.

A voice hailed Amanda from one of the small tables outside a café on the quay, and there was Persis, as decorative as the morning.

'Hi there, honey! I hear you're parked right here in Kyrenia after all? Nice work. I thought nothing of Nicosia from what little we saw of it. Nothing *at* all. Now this! — this is quite a town, and I shall write a romance that will go into half a dozen editions in as many months. Why, it's just made for love! I must get me a beau.'

'Won't your imagination do?' inquired Toby solicitously.

'No, honey. My imagination is Grade A plus, but when it comes to Love, I like 'em over six foot and solid.'

'What about me?' offered Toby.

'That's just sweet of you, honey, but I prefer my beaus to keep both eyes on their work; and if you watch Amanda over my shoulder I can't see myself getting really in the mood. Still, there's a lot of talent lying around; as well as some pretty stiff competition.'

'Meaning me?' inquired Amanda showing her dimples.

'Of course, honey. Who else? Though to tell you the truth I was casting a mental eye over Mrs Norman. That gal is a smooth worker. I am no amateur myself, and Lord knows I count my calories. But when she's around I feel just a shade like Sophie Tucker's twin sister; and say what you like, that is lowering to the morale. Besides, she has the edge on outside operators. It's her own ground and it kinda looks as though she's worked it well. Remember that guy with the beard and an outfit like sunset in technicolor?'

'Lumley Potter,' said Amanda, recognizing the description.

'That's the boy. The one who beat it with your pal Barton's ball and chain. Well, who do you suppose was whispering to him on the boat deck at two o'clock in the morning the other night? Lil' Claire, no less.'

Toby said sharply: 'That's impossible! I mean — how can you know?'

'How? By using my great big eyes, Grandma. That two-by-four cabin of mine was as hot as Broadway in a heatwave, and I slid out for a breath of air. I passed No. 31 — that was the Normans' cabin — on my way. George was snoring fit to shift the deck plates and I spared a sympathetic sigh for his life partner. I need not have wasted my sympathy. The little woman was on the boat deck — taking, we must suppose, an intelligent interest in Art. She's quite a gal!'

'But he's run off with Barton's wife!' said Toby indignantly.

'Maybe the guy's a Mormon.'

Amanda said slowly: 'So *that's* how she knew——'

'About Julia? I guess so. The Potter had probably gotten the dirt from the first officer or the doctor or someone by that time. I imagine that there must have been quite a ruckus going on about it, and most of those who were out and about probably got an ear full. Yes, little Claire is certainly stiff competition. I shall have to brush up on my technique.'

'Who are you thinking of starting on?' inquired Toby, interested.

'Well there's always Major Blaine; and though it may be bad taste to pursue a bereaved widower, we heard plenty last night from his hostess about not letting the poor boy mope, so I guess I may as well try my hand at a little light consolation. And then there's Steve Howard. He's quite a guy. Plenty of looks and charm — and has he got that certain something! Claire seems to have noticed it too.'

'He's *not* good looking!' said Amanda with something of a snap. 'His face is out of drawing.'

'Well as far as I'm concerned, honey, it can stay that way. I never could draw anyway.'

Toby said: 'Persis darling, I never remember you sounding so aggressively American when I knew you in the States. Or did you always talk that way?'

'Not when I'm back home,' said Persis placidly. 'I keep it for foreign travel. It amuses the natives.'

Toby laughed. 'You're just a highly coloured fake and I adore you!'

Persis gave him an odd, slanting look and said: 'Do you, honey?

Well maybe you did once. Or maybe you're like this guy Potter — or any other guy for that matter! — just a Mormon at heart.'

For a moment there was an unexpected tinge of bitterness in Persis Halliday's clear incisive tones and Toby said quickly: 'What's that stuff you're drinking? It looks like ammonia.'

'Maybe it is, at that. The boy with the dinky white apron calls it *oozoo* or *ouzo* — and is it filthy! Still, I'm all for trying anything once. Drag up a chair and join me.'

'Do you mean to tell me that you're knocking back drinks alone and unprotected?' demanded Toby, astounded.

'Not quite. I am not entirely lost to all sense of what is due to me. My escort is in back — trying to get something under the counter if you ask me. Ah, here he is. Okay, George?'

George Norman appeared from the interior of the café bearing a bottle of beer. 'Got it!' he announced triumphantly. 'I knew they had some stored away. Good morning, Miss Derington.' 'Morning, Gates. I'm showing Mrs Halliday the sights.'

Toby said: 'Is your wife here?'

'She'll be along in a minute. Alastair had to send off some cables and she went along to the Post Office with him. Here they are now.'

Claire Norman, still in black and wearing a wide-brimmed black hat that shaded her small face in a most becoming manner, appeared round the corner of the quay, her hand through Alastair Blaine's arm. Major Blaine looked tired and grim and as though he had had remarkably little sleep, if any, during the last forty-eight hours.

'Why — Amanda,' said Claire in her soft, light voice. 'How nice to see you. And Toby. Have you two been exploring the harbour?'

'No,' said Amanda. 'We've been exploring the town. I'm going to look at the harbour now, from the sea wall.'

'I'll come with you,' said Toby.

'I don't want you, Toby,' said Amanda perversely. 'I just want

340

to sit and look at it and not talk. I'll be back.' She turned on her heel and walked quickly away.

Toby made a move as though to follow her, but Claire Norman laid a small hand on his arm and asked him prettily to fetch a chair for her, and by the time he had done so Amanda had gone.

A long stone wall with a small lighthouse on the end of it protected the tiny horseshoe-shaped harbour of Kyrenia from the seaward side, and walking along it Amanda looked across the translucent harbour water to the towering walls of the old Crusader castle, golden in the sunlight, and the beautiful curving coastline that faded into the shimmering heat haze beyond the age-old buttresses.

There were several other people on the sea wall, one of whom, a man who was sitting on the edge of the wall at the harbour side with his legs dangling above the water, was surrounded by an interested crowd of children. He was sketching swiftly with quick, bold strokes of a conté pencil on a large loose-leaf drawing block, and Amanda paused involuntarily, attracted by a burst of childish laughter.

The man spoke without turning his head: 'Good morning, Amarantha.'

'How did you know I was here?' demanded Amanda, startled.

Steve turned about and grinned up at her. 'I have eyes in the back of my head. Or perhaps I'm like that chap in *Maud* whose *"heart would hear her and beat, were it never so airy a tread"*.'

Amanda flushed and turned away. Mr Howard spoke one quick sentence in Greek and instantly Amanda found her way barred by half a dozen laughing children, while three more laid hold of her arms and the belt of her grey linen frock. Amanda's sense of humour got the better of her and she laughed.

'Is this a hold-up?'

'It is. Now come off your high horse, Amarantha, and sit down and relax. I want to talk to you. You can sit on this——'

He ripped off a sheet of cartridge paper from the drawing block

341

and laid it on the edge of the harbour wall. Amanda, surrendering to curiosity and *force majeur*, sat down beside him, and looking downwards at the clear harbour water beneath her dangling feet, saw her own reflection and that of the group of children behind her.

'So much for the eyes in the back of your head. You saw my reflection.'

'I did,' admitted Steve.

Amanda turned to look at him and her gaze fell on the drawing block in his hands. The page was covered, surprisingly enough, with quick, vivid sketches of elephants, tigers, a sailor in bell-bottomed trousers, a witch on a broomstick, a horrific dragon, a sea serpent and a pirate brandishing a cutlass.

Mr Howard had the grace to look abashed. 'Not what you would call a hard morning's work,' he remarked, 'but popular with my public.'

Amanda said in a voice of blank amazement: 'So you *can* draw!'

'Why this unflattering incredulity? Or do I look like a painter of Spiritual Aromas, like my brother-of-the-brush, that dashing home-breaker, Mr Potter?'

Amanda flushed and bit her lip. 'I thought——' she began, and stopped.

'You thought it was merely an act,' concluded Steve. 'But no one should put on an act unless they can also put it across.'

He turned over to a fresh page and idly sketched in the outline of a girl's face and figure that turned suddenly into Amanda as she had looked in the cabin of the *Orantares*. Amanda in a nightdress with her long hair falling below her waist and her eyes wide and frightened.

There was a murmur of admiring recognition from the audience of children, and Amanda reached out, and snatching the pencil from his hand, said abruptly: 'What did you want to talk to me about?'

Steve turned his head and spoke briefly to his youthful audience, and received what appeared to be a chorus of assent.

Amanda said: 'What did you say to them? And how is it that you speak this language so well?'

'There is no end to my accomplishments,' said Mr Howard airily. 'And if you really want to know, I told them that I wished to declare my love to this so beautiful lady, and should any of the English approach I relied on them to give me due warning. The gang are with me to a man, so we can now relax and talk without fear of being overheard.'

'Oh,' said Amanda in a small voice.

Steve laughed. 'Don't worry. I only make love by moonlight. At the moment I merely propose to discuss crime.'

He retrieved the pencil and turning over another page began to sketch the houses on the far side of the harbour, but he was no longer smiling and his voice when he spoke again was terse and low pitched.

'The results of the post-mortem show that Mrs Blaine took poison. And I was right about that glass in your cabin. There are only two sets of finger-prints on it: yours and Mrs Blaine's. The bottle has only one set — yours. Which means that it was polished very carefully before it was put there, and probably handled with gloves. And the tablets in it were the same stuff that was in the glass: pilocarpine nitrate.'

'But – but you can't be sure that there was anything more than just lemon juice and water in that glass,' said Amanda, forcing the words past an uncomfortable constriction in her throat. 'I filled it again with water from the tap — to throw over her.'

'I know. But the remains of the original stuff had spilt and soaked into the carpet. I mopped it up with a handkerchief. There wasn't much of it, but with that bit of peel it was enough. The analysis shows that it contained a solution of pilocarpine nitrate which was probably sufficient to kill a dozen people. A single mouthful would have been enough to kill Mrs Blaine, though it would have taken a good bit longer.'

Amanda said: 'But the bottle! No, it can't be true, because don't you see, if Julia hadn't changed cabins with me, there wouldn't have been *any* finger-prints on the bottle and someone would have noticed it.'

'I wonder. How did you find it?'

'I felt it when I lay down. It made a hard lump.'

'So that you found it almost as soon as your head touched the pillow. The chances are that Mrs Blaine would have done the same, and would have touched it, as you did, and probably thought that some previous occupant of the cabin had left it behind by mistake. It only meant something to you because you had seen Mrs Blaine die of poison. Even if she had not found it, it is an even bet that several people would have handled it before it occurred to anyone to see if it had her finger-prints on it. Now let's have your story again. Right from the beginning this time. Anything that you knew or noticed about these people when you were in Fayid, and why they — and you — are in Cyprus, and as much as you can remember of what they did and said in Fayid and on the way to Port Said and on the boat. In fact the whole works.'

Amanda turned her head and looked at him, but his entire attention appeared to be concentrated on the drawing that was taking shape under the leisurely, unerring strokes of the conté pencil.

She said uncertainly: 'Then you *are*—— '

Steve Howard threw a brief glance in the direction of the café on the quay where Persis Halliday, the Normans, Major Blaine and Toby Gates were seated about a small table in the shade, and said curtly: 'Quickly, Amanda!'

There was not much to tell, and what there was seemed to date back to the evening at the Club in Fayid when her aunt had introduced her to Steven Howard. And yet Amanda had a queer feeling that it went farther back than that, and that Steve himself had been in Fayid for some specific purpose that was entirely unconnected with art, and that his presence at the Officers' Club that night had not been accidental.

She told him what she knew, thinking as she did so that it all sounded very trivial and unimportant. But he questioned her exhaustively on a number of points, and seemed interested to hear that Toby had met Persis in the States while visiting a married sister whose husband was attached to the Embassy Staff in Washington. She re-told yet again how she had come to occupy the cabin that had been allotted to Julia, and everything that she could remember of that last hysterical scene.

Steve said: 'What time did she go down to her cabin? Was she still on deck when you left?'

'No. She went quite early. About ten I think. Someone put on a gramophone record and people started dancing. Alastair danced with Mrs Norman, and I think Julia must have left about then. She started making rather a fuss about having a headache, and went off to her cabin.'

'When did you go down to yours?'

'Just about eleven. I remember the time, because I wound up my watch when I took it off to wash.'

'And Mrs Blaine came into your cabin around five or ten minutes later. Is that right?'

'Yes.'

Steve was silent for a moment or two, and then he said: 'Did all of you know that she made a habit of drinking unsweetened lemon juice?'

'Yes. She used to make rather a virtue of it. She took it to take down her weight. People always seem to advertise their dieting fads. She'd never touch a sweet drink, yet she'd eat ice creams and sticky puddings and chocolates by the ton.'

Steve said: 'Are you quite sure that you've told me everything you know?'

'Quite. Oh there is one other thing, but it can't possibly have anything to do with all this.'

'Never mind; let's have it.'

'Persis says that she went on deck much later that night, because her cabin was hot, and that she saw Mrs Norman and Lumley Potter together on the boat deck.'

Steve made no comment, but his pencil checked and he sat quite still, staring across the lovely harbour with eyes that did not appear to see the charm of the scene that lay before him.

After a moment or two he shrugged his shoulders and returned to his work, and presently one of the children called out something in a shrill piping tone, and he looked round.

'I rather think that a search party is about to be sent after you,' he observed, 'so let us talk of other things in a bright and audible manner. What are you doing in Kyrenia, for instance?'

'You know quite well why I'm here,' said Amanda accusingly. 'You were dining at Mrs Norman's house last night, and she seems to have broadcast the whole story.'

'Oh yes — of course. You couldn't stay unchaperoned with the manager of your uncle's Cyprus venture, so this man Barton has parked you instead *chez* Moon. His loss is our gain. Did you have an entertaining journey from Limassol?'

Amanda embarked on an account of her drive, her stop at Nicosia and her arrival at Miss Moon's, and was still talking when a shadow fell across them and Claire Norman's soft fluting voice said: 'Why, *Steve!* I'd no idea it was you who were monopolizing Amanda. We wondered what was keeping her. Have you been here all morning? You're supposed to be meeting us at the hotel at one o'clock, you know, and it's five past now.'

Steve closed his sketch book, pocketed the pencil and stood up:

'Hullo, Mrs Norman. 'Morning, Gates. Yes, I have been pursuing my vocation in an industrious manner. Miss Derington has been offering advice.'

He leant down and pulled Amanda to her feet.

'Do let me see,' begged Claire Norman. 'If you only knew how I envy people who are *really* creative! Do show us what you have been doing.'

346

Steve held up the sketch book to display the drawing of the harbour and Toby Gates said involuntarily: 'Why that's damned good! I suppose you make a packet out of this sort of thing?'

'Alas, no,' sighed Mr Howard regretfully. 'I shall never make a fortune from my art. It contains a fatal flaw: anyone can instantly recognize what it is intended to represent. One can only make a packet nowadays if one's creative efforts are of the type that the purchasing committee can hang upside down without anyone — including the artist — spotting the error.

A sudden and unexpected breath of wind ruffled the quiet water of the harbour and lifted the sheet of paper, disclosing the page that lay beneath it. It was only for a brief moment, but quite long enough for both Claire Norman and Toby Gates to see and recognize that quick, brilliant sketch of a girl with unbound hair.

Tony Gates said in a thunderstruck voice: 'But that's Amanda! How on earth—— ' He stopped, red-faced and scowling, and Claire Norman laughed her light, tinkling laugh and said: 'Why, Steve! How secretive you are! I had no idea that you and Amanda knew each other so well.'

Steve closed the sketch book and tucked it under his arm. He smiled down at Claire with lazy pleasantness, but Amanda was suddenly and vividly aware, without knowing why she should know it, that he was angry.

'I am afraid,' said Steve gently, 'that that was merely an example of what is known as artist's licence. I do not know Miss Derington well. But that, fortunately, is an error that can be remedied. And now what about some food?'

Claire Norman's glance went swiftly from Mr Howard's smiling face to Amanda's entirely blank one and Captain Gates' scowling countenance, and she laughed again: a laugh that this time was not quite so sweet and tinkling:

'Yes, let's!' she said. 'I'm famished.'

She slipped one small hand through Steve Howard's arm and

347

laid the other on Toby's sleeve, and they walked away towards the Dome Hotel, four abreast in the bright glittering sunlight, their shadows foreshortened on the hot stones at their feet.

8

The dining-room of the Dome Hotel was long, spacious and cool, and a little breeze blew in from the line of windows that opened on to the burning blue of sea and sky.

Amanda looked about her with interest and decided that most of the guests were tourists, with a sprinkling of permanent residents. The Normans and Alastair Blaine were seated at a small table just beyond the one occupied by Persis, Steve Howard, Toby and herself: Claire Norman having suddenly decided that owing to Alastair's recent and dramatic bereavement, it might cause comment if he were to appear as one of a large and cheerful luncheon party at the hotel.

Amanda wondered why, in the circumstances, Claire could not have managed to give him a meal in the privacy of her own home? But Claire was a law unto herself, and Alastair, silent and stunned, was in the mood to do anything he was told without question.

Amanda's gaze, wandering farther, stopped at a strapless and backless white sunsuit printed with several huge scarlet roses and apparently remaining in position upon its wearer by faith alone. She was puzzling over the mechanics of this arresting garment when she became suddenly aware of the identity of the owner. The lady in the sunsuit was none other than Mr Glennister Barton's errant wife, while her companion, temporarily hidden from Amanda's view by an attentive waiter, was presumably her partner in guilt, the improbable Mr Potter.

Amanda was both interested and surprised. Somehow she had not expected Anita Barton to flaunt her liaison in such a public spot as the dining-room of the Dome Hotel. The attentive waiter removed himself, giving Amanda an uninterrupted view, and she studied the couple with considerable interest.

Lumley Potter, she decided, was not enjoying himself. He was looking morose, sulky and more than a little apprehensive, and kept darting anxious glances in the direction of the Normans' table. Anita Barton, however, appeared to be entirely at ease. She was laughing and talking — perhaps a shade too loudly.

Mrs Barton was a dark-haired woman of about twenty-five, with an excellent figure and striking good looks that owed much of their impact to a lavish and theatrical use of make-up. Altogether an unexpected wife, thought Amanda, for someone as quiet and fine-drawn as Glenn Barton.

As though she had felt Amanda's interested gaze, Anita Barton turned full face towards her. Her dark, over-bright eyes looked Amanda over with cool and deliberate insolence and her wide scarlet mouth curved in a mocking smile. She made some remark to her companion and shrugged one bare, sunburnt shoulder. And then all at once her eyes became fixed and hard and her red mouth tightened into a thin line. But she was no longer looking at Amanda. She was looking at someone immediately behind her, and, involuntarily, Amanda turned.

Glenn Barton was standing in the doorway, searching the room with anxious eyes. He did not see his wife, but he saw Amanda and came quickly towards her, threading his way between the tables.

'Glenn!' Claire Norman's voice arrested him as he was about to pass their table, and he paused beside her. She looked up at him with large, luminous eyes and said reproachfully: 'Glenn, you've been overworking again. You look as if you've had no sleep for weeks. You don't know Major Blaine, do you? I think you were over in the Lebanon on business when they were here last year, weren't you?'

'No, we haven't met. But of course I heard about you from——'

350

Glenn checked suddenly and Claire said: 'Stay and have something to eat. We've only just started.'

'I'm afraid I can't. I've a lot to do.'

'Then what about tea? Drop in at the house on your way back.'

'I will if I can,' said Mr Barton hesitantly.

'We shall expect you,' said Claire, smiling up at him.

He nodded absently and made his way across to Amanda. Claire's smile faded and her wide childlike eyes were suddenly narrowed and speculative.

Amanda turned in her chair: 'Hullo, Mr Barton. Were you looking for me? Persis, this is Mr Barton. He very kindly collected me at Limassol.'

'Yes. We met,' said Persis, producing her most dazzling smile. 'But I'm just delighted to meet you again, Mr Barton. Any friend of Amanda's is a friend of ours. Say, why not get a chair and join us?'

Mr Barton blinked and his drawn face relaxed in a smile:

'I – I'd like to very much. But I'm afraid I can't just now.'

'Some other time then,' said Persis warmly.

As one angle of the local triangular scandal, Glenn Barton represented copy; and Persis, whose interest had been aroused by the story, had been determined to make his closer acquaintance; though it is doubtful if her interest would have been so great had he proved to be a less personable man.

'Thank you,' said Glenn Barton. He turned rather abruptly to Amanda and said: 'I really came to ask you if you'd be in this afternoon. At the Villa Oleander I mean. Could you spare me half an hour of your time if I came in about three? I—— ' he hesitated a moment and glanced at her three openly listening companions. 'I have had a letter from your uncle. He has some messages that he wishes me to give you.'

'Of course,' said Amanda. 'I'll expect you about three o'clock.'

'I'll try not to keep you waiting.'

Persis said: 'Say, Mr Barton, I hear you run a wine business.

Vineyards and vats and pretty girls treading out the grapes and all the rest of it.'

'He does,' said Amanda. 'Miss Moon gave me some of his wine yesterday. It was delicious.'

Glenn Barton laughed. 'I'm glad you liked it. You were lucky not to get barley water. I thought that was the only thing that she drank.'

'It is. But thank goodness, she doesn't expect her guests to drink the stuff. It always tastes to me like water in which someone has stewed up half a lemon and three yards of flannel.'

Persis said: 'To get back to your vineyards, Mr Barton. I'm just crazy to see the whole works. Would you take pity on a poor foreigner and show me round one day?'

'I'd be delighted to.'

'Then how about tomorrow?'

'You can't go looking at vines and vats tomorrow, Persis,' said Toby Gates firmly. 'We're all going for a picnic to St Hilarion. Amanda's coming too. You know you arranged the whole thing with George Norman only this morning.'

'So we did. I'll tell you what, Mr Barton — suppose you join the picnic? Then we can get together and fix a day for the vines. Tomorrow at two-thirty. You can give me a lift to Hilarion. Is that a date?'

'I ought not to,' said Glenn Barton with a rueful smile, 'I'm rather busy just now, but — all right. I'd like to come. But I shan't be able to give you a lift I'm afraid. I can't get off as early as that. I could be at Hilarion about four o'clock if that's all right?'

'Sure. That's okay by me. Be seeing you then.'

Glenn Barton smiled at her, turned away and then stopped suddenly, his face rigid, and Amanda, following the direction of his fixed gaze, saw that he was staring at his wife. It was obvious that he had not noticed her until then, and highly unlikely that he would in any case have expected to see her lunching openly at the Dome with Lumley Potter.

Anita Barton had turned in her chair so that she faced him directly. Her eyes were bright and defiant and her painted mouth was hard and ugly. The room was noisy with chatter and the chink of glasses and cutlery, but the four at Amanda's table and the three at Claire's were suddenly silent with the silence of embarrassment and curiosity.

There was a queer grey look about Glenn Barton's thin, tanned face, and his mouth had shut hard. A muscle twitched at the corner of his jaw and his hands had clenched so tightly that the knuckles stood out bone white.

He stood there for perhaps a full minute, and then suddenly swung about and walked quickly and unsteadily from the room.

'Well, what do you know!' remarked Persis into the silence. 'Did you see that guy's face? If I had a dollar for every time I've written "*he turned white under his tan*" I'd buy the Koh-i-noor. But, so help me, I've never seen it happen until now. Fiction is certainly no improvement on nature.'

Steve said: 'Tell me, Mrs Halliday, are all American women as ruthless as you are?'

'Persis to you, Steve honey. And why ruthless? Why, I was *charming* to the poor guy.'

'That's what I meant,' said Steve with a grin. 'But what are you going to do with him when you've got him? Gaff him, or throw him back into the pool?'

'Steve *daaarling!* All I want is to get to know him. Can't you see what divine copy he is?'

'I see all right. You're a ruthless vamp and should be kept under lock and key. And don't bat your eyelashes at me — I suffer from extreme susceptibility.'

'But that's just *wonderful*,' said Persis warmly. 'I can see that you and I have a lot in common. You can drive me to Hilarion.'

'It's a date,' said Mr Howard.

Toby escorted Amanda back to Miss Moon's after luncheon and she dismissed him at the gate. She was feeling unsettled and restless and on edge, and the feeling of enchantment that she had experienced on her arrival at the Villa Oleander had vanished. Miss Moon peered over the landing rail as she closed the front door behind her.

'Ah, you're back, dear. Glenn Barton was asking for you. I told him that I thought you were taking luncheon at the Dome.'

'Yes I saw him, thank you, Miss Moon. He's coming to see me this afternoon. I hope that's all right? My uncle has been writing to fuss him about me.'

'Quite all right, dear. I usually rest in the afternoon, so you will have the drawing-room to yourselves. I shall be down to tea about four o'clock. Ask Glenn to stay. He'll let himself in. Euridice is out for an hour.'

She disappeared and Amanda heard her bedroom door shut. A clock in the hall struck three mellow notes, and almost before the echo had died away in the quiet house there was a sound of quick footsteps on the stone-flagged path and Glenn Barton was there, breathing a little quickly as though he had been hurrying.

'I haven't kept you waiting, have I?' he asked anxiously.

'About two seconds,' said Amanda with a laugh. She led the way into the drawing-room and sat down in a straight-backed chair, carved and gilded and upholstered in faded green velvet. Glenn Barton stood looking down at her with a deep crease between his brows and did not speak.

Amanda said: 'Do sit down. What is it? Has Uncle Oswin been devilling you about me?'

Glenn Barton sat down on the sofa and pushed his hands through his hair in the same boyish and despairing gesture that Amanda had seen him use on the previous day.

He said jerkily: 'I haven't heard from your uncle. That was just an excuse; I had to say something.'

He raised his eyes and looked at her wretchedly.

Glennister Barton must have been at least fifteen years Amanda's senior, and his hair was already flecked with grey at the temples. But all at once Amanda felt as maternal as though she were twice his age and he was a small boy in trouble.

She said quickly and warmly: 'What is it? What's the matter?'

'I had to tell you——' his voice had a ragged edge to it — 'I had to. About Anita — my wife. You see I didn't know that she would be here. I hoped that you wouldn't find out. So I — well I said she was ill. It was a lie of course.'

'Look, Glenn,' said Amanda, unconsciously using his name, 'it doesn't matter. You were only covering up for her. You couldn't have done anything else. I do understand, so don't worry about it — please!'

Glenn dropped his head into his hands and said in a low, uneven voice: 'It's all such a mess. Such a ghastly mess! I didn't believe that it could happen. But it did. I didn't mind what other people said or thought, but this involves the good name of the firm, and you are a Derington. I wanted to hush it up, but I see now that it isn't possible. I – I did what I could.'

'Of course you did,' comforted Amanda, distressed. 'But it's no good trying to cover up for your wife if she doesn't care what people say.'

'I don't understand it,' said Glenn tiredly. 'I don't know why she should behave like this. Perhaps it's some sort of defence mechanism. She's such a child really. A spoilt child who is trying to cover up its own naughtiness by accusing other people of worse things.'

'You mean those stories about Miss Ford?' said Amanda.

Glenn looked up, his face haggard. 'So you've heard about that already!'

'Miss Moon told me. But you don't have to worry, Glenn. She says that no one believes it.'

'How can she know?' said Glenn bitterly. 'There are people who will believe anything.'

He dropped his head on his hands again and after a moment spoke in an almost inaudible voice, as though he had forgotten

355

about Amanda and was finding some relief in speaking his troubled thoughts aloud:

'Anita doesn't like Monica — she never has. Monica is efficient and she has brains, but she's not very tactful. Anita is so gay, and so careless about money and housekeeping and things like that. She likes expensive clothes and parties and late nights, and admiration. She's young; it's only natural. And I suppose I was a bit dull — there was always so much work. Monica used to drop hints; very heavy ones I imagine — and it annoyed Anita. Then one day she lost her temper and they had a quarrel. A silly, rather childish quarrel—— '

Glenn sighed and pushed his hands through his hair again: 'Anita told me that either Monica went or she would. She wouldn't see that I *could* not sack Monica — she was Mr Derington's personal nominee for the post, and until she arrived things were in a bit of a mess in the office. Monica got the whole thing into shape and worked like a demon. I couldn't replace her without damaging the firm's interests. I told Anita that she need never see her or speak to her — I would have seen to that — but that I had to keep her. I *had* to. I can't deal with all the stuff she copes with, as well as my own work; it isn't possible. But Anita wouldn't see it. She just went on saying that if I didn't sack Monica immediately she'd go. I – I didn't think she could mean it. But she did. And now that she's gone she's too proud — and too young — to admit the truth, so she has spread it about that she was forced to leave me because I was having an affair with the woman. An *affair!* With Monica Ford of all people! *Monica!* Oh God, if it wasn't so tragic it would be damnably funny!'

Amanda, looking at him with an aching pity beyond her years, was once again reminded of Julia. Julia whose jealous love of her husband had prompted her to accuse him of entirely imaginary affairs with any and every woman he paid the smallest attention to. Was Mrs Barton only another Julia? Did she really love her husband with the selfish, jealous love that Julia had had for

Alastair? and had he, because of his work, neglected her and so driven her to much the same hysterical extremes of behaviour that Julia had indulged in? Could love really do such dreadful things to people? Drive them so mercilessly?

She said quickly: '*Don't*, Glenn! I don't want to sound catty, but anyone who has ever met Miss Ford will know that it's all nonsense. No one would believe it.'

Glenn lifted his head from his hands and looked at her.

'No,' he said with a wry smile. 'I don't suppose they would. But there are a good many people who have not met her, and it makes an unsavoury story. God knows I can't spare her from the office just now, but for her own sake I've tried to make her go. I can't let her name be spattered with mud by every gossip in the Island. It isn't fair on her. I have got some sort of duty towards the woman — and to your uncle for that matter. But she won't go. She says that if she went now it might look like an admission of guilt, and that anyway she will not be forced to leave by an entirely baseless scandal. I've done my best to persuade her, but it's no use.'

'She's quite right,' said Amanda warmly. 'If you wouldn't sack her because she had a row with your wife, I don't see why she should lose her job now, just because your wife is telling everyone that she was your—— ' She stopped abruptly and flushed.

'Mistress,' finished Glenn Barton wryly. 'I suppose not. But she is the only one I worry about. The others can not only take care of themselves, but give as good as they get.'

'What others?' asked Amanda, puzzled.

'Didn't Miss Moon tell you that too?' inquired Glenn Barton bitterly. 'Monica is not the only one I am supposed to have carried on with. Anita has been very generous with her accusations. I am supposed to have made love to half a dozen women — Mrs Norman for one. In fact it seems that no woman is safe from me. You wouldn't think it to look at me, would you?'

He laughed again. A short, harsh laugh that was entirely devoid of amusement.

'Why don't you strangle her!' demanded Amanda indignantly. 'Anita?'

'Yes. It sounds to me as if it would be justifiable homicide!'

Glenn smiled a curious, twisted smile. 'You don't understand. You see she doesn't really mean it. She's just a spoilt kid who has found that the party isn't as much fun as she thought it would be. She drinks a little too much, and that doesn't help. She's only hitting about her because she's bored and disappointed — with me and marriage and Cyprus.'

'She sounds to me,' said Amanda candidly, 'as if she needed a dozen with a good solid slipper. It's a pity you didn't try it.'

'Perhaps,' said Glenn wryly. 'But it's too late for that now. She wants me to divorce her.'

Amanda said: 'Of course you're going to?'

Glenn Barton got up suddenly and walked over to the open french windows that gave out onto a small covered verandah shadowed with jasmine and climbing roses. He stood with his back to Amanda and his hands in his pockets and spoke without turning his head.

'I *can't!*'

'Why, Glenn? Do you mean because of your job? I know that Uncle Oswin is pretty rabid on the subject of divorce, but it's not your fault.'

'It isn't the job,' said Glenn Barton, still without turning. 'I don't care a *damn* about the job. It's Anita. You see I – I love her so much.'

He swung round suddenly to face Amanda and said harshly, 'I suppose you find that difficult to believe? It's absurd, isn't it, to go on loving someone who can do that to you, and to be unable to stop? I know it doesn't make sense, but it's true all the same. I want her back — on any terms. I don't believe that she loves Lumley Potter. It's only a silly escapade, and if I don't divorce her she'll get over it one day and – and come back to me.'

He looked appealingly at Amanda; his tired, desperate eyes

358

pleading with her to agree with him; to reassure him. Amanda got up swiftly and went to him, gripping his arm:

'Don't look like that, Glenn! Please don't. I'm sure it will all come right in the end. Oh, Glenn, I am so sorry! Isn't there anything I could do? Perhaps if I saw her? — talked to her?'

A sudden light leapt into Glenn's grey eyes and for a moment his whole face seemed to change and the lines in it to alter; the avid, incredulous look of a cornered animal who is suddenly presented with an avenue of escape. It faded as quickly as it had come and his eyes fell.

'No. No, I couldn't possibly ask you to. I shouldn't have alked to you like this. I didn't mean to — honestly I didn't. I only thought that you should know something about it because — well because you're a Derington, and because I'd lied to you. I apologize. It was unforgivable of me to go to pieces and bore you with my sordid private affairs. Will you forgive me and – and try and forget about it?'

He covered her hands with one of his own, and despite the warmth of the hot Mediterranean day she could feel that it was cold and quivering.

'Now you're being silly,' said Amanda with a light laugh. 'You know very well that you don't have to apologize for anything. I'm the one who should do that. Here you are, in the thick of a perfectly beastly crisis in your life, and on top of everything else Uncle Oswin orders you, practically at pistol point, to put me up and show me round. You must have wanted to murder me!'

Glenn's cold fingers tightened convulsively on hers and he said quickly: 'Don't talk like that. You weren't to know. If I'd had any guts I'd have written and explained the whole thing, but – but I couldn't believe that she wouldn't come back. I couldn't think about anything else. My brain seemed to have stopped working, and if it hadn't been for Monica Ford I'd probably be without a job by now as well as without a wife. You've helped me quite enough by letting me talk to you, and I can't let you get involved any further in an affair like this. There's a proverb about touching pitch, and I won't have you touching it.'

'What nonsense!' said Amanda warmly. 'You told me yourself that this involved the good name of the firm. Well, I am a Derington, so you can't keep me out of it. If you'd like me to see your wife, I will.'

Glenn dropped his hand and turned away to stare once more at the sunlit garden beyond the shadowy verandah.

He said slowly: 'I don't know. I simply do not know. You see she refuses to see me, and I don't think she even reads my letters. She says that until I agree to a divorce she has nothing to say to me. If I could only talk to her! — but perhaps she might talk to you.'

'It's worth trying anyway,' said Amanda. 'At the worst she can only show me the door, and after being brought up by Uncle Oswin I am practically immune to snubs!'

Glenn Barton turned quickly and took her hands in a brief hard grasp:

'You're a brick, Amanda. I can't thank you enough. I know I shouldn't let you do this, and probably no good will come of it, but I've reached the stage where I feel I'd try almost anything!'

'Then that's settled,' said Amanda. 'When would be the best time to see her? Now?'

'A good bit later I should think. She's sure to be out bathing or watching Lumley paint during most of the afternoon and evening. Lumley's the snag, of course. He'll be there.'

'I'll go down after supper tonight,' decided Amanda, 'and just walk in. And you're right about Mr Potter. He's going to be terribly in the way. Couldn't we think up some method of getting rid of him, just for an hour?'

Glenn Barton frowned thoughtfully. 'Yes,' he said hesitantly. 'I think it might be done. I could send him a message or something.'

'That's it!' said Amanda with enthusiasm. 'We'll pretend that someone at the hotel wants to see his pictures with the idea of buying one. That's sure to fetch him. I'll get Toby to do it.'

Glenn Barton said uncertainly: 'I think I'd better do it myself. I don't quite feel like explaining this whole sordid set-up to anyone else.'

'We don't need to. But Mr Potter probably wouldn't come for you, and I shall merely tell Toby Gates that I have a date with your wife and as I do not want Lumley Potter around, will he be an angel and decoy him away for an hour? I know he'll do it if I ask him. How do I find the house?'

'It's on the harbour,' said Glenn Barton; and gave directions in detail.

'I'll go down about half past nine,' said Amanda, 'and wait until I see Mr Potter leave, and then go straight up. And as Toby is far too rich for his own good, it won't hurt him at all if he finds that he has to end up by buying a genuine Potter Masterpiece.'

The tense lines around Glenn Barton's mouth relaxed and he laughed.

'How nice to hear you laugh again,' said an approving voice from the doorway. They had not heard Miss Moon's approach and they turned, startled and looking a little guilty.

'I see that dear Amanda has been cheering you up,' said Miss Moon cosily. She was wearing today a linen skirt patterned in shades of cerise, with a blouse of cerise organdie copiously ornamented with narrow frills of lace. Her improbable hair was adorned with a gay bow of tulle in the same shade, while a scarf composed of several yards of the same material encircled her thin neck and floated behind her. The amethysts and opals of yesterday had been replaced by a set of garnets that did not tone well with the prevailing colour scheme, but the chains of silver filigree were the same and the scent of heliotrope accompanied her in an almost visible wave.

She reached up and patted Glenn Barton's thin, tanned cheek with a be-ringed hand: 'Dear boy! It does me good to see you in spirits. Amanda dear, I trust that you will insist on Glenn showing you some of our beauty spots. He should get about more.'

'He's going to,' said Amanda. 'He's coming on a picnic to St Hilarion tomorrow. But I can't take the credit for that, I'm afraid. He was shanghaied into it by a glamorous American authoress. We're all going. Come with us Miss Moon — do!'

'You're a dear child,' said Miss Moon approvingly. 'I wish I could. Although I must admit that I have never enjoyed picnicking. Ants, you know. Not to mention wasps. But I shall be out tomorrow. Lady Cooper-Foot is giving a small afternoon bridge party and tea. Three o'clock to six-thirty. Rather a nuisance, as Andreas and Euridice will both be out for most of the day, though they have promised to be back by seven-thirty at the latest. There is some festival or fête at Aiyos Epiktitos that they wish to attend. There is always some fête somewhere that they cannot miss. Very trying. Though why should they not be gay? So it is probably just as well, now I come to think of it, that we shall both be out for the afternoon. Here is Euridice with the tea. Glenn dear, you will stay and have tea with us, will you not?'

'I'm afraid I can't. I have to get back to the office. Monica has one or two things on the files that have to be dealt with before the post goes tomorrow. Any letters I can post for you, Amanda?'

'I haven't had time to write any yet,' confessed Amanda with a laugh.

Mr Barton bent to kiss Miss Moon's hand — evidently an established ritual that pleased the old lady enormously — and Amanda accompanied him to the front door.

'I'll hunt up Toby after tea and explain about Lumley Potter,' she said in a conspiratorial whisper.

'Bless you!' said Glenn Barton with a catch in his voice.

He turned and ran quickly down the steps and a moment later the front gate clanged behind him and Amanda heard his car start up and purr away up the long rising road that led to Nicosia.

9

It was close on half-past nine when Amanda walked quietly down one of the narrow lanes that led to the harbour, and paused in a patch of deep shadow near the quay.

The warm night was milky with moonlight and the air smelt richly of dust and garlic and fishing nets, and fragrantly of flowers. The streets and the quay were full of idlers and no one turned a head to see Amanda pass. Her short, full-skirted frock of coffee-coloured poplin blended equally well with the white moonlight and the dark patches of shadow, and she had tied a scarf of matching chiffon loosely about her head, peasant-wise, that helped to conceal her face.

She did not expect to meet anyone she knew in the narrow lanes at that hour, but she preferred to be on the safe side as she did not in the least wish to explain her mission to any of her friends or acquaintances.

Alastair Blaine had passed her as she crossed the main road. He was hatless and walking very slowly, his hands in his pockets, and the light from a street lamp had glittered for a moment on his blond hair. But Amanda did not think that he had seen her, for his eyes had been blank and unobservant and he had passed her without pausing.

Thanks to Glenn Barton's directions she had no difficulty in locating the house on the harbour where Lumley Potter had rented a studio flat, and she waited in the shadows of an alleyway, sniffing the spicy air and revelling in the warm beauty of the moonlit night.

Presently she was aware of muffled footsteps clattering on a wooden stair near-by. A door creaked and a moment later Lumley Potter hurried past clutching a large portfolio under one arm, his ginger-coloured beard looking grey in the moonlight.

Dear Toby! thought Amanda gratefully. She waited until Mr Potter turned the corner of the quay, and then left the shadowed alleyway and walked quickly up to the door that Lumley had left open behind him.

A single oil lamp dimly illuminated a narrow hall with flaking plaster walls and a long flight of rickety wooden stairs that led up into darkness. Amanda squared her slim shoulders and started upward.

She passed several landings giving on to rooms that appeared to be unoccupied, for no chink of light showed from under any door and their sole illumination came from the moonlight beyond the grimy landing windows. Glenn had said the top floor. Then this must be the Potter Love-Nest . . .

A strip of light showed from under an ill-fitting door, and a single guttering candle, in a ship's lantern hanging from an iron bracket on the wall, provided a faint, flickering illumination. On the other side of the door a gramophone or a wireless was playing dance music, and Amanda took a deep breath and knocked on the door. She did not wait for an answer but turned the handle and walked in.

The big oblong room was ablaze with light, and Amanda blinked, momentarily dazzled by the contrast from the dimness of the landing and the dark flights of stairs outside.

The room had been colour-washed a vivid shade of salmon pink and there were thick white hand-woven curtains by the open windows. The floor was covered with rust-red matting, and enormous canvases, presumably the work of Mr Potter, hung against the salmon-pink distemper or were stacked in rows against the walls. Mr Potter evidently believed in Paint, and applied it by the pound with the aid of a palette knife or possibly a small trowel. He also, apparently, believed in Gloom and Prussian blue.

A voice said '*Pios ine?*' and Amanda turned quickly and saw Anita Barton.

Mrs Barton presented an incongruous picture in that setting. She was lying face downwards and at full length on a large divan, putting records on a gramophone that stood on the floor beside her. She turned over lazily, and seeing Amanda, came suddenly to her feet.

She was wearing a subtle, clinging dress of black chiffon that breathed Paris in every line, and there were pearls in her ears and at her throat. Her dark hair was cut short and brushed back in smooth shining waves and she looked like a professional fashion model waiting for the photographer.

She stood quite still and stared at Amanda while the record on the gramophone ground to a stop.

'Well I'm damned!' said Anita Barton loudly. 'What are you doing here? Who let you in?'

'I let myself in,' said Amanda apologetically. 'I do hope you don't mind. The downstairs door was open; and I wanted to meet you.'

'I suppose Glenn sent you,' said Mrs Barton, her voice suddenly strident. 'Well in that case you can just turn round and walk right out again!'

'No one sent me,' said Amanda composedly. 'It was my own idea. May I sit down?'

'It's a free country,' said Mrs Barton. She sat down herself with some suddenness on the divan, and Amanda realized with a sharp stab of dismay that she had been drinking and was not entirely sober.

'Well, what is it?' demanded Anita Barton. 'Sob stuff? or Good-Name -of-the-Firm? And where do you come in on this — that's what I'd like to know.'

Amanda said abruptly: 'Are you in love with Mr Potter?'

It was not at all what she had intended to say and the moment the words were out she would have given much to recall them, for

365

Anita Barton flung her head back and went off into a peal of laughter.

'With *Lumley!*' Mrs Barton controlled herself and looked at Amanda with frowning brows:

'Listen — you look a good kid. I don't know what you're after, but whatever it is I bet Glenn's behind it. Have a drink — come on, have one.'

She filled a glass and handed it to Amanda. 'Ouzo. Local poison. Go on, drink it. It won't kill you. They say it's an acquired taste. Well now's your time to acquire it.'

Amanda sipped it with repugnance and suppressed a shudder of distaste.

'What were we talking about?' demanded her hostess, refilling her own glass. 'Lumley! So we were. Dear Lumley. No one could love Lumley unlesh – unless – it were his mother. And do you know what *she* christened him? Well I'll tell you: Alfred! Alf Potts. He didn't think that was dish – distinguished enough, so he changed it to "Lumley Potter". Shall I tell you why he let me run away with him? Two re – reasons. To annoy Claire, and because he wanted to show off. The "Free Life" — t'hell with the conventions! The Creative Artist is above the laws that g – govern the uncreative herd. Long live the Revolution!'

Mrs Barton described an airy circle with her glass, splashed a generous proportion of its contents on the floor and drank the remainder.

'No,' she said, scowling. 'I don't love Lumley. Lumley loves Claire. Claire de la lune! They all love Claire — or that's what *she* thinks. And what a surprise she's going to get one day!'

She dropped her empty glass on to the floor where it rolled in a circle on the matting, and for an appreciable interval she sat staring at it with fixed unseeing eyes, and at last she said in a half whisper: 'But I had to run away with someone. I had to get away from Glenn. You don't know what it was like. You don't know! I want to *live*. I must get away. Right away from this narrow deadly little island — escape. I'd have divorced him if I could, but there wasn't any evidence. What's the good of telling people things? It hurts him and he hates it like hell, but it isn't evidence in court. So I have to make him divorce me. He'll do it. He *must*. I sh – shall make such an exhibition of myself that in the end he'll have to do it f' his own sake' — she appeared to have forgotten Amanda — 'I've got to get away. Right away——'

Amanda said tentatively: 'If you hate the life here so much couldn't you persuade him to get a job somewhere else? Wherever you *would* like to live? I'm sure he could get a transfer. If you went back to him I'm sure he'd try. He said that he only wanted you back — on any terms.'

Anita Barton lifted her head and stared at Amanda. She said loudly and harshly: 'You don't understand. I don't want to be dead and buried. I want to live! I want to have fun. I want to laugh and enjoy myself; and I will – I will! If I had to go back to Glenn I should die. Thash what — die! Nice, quiet, hard-working, dull, *deadly* little Glenn——!'

With a sudden violent gesture she picked up the fallen glass and hurled it at the wall, where it smashed against one of Mr Potter's eccentric canvases and fell in a shower of broken fragments on to the rust-red matting.

'And now,' said Mrs Barton, rising unsteadily, 'I think you'd better go. So nice of you to call. Good-bye.'

Amanda rose. There seemed to be no point in prolonging the interview, as Mrs Barton was obviously in no condition to listen to reasoned arguments that night. But the interview had at least produced some interesting information, even if it had done little towards helping Glenn Barton. She said good-bye and left.

The candle in the ship's lantern had evidently burned out, for the landing was in darkness and she wavered, wondering if she should turn back and ask Anita Barton to lend her a torch or a box of matches. But Mrs Barton had put another record on the gramophone and Amanda could not face a return to that room.

She lingered on the landing for a moment or two, waiting until her eyes should accustom themselves to the gloom, and aware of an inexplicable reluctance to return down that narrow dark staircase.

Presently she walked cautiously forward, and groping for the stair-rail began to move downwards, feeling for each step.

The moonlight beyond the small window on the landing below provided a faint light, but Amanda, peering down the well of the staircase in expectation of seeing the glow of the oil lamp in the hall, could see nothing but blackness below her. Had the hall light too burned out, or had someone blown it out? Or were there three more landings between her and the hall? She could not remember.

Amanda hesitated at the top of the next flight of stairs. Above her she could hear a voice from Mrs Barton's gramophone singing a familiar, lilting French song. *La Mer: 'Voyez — ces oiseaux blancs — et ces maisons rouillées ...'*

It should have been a friendly and encouraging sound, but somehow it was not, and quite suddenly and for no reason Amanda found that she was shivering, and that her heart was beating in queer uneven jerks as though she had been running. She looked quickly over her shoulder, but beyond the faint square of moonlight the landing stretched away into dusty blackness, and if there had been anyone there she could not have seen them. But of course there was no one there! It was absurd to imagine such a thing. She was being ridiculous and childish — afraid of walking down a staircase in the dark!

There was nothing to be frightened of, for she had only to keep one hand on the stair-rail and walk straight down, and in less than a minute she would be out on the open quayside in the bright moonlight. Amanda straightened her shoulders and gripping the flimsy rail, felt for the top step and moved downwards once more into blackness.

She began to count the steps — *four* — *five* — *six* — *seven*. Then all at once she stopped, and stood frozen and still.

There was someone on the stairs behind her. She was quite sure of it. She listened intently, every nerve strained and alert, but she could only hear the muffled music of the gramophone two floors above her. There *could* not be anyone on the stairs behind her! It had only been an echo — or imagination. She must go on — *eight — nine — ten——*

'... *La Mer — a bercé mon coeur — pour la vi-e* ...' The music stopped on a last, long note, and in the silence she heard the stairs above her creak to the soft footsteps of someone who was following her down.

Amanda fought down a rush of blind panic. How many steps to the next landing? *Was* there a next landing? Surely there should be a window? The footsteps behind her had stopped when she stopped, and the house was deathly quiet. But in that stillness she could hear someone breathing in the blackness above her. Or was it only her own frightened breathing?

From somewhere outside the house someone approaching along the quay was singing the tenor part of the love duet from *Butterfly* in a loud and tuneful voice that somehow conveyed the impression that the singer, if not exactly intoxicated, was somewhat elevated by liquor. Amanda took courage from the sound. There were people out there on the quay. Nothing could harm her. She had only to reach the quay——

She went on again, quickly; stumbling in the dark. And instantly those other soft, furtive footsteps followed her. They were quicker now, and closer; and it was not her own frightened breathing that she could hear, but the short hard breathing of someone who followed her. Someone who breathed as an animal breathes, avid and panting, and who, in another moment, would reach out and clutch her——

Amanda stumbled and came hard against the turn of the stair, and turning, pressed frantically back into the angle of the wall, trying not to breathe. She heard a groping hand brush against the rough plaster within a foot of her head ... and then suddenly, in

369

the hall below her, the heavy door was flung wide and the bright glow of a torch showed in the well of the stairs.

Amanda heard a short hard gasp above her, and then the quick pad of running footsteps that retreated into the darkness.

She turned swiftly, but the stairs above her were empty, and whoever had entered the hall below was coming up the staircase towards her, humming softly. It was, oddly enough, the same song that Anita Barton's gramophone had played so short a time ago:

'... *Et d'une chanson d'amour — La Mer — a bercé mon coeur——*'

The beam of a torch fell full on her face, blinding her, and the song stopped short.

'Amarantha! — well, well! And who has been dishevelling your hair this time?'

Amanda spoke in a breathless, sobbing whisper: 'There – there was someone on the stairs! Behind me. I—— '

Steve caught her wrists in a painful grip that spoke as clearly as any words.

He raised his voice a little and said: 'I suppose you've been visiting the Potter studio? Then you can introduce me. Met a fellow at one of these cafés who says that Potter is a newer and bigger and better Picasso — and how! I told him that Potter was probably a mere painter of pot-boilers, but as a brother of the brush' — Mr Howard was slurring his words a little — 'it behoved me to prove his worth before presuming to criticize. I say, that's pretty good, isn't it? Let's go up and see him. There is no time like the present — Napoleon said that. Or was it Josephine?'

'He's out,' said Amanda, still breathless.

'Out? Then don't let's waste our time on the chap. Probably can't paint for pineapples. Let's go out and paint the town instead!'

'But—— '

'*Shut up!*' said Steve softly and savagely.

He pulled her arm through his own, and holding it hard against him, turned and went back down the stairs, singing *'Dolce notte! Quante stella'* in a loud and cheerful voice.

The door banged behind them and Mr Howard, still retaining his hold on Amanda's arm, walked rapidly away along the quay and continued to sing.

He did not turn towards the town, however, but swung instead down the sea wall of the harbour, dragging Amanda with him. The loiterers whom she had observed earlier that evening were gone and the wall was deserted. Half-way along it he stopped and jerked her round to face him. She saw his gaze search the length of the wall, the open sea on one side and the dark harbour water on the other. But there was no boat anchored near them and the wall itself lay white and empty in the brilliant moonlight.

Steve drew a quick breath of relief and his voice when he spoke was no longer either loud or slurred, but low pitched and incisive:

'At least we can't be overheard here; which is more than I can say of any other spot in this damned town! However just in case anyone has a pair of night glasses and is curious, I propose to convey the impression that conversation is not what is on my mind. Stand still!'

The next minute his arms were about Amanda and his cheek was against her hair: 'And now,' said Steve tersely, his voice hard and curt and entirely devoid of any emotional content, 'perhaps you'll tell me what the hell you were doing in that house! Toby Gates told me that you'd gone to see Mrs Barton, and I got down there as quick as I could. What were you doing there?'

His shoulder was warm and firm and smelt comfortingly of shaving soap, clean linen and Turkish cigarettes, and Amanda struggled with a childish desire to turn her head against it and burst into tears. It is possible that Mr Howard was aware of this, for he said sharply: 'Take a pull on yourself, Amanda!'

Amanda steadied herself with an effort and said: 'It was Glenn——'

'*Glenn?* You mean Barton? Was he there?'

'No. He came to tell me about her — Anita. Because he'd pretended that she was ill, and when he heard that she was in Kyrenia he knew that I'd find out ...'

She told him the story as Glenn had told it to her that afternoon, and how she had offered to see Anita Barton and had arranged with Toby Gates to get Lumley Potter safely off the premises.

'And what happened when you got there?' demanded Steve brusquely.

He listened without interruption to her account of that unsatisfactory and abortive interview with Anita Barton, and when she had finished he said:

'What was that about someone on the stairs?'

'There *was* someone,' whispered Amanda, and shivered.

'Steve's arms tightened about her momentarily and he said: 'Go on. Tell me.'

She told him of that brief, ugly, terrifying interlude on the dark rickety staircase, and when she had done he said curtly: 'Quite sure you didn't imagine it?'

'Quite sure,' said Amanda, and shivered again.

'Any idea who it was?'

'No.'

'Could it have been Mrs Barton?'

'No,' said Amanda again, entirely positive.

'What makes you so sure?'

'She had the gramophone on. If she had opened the door it would have sounded louder at once.'

'H'mm. Maybe. On the other hand there is probably another door.'

He brooded for a moment or two, absently rubbing his cheek against her hair, and then said abruptly: 'Who knew that you were going there?'

'No one. Only Glenn — Mr Barton. And Toby of course. No one else.'

'And Toby told me — choosing a nice public spot to do it in

372

— and probably half a dozen other people as well. So that's not much help to us.'

Amanda said with a quaver in her voice: 'What's wrong with that house?'

She was aware of a brief, fractional tension of Steve's body, but he only said: 'Nothing that I know of.'

'Then why did you come there as soon as Toby told you where I was?'

'Because,' said Mr Howard with commendable restraint, 'I do not consider it healthy for you to wander around alone after dark. I warned you once that you'd have to watch your step. Well I meant it. In case you're not aware of it, this afternoon, in the absence of any other evidence, a verdict that amounted to "suicide while of an unsound mind" was returned on Mrs Blaine.'

'But — that means it's all over!' said Amanda. 'If the police think it was suicide, then no one would want to——'

'Can't you understand?' interrupted Steve roughly. 'Mrs Blaine was murdered; and as far as the murderer knows, you are the only person who may be aware of it. If you had talked — if you talk now — that verdict would not stand. Use your head, Amanda!'

'Then you think that – that someone in that house meant to stop me talking by——' Amanda's voice died in her throat.

'I don't know about that. You can't say that because you heard someone coming down a staircase behind you it was necessarily someone who meant to harm you. Or, for that matter, that he or she even knew who you were. It is just on the cards that another visitor may have been expected to pay a call on Mrs Barton tonight, and that in the dark you were mistaken for someone else.'

'For – for someone who ... somebody meant to kill? You mean another murder? Oh no!'

'It's possible. An attempt at one, shall we say?'

'I don't believe it. Why? Why should there be?'

'I'm not sure yet. It's just a theory. But it might account for that incident on the staircase. There are, of course, various other possibilities—— ' There was an odd inflection in Steve Howard's voice.

'I know,' interrupted Amanda bitterly. 'One of which is that I might really have murdered Julia Blaine, and then invented a story of someone on the stairs just to make it look as though it couldn't possibly have been me!'

'Yes,' agreed Steve thoughtfully. 'There is always that of course. I hadn't lost sight of it.'

He heard Amanda's quick gasp of rage and continued reflectively: 'Poison, you see, is a woman's weapon. Women do not as a rule use a gun, and hardly ever a knife. They don't like noise or blood. They prefer poison or pushing someone off a cliff — something which produces death, but death at arm's length so to speak. Men don't mind the bang, or the blood getting on their hands.'

'You – you—— ' words appeared to fail Amanda. 'You dare to think that I—— ' She attempted to wrench herself free and Steve tightened his hold.

'There's no need to fly off the handle, Amarantha. One has to look at every angle. It's a possibility. There are, as I said, others.'

Amanda pulled back against his arms and stared up at him; but the moon was behind him and his face was only a dark shadow against the pale sky and the silver sea. She said in a breathless, furious whisper:

'There's something I haven't lost sight of either! *You* told me not to tell about that bottle. And *you* took it away — *and* the glass! How do I know that you didn't do that because your own fingerprints were on both? I don't believe that you were in Fayid, or on the ship, just because you paint. You were there for a reason. Something to do with Julia — or Toby, or Persis, or someone who was on that ship. There's something horrible going on, and you're mixed up in it!'

She stopped, breathless and trembling, and Steve said reflec-

374

tively: 'You look charming when you're angry. Like an infuriated kitten.'

Amanda made another ineffectual attempt to free herself, but the arms about her were suddenly like a vice, hard and painful, and there was no longer any trace of levity in Steven Howard's voice. He said harshly: 'Keep out of this, Amanda! I mean that. Murder is a diabolical thing. You can't risk taking an interest in the private affairs of anyone who was on that boat. It isn't safe.'

'Why?' asked Amanda uncertainly.

'Because it's essential that you avoid any appearance of suspicion or meddling. It's no secret that you were with Julia Blaine when she died, and someone knows that there was a small bottle containing the poison she died of under the pillow in that cabin. That someone is bound to wonder what you thought when you found it, and why you never mentioned it, and what you have done with it. Remember that a murderer always has a guilty conscience, and that a killer knows quite well that even if he kills a dozen people — or twenty — he himself can only hang once.'

Amanda said in a choking whisper: 'But I don't know anything — I don't want to!'

'You know about the bottle,' said Steve grimly. 'You also questioned the stewardess about that glass. I heard you, so the chances are that several other people did as well. And because of that, someone may be interested enough — or scared enough — to keep a pretty wary eye on you and to get unpleasantly upset when you behave as you did tonight.'

'But I only called on Mrs Barton. There's nothing suspicious in that!'

'No? Not when you tell Toby Gates to lure Mr Potter out of the house? Not when you slip out after dark and — I am willing to bet — sneak along in the shadows with a veil half over your face and lurk in some alleyway until Potter has left, and then steal into the house like a stage conspirator in Act II about to plant the time bomb in the Prime Minister's portfolio? You did, didn't you?'

'Well——' began Amanda defensively, and stopped.

'I thought as much,' said Mr Howard, resigned. 'Listen to me, Amanda — and I'm not going to tell you this again. You are in the unfortunate position of being able to produce evidence that what has scraped past as suicide was, in reality, murder. If, on top of that, you start paying elaborately furtive visits to a woman whom you have never met before, but who was a fellow passenger on board the *Orantares*, someone with a guilty conscience and a single-track mind may begin to ask themselves why all this First Conspirator stuff, if your visit to Mrs Barton is just a social call? — or could it be that you are beginning to make discreet inquiries among the passengers, and if so, what are you after? On the other hand, provided you behave in a perfectly normal manner, whoever was responsible for the murder of Mrs Blaine may be led to believe that you made nothing of that bottle after all, but merely threw it out of the porthole and dismissed the incident — maybe! Now do you get the idea?'

'Yes,' said Amanda with a shudder.

'Good. Keep thinking of it. And keep out of it!'

Amanda said haltingly: 'But – but Julia — If somebody killed her it isn't right that they should get away with it just because I – I hadn't the courage to tell.'

'Don't worry; they won't,' said Steve grimly. 'I promise you that. And it wasn't a question of your not having the courage to tell. You'd have told all right, if I hadn't stopped you.'

'Why did you?'

'Because it was too late to do anything for Mrs Blaine by then, and I had an idea or two of my own that I preferred to follow up without the issue being confused by a cat among the pigeons.'

'Ideas about what?'

'Limes, Times and Temperature,' said Steve lightly. 'And now, as I am beginning to get cramp, I think that the sooner we terminate this tender interlude, the better. Look at me!'

Amanda looked up, startled, and Steve bent his head and kissed her.

It was, as Persis would have said, quite a kiss, and indicated if nothing else that Mr Howard must have had plenty of experience in such matters. Amanda, who owing to a strict policy of chaperonage enforced until recently by Uncle Oswin, had not, had the oddest conviction that the ground under her feet was no longer solid and that for a long moment the moon and stars were describing circles about her head.

'That,' said Mr Howard, releasing her, 'was just for the record.'

'Was it?' said Amanda breathlessly. 'Then this is just for——'

Steve caught her hand a fraction of a second before it reached its mark.

'That would have hurt you much more than it hurt me,' he remarked reprovingly. 'Another time use your fist instead of your palm, and go for the point of the jaw. Like to have another shot?'

'Yes!' said Amanda, breathing stormily. 'With a flatiron!'

'Very wifely,' commented Mr Howard. He looked down at her and laughed.

'I apologize — there! But it was quite irresistible. Don't quarrel with me, Amarantha.' He kissed her hand lightly and tucked it under his arm. 'Come on; it's quite time you got back, or Miss Moon will begin to wonder if you really are a nice girl after all.'

He turned her about and walked her back along the sea wall and up through the moonlit town to the gates of the Villa Oleander.

10

Amanda avoided the harbour on the following morning. In the hot, brilliant sunlight that streamed through the open windows of the Villa Oleander and filled the dusty, gracious rooms with sunbeams, the events of the past night seemed unbelievable and unreal, and even faintly ridiculous. Amanda was almost tempted to wonder if she had not, after all, imagined the sound of those furtive feet on the stairs. Had they perhaps been only an echo of her own footsteps, or a trick played upon her nerves by darkness and an unfamiliar and empty house?

There was only one thing about the happenings of the past night that was entirely real. The fact that Steve Howard had kissed her.

Amanda, standing in the hot sunlight of the garden and remembering that kiss with a return of the curious sensation of dizziness that had accompanied it, was inclined to discount all that Steve Howard had told her, and to suspect that it had merely amused him to see how long he could keep her standing in a close embrace in the moonlight. Hadn't he made some flippant remark on the previous morning about only making love by moonlight?

'I wouldn't put it past him to have done it for a bet!' thought Amanda with sudden bitterness. 'He probably makes a habit of it, and I expect he has kissed Persis already!'

The reflection annoyed her unreasonably, and she did not realize that in the process of brooding over Steve Howard's outrageous behaviour she had very nearly lost sight of the terrifying and infinitely more important fact that she had been indirectly involved in what was almost certainly murder, and that she had

378

entirely forgotten to be frightened. An end that Mr Howard may possibly have had in view when he had terminated their macabre conversation on the harbour wall in that particular manner.

Amanda stood among the freckled shadows of the lemon trees, with the pigeons cooing and fluttering in the deep stone arches of the ruined wall behind her and the scent of roses and syringa and sunbaked dust sweet on the windless air, and thought exclusively of Steven Howard and not at all of Julia Blaine ...

Miss Moon, a blaze of emerald green, appeared upon the creeper-covered verandah outside the drawing-room windows and called down to say that Captain Gates was on the telephone asking if Amanda would go bathing with him.

'Tell him I've gone out!' begged Amanda.

'Certainly, dear. Where to?'

'Just out,' said Amanda, seized with an urgent desire for solitude and a feeling of inability to cope with the conversation of Toby Gates or anyone else — with one possible exception.

She ran across the garden and out into the road, and taking the first turning that offered, presently found herself leaving the town behind her.

The houses became fewer and the road wandered between olive groves, dark pointed cypress trees and stony sun-baked fields where goats grazed among the coarse grasses, weeds and asphodel. An ox cart creaked towards her and a black-haired, black-eyed, bare-footed urchin riding a donkey flourished a branch of oleander and grinned at Amanda as he ambled past. The road was hot and white under her feet and she began to wish that she had thought to bring a hat.

A car swept past, covering her with dust. It drew up abruptly some distance ahead, and reversed until it drew level with her.

'Amanda!' said Alastair Blaine, leaning out over the door. 'What do you think you're doing?'

'Walking,' said Amanda. 'Hullo, Persis. Where are you two off to?'

'We are doing our duty as self-respecting tourists,' said Persis. 'According to the Guide Book, we should not fail to see the Abbey of Bellapais. We are not failing.'

'Come on Amanda,' said Alastair Blaine, leaning out to open the back door. 'Get in. You'll get heat-stroke or a peeling nose or both if you wander around the countryside in this sun, and as you'll have to do the sights some time you may as well do this one now.'

Amanda looked back down the hot dusty road and capitulated. She said: 'You will get me back by one o'clock, won't you?'

'Of course. Half an hour is about my limit for looking at ruins. Hop in.' He slammed the door behind her and changed gear.

Persis had not seconded the invitation and Amanda had the sudden and uncomfortable impression that she was not too pleased at the addition of a third person to the party. But it was too late now, for the car was already moving again.

The white road ran parallel to the sea and the long, narrow barrier of the Kyrenia range that lay between the coast and the central plain. The mountains were blue in the hot sunlight; a clear transparent blue that made them look as though they had been fashioned out of Lalique glass, and their pale serrated peaks, shimmering in the heat haze, had the strange beauty of those distant ranges that Leonardo da Vinci has painted as a background to the Mona Lisa and the Madonna of the Rocks.

A light breeze blew in from the sea, turning the olive trees to silver, and Amanda relaxed into a day dream and made no attempt to talk. Even Persis Halliday's clear and incisive voice had softened and slowed as though the warm peace of the morning was also having its effect on her, and she conducted a low-toned conversation with Alastair Blaine to which Amanda, occupied with her own thoughts, paid no heed.

The car changed gear as the road wound up through a village perched on a low hill. A village of white-walled, pink-roofed houses, bell towers and minarets, encircled with olive groves, silver in the wind, and spiked with the sharp dark green of cypress trees.

Persis said: 'Say, isn't this the cutest place you ever saw! Where's that map? ... Aiyos Epiktitos. That'll be it. Do stop, Alastair, I want to take a photograph.'

Major Blaine looked at his watch and said, resigned: 'I'll give you five minutes. And no wandering round the place if you want to see the Abbey and get back by one.'

The streets were full of people in holiday attire and gay with a flutter of paper flags and green branches, and Amanda suddenly caught sight of a familiar face. It was Euridice, the prop and stay of the Villa Oleander, and Amanda remembered that Miss Moon had mentioned a fête at Aiyos Epiktitos that both Euridice and her nephew Andreas, the odd-job man, were to attend that day.

Euridice, however, appeared to be in anything but a festive mood. She was talking to a small group of black-clad women, one of whom was wailing aloud, and her normally cheerful face was full of woe. She looked up and, seeing Amanda, hurried over to the car.

This meeting, it was providential! declared Euridice. Her English was strangely scrambled and interlarded with whole sentences in her native tongue, but Amanda gathered from her flood of agitated speech that neither she nor Andreas would be able to return to the Villa Oleander that day, and that she wished Amanda to convey this information and her apologies to Miss Moon.

'Tomorrow morning, for the breakfast I come,' said Euridice. 'Today, no.' A relative had died, she explained; the husband of a cousin who kept a Taverna on the road beyond Nicosia. Apparently the cousin's husband had got into some bar-room brawl in Nicosia and had ended up in a culvert with a knife in his back.

Ah, these seafaring men! said Euridice, throwing up her hands.

On the ships they would work like oxen at the plough, but on shore they pursued pleasure and conducted themselves in a truculent manner. The poor Almena! — Euridice mopped her eyes — what sadness to lose a husband thus! This had been her home village before her marriage, and her family, together with Euridice and Andreas, were to leave shortly by bus for Nicosia to attend the funeral, and would not be back that night.

Amanda offered her condolences and promised to inform Miss Moon. Euridice thanked her tearfully and departed.

'Who was your lady friend?' demanded Persis, returning. Amanda explained the circumstances as Alastair Blaine restarted the car and they continued on their way.

The ruined Abbey of Bellapais lay on the knees of the hills, its pale stone walls, arches and tall campanile rising up out of a silvery sea of olives so graciously, so softly opalescent, that it seemed more like a mirage than something built by men, and as though a breath could blow it away.

Beyond and above and below the pale gold walls and empty archways lay a wash of blue; the intense cobalt blue of the distant sea, the cloudless blue of the sky and the soft blue barrier of the Kyrenia range.

Major Blaine braked the car in a patch of shade and Amanda said suddenly: 'I don't think I'm coming in. I'd rather look at it from the hillside. If I go inside there's sure to be a guide and instructive notices, and I couldn't bear to turn it from a dream into a string of dates. I shall sit under one of those olive trees and just stare at it.'

Persis laughed. 'You know what, honey? You are too romantic for your own good — or else you must be in love. Well I guess I won't dissuade you. We're only young once. But speaking for myself I do not intend to miss a trick. I've come to Cyprus to see the sights, and I'll see 'em if it kills me. Where's that dam' guide book? Alastair honey, if you think you're going to lie on your back under any olive tree and go to sleep, you have assessed the

situation incorrectly. You were taking me on a conducted tour —
remember? You start conducting right here. Lead on!'

They passed under the shadow of a stone archway and Amanda,
left alone, turned away and climbed the slope above the road, and
presently settled herself in the shade of an ilex with her back
against the rough bark and gave herself up to a fascinated contemplation of the view.

I should like to live here, thought Amanda dreamily; and
remembered what Miss Moon had said about Time ... that in the
Villa Oleander, Time was their servant, and not they the servants
of Time. Perhaps that was true of all Cyprus. Certainly this
shimmering blue day held a timeless and dream-like quality. But
it was a deceptive quality, for Time must move on here as relent-
lessly as it did in colder and harsher countries, and it was only a
pleasant illusion that here it drifted slowly and lazily. One day the
world would catch up with Cyprus. One day politicians and
greedy, frightened, quarrelling factions would engulf the sleepy,
enchanted island — as they had engulfed so many other lazy,
beautiful places — in a wave of Progress, reinforced concrete and
Town Planning.

The sun moved slowly across the sky and the shadow of the ilex
moved with it. The bark of the tree trunk began to feel unpleasantly hard through the thin green cotton of Amanda's frock
and there was an ant crawling down her back and several more
investigating her ankles.

She rose reluctantly and made her way back to the car. There
was still no sign of Persis and Alastair, and abandoning her
decision not to enter the Abbey, she paid over the small entrance
fee to the drowsy custodian at the entrance and walked into the
Abbey grounds.

Only the shell of the gracious building remained. But the old
stone cloisters were cool and quiet and the ruined arches gave on
to soft blue distances and the grey-green of olives on the hillside
below. Bellapais — The Abbey of Peace. It had been well named.

Amanda wandered across a square of emerald green turf surrounded by shadowed cloisters. There was a rose bush growing at one side of it and a single tall cypress tree. The close-cut turf looked more comfortable than the stony hillside, and she lay face down on it, stretched out at full length on the warm grass in the small patch of shade thrown by the scented sprays of the roses that curved above her. Amanda pulled a grass stem and chewed it reflectively, and presently, feeling pleasantly drowsy, closed her eyes ...

She was aroused by a sound of voices from under the arch of the cloisters on the far side of the rose bush. It was Alastair Blaine who was speaking, though it did not seem like his voice, for its slow, pleasant drawl was entirely missing and the words had a sharp, ragged sound:

'My dear, don't! Not now. You don't understand——'

Persis Halliday answered him, and her voice too was almost the voice of a stranger: hurt and uneven and somehow vulnerable.

'I think I do. Cyprus isn't London, this isn't last year, and Time Marches On. That's it, isn't it? You've changed — and I haven't. Once I thought that you might almost walk out on everything — Julia, your career, everything, anything — for me. Almost — not quite.'

'Persis, you knew it wasn't possible.'

'Because you hadn't a penny beyond your pay and the money was all Julia's? But it's different now, Alastair. She's dead, and it's all yours.'

'You don't understand,' said Alastair tiredly.

'What don't I understand? I came out to Egypt because I had to see you. And her. To see what she was like. I knew the minute I saw you together that you didn't even care for her. But you didn't care any more for me either. Who is she, Alastair?'

'She? I don't know who you are talking about.'

'Neither do I. But I feel that there is someone. Is it Claire? You stopped off here, after that fortnight in London, to stay with the

384

Normans. Oh yes, I know that Julia was here too, and that when you were flown home to London for that conference I had a fair field because she couldn't come with you. But a little thing like having your wife around wouldn't stop Claire!'

'Oh God,' said Alastair Blaine. 'You too!'

Persis said: 'Don't fool yourself, darling — it isn't you she wants. She likes men around, but it's George she really relies on. George, who puts up with all her whims and whimsies and provides her with a nice safe respectable background and fetches and carries for her. Things no one else would do. Is it Claire?'

'I don't know what you're talking about,' said Alastair wearily. 'I have no interest in Claire Norman, and George is my first cousin. In fact now that Julia's dead he's my next of kin, so is it likely that I'd even think of — Oh, leave it!'

'Now you're angry. But if it isn't Claire, who is it? Is it Amanda? Have you fallen for those big grey eyes and that wonderful hair, like Toby Gates? You and Toby! And just over a year ago he was tagging round after me like Mary's little lamb. Oh well, who can blame him. She's a sweet kid, and worth anyone's while for half an hour in the moonlight.'

'Don't be ridiculous!' Alastair's voice was both angry and exasperated.

'Then who?'

'There isn't anyone, I tell you. Can't you see that after Julia——'

Persis cut across the sentence sharply and cruelly: 'You didn't give a dam' for Julia! I know. I've seen you look at her. The best turn she ever did you was to kill herself! That's true, isn't it?'

'Yes,' said Alastair Blaine heavily. 'It's true. But – but you can't shrug off death, Persis. She was my wife, and — oh I don't want to talk about it. I don't want to *think* about it. Can't you see that all I want is a little peace and quiet? I've had nothing but scenes for years. Scenes and tears and hysteria, and nagging, senseless, silly accusations. God! I'm sick of it!'

'Alastair, darling——'

'Don't darling me!' Alastair's voice was suddenly ragged with exhaustion and rage. 'All right, you asked for it and you shall have it! I did make love to you in London last year. Would you like to know why? Because you wanted me to. You shouted for it like a spoilt kid banging the table with a spoon. And you were attractive and amusing and you treated the whole thing as a joke. And because I knew — I knew so damnably well! — that when I got back to Julia she would accuse me of having had an affair with some woman, even if I'd spent the entire bloody fortnight locked in the cell of a monastery!'

'But Alastair——'

'Shut up! I'm talking now. I've never had affairs with women. Do you realize that? Julia was the first woman I ever fell in love with, and I married her. In all the years of our marriage I had never been unfaithful to her — never once! Do you know why? Because I'm not built that way. I cannot be rude or curt to women who put themselves out to be pleasant to me, but I don't want to make love to them. And believe me, they don't want it either! But Julia would never believe that. She preferred to imagine that I was some frightful Lothario, instead of a perfectly ordinary, dull sort of chap without an ounce of sex appeal. And now you! — it's too much! I'd put up with Julia's senseless, endless, *futile* suspicions for years, and I suppose there was bound to be a breaking point one day, and——'

'And I was it,' finished Persis quietly.

'Yes! Oh it wasn't you—— No, I don't mean it like that. But it was knowing so well that as soon as I saw her again I should have to listen to the same old sordid accusations. I suddenly felt that I couldn't take it any more.'

'So you said to yourself "What the hell? If I'm going to be accused of playing around anyway, okay, I'll play around!"'

'Yes!'

'And that's really all there was to it? Just – just a ten-day

386

flirtation with someone who was attractive and amusing and who treated it all as a joke?'

'I'm sorry. I didn't imagine for a moment that you——'

Persis' voice interrupted him before he could finish the sentence: 'Don't, dear! You don't have to say any more. And so there isn't even anyone else!'

She laughed; a little bitter laugh. Alastair did not answer and there was silence for a moment or two. Presently their footsteps moved slowly away together, echoing hollowly under the curved stone arches of the age-old cloisters.

A shadow moved on the grass beside Amanda and a quiet voice quoted Puck's words: ' "*Lord, what fools these mortals be!*" '

Amanda started up. '*You!*' she said on a gasp. 'What are you doing here?'

'The same as you,' said Steve Howard amiably. 'Eavesdropping.'

Amanda's face flamed. 'I was not eavesdropping!'

'Perhaps not intentionally, but the result was the same. Very instructive, wasn't it?'

'Why are you spying on us all?' demanded Amanda hotly.

'You sound very cross, my sweet. Why shouldn't I come here if I wish? A good many people do. In fact all self-respecting tourists are urged not to miss it. I have been pursuing my Art.'

'I don't believe a word of it!' said Amanda. 'And I'm not cross and I'm not your sweet!'

'I withdraw the adjective. There is, alas, a distinct trace of acidity in your manner this morning; and you are not only cross but getting crosser every minute.'

Amanda opened her mouth and shut it again without speaking. She had remembered an admirable piece of advice frequently given to her by Miss Binns, her Uncle Oswin's elderly and placid house-keeper. She drew a deep breath and counted twenty.

'Why are you here?' she inquired in a more reasonable voice.

'To keep an eye on you.'

'On *me?*' said Amanda, startled. 'Why?'

'I find you so attractive that I cannot keep away.'

There was a mocking gleam in Mr Howard's eye and once again Amanda felt her cheeks burn, counted fifteen and said coldly: 'Don't talk nonsense.'

'Don't you believe me?'

'No I don't!' snapped Amanda.

'All right then. I have a brilliant theory that sooner or later someone is going to murder you, and I wish to see who does it. Will that do?'

'Don't you ever speak the truth?' demanded Amanda frostily.

'Not if I can help it,' admitted Steve with disarming candour. 'Truth, Amarantha, as your classical studies will no doubt have informed you, is a naked lady who lives at the bottom of a well. It therefore behoves any gentleman who inadvertently dredges her up in his bucket to look the other way or hurriedly shroud her in a mackintosh.'

Amanda looked at him doubtfully. His brown hair was ruffled into disorder and there was a smudge of blue paint on one side of his chin. He was wearing a blue sports shirt and a pair of grey flannels that had seen better days, and there were paint marks on both.

She said abruptly: 'What have you been painting?'

Mr Howard made an airy gesture of the hand towards the surrounding walls. 'This. From a couple of hundred yards down the road.'

Amanda said: 'I'd like to see it.'

'Suspicious little thing, aren't you? All right — come on.'

They walked back through the Abbey and down the road, and he led the way up a goat track to a point on the opposite hillside some fifty yards to the left of the ilex tree under which Amanda had been sitting.

'Where's your car?' asked Amanda.

'On the upper road; it's not much more than a track.'

There was a clutter of painting gear in the shade of some trees, and Steve picked up a canvas that he had left propped against a tree trunk, and held it up for her inspection.

It was a rough sketch in oils, showing the Abbey of Bellapais lifting above a haze of wind-ruffled olives. The thing had apparently been done entirely with a palette knife, for the paint was laid on with a lavish hand; but it in no way resembled the efforts of Mr Lumley Potter. Despite the strength of the technique the unfinished sketch had captured all the dreamlike, ethereal quality of the ruined Abbey that had so forcibly struck Amanda at her first sight of it, and she said again, and unconsciously, almost the same words that she had used on the harbour wall on the previous morning.

'But you *can* paint!'

She lifted her eyes from the picture and looked at Steve Howard, puzzled and uncertain.

'Poor Amarantha,' said Steve softly. 'You don't know whether you're coming or going, do you? Well if it's any consolation to you, I'm not so sure myself. Why did you come to Cyprus?'

The question was abrupt and unexpected, and Amanda looked startled. 'I wanted to come.'

'Why? Any special reason?'

'Yes,' said Amanda slowly, her mouth curving in a reminiscent smile: 'A poem I read at school. Have you ever read something that made you want to see a special place? That – that sort of haunted you?'

Steve's eyes were no longer mocking. 'Flecker,' he said, smiling, and quoted the lines that had captured the schoolgirl Amanda's childish imagination: '"*I have seen old ships sail like swans asleep beyond the village which men still call Tyre, with leaden age o'ercargoed, dipping deep for Famagusta and the hidden sun that rings black Cyprus with a lake of fire.*"'

'Yes,' said Amanda. She turned to look out across the grey-green mist of olives to the far blue sea beyond them, and spoke

389

in the soft abstracted voice of one who speaks a thought aloud:

'"*Famagusta and the hidden sun . . .*" The names are so beautiful. Famagusta — Kyrenia — Hilarion— Paphos.' Her voice changed to every name, lingering on the syllables. 'Do you know what the castle on that peak over there is called? Miss Moon told me. It's called Buffavento. That means "the wind blows". *The wind blows . . .*' Her voice sank to a whisper.

Steve forbore to correct her translation, and just then a car horn sounded from the road below.

'That'll be Blaine,' said Steve. 'You'd better get back. See you at the picnic this afternoon.'

Amanda turned to look at the square of canvas again. She said a little hesitantly: 'Could I buy it? I'd like to have it for my own. You do sell them, don't you?'

'I do,' said Steve. 'But not, generally speaking, off the peg. However, I'd like to give you this one. You can consider it as an un-birthday present. It's only a rough sketch.'

Amanda smiled at him with a sudden glow in her eyes and reached out a hand for it. 'It's wonderful!' she said.

'It's wet,' said Steve, removing it. 'I'll keep it for the moment. You shall have it later.'

Amanda nodded absently, and went slowly back down the hillside between the olive trees. And all the way back to Kyrenia, while Persis laughed and chattered as though that brief, emotional scene in the Abbey cloisters had never taken place, Amanda was silent and thoughtful.

She was remembering something that Steven Howard had said in the cabin of the *Orantares*: 'I paint indifferent pictures and have a passion for meddling in other people's affairs.' She had put her own interpretation on that and had come to the conclusion that he was some sort of private inquiry agent, and that it was even possible that Julia had employed him to watch her husband so that she might have something besides hysterical suspicions with which to confront Alastair, and acquire thereby an additional hold over him.

But Steve did not seem to fit into that role. And he could paint: there was no doubt at all about that. The conté drawings she had seen on the previous morning had betrayed a considerable talent, but the rough sketch in oils of the Abbey of Bellapais was in an entirely different category and Amanda began to wonder if her imagination had not run away with her.

Had Steve Howard after all come to Fayid and to Cyprus by chance, and with the sole object of painting, and had his subsequent proceedings stemmed, as he himself had suggested, from an amused and analytical interest in the behaviour of his fellow men?

Then there was Persis: Persis and Alastair Blaine, who had apparently met and had a brief affair in London during two short weeks the previous summer, when Alastair had been flown to London on the General's staff to attend some conference. Amanda remembered having heard Julia refer to it once. The conference had been delayed and instead of staying in London for a few days, Alastair had stayed two weeks and — probably as a result of some foolish letter from Julia — reached at last that breaking point to which he had referred. And Persis had fallen in love with him.

Amanda was conscious of a sudden intense pang of pity for Persis Halliday, who had proved to be so vulnerable under that surface shell of glittering, cynical sophistication. It was followed by a surge of admiration. If Persis had indeed received a shattering blow to her heart and her hopes and her pride, there was nothing in her manner to indicate it.

What did she see in Alastair Blaine? wondered Amanda. What had Julia seen? He was tall, blond, sun-tanned and blue-eyed, but not particularly good looking. It was an unremarkable, pleasant and entirely Anglo-Saxon face, and he was in fact, as he himself had said, a 'perfectly ordinary dull sort of chap without an ounce of sex appeal'. Women liked Alastair Blaine, but in much the same way as they liked their brothers. They made use of him and discussed their problems with him in a way that they would never have done had their emotions been involved. It was only Julia's jealousy, Amanda realized, that had built up a picture of Alastair as an irresistible charmer.

Julia was probably the only woman who had ever fallen deeply in love with Alastair Blaine — Julia and Persis. What *did* Persis see in him?

It's because she's an American and she writes, thought Amanda with a sudden flash of understanding.

Persis did not see Alastair as other people saw him. He had looked like her idea of a strong, silent Englishman, and his very indifference to women, as women, had probably lent colour to that view. She had fitted him with a ready-made character and attributes of her own devising, and fallen in love with the result. In love with something that was no more the real Alastair Blaine than a tailor's dummy is flesh and blood.

I wonder what he is really like? thought Amanda. But then what was the real Persis like? — or the real Toby? — or jovial, stupid, easy-going, devoted George Norman? Or, for that matter, Steve Howard?

Amanda frowned unseeingly at the olive groves and the sea; puzzled and disturbed for the first time in her twenty-one years by the realization that despite the dictates of John Donne, each man and woman is, in some way, 'an island unto themselves'.

11

Amanda delivered Euridice's message to Miss Moon, and Miss Moon tut-tutted absently and said: 'I only trust that she will return early enough to cook us some breakfast. At what time are you leaving for this picnic, my dear?'

'Half past two,' said Amanda. 'I'm being collected.'

'I,' said Miss Moon with a regretful sigh, 'shall be leaving a quarter of an hour later. Such a pity that I cannot come with you. St Hilarion always gives me such a feeling of spiritual refreshment and affinity with Time. So much more soothing than Lady Cooper-Foot's bridge afternoons. I shall not enjoy myself at all I fear, and I have a headache coming on — I only trust it does not develop into migraine. But one must not neglect one's duties towards society.'

Amanda said: 'How do I get in if I get back before you, now that Euridice isn't in?'

'Oh, I never lock the house, dear. I have always maintained that any dishonest person who wishes to enter a house will do so despite all the locks and bolts in the world. Locks only serve to incommode the innocent and innocuous. You will find the house open.'

Toby Gates arrived with commendable punctuality on the tick of two-thirty, and Amanda fetched a wide-brimmed hat and a pair of sunglasses and called good-bye to Miss Moon. She received no answer and thought it probable that Miss Moon had already left.

'How are we going, Toby?'

393

'I've hired a car for the afternoon. Not a bad little bus. The Normans offered to give us both a lift, but as they're already taking Alastair Blaine and all the tea things, I thought it sounded a bit of a squash.'

He ushered her into the front seat of a small grey saloon car and Amanda said: 'What about Persis?'

'Howard is taking her.'

The car drew away from the kerb and gathered speed on the long rising road that leads up from Kyrenia to the pass in the hills, from where it drops again to Nicosia and the plain.

'I can't think why I'm doing this,' said Toby. 'If I were in my right mind I should not be on speaking terms with you.'

Amanda turned to look at him in frank surprise. 'Why, Toby? What have I done now?'

'I like that!' said Toby forcefully. 'Do you realize, you long-haired hussy, that entirely owing to you I am down a matter of fifty quid and in possession of two of the most god-awful eyesores that ever defaced a wall?'

'Oh Toby!' Amanda was suddenly stricken with guilt. 'I'd quite forgotten. You *didn't* buy a genuine Potter?'

'My dear girl, I couldn't possibly avoid it! I sent along a note as per order, and then I quite forgot about the chap and went for a stroll in the town. It was meeting Howard that reminded me of him. And when I got back, there he was, planted in the lounge with a portfolio the size of Cyprus, still waiting. So of course after that I had to do something about it. He stayed for hours! Fortunately it didn't seem to matter if I said anything or not. I let him do the talking, and he thinks I am a connoisseur of the Arts. Well I'm sending you those pictures as a small present, and you can jolly well hang them on your walls. And what is more, you can dine with me tonight. You owe me that at least.'

'Toby darling, I *am* sorry. Yes of course I will. The staff is out for the day, so Miss Moon will probably be only too pleased to have one less to cook supper for.'

'Good show. How did your party with the erring wife go? Did she give you the inside low-down on the whole affair?'

'No,' said Amanda repressively. 'We — just talked. Are you sure you know the way, Toby?'

'No,' said Toby. 'But the chap who hired me the car said we can't miss it.'

The road wound up and up through olive groves, firs, cypress, carob, and sunbaked grassy slopes, and just short of the pass Toby turned the car right-handed into a side road signposted to Hilarion. As they turned, a car coming from the direction of Nicosia passed them on its way down to Kyrenia. It was a small green two-seater with a sports hood, driven by a woman, and Amanda thought that she recognized Glenn Barton's secretary, Monica Ford.

Their road skirted the mountain side and presently ran between an outcrop of the hills and past a wide saucer-like depression that Toby said had been a tilting ground — adding that his informant was Persis Halliday, who had been reading up on the subject of Hilarion and had evidently held forth during luncheon.

Rising sheer above it on a pinnacle of rock, over two thousand feet above the sea and silhouetted against the cloudless blue of the sky, stood the ruins of the Crusader castle of St Hilarion — the castle to which, legend says, Richard of the Lion Heart brought his newly-wed bride, Berengaria of Navarre. From this castle he went forth to the Crusades. And from its arched windows Berengaria the Queen must often have looked out on to that same sea to watch for the sails of his ships.

There was another car parked in the shade of some trees below the slope that led up the outer walls of the castle. But it did not belong either to the Normans or to Steven Howard.

'Tourists,' said Toby with contempt.

'Tourist yourself!' retorted Amanda, scrambling out of the car. 'Don't let's wait for the others. Let's go and explore.'

They climbed the stony slope in the hot sunlight and passed into

395

the cool shadow of the Keep. A long flight of worn stone steps led upward to the main bulk of the story-book castle that soared above them, clinging to the naked rock whose sheer sides formed many of its walls. At the foot and to one side of the stairway a man in a vividly patterned sports shirt was seated on a small canvas stool before a large easel. It was Lumley Potter. He turned his head as they approached and his scowl turned to a delighted smile:

'Hullo Gates. Just the man I wanted to see. How does this strike you? Early stages yet, of course, but I feel I have captured something of the tempo and perhaps a *hint* of the aura. At the moment the inner essence eludes me — yes, frankly it eludes me — but I feel that I shall ultimately grasp it.'

'Er – yes – I'm sure you will,' said Toby, staring in horrified disbelief at what appeared to be the portrait of a suet pudding in the making, into which someone had inadvertently stirred a generous dollop of schoolroom ink.

'Well?' said Mr Potter.

'Oh – er – terrific!' said Toby Gates hurriedly. 'I don't think you've met Miss Derington. Amanda, this is Mr Potter.'

Mr Potter expressed himself as pleased to meet Miss Derington and plunged into a discussion of his work that was only terminated by the arrival of the Normans, Major Blaine, Mrs Halliday and Steve Howard.

They left Claire and Major Blaine talking to Lumley — Claire it seemed was entirely familiar with the tempo and aura of art — and continued their exploration of the castle, Persis instructing their ignorance with the aid of a guide book.

Some minutes later, turning a corner, they came unexpectedly upon Anita Barton.

Mrs Barton had spread a travelling rug in a shady corner and lain down at full length with a book and a box of chocolates. The pages of the book were fluttering in a light breeze and a colony of ants were investigating the chocolates. Mrs Barton was asleep. She was wearing an exceedingly becoming dress of corn-coloured linen decorated at the hem and the deep neckline with innumerable small flat flowers cut from white linen and loosely attached by their centres. The effect was charming, but conveyed the impression that Mrs Barton must be exceedingly expensive to dress.

Amanda, gazing down at her, thought that she looked much younger than she had seemed last night — younger, and somehow defenceless — and remembered that Glenn Barton had spoken of his wife as being 'such a child'. Amanda could see now what he had meant. Despite the blue-tinted eyelids, the lavish use of mascara and lipstick and the scarlet lacquer on fingers and toes, there was something oddly childlike about the slumbering figure in the absurd and charming frock.

They turned away noiselessly and left her sleeping.

'This,' said Persis when they were out of earshot, 'is quite a situation. Do we warn her husband that his erring wife is among those present? The guy is due at any moment now. It's almost four. Or do we just ignore the whole thing and let him fall over her and the hell with it?'

'The latter,' advised Mr Howard lazily.

Amanda said anxiously: 'I'd forgotten that Glenn was coming. What time did he say he'd be here?'

'Four, if he could make it.'

Amanda peered over the battlements but could see no car on the white ribbon of road far below. Which was not surprising, for Mr Barton had been delayed ...

Glenn had intended to drive directly from Nicosia to Hilarion, but had found it necessary to go into Kyrenia to deliver some documents to a client who was staying at the Dome. He had been additionally delayed by a puncture just short of the town, and had left his car at a garage on the road and walked down to the hotel, discharged his errand and returned.

He was on his way back to collect his car when he saw Monica Ford's small, shabby two-seater cross an intersection ahead of him and turn down the side road that led past the Villa Oleander.

397

He was conscious of a slight feeling of surprise. What could Monica be doing in Kyrenia? He had seen her briefly in the Nicosia office that morning, but his work had taken him out to the vineyards and he had not been back to the office. Monica had made no mention of driving over to Kyrenia, and he had never before known her to leave the office unattended in his absence. Had something cropped up that required his immediate attention and had Monica come over in serarch of him?

Glenn glanced at his watch and saw that it was already a quarter to four. He hesitated on the pavement, puzzled and undecided, and then crossed the road and turned down to the Villa Oleander.

Monica's car was not outside the house, but he caught a glimpse of green paint and realized that she had parked it at the mouth of a narrow lane shadowed by mulberry trees on the opposite side of the road. Monica herself had just crossed the road and he saw her push open the gate of the Villa Oleander and disappear from view.

Perhaps there had been some message from Oswin Derington for his niece? But Amanda would be at Hilarion and Miss Moon at Lady Cooper-Foot's, while Euridice and Andreas were attending a fête at Aiyos Epiktitos. Monica would find the house empty.

Glenn turned in at the gate which Miss Ford had neglected to close behind her, and walked up the short flagged path. The front door swung open on oiled hinges and he was in the welcome coolness of the high, dim hall. He heard a movement from the direction of the drawing-room and walked across the hall and through the open doorway.

Monica Ford was standing near the french window and he checked abruptly at the sight of her face.

'Monica! My dear — what's the matter?'

Miss Ford did not answer him. Her face was ashy white and blotched with weeping; so drawn and haggard and aged with grief and emotion that it was almost unrecognizable.

'Monica!'

He went quickly towards her, but she shrank back and he

stopped. He saw her lick her dry, trembling lips and she said in a harsh, high whisper: 'What are you doing here? I – I thought you were in Limassol.'

'Monica, what is it? Has anything happened?'

She stared at him for a long moment, her red-rimmed eyes wide and fixed, then turning away she walked stumblingly to the sofa and sank down upon it with her back to him and her head in her hands, and burst into tears.

Oh God! thought Glenn despairingly. Another emotional woman! Anita — and now Monica. For Monica had begun to talk; a flood of hysterical words that fought with her sobs; jumbled, desperate, incoherent, from which a few words stood out, constantly repeated. Her dead brother's name; Anita's; his own — Glenn — Glenn — Glenn.

'. . . I didn't realize . . . I – I loved you, Glenn. I loved you . . .'

Glenn shut his eyes and tried to shut out the sound of her gasping voice; aware of a feeling of sick disgust and cold anger. But Monica's voice went on and on. Thick, ugly, choked with tears: '. . . I didn't realize it until today. I didn't know . . . I wouldn't face it. I've always felt that there was something — something I shouldn't . . . But I wouldn't admit it. And today you were away and Pavlos came to the office about a damaged case. He said you had gone to Hilarion with – with Claire Norman . . . and – and then – then I knew. I loved you . . .'

Glenn opened his eyes and looked at the huddled jerking shoulders with rage and despair. A faint scent of jasmine drifted in through the open windows and mingled with the cheap violet scent that Miss Ford affected, borne on a little breeze that billowed the curtains and fluttered the ends of a vivid green *crêpe de Chine* scarf that Miss Moon had left hanging over the back of the sofa. 'Thursday' thought Glenn automatically, noting the colour.

He tried to speak, but could find no words. There was nothing he could say. Nothing that could do any good now. He ought to have sent her away. He ought to have made her go. The ragged, sobbing voice went on and on and he winced at the sound of his wife's name.

'Anita ... Anita must have known. That's why she left you. I should have known too. But I wouldn't let myself know! I wouldn't face it. It's all my fault ... I pretended that everything was all right. But Anita must have known——'

Anita, thought Glenn with a sudden twinge of almost physical pain. Was it true? Had she known? He had always suspected that she did not really believe the things she had said about himself and Monica Ford — that there was something else behind her sudden defection, and that Monica Ford had been only an excuse. Now Monica herself said that she must have known. And so she had run away. Anita——

The gasping, weeping voice filled the quiet room with ugly sound: 'I don't know what to do! If only it hadn't been for Bobby I could have borne it. But I had to talk to someone — I had to! Glenn! ... Glenn ...'

Monica Ford's voice choked and stopped at long last, like a gramophone record that has run down, and silence flowed back into the dusty, gracious room.

The sun had moved down the sky and now it shone in through the french windows and lay in a bright square of gold on the faded carpet, illuminating Monica Ford's ungainly body and filling the room with a mellow glowing warmth.

Glenn looked down at the slumped, twitching figure with sick distaste. And presently, realizing that there was nothing else he could do, he turned abruptly away from her and walked quickly out of the room.

A clock struck the quarter hour as he crossed the hall, and his hand was on the latch of the front door when he thought he heard a soft sound from somewhere on the bedroom floor.

He turned quickly and looked up. But there was no one on the stairs and nothing moved on the shadowed landing above. Miss Moon was out, and so were Andreas and Euridice, and the upstairs rooms should have been empty. There could be no one there. Perhaps the sound he had heard had been caused by a pigeon or Euridice's grey cat. He hesitated, frowning and uncertain, his nerves on edge and a cold tremor running down his spine. But there was no repetition of the sound and he did not wish to remain any longer under the same roof as Monica Ford. He turned away and left the house, shutting the door quietly behind him. And it was almost a quarter to five by the time he reached Hilarion ...

He found the picnic party seated about the remains of tea on a grassy space by a ruined buttress, and because he was disturbed and preoccupied he did not notice — or at least did not recognize — Lumley Potter's ramshackle car among the cars parked beside the road.

'So you finally made it,' remarked Persis, making room for him beside her. 'We'd given you up.'

Glenn subsided wearily on to the grass and accepted a lukewarm cup of tea which he drank thirstily.

'I'm sorry I'm late,' he apologized. 'I had to go into Kyrenia first, and I had a puncture just short of the town. And then I met Monica, and that held me up a bit.'

He frowned at the recollection of that interview, and for a moment his mouth twisted in a wry grimace of distaste.

Claire said: 'Monica? What was she doing in Kyrenia?'

'Nothing much. She thought she'd pay a call on Miss Derington, but of course there was no one in the house.'

'On me?' said Amanda, surprised. 'I hope you explained that I was out on a picnic and that the house would be empty until after seven, what with Miss Moon and the servants both out. She won't even get any tea! You ought to have brought her along with you.'

The frown in Glenn Barton's eyes deepened. He said uncomfortably: 'She wasn't really in a picnicking mood. She's feeling pretty upset, what with her brother's death and—— ' He broke off and after a short pause said heavily: 'You'll probably be seeing her later anyway. She may wait if she's nothing else to do,' and changed the subject.

They cleared away the tea things and repacked the picnic baskets, and Amanda seized the opportunity of drawing Mr Barton apart and telling him something of her abortive mission on the previous night.

'I'm sorry it was so useless, Glenn,' she finished, 'but I'll try and see her again when – when she's feeling a bit better. At least you know that you were right and that she's not a bit in love with Lumley Potter.'

'Yes,' said Glenn slowly. 'I suppose that's something; though I was always sure she couldn't be. She's too – too fastidious for such an untidy, messy sloppy sort of chap as Potter.' He smiled at Amanda and added a little awkwardly: 'Anyway it was more than kind of you to go, and I'm very grateful. I am really.'

He took her hand and held it for a brief moment in a hard grip, and Amanda's fingers returned the pressure sympathetically. She smiled warmly at him, and in the next instant became suddenly aware that Steve Howard was watching them with an odd look in his eyes. A hard, bright, speculative look that held more than a hint of anger, and that for no reason at all caused Amanda's heart to give a queer little lurch and brought the bright colour up into her cheeks.

Claire called out: 'Glenn, come and give a hand with these baskets and things,' and Mr Barton dropped Amanda's hand and turned away. Presently he and George Norman carried the baskets and rugs down to the cars, Persis accompanying them.

The sun was low in the sky and the ruined walls threw long purple shadows on the grass and the wild thyme and the sheer rock faces that fell away almost vertically to the olive groves and the quiet blue sea far below.

The sea was as smooth and unwrinkled as polished steel, but high above it the breeze had strengthened with the approach of sundown and blew strongly about the castle, whistling shrilly

402

through the stone arches and along the deserted battlements.

Claire and Toby had walked away together deep in conversation, and Amanda, leaning against a parapet of stone and looking downwards, saw Alastair Blaine standing in an embrasure of the battlements below, talking to Anita Barton. She wondered idly if Alastair too would shortly be the possessor of another Potter masterpiece in Prussian blue, and hoped that Glenn would not meet his wife on his return from the cars. He had looked tired and ill and quite incapable of coping with a situation that involved being faced with a runaway wife and her lover.

Amanda turned her attention to the tilting ground that lay far below, and tried to imagine what it must have looked like when banners and pennants had flown there, and knights in armour had jousted before Richard of England and Queen Berengaria on their wedding day in Cyprus almost eight hundred years ago ...

'What are you thinking of, Amarantha?' inquired Steve Howard coming to lean against the wall beside her. She had not heard him approach because of the croon of the wind, and she turned quickly, considerably startled.

'Penny for them,' offered Steve. 'Or are they worth more?'

'If you really want to know, I was thinking that you and Toby and Glenn and the rest of them ought to be in armour, and Persis and Claire and I should be wearing wimples and "camises of fine white linen" and – and ermine lined pelicons — or do I mean surcotes?'

'Anyone mad enough to wear armour in this climate would be toasted to a crisp inside ten minutes,' observed Mr Howard prosaically. 'And you are wrong about the wimple. You should by rights be leaning out of the nearest window letting your hair down — like Rapunzel. How long have you known this man Barton?'

The question took Amanda by surprise. 'Glenn? I met him at Limassol. You know all about that. Why do you ask?'

' "*Glenn*",' murmured Steve, and went on to observe with some asperity that considering the shortness of their acquaintance they appeared to be on remarkably intimate terms with each other.

'Hardly that,' said Amanda sweetly, 'though he, like me, is probably worth anyone's while for half an hour in the moonlight.' She saw with satisfaction that she had made him angry, and added with deliberate provocation: 'I must find out.'

'Try it!' said Steve, smiling unpleasantly.

Something clattered on the stone behind them and a mangled tube of Hooker's Green fell at Amanda's feet. Lumley Potter had joined them.

'Damn!' said Mr Potter fretfully.

He deposited a folding easel and a virgin canvas on the ground and stooped to retrieve half a dozen tubes of paint that had fallen from an insecurely fastened box under his arm.

'Thought I'd make a quick study from here,' said Mr Potter. 'Hullo, Howard; you working on anything here?'

Amanda turned to look at Steve in some surprise. She had not realized that he had made Lumley Potter's acquaintance.

'No, alas. I find that it has nothing to say to me,' said Steve with perfect gravity. 'To the eye perhaps; but spiritually, no.'

'Now that's very interesting,' said Mr Potter earnestly. 'I, on the other hand——'

He plunged with enthusiasm into a pond of theory, and Amanda, who considered that Steve had asked for it, wandered away and left them to it.

She had already been up to the topmost part of the castle, but she thought that she would go again, and alone, to sit by the Queen's window where Berengaria must so often have sat, and watch the sun go down. She climbed a long flight of ruined stone steps with a high curtain wall above her and a steep grassy slope falling away below, and passed under an arch of lichened stone and through small, walled enclosures, partially roofless, that had once been guardrooms, granaries, galleries and *garderobes*.

The Queen's chamber was open to the wind and the evening sky, and a large part of the outer walls had fallen away, so that from the edge of the stone-paved floor one looked down on to tree tops and a yawning gulf where the rocky peak on which the castle of St Hilarion was built fell sheer away in a drop of well over two thousand feet.

Only one portion of the outer walls still remained, and from this the Queen's window, a graceful double arch in stone, looked out across the dreamlike landscape spread far below.

The sky and the sea had lost the deep, intense blue of the earlier afternoon and were pale in the evening light, and along the far horizon lay a faint lilac shadow that was the mountains of Turkey.

Amanda turned from the window and wandered away to where the weather-worn stone gave on to nothingness.

The evening wind whistled shrilly past her, whipping back her thin frock and tugging at her hair so that the heavy coils were loosened and fell upon her shoulders, tumbling down her back. Amanda put up a hand to arrest them, and yet another hairpin slid out, bounced upon the stone and fell into the void.

The song of the wind drowned the sound of footsteps behind her. A hand thrust hard against her and she fell forward and plunged downward into that horrible gulf, her scream of terror whipped away on the wind.

It was her hair that saved Amanda. Those long, thick, golden-brown tresses. Her hair and an aged and twisted fir tree that grew outwards from a fissure in the rock-face below the castle wall.

The branches whipped her face and broke under her, but they caught her hair; tangled it and wrenched at it, but held it as Absalom's had once been held. It checked her fall and gave her just time to clutch at a stronger bough.

Amanda hung there, blind and breathless with terror, her hands clinging frantically to the creaking bough, her long hair dragged taut above her and her feet swinging over emptiness.

She heard a shout above her, but she could not turn her head and she dared not move. The muscles in her arms hurt agonizingly, her clutching fingers were numb from her weight, and the wind sang through the pine needles and drowned out all other sounds.

She heard the bough crack, but it did not break, and she knew that she should move her hold and try to swing herself backwards on to the tree trunk; but she could not do so. If she attempted to relax her hold, she would fall.

The tree shuddered as though something heavy had struck it and a voice that she did not recognize shouted to her to hold on. It seemed to come from somewhere close behind her. But no one could climb down that rock-face below the wall — it would be suicide. Someone else was shouting now and a woman was screaming. Amanda felt the tree shake again and the bough to which she clung cracked ominously. And then hard fingers closed about one wrist and a voice said breathlessly:

'Try and get your food on to the branch behind you. Your left foot. Swing it straight back.'

She obeyed automatically, and could not afterwards remember how she had got from the tree trunk to a narrow ledge of rock that had been concealed from above. Once there, with an arm steadying her, it had not been too difficult to reach the level of the ruined battlements.

Someone above her leaned down and caught her hands, and a moment later her feet were on level ground and she had fainted for the first time in her life.

12

Amanda swam slowly up out of blackness into the warm golden glow of the evening sunlight.

Someone was pouring an unpleasant and fiery liquid down her throat and she choked and coughed; swallowed a considerable quantity of the stuff in the process, and choked again.

Steve Howard, very white about the mouth, was looking down at her with a grim anger that startled her. Amanda stared up at him, puzzled and shaken, and momentarily at a loss to know where she was or what she was doing, and why Steve should be in a rage.

She shut her eyes for a brief moment and opened them again. They were all still there, staring at her with pale excited faces. Claire and George Norman, Persis, Toby, Alastair and Glenn.

'What happened?' asked Amanda. 'Did I——'

And then suddenly she remembered, and stopped on a harsh gasp.

'You fell,' said Steve grimly. 'And I'd like to know what the hell you mean by wandering along parapets that a child of two would realize were unsafe! It's not your fault that you are not unpleasantly dead at this moment.'

It is possible that Mr Howard had a sound knowledge of psychology, for sympathy at this juncture would undoubtedly have reduced Amanda to tears and a return of terror. His curtly callous observation had an entirely opposite effect.

Amanda sat up, her breath coming short, and opened her mouth with the intention of informing him furiously that she had not fallen, but had been pushed.

But she did not say it.

She sat quite still, realizing, with a sudden, appalled clarity, that except for the Cypriot caretaker, Lumley Potter, Anita Barton and herself, there had been no one else at Hilarion that evening but the seven people who faced her.

Then one of nine people — seven of whom stood looking down at her, so close to her that by merely reaching out her hand she could touch any one of them — had meant to murder her. *Her* — Amanda Derington! What was it that Steve had just said? 'It's not your fault that you are not unpleasantly dead at this moment.' It was not someone else's fault either, for one of these people had meant her to be dead. Had tried to kill her——

Amanda shrank back against the sun-warmed stones of the wall, her wide, terrified eyes going from face to face in that circle.

Claire — Alastair — Toby — Glenn — Persis — George — Steve——

No. Not Steve! He was the only one she could be sure of. The only one. Her frightened eyes turned to him and she reached up and clutched at his sleeve.

Steve leant down and jerked her ungently to her feet, and Amanda said breathlessly: 'Please will you all go away. Please! I'm all right. I am really. I'm sorry I gave you all such a fright. I – I think I'd just like to sit here alone for a bit until I feel less peculiar. Please go!'

Her frantic fingers on Steve Howard's arm said *not you! not you!*

Persis said: 'Nonsense! Now see here honey——'

'Persis honey,' remarked Steve pleasantly, 'Scram! I'll see that she doesn't trip over any more walls.'

He glanced at his wrist watch and turned to Toby Gates:

'Would you mind giving Mrs Halliday a lift home, Gates? I'll drive Miss Derington back when she's feeling less scrambled.'

'Of course,' said Toby, looking uncertainly from Persis to Amanda and back again.

'Good idea,' said George Norman, his ruddy features resuming their normal hue. 'Beastly shock for her. Might have been a nasty accident. They really should rail off these dangerous spots. It's a scandal!'

They departed and Amanda was alone with the wind and Mr Howard.

She relaxed her grip on his arm, turned her back on him and said in a muffled voice: 'Would you mind going to the other side of that wall.'

'Why?' inquired Steve. 'Are you going to cry?'

'No,' said Amanda indistinctly. 'I'm going to be sick.' And was.

Mr Howard bore this unalluring spectacle with commendable fortitude, and having provided assistance in the form of a clean handkerchief, remarked that it was a waste of a good brandy and that he hoped for the sake of subsequent visitors that it would rain during the night.

'Feeling better?' he inquired presently.

'Yes thank you. Could we go somewhere where there are four walls and no edge, do you think?'

'Nothing easier.' He drew her hand through his arm and walked her away, keeping her between him and the solid inner wall. They had gone less than half a dozen yards when he checked suddenly and bent down to pick up something that lay wedged between two slabs of stone. It was a small, twisted tube of oil paint from which the top was missing. He turned it over in his hand, looking at it thoughtfully, and then slipped it into his pocket without comment.

They walked back through the roofless rooms, and once again the steep flight of stone steps lay below them.

Amanda stopped and shut her eyes. She had never been in the least affected by heights, but now she knew that she would never be able to look down from any height again without being afraid. She knew that it was ridiculous and absurd; the ruined stairway was wide and safe and the slope that fell away along one side of it was covered with grass and shrubs, trees and fallen boulders. But the fear of falling was on her and she could not move.

Steve Howard picked her up without ceremony and carried her down the long, uneven flight to the quiet and shelter of a grass-grown level, where the solid walls of the Outer Bailey towered comfortingly above them and the last of the sun turned the dry grasses to bright gold.

'All right here?'

'Yes,' said Amanda gratefully. 'I'm sorry about that.'

'You'll get over it,' said Steve, striking a match against the stones and lighting himself a cigarette.

Amanda sank down cross-legged on the warm grass and said in a voice that she tried to keep steady: 'I haven't thanked you yet for – for saving my life. That branch wouldn't have held much longer.'

'You don't have to thank me,' said Steve shortly. 'Barton got you out of that.'

'Glenn?'

'Yes — Glenn.'

Steve's mouth twisted a little wryly on the name. 'He's the one you have to thank. He thought he heard someone scream, and ran out and saw you. I was on my way up, and he yelled out to me, and the next thing I knew he had lowered himself down over the edge and found some sort of a foothold and dropped down onto the trunk of that tree. He must have plenty of nerve. I wouldn't have cared to do it myself.'

'And I let him go without saying anything!' said Amanda, distressed. 'I thought it was you——'

'Alas, no,' said Steve satirically. 'I was merely among those present. How did you happen to do it?'

'I was pushed,' said Amanda in a whisper.

'*Say that again!*'

'S – someone pushed me.'

Steve stood very still, looking down at her, his mouth a tight line and his eyes blazing.

Presently he said quite softly: 'Who?'

'I – I don't know,' said Amanda, a terrified break in her voice. 'The wind was so loud — I didn't hear any other sound. And then suddenly someone pushed me hard and – and I fell . . .' Her voice died out in a whisper and she shuddered uncontrollably.

'You are quite sure it wasn't a sudden gust of wind?'

'Don't be ridiculous!' said Amanda, retreating from the verge of tears. 'It was a *hand*.'

'Man or woman?'

'I tell you I don't *know!* I didn't hear or see anyone.'

'Come on, Amanda — think! Try and remember what it felt like. Was it a small hand or a large one? Hard? Thin? Warm? That dress you're wearing is pretty flimsy, you must have some idea.'

'But I haven't! You see my hair had come down and it was all over my back.'

'*Hell!*' said Steve softly.

He dropped his cigarette on the grass, put his foot on it and sat down beside her with his hands clasped about his knees, and stared fixedly ahead of him at the massive walls of the Outer Bailey. Amanda, watching him, saw that there were harsh lines on his forehead and about his mouth that she did not remember having noticed before, and that his eyes were blank and unseeing.

After a time he said curtly and without turning his head: 'What made you keep quiet up there? — about being pushed?'

'I was just going to say it, and then—— ' Amanda's voice seemed to dry in her throat and she swallowed convulsively.

'And then—— ?' prompted Steve.

'Then I suddenly realized that it might have been one of them. People I know—— ' Amanda's voice wavered and she said desperately: 'Why? I haven't said anything to anyone. Why should someone want to kill me now that it's all over?'

'It isn't all over,' said Steve curtly. 'Not by a long chalk.'

He dropped his chin on his knees and relapsed into silence, brooding with the concentration of a Buddhist considering infinity.

The shadows lengthened and soon the ruined walls of Hilarion would no longer be warmly gold but a cold forbidding grey. The sky above the battlements had already turned to a pale clear green, and the level floor of the tilting ground below the castle began to fill with soft purple shadow.

Steve sighed and moved at last. He stood up, stretching himself, and leaned down to pull Amanda to her feet:

'Come on; it's time we got going. If we don't watch it we shall find ourselves being locked in for the night.'

He put out a hand and lifted a long shining strand of the hair that tumbled in tangled disorder to well below Amanda's waist.

'Beautiful stuff,' observed Steve reflectively. 'I wonder why women will cut it off? Well you can thank your lucky stars you didn't. A crew-cut wouldn't have saved you today, Amarantha. Go on — plait it up or get it out of the way. It gives me ideas — and this is no time for ideas; at least not of that category.'

Amanda's white face flushed with colour and she jerked her head away and plaited her dishevelled hair with quick, unsteady fingers into two heavy schoolgirl plaits.

'You look about six,' commented Steve. 'Can you manage the rest of the way on your own feet?'

'Of course I can,' said Amanda with dignity. 'It was only those stairs.'

He turned on his heel without further comment and walked down ahead of her, whistling abstractedly, his hands deep in his pockets.

There was only one car left beside the roadside at the foot of the slope below Hilarion. The others must have left at least half an hour before.

'Twenty past six,' observed Steve, releasing the clutch and glancing at the dashboard clock. 'You'll just make it.'

'Make what?'

'I gather that you are dining out with young Gates; drinks at seven. He mentioned it during tea.'

'Oh!' said Amanda blankly. 'I'd forgotten. Perhaps he could dine with Persis instead.'

'Going to cut your date?'

'Yes. I – I don't think I feel like facing any of them just now. I feel like getting back to my bedroom and looking under the bed and inside and behind all the furniture, and locking every door and window and then getting into bed and pulling all the bedclothes over my head. And that's just what I'm going to do!'

'A very sound programme,' approved Steve. 'You'll feel braver in the morning. Want me to make your excuses to Toby Gates?'

'Would you? Tell him that I — No; don't tell him anything. I'll write a note if you don't mind waiting while I write it. Then you could give it to him. Would you do that?'

'A pleasure, Amarantha.'

Kyrenia and the coast were still bathed in the last warm glow of the sunset when they turned into the quiet side road and stopped before the Villa Oleander. But the shadows were moving swiftly across the garden and up the face of the house, and only the tops of the tallest cypress trees were still touched with gold.

The water trickling from the mouth of the bronze dolphin made a cool, pleasant sound in the silence, and now that the sun had left the garden the scent of roses and jasmine and dust filled the windless air with fragrance. In the embrasures of the old wall behind the house the pigeons cooed and fluttered as they settled down for the night, and the drowsy hum of the town rose murmurously from beyond the trees and the garden wall. But the house itself seemed strangely silent.

Amanda pushed open the heavy front door and stood in the cool, shadowed hall, listening to that silence.

Miss Moon could not be back yet. She was not given to silence except when resting, and the sound of her voice and her jingling jewellery was almost an integral part of the Villa Oleander.

'What is it Amanda?' inquired Steve Howard, watching her face.

413

'Nothing. It – it's very quiet. I thought perhaps that Miss Moon would be back.'

'Scared?'

'Yes!' said Amanda with a shiver. 'Steve——' she turned to him quickly, unaware that she had for the first time used that familiar abbreviation of his name that Persis and Claire used so lightly — 'would you – would you stay until she comes back? I know it's ridiculous of me, but the house feels so empty.'

'Yes of course,' said Steve, in the manner of one who has been asked to pass the salt. His tone was entirely matter-of-fact and oddly steadying. 'Like me to go upstairs and look under the bed for you?' he suggested with a satirical gleam in his eye.

'Do you think I'm being very silly?' demanded Amanda abruptly.

Steve smiled at her. 'No dear. In fact for a girl who has just escaped a particularly messy end by inches, you are behaving like the entire George Cross Island rolled into one, and I'm proud of you, Amarantha. Do you realize that nine hundred and ninety-nine women out of a thousand would have had shrieking hysterics, burst into tears, died of heart-failure and then rushed screaming to the telephone to book an immediate passage to Baffin Bay or North Borneo?'

Amanda laughed a little shakily. 'I've wanted desperately to do all those things,' she confessed. 'In fact with any encouragement at all, I'd have done them!'

'I know,' said Steve with a grin. 'That's why you didn't get any!'

'You've been quite beastly!' said Amanda accusingly.

'The situation,' observed Steve caustically, 'is sufficiently unpleasant as it is, without being further gummed up with tears and hysteria. Is there by any chance a lavatory in this building?'

'Yes of course. Down that passage and first door on your left.'

'Thanks.'

He departed and Amanda, remembering her decision to write

414

a note to Toby Gates, crossed the hall and went into the drawing-room.

The last of the sunlight had only recently faded from the room, but except before the french windows that gave on to the verandah the green wooden shutters were still closed, and the room was hot and airless and very dark. Amanda threw open the shutters to let in the fast vanishing daylight, and sitting down at Miss Moon's cluttered ormolu desk, reached for writing paper and a pen.

She began to write, aware as she did so that the scratching of the pen sounded astonishingly loud in the quiet room. But after completing no more than two lines she paused: listening, as she had listened in the hall, to the silence.

The windless evening was quiet and very still, and there was no sound in the darkening house. But she was not alone in the room. It was not a suspicion but a certainty. There was someone else in the room besides herself. Someone was hidden there ...

Amanda sat rigid while her blood seemed to turn cold and run slowly. She dared not move, and it seemed that she had lost the power to breathe. She knew that she should turn — she would be safer, surely, with her back to the wall? But she could not move. She must call out; scream for Steve Howard——

Steve! Why of course! it was Steve who had returned across the hall without her hearing him.

She whirled round on a gasp of relief. But there was no one there. The dusty beautiful furniture looked back at her, composed and calm and watchful with that curious sense of watchfulness that many old and inanimate objects possess. The open doorway gaped emptily on the dark and silent hall, and there was no sign of Steven Howard.

It was imagination, Amanda told herself — imagination and the silence of an empty house. There was no third person in the Villa Oleander; no one in the room but herself. She forced herself to turn and face the desk; to pick up the pen. But she could not force her hand to write. She could only sit still; and listen——

The scent of roses and jasmine and violets filled the airless room with a cloying sweetness: odd that she should not have noticed that there were violets growing in the garden. Amanda laid down her pen very carefully. She seemed to be under some curious compulsion not to make any sound that might break that alert and listening silence. There was — someone else in the room — there was.

She stood up quickly and turned, gripping the carved chairback with cold hands and fighting to control a rising panic. Her wide, frightened eyes searched the darkening room, but except for the solid back of the sofa that stood between her and the french windows the furniture was either too frail or so placed as to afford no opportunities for concealment. The glass-fronted cabinets of buhl and marqueterie stood backed against the corners of the room, their cluttered contents making splashes of pure, gleaming colour in the shadowy room. The fading light glinted on carved jade and ivory, enamelled snuff boxes, bottles cut from rose quartz, chrysoprase and lapis lazuli, and on the tiny, twinkling diamonds that formed the cypher of a murdered Empress on a fabulous Fabergé egg of crystal.

The faded brocade curtains hung straight and motionless and it was not possible that anyone could be standing concealed behind them. An ornately framed looking-glass that hung above the writing table reflected another and similar mirror on the opposite wall, and Amanda could see herself in it; endlessly repeated. A long line of slender, frightened girls standing in a dim, silvery corridor in the disk.

But it reflected something else as well. Something that lay beyond the range of her vision, though not beyond the compass of that glimmering oval. A hand——

There was someone crouching on the floor in front of the french windows, concealed by the sofa.

Amanda froze into stillness; her wide eyes fixed upon the reflection of that hand whose fingers were crooked, claw-like, on the faded carpet; waiting for it to be withdrawn — to slide quietly back into hiding. But it did not move.

A sudden stabbing thought broke the web of terror that held her. It's Miss Moon! She turned and leapt across the narrow space that lay between the writing table and the sofa, reached it and was round it.

But it was not Miss Moon. It was someone who lay sprawled face downwards on the floor. A woman in a tight blue cotton frock patterned with rosebuds, who wore a vivid scarf of emerald green *crêpe de Chine* tied about her neck.

Amanda dropped on her knees and touched that outstretched hand. It was slack and warm, and a wave of incredible relief engulfed her. What a fool she was! This must be some visitor who had waited for Miss Moon, and had fainted. She tugged at the limp, warm bulk and turned it over ...

There was nothing she could recognize in that swollen, horribly discoloured face with its glazed, protruding eyes and lolling tongue. Nothing except a necklace and ear-rings of garish plastic flowers and the odour of a cheap violet scent that suggested hair oil.

Amanda let the heavy, lifeless body drop back on to the floor and sprang to her feet, backing away from it, her hands at her throat.

There was a sound of leisurely footsteps crossing the hall and then Steve was standing in the doorway——

The next second he had crossed the floor in three strides and his hands were gripping her shoulders so tightly that they hurt.

'What is it!'

Amanda did not speak but her head turned and Steve's eyes followed the direction of her frozen gaze.

His fingers tightened convulsively on her shoulders so that she winced with pain, and then he had thrust her roughly to one side and was on his knees beside that appalling figure.

He touched it once only, noting, as Amanda had done, the warm

417

slackness of that outstretched hand, and after that only his eyes moved, quickly and intently.

He looked up at Amanda and said harshly: 'Did you touch her?'

Amanda wet her dry lips with her tongue. 'I – I turned her over. I thought she had fainted.'

'You know her?' It was less a query than a statement of fact.

'Yes. It's – she's Glenn Barton's secretary. Monica Ford. He – he said that she had called to see me.'

'I remember. That must have been somewhere between four and half-past. Three hours ago,' said Steve thoughtfully.

Amanda said shuddering: 'Then – then she did wait for me. She's warm. She can't have been dead for three hours!'

'Probably less than half an hour, at a guess.' He looked down at the distorted face and said slowly: 'Both you and Barton mentioned at the picnic that this house would be empty. Someone who did not really believe that Miss Ford would wait for you may have seized the opportunity to slip in here and look for something — perhaps that bottle, or the glass — and been surprised by her on their way out.'

Amanda said in a high, breaking voice: 'But I haven't got them! I haven't got them! — I—— '

Steve stood up swiftly and caught her clutching hands in a hard and exceedingly painful grasp.

'Stop that, Amanda. I'm not standing any nonsense from you! Come on, George Cross Island — pull yourself together!'

Amanda gasped, gulped, and clenched her teeth on her trembling lip, and her breathing steadied.

'That's better,' approved Steve. 'Is there a telephone here?'

'Y – yes. At the end of the passage off the hall.'

'Afraid to go there by yourself?'

'No!' Amanda wrenched her hands from his hold and her chin came up with a jerk.

'That's the girl. All right; go and ring a number for me—— ' He gave her a number and made her repeat it. 'Tell whoever answers

418

it that Steven Howard would like to see Mr Jurgan Calder at the Villa Oleander in Kyrenia and that it will be a late party. Got that?'

'Yes.'

'Repeat it ... That's right. Don't say anything else. Only that, and ring off. And when you've done that you'd better get through to the Dome and leave a message for Toby Gates to say that you will not be able to dine with him tonight. Otherwise we shall have him turning up here to fetch you before we know where we are. Cut along.'

He did not watch Amanda go, but turned back immediately to the huddled, hideous figure on the floor. He was on his knees beside it when she returned, but he had switched on two of the lights, and he did not look up or trouble to inquire if she had done as he asked. It was after seven, but Miss Moon had still not returned. They had been back for just over twenty minutes, thought Amanda numbly — how was it possible to live through so much in so short a space of time?

The sun had set and the sky was green with gathering dusk and pricked with the first stars. The house was very still again. And in that stillness Amanda heard the soft, unmistakable pad of shoeless feet in the room above them.

Steve had heard it too, for his head came up with a jerk and his eyes were wide and bright and intensely alert. Presently the sound was repeated and all at once he was on his feet and at the door. He seemed to move with a swiftness and lack of noise that was, in its way, remarkable.

He swung round suddenly and looked at Amanda. His eyes went from her to the open windows and the garden beyond the verandah, and she saw that he was holding something in his left hand. That same small gun that she had seen once before in the cabin of the *Orantares*.

He said curtly: 'You'd better come with me,' and turned away again without looking to see if she followed him or not.

They went up the stairs swiftly and — on Steve's part — silently.

But Amanda's white, flat-heeled sandals clicked on the polished treads and she stumbled and clung to the stair-rail.

It was Miss Moon's bedroom that lay directly above the drawing-room, and Steve glanced over his shoulder at Amanda, and pushing her back against the landing wall with one hand, turned the handle and kicked the door open with his foot.

There was a shrill, feminine shriek and a familiar clash of silver filigree bracelets, and Amanda said on a sob: 'It's Miss Moon!' and brushing past him she ran into the room.

Miss Moon was standing at the foot of her tumbled bed, wrapped in an elderly cotton kimono patterned with a design of storks and chrysanthemums that suggested that its origin was Manchester rather than Matsumoto. She was wearing what at first sight appeared to be a hat, but which, on inspection, turned out to be an ice-bag of antediluvian design tied on to her head bonnet-wise with a black silk stocking. Bedroom slippers of scuffed kid and an assortment of bracelets completed the ensemble.

'Who is this man?' demanded Miss Moon in outraged tones. 'Amanda, send him away at once! I will not have strange men in my bedroom!'

Amanda flung her arms about Miss Moon and burst into over-wrought tears. Miss Moon enfolded her in a protective clutch that smelt of mothballs, menthol and heliotrope, and glared at Mr Howard. Mr Howard looked thoughtfully back at her. The gun was no longer in evidence and he looked entirely relaxed and innocent of guile.

'There, there, dear!' said Miss Moon, patting Amanda's shuddering shoulders. 'Has he been annoying you? Well I shall know how to deal with him. Sir — you should be ashamed of yourself!'

'I must apologize,' said Mr Howard. 'I didn't know that you were in.'

'That,' observed Miss Moon haughtily, 'is quite evident!'

'How long have you been back, Miss Moon?'

'I cannot see that it is any concern of yours, young man. But if it is of any interest to you, I have not been out.'

'*What?*' Amanda lifted a tear-wet face from Miss Moon's bony shoulder. 'But the bridge party ...'

'I was compelled to send my excuses,' said Miss Moon. 'I am subject to sudden and severe attacks of migraine, and it proved quite impossible for me to go.'

Amanda said: 'Then – then you have been here all the time?'

'I have.'

'That's very interesting,' said Steve.

Miss Moon bristled. 'Interesting? Why should it be interesting?'

'Because,' said Steve gently, 'it means that someone is due for the shock of their life, and I would most earnestly advise you, Miss Moon, not to mention to anyone that you did not go out this afternoon.'

'Young man,' said Miss Moon, drawing herself to her full height, 'I do not understand you. Naturally Lady Cooper-Foot and all those who attended her bridge party are fully aware that I remained at home.'

'Then that's torn it!' said Steve.

Miss Moon looked from Amanda to Steve, and her eyes, despite the heaviness that pain and drugs had lent them, were suddenly sharp and shrewd:

'Tell me what has happened,' she demanded crisply. 'Why would it have been advisable to conceal the fact that I have not left the house?'

'Because,' said Steve softly, 'less than an hour ago a woman was murdered in the room directly below this one — by someone who had every reason to believe that there was no one else in the house.'

13

Awaking late on the following morning, Amanda lay for several minutes staring idly at the misty folds of the mosquito net and wondering why the room seemed so airless. She felt drowsy and relaxed and curiously stupid. It can't be more than six, she thought; the room is still dark.

But the air was always cool and fresh in the early morning, not hot like this. Turning her head she saw that the dimness of the room was due to the fact that the shutters, which were always thrown back at night and only used during the heat of the day, were closed and bolted, and she frowned at them; realizing, from the bright chinks of sunlight that showed between the slats, that it was far later than she had supposed, and puzzled by a vague recollection that it was she herself who had insisted on closing those shutters.

A moment later she was sitting bolt upright with all trace of drowsiness gone, for she had remembered why it had seemed so necessary to lock herself into her room last night.

Amanda pushed back the mosquito net and went over to open the shutters, aware as she did so that it was at least midday. And also that someone must have given her a strong sleeping draught, for her head felt unaccountably heavy.

Steve Howard, of course! He had made her drink a cup of coffee. It had been black and sweet and had left a faintly unpleasant taste on her tongue. That must have been late last night, after the police and the doctor had left and an ambulance had taken Monica

Ford's body away to the Nicosia General Hospital, and the endless questions were over at last.

There had been so many questions.

The man she had telephoned for, the man with an odd name, had arrived while they were still explaining the ugly situation to Miss Moon. Steve had gone down to meet him, and Amanda, who had remained with Miss Moon, had not been present at that interview. She had come out onto the upper landing just as he was leaving and had heard him say: 'All right; we'll play it on those lines. It's your deal. I can stack the deck at my end, and——' He had heard Amanda's sandals click on the stairs and had stopped.

'This is Miss Derington,' said Steve. He did not complete the introduction and Amanda found herself shaking hands with a slim, quiet man who seemed a little shy and very ordinary. The sort of man, thought Amanda, whom one might meet a dozen times and still not remember. There was nothing in any way remarkable about him except perhaps his eyes, which were as cool and quiet and yet as disconcertingly observant as Steve Howard's own.

A moment later he had gone. It was after that that Steve had telephoned for the police and the doctor, and when they arrived he had gone into the drawing-room with them and shut the door. After what seemed a very long time they had sent for Amanda and Miss Moon and had questioned them. Two of the police officers had been British. C.I.D. men from Nicosia. The third had been a Cypriot who spoke excellent English.

Miss Moon had little to tell them. A migraine had descended upon her with sudden and all too familiar severity, and she had telephoned her excuses to Lady Cooper-Foot and retired to bed in a darkened room with an ice-pack and sedatives. Yes, she had been aware of voices in the drawing-room some time during the afternoon. She could not say when. Three-thirty perhaps? Four? She had been in considerable pain and had paid little attention beyond wishing that whoever was speaking would use a less hysterical tone. Oh yes, it had been a woman, and she had sounded upset. No: Miss Moon had not gone down. She had imagined that it must have been Euridice returned unexpectedly, but soon afterwards the drugs had taken effect and she had slept until past seven o'clock and had barely arisen when Amanda and Mr Howard had burst into her room.

But surely, said a police officer, she must have been aware of some sounds, however slight? The woman had been murdered——

'"*Strangling is a very quiet death*,"' murmured Steve Howard meditatively.

Apparently Miss Moon was familiar with *The Duchess of Malfi*, for she had looked at Mr Howard with a distinct gleam of appreciation in her eye and said: 'Exactly! No, I not only heard no other sounds, but I have no idea — if the woman whose voice I heard was indeed Monica Ford — whom she can have been addressing.'

'Glenn,' said Amanda. And explained that Mr Barton had mentioned meeting his secretary and had added that Miss Ford had wished to see her — Amanda — and that she had seemed upset.

They had questioned her as to her previous meeting with Miss Ford on the day of her arrival in Cyprus, and made her repeat as much of their conversation as she could remember. And then they had asked her to tell them again exactly what Glenn Barton said on the subject of his secretary at the picnic that afternoon, and having received corroboration from Mr Howard, they had sent for Mr Barton.

Glenn had arrived shortly after half past nine, having driven from Nicosia at a speed considerably in excess of the recognized limits. He had looked grey and drawn and somehow apathetic. Steve had poured him out a stiff portion of Miss Moon's liqueur brandy and he had swallowed it gratefully.

Yes, he had been to the Villa Oleander that afternoon and had spoken with Miss Ford in this room. He explained the circumstances and agreed that his secretary had been upset. She had recently lost her only brother and sole close relative. And there had been other things on her mind—— He checked abruptly and frowned.

What other things?

Glenn's tired face seemed to grow greyer and he had explained in a halting, difficult voice something of what he had told Amanda in that same room on the previous afternoon: of Anita's suggestions concerning the relations between Miss Ford and himself.

'Of course there was nothing in it,' he explained wearily. 'My wife could never believe such a thing. She only spread that story in order to — well, to make trouble I suppose. They had quarrelled and Miss Ford had probably been rude to her.'

'Anita,' put in Miss Moon crisply, 'was well aware that people would be only too willing to believe that Monica had fallen in love with her employer, but that no one in their senses would believe that he was in love with her. So that from Monica's point of view the story would be doubly wounding.'

'Was she in love with you?' asked a police officer.

The colour came up into Glenn's haggard face and his mouth tightened and set hard. He looked at the man who had asked the question and his eyes did not waver.

'No.' The single word was curt and entirely final.

But they had not finished with him. They went back again to the quarrel between his secretary and his wife, and again and again to his conversation with Miss Ford in the Villa Oleander that afternoon. Was he quite sure of the time? Why was he sure? So he had seen the green scarf? Why, having heard a sound from one of the upper rooms, had he still said at Hilarion that the house was empty?

'I didn't know that Miss Moon was in,' said Glenn wearily. 'I thought it must be a pigeon or the cat.'

He turned to look at Miss Moon. 'I'm sorry, Mooney. If I'd known you were ill I'd have come up.'

'I wouldn't have let you in,' said Miss Moon tartly, and departed to cut sandwiches and brew hot coffee.

They turned back to the picnic at Hilarion:

How many people had been present when Mr Barton had spoken of his secretary and mentioned that there was no one at home in the Villa Oleander? At what time had Mr Barton left Hilarion, and where had he gone?

'To Nicosia,' said Glenn tiredly. 'Prove it? Well as a matter of fact I can. The Normans saw me go. We all left at the same time — except Howard and Miss Derington. There were only four cars there. Gates and Mrs Halliday went ahead of my car and turned left for Kyrenia. I turned up right, and the Normans and Major Blaine were behind me and must have seen me turn. They went down to Kyrenia too, of course. I drove straight to the Nicosia office, and as it happens I can prove that too, because I gave a lift to a couple of troops. You can probably check with them. I dropped them off in the centre of the town just after six. Anything more you want to know?'

There appeared to be a great deal more. But they left at last, and it was just as they were leaving that one of the police officers found the little linen flower.

There was a massive carved chest in the hall, black with age and decorated with medallions of beaten silver, and the small white flower had caught on a rough edge of metal at a level where the hem of a woman's skirt might have brushed past it.

The officer reached down and removed it and turned it over between his fingers. There was a thread hanging from the centre of it as though it had been torn from something.

Amanda said incredulously: 'But that's—— ' and saw Glenn Barton's face, and stopped.

Glenn was staring at her with a tense and desperate appeal in his eyes. Amanda looked away quickly and became aware that Steve had been watching them.

The police officer said: 'This is yours, then?'

426

'Yes,' said Amanda without hesitation. She saw Glenn shut his eyes for a brief moment and catch at the edge of the chest as though to steady himself, and she held out her hand for the flower.

The police officer looked at her long and thoughtfully, and then put it into his pocket. 'If you do not mind, I will keep it. It will be returned of course.'

And then they had gone. Glenn first, and the three police officers perhaps five minutes later. The doctor had already left in the ambulance that had taken Monica Ford's body to Nicosia an hour earlier.

Miss Moon departed to the kitchen to make more coffee and Amanda would have followed her except that Steve Howard stood between her and the door that led through to the kitchen, and he did not look as though he intended to move aside for her as he had moved for Miss Moon.

'Amanda,' said Steve softly, 'you are a damned bad liar and several kinds of a fool into the bargain. What possessed you to do such an idiotic thing?'

Amanda did not pretend to misunderstand him. 'I couldn't do anything else,' she said unhappily. 'You didn't see his face—— '

'Oh yes I did,' interrupted Steve brusquely. 'But that is no reason why you should have laid claim to the thing.'

'What else could I have done? If I'd said it wasn't mine, they'd have asked Miss Moon; and as it wasn't hers, they would have traced it.'

'They'll trace it all right,' said Steve grimly. 'And when they do you are going to find yourself in an exceedingly unpleasant position.'

'Why?' said Amanda defensively.

'There is such a thing as being an accessory after the fact,' pointed out Steve dryly.

'I can't help it,' said Amanda. 'I – I owed him something.'

'For saving your life?' said Steve with an edge to his voice. 'Perhaps. But he had no right to let you do it.'

'You don't understand,' said Amanda. 'He's in love with her.'

'And are you by any chance in love with him?' inquired Steve unpleasantly. 'Is that the real reason for this quixotic gesture?'

Amanda hit him.

She had not meant to do it or known that she would do so. The gesture had been an entirely unexpected and instinctive reaction born of the accumulative terror and shock and emotional strain of the past hours and the last few days. This time he either did not anticipate the action or did not trouble to avoid it.

Amanda stared in stunned dismay at the red mark that her palm had left on Steven Howard's hard cheek; her grey eyes very wide and young.

'I – I'm sorry,' she said in a small, unsteady voice. 'I didn't mean to do that. I—— '

'Don't apologize,' interrupted Steve sardonically. 'After all I did offer you a second try, didn't I? — and they say that practice makes perfect.'

'You're very angry, aren't you?' said Amanda in a subdued voice.

'If I am, it's probably with myself,' said Steve curtly.

And then Miss Moon had reappeared with a fresh pot of coffee and they had drunk it sitting round the dining-room table because none of them wanted to go into the drawing-room again, and because Amanda flatly refused to go to bed.

Amanda had not wanted the hot coffee either, and had asked for a cold drink instead. Steve had ignored the request and had poured out a cup of black coffee to which he had added sugar and, undoubtedly, some drug that he had presumably obtained off Miss Moon or the doctor, and had handed it to her without further words. Amanda had looked at his coolly unemotional eyes and uncompromising mouth and had been too tired to argue. She had drunk it, and it had left an unpleasant taste on her tongue.

Steve had embarked on a long conversation with Miss Moon who, it was soon obvious, had entirely revised her first opinion of him and was already addressing him as 'dear boy'. He had not spoken directly to Amanda again, and presently his voice and his face had begun to fade into a misty background in which only a flight of pseudo-Japanese storks and the jingle of Miss Moon's bracelets stood out at all clearly.

Amanda's eyelids had begun to feel strangely heavy and she found that she could no longer prevent them from closing. She slid down a little lower in her chair and a voice that seemed to come from the other end of a long tunnel had said faintly but distinctly: 'I think, dear boy, that she is almost asleep now,' and another voice, equally far away said: 'And about time too!'

Amanda had forced open her eyes in order to see who was asleep, and had looked up into Steven Howard's face and remembered that he had been angry about something; something to do with Glenn Barton. She must explain about that. Steve had not understood. She found that it was an effort to speak, and said drowsily and with difficulty: 'Glenn—— ' and the face above her was suddenly blank and hard and completely expressionless.

Then her eyes closed again and Steve had lifted her and carried her up a long dark flight of stairs, and she had turned her face against his shoulder and clung to him with terrified desperation, because these were the ruined stone steps of Hilarion once more, and she was afraid of falling.

The door opened with a faint creak of hinges and Amanda turned quickly to see Miss Moon peering cautiously around it.

Miss Moon, a vision in lemon yellow, brightened at the sight of her and said approvingly: 'So you are awake at last! I have looked in several times, but did not wish to wake you. How are you feeling, my dear?'

'A bit stupid,' said Amanda with an attempt at a smile. 'Is it very late?'

'Ten minutes to one, dear. Luncheon will be ready in a moment. I expect you are hungry. I do trust that you feel no ill-effects from

429

those sleeping powders? I have always found them remarkably effective, although I confess I have never taken more than one. But Mr Howard thought that in the circumstances two would be advisable. *Such* a dear boy! So thoughtful — and so well read. How *few* people one meets who have read *Il Conte de Carmagnola* in the original and can discuss it intelligently! Dear Papa would have enjoyed conversing with him. I will tell Euridice to run you a bath.'

'Miss Moon,' said Amanda in a halting voice, 'I – didn't dream it by any chance, did I?'

Miss Moon's face changed and her mouth closed for a moment into a tight line.

'No my dear. I am afraid not. We have had the police here the whole morning. I would not permit them to wake you, since you could have told them nothing more than you told them last night. Several people called to inquire after you. That young Captain Gates, and a Mrs Halliday — American I think, and very striking. And Glenn has been here too. There will have to be an inquest, of course, but the police have satisfied themselves as to the reason for poor Monica Ford's dreadful end.'

Amanda sat down rather suddenly on the edge of her bed. 'Who – who do they think did it?'

'A thief of course,' said Miss Moon, and wrung her hands so that the bracelets jingled. 'Oh, Amanda dear, I fear it was *all* my fault!'

'Darling!' said Amanda, jumping up and giving her hostess a sudden impulsive hug. 'Don't be silly! How could it possibly be your fault?'

'Well you see, dear, there are a great many valuable things in this house. My dear Papa was a great collector. And of course I have never kept anything under lock and key, and everyone knows that I never lock the house up — except of course at night. Euridice insists on that. It must have been a temptation. I see that now. Some dishonest person must have come to hear that the house

430

would be empty yesterday afternoon, and have crept in intending to steal what they could. They would not have expected to find anyone in the drawing-room, and may not have noticed Monica until she had time to see and perhaps even recognize the thief. They think that he lost his head and picked up the scarf only intending to stop her from calling out, and did not mean to kill her — I do *hope* he did not!'

Amanda said: 'But nothing was missing.'

'Oh yes there was, dear. Several of the smaller and more valuable items from dear Papa's collection had been removed from the cabinets in the drawing-room. There are so many things there that I did not immediately realize it.'

Amanda was aware of a sudden and overwhelming wave of relief.

She could not have told why she should be so inexpressibly relieved. Surely she could not have believed that one of a small group of people who were personally known to her could have deliberately strangled poor, harmless, unhappy Monica Ford? No of course she had not. All the same she felt as if a black, crushing weight had been lifted off her shoulders.

'It will be a lesson to me,' sighed Miss Moon. 'I shall have to send dear Papa's collection to the bank. So foolish. Beautiful things should be looked at and appreciated; not locked away in vaults. I think I hear Euridice in the hall. Luncheon will be ready and here I am keeping you talking.'

She hurried away and Amanda bathed and dressed quickly, and having brushed out her tangled hair, rolled it up and bundled the shining mass into a coarse white net in the style that had been fashionable in the days when the young Empress Eugenie had netted her beautiful tresses in a similar manner. Amanda would not let herself think of those desperate moments at Hilarion when her hair alone had saved her from a horrible and disfiguring death, but some frightened instinct would not allow her to pin it securely. She had to feel that it was free and unbound.

431

She turned to look at herself in the long silvery expanse of looking-glass on the wall. The heavy chignon tilted her head back with its weight and made her face appear smaller and more pointed and her slender neck as long as the stem of a flower. White linen dress. White linen sandals. *White linen* — a small flat, white linen flower clinging to a rough edge of metal on the chest in the hall ...

Amanda caught her lip between her teeth. She had forgotten that sinister little flower. But it couldn't mean anything! Supposing Anita Barton *had* been to the Villa Oleander on her return from St Hilarion? Supposing, even, that she was (as her clothes suggested) extravagant and possibly in debt? That still did not make her a thief, any more than her dislike of Monica Ford made her a murderess. Recalling Anita Barton's relaxed and sleeping face, Amanda was suddenly and comfortingly sure of that.

The police and Miss Moon were right. Some petty thief, snatching the jade and crystal trinkets from the drawing-room cabinets, had been surprised by Monica Ford, and had panicked and killed her.

Amanda applied rose-pink lipstick with a steady hand, made a face at herself in the glass and ran downstairs to join Miss Moon.

The dining-room smelt pleasantly of flowers and fruit and Euridice's special brand of ravioli, and beyond the open windows the garden was brilliant with sunlight and noisy with the coo and flutter of pigeons and the sound of Andreas chopping wood. Euridice was conducting an excitable conversation with a friend in the kitchen and Miss Moon was as talkative as ever.

'No,' said Miss Moon, waving away the barley water: 'I never drink with meals, dear. So bad for the digestion; it dilutes the gastric juices. Only between meals. Though of course one so often forgets to do that, and then so much of it is wasted. It does not really keep in this weather. Try some of this melon, dear——'

Everything was suddenly safe and sane and ordinary again, and the house no longer held its breath to listen but basked comfortably in the hot sunshine. Colour came back to Amanda's cheeks and some of the sparkle to her eyes, and with the resilience and optimism of youth she pushed the recollection of the past few days behind her and felt her spirits rise to meet the challenge of the gay, glittering day. She would forget about all the horrible things that had happened. She would not think of them. She was in Cyprus — in Kyrenia — and the sun was shining. She would go out and bathe with Toby and laugh with Persis, and buy embroidered linen in the shops in the town and photograph the harbour as a hundred thousand carefree tourists had done before her.

Her mood lasted until the end of the meal, and it was Miss Moon who shattered it.

Amanda, admiring a Venetian glass fruit dish, had been suddenly reminded of Miss Moon's stolen treasures. 'And I never even asked you about them,' she said remorsefully. 'How horrid of me. Were they things that you were specially fond of?'

'Oh, but I have not lost them,' said Miss Moon placidly. 'They were all found, you know.'

'*Found*? But where? Then they *have* caught the man!'

'No dear. It was Euridice who found them this morning. Or rather Katina, Euridice's cat. *Not* a very engaging animal. She was playing with something on the path — rolling it about — and Euridice saw it glitter and went to pick it up. It was that crystal egg. The Fabergé egg, you know. And there they all were, in the grass by the path. The thief must suddenly have realized that if he were caught with them it would mean a sentence of death for murder, and dropped them.'

'The — the Fabergé egg?' repeated Amanda in a whisper.

'Yes dear. Such a pretty thing. He made a great many of them. For the poor Czarina, you know. This was a specially beautiful

433

one, and of course the diamonds probably add to its value. There is a jewelled bird in it, that sings. I am not very fond of it. Such a tragic story. It makes one wonder, does it not, if Russians are ever to be trusted?'

But Amanda was not listening. She was seeing again the shadowed drawing-room as she had seen it on the previous evening when, rigid with the terrified conviction that the silent room contained someone besides herself, she had looked about it with panic-stricken eyes. The diamonds on the Fabergé egg had sparkled in the last of the daylight.

The egg had been in the buhl cabinet less than a minute before she had discovered the dead body of Monica Ford. It had not been stolen. Someone had removed it later in the evening, together with a handful of similar small objects, in order to convey the impression that Monica Ford had been murdered by a thief. And quite suddenly Amanda knew who had done it and when.

Steve Howard had sent her out of the room to make a telephone call that he could have made with more speed himself. But it had served a double purpose. He had got her out of the way for at least ten minutes, and it must have been then that he had opened the corner cabinet.

Amanda could see him doing it — moving with that noiseless swiftness that had surprised her. Lifting each small, gleaming object in his handkerchief so as to leave no finger-prints, as he had lifted the small bottle with the red poison label in the cabin of the *Orantares*.

'All right — we'll play it on those lines; it's your deal,' the slim, ordinary-looking man with the odd name had said; and the half a dozen or so trinkets from Miss Moon's cabinet had almost certainly been in his possession as he said it. He had shaken hands with Amanda and gone out into the darkness and had dropped that misleading evidence in the overgrown grass by the edge of the flagged path, to lend colour to the theory that Monica Ford's murder had been a chance occurrence instead of part of a hidden, ugly pattern that had begun to form in Fayid, and that involved that small group of people who had sailed for Cyprus on the S.S. *Orantares* — one of whom must have planned the death of Julia Blaine.

14

Amanda did not do any of the things that she had meant to do that afternoon. She ran up to her room instead, and having looked under the bed and inside the cupboards and behind every piece of furniture, she locked the door and wrote three letters. One to her Uncle Oswin, one to her aunt in Fayid, and the third to the shipping company. After which she threw herself on her bed and wept stormily, and had not the least idea why she should do so.

Whatever the reason, she felt considerably better for it; and more than a little ashamed of herself. Presently she heard the clock in the hall strike four and realized that the afternoon had almost gone, and Euridice would be laying tea in the verandah outside the drawing-room.

Amanda sat up and pushed her tumbled hair out of her eyes. She went over to the dressing-table and stopped with a sudden shock of dismay at the sight of her own reflection in the oval looking-glass.

She stood there for a long time, staring at herself. Her hair had escaped from its confining net and had tumbled about her shoulders and half-way down her back in tangled disorder. Her white face was blotched with tears and her dress crumpled and creased.

Looking at herself, she had a sudden and disturbing vision of Julia Blaine, tear blotched and unsightly, giving way to hysteria in the cabin of the *Orantares*. If she wasn't careful, she, Amanda Derington, would soon be behaving as Julia Blaine had behaved.

There was already something about her tear-stained face that was unpleasantly reminiscent of Julia's.

A familiar, mocking voice seemed for a moment to speak in Amanda's ear: '*Come on, George Cross Island — pull yourself together!*'

Amanda straightened her bowed shoulders with a jerk and set her small jaw, and there was a sudden defiant sparkle in her eyes.

The three letters that she had written lay on the writing table by the window. She picked them up, tore them into small pieces and dropped them into the waste-paper basket, and ten minutes later went down to tea with her head high and her red mouth set in lines of determination.

There were voices on the drawing-room verandah and Amanda suffered a momentary qualm. Could it be the police again?

But it was only George Norman.

Mr Norman, who was holding a tea-cup in one hand and a small plate in the other, stood up hurriedly at the sight of Amanda and instantly dropped a piece of toast butter side down on the matting.

'Mooney's been telling me about this terrible business of Glenn's secretary,' explained George Norman, stooping to retrieve the toast and spilling his tea in the process. 'Ghastly show! I can't tell you how shocked we all were. Told Mooney a thousand times if I've told her once that having all that stuff lying round loose was simply asking for it! Ought to be in a bank. Terrible business! Claire's very upset about it. Couldn't sleep a wink last night.'

'Last *night?*' Amanda's voice was startled and incredulous. Did Claire always get bad news ahead of other people? How could she possibly have known last night about Monica Ford?

'Glenn told her,' said George Norman, spreading bloater paste on his toast. 'He telephoned at about half past ten last night. Extraordinary chap. Actually wanted us to go at once and see Anita about something. Seems he didn't dare go himself. Some silly idea that the police might see where he went. He said he couldn't ask you because the police were in your house, and that only left us. Well of course we've been friends of Glenn's for years, but there are limits! He knows perfectly well that Claire and Anita never hit it off. And since then Anita has been spreading all that scandal about him and Claire. However urgent the matter was I do not feel that he should have traded on our personal friendship for him to that extent. Anita Barton is a thoroughly bad lot and he is lucky to be rid of her.'

Miss Moon said: 'I confess I do not understand Anita. I would never have thought her capable of such crudely vulgar behaviour. It does not seem to be at all in keeping with her character. She has changed sadly of late.'

'Drink,' said George Norman succinctly.

'My *dear* boy!' said Miss Moon in horrified protest, 'I am quite sure you are mistaken. Although of course I have heard rumours——'

'I bet you have! It's true, I'm afraid. Drinks like a fish. And that's the girl who never used to touch anything stronger than tomato juice.'

'Perhaps there is a reason for it,' said Miss Moon with a small sigh. 'I cannot help feeling that despite her brazen behaviour Anita is very unhappy. Perhaps she hoped that drink would give her forgetfulness — or courage. "Dutch courage", my dear papa used to call it.'

'She deserves to be unhappy,' said George Norman. 'Impossible woman!' He drained his tea-cup and helped himself to a slice of cake.

Amanda said abruptly: 'What did you all do yesterday? After you left Hilarion?'

'Eh? Oh yesterday. Nothing much. Came down to the Club, you know. I wanted to see a chap who I thought would be there, but he wasn't. Hardly anyone there. Lumley dropped in for a minute or two. He's not a member as a matter of fact. Came up to show a chap some pictures. Claire went off to do a bit of shoppin' and

438

Alastair went for a stroll, and we all forgathered at the Dome for a drink about eight. Alastair was dining there with Mrs Halliday, and she suggested we all stay, so we did. Didn't get home until half past ten, and then the telephone went and there was Glenn going on about this appalling business. Couldn't believe it when Claire told me. Thought the poor chap had finally gone off his rocker.'

Amanda said carefully: 'What happened to Toby — Captain Gates?'

'Oh, he fetched up too. I think he dropped Mrs Halliday at the hotel and drove the car back to the chap he hired it off. He joined us for dinner.'

Amanda relapsed into silence. So they had all separated. All or any of them could have come to the Villa Oleander and gone away again without anyone else knowing about it. They had all been within five minutes' walk of it, and there were three separate entrances to the garden: the front gate, the gate at the far end of the garden that led to the garage, and the small, sun-blistered door in the old Turkish wall that ran the length of the back garden, and which gave onto a narrow secluded lane.

I won't think about it, thought Amanda. I won't ... It was somebody who broke in to steal ... It must have been ... Ordinary, nice people — people that you know — don't do these things. And yet — there was Hilarion. I won't think of it, Amanda told herself again and with desperation.

Miss Moon was saying: 'Yes, a great many people have called. To offer sympathy of course. And two of Amanda's friends came to inquire after her. Lady Cooper-Foot and Mrs Teenley telephoned. Everyone realizes what a shock it must have been to me. But I could not see them all this morning. The police were here you know. And after luncheon dear Amanda went up to her room to rest, so I told Euridice to say that we were "not at home" and to take the receiver off the telephone. So kind of people; but in the circumstances——'

'Nosey Parkers!' snorted George Norman indignantly. 'All the old gossips dying to get the details.'

'Oh surely not, dear boy,' protested Miss Moon, shocked. 'After all, *you* are here, and although of course we did discuss the whole affair, I am sure that you did not come only for that.'

George Norman's already ruddy countenance turned a rich shade of puce and he said hurriedly: 'No, of course not. I mean Claire told me to — I mean—— '

He floundered into incoherence and Miss Moon, taking pity on him, offered him another cup of tea and urged him to move his chair a little farther into the shade afforded by the climbing roses.

'I always like to take tea out here,' said Miss Moon. 'The view is so beautiful. Quite uninterrupted. I often sit here to watch the sunset, though facing west, it has its drawbacks. Almost too much sun; it has sadly faded my drawing-room carpet. But then I myself am a sun-worshipper. I do not think — except during the real heat of the day of course — that one *can* have too much of it. Do you not agree?'

George Norman sighed, and for a moment his face had a wistful look. 'Yes. I suppose so.'

'You sound rather doubtful,' said Amanda, only too anxious to keep the conversation firmly on the weather. 'Don't tell me that you prefer grey skies and drizzle to this heavenly climate?'

'But of course I do,' said George Norman, surprised. 'England is my own country. This foreign stuff is all very well for a time, but one gets tired of it. The heat and the smell and jabbering foreign voices, and this damnable sun, sun, sun. No; give me Suffolk on a grey day with the wind blowing over ploughed fields, and chaffinches and yellow-hammers in the hedges, and—— ' He broke off with a sharp sigh. 'Oh well; no good talking about it. It doesn't suit Claire. If it wasn't for Claire—— ' His voice trailed off into silence and he sat staring at the slowly cooling tea in his cup as though he had temporarily forgotten Amanda and Miss Moon, his square, ruddy face suddenly bleak and bitter.

Miss Moon, said: 'Try a piece of the gingerbread, dear boy. I made it myself. A recipe of my dear grandmother's.'

George Norman awoke from his meditations with a visible start and said hurriedly: 'No thank you. I must be getting back.' He gulped down the contents of his cup and added that he had not meant to inflict himself on her for tea: 'I really only came to——'

'I know. To collect the details,' finished Miss Moon wickedly. 'Well I hope you have them all. Tell Claire that I am sorry to hear that she is feeling so upset, and that I advise a strong dose of Gregory's powder. My dear Papa used to say that it was a sure cure for all imaginary ills. Good-bye, dear boy. So kind of you to call.'

Miss Moon watched him depart and clicked her tongue impatiently.

'It is frequently a matter of surprise to me,' she remarked tartly, 'what some men will put up with. And the nicest men put up with the most. Look at Glenn! As for George, he puts me out of all patience.'

'Why, Miss Moon?' Amanda was interested in the Normans. She was interested, with a shrinking, frightened, fascinated curiosity, in every one of that small group of people who had known Julia Blaine and who had picnicked at Hilarion.

'Because,' said Miss Moon, 'he has got into the habit — Claire has seen to that! — of putting his own wishes and desires and convenience second to those of his wife. There is nothing wrong with Claire's health and George knows it! But he has to keep up the fiction of believing in it for the sake of his own self-respect. It is, of course, a case of "he who pays the piper calls the tune". The money is Claire's, and that has put her in a position to dictate. All the same, George is able bodied and reasonably intelligent. There is no reason why he should not be able to obtain some remunerative employment in his own country if he insisted on returning there. With or without his wife!'

Amanda said: 'But he's so devoted to her.'

'Is he? I suppose so. But I have frequently wondered of late if

441

perhaps he might not be almost relieved were she to emulate Anita Barton. Poor Anita: I fear she made a bad enemy when she came up against George's wife. So foolish of her! But she was always high-spirited and reckless. Anita will always "rush her fences", as my dear Papa would have said. And that so frequently leads to disaster. Claire is far more subtle. Yes, I am afraid that Claire is a bad enemy.'

Miss Moon sighed and Amanda said: 'You like Mrs Barton, don't you?'

'Well ... yes, dear. One could not help being fond of her. She was such a child.'

'Glenn said that too,' said Amanda slowly.

'He was right. Some adults seem to retain the more endearing qualities of childhood longer than others. Though many, of course, retain the worst ones for ever. Anita Barton was one of the former. A little spoilt perhaps, but very trusting and honest, and not very clever. A woman like Claire Norman, for instance, could make rings round her. It seemed that Anita and Glenn would be perfectly happy. Of course she was gay; she always liked parties and people and pretty clothes. And Glenn, poor boy, was very overworked and perhaps did not take her about as much as he should, so that—— '

Miss Moon stopped suddenly and was silent for a moment or two, frowning.

'What is it?' asked Amanda curiously.

'Well dear, it suddenly struck me that if one hears a thing repeated sufficiently often, one begins to believe that it is true, even if it is not. We have all heard so often of late that Glenn neglected Anita. But now I come to think of it, they appeared to go about together a great deal. One certainly never heard that he was remiss where the social side of life was concerned. Of course she may just have found him dull. One does not know.'

'I don't see that she can have it both ways,' pointed out Amanda. 'If — as she says — he was behaving like a Don Juan

442

and making love to about six different women at once, he can't have been exactly dull. He must have had *something* — plenty of spare time, for a start!'

Miss Moon sighed again. 'One would think so. Although of course women do like Glenn. I am very fond of him myself. And so was Claire. She was not at all pleased when he married Anita. All the same, it was exceedingly foolish of Anita to be rude to her, and I have always had a suspicion — uncharitable of me, I fear — that Claire was in some way responsible for the break-up of that marriage. What is it, Euridice?'

Euridice was standing in the french windows behind them, wearing the patient expression of one who has been waiting for at least five minutes. She made a brief and unintelligible remark and went to collect the tea-cups, and Miss Moon turned to Amanda and said: 'Someone asking to see you, dear. If it is that nice Mr Howard, ask him to stay and dine with us.'

Amanda stood up quickly and put her hand to her hair in a gesture that was purely instinctive and feminine.

Miss Moon smiled at her with warm understanding and said: 'You look exceedingly nice, dear. In fact, if I may say so, quite charming.'

Amanda blushed, laughed and went quickly through the french windows and across the drawing-room into the hall: to check abruptly at the sight of her visitor, aware of a sudden and ridiculous sense of disappointment.

It was not Steven Howard who stood waiting for her in the hall of the Villa Oleander. It was, surprisingly enough, Anita Barton. And Anita Barton was frightened. That fact was immediately and startlingly apparent, and it sent an odd cold shiver of apprehension through Amanda.

In the dimness of the high, dark hall Mrs Barton's face had the appearance of a white paper mask on which a child has scrawled features in crudely coloured chalks. The patches of rouge on her cheeks, the vividly lipsticked mouth, the blue-tinted

443

eyelids and heavily mascara'd lashes, stood out in harsh and painful artificiality in a face that was drawn and drained of all natural
colour, and eyes that were as wide and glittering as a terrified
cat's.

There was no longer any trace of prettiness in that face, but
strangely enough its look of haggard fear was not ageing, and with
the loss of her hard defiant assurance, Anita Barton seemed to
have become all at once younger, and as though she were indeed
only the foolish, frightened child to which both her husband and
Miss Moon had likened her.

Amanda was aware of a sudden pang of pity and an instinct of
protectiveness, and she went forward quickly with her hand outstretched. 'What is it? Did you want to see me?'

'Yes—— ' Anita Barton's frightened-cat eyes darted quick
glances about the hall and the long staircase that stretched up into
the shadows of the upper landing, and her fingers tugged
nervously at a small lace-edged handkerchief so that the delicate
fabric tore with a small ripping sound. She dropped it, startled,
and said breathlessly: 'But not here. Can't we go somewhere else.
Will you walk down the road with me?'

Amanda looked at her, puzzled and disturbed. 'All right. Just
wait a moment while I tell Miss Moon.'

She returned to the verandah and informed Miss Moon that she
would be going out for a short walk. Miss Moon looked interested.
'Anita, you say? I was not aware that you knew her. *Hardly* a
suitable companion for you just now dear. People talk so. Do you
not think that perhaps it would be wiser to decline the invitation
— tactfully, of course?'

'I can't,' said Amanda, distressed. 'I think she's in trouble. I
don't suppose I shall be long.'

Once outside the gates of the Villa Oleander Anita Barton
turned to the right and away from the main road, and as soon as
they were out of sight of the house she clutched Amanda's arm and
spoke in a harsh, breathless voice:

444

'Is it true that something of mine was found in Miss Moon's house last night? — a flower off that dress I was wearing?'

'Yes,' said Amanda briefly.

She heard Anita Barton catch her breath in a hard gasp and the fingers that held her arm tightened convulsively so that the pointed scarlet nails dug painfully into her flesh.

Mrs Barton stumbled and recovered herself and stopped near a group of dusty tamarisk trees by a high, white-washed wall in what appeared to be a deserted cul-de-sac:

'Then it is true! I didn't believe it. I thought that it was only – only a spiteful story. But Lumley said—— ' she stopped, and her wide, hunted eyes searched Amanda's face with a desperate intensity. 'Tell me about it, please. I must know.'

Amanda told her. There was not much to tell, but the bare facts were ugly enough and Anita Barton's white face seemed to grow whiter and more pinched as she listened.

She said at last in a harsh whisper: 'Didn't they ask whose it was?'

Amanda hesitated and once more the lacquered fingernails dug into her arm. 'Didn't they?'

'Yes,' said Amanda unhappily. 'I – I said it was mine.'

'You *what?*' Mrs Barton's voice was suddenly strident. 'Why did you do that? Why should you do a thing like that for me?'

'I didn't,' confessed Amanda. 'I did it because of your husband. You see—— '

'*Glenn?*' Anita Barton relaxed her grip and took a quick step backwards, staring. A stare that changed suddenly to a look of scornful comprehension:

'Glenn,' repeated Mrs Barton, her mouth no longer slack-lipped with fear but twisted and derisive. 'So you've fallen for him too, you silly little fool!'

Amanda's chin came up with a jerk. Her grey eyes were suddenly cold and angry and her voice as scornful as Mrs Barton's own:

445

'I think it is you who are the fool, if you really imagine that I have any interest at all in your husband. Perhaps no one else has ever had any interest in him either, and you are just another Julia Blaine. Someone who imagines that no other woman can speak to her husband without falling in love with him. You do love him, don't you? You're only behaving like this because someone has made you jealous. Julia was like that.'

For a long minute Anita Barton did not speak, but the scorn and bitterness left her face and it was once more frightened and quivering. She put her hand up to her throat and said in a voice that was barely above a whisper: 'Yes, Julia was like that. And Julia died. But I don't want to die!'

She swallowed convulsively and her eyes came back to Amanda:

'If Glenn doesn't mean anything to you, and I don't, why did you tell the police that the flower was yours?'

'Because I owed your husband something. My life,' said Amanda bluntly.

'Your *life?* What do you mean?'

Amanda told her, omitting only the fact that her fall had not been accidental. 'So you see,' she concluded, 'I thought that I owed him something in return.'

'So that's why you said that flower was yours!' Suddenly and without warning Anita Barton threw back her head and laughed. A loud peal of hysterical mirth that was somehow incredibly shocking. It stopped as abruptly as it had begun and she reached out and clutched at Amanda's arm once more:

'Listen, I never went near Miss Moon's house yesterday. Do you hear? I never went near it?'

Her teeth chattered suddenly as though she were cold, and Amanda said quickly: 'If you didn't, you'll be able to prove it, and then——'

'But I can't prove it!' interrupted Anita Barton desperately. 'Someone telephoned the café on the quay and asked them to give a message to Lumley. Some visitor who wanted to know if he would take a few of his pictures up to the Club. But the man never turned up, and Lumley waited and didn't get back until late. I was alone in the flat; but I can't prove it. I might have gone out. The floors below are empty. They're used for storage. And there are two ways out of that house.'

'Perhaps you wore that dress to Miss Moon's house some other time?' suggested Amanda. 'That flower thing could have been there for ages, you know. Euridice doesn't seem to be very good at dusting and I don't suppose that anyone would have noticed it.'

'I haven't been at the Villa Oleander since the winter,' said Anita Barton, 'and that flower couldn't have come off my dress there because I've never worn it to the house. Someone put it there; and I know who it was. I know how they could have got it and why they did it. And then you said it was yours, which might have spoilt it all. But it won't — you'll see! The police and everyone will know soon enough.'

Her voice died out in a frightened, hopeless whisper and Amanda's fingers closed over the hand on her arm in a comforting grasp.

'No they won't. Don't look like that, Mrs Barton. The police think that it's mine; and they won't worry about it any more because Miss Moon says that they think it was a thief who killed Miss Ford.'

Anita Barton drew a long shuddering breath and her eyes seemed to look through and beyond Amanda as though they did not see her. She said in a barely audible whisper: 'I shall have to be careful. I shall have to be very careful ...'

The sky beyond the dusty tamarisk trees was tinged with gold and the deserted lane was in shadow, and high above the tree tops Amanda could see the distant, rocky outline of St Hilarion, bright with the sunset. It would not be long now before the swift tropical twilight would be upon them, to merge once more into another night of moonlight and stars. She heard a cart creak past the end of the lane, and from somewhere behind the high, white-washed

447

wall a woman began to sing a plaintive Turkish ballad that was old when the Empire of Byzantium was young.

Anita Barton's eyes seemed to focus Amanda again and she drew a short, hard breath and said: 'Thank you for trying to help. It was kind of you. I don't think you'd better be seen with me, so I'll go back a different way.'

Amanda said, impulsively: 'If there is anything I can do — to help I mean — I'd like to do it. I really would.'

Mrs Barton smiled crookedly. 'That's nice of you. I'll remember.'

She turned on her heel and walked quickly away, and Amanda, following more slowly, saw her take the turning that led into the narrow lane behind the wall where the pigeons of the Villa Oleander cooed and paraded in the ruined embrasures of the time-worn stone.

15

Amanda walked slowly back to the house, but at the gate she suddenly changed her mind, and instead of going in, went on and turned down towards the centre of the town.

She would go and see Steve Howard and tell him about that odd, disturbing interview with Anita Barton. Steve would know what to do.

There was a man loitering at the corner of the road, and as she passed him Amanda had the odd impression that he had taken note of her; not as a pretty girl, but as one who observes and files away a piece of information.

She looked quickly back over her shoulder, but the man was leaning against the wall, apparently intent upon removing a stone from the sole of his shoe, and she wondered if her imagination had tricked her, or if the police were not so satisfied as Miss Moon supposed with the theory that Monica Ford had been killed by a thief, and were watching the Villa Oleander?

It was an uncomfortable thought, and yet she had to admit that she would sleep easier that night if she could be assured that the police were keeping an eye on the house.

She saw Claire Norman and Toby Gates in the town, but they did not see her. They were talking earnestly outside Karafillides' shop, and as she approached they turned and walked away together.

Amanda saw no one else that she knew, with the exception of several children who grinned cheerfully at her and were presumably among those admirers of Steve Howard's whose acquaintance she had made on her first morning in Kyrenia. And struck by a sudden thought, she did not go directly to the Dome, but turned instead towards the harbour, where the low rays of the setting sun had turned the massive walls of Kyrenia Castle to molten gold, and dyed the long range of the hills with rose and cyclamen and lavender streaked with soft blue shadows.

The quiet water of the sleepy little harbour lay like a vast opal in the shelter of the sea wall, mirroring all the clear colours of the evening and the orange-brown mainsail of a small blue sailing boat whose owner was manoeuvring her to her moorings at the far side of the harbour. It was a picture to delight the eye of the least appreciative: a back-drop for a ballet or the setting for an opera by Puccini. But there was no one painting on the wall that evening and Amanda could see no sign of Steve Howard.

She turned to look at the row of tall, flat-roofed houses that ringed the far side of the harbour, one of which contained Lumley Potter's studio flat. The french windows of the Potter studio gave on to a small iron-railed balcony, and Amanda saw a man step out on to the balcony and peer down on to the quay beneath. The distance was too great for her to be able to make out his features, but against the dark square of the open window behind him the man's blond head stood out in sharp relief, and Amanda wondered if Alastair Blaine — if it was Alastair — was being inveigled into purchasing a companion piece to 'Sea Green Cypriots'?

The man turned and went in again and Amanda's gaze wandered along the quays and over the crowded tables of the little café, but Steve Howard was definitely not among those present, and after a time she turned away and walked slowly back towards the Dome Hotel.

The girl at the desk glanced at an array of keys and said that she was afraid Mr Howard must be out. He had left his key at the desk and had not reclaimed it. Perhaps Amanda would care to wait?

Amanda lingered, uncertain whether to stay or to leave a

message asking Steve to call at the Villa Oleander. But as she hesitated, there was a click of high heels on the floor behind her, a waft of *'Bois des Iles'* and Persis Halliday said: 'Hullo there! Just the girl I wanted to see! Amanda honey, I was round at that old Palazzo of yours this morning trying to see you, and I rang up twice this afternoon. But your phone must be out of order. I hear you've been right spang in the middle of a front page story? Come and have a shot of something and tell me all about it at once. Am I thrilled!'

She took Amanda's arm in an affectionate and possessive clasp and swept her off to a corner of a wide lounge where the lights had already been lit and the windows that looked out onto the placid ocean were filled with the last daffodil glow of the sunset.

Persis, thought Amanda, was showing signs of strain. There were lines about her eyes and mouth that Amanda did not remember having seen before, and she looked less glossy and well dressed than usual. There was a large flake of crimson lacquer missing from one fingernail, and for the first time since Amanda had known her, her gleaming hair was less than immaculately sleek.

She questioned Amanda about the events of the previous evening in a low, eager voice that was entirely unlike her usual gay, high-pitched and incisive tones.

Amanda gave her an outline of the story, but avoided details, and eventually Persis abandoned the catechism and relaxed in her chair.

She had apparently called at the Villa Oleander that morning, after hearing the news of the murder from a hotel acquaintance, and had met Miss Moon.

'She wouldn't let me see you,' explained Persis. 'Seems you were asleep. The place appeared to be crawling with cops and your hostess was dealing with them with considerable firmness. She's quite a character. Glenn was there too. And Toby dropped around to ask after you. We all went upstairs and sat in the boudoir and

451

had a quiet smoke, while the cops milled around in the drawing-room. It was quite a party.'

'Why was Glenn there? Were they——?'

'They'd been doing a bit of reconstructing the crime I gather,' said Persis, hailing a passing waiter and throwing him into temporary confusion by demanding rye-on-the-rocks:

'It seems that Glenn was their Public Enemy Number One, until someone tripped over a handful of valuables on the garden path. Will you have sherry or gin? Okay waiter, make it tomato juice.'

Amanda said: 'You mean they thought that *Glenn* had killed her?'

'Sure. Why not? After all, on his own say-so he was the last person to see her alive, and it seems that his wife's been tooting it all over town that he had an affair with the dame. They had it all doped out. Even the local cops have read that one about the secretary who is seduced by the boss!'

'Did you ever see Monica Ford?' demanded Amanda heatedly.

'Nope. But I've heard plenty from those who had that privilege. I gather that she would not exactly have reached the finals of the Beauty Contest at Mud Flats, Pennsylvania. Am I right?'

'You are. She was plain and efficient and thick and thirty-five-ish, and——'

'I get you, honey. But I guess the cops must have been reading *Candid Confessions*, for they were quite a little taken with their theory. Seems they thought the guy had gotten tired of amorous games around the office and had tried to toss the gal aside like a soiled glove, and she wouldn't toss. So he upped and strangled her, left the corpse in Miss Moon's drawing-room, came on up to Hilarion and callously ate a hearty tea to celebrate. That was their theory and they were crazy about it.'

'They must be mad!' said Amanda. 'She hadn't been dead for any time at all. She was *warm*!'

'Yeah, I know. But they probably thought he just pretended to turn off to Nicosia and really turned back and followed the

452

Normans to Kyrenia, whipped into Miss Moon's, strangled his secretary, sprang for his steed — I mean his Studebaker — and hey, for that mad ride for the border! Could be.'

Amanda said scornfully: 'How was he supposed to know that she would still be there? It sounds a lot of poppycock to me.'

'Well it blew a fuse early on. Seems the guy gave a lift to a couple of enlisted men just back of that turn, and they've turned 'em up and checked the times, and he couldn't have made it. Not unless he's mastered the art of being in two places at once. And then there was all that jade and junk lying around the garden path, and they figured that though he might indulge in a little murder, he'd probably draw the line at theft.'

'How did you hear all this?' demanded Amanda. 'Did Miss Moon tell you?'

'Good grief no! She was too busy telling the police what she thought of them. Glenn told me. I brought him back here with me and we had a few drinks and discussed this and that. I like that guy. It's a pity he's still carrying a torch for that wife of his. She sounds a bit screwy to me. Anyone who could leave a nice guy like Glenn, to elope with a set of ginger whiskers and a smell of turpentine, must be rocking on the rails with their signals mixed.'

Persis sipped her drink in silence for a moment or two and presently said thoughtfully: 'Steve was there too.'

'Where?' asked Amanda sharply.

'At your Miss Moon's this morning. That guy's a smooth operator. He's wasted on art. He ought to be giving Dulles and Eden a few lessons in diplomacy.'

'What do you mean?'

'When I gate-crashed your villa this morning,' said Persis with a reminiscent grin, 'the situation was a little complicated. Glenn was not taking too kindly to the suggestion that this Monica had been his mistress, and your Miss Moon was addressing the senior cop in a manner which many a high-school teacher would have envied. Then that housemaid of hers — or cook or what-have-you

— was having hysterics in the kitchen, and the bootboy was offering to fight a cop who seems to have suggested that he might have tipped off a pal that the villa would be empty yesterday afternoon, so why not slide in and swipe a few trinkets? It was quite a situation and I doubt if UNO could have done much better. Then in strolls Steve like a flock of doves bearing olive branches, and in no time at all everyone is sitting around drinking vino and relaxing, and Miss Moon is calling the Head Cop her dear boy. Yes, it was certainly quite a performance.'

Persis lit a cigarette from a small diamond and platinum lighter and looked thoughtfully at Amanda through the smoke:

'You're in love with him, aren't you?'

'Who? Steve Howard? Don't be absurd! I hardly know him.'

'You sound almost convincing, honey — but not quite. And it isn't necessary to know someone to fall in love with them. In fact the less you know about 'em the easier it is.' There was a trace of bitterness in Persis' voice. 'Has he kissed you?'

She saw the vivid colour flood up into Amanda's face and said dryly: 'I see he has. Ah well, some girls have all the luck.'

'Persis,' said Amanda severely, 'don't you ever think of anything but love?'

'Not if I can help it,' said Persis candidly. 'I'm nuts about love! Romance is my business — and a very paying proposition I have found it.'

'Are you going to use everything that has happened here for one of your books?'

A shadow seemed to pass over Persis Halliday's face, and then she laughed. It was a short and rather bitter laugh.

'No. Not quite everything.'

Amanda looked at her curiously and said suddenly: 'Persis — are we real to you? Or are we — are we all just people acting out parts that give you ideas for stories?'

Persis leant back in her chair and blew a smoke ring at the ceiling. She said in a soft, abstracted voice: 'You know, it's queer that you should ask that. Sometimes I do feel that way. As if I was on the other side of a sheet of plate glass, watching a puppet show and thinking "that's interesting". Sometimes the people I write about seem more real to me than a lot of people I meet, because I know them and I own them. It's — I suppose it's a little like being God. I can make my characters do just what I want. Fall in love, get married, hate each other, jump through hoops. I can kill 'em off or make 'em achieve fame and fortune in a coupla' lines of print. But – but real people won't always do what one wants ...'

Her voice sank to a half-whisper on the last words and she relapsed into silence, leaning back in her chair with her abstracted gaze on the darkening sky and the first stars that lay beyond the open windows, while the cigarette burned out between her fingers.

A soft, fluting voice made itself heard from the direction of the door and Persis dropped the stub of her cigarette into her glass and looked over Amanda's shoulder.

'Here comes Teeny-weeny-me,' she observed. 'Why, hullo Claire. Brought the baseball team with you I see.'

Claire Norman, accompanied by her husband, Alastair Blaine, Toby Gates and Lumley Potter, crossed the room and sinking into a chair, announced that she was exhausted. She appeared surprised at seeing Amanda and murmured a few soft words of sympathy on the subject of the *terrible* ordeal that Amanda must have been subjected to.

'We've just been to see Miss Moon,' she said. 'We thought you'd be there too of course, but Mooney said you'd gone out. She was rather secretive about it. She wouldn't say who with. I thought it must be Steve. I didn't think of Persis. Lumley, you're not going, are you?'

'Afraid I must,' said Mr Potter reluctantly. 'I said I'd be back around six, and it's well after seven, and——'

'*Poor* Lumley!' interrupted Claire in her soft, clear voice. She reached up a small hand and laid it on his arm in a brief gesture indicative of sympathy and understanding, and Mr Potter flushed pinkly.

Persis, who had watched this bit of byplay with considerable interest, caught Amanda's eye and winked, and Amanda bit back a laugh and turned hurriedly to Toby Gates who had seated himself on the arm of her chair was inquiring solicitously as to her health.

Mr Potter removed himself, Alastair Blaine ordered a round of drinks, and George Norman asked Amanda to supper at their house:

'Would have asked you before,' he said, 'but didn't think you'd feel up to it. Be delighted if you'd come. Only pot luck of course. Claire, I've just asked Miss Derington to join the party for supper tonight.'

Claire Norman raised her delicate brows and smiled charmingly at Amanda, but Amanda received the sudden and distinct impression that she was not pleased, and said quickly: 'I'm so sorry, I'm afraid I can't come. I couldn't walk out on Miss Moon at such short notice. She had a horrid time yesterday, and today hasn't been exactly peaceful for her.'

'Of course,' sympathized Claire. 'We quite understand. Some other time perhaps.'

Toby said in a low voice: 'Why didn't you give me a ring last night and tell me what had happened? It must have been hellish for you. You know I'd have come up.'

'Thank you Toby,' said Amanda with real gratitude. 'But there wasn't anything you could do.'

'I gather Howard was there,' said Toby with a trace of resentment in his voice.

'He brought me back from Hilarion, that was why. Toby, did you really all call in on Miss Moon again this evening?' She indicated Claire and her entourage with a brief gesture of the hand.

'We just thought we'd look in and see how you were. We all happened to meet rather by accident up at the top of the town, and

456

as it was only about two minutes' walk we went along. It's an astonishing house, isn't it? The old girl took us all over it. Simply crammed with stuff that would make an antique dealer drip at the mouth. Do you know that there's a Constable sketch in one of those bedrooms? Must be worth a packet. No wonder some enterprising burglar had a crack at it. The only thing I can't understand is why the whole shooting match wasn't pinched years ago. I don't believe the old girl would have noticed it if it had been!'

Claire was saying, '——Toby will tell us. Toby dear, is it true that your Regiment is coming here in the autumn? Alastair is being very cagey and Security-Minded about it. As if it mattered!'

Major Blaine laughed. 'I'm not being in the least cagey. I don't know. And I bet Toby doesn't know either. It is commonly supposed that the policy of the Broadmoor graduate responsible for the placing of units is to decide all changes at the last possible moment with the aid of a pin, in the hope — only too frequently realized — of causing the maximum confusion not so much to the enemy but to the units involved. Amanda, now that you've dealt with that tomato mush, how about trying the effects of a gin and lime?'

Amanda smiled and shook her head. 'No thank you, Alastair. I'm afraid it's time I was going. I don't like to keep Miss Moon waiting.'

'Nonsense. You've masses of time for another drink.'

'This is my round,' said Toby quickly. He rose and went to the bell and Alastair Blaine crossed over, and having removed Amanda's empty glass took Toby's place on the arm of her chair and began to make desultory conversation to which Amanda paid little attention.

She was watching the clock and wondering if Steven Howard had returned, and if he too was dining with the Normans? If so it would be too late to tell him about Anita Barton tonight, and she would have to let it keep until tomorrow.

She became aware that Alastair Blaine had lowered his voice to an undertone and had asked her some question. Amanda jerked her gaze from the clock and looked at him.

'I – I'm sorry, Alastair. What did you say?'

Alastair glanced quickly at the four other members of the party, but George was explaining the intricacies of cricket to Persis, and Claire and Toby were discussing a mutual friend in Alexandria. His gaze came back to Amanda and he asked a low-voiced question that was an echo of one that Amanda had already heard once that evening:

'Is it true,' asked Alastair Blaine, 'that something off Anita Barton's dress was found by the police last night?'

'Who told you that?' asked Amanda, startled. 'Did Miss Moon?'

Alastair shook his head. 'No. Claire told me.'

'*Claire?* How did she know?'

'Seems that Barton told her. He rang up in a bit of a stew last night and wanted her to go down and see his wife or Lumley and warn 'em to burn the dress or bury it or get rid of it somehow. Didn't dare go himself for fear the police were tailing him. But I think he must have been a bit worked up to suggest it, as Claire isn't exactly sympathetic to Mrs Barton. However, she and George have always been pretty good friends of his so I suppose he felt that in the special circumstances she might rally round for his sake, if not for Anita's.'

'And did she?'

'No,' said Alastair Blaine slowly, and frowned.

'She seems to have made it her business to tell a good many other people,' said Amanda tartly. 'Is that why you were down at Lumley Potter's?'

Alastair Blaine looked startled.

'I thought I saw you on the balcony,' explained Amanda.

'I did drop in for a minute,' admitted Major Blaine uncomfortably. 'I thought someone should tip her off. But she wasn't in, and Lumley said he'd already told her. Don't know how he got hold

458

of it. Then we met the Normans and Toby in the town and went up to see you. I thing Claire wanted to find out from Miss Moon if it were true. But your peculiar old hostess wasn't giving anything away. *Is* it true?'

Amanda hesitated, but before she could reply Claire looked up and called out in her sweet, fluting voice:

'Steve! What have you been doing with yourself? You're looking very well dressed. Is this in honour of dining with us?'

Amanda turned quickly, aware of an odd breathlessness.

Mr Howard had not, apparently, been occupying himself with art. His hair was unusually smooth, and in place of his normally somewhat casual attire he wore a thin checked suit. He had, it is true, removed the coat, which he carried slung over one shoulder, but his silk shirt was impeccable and he wore the tie of a famous public school.

'No,' said Steve smiling lazily down at Claire. 'Nothing short of a white tie and tails could do justice to that, but as I omitted to pack 'em, this is the best I can do. And damned hot it is too.'

Persis said: 'Where have you been, Steve?'

'Troodos,' said Steve, and offered no further comment.

'*Troodos?*' exclaimed Claire surprised. 'Do you mean you've been the whole way there and back this afternoon? Whatever for?'

'Oh, just to see a man about a dog,' said Steve amicably.

He pulled up a chair and sat down, stretching his long legs before him and driving his hands deep into his pockets.

Claire smiled archly at him and said: 'I don't believe a word of it! Who is she, Steve? I am quite sure that you would never have dressed up in a suit for any mere male — unless you've been to see the Governor, of course!'

She laughed, as though such an idea was preposterous, and Steve grinned at her and turned to George Norman with some query as to whether there was any fishing obtainable in the Island? George rose to the bait with the alacrity of a trout in May and Claire's question remained unanswered.

Persis stood up and said: 'Well I'm for a bath. Toby, collect me in about half an hour and we'll walk up to Claire's.'

Amanda looked at the clock again and rose hurriedly to her feet. 'I'm afraid I must be going too,' she said, addressing the company in general. 'I hadn't realized it was so late.'

George said: 'Change your mind and come on to supper.'

Amanda smiled and shook her head, and Steve, who had risen, said: 'I'll see you home,' thus checkmating Toby Gates who had been about to make a similar suggestion.

Amanda, catching Persis Halliday's amused and mocking eye, said a little stiffly: 'Please don't bother. It's no distance, I can easily go by myself.'

'I'm quite sure you can,' said Steve equably, 'but as I have sundry messages to deliver to Miss Moon, I might as well go up now as later.'

'What messages?' asked Amanda. 'Can't I take them?'

'One or two things about the inquest. It's for eleven tomorrow in Nicosia, and we shall all have to put in an appearance.' He grinned at Amanda with a good deal of comprehension in his gaze and said: 'Of course if you are averse to my company, I can always give you three minutes' start.'

'Don't be ridiculous,' said Amanda with dignity, and walked towards the door.

'Dinner at 8.15, Steve,' Claire called after him. 'Don't be late.'

'I won't.'

Persis said: 'Goodnight honey. Enjoy yourself!' And then they were crossing the hall and a moment later were out in the warm moonlight under a sky that was thick with stars.

Amanda started off at a brisk pace, but as Steve refused to be hurried she was compelled to slow down as the only alternative to having him wandering up the road a yard or so behind her — a proceeding that must appear more than a little ridiculous.

'That's better,' approved Steve, linking his arm casually through hers. 'I have had a tiring day, and just at the moment a marathon race is not in my line. What did you want to see me about?'

Amanda checked and stumbled. 'How did you know I——?'

'No, I am not omniscient, worse luck,' said Steve regretfully. 'The girl at the desk told me that a young lady had been inquiring for me. She added a description that was flattering but reasonably accurate, and a natural modesty forbade me to suppose that all you required was the pleasure of my company. What is it?'

Amanda hesitated, frowning and uncertain.

'Changed your mind?' inquired Steve.

'No,' said Amanda doubtfully. 'Perhaps there isn't anything in it, but Mrs Barton came to see me this evening——'

Steve Howard's leisurely pace did not alter but Amanda had a fleeting impression that the muscles of the arm that was linked through hers had tightened for an infinitesimal moment.

'Did she indeed? What about?'

Amanda told him, repeating that short conversation word for word as accurately as she could remember it. Steve made no comment, except to ask her if she had mentioned the finding of the small linen flower to anyone.

'No,' said Amanda. 'It was Glenn.'

This time there was no mistaking the sudden rigidity of that arm, and perhaps Steve was aware of it, for he released Amanda's arm and thrust his hands into his pockets.

'Ah, the hero boy,' he remarked satirically. 'So he blew the gaff, did he? Now I wonder why?'

Amanda explained the circumstances, her voice quick and indignant, and Steve said caustically: 'Dear Glenn would appear to make quite a habit of getting his girl-friends to pull his chestnuts out of the fire for him.'

'Why must you always sneer at him?' demanded Amanda with some heat. 'I know you all think he's a fool not to say "good-riddance" to Anita, but he can't help it if he's still fond of her. You

461

can't stop loving people just because you want to. It's nothing to do with sense or logic or——'

She stopped suddenly and Steve gave her an odd sideways look and said: 'You do rush to his defence, don't you? No; love has nothing to do with sense and even less with logic. In fact, taking it all round, it is an infernal nuisance and a booby trap laid by Mother Nature with a view to spreading alarm and confusion, defeating the ends of justice and leading inevitably to over-population and the atom-bomb.'

Amanda laughed and Steve said sadly: 'It is no laughing matter I assure you. Just as it becomes vitally necessary to keep one's eye on the ball, along comes a naked and nauseous infant with a brain suitable to its tender years, whom someone has inadvisedly armed with a lethal weapon in the form of a bow and arrow. And *whang!* — there is a spanner in the works.'

'Are you speaking from personal experience?' inquired Amanda with interest.

Mr Howard sighed. 'Yes, alas!' he looked down at her and grinned. 'In fact you can take it that my recent crispness on the subject of dear Glenn is caused by the demon of jealous gnawing at my vitals. No one ever rushes to my defence or sobs sympathetically over my woes. And neither do I win rounds of applause by risking my neck rescuing damsels from certain death. I find it very discouraging.'

Amanda looked at him doubtfully. There was a derisive gleam in his eye and she was quite sure that he did not mean a word of what he had said. Or was there, perhaps, a grain of truth in it?

They had reached the turn down to the Villa Oleander and Amanda noted that once again there was a man standing in the shadow of the wall, lighting a cigarette. It was not the same one who had been there when she had passed earlier that evening, but there was about him the same indefinable suggestion of deliberate and observant loitering that the other man had had.

The quiet, tree-lined road was white with moonlight, but the pavement was a dark patchwork of shadows and Amanda was suddenly intensely grateful to Steven Howard for insisting on accompanying her. It would not have been pleasant to walk through those black shadows alone.

Steve stopped at the gate, glanced at the luminous dial of his watch and said: 'See you tomorrow at the inquest. Don't let them faze you and don't get led off into side issues. Just answer the questions in as few words as possible and lay off unnecessary detail. Keep it short and you'll be okay. Goodnight.'

Amanda said: 'But I thought you wanted to see Miss Moon.'

'She'll have been told all about it by now. You were being a bit haughty about accepting my offer to escort you, so I had to bring pressure to bear. Be seeing you.'

He turned away and Amanda said: 'Steve——'

Steve Howard stopped and turned rather slowly. 'Yes?'

Amanda said: 'It *was* you who took those things from the cabinet, wasn't it? The——'

Steve took a swift stride towards her and the palm of his hand was hard and warm over her mouth. She saw him throw a quick look left and right into the shadows and draw a short breath of relief. He dropped his hand and said low and tersely: 'What makes you think that?'

'The Fabergé egg,' said Amanda in a whisper. 'I noticed it in the cabinet just before I – before I found Monica Ford. The diamonds glittered——'

'*Damn!*' said Mr Howard softly.

He looked down at Amanda and the moonlight showed a deep crease between his brows.

'Have you mentioned that to anyone?' he demanded curtly.

Amanda shook her head.

'Then don't! Not to anyone at all — do you understand?' His voice held a hard edge of command.

'Yes,' said Amanda in a whisper.

Once again he turned his head to look into the shadows and then

463

he shrugged his shoulders in a faintly fatalistic gesture and turned and walked quickly away, his footsteps audible in the silence long after his tall figure had been swallowed up by the shadows.

16

'Is that you dear?' called Miss Moon, peering over the banisters of the upper hall. 'I shall be down in a moment. Tell Euridice we will dine at once.'

Amanda delivered the message to the kitchen and went upstairs to brush her hair. She came down to find Miss Moon awaiting her in the dining-room, arrayed in a regal robe of yellow velvet and wearing a magnificent parure of topazes that would have been greatly improved by cleaning.

Amanda looked down a little guiltily at her own short cotton frock and apologized for not changing.

'Nonsense dear. You look exceedingly nice as you are, and had you delayed to change, the soup would have been cold. I only change from habit. Dear papa would have considered it most odd had I not, but I often think how foolish I am to continue doing so. What did Anita wish to see you about? Such a pity she should have called just then, for Claire and several of your friends dropped in not so very long afterwards. I had a most social evening. They inquired so kindly after you: although I fear that on Claire's part it was less a visit of condolence than of curiosity. But perhaps I am being unkind. That Major Blaine is a very quiet, pleasant-mannered man. His wife committed suicide I hear — so tragic for him. It seems that she—— But of course dear, you know all about it. You were on the same boat. Quite dreadful.'

'Yes,' said Amanda in a colourless voice. She did not in the least wish to discuss the death of Julia Blaine, and hoped that Miss Moon would not pursue the subject. Miss Moon did not. She was

465

far more interested in the fact that Lumley Potter had had the effrontery to accompany Claire and her friends to the Villa Oleander.

'*Such* impertinence, dear! I have always considered him a most tiresome man. Spiritual aromas indeed! Anyone who can depict our enchanting harbour in a *welter* of dirty browns and blacks — and that particularly unpleasant shade of Prussian blue — I cannot but feel to be lacking in *honesty*. And when he knows quite well how fond I have always been of Glenn — not to mention Anita — his action in calling at this house becomes quite inexplicable. Naturally I could not turn him from the door; particularly as Claire had brought him. But I let him see *quite* plainly that I considered his visit an unwarrantable intrusion. He did not look at *all* comfortable,' added Miss Moon with satisfaction.

Amanda was suddenly reminded of something that Anita Barton had said about Lumley Potter and Claire, and she turned to Miss Moon and said abruptly: 'Do you think he wants to marry Mrs Barton?'

'Marry Anita?' said Miss Moon as though such a thing had never occurred to her. 'I am quite sure he does not.'

'Then why do you suppose he ran off with her?'

'I do not think he did — though of course I may be wrong. I think Anita ran off with him. Just to make a scandal. So that Glenn would divorce her. She is obviously quite determined, for reasons of her own, to obtain her freedom; though I am convinced that her object cannot be marriage with Lumley Potter. But Anita — as I think I told you — has a strangely childish streak. When she wants something, she wants it badly and at once and without counting the cost. And you would be surprised, dear, what silly and quite childish things many people will do when their tempers and emotions get the upper hand of them. Things that they would never *dream* of doing if only they would give themselves time for reflection.'

'No I wouldn't,' said Amanda sadly. 'I'm just as bad. I lost my temper and slapped someone across the face the other day. I didn't think that anyone ever really did things like that.'

'Mr Howard,' said Miss Moon placidly. 'It left quite a mark did it not? I own I was interested. Such a dear boy! What had he done to provoke you?'

Amanda laughed, and followed the laugh with a frown. 'He asked me if I'd fallen in love with Glenn Barton.'

'What a foolish question!' said Miss Moon. 'But then gentlemen are often *so* unobservant, dear. Even the most intelligent of them. And when they are jealous they can behave with quite surprising stupidity. Look at Lumley Potter, who has always been devoted to Claire. Not that I consider *him* intelligent: quite the reverse! I imagine that Mr Howard thought that you had laid claim to that flower of Anita's to please Glenn.'

Amanda said: 'Do you notice everything, Miss Moon?'

'Oh I wouldn't say that, dear — but I hope that I am not *too* unobservant.'

'How did you know that it belonged to Mrs Barton?' inquired Amanda curiously. 'Had you seen her in that dress?'

'No,' said Miss Moon. 'Not to my knowledge. But I was aware that both you and Glenn had recognized it, and when I saw him look at you like that of course I knew at once that it must be something of Anita's. I supposed that you had seen her wear it.'

Miss Moon selected a peach and peeled it while Amanda wondered how many other things Miss Moon had noticed and had kept to herself?

'Claire had heard about it too,' said Miss Moon presently. 'She was trying to pump me. I soon put a stop to that! I imagine Glenn, poor boy, must have asked her to warn Anita. He should have known Claire better. But then, as I have said, gentlemen are lamentably unobservant in such matters, and I do not think that Glenn is a particularly good judge of character, or he would have seen through Claire years ago. Let us take coffee in the drawing-room.'

She rose with a clash of bracelets and jewellery, and over the coffee informed Amanda that a police officer had called earlier to notify her that both of them would be expected to attend the inquest on Monica Ford the following morning.

'Only a formality, my dear,' said Miss Moon. 'Nothing to worry about. I understand that all those who were at Hilarion that afternoon have also been asked to attend. I cannot think why. Corroborative evidence on the times of arrival and departure I suppose. Even Lumley and Anita have been requested to be present. Quite unnecessary I should have thought. So hard on poor Glenn.'

Miss Moon turned the conversation on to general topics and shortly after nine o'clock expressed her intention of retiring to bed:

'I feel that we could both do with an early night, dear.'

Amanda was feeling far from sleepy, but she had no intention of remaining alone in the shadowy drawing-room with those shimmering circles of looking-glass that had reflected Monica Ford's lifeless hand.

Euridice had already retired to bed — Andreas slept out — and Miss Moon turned out the lights, closed and bolted the french windows and went into the dining-room to fetch a jug of barley water off the sideboard, the train of her yellow velvet dress trailing regally behind her and collecting a small wash of dust.

'I usually take a jug of this up with me to my bedroom during the hot weather,' said Miss Moon. 'Can I offer you a glass of anything, dear? No? Then let us turn out the lights.'

Amanda relieved her of the jug and carried it upstairs to her room, and Miss Moon said: 'Thank you, dear. Just put it on the bedside table.'

Amanda did so and turned to look about her. She had not been inside Miss Moon's bedroom before, except for those few frantic minutes on the previous evening, when she had had no attention to spare for her surroundings. Miss Moon's bedroom was worth a second look, comprising as it did a magnificent mixture of

468

French baroque and Victorian mahogany. The massive dressing table and wardrobes belonged to the later period, while the carved and gilded vastness of the canopied bed would have done credit to the Pompadour in her hey-day.

On either side of the bed two marble-topped console tables supported a clutter of books, bottles and other oddments, and on one of them stood a massive silver candelabrum that had been converted into a bedside lamp. Amanda switched it on, and the warm glow illuminated the jumbled contents of the table and glinted on gilded garlands and the worn brocaded hangings of the bed.

Something moved on the pillow and she gasped and took a quick step backwards. But it was only Euridice's grey cat, who had been lying curled up in a warm nest formed by an elderly lace-edged bed jacket.

'What is it, dear?' inquired Miss Moon, looking round. 'Oh it is that dreadful cat! Chase it off, dear. I do wish that Euridice would get rid of it. I suppose that there will now be hairs all over the pillow. How very vexing.'

Amanda scooped up the cat, deposited it in the passage, and returning, shook out the bed jacket and picking up the pillow beat off the few short grey hairs that clung to it.

She bent to replace it and stood suddenly very still, her eyes wide with shock and an icy prickle of panic running down her spine.

Something had been lying under that pillow. An insignificant object that was yet horribly familiar.

A small bottle containing a few white tablets and bearing a red poison label.

But it could not be the same one! It could not possibly be! She had not brought it away with her. Steven Howard had taken it. He had wrapped it carefully in his handkerchief and had put it into the pocket of his dressing-gown. Yet it was the same bottle — or its twin.

Amanda found that she was shivering, and she caught her lip hard between her teeth to stop it trembling.

Miss Moon had seated herself before her dressing table and was engaged in removing various necklaces, bracelets and rings and replacing them in an old-fashioned and much worn morocco jewel case the size of a small hatbox. She was still talking, but the flow of her words slid over Amanda without making any impression on her. She could only stare and shiver.

Discovering that she was still holding the pillow, she laid it down carefully on the bed and reached out a shrinking hand for the bottle. But just before she touched it she remembered what Steve had said about finger-prints, and stopped.

There was a small, crumpled lace-edged handkerchief on the table beside Miss Moon's bed, and Amanda picked it up and lifted the bottle with it, holding it with extreme care.

She looked at Miss Moon's unconscious back and suddenly her brain seemed to clear, and she knew——

She knew that there would be no finger-prints on that bottle and just exactly why it had been placed there.

There was to have been a repetition of a scene that had been planned to take place in a cabin of the S.S. *Orantares*. But this time it would be Miss Moon and not Julia Blaine who would die. Miss Moon who should have been at Lady Cooper-Foot's bridge party, but had stayed at home instead, and who might therefore have heard or seen something or someone at the hour that Monica Ford had died. Miss Moon who knew and noticed so much and who might be waiting her chance to say a word that might lead to the hanging of Monica Ford's murderer ...

She would have laid her head on that single down pillow and have felt the small hard lump of the bottle, and would have removed it, looked at it in some surprise and put it aside until the morning — as Julia would have done.

Amanda could almost hear the coroner's verdict. Elderly and eccentric lady, shocked by Miss Ford's murder and distressed by

470

the consideration that her own refusal to keep her house locked was responsible for it, felt herself unable to face a public inquiry and allowed the tragedy to prey on her mind, and the recent suicide of Mrs Blaine to suggest a way out. Yes, it would have been something like that. And but for Euridice's cat and the fact that Amanda had carried up the jug of barley water for her, Miss Moon would have been found dead in the morning.

The barley water!

Amanda whirled round and stared at it. Someone who knew that Julia drank lemon juice and water had made use of that knowledge to disguise the acidity of a poison. Because Miss Moon drank barley water, had that someone laid the same trap for her? There was no innocent iced drink on Miss Moon's bedside table, but there was an empty glass — and the jug that Amanda herself had placed there.

Amanda forced herself to speak, waiting until Miss Moon ceased talking, and not having heard one word that she had said.

'May I have some of your barley water please?' Her voice sounded high-pitched and like a gramophone record, as though it did not belong to her.

Miss Moon turned. 'Why, of course dear. Help yourself.'

Amanda said: 'There's a glass in my room. I'll take some if I may and bring the jug back.'

'Do, dear.'

Amanda thrust the small bottle in its crumpled handkerchief into her pocket and picked up the jug. Once in her own room she filled her own glass from it, her hands shaking so badly that the liquid splashed on to the table. She poured the remainder out of the window, and ran down the passage to the bathroom where she turned on both taps and rinsed the jug again and again. Having dried it on a towel she half-filled it with cold water, and returned to Miss Moon; her face chalk white and her hands still shaking uncontrollably.

'I'm most awfully sorry,' explained Amanda breathlessly, 'but

471

I'm afraid I've spilt your barley water. I've brought you some water instead.'

Miss Moon tutted indulgently and said that Amanda was not to bother about it.

'I – I have to telephone someone,' said Amanda, finding it difficult to keep her voice under control. 'Something I have to ask about. Do you mind?'

'No dear, of course not. You know where the telephone is, do you not? Now don't stay up too late. You are not looking at all well.'

Amanda said goodnight and left the room hurriedly, shutting the door behind her and standing for a moment with her back to it, fighting off an absurd feeling of faintness and aware that her heart was beating unpleasantly fast.

The stairs stretched down into the blackness below, and she was suddenly afraid to go down into the darkness of the deserted hall and past the open doorway of the drawing-room where Monica Ford had died. Supposing that there was someone hiding there, waiting to make sure that Miss Moon died too? Waiting to make sure that they were safe for ever from Miss Moon's observant eyes and chattering tongue?

But of course that was absurd! Whoever had laid that deadly trap for Miss Moon would make certain of being as far away as possible from the Villa Oleander that night. There was nothing to be afraid of. Nothing except the darkness and the silence ...

Amanda set her teeth and forced herself to walk down that long dark stairway, remembering as she did so that other stairway and the footsteps that had crept down behind her. She groped her way to the electric light switch, and a moment later the hall was flooded with soft light from the few candle bulbs in the dusty crystal chandelier that hung from the high ceiling.

The passage off the hall yawned shadowy and silent, and facing it the door stood open on to the dark drawing-room. Amanda shivered and walked resolutely down to the end of the passage, and after a few moments of ineffectual groping, found the switch of the small lamp that hung above the telephone.

It took an absurdly long time to find the number she required. The pages of the telephone book fluttered in her unsteady hands and her fingers refused to obey her, but she found it at last.

It was George who answered the phone:

'Who? ... Oh, Howard. Yes, he's here. Do you want to speak to him?'

'Yes please,' said Amanda, trying to keep the fear and urgency from her voice; trying to speak quite calmly.

'Who is it?' George's voice was maddeningly loud and slow. 'Who? I can't hear you. Amanda? — Oh, Miss Derington! Sorry; didn't recognize your voice. Like me to give him a message? Or would you rather——'

The receiver was abruptly removed from his grasp and Steve's voice said crisply: 'What is it, Amanda?'

'*Steve!*' Amanda's voice wavered suddenly and she clutched at the edge of the table to steady herself. 'Steve, I must see you! Could you — could you come here? At once. I know it's late but — Steve *please!*'

Mr Howard's voice said cheerfully and surprisingly: 'Oh she does, does she? I can't have made myself clear. Perhaps I'd better come round and have a word with her. No, tell her it's no trouble at all. I'll be right along.'

There was a click and he had rung off.

Amanda stared stupidly at the receiver in her hand and was just about to ring the number again and tell him that he had not understood her, when it dawned on her that Steve was once again manufacturing an alibi for the benefit of those who might be unduly interested.

She replaced the receiver slowly, but she could not return to the hall. There were too many doors leading off the hall into too many

473

dark and silent rooms. Too many old, beautiful, silvery mirrors that reflected her and watched her ... as they had watched Monica Ford.

The passage was narrow and bare and smelt strongly of dust and boot-polish and faintly of garlic, and the house was uncannily silent: it did not creak or stir as many houses do after dark. And outside it the windless moonlight night was as silent and as still as the house.

Amanda was seized with a sudden fear of that silence. Surely she should be able to hear Miss Moon moving about in her room? Or had there been another glass somewhere in that room? A glass that she had overlooked? Was Miss Moon even now lying sprawled face downwards on the floor like Julia Blaine? Like Monica Ford——?

Amanda ran down the short passage and raced up the stairs, taking them three at a time, and burst into Miss Moon's room, white with panic.

Miss Moon, clad in a nightgown reminiscent of the one in which the Princess Victoria was popularly supposed to have received the news of her accession, was seated before her dressing-table rolling her hair up in curl-papers. She said: 'What is it, dear?' without looking round.

Amanda clung to the door handle and strove to regain her breath.

'N-nothing. I – thought I heard you call.'

'Probably someone in the road, dear. Did you put your call through?'

'Yes,' said Amanda, her eyes searching the room and seeing no sign of any other glass. 'Steve — Mr Howard — asked if he could come round for a minute or two. About – about the inquest I think. I hope you don't mind.'

'Of course not, dear. I did not realize that it was Mr Howard you were telephoning. Such a delightful man. You will find biscuits and brandy in the sideboard. Gentlemen usually like

brandy; although I have often wondered why. *So* unpleasant —
except in hard sauce. Do not let him keep you up too late.'

'I won't,' promised Amanda.

She went slowly downstairs again, feeling a little foolish and
wondering if she had not, after all, dragged Steve Howard out on
a fool's errand? Supposing there was nothing in the barley water,
and that the bottle contained some drug that Miss Moon took for
her migraines? She should have questioned Miss Moon about it
instead of leaping to wildly melodramatic conclusions. Her nerves
must be badly on edge and Steve would undoubtedly laugh at her.
She had better go up at once and ask Miss Moon.

She turned back, but as she did so someone came rapidly up the
flagged path and took the six stone steps in two. The fall of the
knocker echoed through the quiet hall and Amanda went slowly
to the door, thinking that if it was Steve Howard he must have run
most of the way.

If he had, he gave no sign of it. He looked very tall and slender
silhouetted against the bright moonlight, and he did not appear
to be in the least out of breath. He studied Amanda's face for a
long moment and the tension went out of his own.

He said amicably: 'Are you coming out or am I coming in?'

Amanda flushed and drew back, and he strolled into the hall
and closed the door behind him. He looked about him, glanced
up at the landing above the staircase, and evidently deciding that
the hall was an unsuitable spot for conversation, moved towards
the drawing-room.

'No!' said Amanda sharply. 'Not in there.' She went past him
into the dining-room and switched on the lights.

The dining-room was friendly and lacked the shadowy corners
and the ugly memories of the drawing-room. Steve followed her
in and shut the door.

'Well, Amarantha? What is it now? Judging from your voice on
the telephone I rather expected to find another body on the doorstep.'

'I'm sorry,' said Amanda uncertainly. 'I found something and I got into a panic. And now I think that perhaps it doesn't mean anything after all, and that I've made a fool of myself.'

'Let's see it,' suggested Steve, and held out his hand.

Amanda drew the small bundle of lace and cambric from her pocket and handed it over. He accepted it without much apparent interest, unfolded it, and then stood very still.

A minute ticked away into the silence and there was no longer any trace of casualness in Steve Howard's face or his tall figure, and his eyes were wide and bright and intent. Presently Amanda heard him let his breath out between his teeth and he lifted his head and looked at her.

'Where did you find this?'

Amanda told him, and he listened without interruption, his eyes on her face, and when she had finished told her curtly to fetch the glass of barley water. Amanda left the room and came back a few moments later, breathing a little unevenly, with the glass in her hand.

Steve was standing where she had left him. He had unscrewed the top of the bottle, and two small white tablets were lying in the full glare of the lamplight on the polished surface of the dining-room table. He took the glass from her hand, smelt it, and then wetted the tip of one finger in the contents and touched it to his tongue.

He made a quick grimace and jerking a handkerchief out of his breast pocket, rubbed it over his tongue. Amanda said breathlessly: 'Then it is poison?'

'H'mm?' said Steve in a preoccupied voice.

Amanda repeated the question and he looked at her as though he had momentarily forgotten her existence, and said impatiently: 'Of course it is.'

He pushed the glass away and sat down on the nearest chair with his elbows on the table and frowned at the two white tablets. Something about the handkerchief caught his attention and he

476

reached out a hand for it and spread it flat. It was, or it had been, an expensive trifle. A monogram consisting of three entwined initials was embroidered in one corner, and the lace had been badly torn along one edge.

'A.B.H.,' said Steve pensively. 'Where did you get this, Amanda? It isn't yours.'

'It was on Miss Moon's table, by her bed,' said Amanda, leaning over to look at it. 'And it isn't A.B.H. The centre initial overlaps the other two. Its A.F.B.'

'Anita F. Barton in fact,' said Steve thoughtfully.

'Why, of course!' said Amanda suddenly. 'I remember seeing her drop it. She had it here, in the hall. I suppose Miss Moon picked it up and took it upstairs, meaning to ask whose it was.'

'Mrs Barton seems to be a bit careless with her possessions,' observed Steve grimly. 'Her husband's secretary is found murdered, and a bit of nonsense off Mrs Barton's skirt is discovered in this hall. And if Miss Moon had been found dead tomorrow morning, that handkerchief wouldn't have looked so good; however innocently it came to be there. 'Unless ... I wonder——'

He twisted it absently about his hand, frowning the while, and after a moment inquired abruptly if Miss Moon always took a jug of barley water up to her bedroom at night.

'She told me that she usually did in the hot weather,' said Amanda. 'She doesn't seem to drink anything else. Euridice makes it fresh every day.'

'Have you ever drunk it?'

'No. Only Miss Moon. But no one else would know that.'

'Oh yes they would. I have a tolerably retentive memory, and someone, either you or Glenn Barton — I think both — mentioned the fact at that lunch party at the Dome. Which means that quite a few people knew of Miss Moon's addiction to barley water, and someone put the knowledge to good use.'

'Like – like Julia,' said Amanda, shivering.

'Julia?'

477

'The lemon juice.'

Steve's face was suddenly blank and unreadable. He looked at Amanda for a moment or two and seemed about to say something, but changed his mind.

Amanda said in a voice that was little more than a whisper: 'You thought that something like this might happen, didn't you?'

'Yes. It had occurred rather forcibly to me that whoever put paid to Monica Ford was going to be scared into next week by the news that Miss Moon had been in the house the entire time. We took certain precautions.'

'Then the house *is* being watched! I thought it was.'

'You could hardly miss it,' said Steve dryly. 'In fact, you were not meant to. The knowledge that the place was bristling with cops would, it was hoped, tend to discourage any rough stuff. And then,' he added bitterly, 'someone walks in right under our noses and plants this neat little booby trap. Mind if I touch you?'

He reached out and laid the tips of his fingers briefly against Amanda's arm.

'What's that for?' inquired Amanda, puzzled.

'For Luck. If it hadn't been for you and that cat of the cook's, Miss Moon would have gone the same way as Julia Blaine. In addition to which you appear to bear a charmed life. You ought by rights to be sliced into small sections and distributed in the form of amulets.'

Amanda said in a small, frightened voice: 'But if there are police watching the house they must know who came in——'

'My dear child,' said Steve impatiently, 'of course they know who came in! And that's the hell of it. I can give you a list myself. Barton was here for most of the morning, and during that time Mrs Halliday and young Gates called round to ask after you and stayed a considerable time. George Norman dropped in to tea and then Anita Barton came in to see you, casually shed her handkerchief on the premises and took you out for a walk. While you were out, a squad of sympathizers that included Claire Norman, Major

478

Blaine and Lumley Potter called round and were actually taken on a conducted tour of the house. That makes quite a nice little list of people, all or any of whom could have easily dropped a slug of poison into the barley water and slipped that bottle under Miss Moon's pillow. The thing was a gift, and I ought to be shot for not thinking of it. I considered a good many other possibilities, but not a repeat performance of a previous flop.'

Amanda said: 'Mrs Barton couldn't have done it. There wasn't time. And she didn't go upstairs.'

Steve lifted his eyes from a contemplation of the exhibits before him and looked thoughtfully at Amanda.

He said: 'Let's hear about that visit of hers again. Details please Exactly when did she arrive and how long was she alone in the hall and where was she standing when you first saw her? Everything.'

Amanda told him all that she could remember; hesitantly but in detail.

Steve leant back in his chair, drove his hands into his pockets and frowned at the ceiling: '*H'mm*. I wonder. She would probably have had plenty of time to doctor the barley water, and as she knew Miss Moon fairly well the odds are that she not only knew about the stuff, but where it was kept. Thirty seconds would have been enough for that job. But from what you say, it sounds impossible for her to have made a quick trip to Miss Moon's bedroom and back in the time. Anyway, the risk would have been too great, for if you'd seen her coming down the stairs you would have been curious, to say the least of it.'

He brooded for a while, rocking his chair gently to and fro until it creaked protestingly, and presently he said in a softly meditative voice: 'I think a few words with the cook-general would be in order. I'll get on to that in the morning. However it begins to look as though Mrs Barton is in the clear, and that means ...'

He did not finish the sentence, and presently began to whistle '*Sur le pont d'Avignon*' very softly through his teeth.

Amanda waited for a minute or two and then, as he did not

speak, asked anxiously: 'What does it mean?'

Mr Howard transferred his gaze from the ceiling to Amanda's white face and said thoughtfully: 'It means that one should not go to Birmingham by way of Beachy Head. In other words, if one wishes to get from A to B with the minimum loss of time and temper, one should stick to the main road and not allow oneself to be lured down intriguing but unprofitable bypaths. An error to which I must regretfully plead guilty.'

'I don't understand,' said Amanda with a catch in her voice.

Steve returned the front legs of his chair to the floor with a crash and stood up:

'God forbid that you should! But I should have known better. I had the whole thing cold, but owing to the entirely fortuitous fact that a varied assortment of emotional crises got mixed into the works, I began to look at this thing from another angle. In fact from several other angles. A mistake, Amarantha. There was only one angle. Just as there was only one person who could possibly have been able to push you over the battlements at Hilarion.'

Amanda said in a small, frightened voice: 'Does that mean that you — you know who it is?'

'I think so,' said Steve soberly. 'But the difficulty is going to be to prove it. The obvious procedure of course is to tie up a kid with the object of luring the tiger. That would probably work all right. But I'm not sure that I'm a good enough shot.'

'You mean – you mean deliberately let a murderer have another try at killing her just so that you could see who it is? Steve, you can't! You can't risk it!'

Steve Howard looked down at her and his face and voice were suddenly and inexplicably raw with anger and bitterness:

'No!' he said savagely. 'I can't risk it. That's the damnable part of it. I should, but I daren't — because I've lost my nerve!'

He stared down at Amanda for a long moment as though he

480

hated her, and then swung round violently and jerking open the door walked out of the room.

A minute or two later Amanda heard him strike a match, and followed him into the hall, bewildered and shaken by his sudden rage.

He was standing with his back to her under the dusty chandelier, the light turning his brown hair to bronze, and he must have heard her but he did not turn.

Amanda waited in silence, studying the back of his head and thinking that she could draw it with her eyes shut, and wondering why this should be so when she had only known him for so short a time? The smoke from his cigarette spiralled up into the still air and the scent of it mingled pleasantly with the smell of beeswax and dust and the tall orange lilies that filled a vast copper jar by the carved chest.

Presently he reached out a hand behind him and drew Amanda absently into the curve of his arm, still without turning his head.

He continued to stand quite still, holding her against him; staring ahead of him and drawing thoughtfully at his cigarette as though his mind were several hundred miles away — as indeed it was.

After a time he looked down, blew a smoke ring at the top of Amanda's head, released her and dropped his cigarette end into the jar of lilies:

'Time you were in bed, Amarantha. And quite time I got back to the Normans'. I am supposedly instructing Miss Moon in the procedure at an inquest, and there is no point in overdoing it. Do you think you can find me an empty bottle that'll take the remains of that barley water?'

'I can try,' said Amanda. She disappeared in the direction of the kitchen and presently returned with a bottle that had once contained cooking sherry.

Steve had gone back into the dining-room and was engaged in

replacing the tablets and wrapping the small bottle in a sheet of paper.

'Is it the same stuff that killed Julia?' asked Amanda in a half-whisper.

'No. That would have been inviting odious comparisons.'

'But there would have been anyway. Because of that bottle——'

'You've forgotten something. You kept quiet about that first bottle. Which is why it was tried again — for the simple reason that having once kept your mouth shut you would have to continue to do so, or else land yourself in an exceedingly nasty spot indeed. An angle which I admit should have occurred to me, but didn't.'

Steve decanted the barley water into the sherry bottle with infinite care and pushed the empty glass over to Amanda.

'Run that under the tap half a dozen times, will you? Oh, and you'd better take this——' He tossed over Anita Barton's torn handkerchief. 'Ask Miss Moon about it in the morning and let me know what she says.'

Amanda nodded and put it in her pocket. She removed the glass and carrying it out into the pantry, rinsed it and left it on the draining board and returned to find Steve waiting for her in the hall.

He glanced at the clock and said: 'See you in court,' and pulled open the front door.

Amanda said with a catch in her voice: 'But aren't you going to call in the police?'

'What for?'

'To tell them about the poison, of course!'

Steve shook his head. 'No. I don't think we'll tell anyone for the moment. Not even Miss Moon.'

'But — but surely whoever did it will try again?'

'Oh, sure to. But not that way. It was a good idea, but it's back-fired twice. Someone is due for an unpleasant headache tomorrow trying to work out what went wrong this time; and because they won't know they will lay off that tack and try another. And I think we can block anything else.'

He saw Amanda throw a quick look over her shoulder at the empty hall behind her and said: 'There's nothing to be frightened of tonight, dear, I promise you. The person who planted that stuff is going to make quite sure of being well in the public eye and surrounded by alibis up to a late hour tonight. Nor are they going to come near the place or ask any questions tomorrow. And in any case, the chaps who are watching this house won't let so much as a bluebottle past them between now and tomorrow morning.'

'They let you in,' said Amanda unsteadily.

'That,' said Mr Howard, 'is different. Word has gone round that I am really Marilyn Monroe in disguise, and they are all hoping to get my autograph.'

He removed himself into the night and Amanda bolted the door behind him and went upstairs to bed; but not to sleep.

17

The inquest on Monica Ford was unexpectedly brief. The jury system did not prevail in Cyprus, and an apparently bored judge listened without much interest to the pathologist's report and an account of the police findings. But Amanda received the unpleasant impression that the perfunctory questions did not add up to lack of interest or any conviction that the comfortable theory that a casual thief had been responsible for the murder was necessarily correct. It seemed more as though the officials involved were acting under orders, and she wondered uneasily if someone was being lulled into a false sense of security.

The proceedings had been too smooth — too suave. The voices too silkily polite and the eyes too hard and watchful.

They were all there. Claire and George, Persis and Toby, Alastair and Glenn, Lumley and Anita, Steve, Miss Moon and herself.

Amanda had found that she too was watching them with furtive, frightened eyes, afraid that one face might betray surprise or fear at the sight of Miss Moon. But she had surprised no such expression and did not know whether to be relieved or sorry.

She and Steve Howard had described the finding of Miss Ford's body, and Glenn had told of his meeting with his secretary earlier that afternoon and explained about her brother's death and her recent agitation of mind. He had not looked at his wife, and no further questions had been put to him beyond asking him for the time of his departure from Hilarion and his arrival at Nicosia. The latter had been corroborated, according to the police, by the two

484

young National Service men to whom he had given a lift, and the various members of the picnic party had confirmed the times of his arrival and departure from Hilarion.

Miss Moon had stated that owing to an attack of migraine she had, in fact, been in the bedroom in the Villa Oleander throughout the afternoon, but had heard nothing beyond the sound of a woman's voice raised in apparent agitation some time during the earlier part of the afternoon.

They had accepted the statement without comment and had returned unexpectedly to Amanda. They had asked her four questions, and this time the suave voices had been considerably less suave.

Was it true that she had seen a great deal of Major Blaine in Fayid?

Was it true that Mrs Blaine had died in her cabin on the way to Cyprus?

Was it true that she had been alone in the drawing-room of the Villa Oleander for several minutes — perhaps five or even ten? — before Mr Howard had found her standing beside the body of Miss Ford?

What dress had she worn that day, and would she describe it?

The room had been stiflingly hot and airless and it was pleasant to get into the open again and feel a faint breath of breeze and smell the scent of sunbaked dust and flowering trees.

Miss Moon declined an invitation from the Normans to return to their house for a glass of sherry, and announced her intention of returning home immediately. Andreas was driving her in her own elderly car, and Toby had offered Amanda a lift. Miss Moon went over to talk to Persis Halliday, and someone touched Amanda's arm and she turned to see Glenn Barton.

'I haven't had a chance to talk to you before,' said Glenn in a low voice. 'I wanted to thank you. For saying what you did. I – can't tell you how grateful I am. I know I shouldn't have let you do it, but — well I think you're a brick!'

485

Amanda said quickly: 'Don't Glenn. Anyone would have done the same; but not many people would have risked their necks for me at Hilarion. And I never even thanked you for that.'

Glenn Barton smiled at her and held out his hand. 'Shall we call it quits?'

Amanda put her hand into his, and an exceedingly dry voice behind them said: 'I'm sorry to interrupt you, but I'd like a word with Miss Derington.'

Amanda snatched her hand away and turning quickly looked up into Steven Howard's face and experienced a sudden shock of dismay.

Steve was looking at her as though she were some complete and not particularly attractive stranger whom necessity compelled him to address, and his voice was cold and remote and entirely devoid of expression.

He said: 'I understand that you have a guardian who is at present somewhere in the Middle East. I suggest that you write to him as soon as possible and ask him to come over.'

Amanda stared at him, bewildered. 'But – but why?'

'Because it looks as though you are going to need some responsible person to advise you. You made a statement to the police two nights ago that was entirely untrue and which looks like leading to a lot of trouble.'

He threw a glance of cold dislike at Glenn Barton, and continued curtly:

'In these circumstances I think that you would be well advised to let your uncle know what is going on, and let him decide if he thinks it is worth coming over or not. You won't find that it is in the least amusing being mixed up in a murder case in this part of the world.'

'But he's in Tripoli!' said Amanda.

'I know. Miss Moon told me. That's why I wanted to speak to you. I have a friend in the R.A.F. here who happens to be flying to Tripoli tomorrow, so if you can let me have a letter before

486

midday tomorrow I'll see that your uncle gets it the same evening. He can probably pull enough strings to get here by Monday or Tuesday at the latest. Think it over.'

Steve turned on his heel and walked away and Amanda stared after him; helplessly aware that there were tears in her eyes, and restraining herself with a strong effort from running after him to catch at his arm and demand to know why he had looked at her and spoken to her like that? He could not be jealous of Glenn Barton! — he could not be. Couldn't he *see*——?

Glenn said soberly: 'He's right you know. You ought to let Mr Derington know about this. Would you like me to cable him instead?'

Amanda winked the tears from her eyes and said: 'I – I'll think about it.'

She did not believe for one moment that she was in any danger of arrest. The idea was too ludicrous to be entertained even for a second. She had not, as Glenn Barton and several others had, taken in the significance of those three final questions, and she did not think of them now. She could only think of Steve's face and voice and feel hurt and bewildered and angry.

A police officer came up and spoke to Glenn Barton and Glenn excused himself and they walked away together and re-entered the building.

There was a jingle of bracelets and Miss Moon patted Amanda's arm with a be-ringed hand and said affectionately: 'There, there dear. You must not mind. He is not in the least annoyed with you. Only with himself. And with Glenn of course. Gentlemen are *so* foolish!'

Amanda laughed a little shakily and said: 'You don't miss much, do you Miss Moon?'

'No dear. It is only the young who seem unable to see what is under their noses. Of course he knows quite well that you cannot really have the slightest interest in poor Glenn, but I think that he has a great deal on his mind and that it annoys him to realize that he cannot prevent his attention being distracted by – by extraneous emotions, shall we say?'

'Not extraneous emotions,' corrected Amanda with a somewhat watery chuckle. ' "Unprofitable by-paths".'

'Is that what he said, dear? Well there you are! What did I tell you. And now, as I understand that Captain Gates wishes to drive you back to Kyrenia, I think I will return home. I shall be seeing you for luncheon.'

She turned away as Persis and Toby, who had been buttonholed by Lumley Potter, detached themselves at last and came towards Amanda. A few yards away George Norman, Alastair Blaine and Claire were standing on the kerb in a patch of shadow talking to Steve Howard who was sitting at the wheel of his car. Amanda noted resentfully that he appeared to be in excellent spirits and that the group beside his car, despite the fact — or possibly in reaction to it — that they had just been attending an inquiry into murder, were laughing at something that he had just said.

Anita Barton was standing by herself, a little apart. She was looking forlorn and unhappy and there were dark shadows under her eyes. Her usual air of defiant disregard for public opinion was entirely lacking and she looked noticeably ill at ease.

Amanda, studying her, saw that she was not quite steady on her feet and suspected that she had been drinking — perhaps to give herself courage to face the curious gaze of those who knew how much she had disliked her husband's secretary.

Persis, looking as usual like an advertisement for Saks, Fifth Avenue, caught Amanda's arm in an affectionate clasp and said in plangent tones: 'Well honey, how does it feel to be Suspect Number One?'

'Shut up, Persis!' said Toby crossly. 'Your humour is misplaced. Come on Amanda darling, we're all going along to the Normans' to get drunk. Only possible course, after a session like that.'

'Who's "all"?' inquired Amanda.

'The gang, honey,' supplied Persis. 'The Associated Society of

Suspects. Little did I think when I decided on visiting the birth-place of Venus that all I should get handed in lieu of Love would be a coupla' corpses. It's time the boys at the Tourist Bureau rewrote that "Come to Sunny Cyprus!" stuff, and urged the prospective visitor to pack a gat and bring a lawyer with them.'

'The trouble with you, Persis,' said Toby sourly, 'is that you can't really believe anything you don't see with your own eyes. None of this is any more real to you than one of your own stories, merely because you never saw the bodies of either Julia Blaine or this secretary woman.'

'And did you, Toby dear?' inquired Persis softly.

'No. But Amanda did.'

Persis turned swiftly to Amanda and said contritely: 'He's right. I keep forgetting what heck and hades it must have been for you honey. What would like me to do? Prostrate myself on the pave-ment as a penance, or dedicate my next book "To Amanda, who stole all my beaux"?'

'Meaning Toby?' inquired Amanda with a smile. 'Was he your beau?'

'He certainly was. But humiliating as it is to own it, I am compelled to classify him as one of the ones that got away.'

'What you really mean is one of the ones you couldn't even bother to gaff,' said Toby, lifting one of her hands and kissing it.

'Toby! What a Continental gesture!' exclaimed Persis in mock admiration. 'I had no idea that——' She broke off and said rather sharply: 'Say, what's bitten Glenn?'

Amanda, turning to follow the direction of her gaze, saw Glenn Barton come quickly out into the sunlight, and realized what had prompted that startled exclamation.

Glenn's mouth was compressed into a tight line and he looked frightened and desperate. He stood for a moment looking about him with his eyes narrowed against the glare, and then seeing his wife walked swiftly over to her and put a hand on her arm.

'Anita——'

Anita Barton whirled about, her face white under its heavy make-up, and almost in the same movement she wrenched his hand from her arm and turned as though to walk away.

Glenn's hand shot out and he caught her arm again and swung her round to face him. 'Anita, please! I've got to talk to you. Just for a few minutes. It's for your own sake. Darling *please*.'

His voice was hoarse and desperate and he appeared to be entirely oblivious of the fact that his words were perfectly audible to everyone within a dozen yards and that at least as many inquisitive, interested or appalled pairs of eyes were openly watching him.

An ugly wave of colour flooded up into Anita Barton's livid face and she wrenched herself from his grasp and struck him across the face with the full force of her arm. She stood there for a moment staring at him, her breath coming fast, and then turned on her heel and walked rapidly away, leaving her husband standing in the bright sunlight with the red marks of her fingers showing clearly against his haggard face.

Persis was the first to recover herself and to rush in where angels might justifiably have feared to tread. She went swiftly across to him and said: 'Why, Glenn Barton — I thought you'd gone!' and slipping her hand through his arm almost forcibly turned him round: 'Have you got a car here? Because if you have, you've gotten yourself a passenger. Will you take me some place to get a drink before I drop dead from sunstroke?'

Glenn looked at her with a dazed expression, and then seemed suddenly to focus her, for he smiled a stiff-lipped puzzled smile and said: 'Why – why of course, Mrs——?'

'Persis,' supplied Persis briskly. 'Is that your car over there? Good. Let's go.'

She led him firmly away, talking animatedly and at random, and the entertainment was over.

Steve Howard's car, followed by the Normans', slid away down the road. Lumley Potter hurried off in the wake of Anita Barton, and Amanda, suddenly deciding that she could not bear the prospect of a social gathering at the Normans', asked Toby to drive her instead to the Villa Oleander.

She was feeling mentally and physically exhausted, and by two-thirty was much inclined to follow Miss Moon's example and retire to her bedroom for a siesta. She was still considering the advisability of this course when she heard someone run quickly up the front steps and walk into the hall without knocking. It was Glenn.

'Amanda——!' He gave a quick gasp of relief at the sight of her. 'Amanda, can I talk to you please? Somewhere where we can't be overheard?'

His voice was jerky and uncontrolled and he appeared driven to the verge of collapse. Amanda looked at him for a long moment and then turned without a word and led the way into the drawing-room.

He came in after her, and shutting the door, leant against it.

'What is it, Glenn?'

'Anita,' said Glenn desperately. 'She won't see me. She doesn't understand! Amanda, I know she didn't kill Monica. I *know* she didn't. She may do rash, silly things, but she *could* not kill. I tell you I *know*. Good God! — who should know, if I don't? I don't pretend to know what she was doing in this house that day; she must have been here I suppose, because of that hellish flower. But whatever the reason, it can have had nothing to do with Monica Ford's death. She probably came in to see you, or Miss Moon, and found Monica dead, and panicked. No one could blame her for that!'

Amanda said urgently: 'Glenn, don't stand there. Come and sit down here and tell me what has happened. There's no sense in tearing yourself to pieces like this.'

Glenn laughed. It was a short, curiously wavering laugh that had no amusement in it. He walked unsteadily to the sofa and sank down on it as though his knees had suddenly given way under him.

Amanda looked at him with an anxious frown and left the room abruptly; returning a moment later with a glass containing a stiff proportion of Miss Moon's brandy. Glenn took it from her hand and gulped it down gratefully.

'You're a brick, Amanda. I seem to have said that a good many times of late, don't I?'

He looked up at her with a crooked attempt at a smile and Amanda said: 'What is it, Glenn? What has happened?'

'The police,' said Glenn wretchedly. 'It's that damnable flower. I think they've found out who it belongs to. They asked me if I'd recognized it. And — they asked a hell of a lot of other questions too. About her quarrel with Monica, and wasn't it true that she had told me that either I sacked Monica or she'd leave me, and – and that when I wouldn't, she had left me. They went over and over it. And then they – they wanted to know if I knew that she was friendly with Major Blaine——'

'With *Alastair!*'

'Yes. Oh, I know they asked you the same thing, but that was just routine. This was far more serious.'

Glenn stood up abruptly, and walking over to the french windows stood staring blindly out across the garden, his back to Amanda.

He said in a harsh, jerky voice: 'They suggested that she knew him rather well and that – that his wife's death had made him a rich man. They pointed out that she — Anita——' His voice failed suddenly and Amanda saw his shoulders jerk in a small shudder. Presently he said in a more normal voice:

'They wanted to know if she could have got her hands on any poisons, and asked if it were true that her father had been a doctor. They – they seemed to know so many things. I got scared then, and I tried to talk to her, but she wouldn't speak to me——'

His voice held a sudden hurt, bewildered note. He turned and walked back to Amanda and stood looking down at her, his hands clenching and unclenching at his sides, and said in a flat, exhausted voice: 'I know I shouldn't ask you — I know it's an unforgivable thing to do, but I can't think of any other way out. Will you help me?'

'Yes,' said Amanda, lightly and quite steadily.

Glenn stooped quickly and lifting her hand, kissed it. 'Bless you!' There was a sudden break in his voice.

'What do you want me to do?'

'Persuade her to go away. Lumley's a useless fool. He'll be no help to her. She must get away for a while; to give them time to find out who really did kill Monica.'

'But Glenn, how can I! Persuade her to go where?'

'Lebanon. We have friends there who I know would take her in. And I've got a good many friends among the local fishermen here. I could arrange all that; if only she could be persuaded to go.'

Amanda looked at him with a crease between her brows. She said slowly: 'Glenn you know that won't work. You must know that if they are suspicious of her, and she disappears, it would only confirm their suspicions, because then they'd be sure that she had done it.'

'Yes,' said Glenn heavily. 'I know.'

'Then – then there must be some other reason why you want to get her away. What is it?'

Even as she spoke she was aware of a sudden suspicion that Glenn, whatever he might say to the contrary, was secretly and terribly afraid that his wife might just possibly be more deeply involved than he would admit.

Glenn lifted his tired, red-rimmed eyes to hers and looked at her for a long moment. And when he spoke it was in a voice that was so low that it was barely audible:

'Yes. There is another reason. There is something about all this that I don't understand, and it frightens me. You see I think – I think there is going to be another murder. An attempt at one anyway. If I'm right, there's got to be.'

He heard Amanda catch her breath and did not know that she

493

was remembering that Steve had said almost those same words that night on the harbour wall.

Glenn said: 'Perhaps I'm wrong. I hope I am. But I'm beginning to think that there's — oh, I don't know — something behind all this. A plan. Something that may even have been worked out a long time ago. But now it hasn't gone right, and someone who still means to go through with it is getting frightened and needs a scapegoat. That's why I want to get Anita away. Because I think that she is playing straight into — someone's hands. Once she is safe with friends in the Lebanon, whoever is trying to hide behind her will have to think of something else. And then, if there is another attempt, we can tell the police at once where she is and why she went there. She'll be safe then. But I can't guard against something that I can only sense and guess at, but not see . . .'

His voice died out in a whisper and Amanda said quickly: 'You think you know who it is, don't you?'

He did not answer, and she repeated the question. Glenn's eyes came back to her again.

'Yes.'

'Who?' There was an odd tremor in Amanda's voice.

Glenn shook his head. 'I wouldn't tell you, even if I were sure — and I'm not. It might be dangerous. And I can't be sure; not yet. I think that there is a way to find out, but I daren't use it as long as Anita is here to – to pin things on. Once it cannot possibly be her, then it must be someone else. You do see that, don't you? That would prove it.'

Amanda was conscious of a sudden stab of fear and a vivid recollection of Steve Howard's words about tying up a kid to lure the tiger. So Glenn intended to use himself to lure a tiger into another killing. And provided Anita was safely out of the Island, even if he failed to avoid death himself, it would at least be proof that she was in no way responsible. But he must not do that! — it was too foolhardy a risk. Steve had said 'a killer knows quite

494

well that even if he kills a dozen people, or twenty, he himself can only hang once'. Someone who had killed twice would not hesitate to kill again.

She said breathlessly: 'You can't do it, Glenn. If it's dangerous for Anita it's just as dangerous for you.'

'Me? Oh I can look after myself. But Anita's got no one but that ass Lumley. I've *got* to get her out of it. If I can only do that, without anyone knowing or even guessing that she's gone, there is a chance.'

'But Glenn! even if you do, don't you see that if someone is really trying to pin this on Anita, and – and nothing else happens, and she has disappeared, their object is achieved?'

'Anita's suicide would achieve it in a far more final and satisfactory manner,' said Glenn grimly.

'*Suicide!*'

'Yes. An artistically staged suicide. It wouldn't be so very difficult to arrange. Anita found dead: verdict, suicide rather than face trial and conviction for murder.'

'*No!*' said Amanda in a whisper. 'Oh no, it couldn't be——'

But she knew that it could. Once again she saw, in an ugly flash of memory, Julia Blaine lifting an innocuous, frosted glass, drinking from it, and dying. Felt again the little hard lump of a bottle under her pillow, and stared down with wide, frozen eyes at a similar bottle that had lain under Miss Moon's pillow only last night.

Glenn was quite right. Someone needed a scapegoat, and Anita Barton's death — supposedly by her own hand — would tie up a good many loose ends in a very neat and final manner.

Glenn said: 'She may refuse to go. If she does — well I shall just have to think of something else. But if you can persuade her——'

'I'll try,' said Amanda unsteadily.

Glenn turned quickly away and began to pace up and down the room, his hands in his pockets and frowning concentration on his face. Presently he came to a stop in front of her again and said abruptly: 'It must be tonight. Tomorrow may be too late. If she agrees, would you help her to go? To see that she is safe.'

'Yes.'

'Can you drive a car?'

Amanda nodded.

'Then this is what we'll do. I'll leave a car on the road tonight — against the kerb by that open bit of ground on the main road about fifty yards below the turn out of this road, opposite that house with the blue shutters. If you can get Anita to agree, tell her to take only what she can carry, and to give out that she's got a bit of a headache and intends to go to bed early. There's a little cove just beyond the five-mile beach on the road to Larnaca. Anita will know it. I'll get Yiannopoulos to be there with a boat not later than ten. It will mean leaving here around nine-thirty, which will give her an alibi from then on, as you would be with her. And as it's in the opposite direction from Nicosia, if anything should happen tonight they can't think——' He checked abruptly and then said: 'As soon as she's away, drive back here and leave the car in the same place. I'll pick it up later. There's only one other thing ...'

Glenn pushed his hand wearily through his hair and his mouth twisted bitterly:

'You'll have to pretend that it's your own idea, or Miss Moon's. If she thinks that I've had anything to do with it, she won't touch it. Just at the moment I really believe that she'd rather be arrested for murder than be beholden to me. You see she doesn't understand. She thinks that she can do what she likes and get away with it. She doesn't realize that murder is a deadly thing.'

Once again the words brought an echo of Steven Howard. Steve standing in the bright moonlight on the harbour wall with his arms about Amanda and saying: 'Murder is a diabolical thing.'

Amanda said: 'I'll do my best.'

'I know you will. Make her see that it's serious. Don't let her brush it aside and take the line that nothing can really happen to her.'

Amanda nodded wordlessly.

Glenn said: 'I can't thank you enough, dear. I shouldn't risk getting you involved in anything; I know that. But I'm in a corner. If I could think of any other way out I'd take it; but I can't.'

He was silent for a moment or two, and then his mouth twisted in a wry smile and he said: 'I did try one other way. But it didn't work and I only made rather an ass of myself.' The smile faded and he said: 'The car will be there at nine o' clock. If Anita won't go, well——'

He shrugged his shoulders and turned away, and a moment later Amanda heard the hall door close behind him.

18

Amanda came out on to the quay and walked slowly in the direction of the café at the corner of the harbour.

She felt curiously exhausted, but her exhaustion was mixed with a feeling of elation. Anita Barton had been difficult and suspicious and more than a little tipsy. But she had been frightened too, and it was her fear that had tipped the scales. She had agreed to go.

Amanda had succeeded in convincing her that she and Miss Moon were responsible for the scheme, and perhaps it was Miss Moon's name that had brought about Anita Barton's sudden capitulation. That, and the fact that Amanda had reported the gist of the questions the police had asked Glenn Barton about his wife, hinting mendaciously that they had been put to Miss Moon. She had also allowed it to be supposed that Miss Moon had arranged with the owner of a fishing boat to convey Anita away from the Island; it being unlikely that she herself would have been able to arrange such a thing.

She was to pick up Mrs Barton at a turn of the road near the Post Office at half past nine. Less than half an hour's driving would bring them to the beach where the boat was to wait, and that would give them an ample margin in which to get from the road to the shore — a matter of less than a hundred yards of rough ground and rocks.

The sun was setting in a blaze of gold and rose and apricot and the tall, picturesque houses that ringed the harbour threw long lilac shadows across the quays and the quiet water. A church bell was ringing and from the minaret of a mosque a muezzin intoned the call to prayer.

Amanda turned down the sea wall of the harbour and sat down tiredly on the warm stone. She wished desperately that she could discuss the coming night's work with someone. Glenn had not bound her to secrecy in the matter; but then he would not have considered such a course necessary. It was so obvious that if danger threatened Anita Barton, her departure must not be known or talked about.

Amanda thought longingly and resentfully of Steven Howard. Steve at least would be safe. She could have gone to him and asked for his advice and help. But she could not forget the caustic words that he had spoken only last night on the subject of Glenn Barton: 'Dear Glenn would appear to make a habit of getting his girlfriends to pull his chestnuts out of the fire for him.'

Mr Howard, apprised of the present situation, would undoubtedly consider that dear Glenn had no right to ask Amanda to involve herself in anything that might conceivably be dangerous, and be correspondingly scathing on the subject. He would, in addition, refuse to allow her to have anything whatever to do with the scheme, and might even take steps to prevent Anita Barton leaving the Island. However, even if she had wished to tell him, she could not, for she had passed him on her way to the harbour. He had been driving up the main road that led out of Kyrenia towards Nicosia, and though he had undoubtedly seen her, he had given no sign of having done so.

Amanda sighed and rested her chin on her hand.

A shadow fell across her and a cheerful voice said: 'What's eating you honey? Is it love — or indigestion?'

Amanda turned quickly. 'Persis you beast! You've nearly made me bite my tongue in half? No it isn't love — *or* indigestion. And nothing's eating me.'

'No? Then you're lucky!'

Persis subsided gracefully on the sea wall beside Amanda and said abruptly: 'Honey, I'm worried.'

Amanda turned sideways to look at her and saw that Persis was staring out to sea, her white forehead wrinkled in a frown.

'What's worrying you?'

'It's Glenn,' confessed Persis. 'You know, I like that guy. I like him quite a lot. He makes me feel all maternal; and that's something I've certainly never felt about anyone before. Maybe it's a sign of old age!'

Amanda said cautiously: 'What has he been doing now?'

'Acting like a fool!' said Persis with unexpected violence. 'Do you know what that crazy guy did this morning? He walked right back to see the police and confessed to murdering his secretary!'

'He *what*? He must be mad!'

'That's right. Plain cuckoo! I tried to drag him out. Told the boys he'd had a brain storm. But he had it all doped out and he was perfectly sober about it. Talked away as cool as a mint julep in July. Said he had not gone straight back to Nicosia from Hilarion after all. He'd lied about it. He'd waited out of sight until George's car had turned down to Kyrenia, and then followed it, gone into Miss Moon's, strangled this dame and streaked for home. So they asked him what about the two hitch-hikers he'd given a lift to? And he had that taped too. Said he'd put back the hands of the dashboard clock to fake an alibi, and the boys had taken their time from that. He said it had been preying on his mind, and asked to be arrested.'

'What happened then?' demanded Amanda breathlessly. 'Why didn't they arrest him?'

'Because they aren't that dumb,' said Persis with a sigh. 'They'd thought of that one too. They turned up the statements of the two guys, and the thing came unstuck at once. Seems the boys hadn't taken their time from any dashboard clock — it's busted anyway. They both had wrist-watches and they swear to the time they got back. Glenn tried to argue it, but the cops threw him out with the greatest charm. I thought he was going to cry, and I don't mind telling you honey that it was all I could do not to put my arms round him and kiss him right there in the roadway and say: "There, there, son! Tell Momma all about it and she'll see that you're arrested for murder if that's the way you want it!" And what I want to know,' said Persis with feeling, 'is am I nuts, or is he?'

'So *that's* what he meant!' said Amanda, enlightened.

'How's that?'

'Nothing much. Just something he said about trying something, but that it hadn't been any use and he'd only made rather a fool of himself.'

'When did he say that?' demanded Persis quickly. 'Have you seen him this afternoon?'

'Yes,' said Amanda hesitantly.

She looked at Persis Halliday, frowning and uncertain. Persis could never have seen or heard of Anita Barton until that afternoon on the S.S. *Orantares* at Port Said, and could not previously have been aware of her existence, or that of Monica Ford. She had never been to Cyprus before, and she could have no possible reason for wanting to pin a murder — two murders! — on Glenn Barton's wife.

Quite suddenly Amanda made up her mind. The terror and strain and emotional tension of the last few days had been too much for her, and she had to confide in someone. It should have been Steve, but Steve had been curt and unkind, and he had apparently gone to Nicosia.

Amanda said: 'Persis, if I tell you something, will you promise me that you won't tell anyone else? — anyone at all?'

Persis looked at her for a long moment with narrowed speculative eyes, and then held out her hand. It was a strong hand, with long, intelligent, square-tipped fingers, and its clasp was comfortably firm and reassuring.

'Shoot!' said Persis laconically.

She listened to Amanda's account of the afternoon's interview with enthralled interest, and when it was finished said: 'Well if this doesn't beat Erle Stanley Gardner! When do we start?'

'We?' echoed Amanda.

'Sure. I'm going with you. You don't really think I'm going to let you stick your neck out like this without standing by with a blackjack just in case anyone tries any rough stuff? Why I wouldn't miss it for a million dollars! I'm in on this, honey, and you can't get me out.'

Amanda laughed, conscious of a sudden and overwhelming flood of relief. She would not have admitted to anyone how little the thought of that coming night's adventure had appealed to her, or how frightening she had found the prospect of that long, lonely drive back to Kyrenia. But now that Persis would be with her the affair lost its terrors, and became instead merely an exciting escapade.

Amanda threw an arm about Persis and gave her a sudden and impulsive hug.

'Persis, you're an angel!'

'So I have frequently been informed,' said Persis dryly. 'And now let's take a stroll up to that villa of yours and break it to Miss Moon that you will be dining with me at the Dome. Then there will no hitch over getting to that car on time. What do you say?'

They scrambled to their feet and carried out this programme, and Amanda, not without some qualms, left Miss Moon to dine alone. She reassured herself, however, with the reflection that Steve Howard would have taken every possible precaution to safeguard Miss Moon from further danger, and was relieved to see that the usual loiterer was industriously engaged in doing nothing at the corner of the road.

They met Alastair Blaine coming out of the Dome. He appeared to be in a hurry and said that he had a date to dine at Antonakis' Restaurant in Nicosia.

'I'm told that the speciality is octopus,' said Alastair. 'I've always

502

wanted not to eat octopus, but life catches up on one. I'll probably be seeing you sometime tomorrow — if I survive!'

Persis said: 'Who's your date with, Alastair?' But Alastair was already striding rapidly away into the dusk, and it is doubtful whether he heard the question.

Claire came out of Zari's lace shop opposite the hotel, and seeing them, waved, but did not come over to speak to them and also appeared to be in a hurry.

They saw no one else they knew, beyond a few hotel acquaintances of Persis Halliday's, and Lumley Potter, who was eating a lonely meal in a far corner of the dining-room, and who left early. Anita had evidently thought it best to send him out for the evening. There was no sign of either Toby Gates or Steven Howard, both of whom were obviously dining elsewhere that night.

The lingered over their meal as long as they could, but the hands of the clock seemed to crawl and stop and crawl again. Even Persis began to be affected by tension, for she lit one cigarette from the next in endless succession, jerking the ash on to the floor with nervous fingers and fidgeting restlessly in her chair.

At last it was nine o'clock and Persis glanced at the tiny diamond-ringed dial of her wrist-watch, checked it with a hotel clock, and rose:

'Let's go.'

They went first to her room where Persis fetched a thin tussore silk coat from the cupboard and peered intently at her face in the looking-glass. She tied a chiffon scarf over her smoothly waved hair, applied some lipstick with careful concentration, and declared herself ready.

They walked up through the town, and were pausing at the junction of two roads when George Norman passed them, driving his car. As he slowed down for the cross traffic, the headlights of an approaching car fell full on him, and they saw that his pleasant, rubicund face was looking as sulky as that of a small boy whose play has been interrupted by a request to help with the washing

503

up. He did not see Persis and Amanda, but drove on up the main road out of Kyrenia.

'A dime'll get you a dollar that Teeny Weeny Claire has sent him out to run errands,' commented Persis with a grin. 'What that guy needs is a nice bellhop's outfit with a dandy set of buttons down the front. Then he'd be right in character.'

They found a car parked in a patch of shadow near the edge of the vacant lot. But it was not Glenn's car.

'Sure this is it?' inquired Persis, speaking entirely unintentionally in a whisper.

'It must be. It's empty and the key's in it. He wouldn't have left his own, because his wife would have recognized it.'

'You're dead right. Okay, get in. I'd better sit in the back and put up a silent prayer that this contraption does not belong to some honest but absent-minded citizen who has chosen an unfortunate spot to park his jalopy. I do not fancy the prospect of spending the rest of my stay in Aphrodite's Island in the can!'

Amanda settled herself behind the wheel and turned on the dashboard lights. The ignition key was already in place, and she switched on the engine and pressed the self-starter. A moment later the car moved softly off down the road.

Anita Barton was waiting in the shadow of a jacaranda tree. She wore a dark linen coat and a scarf over her head, and was carrying a small suitcase.

Amanda threw open the car door and the next moment Mrs Barton was beside her, breathing quickly and shivering with fear or tension. She slammed the door behind her, and as the car drew away from the kerb, caught sight of Persis Halliday's reflection in the windscreen and whipped round with a choking cry that was almost a scream.

'*Who's that!*'

'It's all right,' said Amanda quickly. 'It's only Mrs Halliday. She's a friend of mine. She came along to – keep me company on the way back.'

'I don't think we've met,' said Persis sociably. 'I'm pleased to know you. I hope you won't think I'm butting in, but I thought maybe Amanda could do with a bit of support. It's going to be a long ride home.'

'You're an American, aren't you?' said Anita Barton in a hard voice.

'Dyed in the wool,' said Persis.

Mrs Barton fell silent, but it was not a relaxed silence. She sat tense and quivering, and every now and again she threw a quick, hunted look over her shoulder as if she feared to see the headlights of a pursuing car. Twice a car overtook them and passed in a cloud of dust, and she cowered down in her seat; bending her head so that her features were hidden by the dashboard.

The winding road and the olive groves, and the steep stony sides of the Kyrenia range, were milky with moonlight. The sea was a placid sheet of polished silver, and the night was warm and white and wonderful. The road dipped and turned and climbed through the streets of little white-walled villages and fell away into minia-ture valleys where small stone culverts spanned the stony beds of streams; and the miles unwound behind them ...

'We're nearly there,' said Anita Barton, speaking for the first time in almost twenty minutes. 'Stop here. By those trees. We can see from here if the road is clear and if it's safe to go on.'

Amanda pulled the car to a stop where a ragged clump of scrub and casurina trees made a pool of freckled shadow.

'Turn off the lights,' commanded Anita Barton in a harsh whisper.

Amanda switched them off obediently, but left the engine running softly as Mrs Barton opened the car door and stepped out into the moonlit road and Persis and Amanda followed her.

The shore lay some fifty yards or so to the left of the road and was separated from them by a stretch of rock-strewn ground covered with coarse grasses, stunted shrubs and mulberry trees.

Anita Barton spoke in a whisper: 'I'm going to walk to the turn of the road to see if all's clear. Sometimes there are picnic parties here on moonlight nights. Miss Derington had better stay by the car. You' — she turned to Persis — 'will you go to the cliff edge and see if you can see a boat out there? It should be off the rocks about half a mile ahead. You can see straight across from this point. We won't go on if it isn't there.'

'Okay,' said Persis with a sigh. 'I guess it will ruin my nylons to say nothing of my nerves, but it's all in a good cause.'

She turned away and vanished into the shadows of the casurina scrub, her high-heeled slippers making no sound in the soft, sandy soil beyond the road's edge.

Anita Barton waited for a moment or two and then walked round to the front of the car. She stopped suddenly and bent down and Amanda heard her catch her breath.

'What is it?' asked Amanda sharply.

'*Look!*' said Anita Barton in a frightened whisper.

Amanda ran round to her and bent down, staring at the white dusty road where Anita Barton's trembling finger pointed.

'What is it?' she said. 'I don't see——'

And then she saw the shadow on the moonlit road.

Anita Barton's shadow. A shadow that held something in its hand and swung its arm silently upward and swiftly down again.

Amanda tried to turn, but it was too late. Something crashed with a cruel force on to the back of her bent head and she fell forward into blackness and lay sprawling on the moonlit road.

Anita Barton laughed. A soft, unsteady, hysterical sound in that silver silence.

She looked behind her with wide, panic-stricken eyes, but there was no sound or sign of Persis Halliday, and she turned back to Amanda and stooping down, gripped her by the shoulders and half dragged, half lifted her into the car. She closed the door on her, ran round and climbed into the driver's seat and released the brake.

The car slid away with barely a sound down the moonlit road, its lights still switched off — a grey shadow in the black and white and silver of the night. At the bottom of a long slope the road swung round a curve and began to climb again, and the car, having gathered speed, took the gradient at fifty and roared on down the coast road with the needle of the speedometer touching seventy-five.

The rush of the night air revived Amanda and she stirred and moaned with pain and opened her eyes.

For a minute or two she could not remember where she was, or think of anything but the agonizing pain of her head. It seemed to her that she was looking into a red haze shot with stabbing scarlet lights. Then the haze lifted slowly and the night air was cool and pleasant against her throbbing forehead, and she remembered Anita Barton's shadow on the moonlit road ...

Anita had hit her with something; something hard and heavy and made of metal. But the thick coils of her hair had cushioned her from the full force of the savage blow.

Anita——

Amanda lifted her head slowly and painfully and saw Anita Barton's face in the faint glow of the dashboard light. A white mask of a face, the red lips drawn back over the teeth in a purely animal grimace. There was a touch of froth at the corners of that mouth and the wide eyes were fixed and glaring and bright with fear.

She felt Amanda stir, and turned her head. The next moment she had taken her foot from the accelerator and jammed on the brakes.

The car screeched to a standstill and the shock of its sudden stop flung Amanda's numbed body forward against the dashboard.

Anita Barton drew something out of her pocket, and the moon-light glinted along the barrel of a heavy service revolver.

'Don't do anything silly,' she warned, her voice harsh and high and uncontrolled.

She put up her left hand and tore at the silk scarf that was tied

507

about her head, jerked it free and said: 'Turn round with your back to me and put your hands behind you. Quickly!'

Amanda, with that cold ring of metal thrust against her, obeyed numbly. She felt Anita Barton's hot unsteady fingers winding the silk about her wrists and wrenching the knots painfully tight, and realized that she must temporarily have laid aside the gun.

'That's right,' Mrs Barton's voice was panting and breathless. 'Now your ankles.' She dragged Amanda over roughly and tied her ankles with a length of cord that she must have brought with her and then savagely and unexpectedly thrust a handkerchief into Amanda's gasping mouth and wound another length of material across it, pulling down her hair with a ruthless hand so that it would not impede the tightness of the gag. It was quite obvious that she had made her preparations with some care.

'There!' said Anita Barton with breathless satisfaction.

She stared down into Amanda's wide, terror-filled eyes and laughed long and loudly; a high, hysterical laugh.

'So you're another of Glenn's girls, are you. You planned this with him, didn't you? Darling Glenn! What a fool you must have thought me! So he's going to wait for me with a boat, is he? He's going to get a surprise. The very last surprise of his life. He arranged it all so beautifully, didn't he? But he's the one who is going to disappear. Not me. I've kept this gun for him. I thought of using it on myself once, but I shall use it on him instead. It *was* Glenn who put you up to this, wasn't it? — *wasn't it!* Of course it was. Well it's the last thing he'll do. You thought you'd fooled me, didn't you? All that stuff about doing this for my sake; for my safety; when all the time you were doing it for the sake of dear Glenn. Why you little——!'

She used an unprintable word. Her eyes were not sane and her face was ash-white in the moonlight and contorted with rage and fear — the rage and fear of a hunted animal turning at bay. She glared at Amanda, her breast heaving with her panting breath, and suddenly and unexpectedly she laughed again and turned to release the brake.

She drove more slowly now; and presently, at the top of a rise, switched off the engine and let the car coast down a long, gentle sloping stretch of road, and braked it softly near the edge of a patch of shadow thrown by some tall, windworn rocks.

She sat quite still, listening intently, and after a moment or two opened the car door and slipped out.

She turned and looked back at Amanda and said in a whisper that was barely a breath of sound: 'When you hear a shot you'll know that you've helped dear Glenn to a death that will probably be painful. I've never used a gun before, so I shall make quite sure I don't miss him. You can stay here and listen for it. I'll deal with you later.'

She turned away and moved silently out into the moonlight to vanish down a narrow, sandy track between tumbled rocks that led to a low headland, some fifty yards distant, below which the unseen sea purred softly against a shelving beach.

Amanda turned and twisted frantically, wrenching helplessly at her bound wrists. Glenn would not be there, but since his wife did not believe that, it would be some harmless, friendly fisherman who would die. He would be waiting for her, and she would shoot him down without mercy and without warning — killing him as she must have killed poor, helpless Monica Ford. And because she had never used a gun before she would play for safety and fire at the man's chest or stomach, and he would die horribly, coughing blood.

Anita Barton was not sane. Fear for her own safety had driven her over the narrow line that lies between sanity and madness. Had Glenn really suspected all the time that she might be a murderess? Was that why he had tried to get her away — and used any and every excuse to that end?

Amanda writhed and wrenched and tugged at her bonds in helpless, frantic fear. She must not let Anita kill again. She could

509

not lie there and wait for the sound of a shot, and know that she herself would be the next to die. She tried to get her chin on to the car horn, thinking that if she could sound it, it might cause Anita Barton to take fright; but she slipped and fell to the floor, and hit her head on the steering wheel trying to get upright again.

Then all at once hands were gripping her and dragging her up, and there was an urgent, hissing whisper in her ear:

'For Pete's sake stay still! How in heck can I get you outa this while you're hopping like a jumping bean?'

Persis! Amanda's slim body was suddenly limp with relief. Fingers fumbled at the knot behind her head and Persis' voice whispered: 'Damn and blast this hair of yours! Why the heck you want to——'

And then the bandage was whipped away and Amanda spat out the sodden handkerchief and was breathing in deep gulps of air.

'Persis! — how did you get here?'

'*Ssh!* Keep quiet! Do you want that dame back on us?' Persis started on the knotted scarf that bound Amanda's wrists and explained in a whisper:

'I didn't like the look of the set-up. There was a gleam in that gal's eye that I've seen in the eye of a horse in my day. And I don't buy nor ride those horses! I walked round the back of those trees and counted ten and came right back again, and found you out like a light and the girlfriend making a getaway. So I jumped a ride on the luggage grid, and here I am. A very dusty and unpleasant journey, and I nearly broke my neck when she slammed on the brakes a mile or so back. There you are——'

Amanda's wrists were free. She bent and tugged at the knots about her ankles, and a minute later she was out of the car and standing in the bright moonlight.

'Hey, come back!' hissed Persis. 'This is where we beat it!'

'I can't,' said Amanda desperately. 'She thinks it's Glenn down there on the beach, and she'll take a shot at him. Can't you see, I've got to stop her!'

'Okay,' said Persis, resigned. 'I guess I'll come with you. Let's go.'

She jumped out into the road and gave a brief and muffled yelp of pain.

'Holy cat!' gasped Persis, hopping on one foot.

'What is it?'

'Lost a shoe back there, and I've trodden on a rock.'

'Well you can't come on one foot,' said Amanda in a feverish whisper. 'Stay here and find a spanner or something, and if she comes back, see if you can lay her out!'

She turned and ran in the direction that Anita Barton had taken a few minutes before.

The path came out on the top of a low cliff below which lay a tangle of sea grass and huge tumbled rocks. Amanda could see no sign of Anita Barton and imagined that she must be lying in wait in the shadows of one of the big boulders. She crept forward, grateful that the wash of the sea on the shelving beach blurred the sound of her movements, and reached the level of the shore.

The sand was warm and dry and deep and she edged her way between the high, wind-worn rocks and found herself looking out on a small curving beach bounded on one side by the low headland that she had just descended, and on the other by a long natural breakwater of tumbled rocks.

A boat was drifting in from the shining sea; a boat that had evidently been waiting off the point of the rocks. She could hear the soft splash of oars above the hush of a slow tide that broke gently on the beach with a sound like the rustle of dry leaves in a light autumn breeze. Then a keel grated on wet sand.

There was only one man in the small boat, and Amanda saw him ship the oars and jump out into the creaming surf to draw the prow a little farther up the beach.

He turned and walked towards her, and the moonlight fell full on his face.

It was Glenn Barton.

For a moment the shock of that knowledge deprived Amanda of the power to call out. Then she opened her mouth to scream a warning and stopped — checked by the terrified knowledge that Anita must be somewhere ahead of her, and that if she cried out Glenn would stop and Anita, realizing that she was discovered, would fire.

She edged her way forward, keeping to the shadow of the rocks and nearing the point where Anita must be standing.

Someone moved out of the shadows barely half a dozen yards ahead of her and Glenn stopped and said quietly: 'Anita.'

The single, softly spoken word sounded astonishingly loud in that white silence where the only other sound was the lazy, murmurous whisper of the tide.

Anita Barton moved out into the moonlight, one hand in the pocket of her loose linen coat. She drew the hand out slowly, and Amanda raced forward and flung herself on Mrs Barton's arm, dragging it down so that the shot went harmlessly into the sand.

The small bay seemed full of the echoes of that sound, and Amanda's hands were on cold metal, wrenching it, twisting it free and flinging it away.

Glenn stooped slowly and picked it up, and Anita Barton turned on Amanda screaming; clawing at her like a frenzied cat:

'*You fool!* Oh you fool! Can't you see he'll kill us. *No* Glenn! – no – no! I don't want to die!'

She crumpled at Amanda's feet in a sobbing, shuddering heap.

Glenn Barton looked down at the weapon in his hand and then at his frantic wife. He raised the revolver quite steadily and said in a pleasant, soft voice:

'Yes. I shall kill you. You were really becoming too dangerous altogether. Both of you. No, don't move, Amanda! I am an excellent shot and I happen to have my own gun as well as the one my dear wife — my very dear wife — has so thoughtfully provided me with. I am sorry that you will have to disappear too. You will, of course, have accompanied Anita to the Lebanon and a telegram

512

to that effect will be handed in there in a day or two. Anita, naturally, has left a letter which will explain everything to Miss Moon and to anyone who may be interested: I can really copy her handwriting very well. When, eventually, you fail to reappear, it will of course be obvious that my wife has committed another murder.'

Amanda said breathlessly: 'Glenn! — Glenn, what are you talking about? I don't understand——' Her voice did not seem to belong to her, but to some stranger.

'I think you do,' said Glenn softly. 'You came here to spy on me, didn't you Amanda? To report on me to your uncle. I'm sorry that I shall have to shoot you. It's noisy and bloody, and I dislike noise and blood. But there appears to be no alternative. You seem to be immune to poison. Some friend of yours drank the stuff that was meant for you on the ship, and you wouldn't even touch the drink I offered you at the Inn. I'd got either contingency worked out to look like suicide, and it would have saved a great deal of trouble. Then I had what looked like the chance of a lifetime at Hilarion, but a fluke saved you, and when I tried to get back I found Howard was on his way up behind me. As there was no other way down and no one else up there, the only possible way out of a very sticky situation was to risk my neck and save you. The irony of that should appeal to you.'

'*No!*' said Amanda in a sobbing whisper. 'No Glenn. You're mad. You don't know what you're saying!'

'Oh yes I do. I thought I could get you both once before. You practically handed it to me on a plate. I meant to throw you down Anita's stairs, and then go up and send her after you. They'd have said she must have been drunk and pushed you, and then fallen herself. Those banisters are like matchwood. But that interfering idiot Howard wrecked that too.'

Amanda said chokingly: 'I don't believe it! It isn't true.'

'Anita believes it. Don't you Anita dear? Stand up Anita — stand up my darling. You won't like it if I put a bullet through you

513

while you're on the ground. It might hit you where it would hurt. You won't know anything about it if you stand up. The fish will leave nothing that can be identified if you should ever come up on a trawl. But I don't think you will. I'll weight you well. Stand up Anita——'

Anita Barton grovelled in the sand, sobbing and choking and pleading. She crawled forward on her knees, her face a mask of tears and sand, crazy with terror.

Glenn Barton looked down at her with cold disgust and fired with complete indifference.

Anita screamed at the sound of the shot and leapt to her feet, but Glenn did not fire again.

He stood staring, wide-eyed, at the gun in his hand; then he dropped it on to the sand and whipped a second one from the pocket of his coat.

A shadow moved out of the shadows of the piled rocks: and another, and another, until the moonlit curve of the narrow beach was ringed with silent men, and a familiar voice remarked pleasantly:

'You won't find that one any good either, I'm afraid.'

19

Glenn Barton whipped round on the speaker, gun in hand, and Amanda flung herself frantically between them.

'Steve——!'

There was an orange flash of flame and for the third time that night the quiet cove echoed to the sound of a shot.

Steve Howard removed Amanda's clinging fingers and said: 'It's only blank,' and Glenn Barton flung the useless weapon savagely at his head.

Steve ducked, thrust Amanda to one side, and leapt at him.

Amanda heard the blow go home on Glenn Barton's body and saw him bend double and throw his head up, gasping for air. There was the crack of a second blow to the jaw; a crisp, sharp sound that seemed almost as loud as the report of the useless revolver. Glenn Barton's body appeared to leave the ground, and came to rest a yard or so away, spreadeagled and unconscious on the sand.

'I have been aching to do that for days!' observed Steve, breathing a little unevenly.

He turned to a man who was standing beside him, and Amanda saw with a numbed lack of surprise that it was the man with the odd name whom she had seen once before in the hall of the Villa Oleander on the evening that Monica Ford had died.

'Well there he is,' said Steve. 'He's all yours.'

He turned to Anita Barton: 'If you're feeling all right, Mrs Barton, we'll get back to the car. Amanda, you can't cry here! Save it for the journey back and I'll lend you my shoulder.'

He took hold of Anita Barton's arm with one hand and

Amanda's with the other and urged them up the narrow path towards the car. Someone was limping towards them down the path and Steve checked suddenly.

'It's Persis,' said Amanda.

'Good grief!' said Mr Howard, exasperated. 'What the hell is she doing mixed up in this?'

'She came with me,' explained Amanda.

Persis materialized out of the moonlight.

''Lo Steve. Sugar Ray Robinson in person, I presume? I'm sorry I missed the first two acts and the intermission, but I had a grandstand seat for the finale. It certainly packed a punch.'

She turned and accompanied them back to the car, limping a trifle, and subsided abruptly on to the running board.

Steve produced a flask from his coat pocket, removed the cap, filled it and handed it over.

'Thanks a lot,' said Persis, gulping the contents. 'Boy! did I need that. Sling some into Anita; her need is greater than mine.'

Anita Barton drank with chattering teeth and looked at Steve Howard. Her face was still white and tear-streaked, but her voice was no longer hysterical.

'I can't thank you enough. When did you — how did you know about Glenn?'

'You knew, didn't you?' said Steve gently.'

'Of course. That was why I left him. I tried to warn that fool Monica, but she wouldn't listen. She was crazy about him.'

'How did you find out?'

'Oh — little things. A lot of little things that all added up. Then I began to watch him, and – and in the end I found out. I was frightened then. I knew that if he once realized that I knew, he – he'd kill me. He was always a killer. Quiet and decent and – and *deadly*. He'd been making love to Monica, and I used that as an excuse. I had to get away from him. I *had* to!'

Persis said sharply: 'I'll believe almost anything after what I've seen tonight, but I will not believe that guy ever made a

516

pass at a middle-aged dame with buck teeth and a forty-two inch waist!'

'But he did,' said Anita Barton drearily. 'You see she'd been sent out to see what was going on. Mr Derington sent her. He always believed that women had an instinct over shady business. I think he must have heard a few rumours, so he sent out a competent secretary who was to find out what went on, and report.'

Anita Barton subsided wearily onto the running board beside Persis, and leaned her head back against the car door. She said: 'Glenn made love to her. He could always make women fall for him. He has that "little-boy-lost" look about him that makes fools of the best of them — it made a fool of me too! Monica went overboard about him. He was probably the only man who had ever looked twice at her, and he reduced her to a pulp. After that he could do anything with her and make her swallow any lie. I'd stood for his affairs with half a dozen other women including Claire — Claire used to send and carry messages for him that he couldn't risk sending himself. I don't think she realized what he was doing. He probably told her some convincing lie; and anyway she can look after herself. But the Monica business sickened me. When I tried to warn her she was rude and hysterical, and I got Lumley to let me move in on him. He only did it to score off Glenn and Claire, and because he has an inferiority complex as a result of being a Conscientious Objector during the War, so he feels he must pose as a flouter of public opinion.'

Amanda said helplessly: 'I don't understand! What was Glenn doing?'

'Gun running,' said Steve Howard briefly.

'*What?*' Persis straightened up abruptly and nearly fell on her face on the roadside. 'Why — say Steve, where do you come in on all this?'

'Oh, I'd been told off to find out who was back of the racket,' said Steve. He looked over his shoulder and said impatiently: 'How much longer do you suppose those sleuths are going to be?'

'Never mind them,' said Persis firmly. 'Spill it, honey — you have our undivided attention. I for one am not shifting from this spot until I've got all the dirt, and you can't drive off with a gal on the running board!'

Steve laughed a little grimly. He accepted one of Persis' cigarettes, lit it from her lighter, and said:

'We knew that someone was shipping guns into Africa and we knew that they were coming from a satellite country, via Cyprus. We did not know how it was done, but we narrowed it down a bit and became interested in, among others, Glennister Barton. It seemed just possible that he was using the wine business as a cover for something more profitable. He was. And things were going tolerably smoothly for him until Amanda suddenly put a cat among his pigeons.'

'*I* did?' said Amanda incredulously. 'How?'

'You decided to go to Cyprus, and your Uncle Oswin sent an exceedingly official letter demanding that you be put up and taken round and offered all facilities, and all the rest of it. It was a misleading document, and bearing in mind your uncle's preference for females in the role of snoopers, Glenn Barton imagined that you were being sent here expressly to spy on him — as Monica had been. He might have tried to carry it off, if it hadn't been for his matrimonial mess-up.'

Amanda said: 'But why should that matter?'

'Your uncle,' said Steve Howard, 'is a notorious prude in such matters. A hint from you that his nominee for the post of Barton's secretary was rumoured in love with the Boss — not to mention the rest of the set-up! — and Barton would probably have had the sack by wire. Or — more likely — your Uncle Oswin would have arrived on the next plane in order to clean the matter up.'

'Yes,' said Amanda slowly. 'He might have done. He's a bit rabid about that sort of thing.'

'Exactly. Barton couldn't risk it either way. He had a hell of a big deal coming off, and all he needed was just three more weeks and he'd have been in a position to clear off to some salubrious spot like South America, and keep himself in champagne and caviare until he died. It was as close as that. He daren't say that he couldn't have you, so he tried to stop you getting here. The stuff that Julia Blaine drank was meant for you.'

Persis said sharply: 'Julia! You mean that was *murder*?'

'But — but it was in her lemon juice,' said Amanda helplessly.

'It wasn't lemon. It was sweetlime. And there was plenty of sugar in it as well. The carpet was sticky with it. You merely jumped to the conclusion that it was lemon juice and meant for Julia because you hadn't ordered it, and, by a fluke, had happened to change cabins with Mrs Blaine much earlier in the day. Julia would never have ordered or touched such a thing. But a nice icy lime squash left in a cabin on a hot night was a pretty tempting bait. And when you told me that Mrs Blaine had gone to bed around ten o'clock, it began to look even more as though that glass had not been in the wrong cabin after all.'

'But why, Steve?'

'Ice. You didn't go down until nearly eleven, but there was still ice in that glass. There were chips of it on the carpet when I got there. If that drink had been in your cabin before ten the ice in it would have melted. Yet if it had been meant as a trap for Mrs Blaine it would never have been put there almost three-quarters of an hour after she had left the deck and gone to her cabin with a certain amount of attendant publicity. You, however, were dancing.'

Amanda said on a gasp: 'But – but Glenn! ... Glenn couldn't have done it. He wasn't even there!'

'No. But one of his thugs was. You don't really suppose that anyone could run a racket of that description single-handed, do you? There were a gang of 'em up to their necks in it! This was a man called Kostos who was masquerading as a deck-hand. The husband, incidentally, of a woman who keeps an inn on the road to Limassol where you appear to have almost lost one of your nine lives.'

'It can't have been! Glenn told me that her husband was an old wreck of a man who——' She stopped suddenly and said in a shaken voice: 'I see now. He had to say something to make me turn round and look away from the table, so he said the first thing that came into his head. And then she — the woman — said that her husband had been on the ship. Why didn't I notice that? And Glenn dropped his cigarette into my glass. To make sure that no one else would drink it I suppose.'

'He also,' said Steve grimly, 'arranged for the disposal of the deck-hand. He was taking no chances. The chap was supposedly killed in a bar-room brawl: which was, oddly, enough, the reason why Miss Moon's staff, who were related to the widow, did not return on the day that Monica Ford was murdered and you were so neatly shoved over the battlements at Hilarion.'

Amanda shivered violently. 'But *why* Steve? Surely if – if I'd died here it would have been just as bad for him? Uncle Oswin would have come over then.'

'Would he? From all I've heard of him he doesn't sound like a man who would allow his niece, who was also his ward, to be buried in a place like this. It would have been the Derington Family Vault or nothing! Barton would only have had to cable your uncle that he was arranging to fly your corpse home in a coffin, pronto, and would he please meet? And it's my bet that your grief-stricken relative would have scrubbed the rest of his business schedule and taken the next plane to England, so that he could collect the dear-departed at London Airport, and lay on a suitable funeral. And if he *had* come here, he would have been in no state to start bothering about his wine business. That's for certain!

'If he'd come, it would only have been to collect the coffin from scratch, so that he could escort it home in person. Either way, he wouldn't have had the time or the inclination to start investigating the affairs of Mr Glennister Barton until he'd got your mortal remains parked in the family vault. And by that time, Barton would have been living it up in Buenos Aires or Montevideo, or wherever.'

'Yes, I see,' said Amanda with a shiver. 'You're right about the family vault; and about Uncle Oswin too. He'd never have left me here . . .'

'Exactly. I expect Barton was banking on that. But once you'd arrived in Cyprus — presumably to spy out the land — Barton could not risk letting you leave here alive. It was the time factor. He had to have those extra weeks, and the money involved was worth taking risks for. Any risks! He would have killed you and half a dozen others cheerfully for it.'

Amanda said: 'But why on earth should I have committed suicide? What possible reason could I——'

'Judging from statistics,' interrupted Steve impatiently, 'the average adolescent can decide to "End It All" for any number of footling reasons. Unrequited love coming high on the list — the "I can't live without him" syndrome. That would always have been a safe card to play, since it would have been difficult to disprove, once you were dead. After all, it even occurred fleetingly to me — and a lot less fleetingly to the police! — that you might have bumped off Julia Blaine in the hope of snaffling her husband. It was considered a possibility. And if you'd died of the same poison in that pub; it could have been written off as remorse!'

'Yes, you told me about the "possibility",' snapped Amanda, torn between indignation at remembered outrage, and annoyance at being classed as an 'average adolescent': 'But what about Monica? It wasn't possible for Glenn to have killed her. Not by any stretch of even *your* fertile imagination!'

'Oh yes it was. He saw her going into Miss Moon's that afternoon, and followed her in. She had come to see you.'

'But why? What did she want to see me for?'

'Because both she and Barton, as a result of your uncle's letter, had it firmly fixed in their heads that you were really here as a sort of private agent for him. And she had found out what Barton was up to.'

'But surely, she must have known before?'

'She'd probably always known or suspected that there was something pretty peculiar going on, but I think she deliberately shut her eyes to it and tried to pretend that it was merely a matter of smuggling a few cigarettes. Something on those lines. But that afternoon a case, supposedly containing wine, got broken, and as Barton was out, she opened it herself and realized what he was doing. A week earlier and she might still have looked the other way, for she was about as completely under Barton's thumb as a frustrated spinster can be. But her brother had just been murdered by Mau Mau terrorists — armed by Glenn Barton! It broke her up, and she rushed into Kyrenia to see you and spill the beans. And Barton strangled her.'

Amanda said: 'He can't have done, Steve! He can't possibly have done it. The police proved that he went straight from Hilarion to Nicosia.'

'He did. But he killed Monica Ford before he ever arrived at Hilarion.'

'But she was *warm*!'

'I know. That was what put us all out of step for a bit. He'd left her in front of the french windows, where the sun had been full on her from the time he killed her until just before it set. It had barely gone from the room when we got back; remember? Of course she was warm! It's never as easy as detective fiction would have you believe to fix the exact time of death. It depends on a good many things, and temperature has a lot to do with it. Glenn Barton had his wits about him, and made very good use of the fact that the sun would be on that bit of the room from roughly four fifteen onwards. He came on to Hilarion, mentioned having seen the woman, and provided himself with a nice alibi all round. And when he was telephoned for by the police — as he knew he would be — he arrived complete with that neat bit of evidence against his wife, and planted it as he came through the hall.'

'I knew it was Glenn who had done that,' said Anita Barton with a shudder. 'It couldn't have been anyone else. There were several of those flowers in the house. They were always coming off, and I'd left a lot of my stuff behind. He must have gone through my dressing-table drawers, and found one.'

'I imagine so,' said Steve. 'He then provided an affecting scene by registering sufficient horror at the sight of it to attract everyone's suspicious attention. And Amanda nearly spoilt the whole show by rushing into the breach like Florence Nightingale or Flora Macdonald, and claiming it as hers. However, just in case the police proved bat-witted enough to believe her, he took the precaution of ringing up Mrs Norman and spilling the beans under cover of a distracted plea that she should go and see you, Mrs Barton, and tell you to destroy the dress. He knew dam' well that she'd see you dead first, and also that she could be trusted to spread the story around the whole of Cyprus.'

Anita Barton said: 'He meant to get me hanged for murder!'

Steve shook his head. 'I don't think so. The last thing he wanted was a court case of that sort. He was working up to an artistic disappearing act, so that people would jump to the conclusion that you had lost your nerve and bolted. He worked round to that angle very nicely, and I added the last touch by ordering Amanda to write at once to her uncle. That tore it. If she had done so, and her uncle had arrived by return of post, the whole thing would have blown up in his face. I thought that threat would fetch him, and it did.'

Amanda stared at him, speechless, and Anita Barton said wearily: 'And I thought she was in it with him. That she'd fallen for him too, like Monica and all the other fools. I hit her over the head with that gun, and I thought I'd killed her. I'm sorry, Amanda. I knew he was trying to kill me, and I thought you were helping him.'

523

Amanda was not listening to her. She was clinging to the door handle of the car and looking at Steve:

'You mean you *knew* that he'd do something like this?' demanded Amanda breathlessly. 'You told me to write that letter just to make him — to make him . . .' Words appeared to fail her.

'I had to darling,' said Steve. 'We had to panic him into showing his hand. But if it's any consolation to you, it was quite the most unpleasant thing I've ever had to do. We'd have got him on the gun-running without it. But we might well have failed to pin him with murder. And we did at least go to a great deal of trouble to remove the bullets from any guns he possessed and replace them with blanks. Which wasn't as easy as it may sound. However, I will admit that I had left out of my calculations the possibility that Mrs Barton might crack you over the head with a blunt instrument — although I can sympathize with her point of view.'

Amanda stared at him for a long moment, her face white in the moonlight.

She said in a small, frozen voice: 'If you are thinking of driving us back, I think we'd all like to get home. Persis, are you ready?'

'And how!' said Persis. 'Anita honey, will you sit in front by the driver? And I guess it might be a good idea, when we get back, if you and I doubled up for the night just to keep each other company. We'll get a spare bed put up in my room and order up a bath of hot coffee and a quart of chloroform. This has been quite a party, and the sooner we sleep it off the better.'

Amanda got haughtily into the back of the car and said: 'Come on Persis!'

Persis closed the door on Anita Barton and looked at Steve Howard.

'Steve honey,' she inquired softly, 'how much am I offered to drive this car?'

Steve laughed.

'Persis honey,' he said, 'you will drive this car or else——!'

'Okay,' said Persis. 'It's a stick-up!'

Amanda attempted to descend but Steve was too quick for her. He slammed the door behind him and pulled her very roughly into his arms.

Amanda made a small, sobbing and unintelligible sound that was abruptly silenced, and presently said breathlessly: 'Steve, please——!'

'My heart,' said Mr Howard, 'shut up! You can keep the conversation for later. We are not alone.'

'Don't mind us,' said Persis cordially, starting up the car and backing it expertly on the sandy verge. 'Go right ahead and kiss her.'

'What do you think I'm doing?' inquired Steve with pardonable irritation.

Persis laughed, and having tactfully twisted the driving mirror until it faced the roof, headed the car down the long white moonlit road towards Kyrenia.

DEATH IN KENYA

Remembering TINA and JAY –
With Love

Author's Note

Few people nowadays will remember the Mau Mau terrorist rising in Kenya, and millions more will never even have heard of it. But it was an unpleasant business while it lasted. I happened to be in Kenya towards the end of that period, because my husband's regiment had been sent there to deal with 'The Emergency' – which was the white settlers' name for it. And despite some hair-raising moments, I can truthfully say that I enjoyed practically every minute of my stay in that marvellous and exciting country.

The idea for this story came into my mind one evening when I was standing on our verandah in the dusk, and I heard birds calling down in the papyrus swamp that fringed the shores of Lake Naivasha. But the book itself, originally published under the prophetic title *Later Than You Think*, did not take shape until after we had left Kenya. Em's house, *Flamingo*, is an amalgam of several houses built by early settlers in the Rift or on the Kinangop, but I chose to site it on the same spot as the one we ourselves lived in. The opinions voiced by my characters were taken from life and at first hand. For though the Wind of Change was rising fast, very few of the Kenya-born settlers would believe that it could possibly blow strongly enough to uproot them from a country that every single one of them looked upon, and loved, as a *'Land where my fathers died, Land of the pilgrim's pride ...'*

1

A flock of pelicans, their white wings dyed apricot by the setting sun, sailed low over the acacia trees of the garden with a sound like tearing silk, and the sudden swish of their passing sent Alice's heart into her throat and dried her mouth with panic. The shadows of the stately birds flicked across her and were gone, and she leaned weakly against the gate in the plumbago hedge and fought for control.

It was absurd and childish to allow herself to become so hag-ridden by fear that the mere passing of a flight of birds could set her flinching and cowering. But she could not help herself. She had fought fear for too long, and now at last she had reached the limits of endurance. She would have to leave Kenya: she and Eden. Surely he would see that she could not stand any more. For now, in addition to her fear of the country there was her terror of the house.

Alice had always been afraid of Kenya. It seemed to her a savage and uncivilized land full of brooding menace, in which only Em's luxurious house had provided a narrow oasis of safety and comfort. But now there was no longer any safety anywhere, for strange things had been happening in the house of late. Inexplicable, malicious, frightening things ...

It was the cat, declared Zacharia, the old grey-headed Kikuyu who had served Em for almost forty years, explaining away the first appearance of the invisible vandal who had taken to haunting the house. Who else could have thrown down the K'ang Hsi vase from the top of the cabinet where it had stood for so many years? There had been no wind. As for the bottle of red ink that had rolled, un-stoppered, across the carpet upon which the Memsahib set such store, there had been a bird in the room – see, here was a feather! Pusser must have pursued it, and in doing so knocked over both ink bottle and vase.

But Em had not believed it. She had stormed and raged and questioned the African servants, but to no avail. And later, when other things were broken or defaced, Zacharia had made no further mention of Pusser. He and the other house servants had gone about their duties with scared faces and starting, frightened eyes, and Em, too, had said nothing more. She had only become quieter – and looked grim and grey and very old.

Lady Emily DeBrett – Em DeBrett of *Flamingo* – had come to Kenya as a bride in the Colony's early days, and she and her husband, Gerald, had been among the first white settlers in the Rift Valley.

Gerald had never looked upon Kenya as anything more than a Tom Tiddlers Ground. But the seventeen-year-old Emily had taken one look at the great golden valley with its cold craters and savage lava falls, its lily-strewn lakes and its vast herds of game, and had fallen in love with it as some women fall in love with a man.

Gerald had staked out a claim on the shores of Lake Naivasha: acres and acres of virgin land on which he intended to raise sheep and cattle, and grow sisal and maize and lucerne. And on a rising slope of ground, overlooking the lake, he had built a crude mud and wattle hut that had in time given place to a small stone-built house; square, ugly and unpretentious. Em had named the farm *'Flamingo'* because a flight of those fantastic rose-coloured birds had flown across it on that first evening; and *Flamingo* it had remained.

Kendall, Em's son, had been born in the mud and wattle house and christened in the small stone building that had replaced it. There had been no other children, for when Kendall was three years old his father had been killed by a fall from his horse. But *Flamingo* had already begun to justify all Gerald's hopes, and Em had refused to go home. 'This is my home,' she had said, 'and I will never leave it.'

The estate had prospered, and she had pulled down the ugly stone house that Gerald had built, and raised in its stead a huge, sprawling single-storeyed house to her own design. A thatch-roofed house with wide verandahs and spacious rooms panelled in undressed cedar wood, that defied all architectural rules and yet blended with the wild beauty of the Rift Valley as though it had always been a part of it; and Em loved it as she had never loved Gerald or her son Kendall.

She had been a remarkably pretty woman, and she was barely twenty when her husband died; but she did not marry again. Partly because her absorption in the affairs of her estate left her little time for other interests, and partly because hard and unremitting toil soon dispelled that pink-and-white prettiness. She wore, from choice, trousers and shirt and a man's double-terai hat, and as her abundant hair was too much trouble to keep in order, she cropped it short.

At thirty she might have been forty-five or fifty, and from forty onwards, though she became increasingly bulky, she was merely an elderly and eccentric woman whose age it would have been impossible to guess.

Kendall was sent home to Eton, and from there to Oxford. And it was from Oxford, on his twenty-second birthday, that he sent a cable telling of his marriage to pretty Clarissa Brook.

Clarissa had proved to be a girl after Em's own heart, and as Mr Rycett, Em's manager, had retired that year, Kendall had stepped into his place, and he and Clarissa had moved into the manager's house; a pleasant stone-built bungalow in the grounds of *Flamingo*, barely six hundred yards from the main house, and hidden from it by a grove of acacias and a plumbago hedge. But Eden DeBrett, Em's first grandson, was born at *Flamingo*.

Em had insisted on that. 'He must be born in this house. It will be his one day.' And looking at the baby she had thought with pride: I have founded a dynasty. A Kenya dynasty! A hundred years from now – two hundred – there will be DeBretts living in this house and farming this land when Kenya is no longer a raw new Colony, but a great and prosperous country ...

She was as impatient for grandsons as though *Flamingo* had been a kingdom and the DeBretts a royal house whose succession must be assured.

But there were to be no more grandsons for Em. As there had been no more sons. Kendall and Clarissa had died in a car accident, and there was only Eden. Little Eden DeBrett who was such a beautiful child, and whom his grandmother spoiled and adored and loved only one degree less than she loved the land of her adoption.

After Kendall's death there had been another manager, Gus Abbott, who had lived in the bungalow beyond the plumbago hedge for over twenty years, and died in a Mau Mau raid on *Flamingo* in the first months of the Emergency. His place had been taken by a younger man, Mr Gilbraith Markham, and it was Mr Markham's wife Lisa whom Alice had come in search of on this quiet evening: poor, pretty, discontented Lisa, who loved cities and cinemas and gaiety, and who had been so bored by life at *Flamingo* – until the day when she had had the misfortune to fall in love with Eden DeBrett.

Alice pushed open the gate in the plumbago hedge and walked on down the dusty path that wound between clumps of bamboos and flowering shrubs, thinking of Lisa. Of Lisa and Eden ...

It isn't his fault, thought Eden's wife loyally. It's because he's too good-looking. And just because women throw themselves at his head, and lose their own and make fools of themselves over him, it doesn't mean the he— She stopped suddenly, with a grimace of distaste. But it was a sound, and not her thoughts that had checked her.

The path had come out on the edge of a wide lawn in front of a green and white bungalow flanked by towering acacia trees, and someone inside the bungalow was playing the piano. Gilly, of course.

Gilly Markham was not a conspicuous success as a farm manager, and many people in the Rift Valley had attributed his appointment to his musical rather than his managerial abilities. For it was an unexpected facet of Lady Emily DeBrett's character that she was intensely and passionately musical, and there was probably some truth in the rumour that she had permitted Gilly Markham's musical talent to influence her judgement when Gus Abbott's death necessitated the appointment of a new manager at *Flamingo*.

But it was not Gilly's technique that had checked Alice and produced that grimace of distaste. It was the music itself. The Rift Concerto. As if it wasn't enough to hear Em playing it day after day! And now Gilly too——!

It had been an Italian prisoner-of-war who had written the Rift Valley Concerto. Guido Toroni. He had been sent to work at *Flamingo*, and Em had discovered by chance that he had once been a concert pianist. He had composed the concerto on Em's Bechstein grand, and later, when the war was over, he had gone to America where he had made a name for himself. There he had also made a single long-playing record of the concerto especially for Em, to whom he had sent it as a thank-offering and a memento. Em had been inordinately pleased, and had allowed no one to handle it except herself; but just two weeks previously it had been found smashed into a dozen pieces.

It could not possibly have been an accident. It had been a deliberate and ugly piece of spite that had frightened Alice and infuriated Em. But that had not been the worst of it, for Em had taken to playing the concerto from memory: 'so that I shall not forget it'. She had played it again and again during the last two weeks, until the wild, haunting cadences had plucked at Alice's taut nerves and worn them ragged. And now Gilly too was playing it. Playing it as Em played it, with passion and fury. But with a skill and magic that Em's gnarled, spatulate fingers, for all their love, did not possess.

Alice pushed between the canna lilies and ran across the lawn and up the stone steps that led on to the verandah. The door into the drawing-room stood open, and entering without ceremony she leant across Gilly's shoulder and thrust his hands off the keyboard in an ugly crash of sound.

Gilly spun round on the piano stool and stared at her contorted face.

'God! you startled me! What's up? You look all to pieces.' He rose hurriedly. 'Nothing the matter, is there?'

'No. No, nothing.' Alice groped behind her and catching at the arm of a chair, sat down rather suddenly. Her breathing steadied, and a little colour crept back into her pale cheeks. 'I'm sorry, Gilly. My nerves are on edge. It was only that tune. Em's been playing it and playing it until I can't endure the sound of it.'

'She has, has she?' said Gilly, mixing a stiff whisky and soda and handing it to Alice.

He poured out a second and larger one for himself, omitting the soda, and gulped it down: 'Then I'm not surprised your nerves are in ribbons. She's a bloody bad pianist. She takes that third movement as though she were an elephant charging an express train.'

He sat down again at the piano as though to illustrate, and Alice said in a taut voice: 'Gilly, if you play that again I shall scream. I mean it!'

Gilly dropped his hands and regarded her with some concern. 'I say, you are in a bad way! Have another drink?'

'I haven't started on this one yet,' said Alice with an attempt at a laugh. 'Oh, it isn't that. It's – well that record being broken. You heard about that, didn't you?'

'You mean the poltergeist? Of course I did.'

'It *isn't* a poltergeist! Don't *say* things like that! It must be someone – a person. But Em swears by all her servants. She's had them for years and they're nearly all second-generation *Flamingo* servants. Or even third! She won't believe that it is one of them. But it's worrying her badly. I know it is.'

Gilly poured himself out another three fingers of whisky, and subsiding on to the sofa, sipped it moodily. He was a thin, untidy-looking man in the middle thirties with a pallid, discontented face and pale blue eyes that had a habit of sliding away from a direct look. His shock of fair hair was perpetually in need of cutting, and he wore a sweat-stained open-necked shirt, grubby khaki trousers and a sagging belt that supported a revolver in a well-worn holster. Altogether an incongruous figure in Lisa's over-decorated drawing-room. As incongruous as Alice DeBrett with her neat dark head,

537

her neat dark expensive linen suit, her impeccable shoes and flawless pearls, and her pale, strained, Madonna face that was innocent of all but the barest trace of make-up.

'Won't do Em any harm to worry,' said Gilly, sipping whisky. 'Told her years ago she should throw out all her Kukes. Everyone's told her! But Em's always fancied she knew better than anyone else. "Treat 'em right and they'll be loyal." *Bah!* There's no such thing as a loyal Kuke. We've all learned that – the hard way!'

Alice said uncertainly: 'But she's fond of her Kikuyu servants, Gilly. And they did stay with her all through the Emergency, and now that it's over——'

'Who said it was over?' demanded Gilly. 'Over, my foot! What about this latest caper – the Kiama Kia Muingi? *A rose by any other name*, that's what! Secret ceremonies, extortion, intimidation – same old filthy familiar ingredients simmering away again and ready to boil over at the drop of a hat. And yet there are scores of little optimists running round in circles saying that it's all over! Don't let 'em fool you!'

He reached behind him, and groping for the bottle of whisky refilled his glass, slopping the liquid on to the rose-patterned chintz of the sofa in the process. 'Who's to say how many Mau Mau are still on the run in the forests, or Nairobi, or the Rift? Why, they haven't even caught "General Africa" yet – and they say it's over! Y'know – ' Gilly's words were slurring together – 'y'know Hector Brandon? Course you do! Well, Hector's been doin' a lot of interrogation of M.M. old lags, and he says one of 'em told him that there are still a gang of hard-core terrorists hidin' out in the *marula* – the papyrus swamp. Bein' fed by the African labour of the farms along the lake. And Greg Gilbert says he believes General Africa is still employed by a settler. Why, it might be any of Em's Kukes! Who's to tell? Nice quiet house boy or cook or cattleherd by day – Gen'l Africa in a lion skin hat at night. Might even be one of Hector's. In fact, only too likely if you ask me!'

'Oh no, Gilly! Why everyone knows that the Mau Mau swore they'd get Hector because of his intelligence work. Yet they never did, and if General Africa had been one of his own men it would have been too easy.'

'Maybe,' said Gilly sceptically. 'But I'll tell you something that "everyone" doesn't know! And that is that once upon a time Drew Stratton's lot nearly got the "General" – he walked into one of their ambushes with five of his men, and though he managed to get away, he left something behind him: a hunting knife. It had been in a sort of holster at his belt, and by some infernal fluke a bullet chipped it off as clean as a whistle without harming him. But it was the next best thing to getting the man himself, because it had a set of his finger prints on it. The only clue to his identity the Security Forces had ever got their hands on. And what happened to them? Well, I'll tell you. Hector carefully cleaned 'em off! It's always been my belief that he recognized the knife, and that he wasn't taking any chances of one of his darling boys being accused. "Honour of the House", an' all that.'

'Gilly, no!' protested Alice. 'You shouldn't say things like that! It must have been a mistake – an accident.'

'That's what *he* said. Said he thought it belonged to Greg, and merely picked it up off Greg's desk to doodle with. Greg nearly hit the ceiling. It's no use, Alice. You just don't understand what some of these old Kenya hands are capable of; or how their own little patch of land can end by becoming the centre of the universe to them, just because they made it out of nothing by the sweat of their brow, and starved for it and gave up their youth for it, and sacrificed comfort and safety and civilization and a lot of other trivial little things for it. *Brandonmead* is Hector's pride. No – I'm wrong. Ken's his pride. *Brandonmead*'s his life; and he's always sworn by all his African labour. "Loyal to the core" and all that sort of stuff. It would have damned near killed him if it had turned out that one of his precious Kukes was a star Mau Mau thug. I believe he'd have done almost anything to cover it up, and salved his conscience by thinking he could deal with it himself. They're great ones for taking the law into their own hands out here. Haven't you noticed that yet?'

Alice said uncomfortably: 'But Em says——'

'Em!' interrupted Gilly rudely. 'Em's as bad as any of them. Worse! It was silly old bitches like her who caused half the trouble. "My Kukes are loyal. I'll stake my life on it." So they lose – *Bah!* You're not going, are you?'

Alice had put down her half finished glass and stood up. She said coldly: 'I'm afraid I must. I only came over with a message for Lisa, but if she's out perhaps you'd give it to her.'

'She isn't out. She's only gone down to the shamba with the Brandons and Drew Stratton. Here, don't go! Have the other half of that. I didn't mean to get your goat. I know how you feel about Em. You're fond of the old battle-axe. Well, so am I – when she isn't tearing a strip off me! So's all Kenya. Protected Monument – that's Em! Apologize, if I hurt your feelings.'

'That's all right, Gilly,' said Alice hurriedly. 'But I don't think I'll wait, all the same. It's getting late. And if Lisa has guests——'

There was an unexpected trace of embarrassment in her quiet voice, and Gilly's shrewd, pale eyes regarded her with observant interest. He said: 'Ken's not with them, if that's what's worrying you.'

His laugh held a trace of malice as he saw the colour rise in Alice DeBrett's pale cheeks. 'There's no need for you to blush like that, Alice. We all know that you've done your best to snub the poor boy. That is, all except Mabel. But you can't expect Mabel to believe that every woman isn't crazy about her darling son. He's her blind spot. Funny about Ken: I wouldn't have thought you were his type at all.'

'I'm not,' said Alice with a trace of a snap. 'Don't be ridiculous, Gilly. I'm old enough to be his mother!'

'Here! Give yourself a chance! You can't be much more than thirty-five!'

'I'm twenty-seven,' said Alice slowly. 'And Ken isn't twenty yet.'

'Oh well,' said Gilly, dismissing it, and unaware of the blow that he had dealt her. 'Chaps always fall in love with someone older than themselves to start with, and they always fall hard. He'll get over it. Hector ought to send him away. God, I only wish *I* could get the hell out of this Valley! Did you know that Jerry Coles is going to retire soon? You know – the chap who manages the DeBrett property out at Rumuruti. That's the job I'm after. But Em's being damned obstinate. Suit me down to the ground. Nice home, good pay and perks – and no Em looking over my shoulder the entire time, carping and criticizing. Heaven!'

Alice smiled a little wanly and said: 'Wouldn't you find it rather lonely? I shouldn't have thought Lisa would like living so far away.'

Gilly scowled, and his pale eyes were suddenly brooding and sombre. He said: 'That's another reason. It's far away. Over a hundred dusty, uncomfortable, glorious miles away. Far enough, perhaps, to keep her from making an infernal fool of herself over——'

Alice did not let him finish. She walked towards the door, her face white and pinched, and spoke over-loudly, as though to drown out words that she did not wish to hear: 'I really must go. It's getting late and I ought to get back. Will you tell Lisa that——'

Gilly said: 'You can tell her yourself. Here they are now.'

There were footsteps and voices in the verandah, and a moment later Gilly's wife and her guests were in the room. The Brandons, whose property touched the western borders of *Flamingo* and who were such a strangely assorted pair – small, soft-voiced Mabel with her kind, charming face and grey curls, and her choleric husband, Hector, who lived up to his name and was large, loud-voiced and ruddy-featured. Drew Stratton, whose farm lay five miles further along the shores of the lake. And Lisa herself, her bright brown hair bound by a satin ribbon and her wide-skirted dress patterned with roses.

Gilly rose unsteadily and dispensed drinks, and Lisa said: 'Why, hullo, Alice! Nice to see you.'

Her violet eyes slid past Alice with a quick eager look that turned to disappointment, and was neither lost nor misinterpreted by Eden's wife.

Lisa and Eden – ! thought Alice. She pushed away the thought as though it had been a tangible thing and said a little stiffly: 'I only came over with a message from Em. She said that you'd asked for a lift next time she went into Nairobi, and to tell you that she'd be going in on Thursday to fetch her niece from the airport.'

'Great-niece, surely?' corrected Lisa.

'No,' said Mrs Brandon in her gentle voice. 'It's her sister's child. Good evening, Alice.' She dropped her knitting bag on the sofa and sat down beside it. 'Lady Helen was Em's half-sister, and a good deal younger than her. She came out to stay with Em during the first world war, and married Jack Caryll who used to own the Lumley place on the Kinangop: Victoria, the daughter, was born out here. I remember her quite well – a thin little girl who used to ride a zebra that Jack tamed for her. He was killed by a rhino while he was out shooting, and his wife took a dislike to the whole country in consequence. She sold the farm to the Lumleys, and went back to England; and now she's died. It's strange to think that she must have been about twenty years younger than Em, and yet Em's still so strong. But I am surprised that Em should have decided to bring Victoria out here. It seems rather an odd thing to do in – in the circumstances.'

For a moment her soft voice held a trace of embarrassment, and Alice's slight figure stiffened. She said coldly: 'Lady Emily feels that it is time she had someone to take over the secretarial work and help with the milk records. She has always done those herself up to now, but she is getting old, and it tires her.'

541

'But then she has you,' said Mrs Brandon. 'And Eden.'

'I'm afraid I don't type; and Eden has never been fond of paperwork.'

'Eden,' said Hector Brandon roundly, 'is not fond of work in any form! And it's no use your lookin' at me like that, Alice! I've known your husband since he was in short pants, and if you ask me, its a pity his grandmother didn't dust 'em more often – with a slipper!'

Mrs Brandon frowned reprovingly at her husband and said pacifically: 'You mustn't mind Hector, Alice. He always says what he thinks.'

'And proud of it!' boomed Hector.

Why? thought Alice with a spasm of nervous exasperation. Why should anyone consider it an admirable trait to speak their mind when it hurt other people's feelings? – when it was rude and unkind?

'Rugged individualism,' murmured Mr Stratton absently into his glass.

He caught Alice's eye and grinned at her, and some of her defensive hostility left her. Her taut nerves relaxed a little, and she returned the smile, but with a visible effort.

She liked Drew Stratton. He was one of the very few people with whom she felt entirely at ease. Perhaps because he took people as he found them and did not trouble to interest himself in their private affairs. Drew was tall and fair; as fair as Gilly but, unlike Gilly, very brown from the sun that had bleached his hair and brows. His blue eyes were deceptively bland, and if there was any rugged individualism in his make-up it did not take the form of blunt outspokenness. Nor did he find it necessary, in the manner of Hector, to dress in ill-fitting and sweat-stained clothes in order to emphasize the fact that he worked, and worked hard, in a new and raw land.

Gilly was talking again; his voice slurred and over loud: 'Hear some of your cattle were stolen last night, Hector. Serve you right! Y'ought to keep 'em boma'd. Asking for trouble, leavin' 'em loose. It's men like you who play into the hands of the gangs. If I've heard the D.C. tell you that once, I've heard him tell you a thousand times! Invitation to help themselves – cattle all over the place.'

Hector's large red face showed signs of imminent apoplexy, and Mabel Brandon said hurriedly: 'You know we always kept our cattle close boma'd during the Emergency, Gilly. But now that it's over there didn't seem to be any sense in it. And anyway, Drew has never boma'd his!'

542

'Drew happens to employ Masai,' retorted Gilly. 'Makes a difference. Makes a hell of a lot of difference! Who owned the Rift before the whites came? The Masai – that's who! And in those days if any Kikuyu had so much as put his nose into it, they'd have speared him! That's why chaps like Drew were left alone in the Emergency. But more than half your labour are Kukes. You're as bad as Em! Won't give them up, and won't hear a word against them.'

'There isn't one of our Kikuyu who I wouldn't trust with my life,' said Mrs Brandon, bristling slightly. 'Why, they've worked for us for twenty years and more. Samuel was with us before Ken was born!'

'Then why do you carry a gun in that knitting bag?' demanded Gilly. 'Tell me that! Think I don't know?'

Mrs Brandon flushed pinkly and looked as dismayed and conscience-stricken as a child who has been discovered in a fault, and Gilly laughed loudly.

'Pipe down, Gil,' requested Drew mildly. 'You're tight.'

'*A hit, a very palpable hit*. Of course I am!' admitted Gilly with unexpected candour. 'Only possible thing to be these days.'

Drew said softly: 'What are you afraid of, Gilly?'

The alcoholic truculence faded from Gilly's pale, puffy face, leaving it drawn and old beyond his years, and he said in a hoarse whisper that was suddenly and unbelievably shocking in that frilled and beruffled room: 'The same thing that Em is afraid of!'

He looked round the circle of still faces, his eyes flickering and darting as uneasily as trapped moths, and his voice rose sharply in the brief uncomfortable silence: 'There's something damned funny going on at *Flamingo*, and I don't like it. I don't like it at all! Know what I think? I think there's something brewing. Some – some funny business.'

'What d'you mean, "funny business"?' demanded Hector Brandon alertly. 'Em been having trouble with her labour? First I've heard of it.'

'No. I could take that. This is something different. Ever watched a thunderstorm coming up against the wind? S'like that! Waiting. I don't like it. Alice doesn't like it. Em don't like it either. She's stubborn as a mule – won't admit that anything could go wrong at her precious *Flamingo*. But she's not been herself of late. It's getting her down.'

'Nonsense, Gilly!' Hector said firmly. 'Saw her myself only this morning. Top of her form! You're imagining things. Only trouble with Em is that she's getting old.' He allowed Lisa to refill his glass and added reflectively: 'Truth of the matter is, Em's never been her old self since Gus Abbott died. She never really got over that. Felt she'd murdered him.'

'So she did,' said Gilly. 'Murder – manslaughter – slip of the gun. What's it matter what you call it? She killed him.'

'Gilly, how *can* you!' protested Mabel indignantly. 'You know quite well that it happened in the middle of that dreadful attack. And it was largely Gus's fault. He saw one of the gang going for her with a panga, and jumped at him just as Em fired. She's never been quite the same since.'

'That's right,' said Hector. 'He'd been her manager since Kendall's day, and it broke her up. You didn't know her before – except by reputation. But we did. It did something to her. Not so much Gus's death, but the fact that she'd killed him. The whole thing must have been a pretty ghastly experience all round. She lost a couple of her servants that night, murdered by the gang, and two of her dogs were panga'd, and half the huts set on fire. But she shot three of the gang and wounded at least two more, and held off the rest until help came. It was a bloody fine show!'

'*I grant him bloody* – S-Shakespeare!' said Gilly with a bark of laughter. 'An' you're quite right, Hector. I didn't know her before. Mightn't have jumped at the job if I had! She's a difficult woman to work for. Too bloody efficient. That's her trouble. I don't like efficient women.'

He swallowed the contents of his glass at a gulp and Lisa seized the opportunity to return to a topic that was of more interest to her: 'Tell us about this niece of Em's, Alice. What's she like? Is she plain or pretty or middle-aged, or what?'

'I've never met her,' said Alice briefly. 'She must be quite young.'

Her tone did not encourage comment, but Lisa was impervious to tone. She had, moreover, the misfortune to be in love with Alice's husband, and was therefore interested, with an avid, jealous interest, in any other woman who entered his orbit – with the sole exception of his wife, whom she considered to be a colourless and negligible woman, obviously older than her handsome husband and possessing no attractions apart from money. But this new girl – this Victoria Caryll. She would be staying under the same roof as Eden, and be in daily contact with him, and she was young and might be pretty ...

'I can't think why, if Em wanted a secretary, she couldn't have got a part-time one from among the local girls,' said Lisa discontentedly. 'Heaven knows there are enough of them, and some of them must be able to type.'

'Secretary, nuts!' said Gilly, weaving unsteadily across to the table that held the drinks, and refilling his glass. 'If you ask me, she's getting this girl out with the idea of handing over half the property to her one day. Dividing it up between her and Eden. After all, they're the only two blood-relations she's got. And there must be plenty to leave. Bags of loot – even if it's split fifty-fifty. Bet you Hector's right! Come to think of it, can't see why else she sh'd suddenly want to bring the girl out in such a hurry. Or why the girl was willing to come! Bet you it's that!'

'Perhaps,' said Mabel Brandon thoughtfully. 'But it's more likely to be what Alice says. Em's getting old, and when you're old there are times when you suddenly feel that the years are running out too quickly, and you begin to count them like a miser and to realize that you can't go on putting things off like you used to do – you must do them now, or you may not do them at all, because soon it may be too late.'

'For goodness sake, Mabel!' said Lisa with a nervous laugh. 'Anyone would think you were an old woman!'

'I'm not a young one,' said Mabel with a rueful smile. 'It's later than you think.'

'*Don't!*' said Alice with a shiver. The unexpected sharpness of her normally quiet voice evidently surprised her as much as it surprised Mabel Brandon, for she flushed painfully and said with a trace of confusion: 'I'm sorry. It's just that I've always hated that phrase. It was carved on a sundial that we had in the garden at home, and it always frightened me. I don't know why. I – I suppose it was the idea that everything would end sooner than you expected it to. The day – parties – fun – the years. Life! I used to make excuses not to go near the sundial. Silly, isn't it?'

'No!' said Gilly, harshly and abruptly. 'Do it myself. Make excuses to keep away from *Flamingo*. Same thing. Something that frightens me, but I don't know what. Don't mind a poltergeist that breaks things, but when it begins on creatures, that's different. That's – that's damnable. Working up to something. A sighting shot. Makes you wonder where it will end. What it's got its eye on ...'

His voice died out on a whisper and Mabel surveyed him with disapproval and said with unaccustomed severity: 'Really Gilly, you are talking a great deal of nonsense this evening. And you're upsetting poor Lisa. What are you hinting at? That Mau Mau isn't dead yet and that Em's servants have taken the oath? Well suppose it isn't and they have? There's hardly a Kikuyu in the country who hasn't. But it doesn't mean anything any more. The whole thing has fallen to pieces and the few hard-core terrorists who are still on the run are far too busy just keeping alive to plan any more murders. And if it's the poisoning of that unfortunate ridgeback that's worrying you, I'm sure there's nothing sinister in that. It cannot be wise to keep dogs like Simba who attack strangers on sight, and I am not really surprised that someone took the law into their own hands. I might almost have felt tempted to do it myself, fond as I am of dogs, but——'

'But Simba didn't like Ken; that's it, isn't it?' said Alice, surprised to find herself so angry.

Mabel turned towards her, her gentle voice quivering with sudden emotion: 'That is not kind of you, Alice. We all know that Simba liked you, and of course Em is crazy on the subject of dogs. But considering that he once attacked your own husband——'

'Only because Eden was trying to take a book away from me. We were fooling, but Simba thought he was attacking me. He wouldn't let anyone touch me, and I suppose he thought that Ken——'

She bit the sentence off short, aghast at its implications. But it seemed to remain hanging in the air, its import embarrassingly clear to everyone in the room. As embarrassingly clear as the expression upon Mabel Brandon's stricken face, or Hector's stony tight-mouthed stare.

There was a moment of strained and painful silence which was broken by Drew Stratton, who glanced at his wrist watch and rose. He said in a leisurely voice: 'Afraid I must go, Lisa. It's getting late, and my headlights are not all they should be. Thanks for the drink. Can I drop you off at the house, Mrs DeBrett, or did you drive over?'

Alice threw him a grateful look. 'No, I came over by the short cut across the garden. And I really must walk back, because I promised Em I'd get some of the Mardan roses for the dining-room table.'

Drew said: 'Then I'll see you on your way. Eden shouldn't let you wander about alone of an evening.'

'Oh, it's safe enough now. Good night, Lisa. Shall I tell Em you'll go in with her on Thursday?'

'Yes, do. I want to get my hair done. I'll ring up tomorrow and fix an appointment. Drew, if your headlights aren't working you'd better not be long over seeing Alice back.'

'That's right,' said Gilly. 'Remember Alice's sundial. *"It is later than you think!"'*

He laughed again, and the sound of his laughter followed them out into the silent garden.

2

The sun had dipped behind the purple line of the Mau Escarpment, and the lake reflected a handful of rose-pink clouds and a single star that was as yet no more than a ghostly point of silver.

There had been very little rain during the past month, and the path that led between the canna lily beds and bamboos was thick with dust. Mr Stratton slowed his leisurely stride to Alice DeBrett's shorter step, but he did not talk, and Alice was grateful for his silence. There had been too much talk in the Markhams' drawing-room. Too many things had been said that had better have been left unsaid, and too many things had been uncovered that should have been kept decently in hiding. Things that Alice had never previously suspected, or been too preoccupied with her own problems to notice.

Was it, she wondered, the long strain of the Emergency, and the present relaxing of tension and alertness, that had brought these more petty and personal things to the surface and exposed them nakedly in Lisa's pink-and-white drawing-room? Had she, Alice, displayed her own fears and her own feelings as clearly as Lisa and Gilly and the Brandons had done? Had the brief coldness of her reply to Lisa's questions on the subject of Victoria Caryll been as illuminating as Lisa's own comments?

'Look out,' said Drew. He caught her arm, jerking her out of her abstraction just in time to prevent her treading full on a brown, moving band, four inches wide, that spanned the dusty track. A river of hurrying ants – the wicked safari ants whose bite is unbelievably painful.

'You ought to look where you're going,' remarked Mr Stratton mildly. 'That might have been a snake. And anyway you don't want a shoe-full of those creatures. They bite like the devil.'

'I know,' said Alice apologetically. 'I'm afraid I wasn't looking where I was going.'

'Dangerous thing to do in this country,' commented Drew. 'What's worrying you?'

Alice would have resented that question from anyone else, and would certainly not have answered it truthfully. But Drew Stratton was notoriously indifferent to gossip and she knew that it was kindness and not curiosity that had prompted the query. She turned to look at his brown, clear-cut profile, sharp against the quiet sky, and knew suddenly that she could talk to Drew. She had not been able to talk to anyone about Victoria. Not to Eden. Not even to Em, who had said so anxiously: 'You won't mind, dear? It's all over, you know – a long time ago. But she shan't come if you mind.' She had not been able to confess to Em that she minded. But, strangely, she could admit it to Drew.

'It's Victoria,' said Alice. 'Victoria Caryll. Eden and she – they've known each other for a long time. They're some sort of cousins. Em's her aunt and his grandmother, and he used to spend most of his holidays at her mother's house when he was home at school – and at Oxford. They – they were engaged to be married. I don't know what went wrong. I asked Eden once, but he – wouldn't talk about it. And – and her mother died a few months ago, so now she's coming out here . . .'

Alice made a small, helpless gesture with one hand, and Drew reached out and possessed himself of it. He tucked it companionably through his arm, but made no other comment, and once again Alice was conscious of a deep feeling of gratitude and a relief from strain. She could think of no one else who would not have probed and exclaimed, sympathized or uttered bracing platitudes in face of that disclosure. But Drew's silent acceptance of it, and that casual, comforting gesture, had reduced it to its proper proportions. There was really nothing to worry about. It was, in fact, a direct dispensation of Providence that Em's niece should be free to come out to Kenya, for it was going to make it so much easier to break the news to Em that they must leave her. It would have been impossible to leave her alone and old and lonely. But now she would have Victoria. And with luck, and in time, she might even grow to be almost as fond of Victoria as she was of Eden, and if that should happen perhaps she would leave her not only half of the estate, as Hector Brandon had suggested, but *Flamingo*, and the property at Rumuruti, whole and entire, so that she, Alice, would be free of it for ever, and need never come back to Kenya . . .

A huge horned owl, grey in the green twilight, rose up from the stump of a fallen tree and swooped silently across their path, and Alice caught her breath in an audible gasp and stopped suddenly, her fingers clutching frantically at Drew Stratton's sleeve.

549

'It's all right. It's only an owl,' said Drew pacifically.

'It was a death owl!' said Alice, shuddering. 'The servants say that if you see one of those it means that someone is going to die. They're terrified of them!'

'That's no reason why you should be,' said Drew reprovingly. 'You aren't a witchcraft-ridden Kikuyu.'

He frowned down at her, perturbed and a little impatient, and putting a hand over the cold fingers that clutched at his arm, held them in a hard and comforting grasp and said abruptly: 'Mrs DeBrett, I know it's none of my business, but don't you think it's time you gave yourself a holiday in England? You can't have had a very easy time during the last five years, but you mustn't let this country get you down. Why don't you get Eden to take you home for a few months? It will do you both good, and this niece of Em's will be company for her while you are away.'

'Yes,' said Alice a little breathlessly. 'I – we had thought ...' Her colour was coming back and she breathed more easily. She stilled the nervous shivering of her body with a visible effort and said: 'I'm sorry, Drew. I'm behaving very stupidly. You're quite right; I should go home. I'm turning into a jumpy, hysterical wreck. Do you know what Gilly said to me this evening? He said, "You can't be more than thirty-five." And I'm twenty-seven. Eden's only twenty-nine. I can't look six or seven years older than Eden, can I?'

'Gilly was tight,' observed Drew dispassionately.

He studied her gravely, thinking that Gilly's estimate of Mrs DeBrett's age, though ungallant, was understandable. But Drew had seen nerves and shell-shock and sleeplessness before, and recognized the symptoms. He said: 'You look pretty good to me,' and smiled.

He possessed a slow and extraordinarily pleasant smile, and Alice found herself returning it. 'That's better,' approved Drew. 'You look about seventeen when you smile, not twenty-seven. You should do it more often. Are you and Eden going to this dance at Nakuru on Saturday?'

He talked trivialities until they reached the plumbago hedge that marked the boundary of the Markhams' garden, and Alice dismissed him at the gate:

'I'm not letting you come any further, or you won't get home before it's dark. And I'm perfectly safe, thank you. No one is likely to try and murder me between here and the house! Not now, anyway.'

'Probably not,' said Drew, 'but I imagine that it will be some years yet before half the women out here will feel safe without a gun.'

550

He watched her walk away across the garden and was conscious of a brief and unexpected flash of sympathy for Eden DeBrett. Not really the type for a settler's wife, thought Drew. She'll never stay the course.

A dry twig cracked in the soft carpet of dust behind him and he turned sharply. But it was only Gilly Markham.

'Came out for a breath of air,' explained Gilly morosely. 'Mabel's gone off to pick a lettuce or a pineapple or something, and Hector says he's going to walk home, so Lisa's locked up the booze. Women are hell.'

He leaned heavily on the gate, his eyes following the noiseless flight of a bat which swooped and flittered along the pale blossoms of the plumbago hedge, and said with sudden violence: 'God, what a country! What wouldn't I give to get out of this god-forsaken, uncivilized, gang-ridden hole! Can't think how you can stand it.'

'No reason why you should stand it, Gilly,' observed Drew without heat.

'That's what *you* think!' said Gilly sourly. 'Easy enough for you. But I can't afford to up-sticks and get the hell out of it. D'you suppose I wouldn't if I could?'

Drew said dryly: 'If you're getting the same screw as Gus Abbott got, you can't be doing too badly. By all accounts, Gus left a packet.'

'Gus didn't have a wife!' retorted Gilly bitterly. 'You don't know Lisa. If I were making twenty times what I get, Lisa'd spend it. Thinks I don't know why she's always buying herself new clothes and having her face and hair fixed. Well I may be a fool, but I'm not such a fool as I look! Take my advice and don't ever get married, Drew.'

'I'll bear it in mind,' said Drew solemnly. 'So long, Gilly.'

'No, don't go!' said Gilly urgently. 'Stay around for a bit. Got the purple willies on me this evening and that's a fact. Know why people like talking to you, Drew? Well I'll tell you. It's because you're so bloody detached. You don't give a damn for any of it, do you? But tell anyone else anything, and before you know it it's all round the Colony. Why can't they mind their own business?'

'Why indeed?' said Drew. 'Sorry about it, Gilly, but I've got to go. It's late.'

Gilly ignored the interruption. 'Hector, fr'instance. Never forgiven Eden for marrying a woman who he doesn't consider is "The right type for Kenya". What's it got to do with him? Anyone would think he'd invented the place! Probably thinks that as soon as Em dies

551

Alice'll persuade Eden to sell out to that syndicate of Afrikaners who offered a fortune for *Flamingo* last year. Wouldn't suit Hector one bit to have that sort of concern on his doorstep! Ruin the market for him. And the next thing you know they'd build a decent road round the lake, and how he'd hate that! Hector and his like may talk a lot of hot air about the Colony, but the one thing they're terrified of is development around their own little bit of it. They like it just as it is. Just exactly as it ruddy well——'

He broke off abruptly and lifted his head, listening intently.

There was no breath of wind that evening. The vast stretch of the lake lay glass-green in the twilight, and even the birds were silent at last. But someone in the big rambling house that lay beyond the pepper trees and jacarandas in Em's garden was playing the piano. The quiet evening lent clarity and a haunting, melancholy beauty to the distant sound, and Drew, who had turned away, paused involuntarily to listen, and said: 'What is she playing?'

'The Rift Valley Concerto,' said Gilly absently.

His thin, nervous, musician's fingers moved on the top bar of the gate as though it was the keyboard of a piano, and then clenched abruptly into fists, and he struck at the gate in a sudden fury of irritation and said savagely:

'Why the hell can't she play that third movement as it's meant to be played, instead of hammering it out as though it were a bloody pop tune? That woman 'ud make Bartok sound like "Two Eyes of Grey" and Debussy like "The British Grenadiers"! It's murder – that's what it is! Plain murder!'

He relapsed into glowering silence, slumping down on a square concrete block that stood among the grasses by the gate. His brief spurt of rage gave place to an alcoholic sullenness, and he took no note of Mr Stratton's departure.

Alice was half-way back to the house when she remembered the Mardan roses that Em had wanted for the dining-room table, and she turned off the path and walked across the parched grass, and through a sea of delphiniums that grew waist-high and half wild at the foot of a small knoll that was crowned by a tangle of bushes and the trunk of a fallen tree.

From the crest of the knoll, and between a break in the bushes, she could look out over the lush green of the shamba and the wide belt of grey-green vegetation, dark now in the fading light, which was the *marula* – the papyrus swamp that fringed the shores of the lake with a dense, feathery and almost impenetrable jungle, twice the height of a tall man.

A broken branch of the fallen tree supported a cascade of white roses that were not easy to pick even by day, for they were plentifully supplied with thorns. But Em loved them, and during their brief season she liked to arrange them in the Waterford glass bowls that had belonged to her grandmother. Was that why she had asked for them now? So that she could fill other bowls with them and pretend that she did not care? For the Waterford glass bowls had gone. They had been found one afternoon almost a week ago, broken in pieces, though the house had been quiet that day, and the dogs had not barked ...

'Don't touch them!' Alice had said, looking at Em's drawn, ravaged face. 'There may be finger prints on them. We can find out——'

'And have the police all over the house, trampling all over *Flamingo* and bullying my servants? No!' said Em. And she had gathered up the broken pieces with old, pitiful, shaking hands and given them to Zacharia, telling him to throw them away.

Em had refused from the first to send for the police. She had set a number of traps, but no one had fallen into them. The poltergeist seemed to be able to circumnavigate burglar alarms, trip-wires and similar booby traps, and to avoid by instinct objects smeared with a substance guaranteed to inflict an unpleasant sore on any hand that touched it. But the effects of its depredations had been more demoralizing to the whole household than anything achieved by the Mau Mau during the years of the Emergency. The servants were frankly terrified, Eden was angry and on edge, and Em grim and stubborn.

'If someone thinks that they can frighten me into leaving, they'll find they're wrong,' she said. 'The Mau Mau thought they could frighten us into leaving our farms, but we are still here. I don't know what anyone hopes to gain by destroying things I am fond of, but whatever it is, they won't get it!' And as if to emphasize her defiance she had sat down at the piano and played from memory Toroni's 'Rift Valley Concerto': playing it furiously and loudly and not very accurately.

That had been on the day that the recording of the concerto had been destroyed, and that same evening, looking tired and defeated and very old, she had told them that she had sent for Victoria.

Victoria's mother had died that spring and Victoria was at present sharing a small flat in London with two friends, and working as private secretary to the assistant manager of a firm of importers.

'I have asked her to come out here and work for me,' said Em, not looking at Eden: looking at nothing but the candle flames on the dining-room table and, perhaps, the past. 'I am getting too old to deal with half the work I do. I need someone who can be a confidential secretary, and whom I can work hard. And at this time I would rather it were someone who – who belongs. It will also mean that I am doing something for Helen's child. Giving her a home as well as an adequate salary.'

She had looked at Alice for the first time, her eyes blank and unfocused from the dazzle of the candle flames, and said gently: 'You, who are an orphan too, will know what that must mean to her. But she shan't come if you would rather she did not, my dear.'

Perhaps Alice might have found it possible to protest if it had not suddenly seemed to offer a way of escape. She did not want to meet this girl whom Eden had once meant to marry and with whom he must once have been in love. And she did not want Eden to meet her again. But if Em's niece came to live at *Flamingo* perhaps she, Alice, could persuade Eden to leave Kenya: to take her back to England. It would not be as though they were leaving Em alone. She would have Victoria . . .

Alice looked down at the white roses that filled her hands, and letting them drop to the ground, sat down tiredly on the smooth trunk of the fallen tree and thought with affection and desperation and despair of Lady Emily DeBrett. Of Em and Eden. It was not going to be easy to tell Em that she could endure Kenya no longer. Em had a reputation for impatience, hard-headedness, shrewd business acumen, an iron nerve and a refusal to suffer fools gladly. Yet she had suffered Eden's wife, who according to all her lights must have seemed a fool. She had mothered her, protected her, encouraged her, and stood between her and danger.

Sitting in the dusk on the knoll at *Flamingo*, Alice recalled her first sight of Eden's grandmother, and the shock it had given her. Eden had mentioned casually that his grandmother was inclined to be eccentric in the matter of dress, but he had not prepared her for the grotesque figure that had appeared on the porch steps when the car that had brought them the fifty-odd miles from Nairobi Airport drew up before the big thatch-roofed house on the shores of Lake Naivasha.

The years had thickened Emily's stately figure to more than ample proportions, but had not eradicated her antipathy to skirts. She had never willingly worn feminine attire, but she had a fondness for bright colours and a leaning towards eccentricity. Em's scarlet dungarees and vivid blouses – both of which served to exaggerate her impressive bulk to a distressing extent – and the flamboyant wide-brimmed hats that she habitually wore crammed down upon her short cropped hair, had for more than thirty years been as familiar a sight to half Kenya as the roving zebra herds, the wandering, ochre-smeared Masai warriors, or the snows of Kilimanjaro. But they had done nothing to reassure Alice DeBrett, three weeks a bride and arriving at *Flamingo* dizzy from repeated attacks of air-sickness and dusty and shaken from the last fifteen miles over an unmetalled road – a newcomer to a strange country torn with savagery and violence, where even the women carried guns and all men were afraid of the night, never knowing what darkness might bring.

It was odd, looking back on that day, to think that Em had been the only reassuring thing in all the months that had followed. She had been both mother and grandmother to Alice, who had never known either. It was Eden who had failed her. But then it could not be easy to be Eden, thought Eden's wife. To be so fatally good-looking that women looked once and fell desperately in love – as she herself had done. She had been married to Eden for almost five years now, and she still could not look at him without a contraction of the heart.

She loved him so much, and if he had loved *Flamingo* as Em loved it she would have forced herself to staying there for ever: to fighting her terror, her hatred of the land, and the ill health that constant fear, the height and the climate had inflicted upon her. But she did not believe that Eden's roots were too deep in the Kenya soil, or that the land meant to him what it meant to Em. And lately she had persuaded herself that he would be just as happy in England with an estate of his own. Happier! for it had always been a sore point with him that Em had not made him manager instead of Gilly. 'But *Flamingo* will be yours one day,' Em had said. 'You'll need a manager then, and it's better to have one who knows the ropes. Gilly's not much use at present, but managers are hard to get these days, and he'll learn. Besides, he needs the job.'

'I didn't know we were running a philanthropical society!' Eden had said crossly. 'You're losing your grip, Gran darling.'

'That's where you're wrong. You've got a hold over a man who

555

needs a job. None over one who doesn't. And I like things done my way.'

Eden had laughed and kissed her. 'You do hate to have anyone accuse you of having a soft spot, don't you darling? You gave Gilly the job because he was broke, and you know it – and because he knows the difference between Bach and Brahms!'

Em had made a face at him, but she had not denied it.

It was on Em's account more than Eden's that Alice had tried to reconcile herself to spending the rest of her days in Kenya, for although she had come to believe that she might be able to make up to Eden for the loss of *Flamingo*, she knew that she could never compensate Em for the loss of Eden. But now at last she had reached the breaking point. It had not been Victoria who had proved to be the last straw, but the things that had happened in the house during the last weeks: a situation that Eden had once referred to as 'this silly business'.

'It isn't silly,' Alice had said, and for the first time there had been hysteria in her gentle voice. 'It's horrible! Don't you see – everything that has been broken or spoiled has been something special and irreplaceable. It's as if someone who knew everything about Em, and wanted to hurt her specially, knew just the things to choose. Someone – someone *evil*.'

Eden had said sharply: 'That's nonsense! You mustn't be hysterical about this, Alice. Believe me darling, it'll turn out to be some silly Kuke who fancies he has a grievance, or thinks he's had a spell put on him. You mustn't lose your sense of proportion. After all, even if the things are irreplaceable, they're still only things.'

But two days later it had not been a thing. It had been Simba.

Alice had not thought Em capable of tears, and the sight of her red and swollen eyes had been almost as shocking as the discovery of Simba's stiff, contorted body lying among the crushed geraniums below the verandah. She had been frightened before, but it had never been like this. The wanton destruction of Em's most cherished possessions had been horrible enough, but the poisoning of her favourite dog betrayed a cold-blooded malice that went deeper than mere spite.

Gilly was right, thought Alice, cold with foreboding. The 'things' were only a beginning. Simba was another step. Supposing – it is *someone* next? Someone Em loves. *Eden— !* We must get away. We must! While there is still time ...

It had been a particularly trying day for Alice. Eden had gone

556

to Nairobi and would not be back until late, and Em had been noticeably jumpy and on edge all day. She had apparently had a minor squabble with Mabel Brandon in the course of the morning, and had not been pleased when Ken Brandon had presented himself at the house in the afternoon and had to be asked to tea.

Alice had not been pleased either. She found young Ken Brandon's adolescent and unsnubbable infatuation for her more than a little trying, and had read him a stern lecture on the subject only the day before, which he had not taken well. He had ended by threatening to shoot himself – not for the first time – and Alice had lost all patience with him, and observed tartly that it would be no loss. She had hoped that this would put an end to his adoration, but Ken had turned up that afternoon asking to see her, and evidently intending to apologize for the dramatics of the previous day. Em had saved her from another scene by plying the boy with tea and arbitrarily taking Alice out shooting with her immediately afterwards.

Alice never went out shooting if she could help it, but on this occasion she had accepted gratefully, and they had taken Kamau, one of the boys, and driven out in the Land-Rover to shoot a buck for the dogs. Em had shot a kongoni out on the ranges, and helped Kamau to degut it and hoist the limp ungainly body into the back of the Land-Rover, where it lolled in a sticky pool of blood that smeared the seats, stained Em's hands and clothing with ugly dark splotches and filled Alice with shuddering revulsion. It was one of the many things about Kenya that she could never get used to. The casual attitude of most women towards firearms and the sight and smell of blood.

I haven't any courage, thought Alice drearily, staring into the green dusk. Perhaps I had some once, but it's gone. If only I can get away ... If only I need not go back into that horrible house ...

Em was still playing Toroni's concerto, and the too familiar cadences, muted by distance, plucked at Alice's taut nerves, demanding her attention and forcing her to listen.

She had never been able to understand Em's and Gilly's admiration for the concerto. It had seemed to her a tuneless noise, alternating from the discordant to the intolerably dreary. But tonight she seemed to be hearing it for the first time, and it was as if the Valley itself were speaking. The enormous golden Valley and the great yawning craters of extinct volcanoes – Longonot and Suswa and Menengai. The impassable falls of dead lava: the frowning gorge of Hell's Gate: the vast, shallow, flamingo-haunted lakes, and the long twin ramparts of the Mau and the Kinangop that were the walls of the Great Rift.

Em had told her that Toroni had loved the Valley. But Em was wrong, thought Alice, listening to the music. Toroni had not loved the Rift. He had been afraid of it. As she herself was afraid of it. She shivered convulsively, clutching her hands tightly together in her lap; and as she listened a little breath of wind whispered through the bushes and swayed the hanging trails of roses, and somewhere near her a twig cracked sharply.

Quite suddenly, with that sound, the garden was no longer a friendly place, but as full of menace as the house, and Alice stood up quickly and stooped to gather up the fallen flowers, aware that her heart was thumping painfully against her ribs. She had not realized that it had grown so dark.

Below the knoll and beyond the shamba, from the shadowy belt of the papyrus swamp, birds began to call; their clear piping cries mingling with the sweet clear notes of the distant piano. But the day had almost gone and the sky was already shimmering with pale stars, and there was as yet no moon. There should be no birds calling at this hour. Had something, or someone, startled them?

She remembered then what Gilly had said less than an hour ago. Something about General Africa – still at large despite the heavy price that the Government had set on his head, and suspected of being in the employment of one of the settlers in the Naivasha district. Something about a gang under his command who were rumoured to be still in hiding somewhere in the papyrus swamp, being fed by the African labour of the farms that bordered the Lake.

She had not paid much attention to it at the time, but now she remembered it with alarm, and remembered, too, Em's instructions that she should not stay out after sunset. But the sun had set long ago, and now it was almost dark, and the evening breeze had arisen and was stirring the leaves about her and filling the green dusk with soft, stealthy rustlings.

A twig cracked again immediately behind her, and turning quickly she caught a flicker of movement that was not caused by the wind. Her hands tightened about the roses, driving the thorns into her flesh, but caught in a sudden spider's web of panic she was almost unaware of the pain. Her brain told her to run for the house, but her muscles would not obey her. She could not even scream; and she knew that if she did so no one in the house would hear her, for the music of the piano would drown any sound from outside. But there was someone watching her from among the bushes; she was sure of it——

Alice stood quite still, as helpless and as paralysed with terror as the victim of a nightmare. And then, just as she thought that her heart must stop beating, a familiar figure materialized out of the dusk at the foot of the knoll, and the blood seemed to flow again through her numbed veins.

She dropped the roses, and with a choking sob of relief began to run, tripping and stumbling over the rough grass in the uncertain light. She was within a yard of that dimly seen figure when something checked her. A sound . . .

There was something wrong. Something crazily and impossibly wrong. She stopped suddenly, staring. Her eyes widened in her white face and her mouth opened in a soundless scream. For it was someone else. Someone suddenly and horribly unfamiliar.

3

'And as I was saying, what with Income Tax and strikes and the weather, well it's no wonder that so many people decide to live abroad. In fact, as I told Oswin – that's my present husband – I can't understand why more of them don't do it. Don't you agree?'

There was no answer, and Mrs Brocas-Gill, observing with annoyance that her neighbour had fallen asleep, turned her attention instead to the desolate green and brown expanse of Africa that lay far below her, across which the big B.O.A.C. Constellation trailed a tiny blue shadow no bigger than a toy aeroplane.

Miss Caryll, however, was not asleep. Only an exceptionally strong-minded woman, or one in need of a hearing-aid, could have slept in the company of that human long-playing record, Mrs Brocas-Gill. Victoria was neither; but she had endured Mrs Brocas-Gill's indefatigable monologue with barely a break since the aircraft had left London Airport, and as they had been delayed for twenty-four hours at Rome with engine trouble this meant that she had been compelled to listen to it for the best part of two days. Even the nights had not silenced Mrs Brocas-Gill, who had slept with her mouth open, and snored. And Victoria wanted to think.

She had not allowed herself much time for thought during the last three weeks. Once she had made her decision and cabled her acceptance of Aunt Emily's offer, there was little point in stopping to think; and little time in which to do so, for there had been a hundred things to see to. But there would be the flight to Kenya; twenty-four hours of sitting quietly in an aeroplane with nothing to do. There would be time then to think, and to sort out the turmoil in her mind and face the past – and the future. But she had not calculated on Mrs Brocas-Gill, and now they were flying over Africa, and the Dark Continent lay spread out below them with Nairobi Airport only half an hour ahead.

Half an hour! thought Victoria in a panic. Half an hour in which to sort out her thoughts and prepare herself for meeting Eden. To face all those things that she had cravenly refused to face during the past three weeks, and that she had forced herself not to think of for more than five years. Half an hour ...

It was difficult to remember a time when she had not loved Eden DeBrett. She had been five on the day when she had tried to make Falda, the little zebra which her father had caught and tamed for her, jump the cattle gate by one of the waterholes. Falda had not taken kindly to the idea, and Victoria had pitched head-first into the sloshy churned-up mud by the drinking troughs where, in addition to winding herself badly, she ruined the clean cotton dress in which she was supposed to appear at a luncheon party.

It was Eden, nine years old and spending the weekend with his great-Aunt Helen, who had saved the situation. He had retrieved Victoria from the mud, dried her tears on a grubby pocket-handkerchief and suggested the immediate removal of clothes, shoes and socks, and their immersion – and Victoria's – in the clean water of the cattle troughs.

His suggestion had been followed, with such excellent results that when the gong had sounded she had been able to walk demurely up to the house in a crumpled but undoubtedly clean dress, and no one had noticed that her long brown plaits owed some of their sleekness to the fact that they were damp. Eden's superior male intelligence had saved her from disaster and from that day he was Victoria's hero.

She had been a plain little girl, with a tendency to stammer slightly when shy or upset; thin and leggy and very brown. Brown sunburnt skin, brown eyes and long, lank brown hair. But although her own lack of good looks had not interested her, she had been deeply impressed by Eden's beauty.

Even as a child Eden DeBrett was beautiful, and he did not out-grow that beauty as so many children do. It seemed, in fact, to increase as he grew older, and it had its effect on everyone he met, so that there were few people, if any, who were ever to know what he was really like, or to be quite fair to him: their judgement being invariably swung out of true by his amazing good looks.

He was ten when Em hardened her heart and sent him home to a famous preparatory school in England, and the six-year-old Victoria had wept bitterly and uncontrollably, and greatly to Eden's disgust and her own mortification, on the platform of Nairobi railway station where she had gone with her parents to see him off.

Her gay and charming father had died two months later, and the tragedy of his death, the sale of the farm and the misery of leaving

Kenya – even the parting with her ponies and dear fat friendly Falda – had been mitigated by the thought that she would be seeing Eden again. For it had been arranged between Em and Helen that Eden should spend the Christmas and Easter holidays with the Carylls, and return to Kenya once a year to spend the two months of the summer holidays at *Flamingo*.

In actual fact he had spent all his holidays for the next six or seven years with them, and had seen nothing of Em and *Flamingo*; for tragedy on a Homeric scale had taken over the stage, and the war put an end to countless plans, as it was to put an end to countless lives.

Eden had missed active service, but he had done his National Service with the Occupation Forces in Germany, and followed it by three years at Oxford, during which time he had seen little or nothing of the Carylls, for he spent his vacations with Em in Kenya, flying between London and Nairobi. Victoria had not seen him for over a year when Em suddenly announced her intention of paying a visit to England and staying with her half-sister. She had not seen either for years, and she and Eden would spend July and August at Helen's instead of at *Flamingo*.

Victoria's Aunt Emily, who was Eden's grandmother, was exactly as Victoria remembered her, save for the fact that in deference to the post-war nerves of the Islanders she had refrained from wearing her favourite Kenya garb of scarlet dungarees, and was soberly and somewhat disappointingly clad in a brown coat-frock that whispered of moth balls and the Gay Twenties.

Eden had arrived two days later, and he had looked at Victoria as though he were seeing her for the first time: as though she were someone whom he had never seen before.

She had been picking roses and her arms were full of the lovely lavish honey-pinks of Betty Uprichards; but that had been an unrehearsed and entirely fortuitous circumstance, as Eden had not been expected for another two hours. She had blushed under Eden's startled gaze, and Eden had said foolishly: '*Vicky*—! What have you been doing to yourself? You've – you've grown up.'

And at that they had both laughed, and he had leaned forward and kissed her above the roses and they had fallen in love.

No, that was not true, thought Victoria. At least, it was not true of herself, for she had fallen in love with Eden years and years ago, when he had picked her up out of the mud by the cattle troughs and dried her tears with a handkerchief that smelt of Stockholm tar and chewing gum. And she had never stopped loving him.

It was Eden who had fallen in love that day. Or had he? Had it only been affection for someone he had known all his life? Sentiment and a summer evening, and a pretty girl in a yellow dress with her arms full of roses? *Any* pretty girl? No! thought Victoria. No. It isn't true. He did love me. He did! I couldn't have been mistaken.

It had been an enchanted summer. They had danced together and dined together, and walked and talked and planned their lives together. Em had been pleased; but Victoria's mother had not approved of the cousins marrying, and she had been against it from the first.

'I might agree, if they were first cousins,' Em had said, 'but they are not.'

'Eden has Beaumartin blood in him,' said Helen unhappily.

'And Carteret and Brook and DeBrett blood too! It will be a great success.'

But Helen had counselled delay. Eden was only twenty-three, and Victoria four years younger. They could afford to wait. Eden was to do a year's course at an agricultural college so as to fit him for taking over *Flamingo* – as his years at Oxford would fit him, so his grandmother hoped, to hold political office one day in the country of his birth and her adoption.

'He is a second-generation Kenya-ite,' said Em, 'and there are not so many of them. The Colony needs men who love the country to run its affairs.'

By Helen's wish there had been no formal engagement, and no announcement to friends. Em had gone back to Kenya when the summer was over and Victoria had gone on with her secretarial course, because, she told Eden, it would be a help in the running of *Flamingo*.

They were to be married when Eden was twenty-four, and he had actually married when he was within a week of his twenty-fourth birthday. But it had not been to Victoria. It had been to Alice Laxton. Five years ago ... Yet even now, to think of it brought back some of the suffocating, agonizing pain of those days.

It had happened suddenly and without warning. Eden had arrived one afternoon to see her mother, and left again without waiting to see Victoria, who was out. Helen had looked pale and upset but had said nothing more than that Eden had been unable to stay as

563

he had to spend the weekend with friends in Sussex, but that he would be writing.

The letter had come three days later, and Victoria could still remember every line of it as though it had burned itself into her brain. They had made a mistake, wrote Eden, and confused cousinly affection and friendship for something deeper. Nothing could alter that fondness and friendship, and he knew her too well not to know that if she did not agree with him now, she would one day. One day she would fall in love with someone else, as he himself had done, and then her affection for him would fall into its proper place. And as they had never really been engaged, neither of them need suffer any public embarrassment.

As he himself had done ... In the face of that statement there was nothing for Victoria to do but write an unhysterical letter accepting the inevitable and agreeing that his decision was the right one. She had saved her pride, and probably salved Eden's conscience, by doing so; if either of those things were worth doing.

Helen had been relieved and had not attempted to disguise the fact. 'I never think that marriages between cousins are a good idea,' she said. 'Inbreeding never did anyone any good.'

Em had written from Kenya. She had quite obviously accepted Eden's view that the break was mutual, and the letter had been charming and deeply regretful, and had ended with the hope that they might both think better of it. But on the same morning as its arrival *The Times* and the *Telegraph* had published the announcement of Eden's engagement to Alice Laxton, and less than a month later they had been married.

Oh, the agony of those days! The tearing, wrenching pain of loss. The shock of casually opening an illustrated paper at the hairdressers and being confronted with a full page photograph of Eden and his bride leaving St George's, Hanover Square. Eden, grave and unsmiling, and as heart-breakingly handsome as every woman's dream of Prince Charming. And Alice, an anonymous figure in white satin whose bridal veil had blown across her face and partially obscured it.

'Better looking than Robert Taylor or any of those,' said the hairdresser's assistant, peering over her shoulder. 'Ought to be on the films, he ought. It's a waste. Don't think much of her, do you? Can't think how she got him. Money, I expect. The papers say she's got any amount of it. Wish I had! What about just a touch of brilliantine, Miss Caryll?'

Any amount of money ... Had that been why Eden had married her? No, he *could* not be so despicable! Not Eden. But *Flamingo*, she knew, had been losing money of late, and Eden had expensive tastes. Em had spoilt him. It would be nice to be able to think that he only married Alice Laxton for her money, for then she could despise him and be sorry for his wife, and apply salve to her own hurt pride. But what did hurt pride matter in comparison to the pain in her heart? I won't think of him any more, decided Victoria. I won't let myself think of any of this again.

It had not been easy to keep that vow, but hard work had helped, and at last there came a time when memory did not rise and mock her whenever she was tired or off-guard. She had not thought of the past, or of Eden, for months before Helen died, and afterwards she had been able to read his letter of condolence, and reply to it, as though he had meant no more to her than the writers of a dozen other such letters. She had sold the house and taken a secretarial post in London. And then that unexpected letter had arrived from Kenya.

It was not the sort of letter than Em had ever written before, and there was an odd and disturbing suggestion of urgency about it. The same urgency that Helen had sometimes betrayed when she had wanted to do something, or to see someone, and had been afraid that she would not have time to do it before she died. A fear that was both harrowing and pitiful. But there was something else there too. Something that Victoria could not quite put her finger on, and which disturbed her even more.

The letter had contained only one reference to the past: 'You know that I would never have suggested your coming if I had not been quite sure that you and Eden could meet as friends. And I know that you will like his wife. Alice is such a dear girl, but we are neither of us strong, and I fear that I am getting old. I need help.'

Em had provisionally booked a passage for her on an air liner leaving for Nairobi on the twenty-third of the month. Which meant that she would have to decide at once, as the company would not keep the reservation for long. Was that why Em had done it? So that she would be forced to make up her mind quickly, and could not waver and hesitate? Was Em, too, afraid of dying too soon, and aware, as Helen had been, that it was later than she had thought?

England had been enduring an exceptionally cold and wet spell that year, and Victoria, clinging to a strap in a crowded bus on her way to work, the letter in her pocket, had looked out over the damp, bedraggled hat of a stout woman in a wet mackintosh, to the damp, bedraggled London streets that streamed past the rain spotted windows, and thought of the Rift Valley——

The enormous sun-drenched spaces where the cattle grazed and the herds of zebra and gazelle roamed at will under the blue cloud shadows that drifted by as idly as sailing ships on a summer sea. It would be wonderful to see it again. It would be like going home. And *Flamingo* would be a home to her. Aunt Emily had said so. Aunt Emily needed her, and it was so comforting to be needed again. As for Eden, he was happily married, and Alice was 'such a dear girl'. The past was over and done with. She need not think of it.

The stewardess of the air liner said: 'Fasten your safety belts please,' and Mrs Brocas-Gill said: 'Wake up dear. We're going down to land. Are you feeling all right? You're looking very pale.'

'No,' said Victoria a trifle breathlessly. 'No. I'm all right thank you. It's just that——'

The plane tilted on one shining wing and the ground rushed up to meet it. And then they were skimming low over roof-tops and trees and grass and bumping down a long runway, and Victoria was thinking frantically and desperately and futilely: I shouldn't have come! I shouldn't have come! What shall I do when I see Eden? It isn't all over – it won't ever be all over! I shouldn't have come ...

4

The sun was blindingly bright on the white walls of the Airport, and there seemed to be a great many people meeting the plane. But there was no sign of Lady Emily. Or of Eden.

A small stout man with a red face and a bald head, wearing a singularly crumpled suit and, somewhat surprisingly, a revolver in an enormous leather holster, waved a white panama enthusiastically from beyond the barrier and yelled a welcome to someone called 'Pet'.

'There's Oswin,' said Mrs Brocas-Gill.

'You're late!' shouted Mr Brocas-Gill, stating the obvious. 'Expected you yesterday.'

He embraced his wife and was introduced to Victoria. 'Bless my soul!' said Mr Brocas-Gill. 'Jack Caryll's girl. I remember your father when— Why, dammit, I remember *you*! Skinny little thing in plaits. Used to ride a zebra. Glad to see you back.'

He relieved his wife of a dressing-case and an overnight bag and trotted beside them into the comparative coolness of the Airport building:

'Who are you stayin' with? Oh, Em. Hmm. Isn't here, is she? Can't understand it! Bad business. Just shows that it doesn't do to get too complacent. Who's meetin' you?'

'I don't know,' confessed Victoria uncertainly.

'Oh well, they're sure to send someone. We'll keep an eye on you for the moment. Hi! Pet——!' He plunged off in pursuit of his wife who had departed to greet a friend.

Left alone Victoria looked about her a little desperately, searching for a familiar face, until her attention was arrested by a man who had just entered the hall and was standing scanning the newly arrived passengers as though he were looking for someone.

He was a tall, slim, sunburnt man in the early thirties, who carried his inches with a peculiar lounging grace that somehow suggested the popular conception of a cowboy. An effect that was heightened by the fact that he, like Oswin Brocas-Gill, wore a belt that supported a revolver. But there the cowboy resemblance ended, for the cut of the carelessly careful coat, in contrast to Oswin's crumpled attire, spoke almost offensively of Savile Row, while his shoes were undoubtedly handmade – though not in Kenya.

It was not, however, his personal appearance that had caught Victoria's attention, but the fact that he was now observing her with interest and a distinct suggestion of distaste. Men were apt to look at Victoria with interest. They had been doing so in increasing numbers since somewhere around her sixteenth birthday, so there was nothing new in that. What was new was the distaste. No man had ever previously regarded her with the coldly critical lack of approval that was in the blue gaze of the gentleman by the doorway, and Victoria involuntarily glanced down to assure herself that she was not showing six inches of petticoat or wearing odd stockings. She was engaged in this apprehensive survey when he crossed the hall and spoke to her:

'Are you Miss Caryll?'

It was an agreeable voice – or would have been agreeable if it had not been for her conviction that for some reason its owner disapproved of her.

'Y-yes,' said Victoria, disconcerted by that disapproval and annoyed to find herself stammering.

The man reached out and calmly possessed himself of the small suitcase she held. 'My name's Stratton. Lady Emily asked me to meet you. You'd better give me your passport and entry permit and all the rest of it, and I'll get someone to deal with it. Got any money on you?'

'A little,' said Victoria.

'You'll have to get it changed into local currency.'

He held out his hand and Victoria found herself meekly surrendering her bag.

'Stay here. You'd better sit on that sofa,' said Mr Stratton, and left her.

Victoria took his advice and sat staring after his retreating back with a mixture of indignation and relief. She could not imagine why Aunt Emily should have sent this disapproving stranger to meet her, but at least it was not Eden.

She had not realized that she could feel like this. So shaken and unsure of herself and so afraid of being hurt. Well, it was entirely her own fault. She had refused to face facts while there was still time, and now it was too late. She leaned back on the sofa and rested her head against the wall behind it, unaware that she was looking exceedingly pale and shaken.

A stout figure bore down upon her, exuding an overpowering wave of expensive scent, and Mrs Brocas-Gill was with her once more, breathing heavily as though she had been running.

'Ah, I see you've heard,' said Mrs Brocas-Gill, panting a little. 'What an appalling reception for you. *Too* dreadful!'

Victoria struggled to her feet, endeavouring to collect her scattered thoughts, and said: 'Aunt Emily's sent someone to meet me. A Mr Stratton.'

'Oh, Drew,' said Mrs Brocas-Gill. 'I wonder she didn't send Gilly Markham. He's her manager, you know. I was telling you about him. I should have thought he was the obvious person to – but then I don't suppose any of the *Flamingo* people could get away today. Too ghastly for you, my dear. Oh, there you are Oswin. Isn't it *too* dreadful?'

'Yes, yes, yes!' said Mr Brocas-Gill, thrusting passports and permits into his wife's hands. 'Don't let's go over all that again. Hullo, Drew. What are you doing here? Oh, you're collecting Jack's girl, are you? Splendid. Splendid! Was going to keep an eye on her myself until someone turned up. Knew Em wouldn't be here, of course. You'll be all right with Drew, m'dear. We shall be seeing you. Come *on*, Pet! Damned if I'm going to hang around here all day!'

He seized his wife's arm and hurried her away, and Mr Stratton piloted Victoria into the customs shed and said: 'Here's the rest of your luggage. Have you got the keys? You may have to open them.'

Five minutes later she was out in the bright sunlight again and being driven away from the Airport through an area of ugly slums and unattractive bazaars.

There was nothing in these mean, crowded streets that was in any way familiar to Victoria, or that struck any chord of memory. And as they left the town behind, and eucalyptus trees and vivid masses of bougainvillaea replaced the squalid huts and shop fronts, she caught glimpses between the green trees of neat, white, red-roofed houses – primly British and more suggestive of Welwyn Garden City than Darkest Africa – that could not have been here when she had last driven through Nairobi over sixteen years ago.

Mr Stratton spoke at last, breaking a silence that had lasted since they left the Airport:

'I take it that you didn't get your Aunt's cable? She was afraid you might not. That's why she asked me to call in at the Airport, in case you were on the plane.'

'In *case* I was? I don't understand. What cable?'

'I gather she sent one care of your bank, as she thought you might be spending the last few days with friends.'

'I was,' admitted Victoria, bewildered. 'But why did she cable? Didn't she want me to come?'

'Well, hardly, at a time like this. After all, it's a fairly nasty mess to land you into.'

'What mess?' demanded Victoria. 'Is Aunt Em ill?'

Mr Stratton's head came round with a jerk and the car swerved on the road as though his hands had twitched at the wheel. He said incredulously: 'Do you mean to say you don't know? But surely the Brocas-Gills— Look, wasn't it in the home papers?'

'Wasn't what in the home papers?' Victoria's eyes were wide with apprehension. 'Aunt Em ... *Eden*! He isn't——'

'No,' said Mr Stratton shortly. 'He's all right. It's his wife. She was murdered three days ago. I'm sorry. I thought you'd know. It was on the B.B.C., and it must have been in the home papers.'

'No,' said Victoria unsteadily. 'I mean – I didn't listen to the news. There was so much to do. And I – I missed the papers. How did it happen? Tell me about it, please. I'd rather hear now. Before I meet ... Aunt Emily.'

She had hesitated for a moment before speaking her aunt's name, as though she might have intended to use another one, and Mr Stratton, who was at no time unobservant, did not miss it. He turned his head and looked at her, and there was once again, and unmistakably, dislike in the hard line of his mouth and the cold glance of his normally bland blue eyes.

He looked away again and said curtly: 'Alice – Mrs DeBrett – was murdered in the garden of your aunt's house. Someone killed her with a panga – a heavy knife that the Africans use for chopping wood and cutting grass. Your aunt found her. It can't have been a pleasant sight, and though she's bearing up pretty well she was in no state to drive over a hundred miles into Nairobi and back in order to meet you. And neither was Eden. What with the shock, and the police and press swarming all over the place, they've both had a pretty bad time of it. And in any case the funeral's this morning.'

Victoria did not speak, and presently he glanced at her again and suffered a momentary pang of compunction at the sight of her white face. She looked a good deal younger than he had expected her to be, yet she must be at least twenty-four if she had been engaged to Eden DeBrett before he had married Alice. Quite old enough to appreciate the feelings of his wife, who could hardly be expected to welcome the idea of her husband's ex-fiancée as a permanent fixture in the home.

Drew had liked Alice, and he had been sorry for her. And remembering her haggard, defenceless face and haunted eyes, he took a poor view of Miss Caryll, whose arrival seemed to him vulgar and tactless, if not intentionally cruel.

Victoria spoke at last, and in a voice that was barely audible above the hum of the engine:

'I thought it was all over. The Emergency, I mean. Mrs Brocas-Gill said it was. But if the Mau Mau are still murdering people——'

'I see no reason to suppose that it was a Mau Mau killing,' said Drew shortly. 'It merely makes a better headline in the press that way.'

'Then who——?'

'God knows! A maniac. Or someone with a fancied grievance. You never can tell what goes on in an African's head. And there have apparently been a lot of odd and unpleasant happenings at *Flamingo* lately.'

'I knew there was something wrong,' said Victoria in a whisper, and once again Drew's head turned sharply.

'Why do you say that?'

'It – it was Aunt Em's letter. She wrote and asked me if I would come out. She said she was getting too old to do without someone to help her, and that Eden wasn't – and she would rather have someone who belonged, than a stranger. My mother was her only sister you see, and they were fond of each other. But there was something in the way she wrote. As if she had something on her mind that was – Oh, I don't know – But it was an odd letter. A rather frightening one.'

'Frightening in what way?'

'Well – perhaps not frightening. Uncomfortable. She sounded as though she really did need me. Badly. And she'd always been very good to me. My father didn't leave much money, and I know Aunt Em helped with the school bills. So I came.'

'Was that your only reason?'

'No,' said Victoria. She looked up at the blue sky and the blaze of sunlight, and thought of the London rain and fog, and of her longing to live once more under that hot sun and that wide sky. Her lovely mouth curved in the ghost of a smile, and she said softly: 'No. There were other reasons.'

'So I inferred,' said Mr Stratton unpleasantly.

Victoria turned to look at him in surprise, puzzled by his evident hostility, and after a moment or two she said a little diffidently: 'What did you mean about odd and unpleasant things happening at *Flamingo*? What sort of things?'

'Some person or persons unknown has been smashing up your aunt's possessions in a manner usually associated with poltergeists – or ham-handed housemaids.'

'A p-poltergeist! You can't believe that!'

'I don't. I'll start believing in evil spirits only when someone has eliminated all possibility of the evil human element; and not before! Your aunt must have been mad not to send for the police at once, but she's been fighting a rear-guard action with the authorities over her Kikuyu servants for the last five years, and I suppose she wasn't going to give Greg or the D.C. a chance of having them all up and grilling them again, and jailing a handful under suspicion. Trouble is, she's an obstinate old lady, and once she decides on a course of action she sticks to it. She says now that she realized it must be the work of one of her house servants, but that whoever it was must be acting under orders – or threats.'

'But why? Why should anyone do that?'

Mr Stratton shrugged. 'A Mau Mau gang attacked *Flamingo* during the Emergency, and your aunt stood them off and killed several. One of the dead men was rumoured to be a relative of the man who calls himself "General Africa" and who is still at large; so it's just on the cards that this is a private vendetta on the part of the "General". He was always one of the more cunning of the Mau Mau leaders, and there has been a story in circulation for several years that he was and still is employed on one of the farms in the Naivasha area.'

'You mean – you *can't* mean that someone, a settler, is deliberately hiding him?' said Victoria incredulously.

'Good lord, no! If it's true, you may be quite sure that his employer hasn't a clue as to his identity, and that he is using that as a cover. Playing the part of a faithful and probably dull-witted retainer by day, and organizing prison breaks and thefts of cattle, and planning bloody murder by night.'

572

'Surely that isn't possible!'

'Why not? There is no photograph of him in existence and he wears a mask. A square of red silk with holes burned in it for eyes, nose and mouth. None of the men who have turned informer have ever seen his face, so that it's quite possible that he might be going about openly and quite unsuspected. It's also possible that he may have planned this poltergeist business at *Flamingo* as a prelude to murder, and intimidated someone into carrying it out. From all accounts he is intelligent enough to work out a really subtle revenge.'

Victoria shivered despite the hot sunlight, and said: 'I don't see anything subtle about murdering someone with a panga!'

'It isn't the method,' said Drew impatiently. 'It's the murder itself, coming as the climax of a series of petty outrages. If Mrs DeBrett had been murdered out of a blue sky, so to speak, it would have been ghastly enough. But it wouldn't have had half the impact that this has had. Especially on a woman of Lady Emily's temperament. Em can take a straight left to the jaw and survive it, but there's a kind of creeping, cumulative beastliness about this business that makes it all the more frightening for her. A sort of softening-up process. Starting in a small way and getting progressively crueller. She thought it was only an attempt to scare her into selling up and getting out, but when her dog was poisoned she ought to have been warned. That was what Gilly Markham called a "sighting shot". It seems to have scared *him* all right! He's manager at *Flamingo*.'

They were passing through the Kikuyu Reserve, and the scenery was at last vaguely familiar to Victoria: terraced hillsides and clusters of neat round beehive huts; fields of maize and small white patches of pyrethrum; the spiky foliage of pineapples and the vivid green of vegetables and banana palms. Mile upon mile of native shambas, bright against the red-ochre clay, and interspersed with plantations of eucalyptus. But Victoria had no eyes for the scenery. Even the sunlight had ceased to feel warm and gay, and she felt cold and a little sick. '*A sighting shot . . .*'

She turned sharply to look at her companion, and spoke a little breathlessly: 'Is it the end? Or——'

She found that she could not finish the sentence, but Mr Stratton appeared to have no difficulty in translating her confused utterance. He said:

'I imagine it's that thought that is getting Em down. Ever since it started it's been a case of "What next?" Now I should say it's

573

"Who's next?" '

'*Eden!*' said Victoria in a whisper, unaware that she had spoken aloud.

Drew gave her a cold glance and said curtly: 'Why do you think that?'

'Who else would it be? Unless – unless it were Aunt Em herself.'

'Oh, I don't know,' said Drew with deliberate brutality. 'Anyone she liked – or who was useful to her. Or to *Flamingo*.'

'I don't believe it!' said Victoria suddenly and flatly. 'Things like that don't really happen. Not to real people.'

'They've happened this time,' said Drew dryly.

'Oh, I don't mean that Eden's wife hasn't been killed. That must be true. But the other things. There must be some quite ordinary explanation. After all, things get broken in everyone's houses. And the dog might have picked up poison that was meant for rats – or, something.'

'Have it your own way,' said Drew.

'But don't you think it could have been that?'

'No, I don't. I think someone was getting at your aunt. And very successfully, at that! This isn't merely a question of getting rid of a settler. Even the Mau Mau dupes didn't take long to drive up to the fact that if they killed one white settler another one – and not his Kikuyu servants! – would take over. If Em died tomorrow, and Eden the day after, another white settler would take over *Flamingo*.'

'I should,' said Victoria.

Drew's blond eyebrows twitched together in a sudden startled frown and he said slowly: 'Yes, I suppose so. I'd forgotten that you'd be the next-of-kin. Well, there you are, you see. That's why I don't believe that this poltergeist business was aimed at frightening a large landowner into doing a scuttle. In any case, anyone who knew the least thing about Em would know it wouldn't work; and whoever is at the back of this knows a great deal about her, and just how to hit her where it hurts most. Which is what makes me interested in this "General Africa" theory. The average African gets no pleasure out of just shooting an enemy. He prefers to kill him slowly, and watch him suffer.'

It can't be true! thought Victoria. And yet worse things had happened in this country; far worse things. And he was carrying a gun. He didn't look the sort of person who would carry a gun without a good reason for doing so. She said abruptly: 'What about the police? Surely they'll be able to find out who did it?'

'Smashed Em's bric-à-brac?' enquired Drew.

'No. Who killed Mrs DeBrett. People don't get away with murder!'

'You'd be surprised what they get away with in this country!' said Drew cynically.

'But didn't anyone hear anything? Surely she would have screamed?'

'I expect she did, poor girl. But as luck would have it your aunt was playing the piano, and so no one in the house would have heard her. I should never have left her.'

'You?' said Victoria. 'Were you there?'

'Yes,' said Drew bitterly. 'In fact I was the last person, bar the murderer, who saw her alive. I knew she never carried a gun, and it was getting dark; but it was only a short distance to the house and it seemed safe enough. I could even hear that damned piano! Oh well – what the hell's the use of making excuses for oneself now? It's done.'

He wrenched savagely at the wheel as they swerved to avoid a stray goat, and accelerated as though speed afforded him escape from his thoughts.

'But there must have been *some* clues,' persisted Victoria. 'Foot-marks – tracks – bloodstains. *Something!*'

'You've been reading detective stories,' remarked Drew satirically. 'Possibly in books the body is not moved and no one mucks up the ground, but it's apt to happen differently in real life. Your aunt wasn't thinking of clues when she found her grandson's wife dead in the garden. All she could think of was that she might possibly be alive, and she tried to carry her to the house. She almost managed it, too! But she had to fetch one of the house boys in the end, and by the time the D.C. and the doctor and Greg Gilbert and various other people arrived, the "scene of the crime" had been pretty well messed up.'

Victoria said: 'Didn't they find anything, then?'

'Yes. They found a blood-stained cushion, belonging to one of the verandah chairs, in the long grass about twenty feet or so from where Mrs DeBrett's body was found. It looked as though it had been thrown there. And they found some marks among the bushes that seemed to suggest that someone had been standing there for quite a time, presumably watching her. There's a track that runs through the bushes and that links up at least three of the lakeside estates. It's an unofficial short cut that the labour use, and that the Mau Mau undoubtedly used during the Emergency.'

'So it *was* a gang murder after all!' said Victoria with a catch of the breath.

'Perhaps,' said Drew. 'But not on that evidence. Whoever had been watching from the bushes had never left them. The ground just there is pretty dusty, and it was obvious that he had merely turned and gone back the way he came.'

5

The car had been singing down a long straight stretch of road when it brought up suddenly with a screech of tortured tyres, and an abruptness that jerked Victoria forward and narrowly missed bringing her head into violent contact with the windscreen.

'Sorry,' said Mr Stratton, 'but I believe that was a friend of mine.'

He put the gear lever into reverse and backed some fifty yards through a dust cloud of his own making, to draw up alongside a stationary car that stood jacked up on the grassy verge where an African driver wrestled with a recalcitrant tyre.

A tall European in shirtsleeves and wearing a green pork-pie hat jammed on the back of his head appeared from the other side of it, wiping dust and sweat off his face with a handkerchief, and came to lean his elbows on the window of Mr Stratton's car:

'I might have known it,' he remarked bitterly. 'My God, Drew, the next time you do that I'll have you up for dangerous driving and get you sixty days without the option if it's the last thing I do! Didn't you see me flagging you?'

'No,' admitted Mr Stratton, unabashed. 'My mind was on other things. Greg, you won't have met Miss Caryll. Miss Caryll, this is Mr Gilbert, our local S.P. – Superintendent of Police, Naivasha.'

Mr Gilbert reached across him and shook hands with Victoria. He was a long, lean man who except for the fact that his hair was streaked with grey at the temples did not appear to be much older than Mr Stratton. His square, pleasant face was less deeply sunburnt than Drew's, and he possessed a pair of sleepy grey eyes that were anything but a true guide to his character and capabilities.

'You must be Lady Emily's niece,' said Mr Gilbert. 'She told me you were coming out, but I understood that she'd sent a cable to stop you.'

'Yes, I know. I didn't get it. I——'

'Do you want a lift, Greg?' cut in Mr Stratton, brusquely interrupting the sentence.

The S.P. threw him a quick look of surprise. 'Are you in a hurry?' he enquired.

'Not particularly, but Miss Caryll could probably do with something to eat. Her plane was late. Where do you want to be dropped?'

'Same place as Miss Caryll. *Flamingo*.'

'Oh. Anything new cropped up?'

'Not much,' admitted the S.P. climbing into the back of the car. He called out a few instructions to his driver and sat back, urging Mr Stratton to abstain from doing more than fifty: 'My nerves are shot to pieces. I thought we'd finished with this sort of thing for the time being, and I find it pretty exhausting when it crops up again. Old James has gone straight in off the deep end. I've never known him to be in such a bad temper. He bit my head off this morning for making some innocuous remark about the weather.'

'Where was this?' asked Drew, re-starting the car.

'Up at the Lab. They'd been doing a test on that ruddy verandah cushion.'

'Any results?'

'Oh, Alice's of course. Or same blood group, anyway. It was unlikely to be anyone else's. But it was just as well to make sure. Odd, though.'

He tilted his hat over his nose, and closed his eyes. Victoria twisted round in her seat to face him, and as though he were aware of the movement he opened them again and said: 'I must apologize for talking shop, but I'm afraid you're in for a lot of this. In fact you couldn't have chosen a worse time to arrive, and I wish I could suggest that you turn right round and go back again; though I can see that it is hardly practicable.'

'I wouldn't go if it was,' said Victoria with decision.

'Why not?' enquired Drew shortly.

Victoria turned her head to look at him, aware for the first time that his antagonism was personal and not a mere matter of irritation or bad temper. She said coldly: 'I should have thought it was obvious. If my aunt needed someone to help her before, she must need it even more now.'

She met his gaze with a hostility that equalled his own, and then deliberately turned her shoulder to him and gave her attention to the view.

The road wound and dipped through hot sunlight and chequered shadows, and swinging to the right came out abruptly on to the crest of a huge escarpment. And there below them, spread out at their feet like a map drawn upon yellowed parchment, lay the Great Rift. A vast golden valley of sun-bleached grass, speckled by scrub and flat-topped thorn trees, and seamed with dry gullies; hemmed in to left and right by the two great barriers of the Kinangop and the Mau, and dominated by the rolling lava falls and cold, gaping crater of Longonot, standing sentinel at its gate.

Nothing has changed! thought Victoria. But she knew that was not true. The passing of a handful of years might have made little difference, superficially, to the Rift, but everything else had changed. And looking out over that stupendous view she was dismayed to find that her eyes were full of tears.

At the foot of the escarpment the road ceased to wind and twist. The forests of cedar and wild olive fell away, and the car touched ninety miles an hour and held it on the long straight ribbon of tarmac that the Italian prisoners-of-war had built in the war years, until at last they could see the shining levels of Lake Naivasha.

'Might I suggest,' said Mr Gilbert gently, breaking a silence that had lasted for some considerable time, 'that you slow down to sixty before you take the turn? I have no wish to provide Naivasha with two funerals within twenty-four hours, and neither am I in any hurry to meet the mourners.'

Drew removed his foot from the accelerator, and as the car slowed down and swung left-handed into an unmade side road that branched off the tarmac of the main Nairobi road to circle the lake, Victoria said huskily: 'When is it – the funeral?'

'Eleven o'clock. Didn't Drew tell you? That's why none of them could meet you. But they'll have got back by now. How long is it since you last saw your aunt?'

'Six years,' said Victoria.

'Then I'm afraid you'll notice quite a change in her. This business has hit her pretty badly. She always seemed to me like a bit of the Kenya landscape – eternal and indestructible. But now she's suddenly an old lady. It's like seeing a landmark crumble. Poor old Em!'

'I can't see why you have to bother her, today of all days,' said Mr Stratton disagreeably. 'You might at least spare them a further grilling on the day of the funeral. It's going to be bad enough for them to have to— Oh, well. It's none of my business.'

'None,' agreed Mr Gilbert equably. 'For which you can be devoutly grateful. Asking personal questions on this sort of occasion, and of people who are your friends, is not exactly a pleasant task, I assure you. But the fact that we now know for certain whose blood was

579

on the cushion opens up a new field of enquiry. It's an odd facet of the case, that cushion. What was it doing there, and why?'

Drew said: 'No one heard Alice screaming, and she must have screamed. I know that was probably because Em was playing the piano, but there might be another explanation.'

'You mean the cushion might have been used to smother her? I don't believe it. It would have been damned difficult to hold a cushion over the face of a struggling woman while hacking at her with a panga. Unless there were two people in it. But— No, somehow I don't think that it was that. I can't get it out of my head that that cushion ought to tell me something if I weren't too stupid to see it. It doesn't fit.'

'With what?' demanded Mr Stratton, swerving to avoid a pothole of unusually outrageous dimensions that added to the hazards of the dusty, unmetalled road.

'With any of the obvious theories. That cushion was removed from the verandah and carried to the spot where Alice was killed, and then thrown away into the long grass. Yet no one will admit to having touched it that day.'

Drew said: 'I suppose it hasn't occurred to you that Mrs DeBrett might have taken it down herself to sit on, and was merely carrying it back? Or is that a too simple solution for you and your sleuths to contemplate?'

'You should know the answer to that one,' said Mr Gilbert amiably. 'You were the last person to admit to seeing her alive. Was she carrying a brightly coloured cushion?'

'No,' said Drew, 'but——'

'But you think that despite the fact that the sun had set, and that it is apt to get a bit chilly around dusk, she went all the way back to the house in order to fetch one off the verandah? I doubt it! Yet someone took it out there, and I'd like to know why. If I did, I imagine we'd be a lot further on. But as it is, I don't know what to think, and all the things I do think of are decidedly unpleasant. I don't like anything about this case, and I wish to God I could wash my hands of it!'

'Why not hand it over to the C.I.D. squad from Nakuru?'

'I've tried that one, but this time it won't work. They happen to have rather a lot on their plate just now, what with the Hansford case and that Goldfarb business, and James says I can dam' well handle it myself – even though half my personal friends are involved.'

580

'You mean *because* half your personal friends are involved,' said Mr Stratton dryly. 'You know us all very well. Too well!'

The S.P. made no reply; which might have meant anything – or nothing.

The cold shadow of a cloud drifted across the sunlit scene, draining the colour from the grass and the flat-topped thorn trees and lending the landscape a fleeting suggestion of aloofness and hostility, and Victoria shivered again and was suddenly afraid: afraid of the valley and of Africa, and of arriving at *Flamingo*, the house that was Eden's home and where Eden's wife had died a horrible death.

What have I let myself in for? thought Victoria in a panic. What does he mean? That someone in the house is a murderer? Eden's wife— She's dead now. He's free. I should never have come ...

The car ran out of the belt of shadow and past two tall Masai warriors, each carrying a serviceable spear; the red-gold of their lean, ochre-smeared bodies and elaborately plaited hair, and the clean-cut lines of their haughty aquiline features, reminiscent of ancient Egypt. Recognizing the car, they saluted gravely: a courteous salute tinged with gracious condescension, such as might have been accorded by the delegates of a powerful state to a member of a small and friendly nation.

'They don't change much either,' commented Mr Gilbert, following up a private train of thought. 'The Masai are the only ones who have looked at the things of the West and decided that they prefer their own ways, and have stuck to them. Who can say they are not right? The modern African youth with his European clothes and his inferiority complexes is not impressive, but it has never so much as crossed the minds of the Masai that they might be inferior to anyone.'

'Boot's on the other foot!' said Drew laconically, and Greg Gilbert laughed.

Victoria said: 'Father used to employ Mkamba. I can still remember most of them by name. They used to carry bows and arrows in those days – poisoned arrows, too!'

'They still do,' said Mr Gilbert with a grin. 'And that despite the fact that it is strictly against the law! I should say that at a conservative estimate several tons of arrow poison are manufactured yearly in this country. Talk about the "Secret Arrow Poison of the South American Indians!" – this has it licked into a cocked hat, for the simple reason that it's no secret. All you need is a saucepan, a box of matches and grandmother's recipe. The ingredients are growing all over the landscape, and——'

He broke off and hurriedly wound up the car windows as a black and grey sedan raced towards them and shot past, enveloping them in a choking cloud of dust.

'Ken Brandon,' said Drew briefly.

'Oh. How's he taken it?'

'On the chin,' said Drew.

'He's a spoilt brat. These conceited, mannerless young egoists bore me to distraction. Hector is pretty hot on the subject of motes in his neighbour's eye, but young Ken is the outstanding beam in his own.'

'You mean in Mabel's,' corrected Drew dryly. 'Ken is Mabel's sun, moon and stars, and always will be. She is devoted to Hector, but she'd probably have walked out on him if he'd laid a finger on her darling boy. She may be half Hector's size, and a dear, but she's quite capable of standing up to him.'

'I still don't think that excuses him,' grunted Mr Gilbert. 'Or his son! What Alice must have gone through with that boy is nobody's business!'

'It isn't ours, at any rate,' said Drew shortly.

'There,' corrected the S.P., 'you are wrong. It happens to be mine. Anyone or anything that had to do with Alice DeBrett is, at the moment, my business. And that,' he added gently, 'includes you.'

'Um,' said Mr Stratton thoughtfully, and refrained from further comment.

Five miles and eight minutes later a square, weather-beaten notice board bearing the single word *'Flamingo'* came in sight, and the car turned off the lake road on to a rough track that crossed a stretch of barren, rock-strewn ground bordered at the far side by a thick belt of trees and a glint of water. The wheels bumped in and out of deep dust-filled ruts and over and around boulders, roots and hummocks of parched grass, and leaving the hard sunlight, ran under the freckled shadows of pepper trees and giant acacias, to emerge on to a wide smooth sweep of ground before a long, rambling, thatch-roofed house whose bow windows and deep verandahs looked out on the glittering expanse of Lake Naivasha, blue and beautiful in the full blaze of the noonday.

What appeared at first sight to be half a dozen dogs of assorted shapes and sizes rushed out to greet them, barking vociferously, followed by two African houseboys wearing green robes and scarlet tarbooshes, who hurried out to remove suitcases and assist the travellers to alight. A door at the far end of the verandah opened, and an arresting figure walked towards them and stood waiting at the top of a shallow flight of stone steps. The Lady Emily DeBrett of *Flamingo*.

Em had worn a dark coat and skirt for the funeral, but she had discarded them immediately upon her return, and had changed back into the scarlet dungarees and vivid blouse that were her favoured wear. Her white closely cropped hair was adorned with a wide-brimmed hat of multi-coloured straw of the type that tourists buy in such places as Ceylon and Zanzibar, and there were diamonds in her ears and on her gnarled and capable hands and imposing bosom. She should have presented a grotesque appearance, but somehow she did not. She might, instead, have been the Queen of some barbaric kingdom. Hatshepsut of Egypt. Old Tzu-hsi, the Dowager Empress of China. Or Elizabeth the First, old and raddled and dying, but still indomitable: still royal.

Em had at no time been demonstrative, but she greeted Victoria with an unusual display of affection which contained, despite herself, a strong suggestion of relief.

'It's so good to see you, dear,' said Em, embracing her. 'And so good of you to come. I am sorry not to have been able to meet you at the Airport; but then Drew will have explained everything. We need not talk of that just now. How well you look. And how like your mother! You might be Helen all over again. Come along into the house. Drew will——'

She stopped as her gaze fell upon Greg Gilbert, and Victoria felt her stiffen. 'Greg! I didn't know you were here. Did you want to see me?'

'I'm afraid so,' said Mr Gilbert, leisurely mounting the verandah steps. 'I'm sorry about this, Em, but needs must. One or two things have cropped up. I won't keep you long. Eden here?'

'You are not,' announced Em with deliberation, 'going to worry Eden with any more questions today. And that is that! I like you, Greg, but there are some things I will not put up with, even from my friends. If you must worry the servants again, I suppose I can't stop you. But you can leave Eden alone. He can't tell you any more than he has already told you. None of us can!'

'I'm sorry, Em,' repeated Mr Gilbert quietly. 'I'm not doing this for choice.'

Lady Emily's bosom swelled alarmingly until the seams of her scarlet blouse appeared to be in imminent danger of parting. And then all at one she appeared to deflate, both physically and mentally. She stretched out a hand to him and spoke in a voice that was no longer measured and autocratic, but pleading:

'Greg, you can't! Not now. Not today. Surely it can wait?'

Mr Gilbert did not reply, and after a moment her hand dropped and she turned away and spoke to Victoria:

'Come dear, you will want to see your room. Drew, you will find drinks in the drawing-room. Help yourself. Greg had better stay to luncheon as he's here. He can ask his questions afterwards.'

The invitation could hardly have been less pressing, but Mr Gilbert said placidly: 'Thanks, I will,' and followed them into the house.

The room that was to be Victoria's was large and comfortable, with windows that looked out on to a wide strip of lawn, a blaze of bougainvillaea and a view of the lake. Em sat down on the edge of the big old-fashioned bed as though she were very tired, and said: 'I hope you will be comfortable here, dear. And happy.'

Victoria said warmly: 'Of course I shall be, Aunt Em! It's so lovely to be back in Kenya. I can't tell you how grateful I am to you for all your kindness.'

'I have not been kind,' said Em heavily. 'I have been selfish. But I needed someone to help me, and I did not want a stranger – some secretary who would spread gossip about *Flamingo* to half the Colony. I thought if I could only keep it to the family ...' Her voice trailed away, and she shivered.

Victoria came quickly across the room and put her arms about her aunt's sagging shoulders and hugged her. 'It wasn't selfish of you, darling. It was wonderful of you to want me. If only you knew how nice it is to feel wanted again!'

Em patted her hand absently and was silent for a moment or two, and then her fingers tightened suddenly about Victoria's wrist and she looked up into her niece's face with eyes that were bright and intent and full of anxiety. She said harshly, and as though she were forcing herself to speak: 'You must choose for yourself, Victoria. I did not – I was not honest with you when I wrote. I did not tell you everything. Perhaps I was afraid that you might not come. But you are Helen's child, and you must have your chance to decide whether you will go or stay. No! – don't interrupt! Let me say what I want, and then it will be your turn——

'I shall not blame you if you decide not to stay. Remember that. I sent you a cable to try and stop you, but it must have missed you.

I do not know how much Drew Stratton will have told you, but I suppose you know that Eden's wife was murdered. There is a rumour that the remnant of a Mau Mau gang are hiding out somewhere near here, but the police cannot be certain that it is they who are responsible, because – because there have been strange things happening in this house for some weeks past. Not very serious things, but – but worrying, of course. It has meant that all my servants are under suspicion, which is not very pleasant. So if you would prefer not to stay, I shall quite understand.'

Victoria said: 'But of course I'm going to stay, Aunt Em. If you'll let me. Or even if you won't. Just try to get rid of me!'

Em's fingers relaxed their hold, and she said approvingly: 'Good girl.' The emotion and the strain vanished from her face and she stood up briskly and said: 'Luncheon will be ready as soon as you are. You will find us in the drawing-room.'

The door closed behind her, and Victoria turned to stare thoughtfully at her own reflection in the looking glass: a slim, remarkably pretty girl in a leaf-green frock.

'Yes of course I'm going to stay!' said Victoria, speaking aloud in the silence. 'I belong in Kenya. And as for Eden, that's all over and done with – so don't let's have any more nonsense about it!'

She nodded severely at her reflected face, and went off to the bathroom to remove the dust of the lake road.

6

There were four people waiting in the large, casual, beautiful drawing-room: Em, Greg Gilbert, Drew Stratton and Eden.

Eden had been standing by the window talking to Drew when Victoria entered, and he had turned when he heard the door open, and stopped in the middle of a sentence, looking at her.

There was a brief moment of silence, and it was Eden who spoke first; his voice an echo from a day six years ago when he had spoken to a girl in a yellow dress who held an armful of roses. *'Vicky——!'*

Victoria closed the door behind her and said lightly: 'Hullo, Eden. I hope I haven't kept you waiting, Aunt Em?'

Luncheon was an uncomfortable meal, full of odd, abrupt silences and patches of forced conversation. No mention was made of the funeral or any of the happenings of the last three days, and it was not until coffee had been drunk in the drawing-room and Zacharia had removed the empty cups, that Mr Gilbert at last referred to the errand that had brought him to *Flamingo*.

'I'm sorry about this,' apologized Greg, 'but owing to one thing and another I'm afraid I shall have to ask a few more questions.'

'I thought every African on the estate had already been questioned *ad nauseam*,' said Eden bitterly. 'What more do you think you'll get out of them?'

'Not much,' admitted Greg equably. 'But then I'm not really interested in them at the moment. I merely want to know a few more things about last Tuesday. Your movements, for instance.'

'My *what*?' Eden's handsome face was suddenly white with anger and he said furiously: 'Are you by any chance suggesting that I might have murdered my own wife? Because if you are——'

'Don't be ridiculous, Eden!' Em's voice was sharp and commanding. 'Of course he doesn't mean any such thing! We all know how you feel, but I presume that Greg has got to ask this sort of question, so at least let us get it over quickly, and without losing our tempers.'

Greg said pacifically: 'No one is accusing you of anything. But if we can tie up everyone's movements on that day it will at least help to fill in the background. So let's start with yours.'

The colour came back to Eden's face and he thrust his hands into his pockets and turned away to stare blindly out of the window at the sunlit garden. He said: 'You already know exactly where I was and what I was doing that day. You've heard it all before.'

'Roughly, yes. "Exactly" – no.' Gilbert broke off and looked at Drew Stratton. 'Thinking of going anywhere, Drew?'

'Yes,' said Mr Stratton, preparing to leave. 'I can't see that I am serving any useful purpose by staying. See you later, Em, and thanks for the luncheon.'

Mr Gilbert said: 'Just sit down again, will you? I was coming to see you later, but if I can get what I want now it will save me a ten mile drive. You too, Miss Caryll.'

Em said haughtily: 'There is no question that you need ask my niece. She was not even here, and she knows nothing about this.'

'There is one question at least that I think she can answer,' said Greg quietly, 'and I would like her to stay.'

He turned back to Eden before Em could speak, and said: 'You went to Nairobi on Tuesday, didn't you?'

'Yes. To see Jimmy Druce about a Land-Rover he wants to sell. We had luncheon at Muthaiga. You can check up with him if you like.'

'We have. And you left here about ten o'clock. Can you by any chance remember if all the verandah cushions were present and correct when you left?'

'Of course I can't! I don't even know how many there are.'

'Four, I believe,' said Greg. 'And they are fairly striking.'

'I still wouldn't have noticed if there were three or six or a dozen! It's not the sort of thing that anyone would notice.'

'Except Zacharia,' said Mr Gilbert thoughtfully. 'He should have known, but he insists that he can't remember.'

'He's getting old,' said Em in extenuation.

'Ye—s. All the same, you'd think he'd notice a thing like that. It's part of his job. And anything in Harlequin checks and primary colours is apt to be eye-catching. Which makes it look as though they were all there. He would probably have noticed if there was one short.'

Em said: 'So you think that someone removed it off the verandah

587

sometime during the day, and you don't think it's likely to have been done by a stray terrorist from some hide-out in the *marula*.'

'Do you?' enquired Mr Gilbert.

'No,' said Em bleakly. 'No.'

She had been sitting regally erect in a large wing-back chair by the piano, but now she seemed to shrink and crumble and change before their eyes from a vigorous and commanding figure into a tired and anxious old woman. 'You are right, of course. It would have had to be someone from this house.'

'Or someone who could come openly to this house,' amended Mr Gilbert. 'And there is always, of course, the possibility that it was taken out for some entirely unimportant and trivial reason. So trivial that whoever did it has forgotten about it. Which is why, if we can work out where everyone was at every moment of that day, it may jolt someone's memory. What did you do after luncheon, Eden?'

Eden started slightly at the abruptness of the question, and said: 'Shopped in the town. Fetched a suit from the cleaners, collected a clock that had been taken in to be mended, bought a couple of shirts and took in a film to be developed. I think that was all.'

Mr Gilbert consulted a small notebook that he had removed from his coat pocket, and nodded as if satisfied. It was obvious that he had been doing quite a bit of checking on his own, and he made no attempt to conceal the fact. He said: 'Where did you have tea, and when?'

'I didn't. I skipped it.'

'When did you start back?'

'Oh – er – around about seven, I suppose. I'm not sure.'

Mr Gilbert said thoughtfully: 'The shops shut at five, and according to Jimmy Druce you left the Club just after two. Were you really shopping for three hours?'

Eden flushed angrily and said: 'No, of course I wasn't. As a matter of fact, I drove out to the Game Park.'

'When was that?'

'About four, I suppose. Might have been a little earlier. But you won't be able to check that, because I didn't get there. I remembered that the Park is infernally crowded these days, so I pulled up by the side of the road instead, and just sat there.'

'Why?'

'I had a few things I wanted to think about,' said Eden shortly.

'And none of them, Greg, if I may say so, are any of your dam' business!'

Mr Gilbert shrugged and consulted his notebook again. He said: 'Any idea as to how long you sat there? And did anyone you know pass you?'

'No. I wasn't paying attention to passing people, and I only pushed off at last because it was getting late. I'd told Alice I probably wouldn't be back until nine or ten, and I'd meant to dine in Nairobi or somewhere on the road. But I decided that I'd get back for a late meal here after all. I got back here about nine o'clock, and found——'

He did not finish the sentence, but turned once more to stare out of the window.

Mr Gilbert said briskly: 'Thanks very much. Now what about you, Em? First of all, have you remembered anything about that cushion? Moving it, or noticing that it was missing – or not missing?'

'No,' said Em doubtfully. 'I – I may have moved it. But I must admit that I don't remember doing so, and I don't think that there is anything I would have wanted it for. Perhaps Alice did.'

'When?' demanded Greg. 'Her day has been pretty well accounted for. She spent the morning shopping in Naivasha, the afternoon in her room, had tea with you on the verandah, and went out shooting with you immediately afterwards – in order to avoid, I gather, what looked like being an embarrassing *tête-à-tête* with young Ken Brandon. And as it was just after you got back that she went across to the Markhams with a message for Lisa, there doesn't seem to be any point during the day when she could have carried a cushion out to the knoll. Now, can you remember what you yourself did on Tuesday, Em? In detail?'

'I think so,' said Em, frowning. 'Let me see – I had breakfast in bed and didn't get up until just before Eden left. I asked him to fetch the clock and to ring up the Airport and check the time that Victoria would be arriving, and we discussed the purchase of Jimmy's Land-Rover. After Eden had gone I saw the cook and told Kamau what I wanted in the way of vegetables, and then Alice and I made out a list of things we wanted from the stores in Naivasha. As soon as she had gone I started on the milk records, and then Lisa came over to see Eden, but Zacharia told her he'd left. She said she wouldn't disturb me, and left a note asking if we'd give her a lift next time either of us went into Nairobi. I heard the dogs barking and went to see who it was, but she was already half-way across the garden by then, so I didn't stop her.'

Greg said: 'Do the dogs always bark when anyone comes to the house?'

'If they're around. But they stop at once if it's anyone they know.'

'What time was it when Lisa came over?'

'About twenty to eleven I should say: Alice had just left. Then at eleven Gilly came over on business and stayed for half an hour, and he'd only just gone when the Brandons dropped in. We had coffee, and Hector went off to see Kamau about some fodder we're selling him, while Mabel and I talked.'

'What about?'

The question was asked so casually that Em had started to answer it before she realized where it would lead her: 'She'd seen Alice's car in Naivasha and knew she wouldn't be here, and she wanted to see me alone because she was worried about——'

She stopped abruptly, her face flushing in the unbecoming and mottled manner of the old, while her lips folded into a tight hard line.

Eden gave a short and mirthless laugh, and finished the sentence for her. 'About Ken. You needn't worry, Gran darling. It's no secret. What did she want you to do. Ship Alice home, or slip some arsenic in her soup?'

'Eden!' Once again Em's voice was sharp and commanding, and this time it was edged with anger.

'I'm sorry,' said Eden impatiently. 'I quite see that under the present circumstances that was a bloody silly remark to make. But you must admit that Mabel's been making a complete cake of herself over her precious Ken. It wasn't Alice's fault that her kid had a hopeless crush on her. Heaven knows she did everything she could to choke him off! But it wasn't at all easy for her, what with Ken threatening suicide and generally behaving like an amateur actor getting his teeth into Hamlet. She ought to have let me deal with him.'

'She was quite right not to,' said Em tartly. 'She took the very sensible view that it was really only like measles or teething – something that everyone gets when young, though some children get it worse than others. He'd have got over it soon enough. But if you'd taken a hand and lectured him, we'd have had a first class Brandon–DeBrett feud on our hands, and we neither of us wanted

590

that. Hector and Mabel are good friends of mine, and good neigh-bours; but Ken is their Achilles heel.'

'Ken,' said Eden morosely, echoing sentiments recently expressed by Mr Gilbert, 'is a spoilt, egotistical pup who fancies himself as a cross between Byron and an Angry Young Man. For God's sake, what's he got to be crazy or mixed up about? He's only had to ask for something, to be given it!'

'Perhaps that's why,' said Em with a sigh. 'He's just finding out that now he is grown up there are a good many things he can't have for the asking, and he feels that someone is to blame for it. He'll grow out of it.'

'Returning to Mabel,' said Mr Gilbert firmly. 'How long did she stay on Tuesday morning, and could she have removed that cushion?'

'No, of course she didn't!' said Em with a snap. 'Why on earth should she?'

'That's not the point. The question was "could she?" Or was she with you the entire time?'

'Well, no,' said Em reluctantly. 'I— Well it was all rather stupid really. I suppose I wasn't very sympathetic, and Mabel was hurt. She said she'd wait in the garden until Hector was ready to leave, and I went back to the office. But if you think that Mabel had anything to do with Alice's murder, you must be going out of your mind! She was a bit upset about this infatuation of Ken's, but that was all. And of course she had nothing to do with that cushion. Unless——'

She paused, frowning, and Greg said: 'Unless what?'

'Well, I suppose she might have taken it up to the knoll and sat there to wait for Hector. I never thought of that. There you are – I expect that's all there is to it. A perfectly simple explanation.'

'Perfectly,' said Greg. 'But if so, why didn't she admit to it? We asked everyone about it the next day.'

'I expect she forgot,' said Em flatly.

'Perhaps. We can always try and jog her memory. What did you do for the rest of the day?'

'Nothing special. Alice got back around one, and after luncheon I rested, and as you already know we had tea on the verandah at half-past four. Ken arrived in the middle of it, so we had to offer him some. He said he wanted to discuss something with Alice, but I said he would have to postpone it as she was coming out in the

591

Land-Rover with me. I was rather afraid that he'd still be there when we got back, but he wasn't.'

'What time did you get back?'

'About a quarter to six. It was only then that I remembered Lisa's note, and Alice said she'd walk over and tell her that I'd be going into Nairobi on the Thursday to meet Victoria, and she could come in then. I shouldn't have let her go. But – how was I to know?'

Em's voice cracked and Eden crossed the space between them in two strides and put an arm about his grandmother's shoulders. 'Don't, Gran! It wasn't your fault. You've nothing to blame yourself for.'

Em said almost inaudibly: 'Yes I have. If I hadn't sent her over — Or if I had only——'

Eden released her and said harshly: 'If! – if, if, if! Why worry yourself over ifs? – If I hadn't married Alice she wouldn't have come to Kenya. And if she hadn't come to Kenya she wouldn't have been murdered. But does that mean that I am responsible for her death?'

He flung away and dropped into another chair, his legs stretched out before him and his hands deep in his pockets, and Mr Gilbert regarded him thoughtfully for a moment or two, and then turned his attention to Drew Stratton.

'Now about you, Drew. I'd like an account – a detailed account, please – of your last meeting with Mrs DeBrett.'

'I'll try,' said Drew, and embarked on a reasonably accurate account of that evening. 'She was,' he ended deliberately, 'very much upset at the prospect of Miss Caryll's arrival.'

Victoria shrank back in her chair as though he had struck her, while Eden flushed a dull red and Em said indignantly: 'That is not true! You are imagining things. I told her that if she would rather Victoria did not come she had only to say so.'

Drew said: 'Lady Emily, I did not know your granddaughter-in-law very well. But I knew her well enough to know that she would not allow her own feelings in the matter to stand in the way of your wishes; and I cannot imagine any normal woman feeling much enthusiasm for having an ex-fiancée of her husband's installed as a permanent fixture in the home.'

'Is that true?' demanded Mr Gilbert of Victoria. 'Were you two engaged?'

'I——' began Victoria, but got no further. Eden was on his feet again, his handsome face ugly with anger.

'No it is not! There was at one time what I believe is termed an "understanding" between us, but it was a purely private matter, and still is. So you needn't think that you're going to wash a lot of dirty linen in public and drag Victoria into this beastly business. You can keep her out of it!'

'My dear Eden, no one is trying to drag Miss Caryll into anything,' said Greg pacifically. 'But, unfortunately, the personal relationships of people who are involved, however inadvertently, in a murder case, are always a matter of interest.'

'Victoria is not "involved" in any of this!'

'Only indirectly.'

Em straightened herself in the wing-back chair, and once again it was an autocrat who sat there; imperious, regal and accustomed to being obeyed. She said: 'I think we had better get this quite straight, Greg. I am not a fool, and I dislike beating about the bush. It wastes time. What you are attempting to discover is whether Eden, or possibly myself, murdered Alice – *be quiet, Eden!* That is it, isn't it?'

'As a matter of fact,' said Mr Gilbert, 'and speaking solely for myself— No. But that is because you are both personal friends of mine and I know you fairly well. Speaking officially, however, it is not outside the bounds of possibility, and therefore it is just as well to consider that angle so that it can be abandoned. Helps clear the decks, if you know what I mean.'

'I know exactly what you mean,' said Em tartly. 'And you will allow me to tell you that I consider the suggestion an impertinence.'

'Impertinence my foot!' blazed Eden. 'It's a damned insult!'

Em said wearily: 'Oh, *do* be quiet Eden. To term it an insult is to take it seriously. I suppose that such a thing might just be possible, but it is in the highest degree improbable.'

Drew gave her an odd sideways look and said reprovingly: 'You ought to count up to ten before you make statements like that, Em. It was, I think, the late lamented Sherlock Holmes who announced that in any problem, if the impossible was eliminated, what remained, however improbable, was bound to be the answer. Or words to that effect.'

'If that is so, Greg had better arrest me at once!' retorted Em with spirit. 'Of course I *could* have done it! I was here, wasn't I? In fact I was the only person who *was* here. Eden was in Nairobi, and as far as I know no one else called at *Flamingo* that evening. However, I assure you that I did not do it. And now perhaps we can terminate this unpleasant interview. Unless of course there are any more questions that Greg wishes to ask?'

'A few,' said Greg placidly. 'These queer incidents in the house – the breakages. Can you remember exactly when they started?'

Em wrinkled her brow in thought and after a moment or two said slowly: 'Let me see – the first thing was the K'ang Hsi vase. We found it on the floor in bits when we came back from a luncheon party. And there was red ink all over the carpet.'

'The Langley's party,' said Eden. 'Eleventh of last month.'

Greg jotted down the date and said: 'When was the next time?'

'Only a few days later,' said Em. 'It must have been a Saturday, because that's the day I give out the *posho*, and I'd just finished doing it when Zacharia came to say that something else had been broken. Mother's Rockingham plates.'

'Fourteenth,' said Greg, who had been checking the dates in a pocket diary. 'I gather you had a good many incidents of this kind. Any sort of pattern?'

'No. After that it was almost every day. Then nothing for several days, and we thought it had stopped, and then it started again. It – it began to get on my nerves.'

Greg said: 'You ought to have reported it to the police at once.'

'I know that – now. But at the time I— Well, you know quite well why I didn't, Greg! I won't have my servants taken away and held for questioning or jailed on suspicion. They couldn't all have been in it, and why should the rest suffer because one man had got some queer, twisted African idea into his head, and imagined himself to be paying off a grudge? I thought it would work itself out. If I'd realized——'

Em's voice failed, and Greg said: 'When did you decide to send for Miss Caryll? Before all this started? Or afterwards?'

'Afterwards. I think – I think on the day the record of the concerto was broken. That – upset me. I found that I couldn't concentrate any more on the things I usually did myself. And Alice was frightened. I felt I must have someone to help me, and I thought of Victoria.'

Greg turned an enquiring look on Victoria and she answered the

594

unspoken question. 'Aunt Em's letter arrived about three weeks ago. It gave me just time to have all the inoculations and things done, and that was all.'

Mr Gilbert nodded absently and turned back to Lady Emily. 'Just one more question. After your dog was poisoned, were there any more acts of vandalism in the house?'

'No.' Em's voice was a hoarse whisper, and Eden spoke harshly, his back still to the room: 'Gilly was right: that was one step further and we ought to have realized it. It started with something quite trivial, and finished with – Alice.'

'If it has finished,' said Greg soberly.

Eden spun round. 'Why do you say that?'

Greg shrugged his shoulders and said: 'It has been fairly conclusively proved that someone who kills once, and gets away with it, will kill again. Either to cover the first killing, or because the snuffing out of a human life is like taking to drugs. Terrifying, but stimulating. That's why the initiation rites of any secret society of the Mau Mau description include a murder. Because it's only the first killing that is difficult. After that it becomes progressively easier and breeds a callousness towards human life and a frightening megalomania. There's no reason to suppose that your wife's death will put a stop to whatever ugly business has been going on here, and that is why we have got to find the murderer if we have to screen every African – and every European! – in the Rift. Which reminds me, Em, did the Brandons bring a driver with them when they came over here on Tuesday morning?'

'Yes. But Samuel has been with them for over twenty years. He would never——'

She was not allowed to finish. 'Why is it,' demanded Mr Gilbert bitterly, 'that none of you, in spite of all you have been through, can be brought to believe that a faithful servant can also be someone who has taken a binding oath to rid the country of all whites?'

He slammed his notebook shut, returned it to his pocket, and rose with a sigh. 'Well I think that's about all for the moment, though I'm afraid we're going to have to interview all your servants and the labour again tomorrow, Em. But Bill Hennessy will be dealing with that. Be gentle with him, won't you? He tells me that ever since you took a stick to him when you caught him playing toreadors in the bull paddock at the ripe age of ten, he's been scared stiff of you.'

'I wish I could believe that,' said Em bleakly. 'But I don't suppose that there is any more truth in it than in your inference that we ourselves shall not be called upon to endure any more of these inquisitions.'

There was the faintest possible suggestion of appeal in her voice, but Mr Gilbert disregarded it. He said: 'Until we find out who killed Mrs DeBrett, I'm afraid we shall have to go on asking questions. And I cannot believe that any of you would have it otherwise.'

He collected his hat, nodded amiably at them, and left.

7

Em leaned forward in her chair listening to the sound of his retreating footsteps, and a minute later, hearing a car start up and purr away down the dusty drive, she sighed gustily and relaxed.

'Thank heaven for that! I was afraid his driver would not have arrived and that he would fill in the next half-hour upsetting the servants. I am too old for this sort of thing.'

She turned to look at the French ormolu clock that stood on a lacquer cabinet at the far side of the room, and said: 'Four o'clock already! I suppose we had luncheon very late. Will you take tea with us, Drew?'

Mr Stratton declined the invitation, saying that he must get back, and Em heaved herself up out of her chair and accompanied him to the verandah, Victoria and Eden following.

There was someone on the path beyond the jacaranda trees, walking at a pace that suggested urgency, and Eden shaded his eyes with his hand and after a brief inspection announced with a trace of annoyance: 'It's Lisa. What do you suppose she wants?'

'You, I imagine,' said Em with some acerbity. 'Go and head her off, Eden. I don't want to see anyone else today. All I want is tea and peace!'

She turned to Drew with some query relating to a rumoured outbreak of swine fever on a neighbouring estate, and Eden went quickly down the verandah steps, and along the narrow path that led across the garden in the direction of the plumbago hedge and the manager's bungalow.

Victoria saw the woman break into a little run as he approached her, and reaching him, clutch at his coat sleeve. They were too far away for their voices to be audible above Em's plangent strictures on the inefficiency of quarantine precautions, but even from this distance it was possible to see from the woman's gestures and the very movement of her head that she was either excited or upset.

Victoria saw Eden throw a quick look over his shoulder in the direction of the house, and it seemed to her that his face was oddly colourless against the tree shadows. The woman tugged at his sleeve as though she were urging him to walk away with her, and Victoria caught the high-pitched urgency of her voice, pleading or arguing. Then suddenly Eden grasped her arm, and turning about came quickly back to the house, dragging her with him.

Em, immersed in farming shop, was not aware of them until they reached the foot of the verandah steps, and hearing the click of high heels on stone and the jingle of Mrs Markham's charm bracelets, she turned with a look of undisguised impatience.

'Well, Lisa? What is it?'

But it was Eden, and not Mrs Markham who replied. There was a white shade about his mouth and his voice was not quite steady:

'Lisa's got something to say that I think you should hear at once. She——'

Em threw up a hand in an imperious gesture and checked him. Her shrewd old eyes went from one face to the other, and then to the silent figures of Zacharia and a house-boy who were laying afternoon tea in a corner of the verandah. She said coldly: 'If it is important – and I take it that it is? – then we had better go back into the drawing-room. Goodbye, Drew. Thank you for collecting my niece. It was kind of you. I'll send Eden over tomorrow to look at those calves.'

She nodded at him and turned away, and Victoria said a little stiffly: 'Goodbye, Mr Stratton. Thank you for all your trouble.'

'It wasn't any trouble,' said Drew shortly. 'I happened to be in Nairobi and this was on my way back.'

He went away down the steps to his car, leaving Victoria, who possessed a healthy temper of her own, with an itching palm and an unmaidenly desire to box his ears.

Em was speaking peremptorily to her grandson:

'My dear Eden, if this is something that concerns us, it must also concern Victoria, since she is now one of the household. By the way, Lisa, you will not have met my niece, Miss Caryll. Victoria, this is Mrs Markham——'

Victoria shook hands and found herself looking into a pair of large violet eyes, expertly enhanced with pencil and mascara and as unmistakably hostile as Drew Stratton's had been. And then Em said: 'Lend me your arm, dear,' and led the way to the drawing-room with a firm step. But her weight pressed heavily upon Victoria's arm as though she really needed that support, and her bulky body was trembling with fatigue.

She lowered herself into the wing-chair once more, and Eden said:

'Look, Gran, Lisa didn't want to worry you with this, but it seems to me that it's something you should know. She says——'

His grandmother turned a quelling eye upon him and said firmly: 'Let her speak for herself, please. Well, Lisa?'

Lisa flumped down sulkily on to the window seat and rubbed resentfully at the marks that Eden's ungentle grip had left on her bare arm. 'I only thought that Eden ought to know, and then he could decide what to do about it. I wasn't going to tell anyone else. Not even Gilly! Though of course everyone's bound to know sooner or later, as Wambui's sure to tell someone else, and once the servants know it – well, you know how they can never keep anything to themselves.'

Em gave a short bark of laughter. 'How little you know this country, Lisa. They may not be able to keep a secret from their own people, but they can always keep it from us. Make no mistake about that! What is it that you have to tell me? If it is just some servant's gossip, you may be fairly sure that it is unimportant.'

'It wasn't gossip,' said Lisa angrily. 'It was serious.' There was a sudden flash of spite in her violet eyes: '*Very* serious! That's why I thought I ought to discuss it with Eden first. But if he prefers it this way, it's his own look out. It was Wambui, if you want to know. My *ndito*. She's been behaving very oddly the last day or two. Dropping things and forgetting things, and jumping as if she's been stung if anyone made a sudden noise. So this afternoon I tackled her about it, and it all came out. She's in a state about Kamau.'

'You mean *my* Kamau?' demanded Em.

'Yes. It seems he's been courting her, and they've been meeting every night in the bushes on the far side of the knoll.'

Em stiffened where she sat, and her expression was no longer one of bored patience. She said sharply and a little breathlessly: 'You mean they saw something? Is that it? They know who did it?'

Lisa shook her head. 'I don't know. You see Wambui couldn't get away on Tuesday evening, but it seems that Kamau waited for her for quite a time, and now he's hinting to her that he knows something about – Alice's murder.'

There was a sudden silence in the room, and in it Victoria heard a soft sound that was something like the click of a latch and seemed to come from the direction of the door that led out of the drawing-room into the hall. But the next moment her attention was distracted, for Em was speaking again:

'But the police questioned all the servants!' said Em. 'They've seen them half a dozen times already. Surely they would have told us if they'd got any information out of them? Why, Greg Gilbert has been here half the afternoon.'

'Wambui says Kamau told the police that he didn't know anything.'

Em made an angry, impatient gesture. 'Then I don't suppose he does. He's probably only showing off for Wambui's benefit.'

'But we know there was someone in the bushes that night,' insisted Eden. 'Why couldn't it have been Kamau? In fact why couldn't Kamau have been the poltergeist? – and the murderer, for that matter!'

'Don't talk nonsense, Eden,' said Em crossly. 'Kamau's father was one of your grandfather's first servants, and Zacharia is his uncle. He would no more harm me than – than Zacharia would! And you seem to forget that he was the one who killed Gitahi. If *that* isn't proof of loyalty, I'd like to know what is!'

'Oh, all right – all right. I know it's useless to try and persuade you that any of your darling Kukes might be anything but a hundred per cent loyal. But what about the man in the bushes? It squares with that, you know. *Someone* was there!'

'If it was Kamau, it is proof that he was not Alice's murderer,' said Em stiff with anger. 'Whoever was there had not approached the body. You know that quite well.'

'Of course I do. But he could have seen something, couldn't he? He could be telling the truth there.'

'If you think that,' snapped Em, 'I suggest you ring up Greg Gilbert immediately and tell him exactly what Lisa has told us. Then the police can deal with it – and with Wambui!'

'But you can't do that,' gasped Lisa leaping to her feet, her eyes wide with dismay. 'They'd take her away and hold her for questioning. You know what they're like. She might not be back for days, and I simply can't manage without her. Oh, I wish I hadn't said anything! I wish I hadn't.'

Her eyes filled with tears and she sat down abruptly and began to search blindly and without success in the inadequate pockets of her linen suit.

'Here,' said Eden, handing over a handkerchief. He patted her shoulder awkwardly and said: 'Don't cry, Lee.' Lisa dabbed at her tears, and groping for his hand, clung to it, looking up at him with eyes that were openly and helplessly adoring.

Eden withdrew his hand with more speed than gallantry, and Em said dryly: 'You would have done better to come straight to me, would you not, Lisa. Although I am aware that as a confidante I am likely to prove less sympathetic than my grandson! However, you are right in one thing. Unless they resort to violence the police will get nothing out of Kamau. And I will not have my servants intimidated. I will talk to him myself. He can do the rounds with me this evening after dinner. That will be the best way. I often take one of the boys with me, so it will arouse no suspicion; and he will talk better in the dark. They always do. And now let us have some tea.'

Lisa could not stay, but Eden did not offer to see her home, and after lingering for a few moments she turned from him with a petulant toss of the head and walked away down the long garden path, and he came back to his chair, and subsiding into it, stared moodily into space while his tea grew cold. He made no attempt at conversation, and Victoria sat silent, covertly studying him.

The passing of the years had not detracted from his spectacular good looks, and although he looked older and thinner, and there were frown lines on his forehead and fine lines at the corners of his eyes that had come from screwing them up against strong sunlight, there was no denying the fact that in appearance at least he was, if anything, more attractive now than he had been six years ago.

It's not fair! thought Victoria resentfully. How can anyone tell what he is really like when they can't get beyond what he looks like? What do I know about Eden? What did I ever know? Am I still in love with him . . .?

Em too had been disinclined to talk, and now she pushed away her almost untasted cup and came to her feet with sudden decision, announcing that she for one did not intend to sit about all evening doing nothing, and that as they needed dog meat again she proposed to take out the Land-Rover and shoot a buck. Victoria and Eden had better come with her.

Eden said: 'You'll only tire yourself out, racketing round in the Land-Rover, Gran. Why don't you stay here and put your feet up for a change? I'll go. Victoria can come with me if she'd like to.'

Em shot a quick anxious look at her niece and said obstinately: 'I don't wish to put my feet up, thank you. I wish to get out of this house and into the fresh air.'

'What you mean,' said Eden, 'is that you're feeling upset. And whenever that happens you work it off by going out and driving round the countryside far too fast. Shooting for dog meat is just an excuse, and you know it.'

'It's nothing of the sort,' snapped Em. 'You know quite well that they get through a buck in about four days – what is left of it after the servants have had the best cuts. And fresh meat doesn't keep in this weather.'

She stumped off down the verandah and Eden turned to Victoria with a rueful grin. 'You'll have to make allowance for us, Vicky. We're all rather badly shaken up by this. It's a pity you had to arrive just now and get involved in it all. I wish I could have kept you out of it.'

Victoria said soberly: 'Eden, I haven't had time to tell you before how sorry I am about – your wife. But——'

'That's all right,' said Eden hastily. 'You don't have to say anything. Listen, Vicky——' He hesitated, flushed, and then said abruptly: 'I suppose this is quite the wrong time to mention it, but I know you must think I behaved pretty brutally to you in the past. I did, of course. There were reasons why— Oh well, there's no point in going into them now. But what I wanted to say is that I'm damned glad that you're here. I had no right to expect that you'd come, but we need a bit of sanity in this place. And you're right about Gran needing you. She's cracking up, and if we don't watch out she'll end up by having a stroke or running off the rails. Try to see if you can't get her to ease up a bit – on the work, if nothing else.'

Victoria said: 'I'll do what I can. You know that.'

'Yes, of course. But it isn't going to be easy. As you can see, you've landed right into the middle of a really nasty situation. Gran *will* have it that everything is over now, and I wish I could believe it. But I didn't like what Greg said about "only the first killing being difficult". Supposing he was right, and that Alice wasn't the end, but the beginning? Look here, Vicky, if you feel that you'd rather not stay, you – you don't have to, you know. I could always arrange a return passage for you.'

Victoria said: 'Aunt Em said that too. Are you trying to frighten me, Eden? Or merely get rid of me?'

'Good Lord, no! From what I know of you, you don't frighten easily, and thank God for it! Believe me, it's going to be a nice change to have someone about the house who doesn't jump every time a door opens or a leaf drops! But I don't want you to feel that you have to stay. That's all.'

He put out a hand and touched the tip of her nose lightly with one finger. It was a familiar, caressing gesture that he had used so often in the past, and which had been peculiarly their own, and Victoria stepped back as swiftly as though it had been a blow, and turning from him went quickly away.

Em and Eden were both waiting for her in the Land-Rover when she reappeared ten minutes later, and they had driven out on to the ranges, where Em had shot a kongoni and a Thomson's gazelle.

It had been dark by the time they returned, and Em had pronounced herself too tired to change for dinner that night, so they had dined as they were, in the candle-lit dining-room where portraits of dead and gone DeBretts and Beaumartins looked down from the walls. But afterwards, as Zacharia was leaving the drawing-room carrying the coffee tray, Em spoke briefly to him in Swahili.

Victoria did not understand what she said, but Eden turned sharply: 'Kamau? You aren't *really* going to see him tonight? You're far too done up! For goodness sake, Gran, leave it for the morning! He won't run away.'

'How do I know that?' enquired Em morosely, moving towards the door. 'Of course I'm going to see him. Besides, Zach says he told him after tea that he was to go round with me tonight, so he will be waiting. I said he was to bring a lamp and meet me at the gate into the shamba, as I wanted to make sure that the hippos haven't broken the wire again. It is too good an opportunity to miss: I have been told things after dark that I would never have heard by day, and I know these people better than you do – even though I'm not Kenya born!'

'For Pete's sake, Gran!' said Eden, exasperated. 'You're surely not going to do the rounds tonight?'

'Why not? I've never missed it yet.'

'But you're tired out! And anyway, it's not necessary any longer. Oh, you needn't remind me about what happened to Alice! Do you think I need reminding? But even Greg doesn't think that was anything more than an isolated attack, and if the Emergency is over – and we keep being told that it is – then what's the point of going round the place every night to see that the labour are all in and the place is properly locked up, and all the rest of this Commando nonsense? We can't keep it up for ever. Look here, I'll go instead. And what's more, I'll talk to Kamau for you.'

'No dear,' said Em gently but quite definitely. 'He wouldn't talk to you as he will to me.'

'Then I'm going with you. You know I've never liked you wandering around alone after dark, but you would do it. It's quite time it was stopped. Victoria——'

He turned towards her as though for support, and Em said crisply: 'Victoria has nothing to do with this, and it's quite time she went to bed. Don't be silly, Eden. You've never tried to stop me doing it before, and I can't imagine why you are doing it now.'

'I did try, but——'

'But your wife wouldn't let you go instead of me, and she wouldn't allow you to go with me because she was afraid of being alone in the house. I know, dear. But you must see that this is no time to relax our precautions. If you really want to take over doing the rounds we'll discuss the matter tomorrow, but if we want to get anything out of Kamau it's important that I see him alone. So don't let's have any more argument about it. Victoria dear, go to bed. You must be tired out. And you too, Eden! There's no need for you to wait up for me. Good night, dear.'

The door closed behind her with decision, and Eden took a hasty step forward as though he would have followed her, and then looked at Victoria and shrugged his shoulders.

'Now you see what I meant when I said you wouldn't find it an easy job – helping Gran! You'd better do what she told you and get off to bed. I expect you could do with a bit of sleep. Good night.'

He turned and went out by the verandah door, leaving Victoria alone in the silent drawing-room.

8

Despite the anxieties and disturbances of the previous day – or perhaps because of them – Victoria slept soundly and dreamlessly, and awakened feeling refreshed and invigorated and capable of coping with any and every one of the problems that life at *Flamingo* might offer.

Breakfast had been laid on the verandah, and Eden, wearing riding breeches and a thin tweed coat, was sitting on the verandah rail and drinking black coffee. He was looking tired and heavy-eyed and as though he had not had enough sleep during the past night – or for several nights.

He slid off the verandah rail and said: 'Hullo, Vicky. No need to ask how you slept. You look offensively well. I hope the dogs didn't worry you? They're apt to be a bit noisy at intervals.'

'They did wake me a couple of times,' admitted Victoria, seating herself at the table, 'but I was too sleepy to bother. What was all the noise about?'

'Nothing. Or anything! Trouble is, they usually run loose about the grounds at night, but the Markhams' spaniel is on heat, and Lisa asked us if we'd keep 'em locked up for the duration, as apparently they sit under her window and serenade her all night. So they've been shut up in one of the spare godowns, and they hate it. Have some coffee. Gran's having her breakfast in bed. She said to tell you she'd like to see you as soon as you're through with yours. I should take your time if I were you. She's not in the best of tempers.'

'Why? Nothing else has happened, has it? I mean – nothing else has been broken, or——?'

'No, nothing like that. It's just that Kamau never turned up last night, and she hung about waiting for him and got chilled to the bone, and lost her temper into the bargain. She doesn't like being kept waiting and she doesn't take kindly to having her orders disobeyed. He probably had an assignation with his girlfriend. Or else he's lost his nerve and gone A.W.O.L. for a few days! Gran's livid, and I can clearly see that this is going to be one of those days when nothing goes right.'

Zacharia appeared with a dish of buttered eggs and bacon, and Victoria helped herself and enquired if Eden was going out riding.

'I've been,' said Eden briefly. He rejected the eggs with every appearance of loathing, and pouring out a second cup of black coffee, returned to his seat on the verandah rail. 'When you've finished I'll take you along to Gran's room. With any luck she may have simmered down a bit, and it mightn't be a bad idea if we ganged up on her and tried to see if we couldn't persuade her to spend the day in bed.'

But neither hope was to be realized. Em was already up, and in an exceedingly bad temper. They found her seated in front of her dressing-table, wearing a pair of grey corduroy trousers topped by what appeared to be a fisherman's jersey in a painful shade of orange.

'Oh, it's you,' said Em without turning, addressing their reflections in the glass. 'Good morning, Victoria. I trust you had a good night – it's more than I had!'

She turned to speak in trenchant Swahili to Zacharia, who was peering into one of the cupboards, and added crossly: 'He's getting too old for the work. That's what it is. I shall have to pension him off.'

'What's he been doing now?' enquired Eden perfunctorily.

'Lost a pair of my red dungarees. And as one pair hasn't been ironed yet and another is in the wash, and the pair I wore yesterday are filthy, I'm reduced to wearing a pair of your father's old corduroys. Sheer carelessness. Oh, do stop rootling round in that cupboard, Zach! If they weren't there five minutes ago they aren't there now. Here, take these ones away and get them washed at once. You'd better boil them. And see that they're dried and ironed by this evening.'

She reached down and picked up the discarded dungarees and blouse that she had worn on the previous day, and making a bundle of them, flung them at the old Kikuyu who caught them deftly and carried them away.

Eden put a coaxing arm around his grandmother's shoulders and said: 'Snap out of it, Gran. You can't tear a strip off everyone in the house on Victoria's first day here. It'll give her a wrong impression. Don't be cross, darling. It's bad for the blood pressure.'

606

'I'm not cross. I'm furious! Zach thinks that Kamau went off to meet that *ndito* of Lisa's last night instead of waiting for me. If he did, then of course she would have told him that she'd talked to Lisa, and naturally he wasn't going to face me after that. Just wait until I get my hands on him, that's all! I gather he's gone to help cut lucerne in the east field this morning; thinks he can keep out of my way, I suppose. I've told Zach I wish to see him the moment he gets back.'

Em pinned on a diamond brooch and catching sight of Victoria in the looking glass, turned about to study her approvingly.

'How nice you look, dear. I'd forgotten that you were so pretty. Have you had some breakfast? Good. Well now I'm going to show you the office and give you some idea of what there is to do, and then we'll do a tour of the house and the gardens, and after luncheon——'

'After luncheon,' cut in Eden firmly, 'I am taking her out in the launch. Unless you propose to keep her nose to the grindstone from the word "Go"?'

'No, of course not. I want her to enjoy herself. Certainly take her out on the lake. She will like that. And we must arrange a few expeditions – picnic parties, so that she can see something of the Rift. I see no reason why we should mope indoors. Let me see – you are going to take a look at the new bore hole this morning, aren't you? Then we shall see you at luncheon. Come along, dear.'

She swept Victoria out, and the remainder of the morning was devoted to the programme she had outlined. Eden had been delayed, so luncheon was late, and young Mr Hennessy of the police, accompanied by two police askaris, arrived halfway through the meal, and was kept waiting. 'It will do him no harm to cool his heels on the verandah,' observed Em tartly; and she had lingered over the coffee until the hands of the grandfather clock pointed at twenty minutes to three, before going out to see him.

'I wouldn't be in Bill Hennessy's shoes this afternoon for all the coffee in Brazil!' said Eden, taking Victoria's arm and hurrying her down a path that wound between a colourful wilderness of plumbago and wild lupins towards the lake. 'She can't forget that she knew him when he was a sticky little schoolboy, and to have him questioning her servants in the name of the Law is adding insult to injury. Look out for those thorns.'

He opened the gate into the shamba and ushered Victoria into a lush, green wilderness where the warm air was heavy with the scent of

607

orange blossom and drowsy with the hum of bees, and the damp ground squelched under her sandalled feet.

'I suppose that's the trouble with Gran,' continued Eden. 'When you get to her age there's hardly anyone left whom you didn't know when they were children. Makes it difficult to take them seriously. She must feel like a governess in a schoolroom full of irresponsible brats. All the same, I get a bit tired of being treated as if I were still in the Lower Fourth. If Gran would only realize that I was now an adult she'd put me in as manager in place of that waster, Gilly. Damn it all, I may as well learn how to run it, considering that I shall own the place one day. That is, unless Gran cuts me out of her will and leaves it to you instead.'

'To *me*?' exclaimed Victoria, startled. 'What nonsense! Why should she do any such thing?'

Eden shrugged his shoulders and preceded her through another gate into a shadowy forest of banana palms. 'Ask me another. Why does Gran do anything? Because she wants to. Besides, she's a bit of a feminist, our Em. She may think you'd do more for *Flamingo* – and for Kenya – than I would. The female of the species being more deadly than the male – and all the rest of it.'

'Rubbish!' retorted Victoria. 'You know quite well that she adores you. She always has. She only snaps at you to try and disguise the fact; and fools nobody.'

Eden laughed. 'Perhaps. All the same, it's quite on the cards that she may have thought that I was taking my responsibilities as Heir to the Throne too lightly, and doesn't think it will do me any harm to realize that if I don't watch my step she can nominate another candidate. She's a Machiavellian old darling.'

'But *you* don't think that?' said Victoria, troubled. 'I mean, even supposing she did – and she wouldn't! – you don't think that I'd do you out of *Flamingo*, do you?'

Eden stopped, and turned to smile down at her, and her heart did a foolish check and leap. He said: 'Wouldn't you, darling? I wonder. You might think that it would serve me right.'

A tide of colour rose to the roots of Victoria's brown hair and she said confusedly: 'Don't be silly, Eden! I never thought – I mean – Well, we made a mistake. That was all. But we're still friends.'

'Are we?' asked Eden soberly. 'Are we really, Vicky?'

'Of course,' said Victoria, making a determined grab at lightness. 'I'm like Aunt Em. I can't forget that we were allies against

Authority in the days when you were a beastly little boy with scratched knees and a dirty neck.'

But Eden refused to follow her lead. He said, unsmiling: 'Thank you, Vicky.' And reaching out he took her hand, and before she realized what he meant to do, he had lifted it and kissed it.

Victoria fought down a strong impulse to snatch it away and run, and an even stronger one to stroke his bent head with her free hand. Heroically resisting both, she said briskly: 'Do you think we could take some of these bananas on the boat with us? It's years since I picked one straight off the bunch.'

'They're not ripe,' said Eden a shade sulkily. He turned and walked on down the path, only to stop again a few minutes later with an impatient exclamation. 'Damn! The hippo have been in again. It's just ruddy idleness on Gilly's part; he won't see that the fences are properly made. What the hell's the use of a single strand of wire, even if you do run a mild electric current through it? It hasn't apparently even stopped the remnants of the Mau Mau gangs from keeping open an escape route round the lake!'

Victoria said: 'Do you think there's anything in it? Gangs hiding out in the *marula*, I mean?'

'No. Though I suppose it's just possible that the odd man who is still on the run spends a day or two there. There couldn't be a better hiding place, could there? Just look at it!'

He waved a hand in the general direction of the papyrus swamps that reared up like a solid grey-green wall between the shamba and the Lake. A weird, waving jungle, so dense that a man forcing his way through it, his ears filled by the noise of his own passage, might pass within a yard of another who stood still, and never know it. It stretched for miles along the lake shore, and during the Emergency the gangs had cut their own secret paths and built solidly constructed hides in it.

Years earlier Gerald DeBrett too had cut a wide pathway through the papyrus, and laid down a duckboard to the lake edge where he had built a wooden boat-house supported on piles and sheltered by the reeds. It was weather-beaten now, and ramshackle, but Em had kept the approach to it in tolerable repair, and it housed a small rowing boat, a battered punt and a neat white motor launch.

'We had to have a guard on this all through the Emergency,' said Eden, casting off and poling the launch down a narrow channel between shadowy walls of papyrus. 'Damned nuisance it was too.

Greg got pretty crisp about it. He wanted it pulled down and the boats holed or dragged up somewhere where they couldn't be used, to prevent the Mau Mau using them. But Gran wouldn't hear of it. She fixed up a roster of guards. Myself, Gus Abbott and half a dozen of the loyal Kikuyu. Even poor old Zach was pressed into service, but he was far more afraid of handling a gun – and of the hippo – than he was of being murdered. Kamau refused to take a gun at all. He pinned his faith to a panga; and got a chap with it, too! Caught him trying to cut a boat loose, and slashed at him in the dark. Cut his head clean off, and carried it triumphantly up to the house in the morning. Alice fainted all over the coffee cups, but Gran didn't turn a hair.'

Victoria said shuddering: 'You don't mean he actually *showed* it to them?'

'He certainly did. He was as pleased as Punch about it. And with reason! For it turned out be one of the top Mau Mau brass, "Brigadier"Gitahi, no less. There was a nice fat price on his head too, which was duly handed over to Kamau, with the result that the entire labour force of *Flamingo* were beautifully tight for at least a week afterwards. Now let's see if we can get this engine to start.'

The launch glided free of the papyrus and the floating weed beds, and they were in hot sunlight again, with the wide expanse of the lake spread out before them. Bright blue lilies spangled the water, and there was a continuous quack and ruffle of birds: stately white pelicans, numerous as swans on the Liffey; spoonbills, dab-chicks, cormorants, wild duck and herons.

A huge head adorned by two wildly agitated ears rose up on the port bow, regarded them with austere disapproval, and sank again. 'Too many hippo in the lake,' observed Eden, frowning. 'It's quite time we shot some. One or two make rather pleasant local colour, but twenty or thirty of them can do as much damage to the lakeside shambas as a plague of locusts. Look – there are some flamingo. They must be on their way to Elmenteita. They don't often come to Naivasha. Beautiful, aren't they?'

'Lovely!' said Victoria on a breath of rapture. 'You know, I used to think of all this, and wonder if it could possibly be as beautiful as I remembered it to be. But it is. Every bit as beautiful!'

'So in spite of everything,' said Eden, 'you're glad you came back?'

'What do you mean? "In spite of everything",' demanded Victoria defensively.

'Me – Alice – Gran rapidly going off her rocker. A resident polter-geist, and the police almost permanently on the premises,' said Eden bitterly.

'Oh, Eden, I'm sorry!' Victoria lifted a flushed and contrite face. 'I keep on forgetting about Alice. I'm a selfish pig!'

'No you're not, dear. You're refreshingly normal. And thank God for it! To tell you the truth, Vicky, I can't quite believe it myself, and when I'm away from the house it all seems like a nightmare that I shall wake up from. It's only when I get back to the house that – Oh, hell! Let's talk about something else, shall we?'

'Yes, *let's*!' said Victoria gratefully. 'Where are we going, by the way? And whose is that house up on the hill over there?'

'Drew Stratton's. Chap who collected you from the Airport yester-day.'

'Oh,' said Victoria in a repressive voice, and after a moment or two of silence enquired: 'Do you mean his house, or where we are going?'

'Both.'

'Oh,' said Victoria again, betraying a marked lack of enthusiasm.

Eden threw her an amused glance. 'You don't sound wildly enthusiastic. Didn't you take to our Mr Stratton?'

'He didn't take to me. In fact I rather think that he went out of his way to be rude. Is he a confirmed misogynist, or something?'

'Not that I know of. And as everyone in Kenya knows everyone else's innermost secrets, you can take it that he is neither.'

'Merely mannerless, I suppose,' said Victoria with some acidity.

'You have got your knife into him, haven't you?'

'I have never,' said Victoria with dignity, 'taken kindly to being disliked and disapproved of at sight and for no reason.'

Eden laughed. 'Don't tell me it's ever happened to you before, because I won't believe it! You must have got hold of the wrong end of the stick. Everyone likes Drew.'

'I can't think why, when he's obviously conceited and egotistical, as well as being boorish and entirely lacking in manners, and——'

'Here! Hi!' said Eden. 'Give the poor chap a chance! You can't knock our local hero-boy, you know. He's one of our leading citi-zens. In fact we point to him with pride.'

'Why?' demanded Victoria frostily. 'Because he lounges around with a gun on his hip and drives too fast, I suppose?'

'Then you suppose wrong. To start off with he's Kenya-born, and his grandparents were two of the real pioneers – like Delamere and Grogan and old Grandfather DeBrett – and in a young Colony that means something! He lost both his parents before he was twenty, and having copped a packet in the way of wounds and decorations during the Normandy landings, came back to find that his manager had let the place go to rack and ruin, and there was a load of debt instead of the fat profits that other farms had been making during the war years. A lot of men faced with that sort of mess would have sold up and got out, but Drew flatly refused to part with a single acre of his land. Said he knew he could pull it out of the red. And did. He must have lived on cattle food and *posho* for God knows how long, and he worked like ten men. And then just as things were really beginning to look up, the Mau Mau business broke ...'

Eden looked broodingly out across the lake and was silent for so long that at last Victoria said impatiently: 'Go on. What happened to him then?'

'Who? Oh Drew. Nothing much, if you mean to his place. The Strattons have always employed Masai, and Drew was practically brought up in a *manyatta*. He's blood-brother to every ochre-painted *moran* in the Colony, and so the Mau Mau gave him a wide berth. But he's one of the *"My country, 'tis of thee"*, brigade, and he handed over the management of the estate to old Ole Gachia, with instructions to keep it on an even keel, and offered his services to the Security Forces. He ended up by more or less running his own show, and used to go out with a pseudo gang, despite the fact that he's as blond as a chorus girl.'

'What's a "pseudo gang"?' asked Victoria, intrigued.

'Didn't you ever read your papers? They were the boys who pretended to be terrorists. Learnt all the jargon and dressed themselves up for the part – and blacked themselves all over, if they were British. They used to push off into the forests to make contact with the gangs. Drew had a hand-picked bunch of his own. Pukka devils, from all accounts. They pulled off some astonishing coups, and had a pleasant habit of cutting a notch in Drew's verandah rail for every kill. It made an impressive tally, and I am credibly informed that although the Emergency is officially a thing of the past, there is still an occasional new notch there. We'll take a look and see. Here we are. Stand by for the bump.'

He switched off the engine, and as the launch lost speed, manoeuvred it expertly alongside a small wooden jetty that thrust out into a narrow bay whose steep banks blazed with flamboyant and vivid cascades of bougainvillaea. A long flight of steps wound upwards from the jetty and passed between banks of roses and flowering shrubs, to come out on a gravel path which followed the curve of a stone wall buttressing a grassed terrace in front of a long, low, single-storeyed house whose wide verandah was shaded by flowering creepers.

Mr. Stratton might employ Masai on his estate, but his house servants were coast Arabs, and a dignified white-robed figure, whose face might have been carved from a polished chunk of obsidian, greeted the visitors, and informed them that the Bwana should be immediately notified of their arrival.

'What a heavenly view!' said Victoria, leaning on the verandah rail and looking out across a vast panorama of lake and tree-clad hills and far rolling grassland ringed by blue ranges that shimmered like mirages in the afternoon sun. Her eye fell on a long row of notches cut into the wood of the rail, and she drew back sharply, the pleasure on her face giving place to disgust.

'What did I tell you?' said Eden, following the direction of her gaze. 'Quite a nice line-up.'

'*Nice!* You call that nice? Why, it's appalling! And – and barbaric! Chalking up a record of dead men!'

'Of dead murderers,' corrected a dry voice behind her.

Victoria whirled round, her cheeks flushing scarlet. Mr Stratton, dressed in impeccable riding clothes, was standing in the doorway of a room that opened on to the verandah. He was looking perfectly amiable, and his bland gaze travelled thoughtfully from Miss Caryll to her cousin.

'Courtesy call, Eden?'

'Business, I'm afraid. Those Herefords of yours. Gran wants me to have a look at them before we clinch the deal.'

'Of course. She said something about it yesterday. They're in the paddock just behind the house. You'll find Kekinai out there. He'll tell you anything you want to know. I'll entertain Miss Caryll until you're through.'

Eden looked doubtfully at Victoria, and then all at once a malicious smile leapt to life in his eyes, and he said: 'Good idea. I won't be long.' And left them.

Victoria made a swift movement as though she would have followed him, but Mr Stratton, either by accident or design, had moved forward in the same moment and barred her way. 'Cigarette?' he enquired, proffering his case.

'Thank you; I don't smoke,' said Victoria curtly.

'You won't mind if I do? Tea will be along in a minute. Or would you rather have a cold drink? It's quite a pull up from the lake on a hot day.'

Victoria disregarded the offer and said, stammering a little: 'I'm sorry that you should have heard w-what I said. About the notches. I didn't mean to be r-rude.'

'There's no need to apologize for your views,' said Drew gravely.

'I'm not. Only for letting you hear them.'

'My feelings,' said Drew, 'are not so easily wounded. So you think I'm appalling and barbaric because I allow the boys to cut a tally of their kills on my verandah rail, do you? You are not the only one. There are uncounted thousands of soft-hearted and fluffy-minded – and abysmally ignorant – people who would agree with you.'

'Thank you,' said Victoria sweetly.

'Don't mention it. Unlike you, I meant to be rude. You see, Miss Caryll, I get a little bored by people who broadcast views on something that is, to them, only a problem on paper, and one which does not touch them, personally, in any way. We each have something that we love deeply and are prepared to fight for and die for, and kill for! and I wonder just how many of the virtuous prosers, if it was the agony of their own child or wife or lover, or the safety of their own snug little surburban home that was in question, would not fight in their defence?'

Victoria said: 'I didn't mean that. I meant this sort of thing – cutting notches. Making a game of killing.'

'It wasn't a game. It was deadly serious. The men we were after had deliberately bestialized themselves by acts and oaths and cere- monies that were so unspeakably filthy and abominable that the half of them have never been printed, or believed by the outside world. If any of us were caught – and a good many of us were – we knew just how slowly and unpleasantly we should die. You cannot conduct a campaign against a bestial horror like the Mau Mau with gloves on. Or you can! – if you have no objection to digging up a grave in the forest and finding that it contains the body of your best friend, who has been roasted alive over a slow fire after having certain parts of him removed for use in Mau Mau ceremonials.'

Neither Drew's face nor his pleasant voice had altered, but his bland blue eyes were suddenly as hard and blank and cold as pebbles, and Victoria was aware with a sense of shock that he was speaking of something that he himself had seen – and could still see.

She said hesitantly and inadequately: 'I – I'm sorry.'

The blankness left Drew's eyes and he tossed the end of his cigarette over the verandah rail and said: 'Come here; I want to show you something.'

He took her arm in an ungentle grasp, and turning her about, walked her over to the far end of the verandah and stopped before the upright post that supported the corner of the roof. There were notches on that too. Each one cut deep into the flat of the wood pillar.

'Those are our losses,' said Drew, and touched them lightly. 'That one was Sendayo. We used to play together when we were kids. His father worked for mine when they were both young men. That was Mtua. One of the best men we had. They cut his hands and feet off and pegged him out where the safari ants would get him. That one was Tony Sherraway. They burnt him alive. This one was Barugu. He was a Kikuyu whose entire family – parents, grandparents, wife and children – were murdered in the Lari massacre, where the Mau Mau set all the huts in the village on fire and clubbed and panga'd the people as they ran out. Barugu worked for us for a year before they got him, and what they did to him is not repeatable.'

He released Victoria's arm with an impatient gesture and said: 'Why go on? They won't mean anything to you. Or to anyone else. But cutting a tally of kills helped the morale of the others. They also got a bit of satisfaction out of chalking up that score, and out of knowing that if one of them went, he would be amply avenged.'

Drew turned away and stood looking out across the beauty that lay below and around him, his eyes narrowed against the sun glare, and presently he said: 'It's no good trying to treat Africans as though their processes of thought were the same as Europeans. That is the way of madness – and politicians!'

Victoria said doubtfully: 'But it *is* their country.'

'Whose?' demanded Drew, without turning his head.

'The – the Africans.'

'Which Africans? All this that you can see here, the Rift and most of what is known as the White Highlands, belonged, if it belonged to anyone, to the Masai. But it is the Kikuyu who claim the land, though they never owned a foot of it – and would have been speared if they'd set a foot on it! The place was a no-man's-land when Delamere first came here, and the fact that cattle and sheep can now be raised here is entirely due to him and men like him. And even they didn't just grab the land. The handful of Masai then inhabiting it voluntarily exchanged it for the enormous territory that tribe now holds.'

'But——' began Victoria, and was interrupted.

'All the chatter about "It belongs to them",' said Drew, 'makes me tired. Sixty years ago Americans were still fighting Red Indians and Mexicans and grabbing *their* land; but I've never heard anyone suggesting that they should get the hell out of it and give it back to the original owners. Our grandfathers found a howling wilderness that no one wanted, and which, at the time, no one objected to their taking possession of. And with blood, toil, tears and sweat they turned it into a flourishing concern. At which point a yelping chorus is raised, demanding, in the name of "Nationalism", that it be handed over to them. Well, if they are capable of running this on their own, or of turning a howling wilderness into a rich and prosperous concern, let 'em prove it! There's a hell of a lot of Africa. They can find a bit and start right in to show us. But that won't do for them. It's the fruit of somebody else's labour that they are after.'

He flung out a hand in the direction of the green lawns and gardens, the orchards, outhouses and paddocks: 'There was nothing and nobody here when my grandfather first saw this. This is the fruit of his labour – and of my parents', and my own. I was born here, and this is as much my home as Sendayo's. I want to stay here, and if that is immoral and indefensible Colonialism, then every American whose pioneer forebears went in a covered wagon to open up the West is tarred with the same brush; and when U.N.O. orders them out, we may consider moving!'

He turned to face Victoria and for the first time since she had met him, he smiled. It was a disquietingly attractive smile, and despite herself she felt a considerable portion of her hostility towards him waning.

He said: 'I apologize for treating you to a grossly over-simplified lecture on the Settlers' point of view. Very tedious for you. Here's the tea at last. Come and pour out.'

He kept up an idly amiable flow of small-talk until Eden returned, and after that the conversation took a strictly technical turn, and Victoria allowed her attention to wander.

'An over-simplified viewpoint.' Perhaps. Yet she could still remember her father telling her tales of her grandfather's early days in the great valley. The gruelling toil under the burning sun. The laborious digging of wells and the struggle to grow grass and crops

616

and to raise cattle. The first glorious signs of success – of the 'wilderness blossoming like a rose'. The years of drought when first the crops and then the cattle died, and ruin faced them – and was stared down and outfaced by men who refused to be beaten. The first roads. The first hospitals. The first railway. The first schools ... It could not have been easy, but the sweat and the toil and the despair and determination that it had cost had made it doubly dear, and Victoria found herself remembering a line from the theme song of *Oklahoma!* – that exhilarating musical about another pioneer state which barely a century ago had also belonged to 'painted savages'.

'We belong to the land, and the land we belong to is grand.'

She was aroused from her abstraction by Eden saying: 'Look, Drew, if you're driving over to see Gilly, why not come back in the launch with us, and let your driver take the car round to *Flamingo*? Then you can have a word with Gran about the deal. Just as well to get it settled.'

Mr Stratton, having agreed to the suggestion, went off to change out of his riding clothes, and Eden cocked an interrogatory eyebrow at Victoria and said: 'How did you get on with the detestable Drew? Sorry I had to leave you like that, but you wouldn't have enjoyed inspecting cows and calves, and I took it that you wouldn't actually come to blows! Do you mind having him as a passenger on the way home? I want him to have a word with Gran, and this seems a good way of seeing that he gets it.'

'Of course I don't mind. Why should I?' enquired Victoria loftily. 'I'm not so prejudiced that I can't sit in a boat with him. And in any case you will be far too busy discussing milk yields and foot-and-mouth for either of you to notice whether I am there or not.'

Eden laughed and reached out to pull her to her feet. 'Did we bore you? Forgive me, darling. I promise to keep off shop in future whenever you're around.'

Something in Victoria flinched at his casual use of an endearment that had once meant so much but which now came so easily and so meaninglessly to his tongue. She removed the hand that he still held, and said lightly: 'If I'm to be of any use to Aunt Em, the more I know about milk yields and foot-and-mouth the better. So don't let me put you off. Do you suppose the police will have gone by the time we get back?'

'If they haven't, I don't suppose we shall get any supper,' said Eden with a laugh. 'The staff are apt to get a bit disorganized on these occasions. I can't tell you how many times during the Emergency we

617

were reduced to bread and cheese because Greg's chaps had been asking questions and the cook was too upset to concentrate on such mundane matters as meals. Here's Drew. If you're ready, let's go.'

9

Day was withdrawing reluctantly from the valley, and the gardens of *Flamingo* were noisy with the chatter and chirrup of birds coming home to roost. But the house itself was silent, and the police had apparently gone.

Conversation during the return journey had been desultory, but now it had ceased altogether, and Victoria, looking round to see why Eden's steps had slowed, surprised an expression on his face that startled her. He was staring at the house as though he hated it, or was afraid of it, and was walking slowly to delay the moment when he must enter it again.

An unexpected and icy little shiver ran down Victoria's spine, and Mr Stratton, who had been strolling beside her with his hands in his pockets and his face blank and apparently unobservant, said: 'Are you cold? Or was that someone jumping over your grave?'

Victoria started as though she had been sleep-walking, and was suddenly angry with an unreasoning and defensive anger born of the sharp unease that had momentarily possessed her.

'Must you mention graves after what has happened here? I should have thought we could at least have kept off——' She stopped and bit her lip.

Drew's eyebrows lifted and his blue eyes were unpleasantly satirical, but his voice remained unruffled. 'I stand corrected. Very tactless of me. My apologies, Eden.'

'What's that?' said Eden, jerked out of abstraction as Victoria had been. 'I'm sorry. I didn't hear what you said.'

'Nothing of any importance. It doesn't look as though your grandmother is in, does it? Or else she's locked the dogs up.'

'More likely that the police have locked up all our labour!' said Eden bitterly. 'There don't seem to be any cars about, so at least Bill and his boys have pushed off – which is some comfort!'

At the top of the verandah steps he paused to listen, his head lifted and his face strained and intent. But no one moved in the

619

silent house, and the normal cheerful noises from the kitchen and the back premises were conspicuous by their absence.

Something of his disquiet communicated itself to Drew Stratton, who said with unwonted sharpness: 'There's nothing wrong, is there?'

Eden's strained rigidity relaxed and he gave a short and rather uncertain laugh. 'No. No, of course not. I was only wondering where everyone had got to. Place seems a bit deserted this evening. I'll go and rout out Zacharia and some drinks.' But he made no move to go, and the hand that he had laid on the verandah rail tightened until the knuckles showed white through the tanned skin.

Somewhere in the house a door slammed and Victoria jumped at the suddenness of the sound.

'Somebody appears to be at home,' observed Mr Stratton dryly. 'Unless that was your poltergeist.'

Eden's hand dropped from the rail and he turned an appalled face. 'But it couldn't be! – not now. I mean——'

He whirled round and had started for the nearest door at a run when Em appeared at the far end of the verandah:

'Eden! Thank goodness you're back! I've been worried to death.' Her voice sharpened as she took in his expression. 'What's the matter? You haven't – heard anything have you?'

'No,' said Eden with a crack of laughter that held more than a trace of hysteria. 'Not a sound. That's what was worrying me. The whole place was as quiet as a tomb and I suddenly got the horrors, wondering if anything had happened to you. Where is everyone? Don't tell me that young Bill Hennessy has arrested the whole boiling – live stock included? What have you done with the dogs?'

'Locked them up,' said Em and sat down abruptly and heavily in one of the verandah chairs. 'They didn't take to the askaris.'

She appeared to notice Drew and Victoria for the first time and nodded absently at them. 'Good evening, Drew. Didn't see you. Eden brought you, I suppose? Well, I can't talk cattle with you today. It'll have to wait. I'm too upset. Did you have a nice trip on the lake, Victoria? Eden, go and tell Zacharia to bring the drinks. I need something. Brandy, for choice!'

'Bill been giving you a bad time, Gran?' enquired Eden. 'You should have let me stay and deal with him. Come on, tell me the worst. Are half our staff behind bars? Is that why the place is so quiet this evening?'

'No. Nothing like that. He only wanted to ask a lot of silly questions, and I let him get on with it. It isn't the police. It's Kamau.'

'Why? What about him? Don't tell me he really *does* know something after all?'

'I don't know,' said Em tiredly. 'Eden, *do* go and call Zach! I'm sure we could all do with a drink.'

Eden departed, and Drew said: 'Kamau? Isn't he the one who scuppered that Mau Mau "Brigadier" and scooped in a fat reward? Do the police think that he knows something about the murder?'

'No. I mean, yes, he's the one who killed Gitahi. Lisa thought he might know something ...' Em recounted the tale, adding that Kamau had failed to meet her on the previous night. 'And when I sent for him this morning – Oh, *mzuri*, Zacharia. Put it down there. No, no, the Bwanas can help themselves.' She waved the old man away, and Eden dispensed drinks.

'Go on,' said Drew. 'You sent for him this morning?'

Em accepted an exceedingly stiff brandy and soda from her grandson and gulped down half of it before replying. 'They said they thought he'd gone off to cut lucerne, and now it doesn't look as if he did.'

'Bolted, I suppose,' said Eden succinctly.

Em lowered her glass and looked at him sharply. 'Why do you say that?'

'Well, it's the obvious conclusion, isn't it?'

'That's what the Police say. In fact they said just what you said yesterday: that he might have done the murder himself, and now that this girl, Wambui, has told on him, he's lost his nerve and run for it.'

'But you don't believe that,' said Drew slowly.

'No.'

Eden banged his glass down on the tray with such violence that the bottles jumped and rattled. 'Why not? The same old reason I suppose. "My Kukes are loyal!" My God, they ought to have that written up in letters of gold right across the Rift – and headed "Famous Last Words"! Why shouldn't it be the answer? *Someone* did it, and it all ties up with the other things that happened in the house – the poltergeist and the poisoning of Simba. Whoever was responsible for that must have been employed here, or working with an accomplice who was, and if Kamau had no hand in it why has he run away? Tell me that!'

'Because he may think he knows who did it, and is afraid.'

'Afraid of what?'

'Of his own life, of course! Really, Eden, you're being very stupid

621

today. Suppose he *was* watching from the bushes and saw everything? Suppose he even recognized the murderer?'

'In the dusk? At that range?' said Eden scornfully. 'Don't you believe it, Gran! The distance between where he was standing and the spot where Alice was killed is well over fifty yards. And it was getting dark. For all we know, the marks he left may have been made hours earlier – or else they were made by an accomplice keeping *cave*. If Kamau really knows anything about this business it's either because he himself did the murder or connived at it!'

'I don't believe it,' said Em obstinately. 'That's just the sort of conclusion the police jump at – and Gilly and Hector and Mabel. Because it's the easiest one that offers. It's my opinion that Kamau *did* know something, and was sufficiently frightened by what he saw to keep his mouth shut, but couldn't resist throwing out hints to his girl. But I didn't think he'd run away, or that the police would immediately leap to the same silly conclusion that you appear to have leapt to!'

She sipped her drink and glared indignantly at her grandson over the rim of her glass. *'Men!'* said Em scornfully, and directed a speaking glance at her niece. But Victoria's attention had been momentarily distracted by the behaviour of Mr Stratton.

Drew had been sitting on the verandah rail within a foot of her, leaning back lazily against one of the pillars. He looked relaxed and at peace with the world, and appeared to be taking no more than a polite interest in the discussion, until something in Em's last sentence had jerked him to attention. Victoria did not know why she was so sure of this, for he had made no noticeable movement. Nevertheless she was aware that he was no longer relaxed but had abruptly stiffened into alertness, and that he was sitting very still.

She glanced sideways at him and saw that his eyes were wide and very bright and that they held a curious look of astonishment, as though some new and startling thought had suddenly presented itself to him. It was a look that for some reason disturbed Victoria, and she turned quickly to stare at her aunt as though she might find there some clue as to what had caused it. But Em's face was as aloof and sulky as an elderly bloodhound's, and there was nothing to be read there but her scornful impatience with the limited intelligence of all people who did not think as she did.

Eden said: 'Oh, all right, Gran. Don't let's argue about it. We shall always be on opposite sides of the fence over this. You are quite prepared to believe that everyone else's Kikuyu servants are untrustworthy, but never your own. Hector and Mabel are just as bad. Look at the way Hector behaved in '54 over that knife.'

Em said sharply: 'I will not have you talking scandal, Eden! It was an accident, and you know it. Hector and Mabel are old friends of mine, and——'

'And like Kamau can do no wrong,' finished Eden. 'I know, darling. Sorry I spoke. Have another drink. You've finished that one. What about you, Drew? Have the other half.'

'I've still got it, thanks,' said Drew. 'Have Hector and Mabel been over here this afternoon, Em?'

'Yes,' said Em, handing over her glass to be refilled. 'Mabel brought me a bottle of her chutney. A peace-offering, I think. Dear Mabel. She's such a kind-hearted, sensible person except when she gets on to the subject of Ken. Which reminds me, Eden; Ken was here just after you left. He wanted to know if that Luger of yours was still for sale.'

Eden looked slightly surprised. 'He must be mad. He knows quite well that I flogged it in Mays only about ten days ago. He was there! Besides, he wouldn't have been able to get any ammunition for it.'

'Oh well, perhaps I got it wrong. He may have wanted to know if Mays still had it. I'm afraid I was a bit sharp with him. I found him riding right across the lucerne patch behind the labour lines. He didn't expect to see me down there – let alone Hennessy! – and he stammered and stuttered like a schoolboy caught with his fist in the cake tin. Mabel ought to send him to the coast for a spell. Or better still, take him there herself. The boy is a bundle of nerves.'

Eden said shortly: 'The further away she takes him, and them, the better. I hope you were sufficiently sharp with him to discourage any more visits for the time being.'

'Ken is unsnubbable. You ought to know that by now. Lisa took him off my hands. She came over to borrow some sugar, and took him back with her. It's odd that two people like Hector and Mabel should have produced a child like Ken. He's not really the right type for Kenya.'

'Judging from his capacity for falling in love with other men's wives,' said Eden acidly, 'I should have thought he had at least one of the necessary qualifications.'

'Don't be cheap, dear,' said his grandmother severely. She selected a cigarette from a box on the table beside her, and Drew slid off the verandah rail and went over to light it for her.

'Gilly been around today?' he enquired idly, snapping on the lighter.

'I expect so. He's around so often that I don't notice any more. Thank you, Drew.'

Drew returned the lighter to his pocket and observed that he had not realized that Gilly was so hard-working.

'It's not always work,' said Em with a short laugh. 'My Bechstein is a good deal better than his own piano. He comes over to play.'

Eden muttered something under his breath that was uncomplimentary to Mr Gilbraith Markham, and a frown passed over Em's face. She said: 'I know you think I'm an old fool to keep him on, but God knows what would become of him if I didn't. He's very little use as a manager, and not really a good enough musician to keep himself in any sort of comfort – let alone Lisa!'

Eden said coldly: 'That's nonsense. He was offered a perfectly good job with a dance band. A more than adequate salary, with accommodation thrown in. What is more, Lisa was all for his taking it: Nairobi is far more her cup of tea than the Rift.'

Em looked at him with mingled affection and regret. 'You haven't inherited a particle of feeling for music, dear, have you? It's odd, when your father and all my mother's side of the family had such a love for it. All the Beaumartins have been musical, but it's missed you. If it hadn't, you couldn't talk like that. Gilly is enough of a musician to consider that playing in a dance band would rank with prostitution. He'd prefer to starve.'

'Don't you believe it! Gilly is far too fond of himself. He'd have taken it all right, if you hadn't fallen for all that high falutin' stuff and offered him Gus Abbott's job in order to save him from "Prostituting his Art". And if he'd put in as little work with the dance band as he has here, he'd have got the sack inside a week. Probably less! Yet he has the nerve to suggest that you put him in to manage the Rumuruti estates now that Jerry Coles wants to retire.'

Em said softly: 'Perhaps his reasons for wishing to remove to Rumuruti are domestic rather than financial.'

'*Domestic*? Why Lisa simply loathes the idea of going there.'

'Quite,' said Em dryly.

Eden stared at her for a moment, obviously puzzled by her tone, and then flushed hotly in sudden comprehension, and turning his back on her busied himself once more with the tray of drinks.

Em said placidly, but with a wicked twinkle in her eye: 'But I am unlikely to give it to him. You see, I should miss hearing him play.'

'Was he playing here today?' asked Drew.

'I don't think so. I didn't hear him. But then I went down to the labour lines with Bill Hennessy and his askaris, and I wouldn't have heard him from there. I'm getting too deaf.'

Em sighed and shook her head impatiently, as though the infirmities of old age were tormenting flies; and then all at once she stiffened in her chair, listening.

A car was coming up the long, rutted drive between the acacias and the spiky clusters of sisal, and Em rose hurriedly. 'If it's anyone else offering condolences, tell them I'm out. Or ill!'

'Don't worry,' said Eden, 'it'll only be Drew's car. His driver was bringing it round.'

But it was not Mr Stratton's car. It was Mr Gilbert's, and a moment later, accompanied by the Markhams, he walked on to the verandah; and at the sight of his face they all came quickly to their feet.

Greg dispensed with formalities and came straight to the point: 'Hennessy tells me that one of your Kikuyu boys has disappeared. Kamau.'

He ignored Drew, Eden and Victoria, and addressed himself solely to Em, while behind him Lisa fidgeted and twisted her fingers, her pretty face sulky and apprehensive, and Gilly leaned against a verandah pillar with a studied negligence that was belied by the avid interest that was plainly visible in his restless eyes.

Em said coldly and defiantly: 'Yes. And I presume, as you have brought Lisa and Gilly with you, that you know why.'

'Hennessy told me why. It seems that you told him of Mrs Markham's visit to you yesterday, and I came down to see what I could get out of this woman Wambui.'

Lisa gave a little whimpering sob. 'I wish I hadn't said anything to anyone! I *wish* I hadn't! I only thought that Lady Emily ought to know.'

Mr Gilbert ignored the interruption. He said: 'I got quite a lot out of her, but before we go any further I'd like to have your own account of exactly what happened yesterday; from Mrs Markham's arrival to the time you decided that Kamau wasn't going to turn up. Also what action, if any, you took about it this morning.'

Em looked at Greg Gilbert's grim unsmiling face, and her shrewd old eyes were puzzled and wary. She said slowly: 'Let me see——' And for the second time that evening described Lisa's visit and the happenings of the hours that followed it, ending with her enquiries that morning as to Kamau's whereabouts, and her discovery, when Hennessy and his askaris had gone down to the labour lines to question the African employees and their families, that no one had seen him since Zacharia had delivered her message to him on the previous afternoon. Except, presumably, Wambui?

'No, she didn't,' said Lisa with an air of conscious virtue. 'I made a point of seeing that she couldn't get away last night. I thought that you should have every chance to speak to Kamau first, and as I said to Hector——'

She checked suddenly, her eyes and her mouth blank circles of dismay.

Greg turned with a swiftness that startled her, and said brusquely: 'You told me that you had not mentioned this to anyone else. Not even your husband.'

'Least of all her husband,' interpolated Gilly with an edge to his voice.

'Shut up, Gilly! Did you tell Hector Brandon, Lisa?'

Lisa's large violet eyes filled with tears and she said querulously: 'Don't bark at me, Greg! There's no need for you——'

'*Did* you?'

'Well – well, yes. But only in the strictest confidence. After all, I've known Hector for years, and I knew he wouldn't let it go any further. And I was very worried. You don't seem to realize——'

'When did you tell him? Before you'd been over here, or afterwards?'

'Oh, afterwards. Because of course by then I was sure that Lady Emily would get it all out of Kamau, and then everything would be all right. I mean, at least we'd all *know*.'

'Hmm,' said Greg disagreeably. He stared at her long and meditatively until she reddened under his gaze, and then turning away abruptly he addressed himself again to Em:

'We've got search parties out looking for Kamau, and with luck we should pick him up without much trouble. He's probably made for the Reserve. But even when we get him I doubt if we'll get much more out of him than we got out of Wambui.'

Em said tartly: 'You certainly won't if you start off by sending out your askaris to arrest him as though he'd done something criminal, when all he is guilty of is telling his girl-friend that he thinks he knows something about the murder.'

'I'm afraid he told her more than that,' said Greg quietly.

Em stiffened suddenly and once again her eyes moved from Greg to Lisa, and she said haltingly: 'But Lisa, you told me——' and stopped.

Lisa dragged at her handkerchief until the fabric tore, and her voice was high and hysterical: 'I didn't know there was any more! I tell you I didn't know! I had no idea – she just said that he – he knew something. But if I'd known what it was I wouldn't have said a word! Eden, you *know* I wouldn't——'

Eden said in an entirely expressionless voice: 'I'm afraid I don't know what you're talking about. Perhaps Greg will be good enough to explain.'

'Yes,' said Em harshly. 'If you have anything to say Greg, let us hear it and get it over.'

Mr Gilbert surveyed her thoughtfully, and there was something in his expression that frightened Victoria. He said slowly and deliberately: 'Wambui told Mrs Markham that Kamau had hinted that he knew someting about Mrs DeBrett's murder. That was not true. He had done a good deal more than hint, but she was afraid to admit to anything else because his story is too fantastic to be believed.'

He paused, as though collecting his thoughts, and Em said grimly: 'Go on.'

'Kamau's story,' said Greg, 'is that on Tuesday evening he waited for Wambui as usual among the bushes near the knoll, and that shortly after he got there he saw Mrs DeBrett arrive and start picking roses; so he lay low and waited for her to go away. But she sat down on the fallen tree and stayed there until it was nearly dark, and he began to get tired of waiting and must have made some movement in the bushes, for she jumped up as though she was alarmed and began to run away. And then, he said, he saw someone coming to meet her. Someone whom she knew, and ran to. And who killed her.'

'*No!*' cried Lisa, her voice shockingly shrill after Greg's quiet and unemotional tones. 'She made it up! She must have done! I don't believe it!' She burst into noisy sobs, but no one had any attention to spare for her, for they were looking with a fixed and fascinated intensity at Greg Gilbert.

Eden said loudly: 'If he saw who it was, why didn't he say so at once? – when he was questioned with the others? Why didn't——'

Em made a swift impatient gesture of the hand, silencing him, and Greg said slowly, frowning down at the matting as though he preferred not to meet the painfully intent stares that were fixed on him:

627

'Wambui says it was because he recognized the murderer, and was afraid.'

'Go on,' repeated Em, harshly and imperiously. 'Who did he say it was?'

Greg removed his gaze from the matting and looked up, meeting her gaze squarely.

He said softly: 'You, Em.'

10

There was a moment of complete and utter stillness, as though everyone on the verandah had been temporarily deprived of the power of speech or movement. The blood drained out of Em's face leaving it yellow and drawn and incredibly old, and she sat down heavily and abruptly as though her legs could no longer support her.

The protesting creak of the wicker-work chair broke the silence with the effect of a stone dropped into a quiet pool, and Eden said furiously: 'What the hell d'you mean by making accusations like that! By God, I've a good mind to——' He took a swift stride forward, and Drew said sharply and compellingly: 'Be quiet, Eden! You're only making matters worse.'

He reached out and caught Eden's arm, jerking him back, and Greg said: 'I am not making any accusations – at the moment. I am merely repeating something that I have heard at second hand. Well, Em? How about it?'

Eden shook off Drew's restraining hand and said: 'Don't answer him, Gran! If he's going to believe every silly fairy story cooked up by a half-witted African farm-hand, you'd better wait until you can see your lawyer!'

Em paid no attention to him. She looked at Greg with eyes that were blank with shock, and said slowly and as though it were an effort to speak: 'What do you want me to say? That I did not kill Alice? But telling you so is not proof, is it? And I was here in the house that evening, so I suppose from your point of view I could have done it.'

'Gran, for God's sake!' begged Eden.

'Oh, Eden dear, *do* stop being so silly! Drew is quite right. It really does not help at all to lose our heads and shout – or collapse into tears, like Lisa. Surely we can behave in a rational manner? Sit down, Greg. You had better tell me what you propose to do about this – this extraordinary statement.'

Mr Gilbert drew up a chair and sat down facing her. He said: 'We can't do much about it until we pull in Kamau and get him to verify

629

it. What I want you to do is to give me an exact account of what happened that evening. Yes, I know we've been into this before, but I want it once again. You'd been out shooting, and got back just before six. What did you do then?'

'I changed,' said Em patiently.

'Into what? That Japanese job with storks all over it that you were wearing when I arrived later that night?'

'No, of course not! That was a kimono. I changed into a house-coat. Yellow, if you want to know. But I had to take it off because——' She stopped suddenly, and after a brief pause said: 'Because it had blood all over it. Yes ... I can see that that doesn't sound good. But I couldn't help it. I'd tried to carry her up to the house, and – well, you saw her.'

'Yes,' agreed Greg briefly. 'What did you do then? After you'd changed into the house-coat?'

'I came into the drawing-room for a drink, and saw Lisa's note asking for a lift into Nairobi – I'd left it on the piano – and Alice went over to tell her that I'd give her a lift when I went in to fetch Victoria.'

'What did you do when she'd gone?'

'Went out to tell Zach and Cookie about cutting up the kongoni, and after that I saw the dogs fed, and gave Majiri the curtains and covers from Victoria's room to wash – the water's always extra hot in the evenings, because of the baths. Zach came round just before half-past six and turned on the lights, and I told him to leave the drinks in the drawing-room. And then I played the piano.'

'Until when?'

'Until around eight o'clock, when he came in to say that Alice was still not back, and should he serve dinner? I hadn't realized it was so late, and I called the dogs and went off to fetch her. *Must* I go over all that part again?'

'No. That's not the really important time from your point of view, as she must have been killed around seven o'clock, and you say you were playing the piano from six thirty onwards. That in itself is a reasonably good alibi.'

'Why?' enquired Em with an attempt at a smile. 'You've only my word for it.'

Greg consulted the notebook they had seen on the previous day, and said: 'Not quite. Seven of your servants stated independently that the "Memsahib Mkubwa" had been playing during that time, and had not stopped for more than a minute or two at most. Certainly not long enough to murder Alice and then change into fresh clothes, as presumably even old Zacharia would have noticed bloodstains on a yellow house-coat! It couldn't have been done in under ten to fifteen minutes, and on a cross-check of the evidence you never stopped playing for anything like that.'

'You've forgotten something,' said Em dryly. 'I have an extremely good radio-gramophone, and not one of my servants would know the difference.'

Eden said hoarsely: 'Gran, are you mad! Listen, Greg, she doesn't realize how serious this may be. She ought to have a lawyer. Drew, can't *you* stop this? Can't you make her see some sense?'

'Your grandmother,' said Drew, 'appears to me to be seeing it with extreme clarity. It would only be a question of time before someone else thought of that one, so she might just as well mention the radiogram herself.'

'Exactly!' said Em approvingly. 'Everyone knows about it – and about such things as long-playing records, too! I can see no point in laying claim to an alibi that is obviously as full of holes as a sieve. Besides I don't need one. I know quite enough about Kenya to know that no jury in this country is going to take such a charge seriously. And so does Greg! Because everyone knows me. If they did not, it might be possible to get a conviction on such evidence. After all, I am still tolerably strong – strong enough to kill a little weak defenceless creature like Alice who would have been too surprised to——'

Em's voice failed suddenly and she covered her face with her hands as though to blot out the horror that her own words had conjured up: the picture of Alice standing helpless and appalled in the dusk, too stunned with shock to scream or run. A strong shudder shook her bulky body and presently she lifted a ravaged face and staring, haunted eyes, and spoke in a voice that was barely more than a hoarse whisper:

'I've seen a lot of bad things in my time. Men who were mauled by lions or trampled by buffalo or rhino. And – and there was Gus Abbott too. But they were men. I suppose that made it different. It's silly to feel like this. But – but she couldn't bear wounds and blood. I used to tell her that she shouldn't mind. But when I saw her that night, I minded too. I minded . . .'

Eden said: 'Don't, Gran! Please——!' His face was as drawn and ravaged as her own, and, for a moment only, ugly with remembered horror. The sight of it seemed to act on Em like a douche of cold

631

water, and she straightened her bowed shoulders with a palpable effort and said remorsefully: 'Forgive me, dear. I'm behaving very badly. But then this is all so absurd. I wish I knew why Kamau should have said such a thing. Perhaps Wambui made it up?'

'I don't think so,' said Greg. 'I can usually tell when I'm being spun a yarn. I'd say she was speaking the truth. But was Kamau?'

'Yes,' said Drew, abruptly and positively.

There was a simultaneous gasp from at least four throats, and Em shrank back in her chair and stared at him in horrified disbelief.

Mr Stratton viewed his audience with undisguised impatience and said: 'There's no need to look at me as though I'd gone off my head. The thing stands out a mile. Of *course* he was speaking the truth – or what he thought was the truth. Just take a look at Em. She's a nice, bright splash of colour, isn't she? And she's been dressing like that ever since I was in rompers! Eden has already pointed out that the distance between the bushes and the spot where Alice was killed is rather more than fifty yards, and it was getting dark. So all that Kamau saw was someone wearing the sort of hat and clothes she wears, and naturally he thought it was Em. Bet you any money you like I'm right!'

'No takers,' said Greg with a wry smile. 'I ought to have seen it myself.'

'But *why*?' demanded Eden vehemently. 'Why should anyone try and pin it on Gran, when she's the very last person who'd be likely to do it?'

Drew shrugged and said: 'Perhaps that was why. Because no one would credit it.'

'No,' said Greg slowly. 'I imagine that the reason was even simpler than that. Anyone, male or female, could wear that sort of outfit and get away with it, because no one would give them a second look. It also provided an excuse for being seen in the gardens at that hour, for if anyone happened to see the wearer, they'd take it for granted that it was Em. It was the perfect disguise. And that of course is the answer to the riddle of the verandah cushion!'

'How do you work that out?' demanded Em, thereby temporarily depriving Mr Gilbert of his composure.

'Well ... er ... I thought – padding?' he suggested cautiously.

Em looked bewildered but Lisa unexpectedly went off into a gale of giggles, and Em, turning to look at her, remarked coldly that they would all like to share in the joke: any joke.

632

'I'm s-sorry,' gasped Lisa, wavering helplessly between relief and hysteria. 'I suppose I shouldn't laugh, but it's so f-funny! He means your b-b-bosom! A man wouldn't have one, but you have! *Ha, ha, ha, ha!*'

Instinctively and simultaneously every eye was focused upon Em's imposing frontage, and the next minute they were all laughing as helplessly as Lisa – and for much the same reason. Only Em, like Queen Victoria, declined to be amused, and announced austerely that she saw nothing to laugh at.

'You wouldn't, darling. You're behind it!' said Eden, and collapsed into renewed mirth.

Em folded her hands in her lap and waited with a dignified display of patience for the laughter to subside.

'I apologize,' said Greg, mopping his streaming eyes and recovering himself. 'On behalf of us all. Extremely silly and unnecessary, but for some reason it's done me a power of good. Seriously, Em, that cushion worried me. But it's quite obvious that whoever impersonated you was too slim to be convincing, and needed a bit of – well, building up. Hence the cushion. Now what about those clothes? How many pairs of those red overalls have you got, and have you lost any recently?'

Victoria gave a startled gasp and Em said grimly: 'I never thought of that! I should have four pairs of them, but one can't be found.'

'Could it have been missing for some time?'

Em shrugged. 'Perhaps. I wouldn't have noticed, and I don't suppose Zacharia would have done either until an occasion like this morning, when three pairs happened to be in the wash at once.'

'Supposing someone wanted to steal a pair, would it have been easy or difficult? For an outsider, for instance.'

'I should say only too easy. All the washing is hung up on the lines behind the kitchen, and anyone could remove something from a line if they waited for the right moment. The odd thing does occasionally vanish – generally dish-cloths. But Zach ought to have noticed something like a pair of my dungarees. Except that he's getting old – like me.'

Mr Gilbert frowned thoughtfully at the small notebook that lay open on his knee, and presently said: 'By the way, in spite of what you said on the subject of alibis, I think you may turn out to have a cast-iron one after all. Can you remember what you were playing on the piano that evening?'

'Yes,' said Em, her face suddenly bleak. 'I was playing Toroni's concerto. *The Rift Valley Concerto*. There isn't any record of that. Not any longer.'

'So I understand. It was broken by the poltergeist, wasn't it? And I also seem to remember that there was only the one record, and that it isn't on sale, or available to the general public. Am I right?'

'Yes. He had it made for me in New York. But then none of my servants would know the difference between one tune and another, I'm afraid.'

Greg said: 'That's where you're wrong. The average African has a better ear for music than one would imagine, and that particular piece not only had a good many tribal tunes and rhythms incorporated into it, but I gather that Toroni composed it here at *Flamingo*, on your piano; and that you yourself have played it pretty frequently of late. Anyway, three of your servants say that you were playing "Bwana Toroni's songs". So you see it's not such a bad alibi after all. We shall have to check it of course, for form's sake: cable New York and make sure that you couldn't have got hold of a duplicate, and that sort of thing. And if their answer clears you, then the thing is buttoned as far as you are concerned.'

'I rather think that it's buttoned without that,' remarked Gilly unexpectedly. 'In fact you can save yourself the expense of a cable, and the F.B.I. a headache.'

'How's that?' demanded Greg, turning quickly to face him.

Gilly abandoned the pose of disinterested spectator, and strolled forward, his hands in his pockets.

He said: 'Drew'll tell you that I met him at the gate in the hedge just after he'd seen Alice off, and we both heard Em playing that thing. He pushed off, but I didn't. I sat on the concrete block just outside the gate for a goodish while. Until it was dark.'

'You *what*?' demanded Greg incredulously. 'Why the hell didn't you tell me this before? You mean that you were there after seven? Surely you must have heard *something*. A cry, or——'

Gilly cut him short. 'I didn't hear anything! You forget that the knoll is away to the right, and there are trees and bamboos and heaven knows what between it and the gate. But there is a fairly clear line between the gate and the house, and I could hear the piano. I sat there for quite a time, listening to Em tackling that piece. I know it a damn sight better than she does; every bar and every note of it! And you can take it from me that it wouldn't make any difference if you discovered that there were half a

634

million of those records in existence, and all of them in Kenya!'

'Why?' demanded Greg tersely.

'Why? Because I'm enough of a musician to tell the difference between Em's rendering of the concerto, and Toroni's. That's why!'

Gilly transferred his gaze from Greg's relieved face to Em's tight-lipped, rigid mouth and basilisk stare, and laughed.

'I'm sorry, Em. I know that touches you on the raw. But let's face it, you're a pretty poor performer when it comes to the piano, while Toroni was in a class by himself. And if you think I couldn't go into the witness box and swear to the difference between your playing of the concerto and his – and be believed – you're even less of a musician than I take you for. Well?'

The fury died out of Em's face but she continued to eye him with considerable hauteur, and after staring at him in disdainful silence for a full minute, she said coldly: 'As both Greg and Eden seem to think that I could do with an alibi, I shall not argue with you.'

'It may be a useful thing to have handy,' observed Greg, and added briskly. 'And now the next thing is to go after that missing pair of overalls.'

'You are not going after them tonight,' snapped Em. 'At least, not in this house. I don't care what you do in the grounds. Or anywhere else! But I have had quite enough alarms and excursions for one day, and I propose to have an early supper and go to bed. Good night.'

She heaved herself up out of her chair and withdrew with the dignity of a Dowager Empress concluding an audience, leaving a somewhat conscience-stricken silence behind her. It was broken by Eden, who opened a bottle of soda water with an irritable violence that sent it frothing over the matting, and informed Gilly that this time he really had put his foot in it.

'If there is one thing that Gran is vain about,' said Eden, 'it's her playing. You may have given her a cast-iron alibi, but she won't thank you for it. She'd probably have preferred to stand trial! So if you find yourself queueing up at the Labour Exchange in the near future, you'll know why. You'd better get yourself a drink while the going's good. It's probably the last you'll get on the house.'

'Rot!' said Gilly. He giggled light-heartedly, and taking advantage of the offer, poured himself out a double whisky, gulped it down neat, and refilled his glass. 'Your grandmother may have been a tolerable amateur pianist in the days of her youth – though personally, I doubt it. But though her appreciation of good music is still Grade A, her performance, when compared to someone like Toroni's, is on a par with a pianola's. As for booting me out, *phooey*! Bet you she gives me a rise! After all, what's injured pride compared to a stretched neck?'

'Point is,' said Eden, 'that as she'll never believe in the possibility of the latter, she will have plenty of indignation to spare for the former.'

'You underrate her intelligence,' grinned Gilly. '*Skoal!* She may be a vain old peacock, but she's no fool. Sheerest stroke of luck that I didn't trot straight back to the house that evening. Very nearly did! But I'd had just about enough of Hector and Mabel for one day, and I didn't want to run into them; so I stayed where I was and listened to Em massacring that concerto. Stroke of luck!'

Greg slid the notebook into his pocket and said: 'Look, Eden, do you think I could have a word with Majiri and Zacharia without running into Em again – about those dungarees? I shall have to send Bill Hennessy down tomorrow to go into the question in more detail of course. That'll turn his hair white!'

'As long as you steer clear of the cook,' said Eden, 'I don't care who you see. But cheese and biscuits for supper on top of all this would be the last straw. All right, come on.' They departed, leaving Victoria to the society of the Markhams and Mr Stratton.

The sun had set and the gardens were no longer gaily coloured and noisy with bird song, but cool and green and quiet, and a bat swooped out from under the eaves and flitted along the silent verandah.

Lisa stood up and said in a bright, brittle voice: 'So it was all a storm in a teacup. I can't imagine why Greg should have insisted on our coming over with him. So embarrassing! And quite unnecessary, as it happened.'

Gilly poured himself out a third whisky and observed dispassionately that it provided an interesting and unexpected sidelight on his wife's character to find that she could refer to a brutal murder as a storm in a teacup, and that she knew quite well why Greg had brought them over. 'Or you should know. After all, you were the one who started this hare. Besides, you were quite prepared to believe that she'd done it. Don't tell me you weren't!'

Lisa said indignantly: 'Gilly, I do wish you wouldn't talk such arrant nonsense. Drew and I know you well enough to know when you're joking, but Miss Caryll might take you seriously.'

'And how right Miss Caryll would be! You also produced a very, very neat little theory as to *why* Em should have done it, didn't you?'

'Gilly, be quiet!' Lisa rounded on her husband, her eyes brilliant with anger.

'And a damned good theory, too, if I may say so,' said Gilly, ignoring her. 'Except for one small but vital point that you have overlooked.'

'Gilly!' Lisa's voice was imploring, and she dragged at his arm. 'It's getting late. Let's go home.'

'Pipe down, Lisa. Drew's interested; aren't you Drew? Interesting case – very. Drew doesn't believe that any stray Mau Mau thug did this, any more'n I do – or Greg, or Em. Much as they'd like to believe it, Lisa my love. But they don't know what I know.'

He began to giggle, and Drew said: 'What do you know, Gilly?' But the question had been asked too sharply, and the slightly vacuous expression that whisky had brought to Gilly's face was replaced by wariness and a trace of malice.

'We aren't discussing me,' said Gilly. 'Discussin' Lisa's theory about Em. Em and Alice. We all think that Em was fond of Alice – in a patronizing Protect-the-Weak the poor-kid-can't-help-it sort of way. But suppose we were wrong? Supposing that underneath all that surface affection she hated her guts? That it was all an act, and she was really jealous of her – because of Eden, or because one day she would be mistress of *Flamingo*? It's no secret that Em's nuts about Eden and dotty on the subject of *Flamingo*. She'd do anything for either of them – even murder! That was Lisa's theory. And mark you, granting the premise, perfectly feasible. I don't suppose that Em has ever heard that song about *You can't chop your momma up in Massachusetts*, but she'd be quite capable of chopping up a granddaughter-in-law in Kenya if she judged it to be necessary. Law unto herself; that's Em! All the same, Lisa doesn't notice things . . .'

'What sort of things?' This time Drew's voice was deceptively casual.

'Oh – this and that. Or maybe she does? She's a sly little thing, Lisa. All women are sly. Ever noticed that, Drew? You will – you will! Take Mabel, for instance . . . asked if she could take a couple of pineapples home on Tuesday evening, just after Alice left, and went off to pick 'em. Lisa never noticed that she came back without any. And shall I tell you why? Because Lisa had been out too. Down to the shamba, *she* says, to get some tomatoes. Though what she wanted 'em for is anybody's guess – we had roast duck and cauliflower for supper. She thinks *I* don't notice things, but I do!'

Lisa made no comment, but Victoria saw her eyes widen in surprise and become fixed and intent. Gilly wagged his head sagely and helped himself to yet another drink, and Drew said curtly: 'Haven't you had enough of that?'

'Enough of what?' demanded Gilly. 'Women – or Em's whisky? If the former, certainly. But no one can have too much of Em's whisky. First because it's good, and secon'ly because it's Em's; on the house! *Prosit!*'

He took a deep gulp, and lowered his voice to a confidential undertone: 'Ever struck you, Drew, that all the time Greg was talking about alibis for Em, he hadn't noticed that no one else has one either? You, for instance. You say you went off home when you left me. Did you? Mabel says she was picking pineapples. Oh yeah? Hector walked home by the path that runs along the top of the shambas – so he says. Eden's supposed to have been driving around somewhere, and Lisa's wandering round the tomato patch. But is there an alibi in the bunch? Not on your life!'

Drew said amiably: 'That's quite a point. We might start with you. Can you prove one?'

Gilly looked startled. 'Prove what?'

'That you sat on that lump of concrete for half an hour or so and didn't hear a thing?'

Gilly put down his empty glass hurriedly. 'Here! Who says I didn't hear anything? I heard Em playing – I heard that damned concerto of Toroni's.'

'That's what *you* say. But Em had already told us what it was that she had been playing, and the evidence of three of her servants confirmed it. You might have decided to use that information as an alibi for yourself. Or you might still have heard it, but from a good deal nearer! See what I mean? So if I were you I'd lay off all these heavy hints that various people are in need of alibis. Because the obvious inference is that they must each have had a reason for wishing Alice dead, and that you know it. Which is dangerous bunkum.'

'But I do——' began Gilly. And stopped. He made a nervous grab at his glass, and then changed his mind and pushed it away so violently that it toppled off the table and splintered into pieces on the verandah floor.

Lisa said briskly and with a trace of satisfaction in her voice: 'Now look what you've done! That's one of Em's crystal set, and she won't be a bit pleased. Or do you think that if we just tiptoe

638

away and leave her to find it she'll put it down to the poltergeist?'

She accompanied the remark with a high-pitched tinkling laugh; but her face as she bent to pick up the broken pieces was white and frightened, and Victoria, stooping to help her, saw that her hands were shaking uncontrollably.

A light clicked on in the dining-room behind them, and a warm yellow glow fell across the verandah from the windows and the open door. And instantly it was evening no longer, but dusk: the garden shadowy with nightfall and the sky already sprinkled with pale stars.

Lisa deposited the bits of broken glass on the tray and said: 'Would you tell your aunt that it was an accident, and that we're so sorry? Oh, and she did say something about a picnic on the twenty-ninth. It was arranged before – before anything happened of course, so it may not be on. Would you ask her to let me know about it, because I'm afraid we must rush. Drew, you're coming over to collect those papers, aren't you? You'd better stay to supper as it's so late. It's only ourselves and Ken Brandon. He's rather in a state, poor boy, and it might take his mind off things if we had some bridge.'

Drew said firmly: 'No thank you, Lisa. An evening spent coping with an adolescent who is "in a state" is not in my line. Besides, I must get back.'

'Don't blame you,' said Gilly feelingly. 'Good night, Victoria.' He nodded absently at her and followed his wife down the steps and out into the violet dusk.

Victoria watched them go, and then turned to look at Mr Stratton, who had not moved. She was unaware that at that moment her face was as white and as frightened as Lisa's had been – or Gilly's. But Drew, looking down at it, was unaccountably disturbed.

He said abruptly: 'You're scared, aren't you.'

'A – a little,' admitted Victoria. And having admitted it was immediately aware of a diminution of that fear.

'Of what?'

'I don't know. The house – the things that have happened in it. But you don't believe in ghosts, do you?'

'Not in this one,' said Drew grimly. 'That is, if you're referring to the poltergeist.'

'I don't either. It all sounds too——'

She hesitated, wrinkling her brows, and Drew said: 'Too un-ghostly?'

'I was going to say, "too planned"; as though someone had worked it all out very carefully to a – a sort of pattern. I think that is what is frightening.'

'Why? Because you think that no African would have planned something like this and carried it through? If that's what you think, you're wrong. It's just the sort of tortuous scheme that would appeal to them. But there's nothing to be afraid of now, for if there ever was a plan, or a pattern, Mrs DeBrett's death completed it. It's finished.'

He had spoken with complete confidence, but almost before the words were out of his mouth he realized with a sudden sense of shock that he did not believe them. How could anyone assert with confidence that Alice's death had put an end to the things that had happened at *Flamingo*, while her killer was still at large? *It is only the first killing that is difficult*. Greg had said that only yesterday . . .

A bird fluttered among the hanging creepers at the verandah edge, and Drew saw Victoria start at the sound and bite hard on her underlip; and was surprised to find himself suddenly and savagely angry. With Em for bringing the girl out here. With Eden for permitting it. With Greg and Gilly and Lisa for frightening her. And most of all with himself – for caring whether they did or not!

11

Breakfast was barely over on the following morning when young Mr Hennessy and his police askaris descended upon *Flamingo*.

Em interviewed them briefly on the verandah and dismissed them to the kitchen quarters and the labour lines in charge of Eden, there to pursue their enquiries into the disappearance of Kamau and a pair of scarlet dungarees.

An hour later Gilly had appeared with a batch of files, and she retired with him into the office, having refused her niece's offer of assistance.

Victoria, left to her own devices, fetched a hat and went out to explore the garden, and she had been following a narrow path that wound through bushes of bougainvillaea, plumbago and orange trumpet flower when she came suddenly upon a stranger. A middle-aged woman in a green cotton dress who wore a battered wide-brimmed double terai hat jammed down over a riot of grey curls, and who appeared to have lost something, for she was bending down and peering anxiously about her.

'Can I help?' enquired Victoria.

The woman jumped violently, and said in a breathless voice: 'Oh dear, how you startled me! I believe there's a puff adder in there. They are such dangerous creatures. You must be Victoria. I used to know your parents – oh, years ago. You wouldn't remember me. I'm Mabel Brandon. Our place, *Brandonmead*, is just over there——' She gestured vaguely to the west with one hand and began to move on down the path, still talking, so that Victoria had perforce to follow her:

'We have a sort of mutual right-of-way between *Flamingo* and our land,' said Mrs Brandon. 'It saves us going miles by road. There's a track that runs right round this side of the lake across at least a dozen estates. I believe it used to be a game track once. There was any amount of big game in the valley when we first came here. Rhino and lion and buffalo, and even elephant. But of course they're gone now. Just as well really. It would have made farming impossible. Of course lions still come over sometimes from the Masai territory, though they get killed off very quickly. I believe one was seen at Crater Lake only last year. We must take you there. Em said something about a picnic. But she will have cancelled that of course.'

Mrs Brandon had quickened her steps as she talked and now she was walking quite briskly. Almost as though she did not want Victoria to linger among the bushes and was hurrying her away from them, talking trivialities to distract her attention from the fact.

The path took a sharp downward curve and came out upon a long belt of open ground, where a narrow trolley line ran parallel with the shamba and carried the heavy piles of maize and vegetables and bananas up to the higher ground where the *Flamingo* lorries were loaded. Mrs Brandon paused irresolutely and murmured something about running up to see Gilly.

'He won't be there,' volunteered Victoria. 'He's up at the house with Aunt Em.'

'Oh,' said Mrs Brandon doubtfully. 'Well perhaps I might call in there: just for a minute or two. No, don't let's go back that way——' She left the path and struck upwards again, following the trolley line, and they came out among a grove of acacias, one of which was being cut up and converted into charcoal.

Mrs Brandon sat down on the fallen trunk, and removing her hat, fanned her hot face with it and enquired conversationally if Victoria was glad to be back in Kenya, and how did she find Em? 'Personally,' said Mrs Brandon, 'I don't think that she is looking at all well. But then all this has been a terrible blow to her. And now I hear that one of her boys has run off. Kamau.' She paused expectantly, but receiving no reply went on to ask what Mr Gilbert had made of Wambui's story.

'What story?' asked Victoria innocently.

Mrs Brandon's pleasant face flushed and she shifted uncomfortably. But she was not to be deflected. 'The one she told Lisa. That it was Em who had killed Alice. Quite ridiculous of course, but – well, it does raise a question, doesn't it? I was never *quite* sure that Em really liked Alice. And Africans are so quick to spot these things. They're very observant. If Kamau thought that Em disliked her, that might have put the idea into his head – that Em killed her. It would have seemed quite natural to him. The wish being father to the thought. If – if you see what I mean.'

'No,' said Victoria, 'I'm afraid I don't. Mr Gilbert says it's quite obvious that Kamau thought he saw her do it.'

'But that's ridiculous!' protested Mrs Brandon.

'Of course it is,' said Victoria cheerfully. 'But Mr Gilbert thinks it was someone wearing the sort of clothes and hat that Aunt Em wears. He says it would have been the best possible disguise, as even a smaller person or a thinner one could have worn it, since no one would have looked twice.'

'A thin person,' repeated Mabel stupidly. And suddenly sat bolt upright, struck by the same thought that had struck Greg Gilbert. 'The cushion! So *that* was why—! Oh no, it isn't possible. It isn't!'

'What isn't possible?' enquired Victoria, puzzled.

'Prints,' said Mabel confusedly. 'It wasn't a plain one. It——' She seemed suddenly to recollect herself, and stopped short, biting her lip, and presently smiled a little stiffly and said: 'It's difficult to know what to think, isn't it? One does not like to think that one's own servants may be under suspicion, and Em's have always been so staunch. It must be heartbreaking for her. For of course it must be one of the *Flamingo* servants. It could be no one else. What does Greg intend to do about it?'

'I don't know,' said Victoria with perfect truth, and firmly changing the subject, enquired: 'What are those odd looking mud heaps with smoke coming out of them?'

'Charcoal,' said Mabel briefly. 'Does Em think——'

'*Charcoal?* But it's mud and turf!'

'The charcoal is inside,' explained Mabel patiently. 'When a tree dies we cut it up into lengths and then put mud all over it in a huge mound – all those trenches are where the earth and turf were dug out – and when it's covered a slow fire is started at one end which burns away for weeks, and when that's out the charcoal is ready. They're really sort of home-made kilns. Does your aunt think that whoever murdered Alice was really wearing a pair of her dungarees? I mean, surely she must know if a pair is missing? It wouldn't be easy to steal them.'

Victoria gave it up. 'But there is a pair missing,' she said, resigning herself. 'And Aunt Em says it would have been quite easy for anyone who wanted a pair to take them off the washing line. I had a look this morning, and it would. In fact you could have had one yourself today if you'd felt like it. That path you were on passes it quite close.'

'Oh,' said Mrs Brandon, momentarily disconcerted. 'Yes, I suppose it would be possible. It's very careless of Em to have her lines where she can't see them. It encourages pilfering. But the hat – is one of her hats missing too?'

'I don't think so. But one floppy hat would look exactly like another in the dusk, wouldn't it?'

Mrs Brandon's gaze fell on the wide-brimmed double terai she held, and she dropped it as though it had stung her, and then stooped hurriedly and picked it up. She jammed it back on her dishevelled curls and stood up, and said in a rather breathless voice: 'It's dreadfully hot here, isn't it? All those kilns—Shall we go back to the house? Em may have finished with the office work by now, and I should like some shandy.'

She led the way between the acacia trees, and across a waste of parched grass strewn with rough lava boulders towards a green belt of trees and bamboos that screened the gardens; and on arrival at the house went off to telephone her husband.

Victoria departed in search of cold drinks and discovered Eden in the dining-room similarly employed – though he appeared to favour something stronger than shandy.

'Hullo, Vicky. What'll you have? Scotch or rye. Or what about a gin and ginger? You'd better get down to some steady drinking, because the odds are once again heavily in favour of a bread-and-cheese luncheon. The entire household staff are having hysterics over the question of Gran's pants. What a party!'

Victoria laughed and said: 'I've got Mrs Brandon here. She's telephoning her husband to fetch her. She says she'd like some shandy, and I'll have some too. Is there any ice?'

'Lots. I've just collected a bowl from the 'fridge. Also some beer, so you're in luck. I presume Mabel is here with the object of collecting all the latest dope. Has she been cross-questioning you?'

'Yes,' admitted Victoria ruefully. 'I tried to dodge it, but it wasn't any use. She's madly curious.'

'She's scared stiff!' corrected Eden, mixing beer and ginger beer in a jug.

'Scared? But why?'

'Because her darling son had a juvenile crush on my wife,' said Eden.

'But that's no reason——' began Victoria, bewildered.

'No?' Eden added ice cubes, and filling a tankard, pushed it across to Victoria. 'You don't know Mabel! She's nuts about her ewe lamb, and it's my guess that she's been bitten with the crazy notion that Alice having repulsed him, he may have seen red and gone for her, preferring to see her dead rather than lost to him. All very dramatic and Othello-ish, and utterly ridiculous! I don't say that Ken mightn't have done that. In fact he's precisely the type of hysterical young ass who from time to time figures in the Sunday papers as having waylaid his ex-love, and bashed her with his own (and identifiable!) spanner, because she'd thrown him over. But what Mabel hasn't the sense to realize is that if he'd done it, he'd have shot himself five minutes later! Unless of course he had some totally different and entirely unsuspected reason for wanting Alice out of the way, which is absurd. If only one could put that to Mabel it would save her making an ass of herself. But of course one can't.'

'Why not?' demanded Victoria with some heat. 'Because "it's not done", I suppose!'

'No, darling. Because I, personally, do not fancy having my eyes scratched out. Just you try hinting to Mabel that she has even allowed such a possibility to cross her mind. She'd deny it with her last breath and never forgive you for having suggested it. But it's there all right – panicking about in her sub-conscious, if nowhere else. Nothing else will explain why she has taken to thinking up excuses for haunting the place and asking endless questions, and generally behaving like a flustered hen. Darling Mabel. The best thing we can do for her is to add a double brandy to her shandy.'

He mixed himself a stiff John Collins and lifted his glass to Victoria. 'Well, here's to you, darling. Don't let any of this get you down. You're too sweet to get involved in such a miserable business. Keep out of it, Vicky.'

Was there, or was there not, a note of warning in his voice? something more than the mere wish to save her from distress? The uncomfortable thought darted swiftly through Victoria's mind like a small fish glimpsed in deep water, and perhaps it had shown in her face, for Eden set down his glass, and crossing to her, put his hands on her shoulders and looked down into her eyes:

'I can't bear the idea of you getting mixed up in our troubles – in any troubles. And if only I were still strong-minded and self-sacrificing, instead of being weak-willed and abominably selfish, I'd insist on your leaving. But I'm not going to, because you are the one bright diamond in my present pile of coke.'

He smiled down at her, and once again, as it had on the previous day, Victoria's heart seemed to check and miss a beat. His hands tightened on her shoulders and the moment seemed to stretch out interminably.

'Oh, Vicky,' said Eden with a break in his voice, 'what a fool I've been!'

He released her abruptly, and picking up his glass and the jug of shandy, said: 'There's Mabel. Let's go and drink outside.'

He turned away and walked out on to the verandah, and Victoria, following more slowly, found Em and Gilly emerging from the hall door.

'Ah!' said Mr Markham enthusiastically, observing the tankard in her hand. 'Liquor! Just what I stand in need of after devoting an entire hour to the subject of milk (a dreary beverage and one I never touch). Would there be anything stronger than beer in the offing, Eden?'

'You'll find all the usual things on the sideboard in the dining-room,' said Eden. 'Help yourself.'

'Thanks, I will. What about you, Em?'

'Nothing, thank you. I dislike drinking at midday,' said Em grumpily, plumping herself down in a wicker chair.

'You don't know what you miss!' said Gilly blithely, and disappeared into the dining-room.

Mabel accepted a tankard of shandy and sat down on a long wicker divan that stood against the wall, its back formed by a row of three boldly patterned cushions – the fourth being presumably still in the possession of the police. She subjected her hostess to a worried scrutiny, and said anxiously: 'You don't look at all well, Em. You ought to get Dr North to give you a tonic.'

'Thank you, Mabel, I have no desire to fill my stomach with useless nostrums. I am merely tired, that is all. Tired of office work and silly questions and having the police permanently on the premises upsetting my servants. Is young Hennessy still here, Eden?'

'No,' said Eden. 'Having thrown the cook-house into hysterics he has retired to write up a report, and we shall probably have Greg here as soon as he's read it.'

'Did he get anything out of the servants?'

'Nothing but indignant denials and a suggestion that the dogs are responsible. Oh, and several missing dish-cloths that turned up in one of the huts. One of the *totos* had evidently been making a collection of them. No sign of your dungarees, however.'

'Where are the dogs today?' enquired Mabel, bending to peer along the verandah as though she expected to find them concealed under the chairs.

'Locked up,' said Eden. 'And they can stay there! They don't take to police on the premises, any more than Gran does.'

'Sensible animals,' observed Em morosely. 'Gilly, here's your wife. Get her a drink. Good morning, Lisa. What is it now?'

Gilly, who had emerged from the dining-room with a glass in one hand and a bottle of gin in the other, returned to fetch a second glass as Lisa came up the steps looking cool and spruce and pretty in a full skirted dress of pale blue poplin patterned with daisies. He returned with a gin and lime for his wife, and Lisa said: 'I only came over to ask about the picnic. I suppose you *are* postponing it?'

'What picnic?' enquired Em. 'Oh, yes. I remember. We were going to take an all-day picnic tomorrow to show Victoria something of the Valley. No, I see no reason why we should postpone it. It will do us all good to get away from the house for a day – and from the police! Mabel, you and Hector were coming, weren't you? And Ken. Then that's settled. Where shall we go?'

'Crater Lake,' suggested Mabel. 'I was telling Victoria about it just now. It's rather a fascinating spot, Victoria. A lake in the crater of an old volcano. They say it's bottomless, and——'

She was interrupted by the arrival of a Land-Rover containing Hector Brandon and a slim youth wearing the familiar garb of the Angry Young Men – a pair of exceedingly dirty grey flannels and a polo-necked sweater. A lock of his dark hair flopped artistically over a forehead not entirely innocent of the spots that adolescence is apt to inflict upon sensitive youth, and he possessed a pair of hot brown eyes, thin and passably attractive features, and the general air of a misunderstood minor poet.

So this, thought Victoria, was the boy she had caught a glimpse of driving furiously along the lake road on the morning of her arrival, and who had reportedly fallen so disastrously in love with Alice DeBrett.

She had been so intrigued by the unexpected arrival of Ken Brandon that she had not noticed that there had been a third man in the Land-Rover, and only became aware of it when Drew Stratton sat down beside her and observed amiably that it was a nice day.

Victoria started and bit her tongue. 'What? Oh, it's you. I didn't know you were here. What did you say?'

'I made the classic opening remark of the sociably disposed Englishman. I said it was a nice day. It's your move now.'

Victoria eyed him with some misgiving and said: 'I didn't know you were coming here this morning.'

'Would you rather I hadn't? I'm afraid it's a bit late to do much about it now, but I shan't be staying long.'

Victoria flushed pinkly. 'You know quite well I didn't mean it like that. I was only surprised to see you.'

'Pleasantly, I hope?'

'No!' said Victoria, regarding him with a kindling eye. 'I don't think it's ever particularly pleasant to meet people who dislike you; and you don't like me at all, do you? You made that quite clear from the moment you first saw me. Why don't you like me?'

Drew returned her indignant gaze thoughtfully and without embarrassment, and paid her the compliment of disdaining polite denial. He said: 'Because of Alice DeBrett.'

'*Alice?* But I didn't even know her! I don't think I understand.'

'Don't you? I thought I'd been into this once already. You are a very pretty girl, Miss Caryll, and you were once engaged to her husband. I don't know why you broke it off, but whatever the reason, you cannot really have supposed that she would welcome your arrival as a permanent fixture in the household?'

Victoria stiffened and found that her hands were shaking with anger. She gripped them together in her lap and enquired in a deceptively innocent voice: 'And were Mrs DeBrett's feelings so important to you, Mr Stratton?'

She looked with intention at Ken Brandon, who was talking moodily to Lisa Markham, and Drew noted the look and interpreted it correctly. He said dryly: 'I wasn't in love with her, if that is what you mean. Can you say the same about her husband?'

The angry colour drained out of Victoria's face and once again, as on the previous night, she looked young and forlorn and defenceless – and frightened. The indignation and the rigidity left her, and she said in voice that was so low that he barely caught the words: 'I don't know. I wish I did know. Did you think that I came out here to try and take Eden away from her?'

'No,' said Drew, considering the matter. 'She told me that your aunt had asked you to come. But I thought that knowing how she herself must feel about it, you might, perhaps, have refused.'

'You're quite right,' said Victoria, still in a half whisper that appeared to be addressed more to herself than to Drew. 'I should never have come. But— I wanted to come back to Kenya.

648

Mother was dead and I had no one but Aunt Em. I wanted to – to belong again, and come home; and I wouldn't let myself think about Eden. He was married, and it was all over. I don't think I ever thought at all about Alice as a person. She was just something that proved it was all over, and made it safe to come. But now it's different . . .'

Drew looked away from her to where Eden's unstudied grace and startlingly handsome profile were outlined against the brilliant sunlight of the garden, and was startled to find himself wrenched by a physical spasm of jealousy and dislike. He said disagreeably: 'Because now he is free? Is that what you mean? But that should make everything pleasantly simple for you.'

Victoria shook her head without lifting it. It was only a very slight gesture, but somehow it revealed such a gulf of unhappiness and bewilderment that he was shocked out of his anger. He said: 'I'm sorry. That was rude and officious of me. And none of my business. Shall we talk about something else?'

He began to tell her about a film unit that had recently arrived in Nairobi, until Em interrupted him with an enquiry relative to the picnic and the rival merits of Thermos flasks and kettles.

'Not kettles,' said Hector. 'Don't care for lighting fires. Weather's been pretty dry, and we might do no end of damage. Are we going to do any shootin'? Have to bring a gun if we are. Just as well to bring one or two anyway, just in case. After all, one never knows. May be the odd hard-core terrorist hidin' out in those parts. There was always a rumour that the gangs had a hide somewhere near Crater Lake. Better to be on the safe side. And we might get a pot at a warthog or a guinea-fowl.'

'We must make a list,' announced Mabel, 'so that we don't leave anything behind. Has anyone got a pencil and paper?'

'Why worry,' enquired Eden lazily. 'As long as we take plenty of food and drink and enough rugs to go to sleep on afterwards, that's all we're likely to need.'

Mabel regarded him with friendly contempt and remarked that that was just like a man. There were dozens of things that must be taken on a picnic: a flit gun and a fly swatter, a first-aid kit, matches, snake serum——

Eden laughed and turned to Victoria. 'So now you know what you are in for, Vicky. Snakes in the grass and warthogs in the undergrowth, and the odd terrorist lurking on the skyline. A nice, peaceful, Kenya afternoon! You needn't bother with the first-aid kit, Mabel. We always keep one in the Land-Rover. Bandages, lint, bottle of iodine – the works! I don't think we run to morphia and forceps, but possibly you can provide those.'

'As a matter of fact, I can,' retorted Mabel, unruffled. 'I don't believe in being unprepared for emergencies in a country where emergencies are apt to arise, and I always carry a bottle of iodine with me in my pocket. You've no idea how easily a scratch can turn septic in this country. But so far neither Hector nor I have ever had blood-poisoning.'

'Well neither have I, if it comes to that,' said Eden with a grin. 'And without the benefit of iodine! Don't tell me that Hector and Ken carry round the stuff too?'

'Of course they do. It's an elementary precaution that I insist upon. One should really carry permanganate as well.'

'What for? Medicating the drinking water, or washing the salad?'

'Snake-bite, of course. Serum is a bit bulky to take around, syringe and all. But permanganate is better than nothing. If you cut the wound across and rub the crystals in at once it can be very effective.'

'Look, Mabel,' said Eden earnestly, 'let's call off this picnic and go to a cinema instead. The whole thing sounds far too hazardous to me. My idea of a picnic is a peaceful afternoon spent flat on my back in the shade, after eating heartily of cold chicken, stuffed eggs, sausage-rolls and salad, topped off with coffee cake and several pints of beer. I am prepared to put up with flies and ants, but not with having myself carved up with a penknife and doctored with permanganate of potash!'

'Not in the least likely to happen,' said Hector reassuringly. 'Hundred-to-one chance. Though I'm not saying that Crater Lake hasn't got a bad name for snakes. Saw a mamba there once when I was a youngster. Came at me like the wind. Ugly brute. Fortunately I had m'shot-gun. Blew its head off. Very lucky shot.'

Eden covered his eyes and bowed his head on his knees, and Gilly burst into a roar of laughter to which Em added her rich chuckle, while even Ken Brandon momentarily abandoned his Byronic gloom and permitted himself to smile.

Hector said huffily: 'It was not in the least amusing I assure you. If I'd missed it – well, that would have been the end of me. And it's very painful way to die, let me tell you! Seen a chap do it. Blue in the face – writhing and twisting. Not at all funny.'

650

His son's reluctant smile broadened into a grin, and he said: 'Come off it, Dad! You're terrifying the girls. Lisa doesn't like snakes. Do you, Lisa?'

'No,' said Lisa with a shudder. 'Horrible things! Mbogo says that there are a pair of puff adders in a hole under the big acacia by the gate. He says he's seen their tracks in the dust. *Ugh!*'

Mabel gave a sympathetic shiver and said: 'There seems to be a plague of them this year. We're always passing dead ones on the road that have been run over by cars. It's the only thing I don't like about the Rift – the snakes. Hector and Ken don't seem to mind them. They collected them for the venom centre once. That place where they keep snakes and collect the poison for serums.'

'In that case,' said Gilly, 'any intelligent snake should give us a wide berth on Wednesday.' He waved his glass and chanted:

> '*You spotted snakes, with double tongue,*
> *Thorny hedge-hogs, be not seen;*
> *Newts, and blind-worms, do no wrong;*
> *Come not near* — there are Brandons about!'

'I can't see what you've got to be so cheerful about this morning,' said Lisa crossly.

'Can't you, my sweet? Well I'll let you into a secret. I've got a lovely surprise for you. Em's sending us off to Rumuruti when Jerry Coles leaves. How do you like that?'

There was a sudden startled silence. Eden sat bolt upright, while Lisa stared at her husband in open-mouthed, ludicrous dismay, and Drew's blond brows lifted in surprise. Even the Brandons seemed taken aback, and only Em remained tranquil.

The effect of his pronouncement appeared to afford Gilly considerable amusement, but Lisa's gaze had flown to Eden and she said involuntarily: 'Oh no! it isn't true! We can't——'

'Of course it's true,' said Gilly cheerfully. 'Why are you all looking so surprised? I've been trying to blarney Em into nominating me for the job for weeks, and she's seen reason at last. I received the accolade this morning. Manager of DeBrett Farms, Rumuruti. That's me. Or it will be. Aren't you going to congratulate me, Eden?'

Eden's mouth tightened into a narrow and ominous line and he stared at Gilly for a dangerous minute, and then turned to his grandmother. 'Is this true?' he demanded harshly. 'Have you really promised him Coles's job? *Have you?*'

'Come, come, my dear boy,' reproved Hector, intervening with all the tact of a charging rhinoceros. 'Must remember that you're speakin' to your grandmother!'

Drew said very softly: 'Ware wire, Hector!' but Eden did not appear to have heard the interruption. *'Have you?'* he insisted, his eyes on Em.

Em looked long and deliberately from Eden to Lisa, and back again, and said calmly: 'Certainly, dear. On consideration it seemed to me an excellent idea. I admit that I once thought otherwise, but circumstances alter cases. And in the present circumstances I consider that it may prove to be a very satisfactory arrangement after all. To *everyone*. Victoria dear, you have not yet told us if there is any particular spot that you would prefer to visit rather than Crater Lake?'

Victoria, disconcerted at finding herself suddenly drawn into the conversation, disclaimed any preferences, and was perhaps the only person present who interpreted Em's apparently inconsequent query as an attempt to change the conversation. Eden glanced quickly at her, and then at Lisa, whose desperate gaze was still fixed on him, and there was, suddenly, comprehension and something that might almost have been relief in his face.

The rigidity went out of his slim figure and he relaxed in his chair, and Gilly, who had been watching his wife with bright observant eyes and a smile that was tinged with malice, said: 'Aren't you pleased, dear? I thought you'd be delighted! Promotion. More pay. Nice house. New faces – I hope. You'll love it!'

Lisa said nothing. She looked away from Eden at last, her face white and wooden and her mouth a tight scarlet line, and it was Hector who spoke.

'Must say,' said Hector judicially, 'I'm surprised. Shouldn't have said you were up to it, Gilly. If you don't mind my speakin' frankly.'

'But I do mind,' said Gilly. 'And, speaking frankly, I don't consider that it is any of your dam' business. Which reminds me——' He turned his back on Hector, and addressing Ken said conversationally: 'I've been meaning to ask you, Ken. Was that Kerry Lad you were riding on Tuesday evening? Because if so, you really should enter him for the open jumping at the Royal Show. There can't be many hunters who can clear that hedge and the wire on the boundary side of my garden without coming to grief. You should have a walk-over.'

Ken Brandon did not reply, and for the second time that morning a stricken silence descended upon the verandah. But now it was the boy's face that was as white and still as Lisa's had been, and the affectation and the Byronic pose fell away from him. He stared at Gilly like a hypnotized rabbit and licked his dry lips, and then Mabel had risen swiftly and was standing between them, her cheeks pink and her grey curls quivering:

'I don't know what you're talking about, Gilly,' she said in a calmly cheerful voice. 'Ken was riding White Lady on Tuesday. Wasn't he, Em? And she's no good over the sticks.'

'I didn't mean when he came over the first time,' said Gilly softly. 'I meant later on.'

'He wasn't out later on,' said Mabel positively, and turned to Lady Emily: 'We really must be going, Em. Thank you for the shandy. It was delicious. Where are we going to meet tomorrow? I suggest you all come along to us about eleven, as we're on your way, and then we can sort ourselves out and go on from there. Drew, you'll come won't you? Yes, of course you must. We won't take no for an answer. We fixed up who brings what food, didn't we? Then that's all right. Come on, Ken dear. Goodbye, Victoria. It's nice to have met Jack's girl. Can we give you a lift, Drew? Oh – but that's *your* Land-Rover, isn't it?'

'Yes,' said Drew, rising and stubbing out his cigarette. 'I am an uninvited guest at this party. I would appear to have the only transport that does not break down at awkward moments. Which has its disadvantages.'

His smile robbed the words of any offence, and the tension in the atmosphere decreased almost visibly. 'That's right,' confirmed Hector. 'Afraid we broke down. That damned clutch again. Drew picked us up. Wasted his morning, I'm afraid. Hope you won't mind givin' us a lift back, Drew?'

'Not at all, sir. Delighted. Goodbye, Em. Are you really expecting me to turn up at this picnic tomorrow?'

'You heard what Mabel said,' retorted Em with something that in anyone else would have been described as a sniff. 'She "won't take no for an answer". So naturally I shall expect to see you there.'

'All right,' said Drew resignedly, 'though frankly – if I may borrow a favourite word of Hector's – if I had any sense I'd remove myself to Nyali or the Northern Frontier until the situation here was less electric.'

'Greg wouldn't let you go,' announced Em a trifle grimly. '*You* haven't got an alibi either!'

The Land-Rover departed in a cloud of dust, and Eden, who had been watching the Markhams as they walked away across the garden, said slowly: 'What was Gilly getting at – about Ken riding across our land on Tuesday evening? Do you suppose he was here?'

'Yes,' said Em shortly. 'I imagine he did it fairly frequently, and for no better reason than the time-honoured one of passing the house in which his lady lived. Infatuated youth has done that sort of thing – and will go on doing it! – for centuries. But Ken is young enough and foolish enough to try and hide the fact, and Gilly is trading on that to tease him – and Mabel. It's a very silly thing to do, and I shall have to speak to Gilly. Drew is quite right. Too much electricity. I don't like it. I don't like it at all!'

She sighed heavily, and rising from her chair walked away down the verandah, muttering to herself after the manner of the old.

The remainder of the day had passed peacefully enough, but Victoria slept little that night. She lay awake hour after hour, worried at first by personal problems, but later by fear. For as the slow hours ticked away, the house that had seemed so silent began to fill with innumerable small stealthy sounds, until at times she could have sworn that someone was creeping about the darkened rooms – tiptoeing across the floors and easing open doors very softly so that the hinges should not creak.

She had locked her own door when she went to bed, and had been ashamed of herself for doing so. But as she lay awake in the darkness, straining her ears to listen, it occurred to her that it was no use locking your door against a ghost, and that if there were such things as poltergeists it might be in her room at the moment, watching her and chuckling at her fear.

Beyond her window the garden had been white with moonlight, but even there it had not been silent, for down in the papyrus swamps birds were calling; crying like gulls on a windy day; though there was no wind, and it was night.

Were there really still remnants of the Mau Mau gangs hiding in the swamp? – desperate, hunted, hungry men who were being fed in secret by those who were, by daylight, faithful and trusted servants of the settlers whose estates bordered the lake?

Several times during that long night the dogs had growled and barked and scratched at the door of the disused storehouse in which they were locked, and though there might be a trivial reason for that – a rat scuttling in the roof, or a prowling cat – might they not be barking at a man creeping out from the labour lines with food in his hands, to meet a shadow who had come up through the darkness of the shamba and the papyrus swamp? A shadow who had perhaps killed Alice DeBrett——?

12

The Land-Rovers bumped and bounced and jolted over the unmade lake road, trailing the inevitable dust clouds behind them like smoke from an express train, and the morning was hot and blue and brilliant.

The country was more rugged here, near the foothills of the Mau, and oddly shaped hillocks that had once been the cones of volcanoes jutted up out of the plain, turning from green to darkest midnight blue as an idling cloud shadow would engulf one and silhouette it blackly against the surrounding blaze of sunlight.

There was little game to be seen at this hour of the day, for in the hot noonday the great herds of zebra and gazelle that grazed across the open ranges in the early morning and the late afternoon had retired to the shade of the trees. But in a grove of acacias outside a small village a troop of baboons howled and leapt and danced among the branches as the Land-Rovers passed.

The picnic party had arrived separately at the Brandons' farm, and had there sorted themselves out into three Land-Rovers. Ken Brandon and Lisa in Drew Stratton's, Em with Mabel and Hector, and Victoria and Gilly with Eden.

Eden's complement had also included Thuku, Em's African driver, and old Zacharia who had been brought along to deal with such tedious but necessary chores as the cleaning of dirty knives and dishes, the disposal of debris and the repacking of depleted baskets. The Brandons had also brought their driver, Samuel, for it was still not considered safe to leave a vehicle unguarded in the remoter parts of the Rift, and both Samuel and Thuku carried loaded shot-guns.

'There's Crater Lake,' announced Gilly, breaking a silence that had lasted for several miles. 'Or rather, there's the rim of the crater. Over on the right——'

'But there's no road,' objected Victoria.

'Lor' bless you, we don't need roads in this country,' said Gilly. 'What do you take us for? Sissies? I admit that this appalling chain of rocks and potholes that we have been bouncing along for the last umpteen miles or so calls itself a road, but you won't notice any appreciable difference when we take to the open range. Here we go!'

As he spoke, Eden drove the Land-Rover off the dust-laden road and across a long stretch of open country that sloped upward towards high ground crowned with rocks, candelabrum trees, thorn scrub and thickets of wild olive.

'See what I mean?' demanded Gilly, returning violently to his seat from hitting his head on the canvas roof. Victoria, who had inadvertently bitten her tongue, nodded dumbly and braced herself to withstand a sharp list to starboard as they roared up a steep cattle track that climbed over rocks and roots, and came at last to a stop in a small clearing where the two Land-Rovers that had preceded them were already parked.

'Well, that's as far as we can go,' said Eden, applying the brake and wiping the dust out of his eyes. 'We walk from here.'

Gilly descended and went round to the back of the car to superintend the removal of the beer, and Eden jumped out and reached up to lift Victoria down.

He held her for a full half-minute before he released her, and Victoria, looking into the grey eyes that were so near her own, was astonished to realize that her pulse had not quickened nor her heart missed a beat, and that for the first time in her life she was looking at him as though he were a friend, or a cousin, instead of the glamour-gilded Hero of all Romance that he had been to her for so many years.

Her feet touched the ground, and feeling it rough and solid under her shoes it was as if she had touched reality at long last and relinquished her grasp upon illusion.

Eden released her, but she did not move away. She stood in the hot sunlight looking at him gravely and intently, and he smiled his charming quizzical smile and said lightly: 'What is it, Vicky? Learning me by heart?'

'No,' said Victoria slowly. 'I know you by heart. I think that's always been my trouble. I've never known you any other way.'

'You mean, never with your head? Then don't start now, darling. You mightn't like me with your hard little head, and I couldn't bear that.'

He lifted her hand and kissed it, and then suddenly his face changed. The warmth went out of his eyes and he dropped her hand, and Victoria, turning, saw that Lisa and Drew had walked back to the cars and were standing within a few yards of them, having

657

obviously witnessed the brief scene. It was also equally obvious that neither of them was pleased. Drew looked blank and bored and thoroughly disagreeable, and Lisa looked frankly furious.

It was, somehow, a deeply embarrassing moment out of all proportion to the triviality of the occasion, and facing Lisa's white-faced, tight-lipped jealousy and Drew's cold eyes, Victoria found herself blushing as hotly as though she had been guilty of some gross impropriety. She looked away and became aware that Gilly too was an interested spectator. He had come round from the back of the car and was leaning against it, studying his wife with detached interest as though she had been some stranger whom he had not previously met. His gaze took in her ultra-feminine and un-picnic-like garb, and once again there was comprehension and malice in his face, as though he were perfectly aware for whose approval she had dressed.

His glance slid past her and came to rest on Victoria, neat and slim in slacks and shirt, and he said meditatively and in the manner of one speaking a thought aloud: 'You know, she's good, this girl: she uses her head. Lisa'll have to work fast. Very fast!'

Eden said coldly: 'What are you babbling about, Gilly? Have you got the stuff unloaded?'

'I was musing, like Polonius, on the frailty of human nature,' said Gilly. '*Whose violent property fordoes itself, and leads the will to desperate undertakings, as oft as any passion under heaven* – and if you were referring to the beer, yes. I have unloaded it and it is on its way up. Hadn't somebody better stay and keep an eye on our transport, just in case the odd terrorist is still using this salubrious spot as a hide-out?'

Drew said briefly: 'Thuku can stay around.' And taking Lisa by the arm he turned her about and started back up the steep slope, the others following in single file behind him.

Lisa had not spoken, but Drew, holding her arm, could feel that she was shivering as though with ague, and he said sharply: 'Hold up, Lisa! If you don't look where you're going you'll end up with a broken ankle. Here we are——'

They had come out on a bare expanse of broken rock, and below them, ringed by the steep sides of the crater and bordered by a jungle of scrub and acacias, lay a little green lake. The eeriest place, thought Victoria, looking down on it, that she had ever seen. And the most silent.

The sky overhead was clear and blue, but the lake did not reflect it, and the whole cup of the crater was as green and dark and still as though a cold cloud shadow had fallen directly upon it. Victoria shivered, and drawing back from the edge of the cliff, said doubtfully: 'It looks rather an unfriendly place, doesn't it?'

'*A Daniel come to judgement!*' said Gilly. 'My opinion exactly. A morgue. However, don't worry, a few drinks will brighten your viewpoint considerably – and mine. And if you're worrying about the dangers of the African bush, Hector, Eden and Ken are all Grade A marksmen, while Drew has Annie Oakley beat to a frazzle. Anything she could do, he can do better. You are as safe as houses – except for the flies. And Mabel and her flit gun will probably be able to repel those. Let's go.'

Victoria laughed a little shamefacedly, and Drew, after favouring her with a brief, frowning glance, turned and led the way along the rim of the crater to a point where there was a fairly easy route down the cliff to the trees and the lake edge.

They met the Brandons' driver, Samuel, coming up the narrow track having helped carry down the baskets, and found Em, Mabel and Hector comfortably ensconced on rugs and ground sheets in the shade while Zacharia unpacked the luncheon.

Ken Brandon, who had been on a solitary ramble, reported that he had seen the pug marks of a leopard in a patch of wet mud at the far side of the lake, and that there was the skeleton of a big warthog among the bushes. He exhibited one of the enormous curved tusks, and said: 'Look at that! Must have been the great-grandfather of all warthogs. I've never seen tusks that size before.'

The air of embittered gloom had temporarily left him, and he looked boyish and refreshingly normal as he handled the yellowed chunk of ivory.

'Leopard kill?' enquired Drew.

Ken shook his head. 'No. The bones are complete. Old age probably. Or perhaps he was wounded somewhere on Conville's range, and came here to die.'

'Or got bitten by a snake?' suggested Gilly.

Ken dropped the tusk on to the ground and the animation went out of his face. He said: 'Perhaps,' in a colourless voice, and went to sit beside Lisa, who moved over to make room for him.

It was well past two o'clock by the time Zacharia had washed up in the scummy water of the lake, and assisted by Samuel had carried the picnic baskets back up the cliff path to the cars.

Hector departed to inspect the leopard's spoor and the skeleton of the warthog, while his wife produced a voluminous cretonne bag and settled down to some knitting, and Em, who had thoughtfully provided herself with a cushion, announced her intention of resting for at least an hour.

The remaining members of the party had gone off to explore the crater – with the exception of Gilly who, having drunk two bottles of beer on top of seven pink gins, had quarrelled with Hector, been offensive to Ken Brandon and been spoken to sharply by Em, and had retired with a rug and a flit gun to sleep it off behind a clump of bushes. Lisa's sandals, however, were not made for exploring, and she had clung to Eden's arm and they had fallen back and got separated from the others, so that Victoria found herself left with Drew Stratton and young Mr Brandon. Neither of her companions evinced the slightest desire to talk, and Victoria only noticed that Ken had removed himself elsewhere when they had made an almost complete circuit of the crater and she had turned to ask him where he had seen the leopard's pug marks.

'He left us about ten minutes ago,' said Mr Stratton, bored. 'Is there anything else you want to see?'

'Not here,' said Victoria with a shiver. 'I don't think I like this place. And I don't think it likes us. It's too quiet.'

She turned her head, listening, and in the silence they could hear faintly but distinctly, and coming from somewhere twenty or thirty yards ahead and out of sight, a sound that after a moment or two she identified as snores. That would be Gilly Markham – or Em! The snores ended on a loud snort, and after an interval of silence began again, and Victoria turned back to Mr Stratton and enquired uneasily if he really thought that there might be a leopard in the crater?

'Possibly,' said Drew, without interest. 'There are hundreds of hiding places among the rocks, and those pug marks were fairly new. Which is one reason why you can't be left to wander round here on your own.'

Victoria stood still and stared at him for a fulminating moment. 'If that means that you feel that you have to stay around in order to protect me, you needn't bother. I shall be quite safe, and I don't want to explore any more.' She sat down on a convenient boulder, with her chin in the air, and added coldly: 'Don't let me keep you.'

Drew looked at her thoughtfully for a full half-minute, and then he shrugged his shoulders slightly and turned away.

Victoria watched him go with a mixture of resentment and

apprehension, and was strongly tempted to call him back. Not because she anticipated any danger from leopards or terrorists, but because she did not like being left alone in this eerie and disquieting spot, even though she knew that nine other people were presumably within call, and at least three of them – Aunt Emily, Mrs Brandon and Mr Markham – less than thirty yards away. But Drew had disappeared among the thick belt of trees and she could no longer hear the bushes rustling as he moved. She sat quite still, listening; but no one seemed to be moving anywhere in the crater, and the silence flowed back into it, filling it as a cup is filled with water.

It was not in any way a peaceful silence, but a stealthy, all-pervading stillness that contained a disturbing quality of awareness. And suddenly, and for no reason, she was afraid. Where had everyone else got to? Had they all stolen away and left her alone in this horrible place? She must find them again. She would walk over to the trees where they had picnicked, and sit beside Aunt Em and Mrs Brandon and listen to the comforting click of Mrs Brandon's knitting needles.

But she found that she could not make the first move to break that brooding silence, and when at last she heard movements among the trees the sounds were as frightening as the silence had been, for there was about them the same disquieting suggestion of stealth; as though someone – or perhaps several people? – were moving within the crater with infinite caution and the minimum of noise.

Once a stone rattled down from the cliffs with a small metallic clatter that was uncomfortably reminiscent of the chatter of teeth, and then a twig cracked, and Victoria turned quickly: but there was no one there. Only the trees and the shadows and the rank grass – and a flicker of movement that might have been imagination or a bird flitting between the leaves.

'Who's there?' called Victoria, astonished at the huskiness of her own voice. 'Is anyone there?'

The words seemed astonishingly loud in the silence, but no one answered her, and a minute or two later the undergrowth rustled as though something or someone was moving stealthily away. The soft sound grew fainter until it was submerged at last by the silence, and though there were no more sounds Victoria did not move. She sat quite still, listening intently, while the sun moved slowly down the sky and the deep blue shadow of the cliff crept forward across the cup of the crater. Only when it touched her did she give herself a mental shake and stand up.

I'm behaving like an idiot, thought Victoria with disgust: sitting here working myself into a panic over nothing, just because everyone else has very sensibly done what Aunt Em and Mrs Brandon have – gone to sleep! And with that thought courage flowed back and her fears seemed childish, and she began to walk along the marshy margin of the lake towards the spot where they had picnicked. She had almost reached it when a sound that was painfully associated with her recent flight out from England assaulted her ears, and she stopped in sudden distaste. Mr Markham, having awoken from sleep, was obviously – and regrettably – engaged in parting with his lunch and the excess of alcohol with which he had insulted his long-suffering stomach.

Victoria turned and tiptoed away again, feeling for the first time deeply sorry for Gilly's wife, and she was halfway round the far side of the lake when Hector Brandon came out of the bushes a few yards ahead of her and waved cheerfully, and a moment later Lisa Markham joined them. They found Ken Brandon taking photographs with a large box camera, and as they reached the little clearing where they had picnicked, Drew came down the cliff path and Eden strolled out from between the tree trunks.

Em was asleep – her hat tilted well over her nose – and Mabel's busy needles were silent while their owner snored gently.

'A pretty and peaceful picture,' commented Eden. 'But unless we're going to have tea here, it's time we moved on. Wake up, Gran darling!'

Em grunted like a startled warthog, and sitting up with a jerk that dislodged her hat, glared at her grandson.

'I wish,' she said crossly, 'that you would all go away and let me have a short rest. Surely you can amuse yourselves somewhere else for half an hour?'

'You've been resting, darling. And for well over an hour! It's getting on for half-past three.'

'That's right,' confirmed Hector, who had been rousing his sleeping wife. 'Time we were makin' tracks. Here are Zach and Samuel to carry up the rugs. Better let 'em take your cushion too. Hope we haven't left any bottles about. Where's Gilly?'

'Still sleeping it off, I expect,' said Eden. He raised his voice and called out: 'Hi, Gilly, wake up! We're off! Ken, go and rout him out.'

'Rout him out yourself,' said Ken sulkily.

Eden raised his brows, and the boy coloured hotly and said: 'Oh, all right,' and plunged round the clump of bushes behind which

Gilly had retired for his afternoon nap. They heard him give an exclamation of disgust and mutter in an undertone, 'Tight again!' and then, loudly: 'Hi, Gilly – we're going: wake up! *Gilly——!*'

There followed an indescribable gasp, and the next minute he was back again, his face a sickly white and his eyes wide and staring. 'I – I can't wake him! I think he's having a fit.'

Drew departed at a run, closely followed by Hector, and the remainder of the party, rounding the bushes, found him on his knees beside Gilly's recumbent body.

Gilly was shivering violently, and Drew looked up and said curtly: 'It looks like an attack of fever. Has he ever had malaria, Lisa?'

'No,' said Lisa, staring in white-faced distaste at her husband's shuddering body. 'I don't think so. But he did once have——' She checked herself abruptly and bit her lip.

'D.T.'s,' finished Hector bluntly. 'Yes, we know. Perhaps you're right.'

'Nonsense!' said Em crisply. 'He may have had too much to drink, but he certainly wasn't *that* drunk. Must be malaria.'

'He's not hot,' said Drew, laying a hand on Gilly's sweating forehead.

Em bent down to touch him, and drawing back with a gasp, struck with her stick at something that had lain concealed by a fold of the rug.

'Look out!' shouted Hector, leaping forward. *'Snake!'* He snatched the stick from her hand and beat at the puff adder that had been curled up near Gilly's arm, and Ken Brandon ran in with a broken branch, and lifting the limp, battered thing, flung it far out so that it fell with a splash into the silent lake.

Mabel said: 'He's been bitten – *look!*' And plumping down on her knees she pointed a trembling finger at two small purplish punctures on Gilly's bare forearm, from one of which hung a small drop of blood, already congealed. 'Get the serum, Ken! Run——! It's in the pocket of the car. Quickly!'

Ken turned and ran, stumbling through the bushes and panting up the cliff path, and Drew, who had not spoken, pulled back the lid from Gilly's eye, and after a quick look, thrust his hand inside the open-necked shirt, feeling for the heart beat. He said: 'Have we any brandy?'

Hector jerked a small silver flask from his pocket and handed it over without a word, and Drew forced the liquid between Gilly's quivering lips while Em, who had torn the chiffon scarf from her hat, wound it tightly above the puncture marks in a tourniquet, and demanding a sharp knife, made a deep cross-cut from which the blood welled sluggishly.

Gilly made no sound beyond the shuddering breaths that another attack of shivering forced from him, and Em dropped the knife into the grass and said frantically: 'What on earth is Ken doing? Mabel, where's that permanganate you talked about? He'll die before Ken gets back with the serum! Do something, can't you!'

'It's in the car,' gulped Mabel. 'With the rest of the first-aid kit. But I've got some iodine——' She fumbled in the pocket of her skirt and produced a small bottle.

'It may be better than nothing,' said Em, and poured the contents over the cut.

The minutes ticked by, and except for Gilly's laboured breathing the afternoon was so quiet that it seemed to Victoria that those who watched him must be holding their breaths; and in the silence she heard someone's teeth chatter.

Em burst out desperately: 'Eden, for goodness sake go and see what's keeping Ken. He must have——' And then Ken slithered down the cliff path bringing a young avalanche of stones with him, and crashed through the bushes to arrive hot and panting.

Em snatched the syringe from him, and filling it, plunged it into Gilly's arm above the wound, and they waited breathlessly, watching the pallid face, while Mabel chafed his limp hands and the shivering lessened until at last he lay still. His colourless face twitched, and the brandy that Drew had been forcing down his throat trickled from the corners of his mouth.

Drew put down the flask and felt for Gilly's heart again, and after a full minute he stood up and brushed the broken grass from his knees.

'He's dead,' said Drew curtly.

Mabel gave a hoarse cry and Lisa broke into shrill hysterical laughter that was somehow worse than any screaming or tears would have been.

Em stood up swiftly and slapped her across the face with the flat of her palm, and the laughter broke off in a choking gasp.

'Take her away, Mabel!' said Em sharply. 'Take her back to the car.' She turned on Drew and said: 'Don't talk nonsense! Of course he isn't dead. It's only the reaction from the serum.'

'Yes, I should say that was probably the last straw. His heart couldn't stand any more. He's dead all right.'

'No!' said Em hoarsely. 'No!' She looked dazedly at the syringe that she still held, and then threw it from her in a sudden convulsion of horror, while Eden, pushing her aside, went down on his knees beside Gilly, feeling for his heart as Drew had done.

After a minute or two he lifted a drawn and ravaged face, and Lisa, seeing it, said hysterically: 'He is dead, isn't he? *Isn't he!* Oh God, what a fool I've been! Gilly! – Gilly!'

Em said angrily: 'Mabel, I asked you to take her away! *Is* he dead, Eden?'

'Yes,' said Eden briefly, and got slowly to his feet.

They stood looking down at Gilly's thin, bony face with its clever forehead and weak chin, and it seemed to sneer up at them; the mouth half open and pulled down at one corner, and the pale eyes glinting through their lashes as maliciously as they had in life.

Lisa said in a sobbing whisper: 'He isn't dead. He's laughing at us! He's laughing——'

Mabel put an arm about Lisa's waist. Her pleasant gentle face was grey and shrunken, and she looked as though she were going to be sick. She said in a quavering voice: 'Come away, dear. Drew, give me that brandy.'

Drew picked up the flask and handed it over, but Lisa refused to drink from it. She wrenched herself free, gasping and panting. 'No – no, I won't! How do I know it isn't poisoned? Drew gave it to him and he died! How do I know it didn't kill him?'

'Oh, for God's sake, Lisa!' said Eden, exasperated. 'Pull yourself together! Here, Vicky, give Mabel a hand and get her away from here.'

But Victoria was not listening to him. She was watching Drew who was looking at Gilly as he had once looked at Em on the verandah at *Flamingo*. As though some new and startling thought had suddenly presented itself to him. It was a look that had disturbed her then; but coming on top of the shock of Gilly Markham's death it frightened her as Gilly's death had not done, and she backed away from him, and groping for support, found a tree trunk behind her and leant against it, cold and shivering.

Drew turned abruptly away and stooped to search among the grasses, and when he straightened up again they saw that he was holding the syringe that Em had thrown away. The needle was broken and the glass appeared to be smashed, but he handled it with the extreme caution of a man who holds a live bomb, and wrapping it in his handkerchief, put it very carefully into his pocket and bent again to hunt very carefully in the tangled undergrowth.

Em said tersely: 'What is it, Drew? What are you looking for?'

'The needle,' said Drew. 'We may need it.'

'What for?' demanded Hector impatiently. 'Can't use that thing with a broken needle! Stands to reason. Come on, let's get out of here. How are we going to get him up the cliff?'

Drew paid no attention and continued his search, and Em said heavily: 'Eden and Ken should be able to manage it. The rest of us had better get back to the cars.'

She turned away, and pushing Mabel and the sobbing Lisa ahead of her, moved off through the bushes, walking very slowly and as though she were feeling for each step.

Victoria did not move. Partly because she felt incapable of movement, and partly because horrified curiosity had rooted her to the spot. Why should Drew think that it was important to find a useless thing like a broken piece of needle? And why were Hector and Eden watching him with such rigid apprehension? Why didn't they take Gilly back quickly to the cars? Surely they should get him to hospital as soon as possible? He *could* not be dead! Not just like that. There must be something that a doctor could do. Why didn't they do something – instead of watching Drew Stratton and looking so – so tense and strained and wary?

Something moved just behind her, and she whipped round, her heart in her mouth, but it was only old Zacharia calmly collecting the rugs and the ground sheets and various odds and ends that had not been taken away earlier with the picnic baskets.

Drew gave up at last, and turning to the three silent men who had watched him, he said curtly and incomprehensibly: 'They'll want that clasp knife, too. Where has it got to?'

The remark was meaningless to Victoria, but it was instantly obvious that it was clear to Eden, Hector and Ken. Eden's face took on a blankly wooden look that Victoria knew, and Ken gave an audible gasp, while Hector's bronzed features flushed darkly and he said explosively: 'Now look here, Stratton – you keep out of this! We don't want any more hysterical nonsense of that sort. I'll forgive it in Lisa. She's his wife – bound to be upset. But I'm damned if I'll stand it from you! Now, let's get the hell out of here.'

Drew said: 'I'm sorry, Hector, but it isn't as simple as that, and you know it. We must have that knife.'

666

But the knife was not there. They searched the grass and the bushes and shook out the rug on which Gilly had lain, but there was no sign of it.

'We're wasting our time,' said Hector angrily. 'It's probably in Em's pocket. Let's stop fooling about and get the body away. That's the most important thing to do.'

But when they at last arrived at the cars, after a slow and difficult ascent out of the crater, neither Em, Mabel nor Lisa knew anything of the clasp knife.

'I left it down there,' said Em. 'I think I dropped it on the grass. You can't have looked properly.'

'We looked everywhere,' said Drew. 'Who did it belong to? Was it yours?'

'No. I asked for a knife and someone handed me one.'

'Who?'

'I don't remember. And what does it matter, anyway? Why are they putting Gilly in your car?'

Drew said: 'We decided that Eden and I had better take him into Naivasha. You'll have your hands full with Lisa.'

He turned to Mabel and asked if she still had Hector's flask of brandy.

'Yes,' said Mabel, handing it over. 'Though I'm afraid there isn't much left. I think there's a bottle of whisky somewhere if you'd rather have that.'

Drew pocketed the flask without replying, and was turning away when Em spoke softly behind him.

'You've forgotten the iodine,' she said.

13

It was close on five o'clock by the time they arrived back at *Flamingo*, and Em had sent for Dr North and attempted to put Lisa to bed in one of the guest rooms.

But Lisa had refused flatly and with hysteria to sleep at *Flamingo*. The prospect of spending a night in a house that harboured a poltergeist appeared far worse to her than that of returning alone to her own empty bungalow, and eventually it was decided that Mabel should go back with her and stay the night.

Em and Victoria had eaten supper in the candle-lit dining-room, and it was towards the end of that silent meal that Victoria had asked a question that had been troubling her for several hours:

'Aunt Em, what did you mean when you told Drew – Mr Stratton – that he had forgotten the iodine?'

Em looked up from the food that she had barely touched, and her face in the soft light was grey and bleak. As grey and bleak as her voice:

'Because he does not happen to be a fool.'

She pushed her plate away and stared unseeingly at the candle flame that wavered in the faint draught made by Zacharia as he passed silently around the table, and Victoria said uncomfortably: 'I don't understand.'

'No,' said Em slowly. 'You wouldn't, of course. There are so few poisonous snakes in England. But I expect Drew has seen someone die of snake-bite, and that is why he thinks that Gilly Markham was murdered.'

She had spoken the word quite softly and casually into the quiet room, but it seemed to Victoria as though she had shouted it, and that the whole house must echo with it. *Murdered* . . .

Em waved away the dish that Zacharia was proffering, and selecting a cigarette from a box in front of her, lit it from the nearest candle and leant back in her chair, her bulky figure slumped and shapeless.

Victoria said with a catch in her voice: 'But why? How can he think that? It *was* a snake, wasn't it? We all saw it. Does he think

668

that someone put it there? But no one could have— He didn't say so. He didn't say anything! I was there the whole time, and he never said anything about it being – being——'

'Murder,' said Em. And once again the word was like a stone dropped into a quiet pool. 'He may not have used that word; but all the same, that was what he meant.'

'No!' said Victoria breathlessly. 'I don't believe it. If anyone had put a snake there on purpose it might not have bitten him. Or it might have bitten *them*! No one would risk it.'

'Oh, I don't suppose Drew thinks it was put there on purpose,' said Em impatiently. 'I imagine he thinks that someone who happened to have the means was quick enough to seize the opportunity, and make quite sure that Gilly did die. Stupid, really, because if he had been bitten the chances are that he would have died anyway. Personally, I think Drew is wrong. I think Gilly had a heart attack, and that is why he didn't cry out. But if I'm right, then either I killed him, or Drew did. And – and that is not going to be a very pleasant thought for either of us to live with.'

'*You!* You mean he thinks— You think——' Victoria's voice stopped on a gasp and she pushed back her chair and stood up, gripping the edge of the table. 'Aunt Em, you can't think he did it! You *can't*!'

'No, of course I don't,' said Em with a return of impatience. 'Sit down, child. I will not have hysterics. They do not help at all, and after Lisa I have had enough of them to last me a good many years. Neither does Drew think I did it – on purpose. But only two people touched Gilly. Myself and Drew. I made two cuts in his arm and gave him a full strength dose of snake serum, and Drew gave him a great deal of brandy. You cannot do that sort of thing to a man who is having a heart attack without killing him. And then again, if someone did give him poison to ensure that he died, then it was given in one of four ways. It might have been on the blade of the knife, or in the iodine, or the syringe, or in the brandy. Though of course there is always a fifth possibility: that he was given something at luncheon. But Zacharia had washed up all the glasses in the lake I asked.

Victoria sat down again and stared at her aunt. She said imploringly: 'It isn't true. They'll find out that it was only snake-bite, won't they? The doctors will know. It *must* have been snake-bite.'

Em shook her head. 'People who have been bitten by poisonous

669

snakes do not die like that. It's a pity Drew was there. Probably no one else would have noticed details. Or if they had, they'd have kept their mouths shut.'

'But if it was murder——'

'There are some things that are worse than murder,' said Em wearily. 'Trials, hanging, suspicion, miscarriage of justice.' She stubbed out her cigarette and quoted in an undertone: '*Duncan is in his grave; After life's fitful fever he sleeps well; Treason has done his worst: nor steel, nor poison, Malice domestic, foreign levy, nothing, Can touch him further*. Hmm. Gilly was fond of quoting Shakespeare. That would have appealed to him I imagine. *Malice domestic* ... I wonder——'

She relapsed into brooding silence, looking exhausted and ill, and Victoria eyed her in some disquiet and wished fervently that Eden would return. But although it was by now well past nine o'clock there was still no sign of him, and when Em had gone to bed Victoria went out into the dark verandah to listen for the car.

The moon was already high and the lawns and the trees were silver-white and patched with black shadows, and once again from somewhere down by the shamba and the papyrus swamp, birds were calling.

A bat flickered along the verandah almost brushing Victoria's head, and something moved in the shadows and sent her heart into her mouth; but it was only Pusser, the *Flamingo* cat, who had evidently been asleep in one of the wicker chairs.

Victoria was annoyed to find that her heart was racing and that she was breathing as quickly as though she had been running. Why didn't Eden come back? What were they doing – he and Drew? It was hours since they had left Crater Lake with Gilly Markham's body.

Somewhere in the house a clock struck ten, and the light in the dining-room, where Zacharia had been putting away the silver, was turned out. Victoria heard his shuffling footsteps retreating down the hall and then the sound of a door closing. And all at once the house was deathly quiet and only the night outside was full of small sounds.

Victoria clutched at the sides of her chair and glanced quickly over her shoulder at the open doorway that led into the hall, but the silent house seemed more frightening to her than the moonlit garden, and she stayed where she was, tense and listening, until at last she heard the faint, far-away purr of a car.

The sound grew louder and nearer, and presently the yellow glare

670

of headlights lit up the pepper trees and threw long black shadows across the sweep of the drive, and Eden walked up the verandah steps and checked at the sight of Victoria.

'Vicky! What are you doing here! You ought to be in bed. Did you wait up for us?'

'Us?' said Victoria. And saw then that Drew Stratton and young Mr Hennessy of the police were with him.

'Drew brought me back. It was his car. And Bill has been sent along to keep an eye on us and see that none of us makes a break for the border. They're staying the night. We thought it would be more convenient, as Greg wants to see us all in the morning. They can share the double bed in the blue room, and I hope one of them snores!'

He stopped by the hall door and said suddenly: 'There's nothing wrong, is there? Is Gran all right?'

'No. I mean, there's nothing wrong. Aunt Em went to bed. I stayed up because – because I didn't feel like going to sleep.'

'You look as though you could do with it, all the same,' said Eden as the light from the hall fell on her face. 'How's Lisa?'

'All right, I think. Aunt Em wanted her to stay here, but she wouldn't. Mrs Brandon is spending the night with her.'

'Good for Mabel. She won't enjoy it!'

There was a solitary table lamp burning in a corner of the drawing-room, and Eden switched on every other light and said: 'That's better! Vicky, I suppose you couldn't be a darling and rustle us up some coffee and sandwiches, could you? We've just driven back from Nairobi. I ought to have 'phoned, but I didn't want Em asking all sorts of awkward questions with half the Valley listening in on the party line.'

Victoria said: 'There's both in the dining-room. Aunt Em said you'd probably need something when you got back. Wait, and I'll fetch it.'

'Bless you,' said Eden, sinking gratefully into an arm-chair, 'and her. God, I'm tired!'

He lay back and shut his eyes, and looking down at him Victoria felt protective and maternal and as though, in some strange way, she had suddenly grown up.

She became aware that she herself was being watched, and turning her head met Drew Stratton's cool, level gaze. But tonight there was no hostility in his blue eyes; only interest and a faint trace of surprise. Victoria returned his look gravely, and then went away to

671

fetch the Thermos flasks and the chicken sandwiches that Zacharia had left on the sideboard in the dining-room.

There was a light on in the hall, but the two long passages that led off it were full of shadows, and the house was as quiet as Crater Lake had been. Was it waiting for something to happen, as Crater Lake had waited? But that was absurd! thought Victoria impatiently. There was nothing wrong with the house; only with herself and her unruly imagination. *The fault, dear Brutus, is not in our stars, But in ourselves, that we are underlings* – Gilly ... Gilly had been fond of quoting Shakespeare, and Gilly was dead. What was it that Em had said? *Nor steel, nor poison, malice domestic ... nothing can touch him further.* Yes, he was safe – if death were safety. But Eden and Aunt Em? and she herself, Victoria? – what about them?

Victoria shivered again, and setting her teeth, opened the dining-room door and groped for the light switches.

A single bulb in a red shade illuminated the sideboard but left the remainder of the room in shadow, and without waiting to turn on any more, Victoria collected a laden tray, and turned to see Drew Stratton standing behind her.

She had not heard him enter, and she was so startled that she would have dropped the tray if Drew had not taken it from her. He frowned at the sight of her white face and wide eyes, and said: 'What's the matter? Didn't you hear me?'

'No,' said Victoria breathlessly. 'You startled me.'

'I can see I did. You ought not to have stayed up. I suppose you've been sitting around alone, frightening yourself stiff?'

'Something like that,' admitted Victoria with a wan smile. 'What are you doing with that tray?'

'Making quite sure that the contents are as advertised,' said Drew. 'Though as I see that it wasn't only Eden who was expected, I imagine it's safe enough. Who made this? You?'

He had put the tray back on the sideboard and was un-screwing the cap of the Thermos.

'No. I suppose Zacharia did. Or the cook. Why?'

Drew did not reply. He removed the cork and poured a small quantity of coffee into one of the cups, smelt it suspiciously, and then put the tip of his finger into it and touched it cautiously to his tongue.

The import of the action was suddenly and horribly clear to Victoria, and she drew back with a gasp and put her hands to her throat: 'You c-can't— You can't think——' Once again she could not finish a sentence, for her breath appeared to have failed her.

Drew said: 'Seems all right.' He replaced the cork and turned his attention to the sandwiches, and after a moment or two said: 'How many people did Em order coffee for?'

'I – I don't know. She just said that Eden might want something when he came back, but she spoke to Zacharia in Swahili, so I don't know what she said.'

'*Hmm,*' said Drew thoughtfully. 'They all knew that as Eden had gone in my car, I'd probably be bringing him back. But there are four cups. If the extra two were Zacharia's idea, it shows that the old gentleman has more on the ball than one would imagine and had realized that someone from the police would come back with us. Which is interesting, to say the least of it.'

Victoria said huskily: 'Why have they sent a policeman here? Why not to the Markhams' bungalow? Why to us?'

'It isn't only to us. By this time there will not only be one at the Markhams' bungalow, but another at the Brandons.'

'Why? Is it— *Was* Gilly murdered?'

Drew replaced the sandwiches and looked up, frowning. 'Now what gave you that idea?'

'Aunt Em said you thought he h-had been. Was he?'

'Yes,' said Drew briefly, and picked up the tray.

Victoria had hardly slept at all during the previous night and had endured a harrowing day, and the effects were telling upon her. She began to shiver violently, and Drew put the tray down abruptly and took her into his arms.

It was an entirely unexpected action, but an astonishingly comforting one, and Victoria found herself clinging to him as frantically as though he had been a life line in a cold sea. His arms were warm and close and reassuring, and presently she stopped shivering and relaxed against him; feeling safe for perhaps the first time since her arrival at *Flamingo*, and suddenly and surprisingly sleepy. She turned her head against his shoulder and yawned, and Drew laughed and released her.

'You know,' he said, 'this is painfully like one of those detective novels in which just as the plot is getting littered with clues and corpses, the heroine holds up the action for three pages with a sentimental scene. Are you coming into the drawing-room to drink coffee with us, or would you rather go to bed?'

'Bed,' said Victoria; and yawned again.

Drew accompanied her down the dark passage to her room, and

having turned on the light for her, subjected the room to a careful scrutiny.

'No one in the cupboards or under the bed. And Bill Hennessy and I will be in the next room, and Eden only a few doors off. So you've nothing to panic about. I must get back or I shall have the police after me. You all right now?'

'Yes,' said Victoria, and smiled sleepily at him.

Drew took her chin in his hand and bent his head and kissed her quite casually and gently, and went away down the long dark passage, leaving her looking blankly at the panels of the door that he had closed behind him.

It was well past eight o'clock when Victoria awoke to the sound of knocking on her door, and unlocked it to admit an aggrieved Majiri who had apparently made several earlier attempts to rouse her.

The day, thought Victoria, blinking at the sunlight, could hardly be a pleasant one, but it was difficult to believe that horrible and frightening things could happen while the sun shone and the breeze smelt of geraniums and orange blossom, and the lake glittered like a vast aquamarine set in a ring of gold and emeralds. And yet Gilly was dead.

Duncan is in his grave ...

She dressed hurriedly and went out to the verandah to find that Eden, Drew and the young policeman were already half-way through their breakfast, and that Em was having hers in bed.

Lisa and Mabel, both looking white and exhausted, arrived just as the breakfast things were being cleared away, escorted by a police officer who left them at the verandah steps and disappeared round the back of the house.

Mabel was wearing the same crumpled cotton frock that she had worn on the previous day, and she did not look as though she had slept at all, while for the first time in anyone's recollection Lisa Markham had paid little or no attention to her personal appearance. It was also equally evident that she was frightened.

Victoria had offered her some black coffee, and she had gulped it down thirstily, her teeth chattering against the rim of the cup, and replacing it clumsily on the table had let it fall to the ground, where it had smashed into half a dozen pieces.

It had been one of the Rockingham cups, but Lisa had offered no apology or even appeared to notice what she had done. Em, appearing on the verandah arrayed like Solomon in all his glory, had glanced at the broken fragments and made no comment. She had nodded at Mabel, Lisa and Drew, bestowed an affectionate kiss on Victoria and a more perfunctory one on Eden, and ignored Mr Bill Hennessy, who blushed pinkly and looked acutely uncomfortable. And then Hector and Ken had arrived with a third policeman who, after a brief colloquy with Mr Hennessy, also departed round the back of the house.

'I suppose you will all be staying to luncheon,' said Em morosely, surveying the assembled company without pleasure. 'If we are going to spend the entire morning being interrogated, we had better——'

She was interrupted by Lisa, who stood up abruptly and announced in quivering tones that she did not feel at all well: certainly not well enough to answer any questions today from Greg Gilbert or anyone else. That she had only come over because Mabel had said she must, but if she had known that Greg was going to be so inconsiderate and unfeeling as to expect her to undergo a police grilling when——

Her spate of words grew shriller and higher, but any idea of her returning home was forestalled by the arrival of Greg Gilbert, two CID officers from Nakuru, several police askaris and an anonymous individual in a brown suit.

Greg confined his greetings to a single comprehensive nod that embraced everyone in the verandah, but the two CID officers were more punctilious. And then the entire party, with the exception of Mr Hennessy and the askaris, moved into the drawing-room, preceded by Em who seated herself regally in the wing-chair.

Greg refused a chair and stationed himself with his back to the windows, facing the half circle of anxious faces. His own face was blankly impersonal and his voice as devoid of emotional content as though he were reading the minutes of a board meeting to an assembly of total strangers.

He said: 'I imagine that you all know why I am here. An autopsy has been performed on Markham's body, and the doctor's report is quite definite. Gilly was not bitten by a snake, and there is the possibility that he was murdered!'

'No!' Lisa leapt to her feet, white-faced and gasping. 'You can't say that! You can't! It *was* a snake – we saw it!'

Mabel put out a hand and pulled her down again on to the sofa, murmuring: 'Lisa, dear. *Please!* Let him speak.'

Greg said: 'You may have seen it, but it didn't bite him.'

'We saw the fang marks,' said Em quietly.

'So Drew says; and Eden.'

'And I say it – and Mabel, and Ken,' put in Hector. 'Plain as the nose on your face!'

Greg shrugged. 'You saw two punctures that may have been made by anything; one of those double thorns off a thorn tree, for instance. Or if they were made by a snake, it was a snake that had either outlived its poison or emptied its poison sac. The autopsy showed no trace of snake venom, and it's my opinion that the snake you saw was a dead one.'

'But——' began Em, and checked; biting her lip.

Greg turned on her swiftly; 'Can you swear to it being alive? Did you actually see it move?'

Em hesitated, frowning. 'I thought I did. It moved when I hit it, but that might have been—'

'Of course it was alive!' boomed Hector. 'Why, I killed it! Dammit, I've got eyes!'

'But you have to wear spectacles for reading, don't you? And strong ones,' said Greg. 'And so does your wife, and Lady Emily.'

'That's different! Look – I wouldn't have wasted my time bashing a dead snake. Broke its neck and smashed its head.'

'And then threw it into the lake. A pity. If we could have got our hands on it, it might have told us quite a lot.'

'But——' began Hector, and stopped, as Em had done.

There was a brief and painful interval of silence, and then Ken Brandon spoke, his voice a deliberate drawl: '*I* threw it away. And what of it? Are you by any chance suggesting that I did it to destroy evidence?'

'Ken, darling!' begged Mabel in a strangled whisper. 'Don't be silly. *Please* don't be silly, darling.'

Greg favoured the boy with a long coolly critical look and said softly: 'No one is accusing you of anything – yet.'

Mabel caught her breath in a small sobbing gasp and Hector took a swift stride forward, his chin jutting and his hands clenched into fists. 'Now look here, Greg,' he began belligerently.

Mr Gilbert turned a cold gaze upon him, and though he did not raise his voice it held a cutting quality that was as effective as the crack of a whip: '*I* am conducting this enquiry, Hector, and I will do it in my own way. All of you here are required to answer questions, not to ask them; and I would point out that there is a well-known saying to the effect that he who excuses himself, accuses himself. I have not, I repeat, accused anyone – yet. Will you sit down, please? No, not over there. Eden, give him a chair behind Mabel, will you. Thank you.'

Hector seated himself reluctantly, muttering under his breath, and Greg turned his attention back to Em:

'You were answering a question when Hector interrupted you. Are you quite certain that the snake was alive when you hit it?'

'No,' said Em heavily. 'It may have been, and it never occurred to me that it wasn't. I suppose we were all too worked up about Gilly to notice details, and puff adders are often sluggish creatures. But I wouldn't like to swear to it, because——' She hesitated for so long that Greg said: 'Because of what?'

Em sighed and the lines of her face sagged. 'Because I realized later that whatever he died of, it wasn't snake-bite.'

'Why?'

Em threw him a look of impatient contempt and said irritably: 'There is no need to treat me as though I were senile, Greg. You must know quite well that I have seen people die of snake-bite – and before you were born! It is, to say the least of it, an unpleasant death. Gilly didn't die that way; and if you want to know what I think, I think he had a heart attack; but because we saw the snake we jumped to the conclusion that it was snake-bite – and killed him.'

'By giving him that injection?'

Em nodded. 'Drew said it was probably the last straw, and he may have been right. If we'd left him alone he might have pulled through: people do survive heart attacks. But he didn't have a chance. It was seeing the snake – I didn't even think of it being anything else.'

'It wasn't your fault, Gran,' said Eden roughly. 'If you hadn't done it, someone else would. We all thought he'd been bitten. What did he die of, Greg?'

'Heart failure,' said Mr Gilbert calmly.

14

'What!' bellowed Hector, bounding to his feet and stuttering with wrath. 'Then what in thunder do you mean by interrogating us in this fashion? By God, Gilbert, I've a good mind to take this straight up to the Governor! You have the infernal impertinence to post one of your men in my house, and another to keep an eye on my wife and on poor Gilly's widow, when all the time Markham died a natural death from heart failure!'

Mr Gilbert waited patiently until he had quite finished, and for at least a minute afterwards, and his silence appeared to have a sobering effect upon Hector, for he said with considerably less truculence and a trace of uncertainty: 'Well? What have you got to say for yourself?'

'Quite a lot,' said Mr Gilbert gently. 'For one thing, most deaths are due to failure of the heart. What we do not know is *why* Markham's heart stopped beating. It is of course just possible that he was suffering from a heart attack when you found him. He drank fairly heavily – I'm sorry, Lisa, but that's true, isn't it?'

'Yes,' said Lisa. She had ceased to slump in a frightened heap in a corner of the sofa, and there was a look on her pale face that was curiously like eagerness. 'He always drank too much, but in the last few months he seemed to be much worse. I told him we couldn't afford it, and – and that it would kill him if he went on like this; but he only laughed.'

Greg nodded, but said: 'All the same, I don't believe he had a heart attack.'

'But surely – the doctors,' urged Mabel distressfully.

'The doctors say that his heart was flabby and full of blood, and that the symptoms described by Drew and Eden square with a heart attack. But they also square with something else – Acocanthera. *Msunguti.*'

Once again the words meant nothing whatever to Victoria, but in the sudden silence that followed them she became acutely aware that they held a meaning – and a singularly unpleasant one – for

678

every other person in the room. Knowledge and shock – and wariness – was written plainly on six faces. Only Drew showed neither surprise nor wariness, but it was quite clear that he too knew the meaning of those two words.

Greg Gilbert looked round the room as though he expected someone to speak, but no one moved or spoke. They did not even look at one another. They looked at Greg as though they could not look away, and their bodies were still with a stillness that spoke of tensed muscles and held breath.

Greg said slowly: 'I see that you all know just what that means. Except Miss Caryll; which is possibly a good thing for her. For your information, Miss Caryll, I am talking of arrow poison. Something that is only too easy to come by in this country and which produces death – by heart failure – in anything from twenty minutes to two hours. Unfortunately it also produces no detectable symptoms, so unless we can produce other evidence the autopsy verdict on Markham will have to stand as "heart failure due to unknown causes". A verdict with which I, personally, am not prepared to agree.'

'Why?' demanded Em harshly. 'He might well have had a heart attack. He'd been drinking far too much, and he was three parts drunk by lunch-time yesterday – the autopsy must have shown that, too! And he was too thin and too highly strung. He lived on his nerves. Why do you have to believe the worst, when there is no shadow of proof to support it?'

'But there is a shadow of proof,' said Greg gently. 'The fact that three things which might have proved that it was a heart attack are all missing. We had a squad of our men down at Crater Lake at first light, and they went over the ground with a small tooth comb – and a magnet. But though they found the broken half of the needle, they didn't find the knife you slashed Markham's arm with, or the bottle of iodine you doctored it with. Or the snake that may or may not have bitten him. Odd, to say the least of it.'

Ken Brandon leant forward, his hands gripping the arms of his chair so tightly that his knuckles showed white, and said in a high strained voice that had lost all traces of a drawl: 'Why do you keep harping on that snake? What would *you* have done with it? Put it in your pocket? I didn't even know that it would fall in the lake! It was a fluke, I tell you! I——'

Hector said brusquely: 'Shut up, Ken! I'm not letting you say anything more without a lawyer. And if the rest of you have any sense you won't answer any more questions either! If Gilbert is accusing one of us of murder – and it looks damned like it to me! – then he's got no right to expect us to answer questions until we have had legal advice.'

Greg surveyed him thoughtfully, and then turned to look at Em. 'That your opinion too, Em?'

'No, of course not,' said Em crossly. 'I'm no fool. Or at least, not so big a fool as Hector is making himself out to be. Lawyers! *Bah!* The only useful advice that any lawyer could give any of us is to speak the truth and stop behaving as though we had something to hide.'

'If that is to my address,' flared Hector, 'I have nothing to hide! *Nothing!* But I still say——'

'Be quiet, Hector.' Mabel had not raised her voice, but the three softly spoken words were drops of ice, and they froze Hector's torrent of words as ice will freeze Niagara.

No one had ever heard Mabel use that tone before; or had believed her capable of it. And Hector's instant and instinctive reaction to it was equally surprising. He stood for a moment with his mouth open, looking like some large and foolish fish, and then he shut it hurriedly and sat down, and thereafter only spoke when he was spoken to.

Mabel said composedly: 'You must forgive us, Greg. We are all a little upset. Of course we will answer any questions that we can. We all know that you are only here to help, and that it cannot be any less unpleasant for you than it is for us. I suppose you want to know all about the picnic? Why we went and how we went, and when. And what we ate, and things like that.'

Greg shook his head. 'I know that already. I heard it last night from both Drew and Eden. No. I want to know about the knife. And about the bottle of iodine. Em, you used the knife on Markham's arm, didn't you? Whose was it?'

Em met his gaze squarely and with composure, and replied without the least hesitation. 'My own.'

The two words were as coldly and quietly spoken as Mabel's had been, but they produced an even more startling effect. There was an audible and almost simultaneous gasp from several throats: a sound that might have been relief or apprehension or shock, and Eden spoke for the first time since they had entered the drawing-room:

'Gran, are you sure?'

'Of what?' enquired Em, continuing to look blandly at Greg

Gilbert. 'That it was my knife, or that I know what I'm doing? The answer to both is "yes".'

For the first time that morning Mr Gilbert lost his calm. A flush of colour showed red in his tanned cheeks and his mouth and eyes opened in angry astonishment. 'Then why,' he demanded dangerously, 'did you say yesterday that you didn't know whose it was?'

'Did I?' enquired Em blandly. 'I can't have been thinking. We were all a bit——'

'*Upset!*' interrupted Greg savagely. 'So I have already heard. Now look here, Em, I'm not going to have any of this nonsense. That wasn't your knife, and you know it. Whose was it? You won't do any good to anyone by playing the heroine and telling lies to cover up for someone else.'

'You mean for Eden,' said Em calmly. 'But he never carries a knife. Only a silly little gold penknife arrangement on a chain that Alice gave him one Christmas. And I doubt if you'll find any bloodstains or arrow poison on that.'

For a moment it looked as though Mr Gilbert were about to lose his temper as explosively as Hector Brandon had done, but he controlled himself with a visible effort, and said quite quietly: 'I am not going to warn you of the consequences of deliberately obstructing the police, because you must be well aware of them. You also don't give a damn for the police or anyone else, do you? You're like too many of the Old Guard in that. You think that you can be a law unto yourselves. But that's where you're wrong. You can't have your cake and eat it too.'

He looked round at the ring of strained faces and added grimly: 'And that goes for all of you. You cannot let a murderer escape justice just because you happen to know him, or he is a relative or a friend. I do not believe that knife belonged to Lady Emily. The way I heard it, she asked for a knife and was handed one. Quite possibly she did not notice at the time who handed it to her, and she certainly told Stratton yesterday that she did not know whose it was. She has now, for reasons of her own, decided that it was hers. But there were half a dozen of you watching her, and one of you must remember where she was standing and who was next to her; and if the knife was not her own, one of you must have given it to her. That person had better speak up at once.'

No one spoke, and the silence lengthened out and filled with sullenness and strain and taut emotions, until suddenly and un-

expectedly Eden laughed. It was an entirely genuine laugh and therefore the more startling. He leant back in his chair with his hands
in his pockets, and said lightly:

' "Hands up the boy who broke that window!" It's no use Greg.
This isn't the Fifth Form at St Custards, and you can't gate the entire
class for a month if the culprit won't own up. Maybe that knife
really was Gran's.'

'Maybe,' said Greg sceptically. 'Very well, then. If it was, let's have
a description of it.'

'Certainly,' said Em briskly. 'It was a three-bladed knife that once
belonged to Kendall. It had a horn handle with his initials cut on it,
and the small blade had been broken off short. I often take it with
me when I go picnicking or shooting. It's very useful. I had it in
my pocket.'

'I see,' said Greg through shut teeth. 'Can you confirm that,
Eden?'

Eden had been looking at his grandmother with an expression
that was something between doubt and the effort to recall an
elusive memory, and he started slightly on being addressed, and said
hurriedly: 'Yes. Yes of course I can. It generally stays in the hall
drawer. I've seen it a hundred times.'

'And it was the knife your grandmother cut Markham's arm
with?'

Eden's face changed as though a mask had dropped over it, and
he said in an entirely expressionless voice: 'I'm afraid I don't
remember. If she says it was, then presumably it was. We were
all looking at Gilly at the time.'

'Were you!' said Mr Gilbert grimly. And he turned again to Em:
'What did you do with it after that?'

'I put it down – or else I threw it on one side. I'm not sure.'

'And poured iodine on the wound? I'd like to hear about that.'

Em described the incident in some detail, but professed not to
remember what she had done with the bottle.

'Then you didn't hand it back to Mrs Brandon?'

'I don't think so. I probably just dropped it too. It was empty.'

Mabel Brandon dabbed her eyes with a handkerchief and blew
her nose with determination, and looking across at Em she smiled
a little tremulously and said, 'Thank you, Em. I – I know you
do remember, and that you're only saying that to keep me out of it.
But I'm not going to hide behind you. She did give it back to me,
Greg. I took it from her and put it down somewhere, and

I didn't think of it again until Drew asked me what I'd done with it.'

Greg turned slowly and looked at Em, and it was noticeable that she returned his look with less assurance.

'Well, Em?' said Greg softly.

Em's mouth twisted into a wry and somewhat shamefaced smile.

'I'm sorry Greg. Yes, I knew Mabel had taken it. But I also know that she didn't kill Gilly, and I can't see that she need get mixed up in this horrible business just because she always carries around a bottle of iodine in case of accidents.'

'That,' said Greg, still softly, 'is the point. She always carries one, and everyone knows it. And that is why this may be a Mau Mau killing after all.'

'What!' The exclamation came loudly and simultaneously from half a dozen throats, and in a flash the atmosphere in the room changed as though a current of electricity had been switched off, and muscles that had been tense with strain and apprehension relaxed in sudden relief.

'I knew it!' cried Lisa; and began to sob loudly. 'I knew it would be all right!'

Em turned to gaze at her in disapproval, and observed coldly that she was glad that Lisa considered that everything was now all right: it was at least an original view of the case.

'I didn't mean Gilly being dead,' sobbed Lisa. 'Of course that's awful. It's just that I thought Greg might find out——'

'Lisa!' said Drew sharply and compellingly.

He had not spoken before, and his intervention checked Lisa, who gulped and turned to look at him.

'Whatever you were going to say – don't,' said Drew; and grinned at Greg Gilbert's furious face. 'Sorry, Greg, but I'm against shooting sitting birds. And in any case, from your last remark I gather we may all be out of the red, though I don't quite see how you can involve the Mau Mau in this one.'

Mr Gilbert said ominously: 'If you prompt anyone, or interrupt anyone again, Stratton, I shall get you ten days in the cells, if I get the sack for it!'

'And I'll go quiet,' promised Drew equably. 'What is this Mau Mau angle?'

'I should have thought it was obvious enough,' said Greg coldly. 'Hector is still doing a lot of useful interrogation work, and someone may have been laying for him – or for his wife or son. It would have

683

been easy enough to substitute a solution of arrow poison for the iodine, and the next time any of them had a cut or a scratch Mabel would have doctored it from that bottle, and that would have been that. It's a possibility that we can't ignore.'

'And the knife?' enquired Em crisply.

'Same thing. Except – if it *was* your knife – it might conceivably have been a trap laid for either you or Eden.'

'No. Not for us,' said Em thoughtfully. 'The dogs. I have often used it to cauterize sores on the dogs, and it would have got one of them. Like – like Simba.'

Mabel said: 'So Gilly was killed by mistake. It should have been Hector or Ken – or me! Or one of Em's dogs.'

'Or the first person you happened to doctor with iodine or who happened to cut themselves on my knife – and who might just as well have been an African,' pointed out Em dryly. 'It sounds very far-fetched to me, and it still doesn't explain the disappearance of the knife and the bottle. Where does that fit in?'

'It doesn't,' confessed Greg. 'It doesn't even fit in with my own theory of the crime.'

'And what is your theory? Or do you prefer to keep us in the dark?' enquired Em acidly.

Greg looked meditatively at the carpet for a minute or two without speaking, and then allowed his gaze to travel with deliberation along the half circle of intent faces that watched him so anxiously. And it is doubtful if he missed even the smallest change in any one of them.

He said slowly: 'No. There is no reason why I should not tell you, for although I believe that I am right, I can't prove it. I think that Gilly Markham died from the effects of arrow poison, and that his murder was carefully planned in advance. Everyone here, and everyone in the Rift for that matter, knew that he drank too much and could be trusted to drink too much even at a picnic, provided the drink was there; which it was. I believe that someone took a dead puff adder to Crater Lake yesterday, and sometime during the afternoon, while Gilly was asleep, placed it beside him and gave him a jab in the arm with some sort of pronged instrument that had been liberally coated with arrow poison. Something that would leave a wound similar to the mark of a snake's fangs.'

Lisa was the first person to speak. She said in a strained voice that was barely a whisper: 'But – why that way? The snake?'

'Because although arrow poison is not detectable in an autopsy, there might well have been some of it left outside the wound. Enough to prove that it had been used. But the first thing anyone does when dealing with a snake-bite is to make a deep cut on or just above it. That's why it had to be a snake; because the murderer could count on someone removing the evidence in double quick time. It would not matter who did it as long as it was done – and of course it was done. That disposed of any superfluous poison, and the snake was an equally easy bet. No one stops to see if a snake is alive if it is found lying curled up in a life-like attitude beside a sleeping person. They take a bash at it with the first thing that comes handy, and the blows would have made it appear to be moving. Also, no one is going to pay very close attention to it when there is a dying man to attend to. So you see, it would have been fairly foolproof.'

'But you said it could have been the knife,' whispered Lisa. 'Or the iodine. You *said* so!'

'It could have been. Because those two things have inexplicably disappeared. But it is far more likely that the poison was administered at least half an hour before either of those things were used. Acocanthera frequently produces vomiting, and your husband had been sick. He was also found in a state of coma just after three-thirty.'

Mabel's hands twisted together against the skirt of her crumpled cotton frock, and she said distressfully: 'Oh no! – Oh, I do hope not! I mean – I heard him. Being sick. If I had gone to him at once I might have been able to do something. But I thought – well, he *had* had too much to drink, and I thought it would be better to keep away. If *only* I had gone!'

'It wouldn't have done any good. Not if my theory is correct. There's no antidote.'

'But you can't be right!' said Mabel, suddenly sitting bolt upright. 'No, of course you can't be. You can't jab someone in the arm without waking them up. He would have cried out. I should have heard him. And,' she concluded triumphantly, 'I didn't! I didn't hear a *sound*, and neither did Em. Did you, Em?'

'I'm afraid I was asleep,' confessed Em reluctantly. 'I didn't even hear him being sick, and I certainly wouldn't have gone to him if I had.'

Greg said: 'Markham was sleeping off a fairly outsize dose of alcohol; and before the discovery of anaesthetics it was the accepted thing to give a man half a bottle of whisky to drink before an operation or an amputation – to deaden the pain. If the jab was a quick one it might have done no more than jerk him awake for a few seconds, and the chances are that he would have dozed off again at once. What is it, Miss Caryll?'

'N-nothing,' stammered Victoria, startled. 'I d-didn't say anything.'

'But you thought of something, didn't you?'

'Yes. I – it was nothing, really. It was only that while I was standing by the lake yesterday I heard someone snoring, and then they made a noise as though they had been woken up suddenly. You know. A – a sort of snort. I thought it was Gil – Mr Markham. But after a bit the snoring started again.'

'Hmm,' said Greg. 'What time was that?'

'I've no idea. Somewhere between half-past two and three I suppose.'

Greg turned to Mabel and asked her if she had also heard such a sound, and Mabel, looking a trifle conscience-striken, admitted to having dozed, though she had been woken later by hearing Gilly retching. 'But I didn't do anything about it. I remember thinking "*Really!* Poor Lisa." Or something like that, and the next thing I remember was Hector telling me to wake up because it was time we were going.'

'Hmm,' said Greg again, and was silent for so long that the tension became too much for Ken Brandon. His control cracked under the strain of that silence and his voice cracked with it:

'It's no good looking at me! I didn't go near him. I swear I didn't! I didn't even touch him. None of us did – only Stratton and Lady Emily. I'm not going to sit here and be accused of – of things, just because I threw away a dead snake! Dad was quite right. You haven't any right to do this. We aren't under arrest, and I'm going!'

He stood up clenching and unclenching his hands, and looking, for all his nineteen years, less like an Angry Young Man than a small boy who has flown into a temper to hide his fright.

'Oh *no*, Kennie darling!' moaned Mabel, wringing her hands. '*Don't* talk like that. Of course you didn't go near Gilly, darling. Greg knows that. We all know it. Stay here, darling. *Please!*'

Greg said patiently: 'Sit down, Ken. You're only making an ass of yourself, and I haven't accused anyone of anything.'

'*Yet!*' mimicked Ken savagely. 'That's what you said before, isn't it? *"Yet!"* But you will, won't you? Even though you haven't a shred of evidence! Even though you admit yourself that Gilly may have died of a heart attack. And what do you base your precious theory on? The fact that a knife and an empty bottle have been lost or mislaid.

Why, they're probably both still there, trodden into the grass by your flat-footed, bone-headed askaris!'

'Oh no, Kennie. Don't, dear,' sobbed Mabel in a monotonous moaning whisper. But Ken Brandon was beyond listening to reason or his mother's pleas, and the words poured out of him in a childish spate of nervous rage:

'What the hell does it matter if they aren't found? You've as good as admitted that there's nothing wrong with either of them, haven't you? *Haven't you?* And that if Gilly was poisoned, it was done half an hour before anyone used the knife or the iodine on him, which means that it doesn't matter a damn if they're found or not. And yet you can produce a footling thing like that and call it evidence of murder! If that's all the evidence you've got, then you haven't got a case at all. Not a shadow of a case! – and no right in the world to haul us in here and talk like this to us.'

He paused for breath, and Greg said mildly:

'I told you that the disappearance of those two things didn't square with any theory. But that is why I am interested in them: or rather, in why someone thought fit to remove them, and is now lying about it. There must be a reason for that, and it is my guess that whoever made away with them suspected murder – and the murderer – and having a shrewd idea as to how it had been done, jumped to the same conclusion that both Stratton and Lady Emily arrived at: that if it was Acocanthera, it was either on the knife or in the iodine bottle – and therefore hid them. But if it *was* murder, then the one person who would *not* have done that is the murderer; because such an action could only lead to suspicion of murder in what might possibly have passed as death from snake-bite, or, if questions were asked and an autopsy performed, from a heart attack due to heavy drinking. I am quite sure in my own mind that there was nothing wrong with either the knife or the iodine, and when we eventually find them we shall be able to prove it. That is why I am asking whoever made away with them to own up to it now. It must be one of you, and as it cannot possibly be the murderer, all that you are being asked to do is to clear yourself. And at the same time to help clear whoever it was that you suspected of doctoring either of those two things.'

Once again there was a strained silence in the room when he had finished speaking, but if anyone had intended to admit responsibility they were forestalled by Ken Brandon, who said loudly and scornfully:

687

'Oh no, you're not! You're not asking anything of the sort. We're not all fools, though you're treating us as though we were. What you're trying to do is to get one of us to implicate someone else. That's it, isn't it? Maybe there wasn't anything wrong with that knife or the iodine. But someone thought there might be, and they must have had a damned good reason for thinking it. You'd want to know that reason, wouldn't you? Well we're not falling for that one. You can do your own dirty work! I'm going, for one. Come on, Mother, let's get out of here.'

Mabel stood up, pale and trembling, and behind her Hector too had risen; but slowly and reluctantly.

Mr Gilbert moved deliberately and without haste, and placed himself between Ken and the door. He said quietly: 'I'm sorry, Ken, but you can't go just yet. Don't make this any more unpleasant than it need be. Because if you try and leave, I shall have to put you under arrest for obstructing the police.'

'*Try* and leave? I'm going to do more than try! I'm not putting up with this any longer, and that's all there is to it. And just *you* try and stop me!'

He whirled round and made a dive for the open window, and Drew rose swiftly and hit him once and scientifically.

Ken Brandon crumpled at the knees and collapsed upon the floor, his nose bleeding profusely and a foolish smile fixed upon his face. And peace reigned.

'Oh, thank you, Drew!' gasped Mabel with real gratitude.

15

The remainder of the morning was as unenjoyable as the beginning, though less full of unpleasant surprises, and although Mr Gilbert and his entourage had departed shortly before one, the respite had been brief, for they had returned an hour and a half later.

This time the two C.I.D. officers as well as Mr Gilbert faced their audience, while the unobtrusive gentleman in the brown suit sat behind them, and judging from the soft and ceaseless scratching of pen upon paper, occupied himself in taking down their replies verbatim and in shorthand.

The questions that afternoon were mainly concerned with movements. They appeared to be merely routine ones, and often pointless, but one thing at least emerged from them. No one could produce an alibi that covered the period of time in which Gilly Markham could have been murdered, for the entire party, with the exception of Em and Mabel, had separated after luncheon. And even Em and Mabel could not alibi each other, since both at different times had vanished into the bushes for, as Em observed frostily, 'obvious reasons', and later both had slept.

Eden and Lisa, who had departed together, had quarrelled and separated. Not that either admitted to quarrelling, but it took very little intuition on anyone's part to fill in the gap in their respective stories. Lisa said she had 'just strolled about', and Eden said he had sat on a fallen trunk and 'thought he might have dozed'.

Ken Brandon asserted that he had left the crater to explore the far side of it, and had only returned just before the party re-assembled, while Hector said that he had spent the best part of an hour searching among the rocks to see if he could pick up the track of the leopard whose pug marks they had seen at the lake edge.

Drew also had left the crater and gone for a walk, and Victoria, answering endless questions as to the sounds she professed to have heard that afternoon, could only insist that she had seen no one for half an hour after his departure, and thought that they might have been caused by some animal.

No one appeared to have paid much attention to time until well after three o'clock, and though Greg went over and over the details of that last twenty-five minutes of Gilly's life, it had proved impossible to build up an accurate picture of exactly where everyone had stood, or who had been standing next to whom, for only Em, Victoria and Drew had remained in approximately the same position throughout, and they and everyone else had been far too intent on the life-and-death drama that was taking place under their eyes to note the movements or expressions of other people.

'Can't you understand?' said Em, her voice flat with exhaustion. 'He was dying! And we knew he was dying. It never occurred to any of us that it was murder. Why should it? Perhaps if it had we would have watched each other instead of him. But it didn't.'

'Oh, yes it did!' Greg contradicted grimly. 'Three of you at least thought that it might be murder. Otherwise Stratton would not have hunted for that broken needle, or Mrs Markham refused to drink the brandy. Even you knew that something was wrong!'

Em said wearily: 'But I didn't think of murder until much later. Not until Drew started asking questions about the knife and said we must go back and look for it. I'd thought it was a heart attack, and that I'd killed him.'

'I wasn't thinking of you when I said "three people". The third was whoever removed the knife and the iodine bottle. Or if two people were involved in that, then that makes it four. Four people out of seven suspected that Markham had been murdered, and I'd like to know why. Perhaps you can give me your reasons, Mrs Markham? Why did you think that your husband might have been murdered?'

Lisa clutched the arms of her chair and half rose from it. 'I didn't! You can't say I did. You're just trying to get me to admit things I never said. You're twisting things! I – I'd seen Gilly die. Drew gave him brandy, and he died. I wasn't thinking straight. I didn't mean it that way. I only didn't want to drink because – because Gilly had drunk from it – and – and died.'

Greg shrugged his shoulders, and somewhat unexpectedly did not press the question. He turned instead to Drew and demanded his reasons for suspecting murder, but was interrupted by Eden who observed with some asperity that considering Drew had, to his certain knowledge, already answered that question at length on the previous night, and had, moreover, been asked to sign a typed copy of his statement, it appeared to him to be a pointless question and a waste of time.

690

'I never ask pointless questions,' said Mr Gilbert without heat. 'Well, Drew?'

Drew said. 'I knew it couldn't be snake-bite for the same reasons that Em gave you. I've seen men die that way. I've also twice seen a man die from the effects of a poisoned arrow, and as I did not know that the symptoms of heart attack were similar, heart did not occur to me, but *msunguti* did. Gilly had been perfectly well, though a bit tight, an hour earlier, and now he was dying. That was all there was to it.'

'Thank you,' said Greg briefly.

The remainder of the afternoon was merely a repetition of the beginning, with the sole difference that the questions were asked again, and answered, individually and behind the closed door of the dining-room.

It was well after five when Greg had finished with Victoria, who had been questioned last. He looked tired and grim and driven, for excepting only Victoria, these were all his personal friends: people he had known for years, and had dined with and danced with, and suffered with during the harsh years of the Emergency. But he faced them now with the bleak impersonal gaze of a stranger, and his voice was as detached and unfriendly as his eyes:

'I shall probably have to see you all again during the next few days, and until this business is settled I'd be grateful if you'd arrange not to be out, or anywhere where I can't get in touch with you at short notice.'

And then he had gone.

'Well thank goodness that's over!' said Em with a gusty sigh. 'And at least he isn't likely to be back tomorrow, which means that with luck we should have one peaceful day.'

But the following day could hardly have been termed peaceful.

Gilly's body had been brought back for burial, and having notified Mr Gilbert of their intentions, they had all attended the funeral, which had been marred by the behaviour of Lisa and, in a lesser degree, Ken Brandon. Lisa had gone off into screaming, shrieking hysterics and had had to be forcibly removed, and Ken Brandon had quietly and unobtrusively fainted.

Drew had caught him as he fell, and had driven him back to *Flamingo*, together with Mabel. And Em, Eden, Hector and Victoria had returned some twenty minutes later, with the information that Lisa was back in her own bungalow under the care of the doctor's wife, and had been given a strong injection of morphia.

'What was it all about?' demanded Mabel, pallid and shivering. 'You – you don't think she can possibly have ... No! No, of course not! One should not even *think* such things!'

'That Lisa might have done it?' supplied Drew. 'Who is to say what anyone else is capable of under certain pressures? Or even where one's own breaking point lies? But personally I'd cross Lisa off any list of suspects, because unless she's a remarkably good actress, that performance of hers at Crater Lake was genuine. She thought someone had murdered her husband all right, whatever she says now, and she thought the stuff might be in the brandy. Q.E.D. – she didn't do the job herself!'

'My dear Drew,' said Em with asperity, '*all* women are excellent actresses when circumstances force them to it; and the sooner men realize that, the better! But of course Lisa did not murder her husband – though I have no doubt there were times when she wanted to. There were times when I myself felt like it, and I, let me point out, was not compelled to put up with Gilly's company as Lisa was. She could quite possibly have been another Mrs Thompson. Someone who might talk or dream about doing away with an unwanted husband, in the way a child will invent long and improbable stories, but who would never really *mean* it.'

Drew said softly: 'They hanged Mrs Thompson.'

He refused an invitation to stay to luncheon, and left, followed shortly afterwards by the Brandons; and Em, watching them go, had expressed a hope that they – and the police – would stay away from *Flamingo* for at least a week.

But it was a hope that was not to be realized.

Eden and Victoria had spent the afternoon out on the lake, and had returned in the peaceful, pearl-pink evening to find both Drew and the Brandons in the drawing-room again, and the house once more full of policemen. For Kamau, the lover of Wambui, had been found.

'It was the dogs,' said Em looking oddly shrunken in the depths of the big wing-chair, and hugging a woollen shawl about her shoulders as though she were cold. 'They've been kept shut up for days and only taken out on a leash, because of Lisa's bitch. But I – I couldn't keep them shut up for ever, could I? I suppose they smelt him ...'

It had happened barely half an hour after Eden and Victoria had left. Em had heard the barking and had gone out with a whip and tried to beat them off. The dog boy had run out with the leashes, and Em had sent him for the askaris, and having left them on guard had returned to the house and telephoned Greg.

Mr Gilbert and several policemen had arrived within the hour, and what the ants had left of Kamau had been disinterred from a shallow grave among the charcoal kilns.

Greg's temper had not been improved by the discovery that Eden was out in the motor launch and could not be reached, and he had sent for the Brandons and for Drew, who had been questioned severally and separately as to their movements on the night of Kamau's disappearance.

'But why you and the Brandons?' demanded Victoria of Drew.

She had spent an unnerving half-hour in the dining-room answering endless questions, and had come out into the twilit verandah to discover Drew Stratton leaning against one of the creeper-covered pillars and smoking a cigarette.

Drew said sombrely: 'Because whoever killed Kamau presumably killed Alice DeBrett – and then killed Kamau because he had not only seen it done, but had talked about it.'

Victoria said in a small, shaken voice: 'But – but that's just what makes it so pointless. It would have been different if he'd been killed to stop him talking. But he'd talked already. He said it was Aunt Em!'

'I know. But we didn't hear that until the next day, did we? And by that time he was dead. If his girlfriend had only come clean straight away, instead of pretending that he'd merely hinted at knowing something, he might still be alive – though I doubt it. As it was, someone evidently thought it was worth while stopping his mouth permanently, and if it hadn't been for the fact that by a fluke, and because he was no mean pianist, Gilly was able to blow a hole through Wambui's story, your aunt would have been left in a very sticky position. She won't be in too good a one now. Not now that Gilly is dead.'

'Why not?' demanded Victoria anxiously.

'Because Gilly giving evidence on the one subject that he was really at home in would have been able to convince any jury that he knew what he was talking about. But the same evidence, given at second hand by Greg, isn't going to sound nearly so convincing. And now there's this business of Kamau. God, what a mess!'

Victoria said: 'But they couldn't think Aunt Em had killed Kamau! No one could!'

'Why not?' enquired Drew impatiently. 'She had the best opportunity of anyone. She was meeting him that night by the gate into the shamba.'

693

'How can you say that!' blazed Victoria, stiff with anger. 'You haven't any right to! You're just being s-stupid and – and——'

'*Shh!*' said Drew with the flicker of a grin. 'There's no need to fly off the handle. You're not looking at this from the police viewpoint, which is purely concerned with hard facts and is not swayed – or is trying not to be – by the personal angle. You are only thinking of your aunt as someone you know and are fond of. But they have got to think of her as "X", who allied to B, or minus Z, may equal Y.'

Victoria said scornfully: 'Then they're just being stupid too! Suppose she did meet Kamau that night, and kill him? All right, how did she carry him from the gate right up to the place where they found him? And when she got him there, how did she manage to dig a grave and bury him? She's over seventy!'

'Seventy-two, I believe – and as strong as a carthorse. But that's beside the point. You're not using your head, Victoria. If Em had done it she wouldn't have needed to kill him by the gate. She could have invented a dozen excuses to get him to walk with her to the kilns, and dealt with him on the spot. And she wouldn't have needed to dig a grave. There were several there already. It must have been only too easy to topple a body into one of those trenches and cover it up with some of the loose earth that was lying around, and the fumes from the charcoal kilns would have interfered with the scent if tracker dogs were used.'

'But it was Aunt Em's dogs who found him!'

'Ah, that was different. He'd been underground for quite a few days by then.'

Victoria flinched, and Drew said quickly: 'I'm sorry. This is a beastly business for all of us, but the rest of us have at least seen or heard or worse things in our day. The Emergency wasn't a picnic! – though now I come to think of it, that's an unfortunate simile, isn't it? But you've been pitchforked into this from a safe and orderly existence, and it must be pretty unnerving for you. Wishing you hadn't come?'

'No – o,' said Victoria hesitantly. 'I don't think I could ever wish I hadn't come back to Kenya. But I wish I hadn't . . .'

She did not complete the sentence, but come to lean on the verandah rail beside him, looking out into the deepening dusk. There was something about Drew's mere physical presence that was reassuring, and as long as he was here the house seemed less frightening. She turned to look at him and said abruptly:

'Are you staying here tonight?'

'Yes. Greg wants all his suspects under one roof. Or rather, under two: the Brandons are reluctantly parking out at Lisa's. Just as well really, as he seems to have roped in our respective house servants for questioning, and turned all our labour lines into the nearest thing to a concentration camp that I've seen outside one.'

'Then he does think it may possibly be an African after all?'

'Of course he does. He's no fool. They've been getting a far stiffer grilling than we have. You mustn't think that just because Greg has been hauling us over the coals that he hasn't had a squad of his boys doing exactly the same thing to every single African who works on this estate, or on mine or Hector's. There were even two of them who might have pulled off that picnic business. Zach and Samuel were actually down in the crater. And there is still "General Africa" – who is still at large and still unidentified, and who may yet turn out to be the snake in the grass. I don't believe that Greg has lost sight of that possibility for a moment. In fact he's quite capable of making all this display of suspecting one of us with the sole object of confusing the issue and making it look as though the enquiries in the labour lines are merely routine, and that it is the Bwanas who are really under suspicion.'

Victoria gave a little sigh that was partly relief and partly weariness. 'I didn't think of that. You must be right. After all, we couldn't *really* be suspects. Not you or the Brandons, anyway.'

'Why not? We all happened to be here or hereabouts on the night Mrs DeBrett was killed. *And* on the night that Kamau disappeared.'

'But the Brandons weren't even here then!'

'No. But they called at the Markhams' bungalow that evening. Gilly was out, but Lisa had just got back from here, and it seems that she spilt the works. Which means that any one of them could have got over here in time to head off Kamau. It's no distance at all by the short cut between *Flamingo* and *Brandonmead*, and there was a moon that night.'

Victoria said: 'But they wouldn't have got him to go with them. You said that Aunt Em could have made an excuse to get him to walk to the kilns, but he might not have gone with one of the Brandons.'

'Ever noticed that there's a trolley arrangement that runs from the shamba to the road, and passes within a few yards of the kilns? No one would have needed to do any carrying of corpses. Even you could have managed it without much difficulty.'

695

'*Me!* But——'

'No, I'm not accusing you of running amok with a hatchet, so there's no need to glare at me. Though I daresay Greg has had to consider that possibility.'

'What possibility?'

'That you and Eden might have cooked this up between you.'

Victoria looked at him, meeting his bland blue gaze thoughtfully and without anger. Studying his face in the dusk as if it had been a letter held up for her to read: a very important letter.

She said at last: 'And what do you think?'

'Does it matter?'

Victoria did not answer, and presently Drew said slowly and as though he were thinking aloud:

'People who are desperately and deeply in love are probably capable of anything. There are endless examples in history and the newspapers to prove that love can be a debasing passion as well as the most ennobling one; and a stronger and more relentless force than either ambition or hate, because those can be cold-blooded things, but love is always a hot-blooded one. Men and women have died for it – or for the loss of it. They have committed crimes for it and given up thrones for it, started wars, deserted their families, betrayed their countries, stolen, lied and murdered for it. And they will probably go on doing so until the end of time!'

He stubbed out his cigarette against the rail and dropped it among the geraniums, and after a moment or two Victoria said meditatively and without turning her head:

'And you think I might be – capable of anything?'

Drew gave an odd, curt laugh. 'Not of murder. Or even of conniving at it. But of covering up for someone you were in love with, or even very fond of, yes.'

'Even if I knew they had committed a murder? A horrible murder?'

'No. Because you would never love anyone like that.'

Victoria turned to look at him. The last of the daylight was running out with the swiftness of sand in an hour glass, and now it was so dark that she could no longer see the lines in his face.

She said: 'Then at least you don't believe that Eden could have done it.'

'I didn't say that. For all I know, he may have done it; though I shouldn't say it was in the least likely. But then you aren't in love with Eden.'

Victoria did not say anything, but she did not turn away, and Drew said: 'Are you.'

It was an affirmation rather than a question, and as she still did not speak he took her chin in his hand, as he had done once before.

Victoria stood quite still, aware of a crisis in her life: of having reached the end of a road – or perhaps the beginning of one. And then a door at the far end of the verandah opened and the shadows retreated before a flood of warm amber light, and it was no longer dusk, but night.

Drew's hand dropped and he turned unhurriedly:

'Hullo, Eden. Has Greg finished with you at last? How much longer is he likely to be around?'

'God knows,' said Eden shortly. 'What on earth are you two doing out here in the dark?'

'Talking,' said Drew pleasantly. 'Any objection?'

'No, of course not! But there are drinks in the drawing-room if you want one. I've sent Gran to bed.'

'Did she go?'

'Yes, surprisingly enough. She's going to be the next person to have a heart attack if we don't watch it.'

'A genuine one?' enquired Drew. 'Or one of the kind that hit Gilly?'

'Oh, for Pete's sake!' said Eden angrily, and turning his back on Drew he took Victoria's arm. 'Come on, Vicky darling. You must be cold. Come and have a glass of sherry. Or let's finish off the vodka and get really tight.'

They found Mabel in the drawing-room, sipping a brandy and soda and watching the door. Hector, accompanied by Bill Hennessy, had returned to *Brandonmead* to collect various necessities for a night's stay at the Markham's bungalow, but Ken was still being questioned, and Mabel would not leave without him.

'What *are* they doing with Kennie?' she demanded unhappily. 'He's been in there for hours! They must know that he can't know anything at all about this. It isn't kind of Greg – and after all the years we've known him! Drew, don't you think you could go and tell him that we're all very tired, and couldn't he let us go home?'

'No, Mabel. I couldn't,' said Drew firmly, collecting himself a stiff whisky and soda and sinking into an arm-chair. 'It would not only be a pure waste of time, but I have no desire to receive a blistering snub. He'll stop when he feels like it, or when he's got what he wants, and not before.'

'But we shall all be here tomorrow, and the next day.'

697

'We hope,' said Drew dryly. 'Well, here's to crime.'

He lifted his glass and drank deeply, and Eden said furiously: '*Must* you make a joke of it?'

'Sorry,' said Drew mildly.

But Eden refused to be placated. His handsome face was taut with strain and his voice was rough with fatigue, anxiety and anger: 'In the present circumstances, that sort of remark is in bloody bad taste, besides being entirely un-funny!'

Drew raised his eyebrows and pulled a faint grimace, but forebore to take offence. He said amiably: 'You're quite right. I can't have been thinking. My apologies. Have an olive, Mabel; and stop watching that door. Ken will be along any minute now. Hullo, here's another car. Who do you suppose this is? the D.C.?'

But it was only Hector, returning from *Brandonmead* with an assortment of pyjamas, tooth brushes and bedroom slippers. He accepted a drink, and after a nervous glance at his wife said in a subdued voice that contained no echo of his former booming tones: 'Is Kennie still there? They're keeping him a long time. Surely they know the boy isn't feeling fit. Never known him to pass out like that before. He ought to be in bed, not being badgered with silly questions.'

'Then why don't you put a stop to it?' demanded Mabel, wavering on the verge of tears. 'You're his father. They're bullying him: I know they are. Oh, if *only* he'd never met her! Why did this have to happen just when it seemed that everything was going to be peaceful and happy again? I'll never forgive Greg for this – never!'

Hector said uncomfortably: 'He's only doing his duty, dear. Why don't you come over to Lisa's with me now? She won't have given any orders about supper, so we'd better go and see about it.'

Mabel burst into tears and said wildly that is was just like a man to think of his own stomach before the welfare of his son, and Drew got up and left the room.

He returned a few minutes later, looking particularly wooden and accompanied by a white and subdued Ken Brandon, and the reunited family removed themselves into the night.

'How did you work that?' enquired Eden with grudging respect.

'Stuck my neck out,' said Drew morosely, 'and was duly executed.' He drew his index finger across his throat in a brief expressive gesture. 'Greg is in no very pleasant temper, but at least it was preferable to having Mabel going on a crying jag.'

Mr Gilbert appeared in the drawing-room on the heels of this remark, and informed them curtly that he was leaving, but would be back at nine o'clock on the following morning. He would be obliged if they would all be in the house and available at that hour, and he was leaving Bill Hennessy to see to it.

He had refused a drink, and had left; and they had dined frugally on soup and sandwiches, for the majority of the house servants had spent the day being questioned at police headquarters, and Zacharia and Thuku, together with the cook, were being kept there overnight.

Victoria had retired to bed immediately afterwards, and had been accompanied to the door of her room by Eden. He had not searched her room as Drew had done, but he had asked her if she had any aspirins, and on hearing that she had, advised her to take two and get a good night's rest. And then he had kissed her. Not lightly, as Drew had done, but hard and hungrily, holding her close.

She had made no attempt to avoid his embrace; but neither had she returned it. And when he released her at last she had put up a hand and touched his cheek in a fleeting caress that was purely maternal, and there was relief and pity and sadness in her smile; as though she had been a much older woman who has found a page of a forgotten love letter, and is smiling a little ruefully at herself because she cannot remember the name of the boy who wrote it.

16

Mr Gilbert was not only true to his word, but regrettably punctual. It was exactly one minute past nine, and breakfast was still in progress, when the now familiar squad of police and C.I.D. men arrived at *Flamingo*.

But this time the proceedings were brief. Typewritten copies of statements made on the previous day were produced and they were asked to sign them, and that being done Mr Stratton and the Brandons were curtly informed that they could return to their own houses, with the proviso that they must stay within reach of a telephone and not leave the Rift until further notice.

'And that means that you can't suddenly decide to go off on safari to the Northern Frontier, Stratton. Or take a holiday to Malindi, Mrs Brandon. I want you where I can get in touch with you at short notice. I hope that is quite clear.'

'Painfully, thank you,' said Drew.

'Are we under arrest?' demanded Hector, who appeared to have recovered some of his former truculence.

Greg favoured him with a bleak stare and said: 'No,' and went away, armed with a stop watch and a pair of binoculars, to head what appeared to be a conducted tour of the grounds and the short cut between *Flamingo* and *Brandonmead*.

It had been decided after some discussion that Mabel would remain with Lisa for a few days, and Eden had escorted her back to the Markhams' bungalow. Em had gone off to deal with some domestic crisis, pausing only to say morosely: 'I won't ask you to stay to luncheon, Drew, because there probably won't be any. But you should find some beer in the dining-room – if the C.I.D. haven't removed it for analysis to make quite sure we haven't added arsenic to it!'

The door slammed behind her, and Drew laughed. But Victoria did not. Victoria was standing by the bow window, watching Eden and Mabel Brandon as they walked away down the narrow dusty path that led across the garden towards the plumbago hedge and

700

the Markhams' bungalow, and presently Drew said: 'What are you thinking about?'

He had spoken very quietly, as though he did not wish to break her train of thought, and Victoria answered him as quietly:

'Eden.'

A bee flew into the room and buzzed about it, and when it flew out again into the sunlight the room seemed strangely silent.

Victoria said, still looking out of the window: 'You said last night that Eden might have killed his wife; and Kamau. You don't really think that, do you?'

'No. In fact I should say that the betting is about a hundred to one against, despite the fact that the first question that is asked in a murder case is *cui bono*? – who benefits? and, financially at least, Eden does. But then I've known him, on and off, for a good many years, and this affair doesn't fit in with anything I know about him. Eden isn't a fool. He's got plenty of intelligence, and despite all that sunny surface charm, a cool brain and more stubborn determination than most people would give him credit for. He would have known quite well, for instance, that he was bound to be the number one suspect; and why. And that being so he would, if he were guilty, have provided himself with a reasonably cast-iron alibi. Whoever murdered Alice DeBrett planned it pretty carefully – the fact that Em's red trouserings were stolen is proof enough of that! – and only someone who did not need an alibi would have failed to provide one. That, to my mind – and I think, to Greg's – washes Eden out. But I don't know what it leaves us with.'

Victoria said: 'Aunt Em, Mrs Markham, the Brandons, "General Africa"— and you.'

Drew laughed: a laugh that was singularly devoid of amusement. He said: 'I asked for that one, didn't I?'

And then the door opened and Em was back, looking tired and cross and harried, and addressing someone in the hall in vituperative Swahili.

She broke off on seeing Drew and Victoria, and shutting the door with a defiant bang, sank gratefully into the depths of the wing-chair and observed that had she but died an hour before this chance, she had lived a blessed time.

Drew turned his head rather quickly and looked at her with frowning intentness, his blue eyes narrowed and his brows making a straight line across his forehead, as though he were trying to recall some tag-end of memory. Victoria, who had forgotten any Swahili

701

she had ever known, said: 'Who were you talking to, Aunt Em?'

'Myself,' said Em. 'It's the privilege of the aged.'

'In Swahili?' enquired Victoria with a smile.

'Oh, that. That was only Samuel: Hector's gunbearer-cum-driver-cum-general factotum. I found him wandering round the hall, hunting for Mabel's knitting bag that he seems to think she left here. I told him that it wouldn't be here, it would be over at Lisa's if anywhere. He must have misunderstood her. What are you scowling about, Drew?'

'Hmm?' said Drew in a preoccupied voice. 'Oh – nothing much. Just an idea. I must go. Thanks for your enforced hospitality, Em.'

He walked to the door, opened it, and then hesitated as though he were reluctant to leave, and turned to look back at them, the frown still in his eyes and a strange unreadable look on his face that was oddly disturbing. As though he were puzzled and disbelieving – and afraid.

He stood there for at least a minute, looking from one to the other of them; and then he had shrugged his shoulders and gone away without saying anything, and they heard his car start up and purr away down the drive.

Em said uneasily: 'Something's worrying Drew. I wonder— Oh, well, I suppose this wretched business is getting us all down.'

It was shortly after his departure that they heard Greg's car drive away, but it was almost two o'clock by the time Eden returned. He had replied to Em's questions in monosyllables, been uncommunicative on the subject of Lisa, and refusing the dishes that Zacharia proffered, had lunched frugally off a biscuit and several cups of black coffee.

Em had retired to her room to rest, having advised Victoria to do the same. But Victoria had seldom felt less like resting, and she had wandered into the drawing-room, and sitting down at the piano had played scraps of tunes: playing to keep herself from thinking, not of the frightening happenings of the last week, but of the past and her own personal problems. But when she lifted her hands from the keys the thoughts were there waiting for her, and even her hands betrayed her, for they turned from Bach and Debussy to the trite, sweet sentimental melodies of songs that she had once danced to with Eden: 'Some Enchanted Evening' ... 'La Vie en Rose' ... 'Hullo, Young Lovers' ... And an older tune that an older generation had danced to in the days before the war, and that Eden had taken a fancy to. *I get along without you very well* ...

> *I get along without you very well;*
> *Of course I do.*
> *Except perhaps in spring——*

But she had not got along without him very well. Not in spring or summer, autumn or winter ...

> *'What a fool am I ... !'*

Her fingers stumbled on the yellowed keys in a jarring discord, for she had not heard Eden enter and she started violently when he touched her; spinning round on the piano stool so that she was in his arms.

He had not meant to touch her. He had been through a horrible and harrowing week, and had endured a recent interview with Lisa Markham that he did not want to think of ever again – and knew that he would never forget. He supposed that he deserved it, although all the initial advances had been made by her, and he had thought that she knew the rules and would keep to them. But it had been a mistake from the beginning, and now that he had seen Victoria again, it was a calamity.

He had not expected to see Victoria again, or wanted to. But he had not been able to protest against her coming, because to do so might have led to questions, and he had never discussed Victoria with either Alice or Em, and he would not do so now. He had tried to shut Victoria out of his mind and his heart, but it had not been easy. That sentimental song of the 'thirties, that they had discovered and played light-heartedly in the sober post-war years, had indeed proved prophetic. *I get along without you very well – of course I do – except perhaps in spring* ... Or when a tune was played to which they had once danced. Or a girl wore a yellow dress. Or when a rose, or a scent, or a sound recalled Victoria ...

And then Em had sent for her, and he had not had the moral courage to explain to Em why she must not come; though knowing that he would see her again he had realized at last, and with blinding clarity, that neither Alice nor any of the shallow, foolish affairs with which he had attempted to fill the void in his heart meant anything to him; that only Victoria mattered, and despite any barrier of blood he must have her. That he would risk anything to have her! If only he were free——

Victoria had arrived at *Flamingo*, and Alice was dead. He was free. But he knew that he must behave circumspectly. He could not court another woman, even one to whom he had once been engaged, within a few days or even a few months of his wife's death. He would have to wait. He would persuade Em to send him to Rumuruti, and when enough time had elapsed to blur the raw memory of Alice's death he would come back and ask Victoria to marry him, and take her away from the Rift and all its tragic associations until people had forgotten. Until then he would not even touch her again.

But he had walked into the drawing-room and found her playing the tune that had been peculiarly their own, and had touched her almost without meaning to. And she had whirled about and was in his arms, and he was holding her hard against him: decency, convention, common sense thrown to the winds and forgotten. Kissing her hair and whispering broken endearments; telling her that they would get married at once – they could keep it a secret and no one need know except Em. That he could not wait, and that nothing mattered now that they were together again.

He was not aware for several minutes that Victoria was struggling to free herself, and when he realized it at last, and released her, he thought that it was emotion that had driven the blood from her face, and shyness and surprise that made her jump up and back away from him.

Victoria said breathlessly: 'No, Eden! No, please don't! It's no good saying I don't care for you any more, because I suppose I always shall. But not in that way any more. It's all over, and I never realized it. Not even when someone told me so. I still didn't believe it. Until you kissed me last night. I wanted you to kiss me——'

Eden took a swift step towards her, his hands outstretched, and once again she backed away from him.

'No! Oh Eden, I'm so very sorry! But how was I to know that you meant it? You hadn't meant it before, and——'

Eden said: 'Darling, I don't know what you're talking about, and I don't care. But I always meant it – with you. Right from the beginning. And I mean it now.'

Victoria wrung her hands and her face crumpled like a child's when it is going to cry. She said pleadingly: 'No you don't. Please say you don't! You see, I thought you were only kissing me because – because you like kissing girls. Because it was a sort of – of game, and didn't mean anything. I knew that if you kissed me I'd know. And I did. He was quite right. It's all over. It's – it's as if I'd grown up at last. That's silly, at my age. I should have done it before. But I didn't. I'm so fond of you Eden, but I don't love you any

704

more, and I'm not sure that I ever did, in – in the way that matters.

'Who was right?' demanded Eden, white-lipped and seizing on only three words out of all those that she had said.

Victoria looked bewildered, and he repeated the question in a voice that startled her: '*Who was right!* Who have you been discussing me with? Drew?'

A tide of colour flooded Victoria's pale cheeks and her eyes widened in dismay. 'No – I mean – I ought not to have said that. I didn't mean to. Eden, don't look like that! I wasn't discussing you with him. Not in that way.'

'In what way, then? Since when have you been on such intimate terms with Drew Stratton that you can discuss your love affairs with him? No, I don't mean that! Don't let's quarrel, darling. I know I treated you abominably once – over Alice. But I had to do it. At least – I thought I had to, and that it would be the best thing for both of us. I can explain, if you'll let me. And I know that I can make you happy.'

Victoria shook her head and her eyes filled with tears.

'No you can't. Not now. I meant what I said, Eden. I don't love you any more. I'm free too. I realized it when you kissed me last night.'

Eden said harshly: 'Or when Stratton did? Has he kissed you?'

He saw the bright colour deepen in her cheeks and was aghast at the tide of sheer physical jealousy that rose and engulfed him, and over which he had no control. He had always had a quick temper and now he had to hit back: to hit blindly, and to hurt as badly as he himself had been hurt. He gave a curt, ugly laugh:

'So you've fallen for our Mr Stratton, have you? Very amusing! And after all those vows of deathless devotion you used to write me. Remember them? A letter a day – sometimes two. I kept them all. A whole box full. I couldn't bear to part with them, but I might as well send them to Stratton for a wedding present. Or you might like to send him a few? Any of the undated ones would do. It will save you time and paper, and the sentiments you addressed to me will do just as well for him, won't they? After all, if he's getting a second-hand love, he may as well get his love letters at second hand too!'

He laughed again, seeing the disgust and contempt in Victoria's white, frozen face and sparkling eyes, and having begun to laugh, found that he could not stop. He dropped into a chair and hid his face in his hands, pressing them over his eyes as though he could blot out the desperate weariness, the shamed despair and the savage jealousy; and shut out the horrifying sound of his own senseless mirth.

It stopped at last, and he said tonelessly: 'I'm sorry, Vicky. That was a filthy thing to say. I didn't mean it. I don't know what got into me. I'm going to pieces these days – not that that's any excuse. Forgive me, dear.'

He dropped his hands and lifted a haggard face, to find that he had been talking to himself. The room was empty and Victoria had gone.

Fifteen minutes later, leaning against the window-sill of her bedroom, Victoria heard the sound of horses' hooves and saw Eden gallop past, heading for the open country and riding as recklessly as though he were in the last lap of a race. It was a relief to know that he was no longer in the house, and she hoped that he would stay away for an hour or two and give her time to think.

One thing at least was clear. She would have to tell Aunt Em that she could not remain at *Flamingo*. How *dared* Eden talk like that! How could he turn on her like a spoilt, vindictive character out of a third-rate novel? Had he really kept her letters? She had a momentary vision of Drew Stratton reading one, his blue eyes cold with scorn, and her face flamed at the thought.

'But Eden isn't like that!' said Victoria, speaking aloud in the empty bedroom.

He couldn't be like that! He couldn't have changed so much in just five years. She was used to his brief outbreaks of black rage. They had never lasted long and they had never meant anything; and when they were over he had always been desperately ashamed and deeply apologetic. No, he would never do such a cruel, vulgar thing as this.

But the thought of the letters persisted. Not so much because she was afraid that Eden would carry out his preposterous threat, but because of Greg Gilbert.

Who was to say that Mr Gilbert would not order another search of the house, and this time find her letters – and read them? There must be many undated ones, and he might well jump to the conclusion that she had continued to correspond with Eden long after his marriage. He might even think what Drew himself had suggested – that she and Eden had planned Alice's death between them. That Eden, and not Aunt Em, had sent for her.

Seized with sudden resolution, Victoria left the room and walked quickly down the corridor to pause outside the door that led into the wing that had been Alice's and Eden's, and where Eden now slept alone. But with her hand on the door knob, she hesitated.

These were the only rooms in the big, rambling house that she had not as yet seen. She thought fleetingly of Bluebeard's chamber, and found the thought a singularly unpleasant one. Supposing that there was something waiting for her on the other side of that door? The poltergeist, who had ceased its vandalistic pranks with the first taste of blood?

I mustn't go in, thought Victoria with sudden conviction. If I do, I shall be sorry. They are Eden's rooms. I haven't any right to search someone else's rooms. Not even for my own letters——

And yet Mrs Thompson had been convicted on the strength of her letters to her lover, and they had, as Drew had pointed out, hung Mrs Thompson ...

Victoria set her teeth and turned the handle of the door.

17

Alice's bedroom was a long, blue-and-white room that looked out over the rose garden. An impersonal room: neat and cool and without emphasis. A room very like its owner.

There was a blue-and-white bathroom, a small writing room containing a roll-top desk in addition to a rosewood writing table, and, finally, Eden's dressing-room, in which he apparently slept, for there was a camp bed made up in it. There were no photographs of Alice in the room, but a single small snapshot in a battered leather frame adorned the dressing-table. It was badly faded, for it had been taken many years before with a Box Brownie, and Eden had developed and printed it himself. A snapshot of a skinny little girl riding on a zebra.

Looking at it Victoria's resolution wavered. There was surely no need for her to hunt through Eden's belongings for her letters. She had only to ask for them, and he would give them to her. Unless Greg Gilbert found them first——

It was a sobering reflection, and Victoria abandoned hesitation. But fifteen minutes later she was compelled to admit that either Eden had lied about keeping her letters, or they were not here, and she was about to leave the room when her eye was caught by an inequality in the panelling on the wall behind the camp bed. She turned back, and pulling the bed away from the wall, saw for the first time that there was another cupboard in the room: a long low cupboard built into the wall, and probably intended as a toy cupboard for a small boy.

Victoria went down on her knees and opened it, to find that it ran back far farther than she had supposed, and was stacked with old boxes and suitcases. She regarded them with some dismay, for if they were full it was going to take her hours to go through them. But the first two or three that she pulled out were empty, and it seemed likely that the remainder would be.

A small cabin trunk, dragged out to the light of day, revealed a battered collection of birds' eggs and an old box camera that was undoubtedly the one with which Eden had taken the photograph of Victoria on Falda. Victoria shut it with a sigh and pulled out an incongruous and outmoded piece of luggage that could only have belonged to Eden's grandfather, Gerald DeBrett: a tin hat box of antediluvian design. It was empty except for a quantity of yellowing tissue paper, dead moths and D.D.T. powder, but Victoria regarded it with interest, remembering a similar relic of vanished days that had stood in a schoolfriend's attic: a hat box that had possessed a false bottom to it, in which, she had been told, ostrich plumes could be packed. This one too was made to the same pattern, and without thinking, she pressed the almost invisible catch that revealed the hidden space.

There were no ostrich plumes, but there was something else. A flat package wrapped very carefully in several folds of soft silk.

Victoria never knew why she should have unwrapped it, for it could not have been what she was looking for. The action was purely automatic, and for a moment the object that lay revealed merely surprised her, and she was about to replace it when her hands checked and her heart seemed to stop, and she sat back on her heels, staring at it, wide-eyed and rigid, while a hundred frantic thoughts whirled round in her brain, falling into fantastic patterns and breaking up into chaotic fragments that did not make sense.

The poltergeist ... Who was it who had said: 'I'll start believing in evil spirits only when someone has eliminated all possibility of the evil human element.' Drew——! And Drew had said too, 'Who can say what anyone is capable of under certain pressures?'

A dozen things that she had seen or heard during the past week, isolated incidents that had seemed to have no connection with each other, took on shape and meaning: a horrible meaning. But it was the malice in it that frightened her most. Em must be made to suffer the loss of her dearest possessions, starting with the small but cherished things and working up to greater things. Her dog. Her grandson's wife. Her pride and her good name. And at the last there would still be blackmail.

But would Em allow herself to be blackmailed? From what Victoria knew of her, Lady Emily, faced with such a threat, would be just as likely to take the law into her own hands, and shoot the blackmailer and take the consequences, rather than submit. Had the 'poltergeist' thought of that? Or had that malicious brain over-reached itself?

Victoria re-wrapped the package in its folds of bright silk, her

709

hands trembling so that she could barely hold it, and replacing it in its hiding place, closed the hat box and pushed it back into the cupboard. And as she did so she heard a faint sound outside the open window; a scrape and rustle that might have been a bird among the creepers. Or had someone been watching her? She started up, shaking with panic, and pushing the camp bed into place, ran from the room.

Em was walking slowly across the hall at the far end of the corridor, supporting herself on a stick and evidently on her way to the verandah and tea, but Victoria pretended not to have seen her and took refuge in her own room, banging the door behind her and locking it. She did not want to face Aunt Em's shrewd old eyes just yet.

She leant against the closed door, panting and shivering and fighting a panic desire to run out of the house and keep on running until she had put as much distance as possible between herself and *Flamingo*.

She must tell Drew. He would know what to do. Or Mr Gilbert. No, not Mr Gilbert! – he was a policeman first and he would not be able to remember that he was also a friend. She could not do it. She was as bad as Em or Mabel, or any other woman, when it came to that.

It was at least a quarter of an hour later that she went out on the verandah and found tea and her aunt waiting for her.

Em did not look as though her afternoon's rest had benefited her, but her old eyes were as sharply observant as ever, and she dismissed Zacharia with an imperious wave of the hand, and said: 'What has happened, dear? You look as though you had seen a ghost.'

'Not a ghost,' said Victoria with a shiver in her voice. 'A poltergeist.'

'What on earth do you mean!'

'N-nothing,' said Victoria. 'I didn't mean – Aunt Em, I have to tell you something. I can't stay here any longer. I'd like to go as soon as possible. I know I'm being ungrateful, and – and – ungrateful, but I must go!'

Em said gently: 'Sit down, dear. I can see that something has happened to upset you. Here – have some tea. No, drink it up first ... That's better. Now tell me what is the matter. Is it Eden?'

The cup in Victoria's hand shook so badly that the tea slopped into the saucer, and she put it down hurriedly and said breathlessly: 'Why do you say that?'

Em sighed a little heavily and shrugged her shoulders: 'I don't

710

know. You were engaged to him once, and though I thought that was all over, I have not been so sure during the last few days. I know him very well, you see, and I am not unobservant – even though I may be a silly old woman! Has he asked you to marry him? Is it that?'

'Y— yes,' said Victoria. 'But it isn't that. And I couldn't marry him. *Ever!* Not even if he were the – the last person on earth!'

She shuddered so violently that her teeth chattered and she could not go on.

Em's brows drew together in a grimace of annoyance and she said tartly: 'Really, I had credited Eden with more intelligence! I am not surprised that you should feel disgusted. It can hardly be pleasant to receive a proposal from a man whose wife has just been murdered. In the worst *possible* taste! He must have taken leave of his senses. But he has been under a great deal of strain, and you must make allowances, dear. He is not himself just now. I will send him away for a month or so. To Rumuruti perhaps; just as soon as this dreadful business has been cleared up. There is no reason at all why *you* should leave.'

Victoria said desperately: 'You don't understand! It isn't that. It's – it's something else. I can't explain! But this afternoon I found out something that has – has made me realize that I must either go away, or go to the police. Th – that's all!'

She pushed back her chair and stood up, trembling with the effort not to burst into tears, and would not meet Em's shocked gaze.

Em said on a gasp: *'Victoria!'*

'I'm sorry,' said Victoria, her voice high and strained. 'I shouldn't have said that. I didn't mean to. I won't say anything else. But I must go away. I must! I know it's cowardly of me, but I can't help it.'

Em's face was grey and drawn and bleak with anger, but she spoke in a strictly controlled voice, as though she were some efficient governess dealing with a naughty and hysterical child:

'I do not know what you are talking about, but I can see that you are in no fit state to make any rational decisions at the moment. I am afraid it is quite out of the question for you to leave for Nairobi immediately. Greg Gilbert would never permit it, and we cannot reach him at the moment to explain that you refuse to stay here. If you are of the same opinion tomorrow morning you can talk to him yourself, and perhaps you will be able to persuade him to let you leave. But you will have to resign yourself to staying under my roof for at least one more night.'

Victoria's heart sank. She had forgotten Mr Gilbert. She found that she was staring at her aunt in helpless dismay, and she sat down again slowly, feeling weak and boneless and very frightened.

'No,' said Victoria in a whisper, 'I can't go away, can I? I had forgotten that. I shall have to stay.'

'For the moment, anyway,' said Em coldly. And went away, walking very stiffly and upright.

She returned some ten or fifteen minutes later, looking grim and implacable and inconceivably old, and ordered Zacharia to send Thuku round with the Land-Rover. Victoria had not moved. She was still sitting huddled in one of the verandah chairs, staring into vacancy.

'I'm going out to shoot something for the dogs,' said Em without condescending to look at her. 'I shall not be long. Zach tells me that Eden has gone up to see the new bore hole, so I will drive in that direction and tell him that you would prefer not to see him just now.'

She stumped off down the verandah as the Land-Rover drove up, and Victoria saw her climb in stiffly, hoisting her bulk into the driver's seat, and remembered Eden saying that Em invariably worked off her feelings in this manner when she was upset. Poor Aunt Em! However fast she drove, she would not be able to drive away from this!

The Land-Rover bucketed away at a dangerous pace and vanished in a whirling cloud of dust, and silence settled down on *Flamingo* like a grey cloud on a hilltop.

Em had taken the dogs with her, and Pusser, who had been lying on the wicker divan posed against the vivid background of the three harlequin-patterned cushions that Zacharia had arranged in a neat row, rose and stretched elaborately, and jumping down with a flump on to the matting, stalked away and vanished down the verandah steps into the garden.

The low sunlight painted the acacia trees a warm orange and the shadows began to stretch out long and blue across the rough Kikuyu grass of the lawns. Now was the time to telephone Drew, while the house was empty and there was no one to hear.

But Victoria had underestimated the difficulties of getting a number on a party line, and when at last she got the Stratton number Drew was out and the servant who answered the telephone spoke the minimum of English, so that after a brief but tangled conversation she was forced to abandon the attempt to make herself understood.

Returning to the verandah she was startled to find Zacharia there, patting the cushions into place, straightening chairs and emptying ash-trays. He must have been in the dining-room, and he gave Victoria the blank, disinterested glance of an elderly tortoise, and went away down the front steps and round the corner of the house.

Em returned just over half an hour later, but it was obvious that the exercise and exertion had not on this occasion produced a particularly mellowing effect upon her. She looked grim and exhausted and her clothes were stained and dirty and clotted with the dust of the ranges. She slapped it off in clouds, and having wiped her face with a handkerchief on which she had obviously cleaned her hands after assisting to degut the gazelle that was being removed from the back of the Land-Rover, said shortly:

'Eden won't be back tonight. He's ridden over to Hector's and he'll put up there.'

She made no further mention of their previous conversation, but talked instead of the progress of the new bore hole and the unusual dryness of the season. It seemed that she had met Mabel and Lisa out on the ranges. They had driven out more for something to do than for any specific purpose, and Em reported that Lisa looked more her old self.

'She says that she has got some of the account books that Gilly had brought up to date, and she asked if I'd send you over for them, as she can show you which sections will have to be completed, and which ones only need to be checked. I'd appreciate your help with them, if you feel up to it; I'm afraid I don't.'

Victoria said gratefully: 'Of course I will. I'll go now. It will be nice to have something to do.'

'That's what I thought,' said Em. 'Work is a very useful thing in bad times: it has to go on, and so one goes on too. Don't stay too long. It gets dark very quickly once the sun is down. You might pick me some of those delphiniums if you're not too late. I've done nothing about the flowers for days. I haven't had the heart to. But I suppose one has got to start again sometime. You'll find a pair of secateurs somewhere on the bottom shelf of the book-case in the office.'

Em's office was not noted for its tidiness, for she was in the habit of using it as a junk room, and Victoria discovered the secateurs among the welter of raffia and old seed catalogues; dislodging in the process a pyramid of dusty cardboard boxes that cascaded to the floor. She was stacking these back again when one of them fell open,

713

spilling out several dozen wooden slips of the type used for marking seed beds, and, from beneath them, a heavier object that slid out with a dull thud.

It was a very ordinary object to find in such a place: a well-worn and somewhat old-fashioned clasp knife faced with horn. But Victoria, touching it with shrinking fingers, saw that the small blade had been broken off short, and that there were initials cut deep into the horn. K. D. B.

So Em knew! Or if she did not know, she had suspected. She had palmed the knife that Eden had given her – his father's knife – because she had realized that Gilly Markham had not died from snake-bite, and she had been afraid. And later, when she had realized her mistake, she could not explain why she should have hidden it, so had blandly insisted that she herself had taken that knife to Crater Lake. She would not have done that for anyone but Eden.

Victoria lifted it with an unsteady hand and put it back quickly into the box, covering it again with the wooden slips and thrusting the box at the back of the shelf and at the bottom of the pile.

She stood up, breathing quickly as though she had been running, and taking up the secateurs, left the office; closing the door very carefully behind her as though it were vital that she should make no noise that might remind Em of where she had been.

But Em would not have heard anything, for she was sitting at the piano and drowning her troubled thoughts in a flood of melody. The music filled the room and flowed out through the open windows into the quiet garden, and Victoria paused on the verandah to listen to it, and being no more than an average performer herself was not critical of her aunt's execution, as Gilly would have been. Em was playing a Bach fugue, and playing it, in her niece's opinion, remarkably well. Victoria listened, soothed and enchanted.

She did not know at what point she began to be aware that there was something missing from the verandah, or why she should have noticed it at all – or been worried by it. But some elusive fragment of memory nagged at her brain; a sixth sense that whispered words she could not quite hear and drew her attention to something that she could not see.

She looked about her uneasily, but nothing had changed. The shabby wicker chairs and table stood where they had always stood, and Pusser's food and milk were still untouched. Why should she think there was something different about it? Something missing?

She gave an impatient shrug of her shoulders and turned away,

714

and it was not until she had reached the gate in the plumbago hedge that the answer dropped into her mind as though it had been a dry leaf falling from the acacia trees above her – and with so little impact that she could smile at it, thinking only that it was a trivial thing after all . . .

One of the three remaining verandah cushions had been missing. There had been only two brightly patterned squares on the long wicker divan against the wall, though there had been three earlier in the day.

18

The Markhams' bungalow appeared to be empty, and Victoria could hear no voices, though from somewhere in the silent house there came a faint, intermittent sound that resolved itself into the plaintive whining of a dog.

There was no bell, and as no one answered her tentative calls Victoria went through an open doorway and found herself in Lisa's drawing-room.

It was an essentially feminine room. Pink and white and be-ruffled, with the accent on ribbons and roses. But at the present moment it bore a forlorn aspect, for the flowers in the white vases were fading or dead, there was a film of dust on the piano and the occasional tables, and the ash-trays did not look as though they had been emptied for days.

A familiar object lay upon the sofa and provided an incongruous note of colour against the chintzy prettiness: a large cretonne knitting bag in excruciating shades of blue and orange – the property of Mabel Brandon. But there was no sign of its owner, or of Lisa, and after a hesitant interval Victoria opened one of the doors leading out of the drawing-room and found herself on the threshold of an untidy office. If the account books were anywhere they should be here, and she was looking doubtfully about her when she became conscious of being under surveillance, and turned swiftly.

Lisa had entered the drawing-room by the verandah door and was standing quite still, watching her.

For a moment Victoria did not recognize her, for she had never seen Lisa dressed in this fashion before. She was wearing slacks and a shirt of faded khaki, both of which looked as though they might have belonged to her late husband, and in place of her usual high-heeled sandals she wore a shabby pair of tennis shoes, which accounted for the fact that Victoria had not heard her approach.

The room was already growing dark, and as Lisa was standing with her back to the windows Victoria could not see her face very

716

clearly; but there was an expression on it that even in the uncertain light was sufficiently disconcerting to make Victoria regret that she had not waited until the morning before coming over to fetch Gilly's account books.

Lisa was smiling – but only with her red, rigid mouth: above it her violet eyes were fixed in a look that was as purely animal as that of a cat who is watching a bird, or a mousehole.

There was a curious moment of silence that had the effect of being loud with suppressed sound, and then Lisa laughed.

It was a gay sound, light and genuinely amused, and she moved forward and said: 'So you did come! I wondered if you would. Em sent you for the account books, I suppose? They're in there. On the table behind you.'

Victoria said confusedly, conscious that she was stammering badly: 'I-I'm s-sorry. About w-walking in like this. It was r-rude of me, b-but there didn't seem to be anyone about.'

Lisa walked past her into the office and picked up a pile of account books from one of the cluttered tables.

'I know. But the servants are all to pieces because of Greg and his boys, and I don't know where that little beast Wambui has got to. She's been in an awful state since her boy-friend was dug up. I shall have to sack her. Here you are – I suppose this is what you want? It'll do to go on with, anyway, *'Tis enough. 'Twill serve!'*

She laughed again, as though at some exquisite joke, and said in a surprised voice: 'You know, Gilly was always saying things like that. Bits of Shakespeare. It used to madden me. But it's odd how those silly remarks seem to fit in.'

She came back into the drawing-room and said: 'Would you like a drink? There's gin and sherry, and there should be some whisky if Hector and Ken haven't drunk it all.'

'N-no thank you,' said Victoria quickly. 'I must be getting back.'

'What's the hurry? It isn't dark yet.'

'It's not that, but Aunt Em's alone. Besides I said I'd cut some delphiniums. We haven't had any fresh flowers for days.'

'Neither have I,' said Lisa, looking vaguely round at the limp and faded stalks that lolled in the flower vases and made a faint, unpleasant smell in the room. 'The best delphiniums grow by the knoll. The tall pink ones——'

She embarked on a long and disjointed account of the difficulties of growing flowers in a dry year, and as she was standing between

717

Victoria and the door it was not really possible to push past her and leave. And yet Victoria discovered that she wanted to get out of that room as badly as she had ever wanted to get away from *Flamingo*: as badly as she had ever wanted anything. But Lisa continued to talk in her light brittle voice, and to keep between her and the door . . .

'I do wish you'd have something to drink. I don't like drinking alone. Mabel will be sorry to have missed you. She thought you'd be along a bit later. She'll be back any minute now. She's taking Dinah for a walk.'

A faint whining sound disproved her words, but she did not seem to have heard it: 'It's so good of her. Mabel is the kindest person. She knows how I hate taking out Dinah when she's like this, because Em's dogs sometimes follow us. You aren't going, are you? I haven't explained about the account books yet.'

Victoria, who had forgotten that she was clasping them, cast them a startled glance, and Lisa said: 'Give them to me, and I'll show you.'

She took them and carried them over to the window seat, where she laid them out carefully and slowly as though she were deliberately wasting time, and after studying them for several minutes announced that the ones with green covers dealt with the sale of fodder and vegetables, the red ones with fruit – mostly oranges – and the black ones with cattle.

'Very simple and kindergarten, isn't it? Gilly's idea. I don't think you'll have any trouble.'

Victoria scooped them up hurriedly and said: 'No. I'm sure I won't. Thank you so much. I really must be getting back.'

Lisa glanced over her shoulder at the sky beyond the window and said: 'Yes. I think you should. Blue is a difficult colour to see in the dusk. The delphiniums, I mean.'

She laughed lightly and stood to one side, and Victoria said: 'Good night. And thank you.' And went quickly out of the room.

The sun had gone and there were bats flittering in an airy ballet among the trees as Victoria hurried down the dusty path that wound between feathery clumps of bamboo, pepper trees and jacaranda. She was out of sight of the bungalow and had begun to walk more slowly when a nightjar flew up with a harsh cry that startled her, and something rustled in the bushes as though an animal, perhaps an antelope, had slipped past her unseen.

She stopped and stood listening, but a vagrant breeze blew in from

718

the lake and rustled the leaves and grasses, drowning all other sounds. And when it died away she could hear nothing but a distant crying of birds from the papyrus swamp, and the sound of Em's piano, sweet in the silence.

She began to hurry again, and turning a corner, reached the gate and found that she must have forgotten to latch it, for it stood open. She closed it carefully behind her and walked on quickly through a grove of acacias, listening to the music that drifted out across the garden from the open windows of Em's drawing-room.

Em had abandoned Bach and was playing something that was unfamiliar to Victoria. A strange, passionate, haunting piece of music that somehow fitted into the scene as though it were a tangible thing and an integral part of the Valley.

The Rift Valley Concerto! thought Victoria. It could not be anything else. Toroni must have loved the Rift – or hated it – to write like that.

She had almost forgotten the delphiniums, but the weight of the secateurs in her pocket reminded her of them, and she turned off the path and walked across the grass to the foot of the knoll, where they made a sea of blue and pink and purple.

She had begun to cut the flowers when another breath of wind blew across the garden, filling the green dusk with soft and stealthy rustlings, and she straightened up and stood alert and listening. Had it really been only the wind that had moved among the bushes?

The secateurs slid from her hand and were lost among the flowers, and she was aware that her heart was thumping painfully against her ribs. She had not realized that it was so late, or that the interval between sundown and darkness was so brief. Down in the papyrus swamp beyond the shamba birds were crying and calling. As though they had been alarmed by something . . .

Victoria stood quite still, held by the instinct that will make an animal freeze into immobility in the hope of being overlooked, rather than draw attention to itself by running. And as she stood there a familiar figure materialized out of the dusk, walking towards her, and her heart gave a great bound of relief.

She called out a little breathlessly: 'I'm sorry I'm so late. It was the flowers——' And bent to pick them up.

Her hands were full of them when something suddenly slid into her mind; icily and with a blinding impact. Something completely impossible.

The piano was still playing.

The flowers fell from her hands and she jerked upright, staring at the figure that stood facing her in the dusk: staring, paralysed, at a stranger, suddenly and horribly unfamiliar.

Her eyes widened in her white face and her mouth opened in a soundless scream – as Alice's had done. But Alice had not fought, or even flinched from the savage sweeping stroke of the sharpened panga.

Victoria saw it coming and flung herself to one side, and the blow missed its mark and grazed her right shoulder, shearing through the short linen sleeve.

She saw the blade flash in the dusk as it lifted again, and then she was struggling and fighting, gripped to something that was soft and yielding and as suffocating as a feather bolster; her hands round a wrist that seemed made of iron, fending it off, and her ears full of the sound of grunting, panting breaths.

She made no attempt to cry out, for she needed her breath and her young strength to fight for her life. Her foot caught in a rough tangle of grass and she stumbled and fell to her knees, and saw the panga lift again. But it did not fall.

There was someone else there. A dark shape that appeared out of nowhere and sprang at her assailant with the silent savagery of a giant cat.

Victoria, crouched on the grass, heard a hoarse gasping cry, and saw the shapeless scarlet-clad figure crumple and fall sideways. And then the green sky and the purple dusk darkened and closed in on her, and she pitched forward on her face into merciful unconsciousness.

There was a light somewhere that was hurting her eyes, and she felt cold and very sick and aware of a burning pain in her right shoulder.

There were voices too, and someone was saying: 'She'll be all right. It's only a flesh wound.'

A hand touched her forehead and Victoria shuddered uncontrollably and opened her eyes to find that she was lying on her own bed and looking up into Drew Stratton's face.

She said in a gasping whisper: '*Drew!*— Oh, Drew!'

Drew said: 'It's all right, darling. It's all over. Drink this——'

He lifted her against his shoulder, and holding a glass to her mouth, forced her to swallow something that tasted exceedingly nasty. But

720

when he would have laid her down again she turned and clung to him.

'Don't go. Please don't go.'

'I won't.' Drew's leisurely voice was quiet and level and completely reassuring. And all at once she knew that she was safe – for always.

Someone who had been standing just out of the range of her vision went out of the room, closing the door, but she did not turn her head, and Drew did not move.

She could hear cars arriving and leaving, and the occasional shrilling of the telephone. The house was full of muffled voices and movement, and somewhere a woman was crying with a hysterical despairing persistency. But none of it had anything to do with her, and presently Drew lifted her head and kissed her, and time and death and violence ceased to have any meaning.

She said at last, with her head against his shoulder:

'It was Aunt Em.'

'I know, dear.'

'Why did she do it?'

'I'll tell you in the morning.'

Victoria said urgently: 'No! Tell me now. I couldn't sleep – not knowing.'

Drew smiled down at her. 'You won't be able to help yourself, darling. Not after that stuff you've just taken!'

'Then I shall dream about it, and that will be worse. Tell me now.'

But Drew only shook his head, and presently she fell asleep, and when she awoke the sun was high, and it was Mabel Brandon, red-eyed with weeping, who had brought her breakfast on a tray, and after putting a fresh bandage on her shoulder, helped her to dress.

But Mabel would not answer her questions. She had only said: 'She's dead. She died at three o'clock this morning. Eden was with her. One should not speak ill of the dead.' And she had gone away, blowing her nose vehemently and making no attempt to disguise her tears.

The drawing-room had been full of sunlight, and Drew had been standing by the window looking out across the garden. He turned and smiled at her, and Victoria said unsteadily:

'Mrs Brandon says she – she is dead.' Even now she could not bring herself to say that name, because to say it was to admit the impossible. 'Drew, what happened? I don't understand. I don't understand anything!'

721

Drew said: 'Greg knows more about it than I do. Ask him.' And Victoria turned quickly and saw for the first time that there was someone else in the room.

Greg Gilbert gave her a brief smile that did not reach his eyes and left his face as grim and drawn as it had been a moment before, and when he spoke it was to ask what appeared to be an entirely irrelevant question:

'Did you ever know why Eden broke off the engagement between you, and married Alice Laxton?'

'No,' said Victoria, considerably taken aback. 'I suppose he— What has it got to do with this?'

'More than you would think,' said Greg tiredly. 'He broke it off because your mother told him that there was insanity in the family.'

'*Insanity!* Do you mean that I——' Victoria's face was white.

'No. Not in yours. Your grandfather married twice. But both Lady Emily's mother and her grandfather died in lunatic asylums, and there was always some doubt about the manner in which Eden's father met his death.'

'But – but it was a car accident!'

'Yes. But an odd one. Odd enough for a rumour to get around that he might possibly have engineered it himself. There was no shadow of evidence that he was abnormal, or even highly strung. But your mother heard the rumours, and because she knew all about Em's family history she believed them. And in spite of everything that the doctors say about insanity not being hereditary, she was very much against your marrying Eden.'

'Yes,' said Victoria in a whisper. 'I remember.'

'In the end she told Eden, as the only way of stopping it. He was young and impressionable, and it came as an appalling shock to him. I gather he went off for a week by himself and drank himself silly, and decided on a heroic gesture. He wouldn't tell you, because you would insist on disregarding it, and he felt he must do something quite irrevocable – burn his boats before he could weaken. He had met Alice Laxton a few weeks before, and through a cousin of hers he knew her history. Alice had had a bad riding accident in her early teens, and she could never have children. That was the deciding factor. He married her in a haze of self-sacrifice, youthful heroics, desperation and alcohol – and pure selfishness! And woke up to the full stupidity of what he had done when it was too late.'

But Victoria had no interest and little sympathy to spare for Eden

722

just then, and she brushed the information aside and demanded bluntly: 'Do you mean that Aunt Em was mad?'

Greg said: 'No; she was sane enough. But she loved *Flamingo* too much and made a god out of it, and she had meant to found a dynasty: a Kenya dynasty. When she realized that Alice could never have children it meant only one thing to her: that there would be no heir to *Flamingo*. She had a shrewd suspicion that Eden was still in love with you, and she thought you were the right kind of girl for Kenya – as Alice was not! I think the seeds of the idea must have been in her mind for a long time.'

Victoria said: 'But the – poltergeist. They were *her* things. The things she liked best. She *couldn't* have done that!'

'Oh, yes she could. Not the first time. That was the cat, who had chased a bird round the drawing-room. But it gave her an idea for an alibi – that and the rumour that "General Africa" was hiding somewhere in the Naivasha area – and she decided to use it as a smoke screen. I think too that it appealed to some twisted instinct in her. She seems to have looked upon it as a – a penance for what she intended to do. A sort of burnt offering upon the altar of *Flamingo*. There was too much of the fanatic in Em's make-up: and plenty of cunning too, for she knew that if the broken things were her own personal treasures she would be the last person to be suspected of destroying them. But it must have been a small martyrdom to do it.'

Victoria said: '*Things*, yes. But not her dog!'

'Ah! The dog was a different matter. It had been her favourite, and it had switched its allegiance to Alice. She couldn't forgive that.'

Victoria shivered and said in a whisper: 'You said once that the first killing was the hardest. Perhaps that was why she had to do it. To – to practise.'

'It wasn't her first killing. She'd killed her manager, Gus Abbott. We always thought that was an accident, but it seems we were wrong. Abbott lost his nerve, and when *Flamingo* was attacked he didn't want to stay and fight. He wanted to save himself, and he thought he could make a break for it and hide in the garden. But to run away, and from a gang of Mau Mau, was to Em an unforgivable sin, and she apparently shot him quite deliberately. I think that afterwards it gave her a sense of power. To have done that and got away with it. Perhaps it swung the balance, and made it possible for her to plan the murder of Eden's unsuitable wife. For she did plan it.

723

She seized on that first accident, for which Pusser was responsible, and kept on with a series of faked ones; and at the psychological moment she sent for you. It had given her a good excuse for doing so.'

Victoria said: 'She sent for me because my mother had died!'

'No, she didn't. If it had been that, she would have sent for you six months earlier. She sent for you because her plans were working out, and she murdered Alice just as soon as you were due to leave England and could not turn back. If she'd done it earlier, you wouldn't have come, would you?'

'No,' said Victoria slowly.

'Because of Eden. Yes, she knew that. You thought it was safe to come because he was married. But by the time you arrived here he would be free, and she was banking on his marrying you.'

Victoria went over to the window seat and sat down on it, staring out at the green lawns and the placid lake, and presently she said without turning her head:

'There are so many things I don't understand. The piano. Gilly Markham. Were there two records of the concerto? I found one, you know. It was in the false bottom of a hat box in Eden's room. I – I thought it must mean that he was the poltergeist, and that he'd kept it to blackmail her with.'

'Did you? That's irony, if you like! Em didn't know that. She said you told her that you'd found something, and you must leave at once, or go to the police. She went straight to Eden's room and realized that you'd been at the cupboard, and knew what it was that you had found. She thought it meant that you knew everything. That was why you had to be killed. She told us a great deal before she died. I think she was afraid that we might suspect Eden, and she had to clear him.'

'Then there *were* two records!'

'No. Only one. She needed it to manufacture that alibi, and she couldn't bear to destroy it. She smashed another one instead. One long-playing record looks much like another when it's in bits, and no one bothered to piece it together to read the label. She had the whole thing worked out by then. She went off ostensibly to shoot a buck, but actually to ensure that she had a good excuse for getting bloodstained – which was a point that had escaped me. And when she came back she sent Alice over to the Markhams', put a house-coat over her stained clothes and started to play the piano. And when

724

she'd got rid of Zacharia she put on the recording instead, removed the house-coat and went out to meet Alice . . .

'She killed Alice with a panga in order to bolster up the "General Africa" angle, and she came back to the house and dropped it, with a piece of twine round the handle, into the rainwater tank outside her window. Then she came back to her room, took off her stained clothes, put on the house-coat again, and went back to the drawing-room where she was found by Zacharia, still playing the piano, half an hour later. After that it was easy. She removed the record, took it back to its hiding place, stopped to pick up her stained clothes and see them put into the boiler – Majiri did most of the washing at night – and went out to search for Alice.'

Victoria said: 'But the cushion! Why should she have needed that?'

'She didn't. That was a mistake. Mine, as much as anyone's! That cushion threw me right off beam, and incidentally frightened the life out of Mabel! Apparently there had been six of those cushions sold at some charity bazaar, and Mabel had bought two; one of which had disappeared only about ten days ago. Ken says he took it on a picnic on the lake and lost it overboard, but Mabel began to add two and two together and make it eighteen.'

'Then why was it there?'

'Someone had left it on the verandah rail by the rainwater tank, and Em knocked it off and it fell against the panga and got badly stained. It couldn't be left there with the stain on it, so she ran back with it and threw it into the bushes. It was the best she could do, and as it turned out it provided her with an alibi that she had never even thought of – which is why she took another with her when she went out to meet you! She thought she'd covered everything, but she hadn't.'

Victoria said: 'You mean Kamau.'

'Kamau – and Gilly Markham.'

'*Gilly?* But he didn't see her! He only heard her playing. He said so.'

'No he didn't. We merely jumped to the conclusion that that was what he meant. But Gilly was doing a very stupid and dangerous thing. He was letting Em know that he knew the difference between her playing and Toroni's. Gilly knew quite well when Em put on the recording of the concerto. And he wanted that job at Rumuruti and thought he could blackmail her into giving it to him. He should have known better.'

Victoria said in a whisper: 'Then – then that was her too.'

'I'm afraid so. It was a fairly easy job I gather, and done in the way I had outlined – She carried a dead puff adder to the picnic inside her cushion. But Mabel threw a spanner into the works by hiding the clasp knife, and Hector by palming the iodine bottle.'

'But *why*?' demanded Victoria. 'Why should they have done that?'

'Because they both knew that Gilly hadn't died from snake-bite, and that Ken had been hanging about *Flamingo* on the evening that Alice was murdered, hoping to see her, and that Gilly knew it. They also knew that Ken had quite a collection of poisoned arrows – they are a dam' sight too easy to come by in this country! And the knife was Ken's. Hector had borrowed it earlier in the day. Mabel threw it into the lake, and Hector apparently did the same thing with the iodine bottle because it had come out of Mabel's pocket. They both seem to have acted on a silly spur-of-the-moment panic.'

'But it wasn't Ken's knife!' said Victoria. 'It was Eden's. Or rather, his father's. It's here. In the office. I found it.'

Greg did not show much interest. He said: 'Did you? Eden said it was somewhere around, but he couldn't remember what he'd done with it. It had been lost; which was why Em said she'd taken it to the picnic, and described it in detail. She thought it wouldn't turn up again, and she'd realized by then that no one thought Gilly's death was an accident, so that laying claim to it made it look as though she were shielding someone. It was quite a good line in double bluff, when you come to think of it. Em was a good poker player.'

'I suppose she killed Kamau too,' said Victoria, looking very white and sick. 'She went out shooting that evening too, after Mrs Markham had been over. Like – like she did that other time; and last night. Did she kill him?'

'Yes. And it was poetic justice, as it happened. Em thought she knew a lot; but she didn't know that she had killed the man who half the security forces in the country have been hunting for years. Kamau was "General Africa".'

'Good Lord!' said Drew, startled. 'Are you sure of that, Greg? How on earth do you know?'

'Wambui told us,' said Greg. 'She knew. And so did old Zacharia. In fact you'll probably find that there's hardly a Kikuyu from here to Nairobi who didn't know it, but they kept their mouths shut. They were frightened stiff of that man. Specially after he'd killed his only real rival, "Brigadier" Gitahi, and actually collected the Government reward for doing so!'

Greg looked from Victoria to Drew and back again, and said 'You don't know how lucky you are, Miss Caryll. If it hadn't been for Wambui, you'd probably have gone the same way as Alice. It was Wambui who knifed your aunt. She'd been laying for her. She said Kamau had told her that it was the "Memsahib Mkubwa" who had killed the small memsahib, and she was sure that she had also killed Kamau; and now he was avenged. I don't know what the hell we're going to do about that one. Technically, she ought to hang for murder; but actually she saved your life. We didn't hear until pretty late that you had tried to ring Drew, and we wouldn't have got here in time.'

'And – and if you hadn't, you would have thought it was someone else,' said Victoria in an almost inaudible voice. 'Eden, or Mrs Markham, or one of the Brandons. Or an African.'

Greg shook his head. 'Not this time. The pattern was becoming too plain and she wouldn't have got away with it again. Also I think Mrs Markham had tumbled to it at last. It seems that Em had told her that she was going to send you over to get some account books that were of no immediate interest. And Em had asked Alice to pick some flowers too: the knoll was out of sight of the house. I think Lisa guessed.'

Victoria nodded, remembering that curious interview in the Markhams' drawing-room and how it had seemed to her that Lisa was deliberately delaying her – until it got darker. Lisa who had loved Eden, and been driven frantic by jealousy.

A car drew up outside the house and they could hear voices on the verandah. Greg Gilbert looked at his watch and said: 'That will be for me. I must go.'

He turned to Victoria and said: 'I'm afraid you're going to find that there are a bad two or three days ahead of you, and a lot of police procedure to be got through before you can put all this behind you and try and forget it. But I've promised Drew that I'll leave you alone until tomorrow. Goodbye.'

He went out of the room, closing the door behind him, and Victoria was silent for a long time, twisting her hands in her lap and staring before her.

She said at last: 'You thought it might be her, didn't you.'

Drew did not answer for a moment or two, and she turned to look up at him.

'I – wondered,' said Drew slowly.

'Why?'

727

'I don't know. A lot of trivial things. But they added up. The first time was when Kamau had disappeared. Even Greg thought that he had just made a bolt for the Reserve, but when Em spoke of him she used the past tense. As though he were dead.'

'Was that all?'

'No. She couldn't stop talking about the things she had done. Remember the times she accused herself of killing Alice – and Gilly? She put it in such a way that we didn't take it seriously. But it was interesting. And then suddenly she said something that was more than merely interesting, and I began to wonder again. She quoted something from Macbeth; do you remember?'

'Yes,' said Victoria. 'Something about if she had died before, she would have lived long enough. I didn't know it was from Macbeth.'

'Had I but died an hour before this chance, I had liv'd a blessèd time', quoted Drew. 'Macbeth says that, when having murdered Duncan, the murder is discovered. I was interested in the workings of Em's mind; and I didn't like it. I was afraid for you then, and I began to consider seriously the possibility of Em being the murderer. I went to see Greg, which was why I was out when you telephoned. I was at his office until about six, and when I rang my house to say that I'd be back late I was told that the new memsahib from *Flamingo* had wanted to speak to me. I knew it must be you, and that you wouldn't have done that unless you had been frightened.'

Victoria nodded without speaking, and turned to look out of the window again; and presently Drew asked a question that he had asked her once before in that room: 'What are you thinking about?'

'Eden,' said Victoria, as she had said then. 'Drew, you don't mind about Eden, do you?'

'Do I have to?' asked Drew.

'No,' said Victoria, 'Not any more.'

She did not turn her head, but she groped for his hand, and finding it, held it to her cheek; and he felt the wetness of it and knew that she was crying: for Eden and Alice – and Em.

Outside on the drive a car started up and drove away with an impatient blare on the horn. Greg and the police had gone, and the house was quiet again. But there was no longer any awareness in its silence. The tension and the trouble that had filled it had departed from it at last. It had ceased to be a Graven Image demanding sacrifices, for its High Priestess was dead, and it was only a pleasant,

728

rambling house whose windows looked out across green gardens to the wide beauty of Lake Naivasha and all the glory of the Rift Valley.

BY THE SAME AUTHOR

The Far Pavilions

'A *Gone with the Wind* of the North-West Frontier' – *The Times*

The Far Pavilions is a story about an Englishman – Ashton Pelham-Martyn – brought up as a Hindu. It is the story of his passionate, but dangerous, love for Juli, an Indian princess. It is the story of divided loyalties, of friendship that endures till death, of high adventure and of the clash between East and West.

Shadow of the Moon

When India bursts into flaming hatred and bitter bloodshed during the dark days of the Mutiny, Captain Alex Randall and his superior's wife, the lovely raven-haired Winter de Ballesteros, are thrown unwillingly together in the struggle for survival.

'A closely interwoven story of love and war whose descriptive prose is so evocative that you can actually see and – much more – smell India as the country assaults you from the page' – *Sunday Telegraph*

Trade Wind

The year is 1859 and Hero Hollis, beautiful and headstrong niece of the American consul, arrives in Zanzibar. It is an earthly paradise fragrant with spices and frangipani; it is also the last and greatest outpost of the Slave Trade. A passionate opponent of slavery, Hero is swept into a turmoil of royal intrigue, abduction, piracy, smuggling and a virulent cholera epidemic. There in Zanzibar, the most cruelly beautiful island of the Southern Seas, she must choose her love and unravel her destiny.

The Sun in the Morning
The first volume of her autobiography

In this wonderfully evocative autobiography M. M. Kaye recounts her first eighteen years in India and England. Rich in period detail and peopled with extraordinary and unforgettable characters *The Sun in the Morning* is a brilliant and vivid memoir of life under the Raj.

'Although sites, houses, even whole cities may have changed or perished as completely as the Raj itself, those dusty, dehydrated crumbs of memory are freshly reconstituted here in the glowing, shimmering, indelibly bright colours of true romance' – *Daily Telegraph*

BY THE SAME AUTHOR

Death in Kashmir

When a young Sarah Parrish takes a skiing holiday in Gulmarg, a resort high above the fabled vale of Kashmir, she anticipates an amusing but uneventful stay. But the discovery of the grotesque corpse of grey-haired sociable Mrs Matthews casts a dark shadow over the party. On learning the real truth about her death, Sarah is plunged into a deadly intrigue of secret messages, mysterious rendezvous – and murder.

Death in the Andamans

The enchanting islands in the Indian Ocean beckoned irresistibly . . .

Though Copper Randal soon discovers that paradise has a darker side. A sense of foreboding hangs in the hot stillness among the mango trees and coconut palms. But neither she, nor her friend Valerie, stepdaughter of the Islands' Chief Commissioner, could have anticipated the sinister climax to the picnic after the hurricane struck . . .

Death in Zanzibar

To Dany Ashton it seems like the offer of the holiday of a lifetime when her stepfather invites her to stay on the exotic 'Isle of Cloves'. But even before her plane takes off Dany's delight has faded as she finds herself at the centre of a frightening mystery. On her arrival at Kivulimi, the 'House of Shade', her unease turns to terror when she realizes that among the houseguests is a dangerous and ruthless murderer. Dany doesn't know who to trust . . .